THE YEAR'S 25 FINEST
CRIME & MYSTERY STORIES
Fourth Annual Edition

The Year's 25 Finest Crime & Mystery Stories

Fourth Annual Edition

Edited by the Staff of *Mystery Scene*

With an Introduction by Jon L. Breen

Carroll & Graf Publishers, Inc.
New York

First edition October 1995

*Carroll & Graf Publishers, Inc.
260 Fifth Avenue
New York, NY 10001*

Library of Congress Cataloging-in-Publication Data is available.

ISBN 0-7867-0251-6

Manufactured in the United States of America.

95 96 97   5 4 3 2 1

PERMISSIONS

CONTENTS

SHORT NOVEL

EDGAR NOMINEES

Introduction
THE MYSTERY IN 1994

Considering the number of times his name appears below, I would have to call 1994 the year of Lawrence Block. The prize-givings and publication schedules seemed to be one long Block Party. Deservedly so, since the creator of Matt Scudder and Bernie Rhodenbarr has passed from reliable veteran practitioner to certified genius superstar—and on the basis of work, not hype.

On a less happy note, 1994 saw the deaths of more major figures in the crime fiction field than any I can recall, among them Julian Symons, one of the greatest of the all-rounders as author, critic, and historian; Michael Innes (J.I.M. Stewart), last survivor among the top names from Great Britain's Golden Age of Detection; Robert Bloch, who would still be a legendary figure among his fellow writers even if *Psycho* had never been written; and one of the most renowned of mystery editors, Joan Kahn.

Biggest mystery fiction news story to extend outside the boundaries of the field itself was the revelation that novelist Anne Perry, author of two distinguished series of Victorian detective novels, was convicted of murder as a teenager. Perry, born Juliet Hulme, and friend Pauline Parker were tried and convicted for the murder of Parker's mother in a notorious 1954 New Zealand case that was fictionalized in Vin Packer's 1958 novel *The Evil Friendship*, and was also the subject of a 1994 film, *Heavenly Creatures*.

As the year went by, there were continuing rumbles of a shakeout in the mystery field, with some established bylines losing their slots on the publishing lists. Still, if the field was undergoing a contraction, you couldn't prove it by the raw numbers. By my own count, 308 novels were submitted for the best hardcover Edgar Allan Poe Award, and as a reviewer I received at least another 64 hardcover non-firsts that were not submitted for the Edgar. That means at least 372 new novels in the broad genre, not counting first novels and paperback originals. Thus, the numbers remain healthy and may even be up over recent seasons.

BEST NOVELS OF THE YEAR 1994

I had the honor of chairing the Edgar committee for best hardcover novel of 1994. Like all mystery readers, I have often scratched my head wondering how Edgar committees chose some books to honor while over-looking others equally or more worthy. But this year, I thought, surely, for once the committee got it right. Then respected fan critic Barry Gardner wrote in *Mystery & Detective Monthly* (March 1995): "Am I right in thinking that the Best Novel group is the most off-the-wall in recent memory, in terms of what was *not* nominated, as well as some of the ones that were?" Oh, well.

While the five Edgar nominees (see Abrahams, Block, Buchanan, Robinson, and Walker in the list below) were not necessarily my personal top five, I strongly endorse them all as deserving of celebration. And at least my best-fifteen list can be delivered with fewer disclaimers than usual. The following comes closer than ever to representing one reviewer's opinion on the best of 1994—at least those non-first novels published in hard covers.

Peter Abrahams, *Lights Out* (Mysterious): If you admire the suspense fiction of Cornell Woolrich, Abrahams is a contemporary to try. This is a strong variation on the old plot of the framed convict who gets out of jail and tries to discover how he got there.

Lawrence Block, *A Long Line of Dead Men* (Morrow): Though lacking a private-eye license, New York's Matt Scudder is at the very top of the current sleuths-for-hire heap, as this tale of a series of murders of members of a "last man" club demonstrates once more.

Edna Buchanan, *Miami, it's Murder* (Hyperion): The legendary Miami reporter delivers an outstanding journalism procedural in Britt Montero's second adventure.

Dorothy Cannell, *How to Murder Your Mother-in-Law* (Bantam): Cannell lives up to her reputation as one of the funniest writers in the mystery genre in the latest Ellie Haskell novel.

Michael Connelly, *The Concrete Blonde* (Little, Brown): Captivating as both a police and a courtroom procedural, the third novel about L.A. cop Hieronymus Bosch was the choice of many readers as best of the year.

Barbara D'Amato, *Hard Case* (Scribners): The background of a hospital trauma center and a beautifully dovetailed puzzle plot make this one of the best cases for investigative reporter Cat Marsala.

Peter Dickinson, *The Yellow Room Conspiracy* (Mysterious): If anyone produced a mystery fiction classic in the past year, it was the undervalued Dickinson, who mixes past and present in an astonishing puzzle novel.

Dick Francis, *Wild Horses* (Putnam): Though he may not be the only celebrity mystery writer (i.e., one whose original fame was in another field of endeavor) who writes his own books, Francis is surely the most successful in terms of both commerce and quality. Here the ex-steeplechase jockey combines horse racing and movie making in one of his very best novels.

Robert Irvine, *The Hosanna Shout* (St. Martin's): This one ranks near the top among Salt Lake City private eye Moroni Traveler's cases. Irvine returned to the TV news background of his earliest books in his other 1994 novel, *Barking Dogs* (St. Martin's).

Joe R. Lansdale, *Mucho Mojo* (Mysterious): Hap Collins and Leonard Pine return in what may be their talented dark-suspense-inclined creator's closest approach to an Agatha Christie-style whodunit.

Sharyn McCrumb, *She Walks These Hills* (Scribners): With the Connelly and Dickinson books above, this was one of the best novels of the year *not* to be nominated for an Edgar, a masterpiece of story construction and character-drawing.

Dianne G. Pugh, *Slow Squeeze* (Pocket): The latest about investment counselor Iris Thorne is an unusual variation on the amateur detective story that, by the author's own account, readers either loved or hated. Put me in the former camp.

Peter Robinson, *Wednesday's Child* (Scribners): This extraordinary Yorkshire police procedural impressed me so much, I dragged out the biggest gun I could find for comparison: Hillary Waugh's classic *Last Seen Wearing* (1951).

Alan Russell, *The Hotel Detective* (Mysterious): This modular mystery about the hotel business was one of the funniest and most purely entertaining books of the year.

Mary Willis Walker, *The Red Scream* (Doubleday): The deserving Edgar winner features a true-crime writer reconsidering one of her successes. It's a strong performance in all respects.

SHORT STORIES

A number of well-known writers had new collections during the year: Jeffrey Archer's *Twelve Red Herrings* (HarperCollins), Mary Higgins Clark's *The Lottery Winner: Alvirah and Willy Stories* (Simon and Schuster), James Ellroy's *Hollywood Nocturnes* (Penzler), Joyce Carol Oates's *Haunted: Tales of the Grotesque* (Dutton), and June Thomson's *The Secret Chronicles of Sherlock Holmes* (Penzler). A classic collection in a new translation was Karel Capek's *Tales from Two Pockets* (Catbird Press, 16 Windsor Road, North Haven, CT 06473). Strictly for the high-rolling collector's market was Lawrence Block's limited edition *Ehrengraf for the Defense* (A.S.A.P., 23852 Via Navarra, Mission Viejo, CA 92691).

The original anthology market remained strong. Robert J. Randisi and

Susan Dunlap drew new stories from members of Private Eye Writers of America and Sisters in Crime for *Deadly Allies II* (Doubleday). Other new entries in anthology series were the Adams Round Table's *Justice in Manhattan* (Longmeadow) and the British *2nd Culprit* (St. Martin's), edited by Liza Cody and Michael Z. Lewin. Yet more cat mysteries were created for *Feline and Famous: Cat Crimes Goes Hollywood* (Fine), edited by Martin Greenberg and Ed Gorman. Greenberg also edited the matching collections *Murder for Mother* and *Murder for Father* (both Signet) and joined Maxim Jakubowski in gathering *Royal Crimes* (Signet). Sleuthing teams were featured in Elaine Raco Chase's *Partners in Crime* (Signet). Mickey Spillane and Max Allan Collins gathered hitman tales in *Murder is My Business* (Dutton). Combining new stories with reprints were Marvin Kaye's *The Game is Afoot: Parodies, Pastiches and Ponderings of Sherlock Holmes* (St. Martin's) and Michele Slung and Roland Hartman's *Murder for Halloween* (Mysterious).

As usual, the Dell Magazines files of *Ellery Queen's Mystery Magazine* and *Alfred Hitchcock's Mystery Magazine* were mined for several theme anthologies: Janet Hutchings gathered historical mysteries in *Once Upon a Crime* (St. Martin's), while Cynthia Manson edited *Women of Mystery II* and *Death on the Veranda: Mystery Stories of the South* (both Carroll & Graf). Another Manson-edited reprint anthology was *Murder on Trial* (Signet), the first printing of which appeared without one of the announced stories, Lawrence Block's "The Ehrengraf Presumption." In the most ambitious reprint anthologies of the year, Marie Smith gathered Victorian and Edwardian tales in *The Mammoth Book of Golden Age Detective Stories* (Carroll & Graf) and Ed Gorman tracked down some of the best American writers and stories of recent decades in *A Treasury of Great Detective and Murder Mysteries* (Carroll & Graf).

REFERENCE BOOKS AND SECONDARY SOURCES

The book of the year was the Edgar winner, William L. DeAndrea's *Encyclopedia Mysteriosa* (Prentice Hall), a reference work most comparable to the excellent but aging *Encyclopedia of Mystery and Detection* (1976). While the author's selection of entries may raise an occasional eyebrow—why, for example, exclude writers as significant as Jack Ritchie and Dick Lochte while including TV shows as obscure as *Code 3* and *Cop Rock?*—the book is informative, accurate, and (as expected from its author) consistently readable and entertaining.

Other secondary sources of note included two covering similar ground, *Great Women Mystery Writers* (Greenwood), edited by Kathleen Gregory

Klein, and *By a Woman's Hand* (Berkley) by Jean Swanson and Dean James. Rosemary Herbert produced the best volume to date of mystery writer interviews in *The Fatal Art of Entertainment* (G. K. Hall). A new two-volume edition of Allen J. Hubin's *Crime Fiction: A Comprehensive Bibliography* (Garland) extended coverage through 1990 and added valuable new features. Martin Greenberg, along with his fiction anthologizing, edited *The Tony Hillerman Companion* (HarperCollins). The first secondary source on Robert B. Parker was *Spenser's Boston* (Penzler).

SUB-GENRES

I. Private Eyes. Apart from the Block and Irvine titles on my top fifteen, there were plenty of sleuths-for-hire in good form during the year, among them James Sallis's Lewis Griffin in *Black Hornet* (Carroll & Graf), Linda Grant's Catherine Sayler in *A Woman's Place* (Scribners), Maxine O'Callaghan's Delilah West in *Trade-Off* (St. Martin's), Thomas D. Davis's Dave Strickland in *Murdered Sleep* (Walker), Melodie Johnson Howe's Clare Conrad in *Beauty Dies* (Viking), Harold Adams's Carl Wilcox in *A Way with Widows* (Walker), Sue Grafton's Kinsey Millhone in *"K" is for Killer* (Holt), Sara Paretsky's V. I. Warshawski in *Tunnel Vision* (Delacorte), Les Roberts's Saxon in *The Lemon Chicken Jones* (St. Martin's), Parnell Hall's Stanley Hastings in *Blackmail* (Mysterious), John Lutz's Fred Carver in *Torch* (Holt), William Sanders's Taggert Roper in *A Death on 66* (St. Martin's), Max Allan Collins's Nate Heller in *Carnal Hours* (Dutton), Arthur Lyons's Jacob Asch in *False Pretenses* (Mysterious), and (in probably his best adventure to date) Robert J. Randisi's Miles Jacoby in *Stand-Up* (St. Martin's). Ed Gorman's Robert Payne debuted in the memorable *Blood Moon* (St. Martin's) in a year that also saw a limited-edition American publication of Gorman's *Shadow Games* (CD Publications, P.O. Box 18433, Baltimore, MD 21237), nominated for a Shamus Award on the basis of its 1993 publication as a British paperback original.

II. Formal Detection. For one of the most complicated and clever Golden Age-style puzzles in years, try Lawrence Block's semi-parodic *The Burglar Who Traded Ted Williams* (Dutton). Michael Dibdin's *The Dying of the Light* (Pantheon) offers a much darker parody of classical detection. Non-parodic and worth a recommendation are Jean Hager's *The Redbird's Cry* (Mysterious), Minette Walters's Gold Dagger-winning *The Scold's Bridle* (St. Martin's), Robert A. Carter's *Final Edit* (Mysterious), William L. DeAndrea's *The Manx Murders* (Penzler), William X. Kienzle's *Bishop as Pawn* (Andrews and McMeel), Jane Dentinger's *The Queen is Dead*, Nancy Pickard's *Confession* (Pocket Books), Aaron Elkins's *Dead Men's Hearts* (Mysterious), and two from Richard A. Lupoff's

Hobart Lindsey/Marvia Plum series, *The Bessie Blue Killer* and *The Sepia Siren Killer* (both St. Martin's). I was too preoccupied with hardcover Edgar nominees to read many first mysteries in 1994, but one good one in the classical vein was Jeff Abbott's *Do Unto Others* (Ballantine).

III. Police procedurals. Among the strong pure police novels of the year were the first books in new series from L.A.P.D. detective Paul Bishop, *Kill Me Again* (Avon), and Nick Gaitano (a.k.a. Eugene Izzi), *Special Victims* (Simon and Schuster). Michael Gilbert's Patrick Petrella returned in *Roller Coaster* (Carroll & Graf); Donna Leon's Venetian Guido Brunetti had a strong outing in *Dressed for Death* (HarperCollins), and Thomas Adcock's Neal Hockaday took an Irish vacation in *Drown All the Ducks* (Pocket Books). Many series cops don't strictly speaking occupy procedurals: Janwillem van de Wetering's now-retired Amsterdam policemen Grijpstra and De Gier made a notable comeback after eight years in *Just a Corpse at Twilight* (Soho); Julie Smith's New Orleans cop Skip Langdon explored the world of computer bulletin boards in *New Orleans Beat* (Fawcett Columbine); Deborah Crombie's team of Duncan Kincaid and Gemma Jones marked their creator as near the top of the heap of American writers of British-style mysteries in *All Shall Be Well* (Scribners); and H.R.F. Keating's Inspector Ghote appeared in two cases new to American readers, *Cheating Death* (Mysterious) and *Doing Wrong* (Penzler).

IV. Historicals. Here is the opportunity to salute the impossibly prolific English writer, P. C. Doherty, who had (note the carefully hedged language) no fewer than six new books under his own name and at least three pseudonyms: Michael Clynes, C. L. Grace, and Paul Harding. For samples, try Doherty's *Murder Wears a Cowl* (St. Martin's), Harding's *Red Slayer* (Morrow), Grace's *The Eye of God* (St. Martin's), and best of all Clynes's *The Poisoned Chalice* (Penzler), featuring the author's most entertaining character, Sir Roger Shallot. Among the good historicals not by Doherty were Ellis Peters's *Brother Cadfael's Penance* (Mysterious), Lindsey Davis's *Poseidon's Gold* (Crown), Maan Meyers's *The High Constable* (Doubleday), and Anne Perry's *The Sins of the Wolf* (Fawcett Columbine). Caleb Carr's bestselling *The Alienist* (Random) didn't grab this reviewer but was a favorite of many.

V. Suspense. Yes, this is a catch-all for books tough to pigeonhole. Among those titles usually classed as mainstream suspense were Bill Pronzini's *With an Extreme Burning* (Carroll & Graf), Andrew Klavan's *Corruption* (Morrow), Mary Higgins Clark's *Remember Me* (Simon and Schuster), Soledad Santiago's *Nightside* (Doubleday), and Evan Hunter's dazzling *Criminal Conversation* (Warner). If you long for a return to the fiction *noir* of fifties paperback originals, look no farther than George P. Pelecanos's caper novel *Shoedog* (St. Martin's). And no novel was more distinctive and unusual than R. D. Zimmerman's emotionally charged *Red Trance* (Morrow).

VI. Humor. It was a strong year for comedic mysteries, from the Russell and Cannell titles on the best-fifteen list to Donald E. Westlake's take on the country music world in *Baby, Would I Lie?* (Mysterious), Gar Antony Haywood's fresh variation on the husband-and-wife detecting team in *Going Nowhere Fast* (Putnam), Bill Crider's number on political correctness in ... *A Dangerous Thing* (Walker), Richard Hoyt's mock-Bondian World Cup thriller *Red Card* (Forge), Simon Brett's latest Charles Paris adventure *A Reconstructed Corpse* (Scribners), and Gillian Roberts's *Our Miss Brooks*-ish *How I Spent My Summer Vacation* (Ballantine).

VII. The Lawyers. The lawyer sleuths, most guided in their endeavors by lawyer novelists, are always with us. Especially impressive were Ronald Levitsky's Nate Rosen in *The Innocence That Was* (Scribners) and Paul Levine's Jake Lassiter in *Mortal Sin* (Morrow). Among others in solid form were Butch Karp in *Justice Denied* (Dutton) by Robert K. Tanenbaum (with acknowledged collaborator Michael Gruber); Grif Stockley's Gideon Page in *Religious Convictions* (Simon and Schuster), Michael A. Kahn's Rachel Gold in *Firm Ambitions* (Dutton), Lia Matera's Laura DiPalma in *Face Value* (Simon and Schuster), and Frederick D. Huebner's Matthew Riordan in *Methods of Execution* (Simon and Schuster). Joe L. Hensley introduced a new central character, Jim Carlos Singer, in *Grim City* (St. Martin's).

OTHERS MENTIONED IN DISPATCHES

Have we mentioned everybody? Not hardly. Among many well-known writers with new novels were James Lee Burke, Richard Condon, Patricia Cornwell, Susan Dunlap, Nicolas Freeling, Joe Gores, John Grisham, Adam Hall, Carolyn G. Hart, Joan Hess, Reginald Hill, Clark Howard, Faye Kellerman, Jonathan Kellerman, Ed McBain, Gregory Macdonald, Margaret Maron, Walter Mosley, Marcia Muller, Robert B. Parker, Elizabeth Peters, Paco Ignacio Taibo II, Ross Thomas, and Phyllis A. Whitney.

A SENSE OF HISTORY

For several years, Otto Penzler's Armchair Detective Library has reprinted notable novels, sometimes for the first time in hardcover, with new introductions by their authors. In 1994, volumes by Ed McBain, Lawrence Block, and Tony Hillerman were among those added. With the temporary (one hopes) interruption of Penzler's publishing imprint, the series' future is in doubt.

Carroll & Graf continued to revive good out-of-print mysteries, from Warren Murphy's 1982 paperback original *Smoked Out* to the historical mysteries of John Dickson Carr, notably the 1957 time-travel novel, *Fire, Burn*, while Douglas G. Greene launched a new small-press publisher, Crippen & Landru (P.O. Box 9315, Norfolk, VA 93505), with the first book publication of the Carr radio serial, *Speak of the Devil*. Foul/Play Countryman is another source for new editions of older books, including some of Robert Barnard's strong backlist of titles. Bantam continued its reprinting of Rex Stout's mysteries with new introductions by various luminaries; I was surprised to find 1969's *Death of a Dude*, introduced by western writer Don Coldsmith, was a much better book than I remembered. Among the real vintage items in paperback were Paul Cain's Hammett-influenced 1933 novel *Fast One* (Vintage) and Ellery Queen's very different but equally classic 1931 book, *The Dutch Shoe Mystery* (Penzler).

AWARD WINNERS FOR 1994

EDGAR ALLAN POE AWARDS
(Mystery Writers of America)

Best novel: Mary Willis Walker, *The Red Scream* (Doubleday)

Best first novel by an American author: George Dawes Green, *The Caveman's Valentine* (Warner)

Best original paperback: Lisa Scottoline, *Final Appeal* (Harper)

Best fact crime book: Joe Domanick, *To Protect and Serve* (Pocket)

Best critical/biographical work: William L. DeAndrea, *Encyclopedia Mysteriosa* (Prentice-Hall/Macmillan)

Best short story: Doug Allyn, "The Dancing Bear" (*Alfred Hitchcock's Mystery Magazine*, March)

Best young adult mystery: Nancy Springer, *Toughing It* (Harcourt Brace)

Best juvenile mystery: Willo Davis Roberts, *The Absolutely True Story . . . How I Visited Yellowstone Park with the Terrible Rubes* (Atheneum)

Best episode in a television series: Steven Bochco, Walon Green, and David Milch, "Simone Says" (*NYPD Blue*, 20th Century-Fox/ABC-TV)

Best television feature or miniseries: Jimmy McGovern, *Cracker: To Say I Love You* (A & E Mystery)

Best motion picture: Quentin Tarantino, *Pulp Fiction* (Miramax)

Grand master: Mickey Spillane

Robert L. Fish award (best first story): Batya Swift Yasgur, "Me and Mr. Harry" (*Ellery Queen's Mystery Magazine*, mid-December)
Ellery Queen award: Martin H. Greenberg
Raven: Paul Le Clerc, President, New York Public Library

Agatha Awards

(Malice Domestic Mystery Convention)

Best novel: Sharyn McCrumb, *She Walks These Hills* (Scribners)
Best first novel: Jeff Abbott, *Do Unto Others* (Ballantine)
Best short story: Dorothy Cannell, "The Family Jewels" (*Malice Domestic III* [Pocket])
Best non-fiction: William L. DeAndrea, *Encyclopedia Mysteriosa* (Prentice-Hall/Macmillan)

Dilys Award

(Independent Mystery Booksellers Association)

Janet Evanovich, *One for the Money* (Scribners)

AWARD WINNERS FOR 1993

ANTHONY AWARDS
(Bouchercon World Mystery Convention)

Best novel: Marcia Muller, *Wolf in the Shadows* (Mysterious)
Best first novel: Nevada Barr, *Track of the Cat*
Best true crime: Ann Rule, *A Rose for Her Grave*
Best short story: Susan Dunlap, "Checkout" (*Malice Domestic 2* [Pocket])
Best short-story collection: Mary Higgins Clark, ed., *Malice Domestic 2* (Pocket)
Best critical work: Ed Gorman, Martin H. Greenberg, Larry Segriff, eds, with Jon L. Breen, *The Fine Art of Murder* (Carroll & Graf)

Shamus Awards

(Private Eye Writers of America)

Best novel: Lawrence Block, *The Devil Knows You're Dead* (Morrow)
Best first novel: Lynn Hightower, *Satan's Lambs* (Walker)

Best original paperback novel: Rodman Philbrick, *Brothers and Sinners* (NAL)

Best short story: Lawrence Block, "The Merciful Angel of Death" (*The New Mystery* [Dutton])

Lifetime achievement award: Stephen J. Cannell

Dagger Awards

(Crime Writers' Association, Great Britain)

Gold Dagger: Minette Walters, *The Scold's Bridle*
Silver Dagger: Peter Hoeg, *Miss Smilla's Feeling for Snow*
Short story: Ian Rankin, "Deep Hole" (*London Noir*)

Macavity Awards

(Mystery Readers International)

Best novel: Minette Walters, *The Sculptress* (St. Martin's)

Best first novel: Sharan Newman, *Death Comes as an Epiphany* (TOR)

Best nonfiction or critical work: Ed Gorman, Martin H. Greenberg, Larry Segriff, eds, with Jon L. Breen, *The Fine Art of Murder* (Carroll & Graf)

Best short story: Susan Dunlap, "Checkout" (*Malice Domestic* 2 [Pocket])

Arthur Ellis Awards
(Crime Writers of Canada)

Best novel: John Lawrence Reynolds, *Gypsy Sins* (HarperCollins)

Best first novel: Gavin Scott, *Memory Trace* (Cormorant)

Best true crime: David R. Williams, *With Malice Aforethought: Six Spectacular Canadian Trials* (Sono Nis)

Best short story: Robert J. Sawyer, "Just Like Old Times" (*On Spec: The Canadian Magazine of Speculative Writing*, Summer 1993)

Best juvenile: John Dowd, *Abalone Summer* (Raincoast)

Best play: Timothy Findley, *The Stillborn Lover* (Blizzard)

Hammett Prize

(North American Branch,
International Association of Crime Writers)

James Crumley, *Mexican Tree Duck* (Mysterious)

THE YEAR'S 25 FINEST CRIME & MYSTERY STORIES
Fourth Annual Edition

Robert Barnard is generally thought to be one of the world's leading practitioners of the pure detective story. While this kind of accolade is nice, it
belies the sheer breadth, not to mention power, of his accomplishments. He
is clever and bitchy in DEATH OF AN OLD GOAT (1977); melancholy, even
poetic, in OUT OF THE BLACKOUT (1985); and detached, even cynical in
BODIES (1986). In other words, while he does write the pure detective story,
he makes the form serve him rather than the other way around. He is at his
best in the following story.

The Gentleman in the Lake
ROBERT BARNARD

There had been violent storms that night, but the body did not come to
the surface until they had died down and a watery summer sun sent
ripples of lemon and silver across the still-disturbed surface of Derwent
Water. It was first seen by a little girl, clutching a plastic beaker of orange
juice, who had strayed down from the small car park, over the pebbles,
to the edge of the lake.

"What's that, Mummy?"

"What's what, dear?"

Her mother was wandering round, drinking in the calm, the silence,
the magisterial beauty, the more potent for the absence of other tourists.
She was a businesswoman, and holidays by the Lakes made her question
uncomfortably what she was doing with her life. She strolled down to
where the water lapped onto the stones.

"*There*, Mummy. *That.*"

She looked towards the lake. A sort of bundle bobbed on the surface a
hundred yards or so away. She screwed up her eyes. A sort of *tweedy* bundle. Greeny-brown, like an old-fashioned gentleman's suit. As she watched
she realised that she could make out, stretching out from the bundle, two
lines . . . *Legs*. She put her hand firmly on her daughter's shoulder.

"Oh, it's just an old bundle of clothes, darling. Look, there's Patch
wanting to play. He has to stretch his legs too, you know."

3

Patch barked obligingly, and the little girl trotted off to throw his ball for him. Without hurrying the woman made her way back to the car, picked up the car phone, and dialed 999.

IT WAS LATE on in the previous summer that Marcia Catchpole had sat beside Sir James Harrington at a dinner party in St. John's Wood. "Something immensely distinguished in Law," her hostess Serena Fisk had told her vaguely. "Not a judge, but a rather famous defending counsel, or prosecuting counsel, or *something* of that sort."

He had been rather quiet as they all sat down: urbane, courteous in a dated sort of way, but quiet. It was as if he was far away, reviewing the finer points of a case long ago.

"So nice to have *soup*," said Marcia, famous for "drawing people out," especially men. "Soup seems almost to have gone out these days."

"Really?" said Sir James, as if they were discussing the habits of Eskimos or Trobriand Islanders. "Yes, I suppose you don't often . . . *get it*."

"No, it's all melons and ham, and pâté, and seafood cocktails."

"Is it? *Is* it?"

His concentration wavering, he returned to his soup, which he was consuming a good deal more expertly than Marcia, who, truth to tell, was more used to melons and suchlike.

"You don't eat out a great deal?"

"No. Not now. Once, when I was practising. . . . But not now. And not since my wife died."

"Of course you're right: people don't like singles, do they?"

"Singles?"

"People on their own. For dinner parties. They have to find another one—like me tonight."

"Yes . . . Yes," he said, as if only half-understanding what she said.

"And it's no fun eating in a restaurant on your own, is it?"

"No . . . None at all. . . . I have a woman come in," he added, as if trying to make a contribution of his own.

"To cook and clean for you?"

"Yes . . . Perfectly capable woman. . . . It's not the same, though."

"No. Nothing is, is it, when you find yourself on your own?"

"No, it's not. . . ." He thought, as if thought was difficult. "You can't *do* so many things you used to do."

"Ah, you find that too, do you? What do you miss most?"

There was a moment's silence, as if he had forgotten what they were talking about. Then he said: "Travel. I'd like to go to the Lakes again."

"Oh, the Lakes! One of my favourite places. Don't you drive?"

"No. I've never had any need before."

"Do you have children?"

"Oh yes. Two sons. One in medicine, one in politics. Busy chaps with families of their own. Can't expect them to take me places . . . Don't see much of them. . . ." His moment of animation seemed to fade, and he picked away at his entrée. "What *is* this fish, Molly?"

When, the next day, she phoned to thank her hostess, Marcia commented that Sir James was "such a sweetie."

"You and he seemed to get on like a house on fire, anyway."

"Oh, we did."

"Other people said he was awfully vague."

"Oh, it's the legal mind. Wrapped in grand generalities. His wife been dead long?"

"About two years. I believe he misses her frightfully. Molly used to arrange all the practicalities for him."

"I can believe that. I was supposed to ring him about a book I have that he wanted, but he forgot to give me his number."

"Oh, it's two-seven-one-eight-seven-six. A rather grand place in Chelsea."

But Marcia had already guessed the number after going through the telephone directory. She had also guessed at the name of Sir James's late wife.

"WE CAN'T DO MUCH till we have the pathologist's report," said Superintendent Southern, fingering the still-damp material of a tweed suit. "Except perhaps about *this*."

Sergeant Potter looked down at it.

"I don't know a lot about such things," he said, "but I'd have said that suit was dear."

"So would I. A gentleman's suit, made to measure and beautifully sewn. I've had one of the secretaries in who knows about these things. A gentleman's suit for country wear. Made for a man who doesn't know the meaning of the word 'casual.' With a nametag sewn in by the tailor and crudely removed . . . with a razor blade probably."

"You don't *get* razor blades much these days."

"Perhaps he's also someone who doesn't know the meaning of the word 'throwaway.' A picture seems to be emerging."

"And the removal of the nametag almost inevitably means—"

"Murder. Yes, I'd say so."

MARCIA DECIDED AGAINST ringing Sir James up. She felt sure he would not remember who she was. Instead, she would call round with the book, which had indeed come up in conversation—because she had made sure it did. Marcia was very good at fostering acquaintanceships with men, and had had two moderately lucrative divorces to prove it.

She timed her visit for late afternoon, when she calculated that the lady who cooked and "did" for him would have gone home. When he opened the door he blinked, and his hand strayed towards his lips.

"I'm afraid I—"

"Marcia Catchpole. We met at Serena Fisk's. I brought the book on Wordsworth we were talking about."

She proffered Stephen Gill on Wordsworth, in paperback. She had thought as she bought it that Sir James was probably not used to paperbacks, but she decided that, as an investment, Sir James was not yet worth the price of a hardback.

"Oh, I don't ... er ... Won't you come in?"

"Lovely!"

She was taken into a rather grim sitting room, lined with legal books and Victorian first editions. Sir James began to make uncertain remarks about how he thought he could manage tea.

"Why don't you let me make it? You'll not be used to fending for yourself, let alone for visitors. It was different in your generation, wasn't it? Is that the kitchen?"

And she immediately showed an uncanny instinct for finding things and doing the necessary. Sir James watched her, bemused, for a minute or two, then shuffled back to the sitting room. When she came in with a tray, with tea things on it and a plate of biscuits, he looked as if he had forgotten who she was, and how she came to be there.

"There, that's nice, isn't it? Do you like it strong? Not too strong, right. I think you'll enjoy the Wordsworth book. Wordsworth really *is* the Lakes, don't you agree?"

She had formed the notion, when talking to him at Serena Fisk's dinner party, that his reading was remaining with him longer than his grip on real life. This was confirmed by the conversation on this visit. As long as the talk stayed with Wordsworth and his Lakeland circle it approached a normal chat: he would forget the names of poems, but he would sometimes quote several lines of the better-known ones verbatim. Marcia had been educated at a moderately good state school, and she managed to keep her end up.

Marcia got up to go just at the right time, when Sir James had got used to her being there and before he began wanting her to go. At the door she said: "I'm expecting to have to go to the Lakes on business in a couple of weeks. I'd be happy if you'd come along."

"Oh, I couldn't possibly—"

"No obligations either way: we pay for ourselves, separate rooms *of course*, quite independent of each other. I've got business in Cockermouth, and I thought of staying by Buttermere or Crummock Water."

A glint came into his eyes.

"It would be wonderful to see them again. But I really couldn't—"

"Of course you could. It would be my pleasure. It's always better in congenial company, isn't it? I'll be in touch about the arrangements."

Marcia was in no doubt she would have to make all the arrangements, down to doing his packing and contacting his cleaning woman. But she was confident she would bring it off.

"KILLED BY A BLOW to the head," said Superintendent Southern, when he had skimmed through the pathologist's report. "Some kind of accident, for example a boating accident, can't entirely be ruled out, but there was some time between his being killed and his going into the water."

"In which case, what happened to the boat? And why didn't whoever was with him simply go back to base and report it, rather than heaving him in?"

"Exactly.... From what remains, the pathologist suggests a smooth liver—a townee not a countryman, even of the upper-crust kind."

"I think you suspected that from the suit, didn't you, sir?"

"I did. Where do you go for a first-rate suit for country holidays if you're a townee?"

"Same as for business suits? Savile Row, sir?"

"If you're a well-heeled Londoner that's exactly where you go. We'll start there."

MARCIA WENT ROUND to Sir James's two days before she had decided to set off North. Sir James remembered little or nothing about the proposed trip, still less whether he had agreed to go. Marcia got them a cup of tea, put maps on his lap, then began his packing for him. Before she went she cooked him his light supper (wondering how he had ever managed to cook it for himself) and got out of him the name of his daily. Later on she rang her and told her she was taking Sir James to the Lakes, and he'd be away for at most a week. The woman sounded sceptical but uncertain whether it was her place to say anything. Marcia, in any case, didn't give her the opportunity.

She also rang Serena Fisk to tell her. She had an ulterior motive for doing so. In the course of the conversation she casually asked: "How did he get to your dinner party?"

"Oh, I drove him. Homecooks were doing the food, so there was no problem. Those sons of his wouldn't lift a finger to help him. Then Bill drove him home later. Said he couldn't get a coherent word out of him."

"I expect he was tired. If you talk to him about literature you can see there's still a mind there."

"Literature was never my strong point, Marcia."

"Anyway, I'm taking him to the Lakes for a week on Friday."

"*Really?* Well, you are getting on well with him. Rather you than me."

"Oh, all he needs is a bit of stimulus," said Marcia. She felt confident now that she had little to fear from old friends or sons.

This first visit to the Lakes went off extremely well from Marcia's point of view. When she collected him, the idea that he was going somewhere seemed actually to have got through to him. She finished the packing with last-minute things, got him and his cases into the car, and in no time they were on the M1. During a pub lunch he called her "Molly" again, and when they at last reached the Lakes she saw that glint in his eyes, heard little grunts of pleasure.

She had booked them into Crummock Lodge, an unpretentious but spacious hotel which seemed to her just the sort of place Sir James would have been used to on his holidays in the Lakes. They had separate rooms, as she had promised. "He's an old friend who's been very ill," she told the manager. They ate well, went on drives and gentle walks. If anyone stopped and talked, Sir James managed a sort of distant benignity which carried them through. As before, he was best if he talked about literature. Once, after Marcia had had a conversation with a farmer over a dry stone wall he said:

"Wordsworth always believed in the wisdom of simple country people."

It sounded like something a schoolmaster had once drummed into him. Marcia would have liked to say, "But when his brother married a servant he said it was an outrage." But she herself had risen by marriage, or marriages, and the point seemed to strike too close to home.

On the afternoon when she had her private business in Cockermouth she walked Sir James hard in the morning and left him tucked up in bed after lunch. Then she visited a friend who had retired to a small cottage on the outskirts of the town. He had been a private detective, and had been useful to her in her first divorce. The dicey method he had used to get dirt on her husband had convinced her that in his case private detection was very close to crime itself, and she had maintained the connection. She told him the outline of what she had in mind, and told him she might need him in the future.

When, after a week, they returned to London, Marcia was completely satisfied. She now had a secure place in Sir James's life. He no longer looked bewildered when she came round, even looked pleased, and often called her "Molly." She went to the Chelsea house often in the evenings, cooked his meal for him, and together they watched television like an old couple.

It would soon be time to make arrangements at a Registry Office.

IN THE PROCESS of walking from establishment to establishment in Savile Row, Southern came to feel he had had as much as he could stand of stiffness, professional discretion, and awed hush. They were only high-class tailors, he thought to himself, not the Church of bloody England. Still, when they heard that one of their clients could have ended up as an anonymous corpse in Derwent Water, they were willing to cooperate. The three establishments which offered that particular tweed handed him silently a list of those customers who had had suits made from it in the last ten years.

"Would you know if any of these are dead?" he asked one shop manager.

"Of course, sir. We make a note in our records when their obituary appears in the *Times*."

The man took the paper back and put a little crucifix sign against two of the four names. The two remaining were a well-known television newsreader and Sir James Harrington.

"Is Sir James still alive?"

"Oh certainly. There's been no obituary for him. But he's very old: we have had no order from him for some time."

It was Sir James that Southern decided to start with. Scotland Yard knew all about him, and provided a picture, a review of the major trials in which he had featured, and his address. When Southern failed to get an answer from phone calls to the house, he went round to try the personal touch. There was a For Sale notice on it that looked to have been there for some time.

THE ARRANGEMENTS for the Registry Office wedding went without a hitch. A month after their trip, Marcia went to book it in a suburb where neither Sir James nor she was known. Then she began foreshadowing it to Sir James, to accustom him to the idea.

"Best make it legal," she said, in her slightly vulgar way.

"Legal?" he enquired, from a great distance.

"You and me. But we'll just go on as we are."

She thought about witnesses, foresaw various dangers, and decided to pay for her detective friend to come down. He was the one person who knew of her intentions, and he could study Sir James's manner.

"Got a lady friend you could bring with you?" she asked when she rang him.

" 'Course I have. Though nobody as desirable as you, Marcia love."

"Keep your desires to yourself, Ben Brackett. This is business."

Sir James went through the ceremony with that generalized dignity which had characterised him in all his dealings with Marcia. He behaved to Ben Brackett and his lady friend as if they were somewhat dodgy witnesses who happened to be on his side in this particular trial. He spoke his words clearly, and almost seemed to mean them. Marcia told herself that in marrying her he was doing what he actually wanted to do.

She didn't risk any celebration after the ceremony. She paid off Ben Brackett, drove Sir James home to change and pack again, then set off for the Lake District.

This time she had rented a cottage, as being more private. It was just outside Grange—a two-bedroom stone cottage, very comfortable and rather expensive. She had taken it for six weeks in the name of Sir James and Lady Harrington. Once there and settled in, Sir James seemed, in his way, vaguely happy: he would potter off on his own down to the lakeside, or up the narrow abutting fields. He would raise his hat to villagers and tourists, and swap remarks about the weather.

He also signed, in a wavering hand, anything put in front of him.

Marcia wrote first to his sons, similar but not identical letters, telling them of his marriage and of his happiness with his dear wife. The letters also touched on business matters: "I wonder if you would object if I put the house on the market? After living up here I cannot imagine living in London again. Of course the money would come to you after my wife's death." At the foot of Marcia's typed script Sir James wrote at her direction: "Your loving Dad."

The letters brought two furious responses, as Marcia had known they would. Both were addressed to her, and both threatened legal action. Both said they knew their father was mentally incapable of deciding to marry again, and accused her of taking advantage of his senility.

"My dear boys," typed Marcia gleefully. "I am surprised that you apparently consider me senile, and wonder how you could have allowed me to live alone without proper care if you believed that to be the case."

Back and forth the letters flew. Gradually Marcia discerned a subtle difference between the two sets of letters. Those from the MP were slightly less shrill, slightly more accommodating. He fears a scandal, she thought. Nothing worse than a messy court case for an MP's reputation. It was to Sir Evelyn Harrington, MP for Finchingford, that she made her proposal.

SOUTHERN FOUND THE ESTATE agents quite obliging. Their dealings, they said, had been with Sir James himself. He had signed all the letters from Cumbria. They showed Southern the file, and he noted the shaky signature. Once they had spoken to Lady Harrington, they said: a low offer had been received, which demanded a quick decision. They had not recommended acceptance, since, though the property market was more dead than alive, a good house in Chelsea was bound to make a very handsome sum once it picked up. Lady Harrington had said that Sir James had a slight cold, but that he agreed with them that the offer was derisory and should be refused.

Southern's brow creased: wasn't Lady Harrington dead?

There was clearly enough of interest about Sir James Harrington to stay with him for a bit. Southern consulted the file at Scotland Yard and set up a meeting with the man's son at the House of Commons.

Sir Evelyn was a man in his late forties, tall and well-set-up. He had been knighted, Southern had discovered, in the last mass knighting of Tory backbenchers who had always voted at their party's call. The impression Sir Evelyn made was not of a stupid man, but of an unoriginal one.

"My father? Oh yes, he's alive. Living up in the Lake District somewhere."

"You're sure of this?"

"Sure as one can be when there's no contact." Southern left a silence, so the man was forced to elaborate. "Never was much. He's a remote bugger ... a remote sort of chap, my father. Stiff, always working, never had the sort of common touch you need with children. Too keen on being the world's greatest prosecuting counsel. ... He sent us away to school when we were seven."

Suddenly there was anger, pain, and real humanity in the voice.

"You resented that?"

"*Yes*. My brother had gone the year before and told me what that prep school was like. I pleaded with him. But he sent me just the same."

"Did your mother want you to go?"

"My mother did as she was told. Or else."

"That's not the present Lady Harrington?"

"Oh no. The present Lady Harrington is, I like to think, what my father deserves. ... We'd been warned he was failing by his daily. Dinner burst in the oven, forgetting to change his clothes, that kind of thing. We didn't take too much notice. The difficulties of getting a stiff-necked old ... man into residential care seemed insuperable. Then the next we heard he's married again and gone to live in the Lake District."

"Didn't you protest?"

"Of course we did. It was obvious she was after his money. And the letters he wrote, or she wrote for him, were all wrong. He would *never* have signed himself 'Dad,' let alone 'Your loving Dad.' But the kind of action that would have been necessary to annul the marriage can look ugly—for *both* sides of the case. So when she proposed an independent examination by a local doctor and psychiatrist, I persuaded my brother to agree."

"And what did they say?"

"Said he was vague, a little forgetful, but perfectly capable of understanding what he'd done when he married her, and apparently very happy. That was the end of the matter for us. The end of *him*."

MARCIA HAD DECIDED from the beginning that in the early months of her life as Lady Harrington she and Sir James would have to move round a lot. As long as he was merely an elderly gentleman pottering around the Lakes and exchanging meteorological banalities with the locals there was little to fear. But as they became used to him there was a danger that they would try to engage him in conversation of more substance. If that happened, his mental state might very quickly become apparent.

As negotiations with the two sons developed, Marcia began to see her way clear. Their six weeks at Grange were nearing an end, so she arranged to rent a cottage between Crummock Water and Cockermouth. When the sons agreed to an independent assessment of their father's mental condition and nominated a doctor and a psychiatrist from Keswick to undertake it, Marcia phoned them and arranged their visit for one of their first days in the new cottage. Then she booked Sir James and herself into Crummock Lodge for the relevant days. "I'll be busy getting the cottage ready," she told the manager. She felt distinctly pleased with herself. No danger of the independent team talking to locals.

"I don't see why we have to move," complained Sir James when she told him. "I like it here."

"Oh, we need to see a few places before we decide where we really want to settle," said Marcia soothingly. "I've booked us into Crummock Lodge, so I'll be able to get the new cottage looking nice before we move in."

"This is nice. I want to stay here."

There was no problem with money. On a drive to Cockermouth Marcia had arranged to have Sir James's bank account transferred there. He had signed the form without a qualm, together with one making the account a joint one. Everything in the London house was put into store, and the estate agents forwarded Sir James's mail, including his dividend cheques and his pension, regularly. There was no hurry about selling the house, but when it did finally go Marcia foresaw herself in clover. With Sir James, of course, and he was a bit of a bore. But very much worth putting up with.

As Marcia began discreetly packing for the move Sir James's agitation grew, his complaints became more insistent.

"I don't want to move. Why should we move, Molly? We're happy here. If we can't have this cottage we can buy a place. There are houses for sale."

To take his mind off it, Marcia borrowed their neighbour's rowing boat and took him for a little trip on the lake. It didn't take his mind off it. "This is lovely," he kept saying. "Derwent Water has always been my favourite. Why should we move on? I'm not moving, Molly."

He was beginning to get on her nerves. She had to tell herself that a few frazzled nerves were a small price to pay.

The night before they were due to move, the packing had to be done openly. Marcia brought all the suitcases into the living room and began methodically distributing to each one the belongings they had brought with them. Sir James had been dozing when she began, as he often did in the evening. She was halfway through her task when she realised he was awake and struggling to his feet.

"You haven't been listening to what I've been saying, have you, Molly? Well, have you, woman? I'm not moving!"

Marcia got to her feet.

"I know it's upsetting, dear—"

"It's not upsetting because we're staying here."

"Perhaps it will only be for a time. I've got it all organised, and you'll be quite comfy—"

"Don't treat me like a child, Molly!" Suddenly she realised with a shock that he had raised his arm. "Don't treat me like a child!" His hand came down with a feeble slap across her cheek. "Listen to what I say, woman!" Slap again. "I am not moving!" This time he punched her, and it hurt. "You'll do what I say, or it'll be the worse for you!" And he punched her again.

Marcia exploded with rage.

"You *bloody* old bully!" she screamed. "You brute! That's how you treated your wife, is it? Well, it's not how you're treating me!"

She brought up her stronger hands and gave him an almighty shove away from her even as he raised his fist for another punch. He lurched back, tried to regain his balance, then fell against the fireplace, hitting his head hard against the corner of the mantel-piece. Then he crumpled to the floor and lay still.

For a moment Marcia did nothing. Then she sat down and sobbed. She wasn't a sobbing woman, but she felt she had had a sudden revelation of what this man's—this old monster's—relations had been with his dead wife. She had never for a moment suspected it. She no longer felt pity for him, if she ever had. She felt contempt.

She dragged herself wearily to her feet. She'd put him to bed, and by morning he'd have forgotten. She bent down over him. Then, panic-stricken, she put her hand to his mouth, felt his chest, felt for his heart. It didn't take long to tell that he was dead. She sat down on the sofa and contemplated the wreck of her plans.

SOUTHERN AND POTTER FOUND the woman in the general-store-cum-newsagent's at Grange chatty and informative.

"Oh, Sir James. Yes, they were here for several weeks. Nice enough couple, though I think he'd married beneath him."

"Was he in full possession of his faculties, do you think?"

The woman hesitated.

"Well, you'd have thought so. Always said, 'Nice day,' or 'Hope the rain keeps off,' if he came in for a tin of tobacco or a bottle of wine.

But no more than that. Then one day I said, 'Shame about the Waleses, isn't it?'—you know, at the time of the split-up. He seemed bewildered, so I said, 'The Prince and Princess of Wales separating.' Even then it was obvious he didn't understand. It was embarrassing. I turned away and served somebody else. But there's others had the same experience."

AFTER SOME MINUTES Marcia found it intolerable to be in the same room as the body. Trying to look the other way, she dragged it through to the dining room. Even as she did so she realised that she had made a decision: she was not going to the police, and her plans were not at an end.

Because after all, she had her "Sir James" all lined up. In the operation planned for the next few days, the existence of the real one was anyway something of an embarrassment. Now that stumbling block had been removed. She rang Ben Blackett and told him there had been a slight change of plan, but it needn't affect his part in it. She rang Crummock Lodge and told them that Sir James had changed his mind and wanted to settle straight into the new cottage. While there was still some dim light, she went into the garden and out into the lonely land behind, collecting as many large stones as she could find. Then she slipped down and put them into the rowing boat she had borrowed from her neighbour the day before.

She had no illusions about the size—or more specifically the weight—of the problem she had in disposing of the body. She gave herself a stiff brandy, but no more than one. She found a razor blade and, shaking, removed the name from Sir James's suit. Then she finished her packing, so that everything was ready for departure. The farming people of the area were early to bed as a rule, but there were too many tourists staying there, she calculated, for it to be really safe before the early hours. At precisely one o'clock she began the long haul down to the shore. Sir James had been nearly six foot, so though his form was wasted, he was both heavy and difficult to lift. Marcia found, though, that carrying was easier than dragging, and quieter too. In three arduous stages she got him to the boat, then into it. The worst was over. She rowed out to the dark centre of the lake—the crescent moon was blessedly obscured by clouds—filled his pockets with stones, then carefully, gradually, eased the body out of the boat and into the water. She watched it sink, then made for the shore. Two large brandies later, she piled the cases into the car, locked up the cottage, and drove off in the direction of Cockermouth.

After the horror and difficulty of the night before, everything went beautifully. Marcia had barely settled into the new cottage when Ben Brackett arrived. He already had some of Sir James's characteristics off pat: his distant, condescending affability, for example. Marcia coached him in others, and they tried to marry them to qualities the real Sir James had no longer had: lucidity and purpose.

When the team of two arrived, the fake Sir James was working in the garden. "Got to get it in some sort of order," he explained, in his upper-class voice. "Haven't the strength I once had, though." When they were all inside, and over a splendid afternoon tea, he paid eloquent tribute to his new wife.

"She's made a new man of me," he explained. "I was letting myself go after Molly died. Marcia pulled me up in my tracks and brought me round. Oh, I know the boys are angry. I don't blame them. In fact, I blame myself. I was never a good father to them—too busy to be one. Got my priorities wrong. But it won't hurt them to wait a few years for the money."

The team was clearly impressed. They steered the talk round to politics, the international situation, changes in the law. "Sir James" kept his end up, all in that rather grand voice and distant manner. When the two men left, Marcia knew that her problems were over. She and Ben Brackett waited for the sound of the car leaving to go back to Keswick, then she poured very large whiskies for them. Over their third she told him what had happened to the real Sir James.

"You did superbly," said Ben Brackett when she had finished.

"It was bloody difficult."

"I bet it was. But it was worth it. Look how it went today. A piece of cake. We had them in the palms of our hands. We won, Marcia! Let's have another drink on that. We won!"

Even as she poured, Marcia registered disquiet at that "we."

SITTING IN HIS POKY OFFICE in Kendal, Southern and Potter surveyed the reports and other pieces of evidence they had set out on the desk.

"It's becoming quite clear," said Southern thoughtfully. "In Grange we have an old man who hardly seems to know who the Prince and Princess of Wales are. In the cottage near Cockermouth we have an old man who can talk confidently about politics and the law. In Grange we have a feeble man, and a corpse which is that of a soft liver. In the other cottage we have a man who gardens—perhaps to justify the fact that his hands are *not* those of a soft-living lawyer. At some time between taking her husband on the lake—was that a rehearsal, I wonder?—and the departure in the night, she killed him. She must already have had someone lined up to take his place for the visit of the medical team."

"And they're there still," said Potter, pointing to the letter from the estate agents in London. "That's where all communications still go."

"And that's where we're going to go," said Southern, getting up.

They had got good information on the cottage from the Cockermouth police. They left their car in the car park of a roadside pub, and took the lane through fields and down towards the northern shore of Crummock Water. They soon saw the cottage, overlooking the lake, lonely . . .

But the cottage was not as quiet as its surroundings. As they walked towards the place they heard shouting. A minute or two later they heard two thick voices arguing. When they could distinguish words, it was in a voice far from upper-crust:

"Will you get that drink, you cow? ... How can I when I can hardly stand? ... Get me that drink or it'll be the worse for you tomorrow.... You'd better remember who stands between you and a long jail sentence, Marcia. You'd do well to think about that *all the time*.... Now get me that scotch or you'll feel my fist!"

When Southern banged on the door there was silence. The woman who opened the door was haggard-looking, with bleary eyes and a bruise on the side of her face. In the room behind her, slumped back in a chair, they saw a man whose expensive clothes were in disarray, whose face was red and puffy, and who most resembled a music hall comic's version of a gentleman.

"Lady Harrington? I'm Superintendent Southern and this is Sergeant Potter. I wonder if we could come in? We have to talk to you."

He raised his ID towards her clouded eyes. She looked down at it slowly. When she looked up again, Southern could have sworn that the expression on her face was one of relief.

Wendy Hornsby has the tart tongue of the Southern California school of mystery writing. But she makes the form her own by adding quirky humor that gives her people depth and not a little modern sorrow. If you want to try her at longer length, start with MIDNIGHT BABY (1993), which takes some real risks with the form of the detective story. It is a wise and savvy novel and not at all what one would expect from a woman whose graduate degrees are in ancient and medieval history.

High Heels in the Headliner
WENDY HORNSBY

"Exquisite prose, charming story. A nice read." Thea tossed the stack of reviews her editor had sent into the file drawer and slammed it shut. The reviews were always the same, exquisite, charming, nice. What she wanted to hear was, "Tough, gritty, compelling, real. Hardest of the hard-boiled."

Thea had honestly tried to break away from writing bestselling fluff. What she wanted more than anything was to be taken seriously as a writer among writers. To do that, she knew she had to achieve tough, gritty, and real. The problem was, her whole damn life was exquisite, charming, nice.

Thea wrote from her own real-life experience, such as it was. One day, when she was about halfway through the first draft of *Lord Rimrock, L.A.P.D.*, a homeless man with one of those grubby cardboard signs— Will Work for Food—jumped out at her from his spot on the median strip up on Pacific Coast Highway. Nearly scared her to death. She used that raw emotion, the fear like a cold dagger in her gut, to write a wonderful scene for Officer Lord Rimrock. But her editor scrapped it because it was out of tone with the rest of the book. Over drawn, the editor said.

Fucking over drawn, Thea muttered and walked up to the corner shop for a bottle of wine to take the edge off her ennui.

In her mind, while she waited in line to pay, she rethought her detective. She chucked Lord Rimrock and replaced him with a Harvard man who preferred the action of big-city police work to law school. He was tall and muscular with a streak of gray at the temple. She was working on a name for him when she noticed that the man behind her in line had a detective's shield hanging on his belt.

She gawked. Here in the flesh was a real detective, her first sighting. He was also a major disappointment. His cheap suit needed pressing, he had a little paunch, and he was sweating. Lord Rimrock never sweated. Harvard men don't sweat.

"Excuse me," she said when he caught her staring.

"Don't worry about it." His world-weary scowl changed to a smarmy smile and she realized that he had mistaken her curiosity for a come on. She went for it.

"What division do you work from?" That much she knew to ask.

"Homicide. Major crimes." *He smiled out of the side of his mouth, not giving up much, not telling her to go away, either. She raised her beautiful eyes to meet his.* No. Beautiful was the wrong tone. Too charming.

"Must be interesting work," Thea said.

"Not very." *She knew he was flattered and played him like a . . .* She'd work out the simile later.

"What you do is interesting to me," she said. "I write mystery novels."

"Oh yeah?" He was intrigued.

"I suppose you're always bothered by writers looking for help with procedural details."

"I never met a writer," he said. "Unless you count asshole reporters."

She laughed, scratching the Harvard man from her thoughts, dumping the gray streak at the temple. This detective had almost no hair at all.

Thea paid for her bottle of Chardonnay. The detective put his six-pack on the counter, brushing her hand in passing. Before she could decide on an exit line, he said, "Have you ever been on a ride-along? You know, go out with the police and observe."

"I never have," she said. "It would be helpful. How does one arrange a ride-along?"

"I don't know anymore." *The gravel in his voice told her he'd seen too much of life.* "Used to do it all the time. Damned liability shit now, though. Department has really pulled back. Too bad. I think what most taxpayers need is a dose of reality. If they saw what we deal with all day, they'd get off our backs."

Thea did actually raise her beautiful eyes to him. "I think the average person is fascinated by what you do. That's why they read mysteries. That's why I write them. I would love to sit down with you some time, talk about your experiences."

"Oh yeah?" He responded by pulling in his paunch. "I just finished up at a crime scene in the neighborhood. I'm on my way home. Maybe you'd like to go for a drink."

"Indeed, I would." Thea gripped the neck of the wine bottle, hesitating before she spoke. "Tell you what. If you take me by the crime scene and show me around, we can go to my place after, have some wine and discuss the details."

Bostitch was his name. He paid for his beer and took her out to his city car, awkward in his eagerness to get on with things.

The crime scene was a good one, an old lady stabbed in her bedroom. Bostitch walked Thea right into the apartment past the forensics people who were still sifting for evidence. He explained how the blood spatter patterns on the walls were like a map of the stabbing, showed her a long arterial spray. *On the carpet where the body was found, she could trace the contours of the woman's head and outstretched arms. Like a snow angel made in blood.*

The victim's family arrived. They had come to look through the house to determine what, if anything, was missing, but all they could do was stand around, numbed by grief. Numbed? Was that it?

Thea walked up to the daughter and said, "How do you feel?"

"Oh, it's awful," the woman sobbed. "Mom was the sweetest woman on earth. Who would do this to her?"

Thea patted the daughter's back, her question still unanswered. How did she feel? Scorched, hollow, riven, shredded, iced in the gut? What?

"Seen enough?" Bostitch asked, taking Thea's arm.

She hadn't seen enough, but she smiled compliantly up into his face. She didn't want him to think she was a ghoul. Or a wimp. To her surprise, she was not bothered by the gore or the smell or any of it. She was the totally objective observer, seeing everything through the eyes of her fictional detective character.

Bostitch showed her the homicide kit he kept in the trunk of his car, mostly forms, rubber gloves, plastic bags. She was more impressed by the name than the contents, but she took a copy of everything for future reference to make him happy.

By the time Bostitch drove her back to her house, Thea's detective had evolved. He was the son of alcoholics, grew up in Wilmington in the shadow of the oil refineries. He would have an ethnic name similar to Bostitch. The sort of man who wouldn't know where Harvard was.

In her exquisite living room, they drank the thirty-dollar Chardonnay. Bostitch told stories, Thea listened. All the time she was smiling or laughing or pretending shock, she was making mental notes. *He sat with his arm draped on the back of the couch, the front of his jacket open, an invitation to come closer. He slugged down the fine cold wine like soda pop. When it was gone, he reached for the warm six-pack he had brought in with him and flipped one open.*

By that point, Bostitch was telling war stories about the old days when he was in uniform. The good old days. He had worked morning watch, the shift from midnight to seven. He liked being on patrol in the middle of the night because everything that went down at oh-dark-thirty had an edge. After work he and his partners would hit the early opening bars. They would get blasted and take women down to a cul-de-sac under the freeway and screw off the booze before they went home. Not beer, he told her. Hard stuff.

"Your girlfriend would meet you?" Thea asked.

"Girlfriend? Shit no. I'd never take a girlfriend down there. There are certain women who just wet themselves for a cop in uniform. We'd go, they'd show."

"I can't imagine," Thea said, wide-eyed, her worldly mien slipping. She couldn't imagine it. She had never had casual sex with anyone. Well, just once actually, with an English professor her freshman year. It had been pretty dull stuff and not worth counting.

"What sort of girls were they?" she asked him.

"All kinds. There was one—she was big, I mean big—we'd go pick her up on the way. She'd say, 'I won't do more than ten of you, and I won't take it in the rear.' She was a secretary or something."

"You made that up," Thea said.

"Swear to God," he said.

"I won't believe you unless you show me," Thea said. She knew where in the book she would use this gem, her raggedy old detective joining the young cowboys in uniform for one last blow out with young women. No. He'd have a young female partner and take her there to shock her. A rite of passage for a rookie female detective.

The problem was, Thea still couldn't visualize it, and she had to get it just right. "Take me to this place."

She knew that Bostitch completely misunderstood that she was only interested for research purposes. Explaining this might not have gotten him up off the couch so fast. They stopped for another bottle on the way—a pint of scotch.

It was just dusk when Bostitch pulled up onto the hard-packed dirt of a vacant lot at the end of the cul-de-sac and parked. A small encampment of homeless people scurried away under the freeway when they recognized the city-issue car.

The cul-de-sac was at the end of a street to nowhere, a despoiled landscape of discarded furniture, cars, and humanity. Even weeds couldn't thrive. She thought humanity wouldn't get past the editor—over drawn—but that was the idea. She would find the right word later.

Bostitch skewed around in his seat to face her.

"We used to have bonfires here," he said. "Until the city got froggy about it. Screwed up traffic on the freeway. All the smoke."

"Spoiled your fun?" she said.

"It would take more than that." He smiled out the window. "One night, my partner talked me into coming out here before the shift was over. It wasn't even daylight yet. Some babe promised to meet him. I sat inside here and wrote reports while they did it on the hood. God, I'll never forget it. I'm working away in my seat with this naked white ass pumping against the windshield in front of my face—bump, bump, bump. Funny as hell. Bet that messed up freeway traffic."

Thea laughed, not at his story, but at her own prose version of it.

"You ever get naked on the hood of the car?" she asked. She'd had enough booze to ask it easily. For research.

"I like it inside better," he said.

"In the car?" she asked. She moved closer, *leaning near enough to smell the beer on his breath. During his twenty-five years with the police, he must have had half the women in the city. She wanted to know what they had taught him. What he might teach her.*

She lapped her tongue lightly along the inner curve of his lips. Thea said, with a throaty chuckle, "I won't do more than ten of you. And I won't take it in the rear."

When he took her in his arms he wasn't as rough as she had hoped he would be. She set the pace by the eager, almost violent way she tore loose his tie, ripped open his shirt. His five-o'clock shadow sanded a layer of skin off her chin.

They ended up in the back seat, their clothes as wrinkled and shredded as the crime scene report under them. At the moment of her ecstasy the heel of Thea's shoe thrust up through the velour headliner. She looked at the long tear. *The sound of the rip was like cymbals crashing at the peak of a symphony, except the only music was the rhythmic grunting and groaning from the tangle of bodies in the back seat. She jammed her foot through the hole, bracing it against the hard metal roof of the car to get some leverage to meet his thrusting, giving him a more solid base to bang against.*

Bostitch seemed to stop breathing altogether. His face grew a dangerous red and drew up into an agonized sort of grimace that stretched every sinew in his neck. Thea was beginning to worry that she might have killed him when he finally exhaled.

"Oh Jesus," he moaned. "Oh sweet, sweet Jesus."

She untangled her foot from the torn headliner and wrapped her bare legs around him, trapping him inside her until the pulsing ceased. Maybe not, she thought. Pulsing, throbbing were definitely overused.

After the afterglow, what would she feel? Not shame or anything akin to it. She smiled with pride in her prowess. She had whipped his ass and left him gasping. Thea buried her face against his chest and bit his small, hard nipple.

"You're amazing," he said, still breathing hard.

She said nothing. That moment was definitely not the time to explain that it was her female detective, Ricky, or maybe Marty Tenwolde, who was amazing. Thea herself was far too inhibited to have initiated the wild sex that had left their automobile nest in serious need of repair.

When they had pulled their clothes back together, he said, "Now what?"

"Skid Row," she said. "I've always been afraid to go down there, but I need to see it for the book I'm working on."

"Good reason to be afraid." *The cop spoke with a different voice than the lover, a deep, weary growl that* something or other. "You don't really want to go down there."

"I do, though. With you. You're armed. You're the law. We'll be safe."

She batted her big, beautiful eyes again. Flattery and some purring were enough to sway him. He drove her downtown to Skid Row.

Thea had never seen anything as squalid and depraved. Toothless, stoned hookers running down the middle of the street. Men dry heaving in the gutter. *The smell alone made him wish she hadn't come along. He was embarrassed that she saw the old wino defecate openly on the sidewalk. But she only smiled that wry smile that always made the front of his slacks feel tight.*

There was a six- or seven-person brawl in progress on one corner. Thea loved it when Bostitch merely honked his horn to make them scatter like so many cockroaches.

"Seen enough?" he asked.

"Yes. Thank you."

Bostitch held her hand all the way back to her house.

"Will you come in?" she asked him.

"I'll come in. But don't expect much more out of my sorry old carcass. I haven't been that fired up since . . ."

"I thought for a minute you had died," she said. "I didn't know where to send the body."

"Felt like I was on my way to heaven." He slid a business card with a gold detective's shield from behind his visor and handed it to her. "You ever need anything, page me through the office."

So, he had a wife. A lot of men do. Thea hadn't considered a wife in the equation. She liked it—nice characterization. Bostitch called home from the phone on Thea's desk and told the wife he'd be out late on a case. Maybe all night.

"No wonder you fool around," Thea said when he turned his attention back to her. "It's too easy. Does your wife believe you?"

He shrugged. "She doesn't much bother anymore believing or not believing."

"Good line," Thea said. More than anything, she wanted to turn on her computer and get some of what she had learned on disk before she forgot anything. She had a whole new vocabulary: boot the door meant to kick it down, elwopp was life without possibility of parole, fifty-one-fifty was a mental incompetent. So many things to catalog.

"Where's your favorite place to make love?" she asked him.

"In a bed."

That's where they did it next. At least, that's where they began. Bostitch was stunned, pleased, by the performance Thea coaxed from him. He gave Thea a whole chapter.

All the next week she was his shadow. She stood beside him during the autopsy of the stabbing victim, professional and detached because female detective Marty Tenwolde would be. The top of the old lady's skull made a pop like a champagne cork when the coroner sawed it off, but she wasn't even startled. She was as tough and gritty as any man on the force. She was tender, too. After a long day of detecting, she took the old guy home and screwed him until he begged for mercy. Detective Tenwolde felt . . .

That feeling stuff was the hard part. Tenwolde would feel attached to her old married partner. Be intrigued by him. She couldn't help mothering him a bit, but she could by no stretch describe her feelings as maternal. Love was going too far.

Thea watched Bostitch testify in court one day. A murder case, but not a particularly interesting one. It was a garden-variety family shootout, drunk husband takes off after estranged wife and her boyfriend. Thea added to her new vocabulary, learning that dead bang meant a case with an almost guaranteed conviction.

Bostitch looked sharper than usual and Thea was impressed by his professionalism. Of course, he winked at her when he thought the jury wasn't looking, checked for her reaction whenever he scored a point against the defense attorney. She always smiled back at him, but she was really more interested in the defendant, a pathetic little man who professed profound grief when he took the stand in his defense. He cried. *Without his wife, he was only a shell occupying space in this universe. His wife had defined his existence, made him complete. Killing her had only been a crude way to kill himself.* If he had any style, he would beg for the death sentence and let the state finish the job for him. Thea wondered what it felt like to lose a loved one in such a violent fashion.

Detective Tenwolde cradled her partner's bleeding head in her lap, knowing he was dying. She pressed her face close to his ear and whispered, "My only regret is I'll never be able to fuck you again, big guy. I love your ragged old ass." Needed something, but it was a good farewell line. Tough, gritty, yet tender.

Out in the corridor after court, the deputy district attorney complimented Bostitch's testimony. Thea, holding his hand, felt proud. No, she thought, she felt lustful. *If he had asked her to, for his reward in getting the kid convicted, she would gladly have blown Bostitch right there on the escalator.* Maybe she did love him. Something to think about.

After court, Thea talked Bostitch into taking her to a Hungarian restaurant he had told her about. He had had a run-in with a lunatic there a year or so earlier. Shot the man dead. Thea wanted to see where.

"There's nothing to see," he said as he pulled into the hillside parking lot. "But the food's okay. Mostly goulash. You know, like stew. We might as well eat."

They walked inside with their arms around each other. The owner knew Bostitch and showed them to a quiet booth in a far-back corner. It was very dark.

"I haven't seen Laszlo's brother for four or five months," the owner said, setting big plates of steaming goulash in front of them. He had a slight accent. "He was plenty mad at you, Bostitch, I tell you. Everybody knows Laszlo was a crazy man, always carrying those guns around. What could you do but shoot him? He shot first. I think maybe his brother is a little nuts, too."

"Show me where he died," Thea said, her lips against Bostitch's jug-like ear. He turned his face to her and kissed her.

"Let's eat and get out of here," he said. "We shouldn't have come."

There was a sudden commotion at the door and a big, fiery-eyed man burst in. The first thing Thea noticed was the shotgun he held at his side. The owner rushed up to him, distracted his attention away from Thea's side of the restaurant.

"Shh, Thea." Bostitch, keeping his eyes on the man with the shotgun, pulled his automatic from his belt holster. "That's Laszlo's brother. Someone must have called him, told him I was here. We're going to slip out the back way while they have him distracted."

"But he has a gun. He'll shoot someone."

"No he won't. He's looking for me. Once I'm out of here, they'll calm him down. Let me get out the door, then you follow me. Whatever you do, don't get close to me, and for chrissake stay quiet. Don't attract his attention." Bostitch slipped out of the booth.

She felt *alive. Adrenaline wakened every primitive instinct for survival. Every instinct to protect her man. If the asshole with the gun made so much as a move toward Bostitch, Tenwolde would grind him into dogmeat. Bostitch was only one step from safety when Tenwolde saw the gunman turn and spot him.*

Dogmeat was good, Thea thought. The rest she was still unclear about. That's when she stood up and screamed, "Don't shoot him. I love him."

Bostitch would have made it out the door, but Thea's outburst caused him to look back. That instant's pause was just long enough for the befuddled gunman to find Bostitch in his sights and fire a double-aught load into his abdomen. Bostitch managed to fire off a round of his own. The gunman was dead before he fell.

Thea ran to Bostitch and caught him as he slid to the floor, leaving a wide red smear on the wall.

His head was heavy in her arms.

"Why?" he sighed. His eyes went dull.

Tenwolde watched the light fade from her partner's eyes, felt his last breath escape from his shattered chest. She couldn't let him see her cry; he'd tease her forever. That's when she lost it. Bostitch had used up his forever.

"It's not fair, big guy," she said, smoothing his sparse hair. She felt a hole open in her chest as big as the gaping wound through his. Without him, she was incomplete. "You promised me one more academy-award fuck. You're not going back on your promise, are you?"

He was gone. Still, she held on to him, her cheek against his, his blood on her lips. "I never told you, Bostitch. I love your raggedy old ass."

Carole Nelson Douglas has distinguished herself as a fantasy writer, a science fiction writer, and a romance writer (if you think intelligent romances can't be written, try hers). Since 1990, however, Carole has concentrated on detective fiction, with one series about diva-detective Irene Adler ("the only woman to outwit Sherlock Holmes") and a second about Las Vegas publicist Temple Barr, and her big black tomcat sleuth, Midnight Louie, whose acquaintance you are about to make. Louie recently made the USA Today bestseller list and is about to become a staple of the contemporary mystery scene.

Coyote Peyote
CAROLE NELSON DOUGLAS

A lot of folks don't realize that Las Vegas is the world's biggest Cubic Zirconia set in a vast bezel of sand and sagebrush. Glitz in the Gobi, so to speak.

Sure, most everybody knows that the old town twinkles, but that is all they see, the high-wattage Las Vegas Strip and Glitter Gulch downtown. Millions of annual visitors fly in and out of McCarran Airport on the big silver thunderbirds, commercial or chartered jets, like migratory flocks of junketing gooney birds equipped with cameras and cash.

They land at McCarran Airport, now as glittering a monument to the Vegas mystique as any Strip hotel, with shining rows of slot machines chiming in its metal-mirrored vastness.

Most stick to Las Vegas's advertised attractions and distractions: they soak up sun, stage shows, shady doings of a sexual nature, and the comparatively good clean fun in the casinos that pave the place. To them, Las Vegas is the holodeck of the good starship *Enterprise* in the twentieth century. You go there; it is like no place on earth; you leave and you're right back where you were, maybe poorer but at least dazzled for your dough.

Nobody thinks of Las Vegas as a huge, artificial oasis stuck smack wattle-and-daub in the middle of the Wild West wilderness like a diamond in the navel of a desert dancing girl. Nobody sees its gaudy glory as squatting on the onetime ghost-dancing grounds of the southern Paiute Indians. Hardly anyone ever harks back to the area's hairy mining-boom days, which are only evoked now by hokey casino names like The Golden Nugget.

Nobody ever figures that the sea of desert all around the pleasure island of Las Vegas is good for anything but ignoring.

I must admit that I agree. I know Las Vegas from the bottom up, and some in this urban jukebox know me: Midnight Louie, dude-about-town and undercover expert. The only sand I like to feel between my toes is in a litter box, and I am not too fond of artificial indoor facilities at that. I prefer open air and good, clean dirt.

I prefer other amenities, such as the gilded carp that school in the decorative pond behind the Crystal Phoenix Hotel and Casino, the classiest hostelry on the Strip, hence carp so pricey that they are called koi. I call them dinner.

For a time I was unofficial house detective at the Crystal Phoenix, and the carp pond was my prime-time hangout. It is always handy to locate an office near a good diner. Location, location, location, say the real estate agents, and I am always open to an apt suggestion from an expert.

I hang out my shingle near the calla lilies that border the carp pond. I do not literally hang out a shingle, you understand. The word simply gets around where Midnight Louie is to be found, and the word on the street is clear on two subjects. One is that Midnight Louie will not look with favor upon any individual messing with his friends at the Crystal Phoenix, whether two- or four-footed. The other is that Midnight Louie is not averse to handling problems of a delicate nature now and again, provided payment is prompt and sufficient.

I am not lightweight, topping twenty pounds soaking wet, and I didn't weigh onto the scales just yesterday, either. Yet my hair is still a glossy raven black, my tourmaline-green eyes can see 20/20, and my ears know when to perk up and when to lie back and broadcast a warning. (Some claim my kind have no color sense, but they have never asked us straight out.) I keep my coat in impeccable sheen and my hidden shivs as sharp as the crease in Macho Mario Fontana's bodyguard's pants.

Despite my awesome physical presence, I am a modest dude who gets along well with everyone—especially if every one of them is female—except for those of the canine persuasion.

This is a family failing. Something about the canine personality invariably raises the hair on the back of our necks, not to mention our spines, and makes our second-most-valuable members stand up and salute.

So you can understand how I feel one day when I am drowsing in my office, due both to a lack of cases and to a surfeit of something fishy for lunch, and I spot a suspicious shadow on the nearest sun-rinsed wall.

The hour is past 6:00 P.M., when Las Vegas hotel pools close faster than a shark's mouth, the better to hustle tourists into the casinos to gamble the night and their grubstakes away. Nobody much of any species is around. Even the carp are keeping low, for reasons that may have something to do with not-so-little me.

So my eyes are slit to half-mast, the sinking sun is sifting through the calla lilies, and life is not too tacky . . . and then, there it is, that unwelcome shadow.

Who could mistake the long, sharp snout, ajar enough to flaunt a nasty serrated edge of fangs, or the huge, long, sharp ears? No doubt about it, this angular silhouette has the avid, hungry outlines of that jackal-headed Egyptian god of the dead, Anubis. (I know something about Egyptian gods, seeing as how a forebear was one of them: Bast. Or Bastet, to be formal. You may have heard of this dude. Or dudette. And you may call me Louie anyway; I do not ride on family connections.)

Right then and there Midnight Louie has a bad-hair day, let me tell you, as I make like a croquet hoop and rise to my feet and the occasion. From the size of the shadow, this is not the largest canine I have ever seen, but it is one serious customer, and it does not take a house detective to figure that out.

"At ease!" the shadow jaws bark out, looking even more lethal. "I am just here on business."

I know better than to relax when I am told to, but I am not one to turn tail and run, either. So I wait.

"You this Midnight Louie?" my sun-shy visitor demands in the same sharp yet gruff voice.

"Who wishes to know?"

"Never mind."

So much for the direct route. I pretend to settle back onto my haunches, but my restless shivs slide silently in and out of my mitts. Unlike the average mutt, I know how to keep quiet.

Above me, a lazy bee buzzes the big yellow calla lily blossoms. I hiccup.

"You do not look like much," my rude visitor says after a bit.

"The opinion may be mutual," I growl back. "Step into the open and we will see."

He does, and I am sorry I asked.

There is no fooling myself. I eye narrow legs with long, curved nails like a mandarin's. I take in eyes as yellow and hard as a bladder stone. The head is even more predatory than I suspected. The body is lean, but hard. The terminal member is as scrawny as a foot-long hot dog and carried low, like a whip.

This dude is a dog, all right, but just barely—no mere domesticated dog but a dingo from the desert. I begin to appreciate how Little Red Riding Hood felt, and I do not even have a grandmother (that I know of) to worry about.

"What can I do for you?" I ask, hoping that the answer is not "Lunch." I do not do lunch with literal predators.

The dude sidles into the shade alongside me. My sniffer almost over-doses on the odor; this bozo has not taken a bath in at least a week, perhaps another reason I dislike the canine type.

He sits beside me under the calla leaves, his yellow eyes searching the vicinity for any sign of life.

"I need a favor," he says.

Well, knock me over with a wolverine. I am all too aware that the dude I am dealing with is normally a breed apart. He and his kind operate on the fringes of civilized Las Vegas, out in the lawless open desert. Some call them cowardly; others, clever. Certainly they are hated, and hunted. Many are killed. All kill. Among other things.

"I do not do favors for those who practice certain unnatural acts."

"Such as?"

"I hear your kin will eat . . . bugs."

"So will humans," the dude notes calmly.

"That is not all. I also hear that your kind will dine on"—I swallow and try not to let my whiskers quiver—"the dead." Why else was Anubis head jackal of the Underground in ancient Egypt? My visitor looks like a lineal descendant.

"We will, when there is nothing living to eat," he concedes with chilling calm. "In the city, such as we are called refuse managers."

I say nothing, unconvinced.

When sitting, this dude looks exactly like an Egyptian statue, and he gazes idly on the lush, landscaped surroundings, so different from his usual arid turf. I realize that it has taken some nerve and a good deal of courage for this popular pariah to venture into the very heart of Vegas. Just to see me. Well, Midnight Louie is a teensy bit flattered, come to think of it.

"When did you last," he asks, "partake of a bit of mislaid Big-o-Burger from down the street?"

"That is different," I begin.

"Dead meat," he intones relentlessly. "Someone else killed it, and you ate it." The yellow eyes slide my way. I detect a malicious twinkle. "What about the contents of the cans so feverishly hawked at your kind?"

I am not misled; this dude is about as twinkly as the mother-of-pearl handle on a derringer.

"I do my own fishing." I nod at the silent pond. "So what is your problem?"

"Murder." His answer sends a petite shudder through my considerable frame. I was hoping for something minor, like road-runner attack.

"Who is the victim?"

"Victims."

"How many?"

"Six, so far."

"And the method?"

"Always the same."

"You are talking serial killer here, pal."

"Oh, are we friends?" Another shrewd golden glint. This dude has Bette Davis eyes, when she played the homicidal Baby Jane.

"Business associates," I said firmly. No dude in his right mind would turn down this character. "Who are the victims?"

"My brothers and sisters."

"Oh."

I do not know how to put it that one—or six—dead coyotes are hardly considered murder victims by the majority of the human population, and, face it, humans run this planet.

For now I know this dude, by type if not name: Don Coyote himself, one of an accursed species, with bounty hunters everywhere ready to clip their ears and tails for a few bucks or just the principle of the thing. It does not take a genius to figure out that any suspects for the so-called crime of killing coyotes are legion.

"If you are so smart," I note diplomatically, "you know that it would be easier to find those who *did* kill coyotes than otherwise."

"This case is different," he says sharply. "We are used to the hunters. We have outwitted them more often than not. We survive, if not thrive, and we spread, even while our cousin Gray Wolf clan has been driven to near extinction. We have evaded steel trap and strychnine poison. We are legendary for defying odds. What kills us now is new and insidious. Not just our green young succumb, but those who should know better. This is not the eternal war we wage with both prey and hunter; this is what I said ... murder."

"That is no surprise, either. You are not exactly Mr. Popularity around here."

His lips peel back from spectacular sharp white teeth, much improved, no doubt, by grinding such roughage as beetle shells and bones. "That is why I seek an emissary."

"Why not try a police dog?"

"Frankly, your kind is more successful at undercover work. Even a domesticated dog"—his tone is more than condescending, it is majestically indifferent; on this subject we agree—"is handicapped. He is assumed to belong to some human, which attracts notice and sometimes misguided attempts at rescue. Your breed, on the other hand, although equally commonplace in human haunts, is known to walk alone by sly and secret ways and is more often ignored."

I shrug and adjust one of my sharp-looking black leather gloves. "Say I was to accept this commission of yours. What would I get?"

His long red tongue lolls out. I cannot tell if he is grinning or scanning the ground for a conga line of ants. Antipasto in his book, so to speak.

"I am head honcho around here," the coyote ruminates with a certain reluctance, like he is giving away the combination to the family safe. "I keep caches of hidden treasure here and there. If you successfully find— or simply stop—the coyote-killer, I will tell you the whereabouts of one. That would be your payoff."

"How much is it worth?" I demand.

The yellow eyes look right through me. "Beyond price."

"How do I know that?"

"I can only say that humans highly prize these objects."

Hmm. Coyotes are scavengers of the desert. I speculate on the array of inedible goodies they might run across in the wide Mojave, but silver comes first to mind, perhaps because Jersey Joe Jackson, the high roller who helped build and bilk Vegas in the forties, also hid huge caches of stolen silver dollars both in town and out on the sandy lonesome.

Then there are plain old silver nuggets left over from mining days. I am not fussy. Or ... maybe jewels. Stolen jewels. I do not doubt for a minute that this wily old dude knows secrets even the wind-singing sands do not whisper about.

I stand and stretch nonchalantly. "Where do I begin?" For a moment I am eye-to-eye with those ancient ocher orbs.

Then the dude also rises, and vanishes into the dark at the back of the calla lilies. "Follow me to the scene of the crimes."

IT IS NIGHT by the time we get there. I have forgotten that dudes of this type are always hot to trot and can keep it up for miles. After I showed him a quick exit from the city, we were off through the boonies.

Miles of surly sagebrush have passed under my tender tootsie pads when we finally stop for good. I huff and puff and could not blow down a mouse house at the moment, but I was loath to let this dancing dog outpace me.

Although I pride myself on my night vision, all I can spy are a skyful of stars the wizards of the Strip might do well to emulate for sparse good taste, towering Joshua trees with their thick limbs frozen into traffic-cop positions, and a lot of low scrub, much of it barbed like wire. Oh, yes, and the full moon floating overhead like a bowl of warm milk seen from a kitchen countertop, and, occasionally, the moonsheen in the coyote's sun-yellow eyes as he gives me mocking glances.

"I forget," he says, "that the city-bred are easily tired."

"Not in the slightest," I pant, hissing between my teeth. "But how can I study the crime scene in the dark?"

"I thought your breed could see despite the night."

"Not enough for a thorough investigation. Where are we anyway?"

"At an enclave of humans away from the city. My unfortunate brothers and sisters ventured near to snag the errant morsel and were cut down one by one."

"Listen, my kind are not noted for longevity, either, so I dig the problem. Still, what can I do about it?"

"Perhaps you can interview the survivors."

With that he steps back, braces his long legs, and lifts his head until his snout points at the moon. An unearthly howl punctuated by a series of yips emerges from between those awesome teeth.

So it is that in a few moments I am making house calls on a series of coyote families. While my guide has not stuck around for the painstaking interviews, soon an unsavory picture is emerging: the victims were indeed primo survivors, too savvy to be silently slain in the current manner.

I speak to Sings-with-Soul, the winsome widow of Yellow Foot-Feathers, the first to be found dead.

I no more advocate cross-species hanky-panky than I do bug-biting, but I must admit that Sings-with-Soul has particularly luminous amber eyes and a dainty turn of foreleg, from what I can tell in the dark.

After several interviews, I remain in the dark myself. Unfortunately, although they sometimes run in impressive packs, coyotes mostly hunt alone. The stories are depressingly similar.

Yellow Foot-Feathers did not return to the den after a night's prowl. When Sings-with-Soul left her kits with a friend to go searching, she followed his scent to find him dead, unmarked by any weapon, beside a stunted Joshua tree.

Sand Stalker was out rounding up a delicacy or two for his mate, Moon-finder, and their two helpless kits. In the morning, his body was found a three-minute trot toward the setting sun from Yellow Foot-Feathers'.

Windswift, a two-year-old female, died a four-minute trot away, two days later. The same distance farther on lay Weatherworn, an elder of the tribe and by far its wiliest member.

"We are used to the high death toll of our kind," Sings-with-Soul tells me with mournful anger, "but these deaths are systematic beyond the bounty hunters' traps and poison, or the so-called sportsmen with guns, or even the angry ranchers who accuse us of raiding their livestock."

I nod. It is not a pretty picture, and I am used to the statistics of my own kind who share the supposed shelter of civilization. Four out of five cuddly kittens born die within a year, often within the environs of a death compound. Still, there is something demonic about these serial slayings. Even in the dark I sense a pattern.

By the wee hours I have settled beside a prickly poppy, counting on my choice of plant companion to keep away such night-roving characters as skunks, large furry spiders who are older than Whistler's mother, lizards, and snakes, although I would not mind meeting a passing mouse or two, for it has been some time since my last snack.

The coyotes have vanished back into the brush. From time to time they break into heartbroken howls that some might take for the usual coyote chorus but which I know express rage and sorrow at their helplessness to stop the slaughter.

I wait for daylight, eager to begin investigating for real. My curiosity has been roused, despite myself. As long as I am all the way out here in this desolate wilderness, I might as well earn my tempting coyote cache and maybe keep the young Foot-Feathers kits from the same fate as their father.

DESPITE THE DESERT CHILL and the forbidding terrain, I manage to doze off. I awake to feel the sun pouring down on me like hot melted butter, softening my night-stiff bones.

I heard an odd tapping sound, as of someone gently rapping, rapping on a door to rouse me. Confused, I force my eyelids open, preparing for an onslaught of bright light.

In the sudden slit of my pupils I see a sight to curl the hair on a bronze cat—a whole city, a settlement, of buildings against the bright-blue morning sky. I sniff sawdust and stucco. I see pale pine skeletons rising into the sky.

I turn so fast I snag my rear member on a prickly poppy. Behind me extends the endless desert I imagined in the dark of last night when I interviewed the coyote crew. Did not their lost ones fall near where we stood, where I stand now?

I turn back to the hub of activity. A banshee saw whines, while men with bandannas around their foreheads and sleeveless T-shirts or bare muscled chests as tan as a Doberman move their blue-jeaned legs hither and yon, climbing, pounding, clamoring.

Stunned, I stick to basics. *A three-minute trot toward the setting sun.* I turn westward and start trotting, allowing for a difference in speed and stride. Indeed, I am soon sniffing a patch of sweet-smelling desert alyssum on which a stronger, sweeter, sicklier scent has settled recently.

The body is gone, no doubt removed by human pallbearers, but the land remembers. Sand Stalker's last stand.

I move on, tracing the path of death and finding the lingering scent where I expect. At no time does my route veer away from the huge clot of buildings under construction. The dead coyotes begin to form a ritual circle around the project, like guardian spirits slaughtered to protect the site.

The head coyote is right. Something stinks in this sequence of events, and it is not merely death.

I dust off my topcoat, quell my protesting empty stomach, and stalk casually toward the humans and their works.

Soon I am treading dusty asphalt, walking on roads, however primitive. Beyond the construction site I discover curving vistas of completed edifices—sprawling two-story buildings big enough to be strip shopping centers, sitting amid fresh-sodded grass. Sprinkler systems spray droplets on the turf like a holy-water blessing. After a while I realize that these erections are each single-family homes.

In an hour's stroll I have mastered the place. I am in the midst of Henderson, Nevada, touring its vaunted housing boom. I have heard that this bedroom community just a hop, skip, and commute southeast of Las Vegas is jumping, but I've never had occasion to see for myself before.

No wonder the coyotes are goners. They were trespassing on some high-end new real estate of the first order. I sit under one of the paired yucca trees that mark the development's entrance to read the billboard, which features colors like trendy turquoise, orange, and lavender, bordered by a chorus line of alternating jalapeño peppers and howling coyotes.

PEYOTE SKIES: A JIMMY RAY RUGGLES PLANNED COMMUNITY, announces angular lettering meant to resemble the zigzags on a Native American blanket. Jimmy Ray's smiling photo discreetly anchors one corner of the sign. Although it is a well-kept secret that I can read, I am having no trouble in looking illiterate as I squint to decipher the tortured script. This is real detective work!

After much study, I know that Peyote Skies is an ecologically engineered environment that sets up no artificial barriers like fences between nature and the community. The words "Sante Fe-like serenity," "untrammeled nature," and "all the amenities" are invoked. No wonder. I have heard that refugees from the Quaker State of California are flocking to places north, south, and west of their unhappy home. Apparently, Henderson is providing a haven for escaping excesses.

I stroll the streets of Peyote Skies unquestioned, even unremarked, just as the coyote predicted. Perhaps my dramatic dark good looks seem right at home in the plethora of pastel colors painting every visible surface. Despite my empty stomach, I am soon ready to puke at the amount of dusty orange, lavender, and Peyote Skies turquoise I am forced to digest.

Earlier I remarked that I was not born yesterday. I am also pretty streetwise, so I know that "peyote" names a blue-green cactus whose flowers produce beads that dry into little buttons of mescal. Bite into one of these babies, and you are soon seeing visions as hallucinatory as the after-dinner-mint-colored development before me.

Mescaline's mind-tripping properties were, and are, used for Native

American religious rites but are otherwise strictly illegal. I do not know if the Paiutes around here were, or are, into mescaline, but I do know that less native Americans definitely are.

As for myself, I take a little nip now and again but keep off the hard stuff in any form. Obviously, the designer of this mish-mash was not so restrained.

The completed houses are occupied but mostly deserted, looking like pages from decorating magazines. Kids are at school, husbands and wives are at work or at play.

I find it macabre that while dead coyotes litter the back fringes of this theme-park development, the front doors and mailboxes bear the colorful image of the howling coyote made ad nauseam familiar of late on jewelry, coffee mugs and fabrics.

Perhaps the surrounding color scheme accounts for the en masse howling, but, like the desert itself, these coyotes are silent, despite their posture. I do not blame them for complaining; my own kind's image has been appropriated for a panoply of merchandise we would not scrape kitty litter over. Humans are especially sentimental about creatures they kill.

Because of the lack of "artificial barriers," I can stroll around these palatial joints unimpeded, although I spot a ton of security service signs and even more discreet warning labels on windows.

The backyards are as manicured as the front, then end abruptly where the desert begins. I move to the verge between green and greige, my sand-blasted pads relishing the cushy emerald carpet of grass. Then a door cracks behind me. I turn to stare.

Something small, blond, and fluffy is flouncing toward me over the grass, barking. I glance to the house across sixty yards of crew-cut Bermuda. It is so distant that Fideaux's high, affected yips are beyond earshot, but I believe I heard a frantic human voice fruitlessly urging the little escapee homeward.

So I show my teeth and hold my place until Fideaux is within pouncing distance. It stops to tilt a head as adorably curly-topped as Shirley Temple's. It sits on its little hind end. It drops its tiny jaw. The big, bad, black pussycat is supposed to be scrambling up a tree or over a fence, but there are only Joshua trees here and they sting like hell, and there is no fence, just desert and the Great Sandy Beyond.

Fideaux's irritating yaps become a whimper.

"You," I tell it savagely, "are coyote meat."

Then I turn and stroll onto the sand—ouch! Still, it is a dramatic exit. I glance back to see Blondie barreling back to the rambling deck, whimpering for Mommy.

Then I ramble myself, out front to civilization, where I finally hitch a ride on a landscaping truck back to Vegas proper. (Or improper.)

I cannot decide which I am happier to escape: the sere, sharp-fanged desert of cactus and coyote, or the rotted-fruit shades of the faux-Southwest landscape at Peyote Skies.

AFTER TAKING A DIP in the carp pool, I avoid the vicinity and any new visits by strange dudes with odd-colored eyes by heading for a secret retreat of mine. Now that I have scouted the situation, I am ready to do some deep thinking.

Luckily, I know just the place: the ghost suite at the Crystal Phoenix. This is room 713, which used to be a permanent residence for Jersey Joe Jackson back in the forties, when the Crystal Phoenix was called the Joshua Tree Hotel. Jersey Joe didn't die until the seventies, by which time he was reputed to be a broke and broken man—and, worse, completely forgotten.

The empty suite stands furnished as when he died, partly because the current management recognized it as a snapshot of an earlier era that should not be destroyed, partly because certain parties claim to have seen a thin, silver-haired dude dancing through the crack in the door now and again.

I have spent many unmolested hours here in recent years. While I may have glimpsed an odd slash of light through the wooden blinds, I cannot say yea or nay to the notion of a ghost. No one bothers me here, but I have never found the door locked to my velvet touch.

I settle on my favorite seat, a chartreuse-green satin chair that happens to make a stunning backdrop for one of my coloring. I do my best thinking when I look particularly impressive, although I am often accused of simply sleeping at such times.

The silence is as potent as Napoleonic brandy (not that I have ever sampled such a delicacy, but I do have imagination). While I lap it, with my eyes closed and my claws kneading the chartreuse satin, certain surly facts darken my mind.

First, how. The lack of marks upon the bodies suggests poison. The victims' wary familiarity with strychnine, the poison of choice for coyote hunters, suggests another toxin. I do not rule out snakebite. It is possible that the hustle and bustle of Peyote Skies has disturbed nests of venomous critters and driven them to the boundaries of the development, which would explain the neat alignment of the bodies.

Snakebite, however, usually results in swollen limbs, and the survivors detected nothing of the sort.

All right. Say the perpetrator is the usual snake of the human sort. Say some other poison was used, which would take in the wiliest coyote.

Why? What is the motive? It cannot be for pelts, because the animals were left where they fell. It cannot be the ancient antipathy of sheep ranchers toward the ignoble coyote, because you can bet that the surrounding land, however vacant at the moment, is all owned by developers like the creators of Peyote Skies. Developments multiply around each other like fire ant mounds, gulping up huge tracts of land.

Round and round I go, mentally retracing the semicircular path of the coyote corpses, my eyes always upon the grotesque hub of housing hubris and hullabaloo whose boundaries are marked with death.

My contact coyote, who was oddly shy about giving his name, no doubt due to a criminal past, said that nearby families have been warned to avoid the area. However, no number of nightly howls will warn off passersby, given the wide range of the average desert dog.

More coyotes could die, not that anybody much would notice, any more than anyone has much noted the current crop of dead coyotes. But I have no personal grudge against Don Coyote, and I do have a deep desire to get a piece of a coyote cache.

Odious as the notion is, I must return to the crime scene—and Peyote Skies—and set up a stakeout. Maybe I can talk Sings-with-Soul into leaving her kits with a sitter and keeping me some feminine company. An ace detective can always use a leggy secretary for dramatic effect.

IT IS NO DICE on the dame, but I do get the loan of Happy Hocks, a half-grown pup with time on his tail. The head coyote himself is nowhere to be seen. I hope he does not pull this vanishing act when it is time to reward Midnight Louie for successfully concluding the investigation. After being forced to hop a ride on a gravel truck to get to the site, I am not in a good mood.

"Keep down and out of sight when I say so," I instruct the gangly youngster.

"Yes, sir, Mr. Midnight. I want to be a famous crime solver like you when I grow up. I will be as quiet as a cactus."

I doubt it. There is too much vinegaroon in this punk.

We work our way closer to the settlement, Happy Hocks bounding hither and thither among the brush and occasionally running out whimpering to rub his snout in the sand.

"Catclaw," I diagnose as I survey the particular cactus patch he has just learned to leave alone. "Did not some elder tell you about those spines?"

"Naw, we have to learn some things on our own, Mr. Midnight." Happy sneezes and then grins idiotically.

"Well, stay out of the flora and stick close to me. You might learn something really useful."

He bounds over and keeps me pretty tight company, close enough so I can see him lower his nosy snout to the sand again, snuffle, and come up smacking an unidentified insect. It is a good thing I skipped breakfast, or I might have lost it right there. I am far from squeamish about the unadorned facts of life, since I have eaten a lot of meals raw in my time, but I draw the line at insects.

I can see that it will be a long day, yet as we creep on our bellies toward the completed houses, plain awe quashes a lot of Happy Hock's more annoying qualities.

"What are these painted canyons, Mr. Midnight?" he asks.

I appreciate a suitably humble tone of address. "Houses, Happy. Modernistic mansions for idle humans with tons of money and a *soup's-on* of social conscience." (I like to expose the young to a little French.)

"Dens, Mr. Midnight?"

"Right. Dens . . . and exercise rooms and wet bars and state-of-the-art kitchens."

Happy frowns at my laundry list of amenities, being a country boy, but grins again. "Dens. Are there kits inside?"

"Sure. Little kits and big kits."

He frowns again. "Is that green that surrounds the dens some fancy water, for safety?"

"No, my lad. That is a moat of the finest Bermuda grass, imported to cushion the humans' bare feet and clipped to permit a few practice golf balls."

"It grows, and they cut it?"

"Strange behavior, I know."

"Can I walk on it?"

I eye the house before us, which is not the one that hosts the obnoxious Fideaux. "I guess it is okay, kid. Just here at the edge, though."

So he trots along the sharp demarcation line between desert and cushy carpet of grass, his long legs pumping on the Bermuda.

"It is cool and soft," he says with another grin.

"But not for you." I gesture him back on the sand with me. If anyone is going to patrol on the emerald plush, it will be the senior member of this team.

Happy Hocks gives a yip only slightly less annoying than Fideaux's and forgets himself enough to bound over to a clump of beaver-tail cactus.

"Watch those spines!" I warn again, beginning to sound like a nanny.

"Look, Mr. Midnight, bonanza!"

I trot over, hoping for a clue. Is it possible the amiable idiot could have stumbled across something important?

I see a bright patch of tissue paper on the ground. Orange. Then my less lengthy nose finally catches a whiff of what roped Happy's attention. The paper is a Big-o-Burger wrapper. Nestled at its center is a nice bit of bun, burger, and exclusive Big-o-Burger Better Barbe-Q Sauce, which I have been known to sample myself.

Happy steps politely back from his find. "You can have it, Mr. Midnight."

Do I detect a glint of hero worship in those bright yellow eyes? Certainly it is unheard of for a coyote to share with a dude of another species, and usually even with his own.

My nose tells me that the Better Barbe-Q Sauce is permeating a thick slab of meat, which is cooked but is also indubitably dead. I am about to partake, when I recall my conversation with the head coyote about superior species spurning dead meat. I cannot go back on my avowed position, at least not within witnessing distance by any of the coyote clan, so I shake a mitt and mince back from the find.

"Go ahead, kid. I prefer sushi."

"Fish!" he says in disgust, wrinkling his long nose. Happy Hocks nails the remaining Big-o-Burger with one bite.

We continue our rounds, observing the activity. Happy Hocks is full of wonder at the ways of humans. I know their ways and am watching for any that are out of the ordinary.

Not much happens here. Any kids too young to be in school are kept in from the heat and nearby construction dangers. I see faces of my kind peering out from windows, never looking as downcast as I would expect at their imprisoned lot.

Except for the escaping Fideaux, I do not spy any dogs, no loss to me personally, except that this breed must go out, whether free or on lines, to do their disgusting duty.

Imagine, leaving such unwanted items in plain view for someone else to pick up and bury! Such vile habits explain why the canine family occupies a lower rung of the evolutionary ladder than the feline.

I express my disdain to Happy, who frowns again.

"But, Mr. Midnight, if we of coyote clan were to bury our water and dung, we would not know where we have been, or who had been there first. We would have no way to mark territory."

"Who would want such tainted territory?" I mutter.

But I get to thinking. Maybe this whole case *is* a matter of marking territory.

In a couple of hours I have toured as much of Peyote Skies as I can stand. I have also had enough of Happy Hocks's prattle. I send the kid home, watching his yellow coat blend instantly with the dung-shaded desert. Our discussion of bathroom habits has definitely colored my outlook.

With relief, I take up a lone outpost under a newly planted oleander bush—no seedlings for these Peyote Skies folks, only expensive full-grown plantings.

Three houses down, workmen hammer, saw, and shout. Here all is peaceful. Too peaceful. Although I welcome a world without dogs, I am uneasy at the absence of these popular house pets in this development. The entire outdoors is dogless, except for the undomesticated coyotes, and any of those that came within howling distance of here are dead.

Is Peyote Skies too pristine for dogs? I know some housing developments rule against many things.

Human voices disturb my reverie. I cringe deeper into the oleander shade. A woman exits the house, wearing slacks and sweater in the same putrid shades that saturate the development. Sure enough, a turquoise coyote is howling on her chest.

The man wears a suit, but the color is pale and the jacket is open. "Which sprinkler isn't working, Mrs. Ebert?"

"More than one, a whole line, down by the oleanders."

"Oh, at the edge of the lot."

He walks my way, but he does not see me, because I am dark as dirt and I shut my eyes to thin green slits. His foot kicks at the small silver spikes poking up like lethal flowers through the expensive grass.

"Looks like a line's out, Mrs. Ebert." He bends down to fiddle with a sprinkler, but his eyes are skipping over the edge of the desert so close you can smell the sweet alyssum on the hot, dry breeze. At least coyotes use room deodorizers.

He is big, overweight like a middle-aged busy man will get, with a fleshy face too tan for an officebound dude. He has thinning brown hair and dirt-brown eyes, sneaky brown eyes. The short hairs on my shoulder blades begin to rise. He acts like he knows someone is watching, but he never notices me, and I am even gladder of that fact now.

His back still to the woman, he reaches into his pocket to pull out something, maybe a handkerchief. Sweat beads on the hairless patches atop his head. His mouth quirks into what would be a grin if he were happy. He looks nervous, intent.

He throws the handkerchief past the oleanders, out toward the desert, as he stands. A good hard throw. Even I know that cloth is too flimsy to carry for a distance like that.

"Just a bum line, Mrs. Ebert. The company will replace it free of charge."

"That's great, Mr. Phelps." The woman expected this, but she makes gratified noises anyway.

"Peyote Skies wants its residents happy with everything." Mr. Phelps is donning a genial face and moving over the thick grass toward the woman. "Jimmy Ray Ruggles didn't develop this concept from the ground up to let a broken water line turn a band of your Bermuda brown."

"Plus, a broken line could be wasting water," she reminds him.

"Right." I heard his smirk, though his broad polyester-blend back is turned to me. "No water wasted here," he says, standing on an ocean of emerald-green grass. "Peyote Skies is a Jimmy Ray Ruggles baby, down to the last leaf of landscaping. It's gotta be perfect."

They smile at each other and amble toward the pale-yellow house together. I do not wait to see them enter. I have turned and streaked into the desert.

Not far away I find the orange handkerchief. A stone the size of a catnip mouse lies near it, but it is not really a handkerchief. I take one look and go bounding into the deeper desert at a coyote pace, thinking furiously. I do not like the idea of a new victim dying while I am on the job.

It is easiest to find Sings-with-Soul's den, next to the big stand of coyote cactus, whose gourds are catnip to coyotes. With the kits yipping serially in the background, I tell her my problem. Her yellow eyes show their whites.

"I can call, but then what?" she asks me.

"Just get him here. I will think of something."

She assumes a position that uncannily mimics the image on the home owner's sweater, lifts her head until her yellow throat aims at high noon, and lets loose an ungodly series of yowls.

Sings-with-Soul has Janis Joplin beat by a Clark County mile. My own ears flatten as much as hers, in self-defense. Even the kits quit yipping and join in with falsetto minihowls. Ouch!

Daylight howls seem out of place, but I figure they will attract attention. Sure enough, soon coyotes spring out of the drab desert floor as if they were made of animated dust. Frankly, they all look alike to me, so I do not recognize any I met the night before.

One comes slowly. My gut tightens as I recognize my quarry, Happy Hocks. The old dude who commissioned me is nowhere to be seen, and I am not unhappy. I do not have good news.

Once I am the center of a circle of quizzical coyotes (it is a good thing I am not the nervous type), I explain.

"I have discovered who is killing your kin—and how. Unfortunately, Happy Hocks ate some poisoned food."

Heads snap toward Happy, whose own head is hanging a trifle low. His big ears are not as erect as before, and I notice his eye whites are turning yellow.

"I was feeling . . . tired, Mr. Midnight," he whimpers. "What can I do?"

"Is there anything you do *not* eat around here?" I ask the others.

"There is little coyote clan will not eat, if they have to," a gray-muzzle answers.

"There must be something that you wouldn't touch on a bet—some cactus, some plant, that makes you sick."

Sings-with-Soul's head lifts. "Of course. We were too shocked to think. An antidote."

"No sure bet," I warn, eyeing the listless happy Hocks. "I have already thought of oleander, but that is so poisonous the cure could kill as well. Whatever this unknown poison is, if we act quickly enough—"

"Alyssum leaves," says the unnamed grizzle-muzzle, "taste hot and harsh."

"Prince's plume," another coyote offers. "Worse taste!"

"Desert tobacco," the oldster suggests again. "Paiutes smoked it. Such stinkweed should make this youngster plenty sick."

"I know!" Sings-with-Soul edges away from the big-eyed, big-eared kits watching our powwow. "Brushtail was sick only a week ago after I nipped her home from that plant there."

We turn as one to regard a modest, foot-high growth covered with tiny dull-green leaves. Small leafless stalks are crowned with seed beads.

Happy Hocks is nosed over to the plant and watched until he bites off several tiny pods. Meanwhile, grizzle-muzzle trots off, returning with a fragrant bouquet of desert alyssum.

Happy Hocks's muzzle develops a perpetual wrinkle as he downs these desert delights, but his eye whites gleam with fear.

"Sharp," he comments with a short bark. "Hot. Burning."

I say nothing. The hot burning, I fear, could be the poison working. I have no love for vegetables, but in the interests of science, I nibble a pod. I am not an expert, either, but I have nicked the occasional burger fragment and I recognize this plant's terrible taste. Ironically, Happy Hocks is having lots of fresh mustard on his death-o-Burger.

We watch the poor pup gum down these tough little taste bombs. Finally, his skinny sides begin to heave. I am surprised to see the gathered coyotes politely turn their heads from this unpleasant sight.

When it is over, the dirty work is left to Midnight Louie.

I amble over to examine the remains. In a pile of regurgitated greens lies the fatal lump of meat. It looks fairly undigested. With one sharp nail I paw the meat. After a few prods it falls open along the fault line. Inside lies a metallic powder.

"Bury it," I growl at the assembled coyote clan.

Happy Hocks's hangdog look lifts. "I think I feel better, Mr. Midnight."

"Keep it that way and, ah, drink lots of liquids and get plenty of rest." What can it hurt?

Amid a chorus of coyote thanks, I flatten my ears and head back to the dangerous turf of Peyote Skies.

I now know the means (if not the brand of poison), and I know the motive. I even know the perpetrator. What I don't know is how to stop him.

SO I SHADOW HIM.

This is no big deal. For one thing, my coloration makes me a born shadow, and I have always been good at tailing. For another, Mr. Phelps is all over this development.

Apparently, he is a troubleshooter for this Jimmy Ray Ruggles. Mr. Phelps inspects deck planking that gapes too much for an owner's aesthetic sense. He orders shriveling bushes replaced. He keeps everybody happy.

And he obligingly confesses to the crime. So to speak.

"My kids are real upset about having to keep Rocky inside," a harried householder in a thousand-dollar suit complains when he buttonholes a passing Mr. Phelps in his aggregate driveway. "We never thought about coyotes running off with our pets. What about stockade fences?"

"Jimmy Ray wants the development open to the desert; that's the whole point. We're working on the coyote problem. Maybe electric fences."

"What about those dead coyotes on the perimeter? That's not healthy, dead animals so close to the houses."

"We clean up the area as soon as they're found."

"What's killing them? They're not rabid?"

"No, no," Mr. Phelps says quickly. You can see the word "rabid" conjuring visions of damage suits and buyer panic. "Just varmints. Pests. Coyotes die all the time. Old age. Gunshot wounds. Don't worry, sir. As soon as the coyotes catch on that this area is populated now, they'll keep their distance."

The busy man in the suit hops into a red BMW convertible and takes off, looking unconvinced.

Mr. Phelps heads on to the biggest house in the completed section, a white stucco job with a high red-tile roof the size of a circus tent.

I follow, the only free-roaming critter in the complex. The feeling is spooky. At the back of the big house is a circular sun room with floor-to-ceiling windows surrounded by a bleached redwood deck.

Mr. Jimmy Ray Ruggles soon comes out with a woman carrying a kid. These Peyote Skies people sure like their backyards and their desert view.

I stay low in the landscaping and edge close enough to hear every word.

"It's going great, Jimmy Ray." Mr. Phelps's hearty, adman voice gives "phony" a gold plating.

"What about the pet-killing problem?" the top man asks.

"We'll be rid of all coyotes, dead or alive, any day now. We're trying low-profile electric fences."

The boss man's face darkens. "That'll ruin the view."

Mr. Jimmy Ray Ruggles is as nice-looking as his picture. Though he is only in his mid thirties, he even smells rich, thanks to some Frenchy men's cologne. Mrs. Jimmy Ray Ruggles, a slender woman with sun-streaked blond hair, wears Chanel No. 5 with her tennis whites.

She puts down the little girl, whose dark hair suggests that Mama's been in the bleach bottle. The kid is a little doll of maybe four, in a pink dress. She grabs on to her mother's shorts and hides behind her.

Mr. Phelps looks nervous again. He glances down the green expanse of lawn to the broad brown swath of desert. Between here and there stands the bright Tinkertoy construction of a kiddie play set that sports enough swings, slides, and monkey bars to outfit a whole playground.

"We're putting the wires real low," Mr. Phelps says.

"The coyotes'll jump 'em if they want to come in bad enough."

"Maybe not," Mr. Phelps adds lamely.

I can smell what he's thinking: not if enough of them die. So the boss does not know about this guy's one-man pest-control plan.

Mr. Phelps suddenly bends down and smiles at the little girl. "How are you, Caitlyn? Want Uncle Phil to take you for a swingsy?"

Caitlyn doesn't look too good. In fact, she looks as down in the mouth as Happy Hocks did not long ago. Her dark eyes are as round as two moons in eclipse, and her precious opposable thumb is stuck in her mouth like a lollipop, where it can do no good whatsoever. What I would give for one of those! Preferably two; I am a balanced kind of dude.

"What do you say, Caitlyn?" her mother prods. "Uncle Phil was awful nice to get you that recreation set." Mrs. Jimmy Ray looks apologetically at Mr. Phelps. "She's so shy for her age."

"That's okay." Mr. Phelps is really turning on the hard sell now. "She knows her Uncle Phil is her best friend. Come on, Caitie, upsy-daisy."

He swoops the little girl up on one arm, and I can see the fear in her eyes. I myself do not care to be swooped up. As for being forced to swish to and fro at a height in the name of fun ... please!

The fond parents smile as Uncle Phil leads little Caitie to the swing set.

I slink under the oleanders until I am level with the gaudy swing set, most unhappy. I will not overhear anything good way down here, but I must follow Mr. Phelps until I get something on him that will stick. At least I now know that his dirty deeds are a solo act.

Mr. Phelps lifts the little girl onto the swing seat. Her clinging mitts turn white-knuckled on the chains. He shoves off. She goes sailing to and fro above his head, down to the ground and up again forward and then down and back.

I shut my eyes. This is worse than watching Happy Hocks lose his Big-o-Burger.

Mr. Phelps looks up as Caitlyn swings over him, her skirt lifting in the wind. Her eyes flash by, terrified.

Then he slows the swing.

"Phil!" Mrs. Jimmy Ray Ruggles is calling from the deck.

Mr. Phelps bends down to whisper something to the little girl. Her fingers do not uncurl from the swing chains.

Mr. Phelps goes up the green lawn to the deck. I turn to follow, but something makes me look back at Caitlyn.

The swing is still. She has bent to pick up something from the grass and is setting it in her lap, gazing at it unhappily. Then, as if taking a pill that will make a bad headache go away, she lifts a hand to her mouth.

I scope the entire scenario in a nanosecond. My mind flashes back to Mr. Coyote-killer Phelps, his hands up, pushing the swing. Again I see his open suitcoat swinging back, side pockets tilted at an angle. I can imagine something falling out and down to the grass, unnoticed.

The little girl, a shy, unhappy kid who is afraid of almost everything. A familiar package, bright orange, with a tasty piece of Big-o-Burger still in it. Maybe she thinks you can swallow fear, push it back down. Maybe some kids will eat anything, just like coyotes.

I am over in a slingshot.

I leap up to paw the too-familiar orange paper, then to push her hand away from her mouth. She is chewing. Now her eyes grow enormous, and her fear erupts in a scream.

"Mommy, Mommy!"

She is still chewing.

I leap onto her lap (claws in), to rap her cheek.

Some half-chewed food falls to the orange wrapper covering her short pink skirt like a napkin.

She is still chewing in dazed reflex.

I pat her cheek until she coughs out something more.

But I have seen her swallow.

Then they come for me, three running figures.

"Caitlyn!" they shriek.

"Shoo!" they shout. "Get away!"

I leap down with the Big-o-Burger wrapper in my mouth, dragging it from the yard.

"Mommy, Mommy!" Caitlyn cries as she is swept into her mother's arms, as the two men in their big shoes come after me.

I could outrun them in the snap of a maître d's fingers, but I dare not leave behind the poisoned Big-o-Burger. It is evidence. Uncle Phil knows now that he has to destroy it.

I drag it into the last oleanders between me and the desert, working myself deep into the shrubbery and shadows.

"Jimmy Ray!" Caitlyn's mother sounds annoyed. "I think she ate some of the food that filthy alley cat dragged into the yard. What was it?"

The men's feet stop pounding beside me. "I saw the wrapper," Jimmy Ray Ruggles shouts back. "A Big-o-Burger."

"Can you imagine how long that was sitting around?" she demands. "Oh, Caitie—"

She turns to retreat to the house, carrying the kid.

I see her husband's feet swiveling to follow her.

I see Mr. Phelps's feet moving closer along the oleanders.

I do not need to see his face to know that he looks even more nervous than ever, and angrier. At this moment, Midnight Louie is one should-be-dead coyote.

"Phil!" The boss is calling. "Forget the cat. We better get Caitlyn calmed down for a nap. Come up to the house, and we'll talk later."

The feet before me do not move, and I know why. I am a hunter myself. Uncle Phil wants to destroy—evidence and me. I do not move. If I must, I will desert my hard-won prize, but not without a fight. This time my shivs are out and my teeth are bared.

Finally, the feet turn and thump away.

I withdraw, but not far. I know what I wait for.

THE MOON IS OUT again, full as a tick.

I watch the dark house.

At what must be my namesake midnight hour, a light blinks on upstairs. I edge forward to watch lights turn on through the house, down to the kitchen.

In five minutes, I can hear sirens. The wash of revolving red lights splash the sides of the big white house like gouts of blood. Soon the sirens wail away, fading, but the house stays brightly lit. Out on the dark, unseen desert, coyotes keep the siren heartfelt company.

Dawn is no surprise. I wait.

Around noon, Mr. Jimmy Ray Ruggles comes out onto the deck. He looks even younger in jeans and a rumpled T-shirt. He walks down the lawn, Mr. Phelps a deferential step behind. Mr. Jimmy Ray Ruggles's face is more rumpled than his shirt. I glimpse in his eyes the same fear that filled his daughter's less than a day ago. I know the swing that Mr. Jimmy Ray Ruggles has been riding for the past twelve hours. I want to know what has happened to Caitlyn.

"It was near here," Mr. Jimmy Ray Ruggles says in a weary, angry voice.

"That cat is long gone, with his booty," Mr. Phelps says. Hopes.

"I've got to look. I've got to know what it was, Phil."

Mr. Jimmy Ray Ruggles gets down on his hands and knees to peer under the oleanders.

I am waiting, where I always was.

"By God, the damn cat's still here!" he hisses. "I can see the wrapper too!"

"There won't be anything left."

"Damn it, Phil! They can analyze even little bits, molecules, maybe.

I've got to know what—" His voice breaks. "That's all right, kitty. I just want the paper."

He sticks his hand under the bush. I see his pale face. I see Mr. Phelps peering over his shoulder, twice as worried.

"Jimmy Ray, that's a big cat. He could have rabies. He could scratch or bite you—"

"I don't care! It's for Caitie." His hand reaches the crumpled orange paper in front of me, with the two lumps of mashed food on it.

I sit very still and let him take it. He slowly draws it away, seeping fear. I am sorry that I am such a scary dude.

Then he is gone and Mr. Phelps is staring at me through the spiky oleander leaves with as much hatred as I have ever seen.

"Black devil!" he says like a curse.

I am not sorry that I am such a scary dude after all.

I WAIT AGAIN. I want to know.

But the house is empty and the hours pass. I am hungry, but I wait. When I am thirsty, I slink out to lap up some sprinkler water. Then I return to my post.

The odds are that I will never know, just as they are one hundred percent that I will never tell. But I wait.

I am rewarded at dusk, when the desert sky bleeds a Southwest palette of lavender and peach ... and orange ... that developers can only dream of.

Two men on the lawn. Lights in the house.

"Tell me," Mr. Jimmy Ray Ruggles is saying, and I think the iron tone in his voice could force even me to talk.

"Tell you what?" A nervous laugh.

"The dead coyotes. You said you were handling it. How? Phil, how!"

"Jim—"

"It was with poisoned food, wasn't it? And somehow Caitie got into it. Listen, you can tell me now. Caitie will be fine, thank God. She's still unconscious, but the doctors say she didn't get enough poison to cause permanent damage. They hope not anyway. Listen, I won't blame you. I know you're devoted to Peyote Skies, like I am. Maybe too much. Tell me."

"All right." Mr. Phelps sounds empty. The men walk toward the oleanders, toward me. "I never dreamed, Jimmy Ray—I just wanted to discourage the damn coyotes, and it was working. We haven't found any dead ones since a week ago. I salted the Big-o-Burgers. Somehow, one of the ... traps fell out of my pocket yesterday and I never knew. Caitie swooped it up, and I never saw—"

"Don't you remember? She's always loved Big-o-Burgers," Mr. Jimmy Ray Ruggles says softly.

Mr. Phelps's voice is breaking now, but this theatrical touch does not break Midnight's Louie's heart. "I was going to stop soon."

"But ... thallium, Phil, an outlawed poison! With no taste, no smell, a poison that never degrades even though it's been illegal for decades. Didn't you realize it could kill more than coyotes—pets, children? Where on earth did you get it?"

"I own some old houses in town. The carpenters back then used it as rat poison, inside the walls. It was still there. I figured it would fool the coyotes; they're too smart for anything else. I swear to God, Jimmy Ray, if I had known it would hurt Caitie I would have cut off my right arm—"

"I know. I know."

Mr. Jimmy Ray Ruggles has stopped directly in front of me. "I suppose that big old black cat is dead from it by now, but thank God he fought Caitie for it. Thank God we found him and a sample of the poison so they could treat her."

His shoes turn, then go. Mr. Phelps's do not.

"Black devil," he whispers to the twilight air.

I accept my plaudits with silent good grace and finally depart.

IT TAKES ME A FULL DAY to recover my strength and placate my defrauded appetite. I am satisfied that no more coyotes will be sacrificed on the altar of Peyote Skies and that the developer's daughter will be well, but I do wish that Mr. Phelps would find the fate he deserves. I fear that the scandal would hurt Peyote Skies too much for even a fond father to pursue the matter.

Then I begin to worry about my payoff. I am, after all, not doing charity work. I dash out to the desert on the nearest gravel truck, to find that Happy Hocks is as peppy as ever (alas!) and that these coyote clan types have never heard of the strange old dude who commissioned me.

So I am soon languishing beside the carp pond at the Crystal Phoenix again, feeling that I have been taken in a shell game, when I spot a familiar profile on the sun-rinsed wall.

"I thought you had headed for the hills."

"Foolish feline," the big-eared coyote silhouette answers. "I always keep my bargains. I merely had to ensure that you had done as agreed."

"And then some. Where is my reward?"

I watch the shadow jaws move and hear the harsh desert voice describe a site that, to my delight, is on the Crystal Phoenix grounds.

"Once all of Las Vegas was desert," the coyote says, "and my ancestors had many secret places. You will find my cache behind the third palm on the east side of the pool."

"Where?"

"In the ground. You will have to dig for it. You can dig?"

"I do so daily," I retort.

"Deep."

"What I can do shallow, I can do deep."

"Good. Goodbye."

With that terse farewell, me and the coyote call it quits.

I spring for the pool area. I dodge stinking tourists basting on lounges, dripping coconut oil between the plastic strips.

I count off palms. I retire discreetly behind one and dig. And dig. And dig.

About a half-foot down, I hit pay dirt. Coyote pay dirt. Excavating further, I uncover my treasure. Then I sit back to study it.

I regard a deposit of small brown nubs. Of pods, so to speak. Of coyote dung intermixed with a foreign substance: the button of the mescal cactus, called peyote by the Indians. I have been paid off, all right. In Coyote peyote, both forms. Apparently this big-eared dude thinks that his leavings are caramel. The worst part is feeling that it serves me right for trusting a coyote.

By nightfall I have retreated to the ghost suite of the Crystal Phoenix to salve my wounded psyche. It does not soothe my savage soul to have been taken to the cleaners by a dirty dog. A yellow dog. By Don Coyote. Maybe the mescaline is worth something, but not in my circles. I do not do drugs, and my only vice, catnip, is a legally available substance. As for coyote dung, it does not even have a souvenir value.

As I muse in the antique air of suite 713, I recall that there is coyote, and then there is Coyote. Coyote of Native American legend is also called the Old Man, the Trickster, the Dirty Old Man who is at times advised by his own droppings. It is said that Coyote takes many forms and that to deal with him is always dicey, for he embodies the worst and the best of humankind.

I contemplate that though I have saved coyote clan from an underhanded attack, I have also saved humankind from the ricochet of that attack upon itself; that I have suffered hunger and thorns in my feet, not to mention threats to body and soul, and I have nothing to show for it but coyote peyote.

My self-esteem is so low that I could win a limbo contest dancing under it.

And then I notice that a console across the room has flipped its lid. I have seen that ash-blond oblong of furniture for many years and never knew that it had a lid to flip.

By the way the light dances inside the lid, like an aurora borealis, the lid interior is mirrored, and in that mirror is reflected an oval image.

The image flickers eerily, then resolves. Sound issues from the bowels of the cabinet. I sit mesmerized, even when I realize that I am watching a late-forties-vintage TV set display a perfectly ordinary contemporary television show I do not normally deign to watch—that exercise in tabloid journalism known as *The Daily Scoop* but which I call the Daily Pooper Scooper in my septic moments. Or do I mean skeptic?

Whatever, what to my wandering eyes should appear but a camera pan across the entry sign to Peyote Skies. An offscreen voice begins saying what a tony development this is and discusses the rash of coyote poisonings, culminating in the tragic poisoning of the developer's daughter. Caitlyn's image flashes across the screen, smiling and happy.

Next I see an image of Mr. Phelps being led away in handcuffs by grim-looking men. Hallelujah!

Then Miss Ashley Ames, a most attractive anorexic bottle blonde with bony kneecaps, comes on-screen with a breathless narrative.

It seems that little Caitlyn Ruggles's poisoning was considered a tragic mistake stemming from a misguided attempt by a Peyote Skies employee to rid the development of pet-napping coyotes ... until the child victim regained consciousness and began speaking of the unspeakable. "Uncle Phil" had been sexually abusing her.

Caitlin's shocked parents called the police. An investigation revealed that P. W. Phelps, a vice president in the Peyote Skies company, had been molesting the child, who was beginning to talk of telling.

"It is alleged," Miss Ashley Ames says in a tone that is most delightfully dubious about the "alleged" part, "that he poisoned the half-dozen coyotes to create a pattern in which the 'accidental' death of young Caitlyn Ruggles would be seen as a tragic side effect.

'Had it not been," she goes on, and I can hardly believe my ears, even though they are standing at full attention, 'for the lucky chance that a starving stray black cat fought the child for the poisoned piece of a major fast-food-chain hamburger, this nefarious scheme would never have been discovered."

I am more than somewhat taken aback by my description as "starving."

The next shot distracts me: Caitlyn and her parents at the Las Vegas Humane Society, adopting a small black kitten, all smiles. Even the kitten is smiling.

I am smiling. Hell, I suspect that somewhere Coyote is smiling.

In fact, as the ancient television's image and sound fade, I believe I glimpse a silver-haired human dude with mighty big ears vanishing through a crack in the door.

I recall that Jersey Joe Jackson hid a few caches around Las Vegas in his time. And that Coyote never changes, and always does. And that he performs tricks, maybe even with vintage television sets.

The best and the worst of both beast and man himself.

Indeed.

Publication of EDWIN OF THE IRON SHOES (1977) started a quiet revolution in contemporary fiction: it introduced the first modern female private investigator. Sharon McCone was (and remains) smart without being harsh; compassionate without being treacly, and liberated without being doctrinaire. Twenty-some books and nearly two decades later, Marcia is finally getting her due not only for launching Sharon McCone (and thus all other female private eyes) but also for being a first-rate storyteller, one who gets better, and richer and deeper, with each new book.

The Lost Coast
MARCIA MULLER

California's Lost Coast is at the same time one of the most desolate and beautiful of shorelines. Northerly winds whip the sand into a dust-devil frenzy; eerie, stationary fogs hang in the trees and distort the driftwood until it resembles the bones of prehistoric mammals; bruised clouds hover above the peaks of the distant King Range, then blow down to sea level and dump icy torrents. But on a fair day the sea and sky show infinite shadings of blue, and the wildflowers are a riot of color. If you wait quietly, you can spot deer, peregrine falcons, foxes, otters, even black bears and mountain lions.

A contradictory and oddly compelling place, this seventy-three-mile stretch of coast southwest of Eureka, where—as with most worthwhile things or people—you must take the bad with the good.

Unfortunately, on my first visit there I was taking mostly the bad. Strong wind pushed my MG all over the steep, narrow road, making its hairpin turns even more perilous. Early October rain cut my visibility to a few yards. After I crossed the swollen Bear River, the road continued to twist and wind, and I began to understand why the natives had dubbed it The Wildcat.

Somewhere ahead, my client had told me, was the hamlet of Petrolia—site of the first oil well drilled in California, he'd irrelevantly added. The man was a conservative politician, a former lumber-company attorney, and given what I knew of his voting record on the environment, I was certain we disagreed on the desirability of that event, as well as any number of similar issues. But the urgency of the current situation dictated that I keep my opinions to myself, so I'd simply written down the directions he gave me—omitting his travelogue-like asides—and gotten under way.

I drove through Petrolia—a handful of new buildings, since the village had been all but leveled in the disastrous earthquake of 1992—and turned toward the sea on an unpaved road. After two miles I began looking for the orange post that marked the dirt track to the client's cabin.

The whole time I was wishing I was back in San Francisco. This wasn't my kind of case; I didn't like the client, Steve Shoemaker; and even though the fee was good, this was the week I'd scheduled to take off a few personal business days from All Souls Legal Cooperative, where I'm chief investigator. But Jack Stuart, our criminal specialist, had asked me to take on the job as a favor to him. Steve Shoemaker was Jack's old friend from college in Southern California, and he'd asked for a referral to a private detective. Jack owed Steve a favor; I owed Jack several, so there was no way I could gracefully refuse.

But I couldn't shake the feeling that something was wrong with this case. And I couldn't help wishing that I'd come to the Lost Coast in summertime, with a backpack and in the company of my lover—instead of on a rainy fall afternoon, with a .38 Special and soon to be in the company of Shoemaker's disagreeable wife, Andrea.

The rain was sheeting down by the time I spotted the orange post. It had turned the hard-packed earth to mud, and my MG's tires sank deep in the ruts, its undercarriage scraping dangerously. I could barely make out the stand of live oaks and sycamores where the track ended; no way to tell if another vehicle had traveled over it recently.

When I reached the end of the track I saw one of those boxy four-wheel-drive wagons—Bronco? Cherokee?—drawn in under the drooping branches of an oak. Andrea Shoemaker's? I'd neglected to get a description from her husband of what she drove. I got out of the MG, turning the hood of my heavy sweater up against the downpour; the wind promptly blew it off. So much for what the catalog had described as "extra protection on those cold nights." I yanked the hood up again and held it there, went around and took my .38 from the trunk and shoved it into the outside flap of my purse. Then I went over and tried the door of the four-wheel drive. Unlocked. I opened it, slipped into the driver's seat.

Nothing identifying its owner was on the seats or in the side pockets, but in the glove compartment I found a registration in the name of Andrea Shoemaker. I rummaged around, came up with nothing else of interest. Then I got out and walked through the trees, looking for the cabin.

Shoemaker had told me to follow a deer track through the grove. No sign of it in this downpour; no deer, either. Nothing but wind-lashed trees, the oaks pelting me with acorns. I moved slowly through them, swiveling my head from side to side, until I made out a bulky shape tucked beneath the farthest of the sycamores.

As I got closer, I saw the cabin was of plain weathered wood, rudely constructed, with the chimney of a woodstove extending from its composition shingle roof. Small—two or three rooms—and no light showing in its windows. And the door was open, banging against the inside wall . . .

I quickened my pace, taking the gun from my purse. Alongside the door I stopped to listen. Silence. I had a flashlight in my bag; I took it out. Moved to where I could see inside, then turned the flash on and shone it through the door.

All that was visible was rough board walls, an oilcloth-covered table and chairs, an ancient woodstove. I stepped inside, swinging the light around. Unlit oil lamp on the table; flower-cushioned wooden furniture of the sort you always find in vacation cabins; rag rugs; shelves holding an assortment of tattered paperbacks, seashells, and driftwood. I shifted the light again, more slowly.

A chair on the far side of the table was tipped over, and a woman's purse lay on the edge of the woodstove, its contents spilling out. When I got over there I saw a .32 Iver Johnson revolver lying on the floor.

Andrea Shoemaker owned a .32. She'd told me so the day before.

Two doors opened off the room. Quietly I went to one and tried it. A closet, shelves stocked with staples and canned goods and bottled water. I looked around the room again, listening. No sound but the wail of wind and the pelt of rain on the roof. I stepped to the other door.

A bedroom, almost filled wall-to-wall by a king-sized bed covered with a goosedown comforter and piled with colorful pillows. Old bureau pushed in one corner, another unlit oil lamp on the single nightstand. Small travel bag on the bed.

The bag hadn't been opened. I examined its contents. Jeans, a couple of sweaters, underthings, toilet articles. Package of condoms. Uh-huh. She'd come here, as I'd found out, to meet a man. The affairs usually began with a casual pickup; they were never of long duration; and they all seemed to culminate in a romantic weekend in the isolated cabin.

Dangerous game, particularly in these days when AIDS and the prevalence of disturbed individuals of both sexes threatened. But Andrea Shoemaker had kept her latest date with an even larger threat hanging over her: for the past six weeks, a man with a serious grudge against her husband had been stalking her. For all I knew, he and the date were one and the same.

And where was Andrea now?

THIS CASE HAD STARTED on Wednesday, two days ago, when I'd driven up to Eureka, a lumbering and fishing town on Humboldt Bay. After I passed the Humboldt County line I began to see huge logging trucks toiling through the mountain passes, shredded curls of redwood bark trailing in their wakes. Twenty-five miles south of the city itself was the company-owned town of Scotia, mill stacks belching white smoke and filling the air with the scent of freshly cut wood. Yards full of logs waiting to be fed to the mills lined the highway. When I reached Eureka itself, the downtown struck me as curiously quiet; many of the stores were out of business, and the sidewalks were mostly deserted. The recession had hit the lumber industry hard, and the earthquake hadn't helped the area's strapped economy.

I'd arranged to meet Steve Shoemaker at his law offices in Old Town, near the waterfront. It was a picturesque area full of renovated warehouses and interesting shops and restaurants, tricked up for tourists with the inevitable horse-and-carriage rides and T-shirt shops, but still pleasant. Shoemaker's offices were off a cobblestoned courtyard containing a couple of antique shops and a decorator's showroom.

When I gave my card to the secretary, she said Assemblyman Shoemaker was in conference and asked me to wait. The man, I knew, had lost his seat in the state legislature this past election, so the term of address seemed inappropriate. The appointments of the waiting room struck me as a bit much: brass and mahogany and marble and velvet, plenty of it, the furnishings all antiques that tended to the garish. I sat on a red velvet sofa and looked for something to read. *Architectural Digest, National Review, Foreign Affairs*—that was it, take it or leave it. I left it. My idea of waiting-room reading material is *People*; I love it, but I'm too embarrassed to subscribe.

The minutes ticked by: ten, fifteen, twenty. I contemplated the issue of *Architectural Digest*, then opted instead for staring at a fake Rembrandt on the far wall. Twenty-five, thirty. I was getting irritated now. Shoemaker had asked me to be here by three; I'd arrived on the dot. If this was, as he'd claimed, a matter of such urgency and delicacy that he couldn't go into it on the phone, why was he in conference at the appointed time?

Thirty-five minutes. Thirty-seven. The door to the inner sanctum opened and a woman strode out. A tall woman, with long chestnut hair, wearing a raincoat and black leather boots. Her eyes rested on me in passing—a cool gray, hard with anger. Then she went out, slamming the door behind her.

The secretary—a trim blonde in a tailored suit—started as the door slammed. She glanced at me and tried to cover with a smile, but its edges were strained, and her fingertips pressed hard against the desk. The phone at her elbow buzzed; she snatched up the receiver. Spoke into it, then said to me, "Ms. McCone, Assemblyman Shoemaker will see you now." As she ushered me inside, she again gave me her frayed-edge smile.

Tense situation in this office, I thought. Brought on by what? The matter Steve Shoemaker wanted me to investigate? The client who had just made her angry exit? Or something else entirely ... ?

Shoemaker's office was even more pretentious than the waiting room: more brass, mahogany, velvet, and marble; more fake Old Masters in heavy gilt frames; more antiques; more of everything. Shoemaker's demeanor was not as nervous as his secretary's, but when he rose to greet me, I noticed a jerkiness in his movements, as if he was holding himself under tight control. I clasped his outstretched hand and smiled, hoping the familiar social rituals would set him more at ease.

Momentarily they did. He thanked me for coming, apologized for making me wait, and inquired after Jack Stuart. After I was seated in one of the clients' chairs, he offered me a drink; I asked for mineral water. As he went to a wet bar tucked behind a tapestry screen, I took the opportunity to study him.

Shoemaker was handsome: dark hair, with the gray so artfully interwoven that it must have been professionally dyed. Chiseled features; nice, well-muscled body, shown off to perfection by an expensive blue suit. When he handed me my drink, his smile revealed white, even teeth that I—having spent the greater part of the previous month in the company of my dentist—recognized as capped. Yes, a very good-looking man, politician handsome. Jack's old friend or not, his appearance and manner called up my gut-level distrust.

My client went around his desk and reclaimed his chair. He held a drink of his own—something dark amber—and he took a deep swallow before speaking. The alcohol replenished his vitality some; he drank again, set the glass on a pewter coaster, and said, "Ms. McCone, I'm glad you could come up here on such short notice."

"You mentioned on the phone that the case is extremely urgent—and delicate."

He ran his hand over his hair—lightly, so as not to disturb its styling. "Extremely urgent and delicate," he repeated, seeming to savor the phrase.

"Why don't you tell me about it?"

His eyes strayed to the half-full glass on the coaster. Then they moved to the door through which I'd entered. Returned to me. "You saw the woman who just left?"

I nodded.

"My wife, Andrea."

I waited.

"She's very angry with me for hiring you."

"She did act angry. Why?"

Now he reached for the glass and belted down its contents. Leaned back and rattled the ice cubes as he spoke. "It's a long story. Painful to me. I'm not sure where to begin. I just ... don't know what to make of the things that are happening."

"That's what you've hired me to do. Begin anywhere. We'll fill in the gaps later." I pulled a small tape recorder from my bag and set it on the edge of his desk. "Do you mind?"

Shoemaker eyed it warily, but shook his head. After a moment's hesitation, he said, "Someone is stalking my wife."

"Following her? Threatening her?"

"Not following, not that I know of. He writes notes, threatening to kill her. He leaves ... things at the house. At her place of business. Dead things. Birds, rats, one time a cat. Andrea loves cats. She ..." He shook his head, went to the bar for a refill.

"What else? Phone calls?"

"No. One time, a floral arrangement—suitable for a funeral."

"Does he sign the notes?"

"John. Just John."

"Does Mrs. Shoemaker know anyone named John who has a grudge against her?"

"She says no. And I ..." He sat down, fresh drink in hand. "I have reason to believe that this John has a grudge against me, is using this harassment of Andrea to get at me personally."

"Why do you think that?"

"The wording of the notes."

"May I see them?"

He looked around, as if he were afraid someone might be listening. "Later. I keep them elsewhere."

Something, then, I thought, that he didn't want his office staff to see. Something shameful, perhaps even criminal.

"Okay," I said, "how long has this been going on?"

"About six weeks."

"Have you contacted the police?"

"Informally. A man I know on the force, Sergeant Bob Wolfe. But after he started looking into it, I had to ask him to drop it."

"Why?"

"I'm in a sensitive political position."

"Excuse me if I'm mistaken, Mr. Shoemaker, but it's my understanding that you're no longer serving in the state legislature."

"That's correct, but I'm about to announce my candidacy in a special election for a senate seat that's recently been vacated."

"I see. So after you asked your contact on the police force to back off, you decided to use a private investigator, and Jack recommended me. Why not use someone local?"

"As I said, my position is sensitive. I don't want word of this getting out in the community. That's why Andrea is so angry with me. She claims I value my political career more than her life."

I waited, wondering how he'd attempt to explain that away.

He didn't even try, merely went on, "In our . . . conversation just prior to this, she threatened to leave me. This coming weekend she plans to go to a cabin on the Lost Coast that she inherited from her father to, as she put it, sort things through. Alone. Do you know that part of the coast?"

"I've read some travel pieces on it."

"Then you're aware how remote it is. The cabin's very isolated. I don't want Andrea going there while this John person is on the loose."

"Does she go there often?"

"Fairly often. I don't; it's too rustic for me—no running water, phone, or electricity. But Andrea likes it. Why do you ask?"

"I'm wondering if John—whoever he is—knows about the cabin. Has she been there since the harassment began?"

"No. Initially she agreed that it wouldn't be a good idea. But now . . ." He shrugged.

"I'll need to speak with Mrs. Shoemaker. Maybe I can reason with her, persuade her not to go until we've identified John. Or maybe she'll allow me to go along as her bodyguard."

"You can speak with her if you like, but she's beyond reasoning with. And there's no way you can stop her or force her to allow you to accompany her. My wife is a strong-willed woman; that interior decorating firm across the courtyard is hers, she built it from the ground up. When Andrea decides to do something, she does it. And asks permission from no one."

"Still, I'd like to try reasoning. This trip to the cabin—that's the urgency you mentioned on the phone. Two days to find the man behind the harassment before she goes out there and perhaps makes a target of herself."

"Yes."

"Then I'd better get started. That funeral arrangement—what florist did it come from?"

Shoemaker shook his head. "It arrived at least five weeks ago, before either of us noticed a pattern to the harassment. Andrea just shrugged it off, threw the wrappings and card away."

"Let's go look at the notes, then. They're my only lead."

Vengeance will be mine. The sudden blow. The quick attack. Vengeance is the price of silence.

Mute testimony paves the way to an early grave. The rest is silence.

A freshly turned grave is silent testimony to an old wrong and its avenger.

There was more in the same vein—slightly biblical-flavored and stilted. But chilling to me, even though the safety-deposit booth at Shoemaker's bank was overly warm. If that was my reaction, what had these notes done to Andrea Shoemaker? No wonder she was thinking of leaving a husband who cared more for the electorate's opinion than his wife's life and safety.

The notes had been typed without error on an electric machine that had left no such obvious clues as chipped or skewed keys. The paper and envelopes were plain and cheap, purchasable at any discount store. They had been handled, I was sure, by nothing more than gloved hands. No signature—just the typed name "John."

But the writer had wanted the Shoemakers—one of them, anyway—to know who he was. Thus the theme that ran through them all: silence and revenge.

I said, "I take it your contact at the E.P.D. had their lab go over these?"

"Yes. There was nothing. That's why he wanted to probe further—something I couldn't permit him to do."

"Because of this revenge-and-silence business. Tell me about it."

Shoemaker looked around furtively. My God, did he think bank employees had nothing better to do with their time than to eavesdrop on our conversation?

"We'll go have a drink," he said. "I know a place that's private."

WE WENT TO A RESTAURANT a few blocks away, where Shoemaker had another bourbon and I toyed with a glass of iced tea. After some prodding, he told me his story; it didn't enhance him in my eyes.

Seventeen years ago Shoemaker had been interviewing for a staff attorney's position at a large lumber company. While on a tour of the mills, he witnessed an accident in which a worker named Sam Carding was severely mangled while trying to clear a jam in a bark-stripping machine. Shoemaker, who had worked in the mills summers to pay for his education, knew the accident was due to company negligence, but accepted a handsome job offer in exchange for not testifying for the plaintiff in the ensuing lawsuit. The court ruled against Carding, confined to a wheelchair and in constant pain; a year later, while the case was still under appeal,

Carding shot his wife and himself. The couple's three children were given token settlements in exchange for dropping the suit and then were adopted by relatives in a different part of the country.

"It's not a pretty story, Mr. Shoemaker," I said, "and I can see why the wording of the notes might make you suspect there's a connection between it and this harassment. But who do you think John is?"

"Carding's oldest boy. Carding and his family knew I'd witnessed the accident; one of his coworkers saw me watching from the catwalk and told him. Later, when I turned up as a senior counsel . . ." He shrugged.

"But why, after all this time—?"

"Why not? People nurse grudges. John Carding was sixteen at the time of the lawsuit; there were some ugly scenes with him, both at my home and my office at the mill. By now he'd be in his forties. Maybe it's his way of acting out some sort of midlife crisis."

"Well, I'll call my office and have my assistant run a check on all three Carding kids. And I want to speak with Mrs. Shoemaker—preferably in your presence."

He glanced at his watch. "It can't be tonight. She's got a meeting of her professional organization, and I'm dining with my campaign manager."

A potentially psychotic man was threatening Andrea's life, yet they both carried on as usual. Well, who was I to question it? Maybe it was their way of coping.

"Tomorrow, then," I said. "Your home. At the noon hour."

Shoemaker nodded. Then he gave me the address, as well as the names of John Carding's siblings.

I left him on the sidewalk in front of the restaurant: a handsome man whose shoulders now slumped inside his expensive suitcoat, shivering in the brisk wind off Humboldt Bay. As we shook hands, I saw that shame made his gaze unsteady, the set of his mouth less than firm.

I knew that kind of shame. Over the course of my career, I'd committed some dreadful acts that years later woke me in the deep of the night to sudden panic. I'd also *not* committed certain acts—failures that woke me to regret and emptiness. My sins of omission were infinitely worse than those of commission, because I knew that if I'd acted, I could have made a difference. Could even have saved a life.

I WASN'T ABLE TO REACH Rae Kelleher, my assistant at All Souls, that evening, and by the time she got back to me the next morning—Thursday—I was definitely annoyed. Still, I tried to keep a lid on my irritation. Rae is young, attractive, and in love; I couldn't expect her to spend her evenings waiting to be of service to her workaholic boss.

I got her started on a computer check on all three Cardings, then took myself to the Eureka P.D. and spoke with Shoemaker's contact, Sergeant Bob Wolfe. Wolfe—a dark-haired, sharp-featured man whose appearance was a good match for his surname—told me he'd had the notes processed by the lab, which had turned up no useful evidence.

"Then I started to probe, you know? When you got a harassment case like this, you look into the victims' private lives."

"And that was when Shoemaker told you to back off."

"Uh-huh."

"When was this?"

"About five weeks ago."

"I wonder why he waited so long to hire me. Did he, by any chance, ask you for a referral to a local investigator?"

Wolfe frowned. "Not this time."

"Then you'd referred him to someone before?"

"Yeah, guy who used to be on the force—Dave Morrison. Last April."

"Did Shoemaker tell you why he needed an investigator?"

"No, and I didn't ask. These politicians, they're always trying to get something on their rivals. I didn't want any part of it."

"Do you have Morrison's address and phone number handy?"

Wolfe reached into his desk drawer, shuffled things, and flipped a business card across the blotter. "Dave gave me a stack of these when he set up shop," he said. "Always glad to help an old pal."

MORRISON WAS OUT OF TOWN, the message on his answering machine said, but would be back tomorrow afternoon. I left a message of my own, asking him to call me at my motel. Then I headed for the Shoemakers' home, hoping I could talk some common sense into Andrea.

But Andrea wasn't having any common sense.

She strode around the parlor of their big Victorian—built by one of the city's lumber barons, her husband told me when I complimented them on it—arguing and waving her arms and making scathing statements punctuated by a good amount of profanity. And knocking back martinis, even though it was only a little past noon.

Yes, she was going to the cabin. No, neither her husband nor I was welcome there. No, she wouldn't postpone the trip; she was sick and tired of being cooped up like some kind of zoo animal because her husband had made a mistake years before she'd met him. All right, she realized this John person was dangerous. But she'd taken self-defense classes and owned a .32 revolver. Of course she knew how to use it. Practiced frequently, too. Women had to be prepared these days, and she was.

But, she added darkly, glaring at her husband, she'd just as soon not have to shoot John. She'd rather send him straight back to Steve and let them settle this score. May the best man win—and she was placing bets on John.

As far as I was concerned, Steve and Andrea Shoemaker deserved each other.

I tried to explain to her that self-defense classes don't fully prepare you for a paralyzing, heart-pounding encounter with an actual violent stranger. I tried to warn her that the ability to shoot well on a firing range doesn't fully prepare you for pumping a bullet into a human being who is advancing swiftly on you.

I wanted to tell her she was being an idiot.

Before I could, she slammed down her glass and stormed out of the house.

Her husband replenished his own drink and said, "Now do you see what I'm up against?"

I didn't respond to that. Instead I said, "I spoke with Sergeant Wolfe earlier."

"And?"

"He told me he referred you to a local private investigator, Dave Morrison, last April."

"So?"

"Why didn't you hire Morrison for this job?"

"As I told you yesterday, my—"

"Sensitive position, yes."

Shoemaker scowled.

Before he could comment, I asked, "What was the job last April?"

"Nothing to do with this matter."

"Something to do with politics?"

"In a way."

"Mr. Shoemaker, hasn't it occurred to you that a political enemy may be using the Carding case as a smoke screen? That a rival's trying to throw you off balance before this special election?"

"It did, and ... well, it isn't my opponent's style. My God, we're civilized people. But those notes ... they're the work of a lunatic."

I wasn't so sure he was right—both about the notes being the work of a lunatic and politicians being civilized people—but I merely said, "Okay, you keep working on Mrs. Shoemaker. At least persuade her to let me go to the Lost Coast with her. I'll be in touch." Then I headed for the public library.

AFTER A FEW HOURS of ruining my eyes at the microfilm machine, I knew little more than before. Newspaper accounts of the Carding accident, lawsuit, and murder-suicide didn't differ substantially from what my client had told me. Their coverage of the Shoemakers' activities was only marginally interesting.

Normally I don't do a great deal of background investigation on clients, but as Sergeant Wolfe had said, in a case like this where one or both of them was a target, a thorough look at careers and lifestyles was mandatory. The papers described Steve as a straightforward, effective assemblyman who took a hard, conservative stance on such issues as welfare and the environment. He was strongly pro-business, particularly the lumber industry. He and his "charming and talented wife" didn't share many interests: Steve hunted and golfed; Andrea was a "generous supporter of the arts" and a "lavish party-giver." An odd couple, I thought, and odd people to be friends of Jack Stuart, a liberal who'd chosen to dedicate his career to representing the underdog.

Back at the motel, I put in a call to Jack. Why, I asked him, had he remained close to a man who was so clearly his opposite?

Jack laughed. "You're trying to say politely that you think he's a pompous, conservative ass."

"Well . . ."

"Okay, I admit it: He is. But back in college, he was a mentor to me. I doubt I would have gone into the law if it hadn't been for Steve. And we shared some good times, too: One summer we took a motorcycle trip around the country, like something out of *Easy Rider* without the tragedy. I guess we stay in touch because of a shared past."

I was trying to imagine Steve Shoemaker on a motorcycle; the picture wouldn't materialize. "Was he always so conservative?" I asked.

"No, not until he moved back to Eureka and went to work for that lumber company. Then . . . I don't know. Everything changed. It was as if something had happened that took all the fight out of him."

What had happened, I thought, was trading another man's life for a prestigious job.

Jack and I chatted for a moment longer, and then I asked him to transfer me to Rae. She hadn't turned up anything on the Cardings yet, but was working on it. In the meantime, she added, she'd taken care of what correspondence had come in, dealt with seven phone calls, entered next week's must-do's in the call-up file she'd created for me, and found a remedy for the blight that was affecting my rubber plant.

With a pang, I realized that the office ran just as well—better, per-haps—when I wasn't there. It would keep functioning smoothly without me for weeks, months, maybe years.

Hell, it would probably keep functioning smoothly even if I were dead.

IN THE MORNING I opened the Yellow Pages to Florists and began calling each that was listed. While Shoemaker had been vague on the date his wife received the funeral arrangement, surely a customer who wanted one sent to a private home, rather than a mortuary, would stand out in the order-taker's mind. The listing was long, covering a relatively wide area; it wasn't until I reached the R's and my watch showed nearly eleven o'clock that I got lucky.

"I don't remember any order like that in the past six weeks," the clerk at Rainbow Florists said, "but we had one yesterday, was delivered this morning."

I gripped the receiver harder. "Will you pull the order, please?"

"I'm not sure I should—"

"Please. You could help to save a woman's life."

Quick intake of breath, then his voice filled with excitement; he'd become part of a real-life drama. "One minute. I'll check." When he came back on the line, he said, "Thirty-dollar standard condolence arrangement, delivered this morning to Mr. Steven Shoemaker—"

"*Mister?* Not Mrs. or Ms.?"

"Mister, definitely. I took the order myself." He read off the Shoemakers' address.

"Who placed it?"

"A kid. Came in with cash and written instructions."

Standard ploy—hire a kid off the street so nobody can identify you. "Thanks very much."

"Aren't you going to tell me—"

I hung up and dialed Shoemaker's office. His secretary told me he was working at home today. I dialed the home number. Busy. I hung up, and the phone rang immediately. Rae, with information on the Cardings.

She'd traced Sam Carding's daughter and younger son. The daughter lived near Cleveland, Ohio, and Rae had spoken with her on the phone. John, his sister had told her, was a drifter and an addict; she hadn't seen or spoken to him in more than ten years. When Rae reached the younger brother at his office in L.A., he told her the same, adding that he assumed John had died years ago.

I thanked Rae and told her to keep on it. Then I called Shoemaker's home number again. Still busy; time to go over there.

SHOEMAKER'S LINCOLN WAS PARKED in the drive of the Victorian, a dusty Honda motorcycle beside it. As I rang the doorbell I again tried to picture a younger, free-spirited Steve bumming around the country on a bike with Jack, but the image simply wouldn't come clear. It took Shoemaker a while to answer the door, and when he saw me, his mouth pulled down in displeasure.

"Come in, and be quick about it," he told me. "I'm on an important conference call."

I was quick about it. He rushed down the hallway to what must be a study, and I went into the parlor where we'd talked the day before. Unlike his offices, it was exquisitely decorated, calling up images of the days of the lumber barons. Andrea's work, probably. Had she also done his offices? Perhaps their gaudy decor was her way of getting back at a husband who put his political life ahead of their marriage?

It was at least half an hour before Shoemaker finished with his call. He appeared in the archway leading to the hall, somewhat disheveled, running his fingers through his hair. "Come with me," he said. "I have something to show you."

He led me to a large kitchen at the back of the house. A floral arrangement sat on the granite-topped center island: white lilies with a single red rose. Shoemaker handed me the card: "My sympathy on your wife's passing." It was signed "John."

"Where's Mrs. Shoemaker?" I asked.

"Apparently she went out to the coast last night. I haven't seen her since she walked out on us at the noon hour."

"And you've been home the whole time?"

He nodded. "Mainly on the phone."

"Why didn't you call me when she didn't come home?"

"I didn't realize she hadn't until mid-morning. We have separate bedrooms, and Andrea comes and goes as she pleases. Then this arrangement arrived, and my conference call came through . . ." He shrugged, spreading his hands helplessly.

"All right," I said, "I'm going out there whether she likes it or not. And I think you'd better clear up whatever you're doing here and follow. Maybe your showing up there will convince her you care about her safety, make her listen to reason."

As I spoke, Shoemaker had taken a fifth of Tanqueray gin and a jar of Del Prado Spanish olives from a Lucky sack that sat on the counter. He opened a cupboard, reached for a glass.

"No," I said. "This is no time to have a drink."

He hesitated, then replaced the glass, and began giving me directions to the cabin. His voice was flat, and his curious travelogue-like digressions made me feel as if I were listening to a tape of a *National Geographic* special. Reality, I thought, had finally sunk in, and it had turned him into an automaton.

I HAD ONE STOP TO MAKE before heading out to the coast, but it was right on my way. Morrison Investigations had its office in what looked to be a former motel on Highway 101, near the outskirts of the city. It was a neighborhood of fast-food restaurants and bars, thrift shops and marginal businesses. Besides the detective agency, the motel's cinder-block units housed an insurance brokerage, a secretarial service, two accountants, and a palm reader. Dave Morrison, who was just arriving as I pulled into the parking area, was a bit of a surprise: in his mid-forties, wearing one small gold earring and a short ponytail. I wondered what Steve Shoemaker had made of him.

Morrison showed me into a two-room suite crowded with computer equipment and file cabinets and furniture that looked as if he might have hauled it down the street from the nearby Thrift Emporium. When he noticed me studying him, he grinned easily. "I know, I don't look like a former cop. I worked undercover Narcotics my last few years on the force. Afterwards I realized I was comfortable with the uniform." His gesture took in his lumberjack's shirt, work-worn jeans and boots.

I smiled in return, and he cleared some files off a chair so I could sit.

"So you're working for Steve Shoemaker," he said.

"I understand you did, too."

He nodded. "Last April and again around the beginning of August."

"Did he approach you about another job after that?"

He shook his head.

"And the jobs you did for him were—"

"You know better than to ask that."

"I was going to ask, were they completed to his satisfaction?"

"Yes."

"Do you have any idea why Shoemaker would go to the trouble of bringing me up from San Francisco when he had an investigator here whose work satisfied him?"

Headshake.

"Shoemaker told me the first job you did for him had to do with politics."

The corner of his mouth twitched. "In a matter of speaking." He paused, shrewd eyes assessing me. "How come you're investigating your own client?"

"It's that kind of case. And something feels wrong. Did you get that sense about either of the jobs you took on for him?"

"No." Then he hesitated, frowning. "Well, maybe. Why don't you just come out and ask what you want to? If I can, I'll answer."

"Okay—did either of the jobs have to do with a man named John Carding?"

That surprised him. After a moment he asked a question of his own. "He's still trying to trace Carding?"

"Yes."

Morrison got up and moved toward the window, stopped and drummed his fingers on top of a file cabinet. "Well, I can save you further trouble. John Carding is untraceable. I tried every way I know—and that's every way there is. My guess is that he's dead, years dead."

"And when was it you tried to trace him?"

"Most of August."

Weeks before Andrea Shoemaker had begun to receive the notes from "John." Unless the harassment had started earlier? No, I'd seen all the notes, examined their postmarks. Unless she'd thrown away the first ones, as she had the card that came with the funeral arrangement?

"Shoemaker tell you why he wanted to find Carding?" I asked.

"Uh-uh."

"And your investigation last April had nothing to do with Carding?"

At first I thought Morrison hadn't heard the question. He was looking out the window; then he turned, expression thoughtful, and opened one of the drawers of the filing cabinet beside him. "Let me refresh my memory," he said, taking out a couple of folders. I watched as he flipped through them, frowning.

Finally he said, "I'm not gonna ask about your case. If something feels wrong, it could be because of what I turned up last spring—and that I don't want on my conscience." He closed one file, slipped it back in the cabinet, then glanced at his watch. "Damn! I just remembered I've got to make a call." He crossed to the desk, set the open file on it. "I better do it from the other room. You stay here, find something to read."

I waited until he'd left, then went over and picked up the file. Read it with growing interest and began putting things together. Andrea had been discreet about her extramarital activities, but not so discreet that a competent investigator like Morrison couldn't uncover them.

When Morrison returned, I was ready to leave for the Lost Coast.

"Hope you weren't bored," he said.

"No, I'm easily amused. And, Mr. Morrison, I owe you a dinner."

"You know where to find me. I'll look forward to seeing you again."

AND NOW THAT I'd reached the cabin, Andrea had disappeared. The victim of violence, all signs indicated. But the victim of whom? John Carding—a man no one had seen or heard from for over ten years? Another man named John, one of her cast-off lovers? Or . . .?

What mattered now was to find her.

I retraced my steps, turning up the hood of my sweater again as I went outside. circled the cabin, peering through the lashing rain. I could make out a couple of other small structures back there: outhouse and shed. The outhouse was empty. I crossed to the shed. Its door was propped open with a log, as if she'd been getting fuel for the stove.

Inside, next to a neatly stacked cord of wood, I found her.

She lay facedown on the hard-packed dirt floor, blue-jeaned legs splayed, plaid-jacketed arms flung above her head, chestnut hair cascading over her back. The little room was silent, the total silence that surrounds the dead. Even my own breath was stilled; when it came again, it sounded obscenely loud.

I knelt beside her, forced myself to perform all the checks I've made more times than I could have imagined. No breath, no pulse, no warmth to the skin. And the rigidity . . .

On the average—although there's a wide variance—rigor mortis sets in to the upper body five to six hours after death; the whole body is usually affected within eighteen hours. I backed up and felt the lower portion of her body. Rigid; rigor was complete. I straightened, went to stand in the doorway. She'd probably been dead since midnight. And the cause? I couldn't see any wounds, couldn't further examine her without disturbing the scene. What I should be doing was getting in touch with the sheriff's department.

Back to the cabin. Emotions tore at me: anger, regret, and—yes—guilt that I hadn't prevented this. But I also sensed that I *couldn't* have prevented it. I, or someone like me, had been an integral component from the first.

In the front room I found some kitchen matches and lit the oil lamp. Then I went around the table and looked down at where her revolver lay on the floor. More evidence; don't touch it. The purse and its spilled contents rested near the edge of the stove. I inventoried the items visually: the usual makeup, brush, comb, spray perfume; wallet, keys, roll of postage stamps; daily planner that had flopped open to show pockets for business cards and receipts. And a loose piece of paper . . .

Lucky Food Center, it said at the top. Perhaps she'd stopped to pick up supplies before leaving Eureka; the date and time on this receipt might indicate how long she'd remained in town before storming out on her husband and me.

I picked it up. At the bottom I found yesterday's date and the time of purchase: 9:14 P.M.

"KY SERV DELI . . . CRABS . . . WINE . . . DEL PRAD OLIVE . . . LG RED DEL . . . ROUGE ET NOIR . . . BAKERY . . . TANQ GIN—"

A sound outside. Footsteps slogging thorough the mud. I stuffed the receipt into my pocket.

Steve Shoemaker came through the open door in a hurry, rain hat pulled low on his forehead, droplets sluicing down his chiseled nose. He stopped when he saw me, looked around. "Where's Andrea?"

I said, "I don't know."

"What do you mean you don't know? Her Bronco's outside. That's her purse on the stove."

"And her weekend bag's on the bed, but she's nowhere to be found."

Shoemaker arranged his face into lines of concern. "There's been a struggle here."

"Appears that way."

"Come on, we'll go look for her. She may be in the outhouse or the shed. She may be hurt—"

"It won't be necessary to look." I had my gun out of my purse now, and I leveled it at him. "I know you killed your wife, Shoemaker."

"What!"

"Her body's where you left it last night. What time did you kill her? How?"

His faked concern shaded into panic. "I didn't—"

"You did."

No reply. His eyes moved from side to side—calculating, looking for a way out.

I added, "You drove her here in the Bronco, with your motorcycle inside. Arranged things to simulate a struggle, put her in the shed, then drove back to town on the bike. You shouldn't have left the bike outside the house where I could see it. It wasn't muddy out here last night, but it sure was dusty."

"Where are these baseless accusations coming from? John Carding—"

"Is untraceable, probably dead, as you know from the check Dave Morrison ran."

"He told you—What about the notes, the flowers, the dead things—"

"Sent by you."

"Why would I do that?"

"To set the scene for getting rid of a chronically unfaithful wife who had potential to become a political embarrassment."

He wasn't cracking, though. "Granted, Andrea had her problems. But why would I rake up the Carding matter?"

"Because it would sound convincing for you to admit what you did all those years ago. God knows it convinced me. And I doubt the police would ever have made the details public. Why destroy a grieving widower and prominent citizen? Particularly when they'd never find Carding or bring him to trial. You've got one problem, though: me. You never should have brought me in to back up your scenario."

He licked his lips, glaring at me. Then he drew himself up, leaned forward aggressively—a posture the attorneys at All Souls jokingly refer to as their "litigator's mode."

"You have no proof of this," he said firmly, jabbing his index finger at me. "No proof whatsoever."

"Deli items, crabs, wine, apples," I recited. "Del Prado Spanish olives, Tanqueray gin."

"What the hell are you talking about?"

"I have Andrea's receipt for the items she bought at Lucky yesterday, before she stopped home to pick up her weekend bag. None of those things is here in the cabin."

"So?"

"I know that at least two of them—the olives and the gin—are at your house in Eureka. I'm willing to bet they all are."

"What if they are? She did some shopping for me yesterday morning—"

"The receipt is dated yesterday *evening*, nine-fourteen P.M. I'll quote you, Shoemaker: 'Apparently she went out to the coast last night. I haven't seen her since she walked out on us at the noon hour.' But you claim you didn't leave home after noon."

That did it; that opened the cracks. He stood for a moment, then half collapsed into one of the chairs and put his head in his hands.

THE NEXT SUMMER, after I testified at the trial in which Steve Shoemaker was convicted of the first-degree murder of his wife, I returned to the Lost Coast—with a backpack, without the .38, and in the company of my lover. We walked sand beaches under skies that showed infinite shadings of blue; we made love in fields of wildflowers; we waited quietly for the deer, falcons, and foxes.

I'd already taken the bad from this place; now I could take the good.

Nancy Pickard has won just about every mystery award there is, and in doing so has set on the shelf ten books that will likely outlast this era. Nancy took the traditional novel and gave it some of the edge of the hardboiled genre. Read the opening pages of MARRIAGE IS MURDER sometime. Hammett was never tougher or angrier or sadder. Nancy is also very, very witty. She has just the right sardonic eye and ear to record our foolishness. And she came do it in the small town (Port Frederick, Mass.) or the big city (New York). The remarkable thing is that one senses Nancy has only just begun. She'll get even better in the future.

Sign of the Times
NANCY PICKARD

Gentleman Joe had worked with some gorillas in his time, but this was ridiculous. This one was three hundred pounds of ugly and her name was Bubba.

"Good evening, dear," Joe said politely as he stepped into her house trailer that Friday night. "How's my girl?"

The nine-year-old lowland gorilla raised her massive head from the comfy nest of blankets where she slept in her cage. She opened one intelligent black eye, lifted the rubbery fingers of one hand and greeted Joe with an easily identifiable and definitely obscene gesture.

Joe's companion stared.

"Did that monkey just do what I think she did?" Melvin asked. His own blue, but not nearly so intelligent eyes widened. "I don't think she likes you, G.J."

"Nonsense." Joe entered his initials and the exact time in the logbook in which the university professors kept minute-by-minute track of the care and feeding of Bubba. She was rarely left alone or unguarded; a gap of only thirty seconds appeared between the time the last graduate student, a woman named Carole, had signed out and Joe signed in. He stepped over to the refrigerator, opened the door and looked over the tasty assortment of gorilla treats and vitamins. "Here, have a banana."

"Thanks." Melvin caught the fruit Joe tossed to him, but paused before he peeled it. "She's looking at me funny, Joe. Is this her banana?"

"Melvin." Joe spoke with the exaggerated patience one uses with the lower orders. "Try to remember she's just an animal. Try to remember who's boss." He grabbed an apple for himself. Bubba's eyes fastened on its shiny red beauty; the thick fingers of her left hand moved in her right palm.

"Yeah, but ain't this the one what can talk?"

"She has a vocabulary, yes," Joe said loftily. "The professors have taught her sign language and she knows about six hundred-fifty words."

"Do any of them include get your hands off my banana or I'll kill you?"

Joe chuckled. He fastidiously picked gorilla hairs off the seat of Bubba's favorite easy chair and sat down. In her cage, Bubba's brows came down over her eyes. "You have the wrong idea about gorillas," Joe explained to Melvin. "They're strong, of course, but they're not mean. Bubba won't hurt you."

"If you say so." Melvin put the uneaten banana on the coffee table. He offered the gorilla a tense but conciliatory grin. She drew back her lips in a wide grin, too, showing off large teeth that were rather more white than Melvin's.

"See?" Gentleman Joe crunched down on the apple. "Now go back to sleep, Bubba, it's past your bedtime."

The gorilla obediently lowered her eyelids, though a glint of white continued to show between her lashes. She was accustomed to Joe's presence as her night guardian now that he'd been on the job a month. It was his probation officer who'd convinced the university to hire him based on the facts of his college degree and his reputation for having a peaceable—albeit greedy—nature.

"She's amazing, really," Joe lectured. "Or so the good professors say. Her 'talk' is not just a simple matter of saying yes, no, and feed me; any dog can communicate that much. Bubba's use of language extends even to abstractions."

He automatically answered the blank look on Melvin's face.

"I mean she can understand concepts like right and wrong, good and bad, happy and sad. You've just seen her insult me. She can also make jokes and even play games of pretend. She actually seems to *think*. She makes up words, she asks simple questions, and answers others correctly. What I find most astonishing is that she has a sense of time—past, present, and future. She can refer back to events and emotions that took place in the past, for instance."

Melvin looked dumbfounded.

"Do you mean to say," he demanded, "that tomorrow she'll remember we was here tonight?"

"Correct factually if not grammatically."

"And she'd be able to tell somebody that?"

"Very good, Melvin. You're nearly as perceptive as Bubba."

Melvin ignored the sarcasm. He grinned broadly and, this time, genuinely. "Well, my God, G.J., that there gives me an idea."

Joe grimaced at the solecism.

"Your last idea got me five years in Leavenworth, Melvin. Don't talk to me about your ideas."

"But you got out for good behavior."

"I *always* get out for good behavior." Joe crossed one leg of his crisply clean jeans over the other. He always had his jeans dry cleaned—hung, no starch—and his shirts professionally pressed, even if the luxury entailed other sacrifices. "A gentleman," as he frequently remarked, "has his priorities." His immaculate appearance was one reason for his nickname. Joe might be a thief, but he always looked the part of a gentleman. He said determinedly, "And now I'm going to stay out on good behavior."

Melvin's small eyes shifted.

"But G.J.," he said in syrupy tones, "there's a charity ball tonight."

"Do not tell me. I do not want to know." His specialty was robbing the kitty at charity fund-raising events; in his trademark tuxedo, Joe moved easily among the rich from whose burdened shoulders he liked to remove the worry of wealth.

"It's a fund raiser for the preservation of English opera. . . ."

"Dear God, who'd want to preserve that?"

". . . And they're having a money tree, Joe."

"You are a manipulative and despicable person, Melvin."

"This money tree is going to be seven feet high and the guests will stick their cash gifts onto it."

"*Cash?*"

"Yeah, no checks. It's a gimmick for publicity pictures. All that beautiful green cash, like a tree budding leaves in the spring."

Joe rolled his eyes at Melvin's flight of poetic fancy. He took the nearly nibbled core of his apple and deposited it in the garbage disposal. From the cage in the corner came a low growl.

"You imply it is harvest time," Joe inquired of Melvin, "and I the happy reaper?"

"No." His companion grinned and sprang his idea. "*I'm* the reaper this time. Listen, G.J., we've got the opportunity here for the world's most unusual alibi. I'll put on a tux and pull the job while you stay here with Bubba. I'll make sure the job has all the earmarks of one of your heists, so the cops will naturally assume it was you."

"Are you *crazy?*" Gentleman Joe's carefully cultivated aplomb shattered for a moment, revealing a hint of pure, unadulterated Bronx.

"Then when the cops come to question you, you'll have a witness to prove you was here all the time." Melvin leaned back in his chair in a most irritatingly superior way.

"Bubba?"

"You said she remembers the past, right? And she answers questions, right? And the professors will back up whatever their monkey says 'cause their scientific reputations are at stake, right? What have we got to lose? They'll never connect this job to me, and you'll have an alibi that's so weird it's got to be true."

Joe picked up Bubba's favorite red ball from the floor and bounced it thoughtfully from hand to hand. The gorilla's eyes followed the ball, back and forth, back and forth. "I really loathe English opera," Joe said finally. "Sixty-fifty split?"

"Agreed." Melvin grinned hugely. "Guess I'd better go climb into my monkey suit."

They laughed uproariously.

In her cozy nest, Bubba grinned, too.

"WE KNOW YOU DID IT, Joe." Approximately twenty-four hours later, the police detective was squeezed into the house trailer with Joe and two university professors, Dr. Andy Kline and Dr. LouAnn Frasier. They'd come quickly in the middle of the night at Joe's request. "This job has your name all over it in capital letters. Not much of a challenge, frankly. You're not as much fun as you used to be, G.J."

The professors stared.

"I was here the whole time," Joe said calmly. He smiled reassuringly at his employers, who smiled uneasily back at him. "I could not possibly have robbed a charity ball."

The detective also smiled. "Prove it."

"I have a witness."

"Who?"

Joe pointed at the gorilla in the cage.

At the cop's incredulous look, the professors hastened to provide a short course on language development and intelligence in the lowland gorilla. They were very convincing.

"Nobody could make this up," the detective said finally. He shook his head. "If that gorilla says you were here, it's just so damned weird, it's got to be true."

"Ask her," Joe said confidently.

"Doctor?" The detective turned to Dr. Kline. "Would you please grill your gorilla?"

"Certainly, officer." The professor sat down on the floor facing Bubba, who glanced alertly at each human in turn, lingering a moment on Joe.

"I'm asking her to identify that man," the professor explained as he began signing.

"Joe," was Bubba's reply, through the professor's translation. The cop looked impressed.

"She's crazy about me," Joe assured the detective.

"I'm asking her if she remembers last night," Dr. Kline continued.

"Yes," Bubba signed. "Bubba sleep."

"I'm asking who she saw last night."

"Carole," Bubba signed, and the professor explained that Carole was the graduate student who had the duty before Joe.

"Who else, Bubba?"

The moving, rubbery fingers paused. Then they signed.

"Nobody."

Gentleman Joe's heart began to pound to strange African rhythms.

"Nobody, Bubba?" Dr. Frasier broke in. "Joe was here last night, wasn't he?"

"No. Bubba alone. Bubba sad."

The professors and the detective stared accusingly at Joe.

"I was here!" he protested desperately. "She's lying!"

The cop turned a skeptical face to the professors. "Is that possible? Can *gorillas* lie?"

"Oh, yes," Dr. Kline said. Joe's heart settled back into a normal rhythm. "Interestingly enough, the ability to lie is proof of advanced capability in language and thought. I'm afraid Bubba can fib with the best—or worst—of us."

"However ..." Something in Dr. Frasier's tone set Joe's palms to sweating again. "... gorillas are individuals, just as humans are, with distinct personality traits. Bubba, for instance, always tells the truth about people she likes."

"Oh, my God," Joe said weakly. An image of a certain obscene gesture floated through his mind, followed by an image of Melvin basking on a beach in Acapulco, followed by an image of a neatly wrapped parcel containing thousands of dollars in cash that was sitting on a shelf in Joe's apartment.

The cop's grin was as wide as Bubba's.

"You said it yourself, Joe." He smirked. "She's crazy about me, you said. So much for this monkey business of an alibi! Let's mosey on down to the station, shall we? And have a nice gentlemanly conversation about all those incriminating clues you left scattered around the scene of the crime."

He led a stumbling Gentleman Joe out the door to the waiting police car.

In the trailer, black rubbery fingers moved quietly in a palm.

"Bye, bye, Joe," they said.

About the time this anthology appears, Baen books will publish Larry Segriff's first novel, a smooth, fascinating adventure story that recalls the wonderful early books of Robert Heinlein. This anthology includes several other mystery writers who've also worked in science fiction—Carole Nelson Douglas, Dana Stabenow, and Ed Gorman among them—so Larry should feel right at home. The name Larry Segriff will be more familiar to you by this time next year when even more of his fine, polished stories have appeared in mystery and science fiction publications alike.

Unkindest Cut
LARRY SEGRIFF

Her sudden lunge caught me by surprise. I rocked back on my heels, but I couldn't get out of range, and her blade *thunked* solidly against my mask.

"Nice shot, Sue," I said.

She grinned. "Not really. If you'd quit looking at my legs so much, you wouldn't be such an easy target."

I shrugged. "Wear knickers, then."

"What, and miss all these easy shots? Are you crazy?"

I had to admit, she had great legs, and as long as she was going to wear those high-cut running shorts, I was going to look. At practice, anyway.

She sketched a brief salute and came at me again.

I couldn't help myself. I grinned, and dropped my gaze to her legs once more.

I was between cases at the moment, a situation I was all too familiar with these days with my little one-man detective agency. I fenced for the enjoyment and the exercise, and for the occasional paycheck I picked up directing at the bigger meets. Once in a great while, I'd help put on a demo somewhere, too, but mostly I fenced for the fun.

We were a university club, and on this Friday evening, the last regular practice of the year, turnout was light. It was the end of finals week, Mother's Day just two days away, and most of the students were gone.

75

Of those who were still in town, most of them were down at the bars, celebrating, instead of sweating on the strip.

I couldn't say I blamed them, of course. My own college days weren't so long ago that I couldn't remember what it was like. Still, I was glad for those few—either too young to drink or too old to get excited about it—who'd show up to fence.

Sue was in that latter category, maybe twenty-five or so. She was a grad student in paleontology, but I hadn't yet been able to interest her in my old bones. We'd gone out a time or two for beers after fencing, as I'd done with almost everyone in the club, but it had never progressed beyond the friendship stage.

She was short, maybe five-three on her tiptoes, well below my nearly six-foot frame. Her hair was dark, as was mine, but hers was more nearly black while mine was a flat brown. She had gray eyes; mine were green, but changed according to the light.

Sue fenced foil, mostly. She was using a saber tonight because it was my birthday, and she wanted to be kind to me. Maybe that was why she wasn't wearing her knickers, too.

She lunged again, and I parried, and she parried. I picked up the remise of her initial attack with a *prise de fer* counterattack, a strong taking of her blade, but she was ready for that. Maintaining pressure on my blade so I couldn't release, she turned her lunge into a flèche and ran by me.

No point either way, but it was a nice phrase, and I said so. She smiled, came back on guard, and lunged again.

Happy birthday.

"So, we going out afterward?" she asked.

I shrugged. "That's up to the rest of you. I'd like to, of course. Maybe out to the East Ender." That was our favorite watering hole, an English-style pub—or as close as you were likely to find here in the heartlands—that served sandwiches and wonderful onion rings until nearly midnight on Fridays and Saturdays.

"Sounds good," she said. "I'll ask around."

Then the fencing got serious, and we had no breath for talking.

AS IT TURNED OUT, there were only eight of us at practice, and half of us went out. Sue and I were joined by Linda and Jeff. They were no more a couple than Sue and I were, though Jeff gave clear signals that he'd like them to be.

Linda was young, just finishing up her first year of classes at the university. I hadn't really tried to get to know her yet, but I thought I'd heard her say she was from Nebraska. Tall and blond, with surprisingly warm brown eyes, she made quite a contrast with Sue when the two of them fenced.

Jeff was a bit older, maybe twenty-one or -two. An engineering student, he was in his junior year and doing quite well from what he said. He was sandy-haired and stocky, and worked out a lot.

We found a table in one of the corners and ordered a pitcher. Linda was underage, but the waitress knew us and brought her a glass anyway. She also brought a pitcher of ice water and a plate of garlic bread, without our having to order them.

We were pretty good customers, even if most of us couldn't afford much of a tip.

"You fencing in the meet next weekend?" Jeff asked me. He was on his third glass of beer already. I was still drinking water.

"Thinking about it," I said. We always liked to kick off the summer with a fun meet. Those of us who lived in town—and there were a surprising number of us, for a university club—got together and fenced and grilled burgers and drank beer. The last couple of years we'd opened it up to other regional clubs, and some of the hotshots, like Jeff, were pressing to make it even bigger. Like me, Jeff was a saber fencer. Unlike me, that was just about all he fenced. If he kept with it, he had a shot at being very good in a few more years. "I might just direct instead."

He nodded. "Be a good thing if you fenced. Might help draw some folks from out of state."

I frowned. I've never liked pressure, even from friends. "Like I said, I'm thinking about it."

He nodded again and took the hint. Helping himself to more beer, he turned toward Linda and asked her the same question.

Sue leaned over to me, and I didn't get to hear Linda's response. Not that I really needed to. She was just learning to fence, still practicing her footwork. I'd be surprised if she felt ready to compete.

"I hate to see him drink so much." Sue spoke in a low voice directly into my ear. "He has a tendency to get mean."

I nodded, remembering a few incidents. Jeff was a stocky guy. He worked out a lot, mostly to keep the beer off his gut, I thought, and there had been several times in the last couple of years when I'd pulled him out of a bar where things were starting to get nasty.

A real nice guy, even on the strip—which was surprising for a saber fencer—but he didn't mix well with booze. Following Sue's eyes, I saw that he had his hand on Linda's arm and was leaning in close to her. She seemed to be handling it all right, though, so I decided not to say anything.

Instead, I flagged the waitress so we could order some food. Most of us didn't eat before practice, and I hoped that putting some food in Jeff's belly would slow him down.

It didn't work. He muttered something about being low on cash and simply ordered more beer. I didn't bother offering a loan. If he could afford to drink, he could afford to eat. Clearly, it wasn't his wallet that was stopping him, it was his priorities, and I couldn't loan him any of mine.

All in all, we had a pretty nice time. Sue and Linda chipped in to buy my beers, but I wouldn't let them pay for my meal, too. My income was small and irregular, it was true, but I could still afford to eat. I couldn't always say the same for them.

We walked out to the parking lot as a group and headed over to Sue's car, a battered old Ford in even worse shape than my Toyota.

Jeff, huddled against the chill of the wind, caught at Linda's arm. "Give you a ride?" He gestured toward his motorcycle, but the leer on his face and the emphasis he'd placed on the last word indicated a different meaning altogether.

My heart went out to Linda. She had to be used to such advances, I knew, but still I felt sorry for her. There was an air of innocence about her that I hated to see sullied.

She handled it well, though. "Thank you, Jeff," she said, answering only his words, "but not tonight. It's too cold, and I'm still sweaty from practice."

"I'll keep you warm," he said with that same disgusting leer.

"No, thanks," she said again, and this time there was an unmistakable edge in her voice. Turning away, she got in the passenger's side of Sue's ancient Ford.

Jeff glowered and stomped off.

"Do you think he should drive?" Sue asked me.

I didn't answer her, I was already walking off after him.

"Jeff!" I called. "Wait up!"

He didn't slow, but he didn't speed up, either, and I caught up with him as he was mounting his bike.

"She's right; it is too cold for that. Why don't you catch a ride with me?"

He put the key in the ignition before raising his gaze to meet mine. "Jax," he said. "Fuck off," and kicked down hard. The engine fired and caught, and he roared off without another word.

I sighed and stared off after him. That kid was getting hard to be around. Zipping up my coat a little higher, I turned and went back to Sue.

"I saw," she said. "God, he was really disgusting, wasn't he?"

"Yeah. Be sure and talk to Linda about it, will you? I'd rather she didn't hate him because of it."

She gave me a hard look. "I don't understand you, Jax. How can you defend him so much?"

I shrugged. "Hell, he's just a kid, Sue. I don't want to see his mistakes follow him for the rest of his life." I looked away, reluctant to add anything further, but after a moment I brought my gaze back to her. "Hell, Sue, I've done some pretty stupid things myself. I'm only glad that most of them are safely in the past."

She frowned, but didn't respond.

"Speaking of stupid things," I went on, "I was going to ask you for a birthday kiss, but he kind of put me out of the mood."

She took an involuntary step backward. "Don't," she said, then stopped. I hadn't moved. "Oh, Jax, I wish—"

She didn't say anything more. Just turned and opened her door and got in. A moment later she was gone, as abruptly, as inexplicably, as Jeff.

Shaking my head, I went to my old Toyota and took myself home. Some birthday.

I SPENT THE NEXT DAY at my small office, riding the desk and hoping the phone would ring. It didn't. No belated cards came either, which was exactly the same amount that had arrived on time. Oh, well.

Sunday turned out no better. Mother's Day: just another square on the calendar, right? Only this one always carried a load of grief and guilt for me. Not that Father's Day was much better.

Sue showed up a little late, looking like she'd been crying. I wasn't fencing at the time. Two novices—young, local kids—were the only ones there, and I didn't feel much like giving a lesson. She didn't say anything. Just slipped her mask on and grabbed a foil. I didn't feel I could ask her what was wrong. I merely nodded and pulled out my own blade and didn't even kid her about leaving her sweatpants on.

On Sundays, practice usually ran from one to about three. Now that we had started our summer schedule, we fenced until nearly five. When Linda hadn't shown up by the end, Sue started asking about her.

"She said she was coming today, didn't she?"

I shrugged, toweling off. I knew she was staying in town for the summer, but I didn't know about this weekend. "I don't know. She talked to Jeff more than to me." Which didn't help much. Jeff hadn't come to practice, either. "You don't think they're together, do you?"

She snorted and shook her head. "Not after what she had to say about him Friday."

I frowned, unable to find anything to say to that. She obviously hadn't tried to stick up for Jeff, but I couldn't really blame her for that.

"So what do you think?" I asked.

"I think I'll drop by Linda's on my way home. Want to come?"

"Sure," I said with no hesitation. I wasn't particularly worried about Linda, but I thought spending some time with Sue might shed a little light on her own behavior.

We drove over separately, Sue in the lead. I knew which dorm Linda lived in, but I'd never been to her room.

It was a large brick building with almost no on-street parking. The U liked to funnel all cars to very large, and very faraway parking lots. Being Sunday, with lots of moms and pops picking up their bright, young progeny, we were unable to find spots together. Finally, pulling over into a quasi-legal space, Sue rolled down her window and yelled, "Eighteen-oh-seven. Come when you can."

The car behind me honked, and I waved and drove off. It took me ten minutes to find an empty spot of my own, and ten more to walk back to Linda's dorm.

The door to 1807 was closed, and no one answered my knock. After a moment, I tried the knob, found it unlocked, and went on in.

A glorified shoe box, like most dormitories, this one was maybe fifteen feet square. There were two beds in it, hardly more than cots, with twin dresser-desk combinations built into one wall. Next to the door, a large, double closet stood, with accordion-fold doors to offer a modicum of privacy.

I saw all that in a glance, filling in details from when I'd lived in a similar room, almost fifteen years before. Then I saw the two women and the blood, and had no more time for sightseeing.

The nearest of the two beds was unmade. Glancing at it, I could see a smear of blood and other stains. I felt immediately I knew what had happened, and a quick look at Linda confirmed it.

She sat in a chair near the window, as far from the door and that bed as she could get. Her knees were pulled up to her chin, her face bore a tortured expression, and she wasn't moving. Sue was kneeling at her side, trying to offer some comfort, but Linda was not responding. She just kept staring at that bed.

I took one look at her face and then looked away, unable to bear the sight any longer. There was some puffiness to her lips, and a darkening ring around her left eye, but it was the suffering in those eyes that made me turn away.

She'd showered—obsessively, I'd have guessed—and was dressed, but that was as far back to normal as she'd come. Her long blond hair was a tangled mess, and she'd made no attempt to cover any of the marks with makeup.

I took one step into the room, Linda's name on my lips, but Sue stopped me before I could say anything. "Go home, Jax," she said. "I'll call you later."

I didn't want to leave, but it was clear I could do no good there at the moment. Feeling woefully inadequate, I nodded once and left.

Perhaps I should have gone straight home. Instead, I went downstairs to a university phone, opened up the directory, and got Jeff's address. Then I took myself there.

He didn't live far away. In fact, his frat house was just up the street. It was a glorious spring day, showing none of the chill we'd had on Friday, but I hardly noticed as I strode down the cracked sidewalk.

Delta Rho was the fourth house from the end, and I went in without knocking. Some pledge looked up from where he was doing scut work in the kitchen and asked if he could help me.

"Jeff Carlton," I said. "He live here?"

"Sure," the dweeb said. "Should I call him for you?"

"I'll go up. Where's his room?"

"You're not allowed—" he began. I cut him off with a look.

"Where's his room?" I repeated.

I don't normally think of myself as a dangerous man, but something of my rage must have shown through because the kid told me. "Upstairs, second floor, last room on the left."

I headed up the stairs without another word. Behind me, I could see him diving for a phone, but I didn't care. I didn't think I'd be there long.

At the first landing I headed left, watching for signs of Jeff. The kid could have lied to me, of course, but I didn't think so. I'd seen his face, and I believed him.

The last door was closed. I kicked it open. Jeff was inside, in a room slightly smaller than Linda's. It had only one bed, but this wasn't bloody and he was sitting on it.

"Jax," he said, looking up at my entrance. "What the hell?"

That was as far as he got. In two strides I was right next to him. Without a word, I swung my fist as hard as I could.

He made no move to protect himself, and my blow landed high on his cheekbone. He cried out and fell back, and then I felt strong hands grip me from behind.

"No!" Jeff cried, struggling to get back up. "Jaws, Ape, it's all right. Really."

At his words the grip on me fell away. I could hear a small crowd gathered behind me, but I didn't turn to look at them. I kept my eyes on Jeff.

"You son of a bitch," I said when his gaze came up to meet mine.

"Jax—"

"I just left her. She's a mess, literally a mess. Friday night she was a nice, pretty young girl, with her whole life ahead of her. Now she's a broken woman with nothing to look forward to but nightmares and terror for years to come. Are you proud of yourself, Jeff? Just tell me that. Are you proud of yourself?"

"Jax," he said, and this time I let him talk. I had nothing more to say, and I didn't feel like hitting him again just yet. "What in the hell are you talking about?"

I almost did hit him again, then. He must have seen that on my face because he lifted his hands defensively. I chose to batter him with words, instead.

"Linda," I said, spitting the name at him. "I just left her, like I said. I saw what you did to her."

He lowered his hands, and I saw confusion blooming on his face behind them. "What I did to Linda? Jax, I'm going to ask you again: what are you talking about?"

"Jesus, Jeff, do I have to spell it out for you? Sue got worried about her, so we went over to check on her. And we found her, just as you left her Friday night."

He was shaking his head. "Jax, I left her at the same time I left you: in the parking lot at the East Ender. I swear, I have no idea what you're talking about."

"Christ, Jeff. You raped her. What do I have to do, search your room for her panties to make you admit it?"

He had gone pale at my words. "Rape? God, Jax, no. I didn't."

My hands formed themselves into fists again, but this time he didn't move. "Come on, Jeff. You weren't surprised to see me, and you weren't surprised to see me furious."

His face grew even grimmer at that. "Yeah, Jax, you're right. I wasn't surprised when you burst in here, but not for that reason." He rose to his feet, and I let him. It would just be that much more satisfying to knock him down again, if I decided to.

Unconsciously, his right hand came up and massaged the beginnings of the bruise I'd given him. "Did she say I did it, Jax?"

I shook my head. "She wasn't talking at all when I was there. But," I added, unwilling to grant him anything, "she didn't have to. It was obvious. My God, man, you were all over her Friday night. Sue and I both saw it."

He nodded. "Yeah, and I'm sorry for that—"

"Sorry!" I broke in. "Jeff, I've stood up for you a lot of times, but this is one situation where an apology just isn't enough."

"Jax," his eyes were boring into mine with a seriousness I'd never seen from him before, "I was picked up Friday night, not more than ten minutes after I left the pub. Drunk driving. I know you're in tight with the cops, so I figured you'd have heard all about it. It was after midnight when they arrested me, so they were able to hold me until today. I got home only a few hours ago." His look was, if anything, even bleaker. "You've got to know how sorry I am about what happened to Linda, but it wasn't me, Jax. It wasn't me."

I felt as if my punch had rebounded and landed in my gut. "Jeff, I—"

He waved it away. "Don't worry about it, Jax. You're right, you've gone to bat for me a lot. I had it coming. Let's just forget about it, okay?"

I shook my head. It was fine if he wanted to forgive and forget. I wasn't going to let me off that easy.

"I've got to go," I said and, without another word, spun on my heel and left.

I don't remember much about the walk to my car. It must have calmed me somewhat, however, because I made it home without any further problems. At least, I didn't have any accidents, and no cops stopped me.

I tried to drink a beer after I got home, but I didn't really want it. I just kept replaying that scene with Jeff. Part of it, of course, was that I was furious—and more than a little disillusioned—with myself for losing control like that, and at the wrong person. Mostly, though, I kept asking myself, *If not Jeff, who?*

There was no answer to that, and the day finally wound down to a dark and cheerless close.

MONDAY EVENING, I returned home from work to find Sue sitting out on my porch. The warmth of yesterday was but a memory, and the bite in the air had turned her cheeks and nose red. Still, she sat quietly, an unopened six-pack on the swing beside her, seeming not to notice the chill.

She moved the cans as I came up the steps, and I took the spot next to her.

"She's going home." Sue handed me a beer and opened one for herself.

I nodded. "How's she doing?" Stupid question. I knew, but there didn't seem much else to say.

"She's shattered, Jax. Absolutely shattered." Sue tipped back her can and took a long, long drink. "I got her to the hospital and called the Crisis Center for her, but it didn't do much good. I only hope she can get some help back home."

I opened my beer and drank some of it. "Call the police?"

She shook her head. "She didn't want me to. Said she just wanted to forget about it." She gave me a dark look. "That was more than an hour after you left. It took me that long just to get her to start talking."

I had to look away. It made no sense, but at that moment I felt partly guilty, as if being a man was enough to incriminate. From what I saw in Sue's eyes, maybe it was. "Did she say who did it?"

That earned me a scornful look. "She didn't have to."

"No, Sue," I shook my head. "That's what I thought, too, but I was wrong." I told her about my visit to Jeff. At first she was unwilling to believe me, but after I showed her the box in the newspaper she had no choice.

"Damn," she said.

"Yeah. It was bad enough when we had someone to blame. Now . . ."

We both drank some more beer.

"Jax?" she said after a while.

"Yeah?"

"I've never told this to anyone."

"Sue." I didn't know what I was going to say. The pain in her voice pulled the word out of me, but she didn't let me go on.

"I was raped once. Back in high school. I'd gone out with this guy, a friend of a friend, and we had a good time. Up until I said no, anyway. We'd been drinking a little, not much, and he decided I didn't really mean it. I did. I pressed charges, but he walked. The jury found it a case of implied consent. Said I'd agreed to go out with him, I'd agreed to go back to his place, even knowing his parents were out of town. Like that meant I agreed to everything else. Bastard. That's why I fence, and why I study martial arts." She trained in Tae Kwon Do, I knew, and Shotokan karate. "That's also why I've never let you . . ."

Her voice trailed off, and there was nothing I could do. I wanted very much to hold her right then, but I didn't think she'd be receptive to the idea.

"I just can't," she finished.

I thought back to yesterday, and how she'd looked when she first walked into the fencing room. Had she gotten pregnant? I had wondered. If so, I had the feeling Mother's Day was even worse for her than it was for me.

My hands had closed around the beer can I held until I was almost crushing it. I looked down at them, surprised, and forced them to relax.

"What happened to him?" I asked, my voice low and rough.

She gave a bitter little laugh. "He went on to college—not this one— and then into business with his father. Last I heard, he had a wife and a couple of kids. Sometimes, I dream about going back and finding some way to make him pay, but I can't, Jax. Anything I do to him would affect those others in his life, the innocent ones. I can't hurt them like he hurt me, Jax."

She finished her beer, tossed the can in one corner of the porch— standard procedure for my place—and stood up.

"Leaving so soon?"

"Yeah. I need to talk to Linda. If she'll talk. You say Jeff didn't do it; I'm going to find out who did."

I rose, too. I didn't offer to help her investigate, and she didn't ask me to. Hell, this wasn't a case. It was a vendetta.

"Call me," I said.

She nodded and was gone, leaving four full beers behind. I looked at them briefly, then took them inside and put them in the fridge.

I made myself a minor dinner, something from the freezer, and was picking at it when the phone rang. It was Sue.

"She's still not saying much. Said her roomy is gone for the summer. She left Thursday, after her last test. No help there. As for who the guy was, Linda wouldn't say. Flat out refused to name him, or even say whether she knew him. She says she's trying to forget about it, and doesn't really want to talk about it. I told her that won't help, but believe me, I understand what she's feeling."

"Okay, Sue. Thanks for letting me know."

"No problem. I'm going to talk to some of the people in the adjoining rooms, see if anyone saw or heard anything. It was pretty late Friday, though. Won't have been many students still around. It's worth a shot, though."

"Yeah," I agreed. "And listen, anytime you want to talk, you know where I am."

Silence for a moment, then she said, "Right. Thanks, Jax. I might take you up on that sometime." And then she hung up.

Something was nagging at me. Something she'd said, maybe, or something I'd seen, but I couldn't put my finger on it. I worked at it for a while, then shrugged and gave up. Tossing the remains of my supper, I helped myself to one of Sue's beers and went looking for a book to read.

THE NEXT DAY was Tuesday, a practice day. We usually met over at the Field House around seven. I still had nothing in the works so I showed up a little early, skipping dinner as was my wont.

Sue was already there when I arrived, and we had a chance to talk, but it turned out there wasn't all that much to say. She'd asked around, but had learned as little as she'd expected. Most of the people on that floor had been gone; the few that were there hadn't heard or seen a thing.

I asked her to fence, but she shook her head. "No, Jax. The mood I'm in, it'd probably be a painful experience. I'll inflict it on somebody else."

It was one of the worst practices I could ever remember. Through it all, I kept thinking about what had been done to Linda. My mind kept replaying the scene in her room, showing me visions of her hunched over in that chair, bloodstained and broken. I raised a few welts that night myself, and spent most of the evening apologizing. Sue and I had decided not to say anything about what had happened, so explaining was out of the question. Like her, I simply had to pick my targets with care.

Jeff didn't show up until 8:45, barely fifteen minutes before we normally knocked off. He had his gear, though, and since I had run out of people to beat on, I offered to fence him. He agreed, and the swelling on his left cheekbone was a strong reminder to me to take it easy.

"How's it going, Jeff?" I asked as he got into his gear.

He shrugged. "I'm not drinking anymore, if that's what you mean."

Well, no, that wasn't what I meant, but I didn't blame him for being a little edgy. "How about some épée tonight? Gear up for the meet."

He nodded, and we grabbed our blades. We didn't speak again until we were out on the strip.

"How's Linda?" he asked.

I stiffened partway through my salute. "She's back home," I said. "And, Jeff, Sue and I agreed that no one needs to know what happened. She deserves that much at least, so let's not talk about it here, okay?"

He nodded, and we started to fence.

Anyone watching would have wondered what the hell was wrong with us. We were both stiff and tentative, a far cry from our normal styles. Fortunately, no one was watching us.

I had just landed a solid shot in his chest, bending my blade. There was a pause in the action while I attempted to straighten it. The time honored but not-recommended method was to run it under a foot, putting weight on it the entire time. As I was doing that, I brought up something that had been bothering me.

"Listen, Jeff, I want to apologize again about poking you on Sunday."

"Forget it, Jax," he began, but I cut him off.

"No. Hear me out. It's not just the poke. Like you said, maybe you had it coming. I still feel bad about it, but I can live with it. The part that's really bugging me is that I was so convinced that you had done it. If you hadn't had that alibi . . ."

My voice trailed off, but he didn't seem to notice anything amiss. "Like I said, Jax, forget it. I was way out of line that night. Anyone would have thought the same thing. Jax?"

I had frozen while he spoke, the tip of my épée still trapped beneath my left foot.

"Jess," I said, and even I could hear the difference in my voice. "That alibi." At those words I could see him stiffen.

"Yeah?"

"What time did you say the cops picked you up?"

"After midnight, Jax."

"Right. Ten minutes after we left the parking lot?"

"Something like that."

I tensed, and felt the tip of my épée break off beneath my foot. "Nice try, Jeff. You know I don't wear a watch to practice. It would have worked, too, on a different night. Friday was my birthday, though, as you may recall, and I was keyed up when I got home, too keyed up to sleep. I turned on the tube for a while, just long enough to see that Jay Leno was still on. It wasn't midnight yet, Jeff, not by at least an hour, and the paper said you were picked up at 1:25 A.M.

"You did it, Jeff. You raped her."

His shoulders fell and so did the point of his weapon. "So what are you doing to do, Jax? Hit me again? Or are you going to turn me in to the police, Mr. Private Investigator?" There was a note of defiance in his voice, an almost childish taunt.

"No, Jeff," I said. "I'm going to fence you. Come to guard."

"It wasn't really rape," he said. "I mean, she never said no or anything."

I stiffened at that, fury filling my limbs with the desire to throttle him. "Did she say yes, Jeff? Did you give her a chance to say anything at all?"

He didn't answer.

"Come to guard, you son of a bitch," I said.

Reluctantly, he did so.

In a few years, he probably would have been a good fencer. On that night, however, he was not good enough. As he came to guard, I brought my own blade up, revealing the jagged end for the first time. I thought I heard him gasp, but by then I was already moving.

I beat once and felt his point slip aside, and then I lunged, full out, putting all my fury, all my pain, and all my sorrow into it. I could have gone for his throat; I could have tried for a weak spot in his mask. I didn't. I aimed much lower than that.

I hit him in the groin, and I felt my blade sink into him a long ways. He cried out, once, and collapsed, my épée still buried in him.

What the hell, I thought as I removed my mask and watched the sudden commotion. What I'd just done could cost me my license, I knew, but at the moment I didn't really care. Besides, I suspected the whole thing would be written off as an unfortunate accident. He'd live, and he had to know that if he tried to bring charges against me, I'd tell the cops what I knew. I only hoped my aim had been good enough to make sure he never raped anyone again.

I wondered if I would ever feel bad about what I'd just done, but I decided I probably wouldn't. After all, I realized, it wasn't really an attack. I mean, he never said no, did he?

Ian Rankin won the 1992 Raymond Chandler Fulbright Fellowship in crime and detective fiction. This season he's won the Golden Dagger for the following story. Rankin is a Scotsman who lives in France with his wife and son. His most recent novel features his Inspector Rebus in THE BLACK BOOK.

A Deep Hole
IAN RANKIN

I used to be a road digger, which is to say I dug up roads for a living. These days I'm a Repair Effecter for the council's Highways Department. I still dig up roads—sorry, *highways*—only now it sounds better, doesn't it? They tell me there's some guy in an office somewhere whose job is thinking up posh names for people like me, for the rubbish collectors and street sweepers and toilet attendants. (Usually they manage to stick in the word "environmental" somewhere.) This way, we're made to feel important. Must be some job that, thinking up posh names. I wonder what job title *he's* given himself. Environmental Title Co-ordination Executive, eh?

They call me Sam the Spade. There's supposed to be a joke there, but I don't get it. I got the name because after Robbie's got to work with the pneumatic drill, I get in about things with the spade and clear out everything he's broken up. Robbie's called "The Driller Killer." That was the name of an old horror video. I never saw it myself. I tried working with the pneumatic drill a few times. There's more pay if you operate the drill. You become *skilled* rather than unskilled labour. But after fifteen seconds I could feel the fillings popping out of my teeth. Even now my spine aches in bed at night. Too much sex, the boys say. Ha ha.

Now Daintry, his title would be something like Last Hope Cash Dispensation Executive. Or, in the old parlance, a plain money lender. Nobody remembers Daintry's first name. He shrugged it off some time back when he was a teenager, and he hasn't been a teenager for a few years and some. He's the guy you go to on a Friday or Saturday for a few quid to see you through the weekend. And come the following week's dole cheque (or, if you're one of the fortunate few, pay packet) Daintry'll be waiting while you cash it, his hand out for the money he loaned plus a whack of interest.

While you're only too happy to see Daintry before the weekend, you're not so happy about him still being around *after* the weekend. You don't want to pay him back, certainly not the interest. But you do, inevitably. You do pay him back. Because he's a persistent sort of fellow with a good line in colourful threats and a ready abundance of Physical Persuasion Techniques.

I think the chief reason people didn't like Daintry was that he never made anything of himself. I mean, he still lived on the same estate as his clients, albeit in one of the two-storey houses rather than the blocks of flats. His front garden was a jungle, his window panes filthy, and the inside of his house a thing of horror. He dressed in cheap clothes, which hung off him. He wouldn't shave for days, his hair always needed washing ... You're getting the picture, eh? Me, when I'm not working I'm a neat and tidy sort of guy. My mum's friends, the women she gossips with, they're always shaking their heads and asking how come I never found myself a girl. They speak about me in the past tense like that, like I'm not going to find one now. On the contrary. I'm thirty-eight, and all my friends have split up with their wives by now. So there are more and more single women my age appearing around the estate. It's only a question of time. Soon it'll be Brenda's turn. She'll leave Harry, or he'll kick her out. No kids, so that's not a problem. I hear gossip that their arguments are getting louder and louder and more frequent. There are threats too, late at night after a good drink down at the the club. I'm leaving you, no you're not, yes I am, well get the hell out then, I'll be back for my stuff, on you go, I wouldn't give you the satisfaction, well stay if you like.

Just like a ballet, eh? Well, I think so anyway. I've been waiting for Brenda for a long time. I can wait a little longer. I'm certainly a more attractive prospect than Daintry. Who'd move in with him? Nobody, I can tell you. He's a loner. No friends, just people he might drink with. He'll sometimes buy a few drinks for a few of the harder cases, then get them to put the frighteners on some late-payer who's either getting cocky or else talking about going to the police. Not that the police would do anything. What? Around here? If they're not in Daintry's pocket, they either don't care about the place anyway or else are scared to come near. Daintry did a guy in once inside the club. A Sunday afternoon too, stabbed him in the toilets. Police came, talked to everyone in the club— nobody'd seen anything. Daintry may be a bastard, but he's *our* bastard. Besides, there's always a reason. If you haven't crossed him, you're none of his business ... and *he'd* better not be any of *yours*.

I knew him of course. Oh yeah, we went to school together, same class all the way from five to sixteen years old. He was never quite as good as me at the subjects, but he was quiet and pretty well behaved. Until about fifteen. A switch flipped in his brain at fifteen. Actually, I'm lying: he was always better than me at arithmetic. So I suppose he was cut out for a career as a money lender. Or, as he once described himself, "a bank manager with menaces."

God knows how many people he's murdered. Can't be that many, or we'd all have noticed. That's why I thought all the information I used to give him was just part of his act. He knew word would get around about what he was asking me for, and those whispers and rumours would strengthen his reputation. That's what I always thought. I never took it seriously. As a result, I tapped him for a loan once or twice and *he never charged me a penny*. He also bought me a few drinks, and once provided a van when I wanted to sell the piano. See, he wasn't all bad. He had his good side. If it hadn't been for him, we'd never have shifted that piano, and it'd still be sitting there in the living room reminding my mother of the tunes dad used to play on it, tunes she'd hum late into the night and then again at the crack of dawn.

It seemed strange at first that he'd want to see me. He would come over to me in pubs and sling his arm around my neck, asking if I was all right, patting me and ordering the same again. We'd hardly spoken more than a sentence at a time to one another since leaving school, but now he was smiles and reminiscences and all interested in my job of work.

"I just dig holes."

He nodded. "And that's important work, believe me. Without the likes of you, my car's suspension would be shot to hell."

Of course, his car's suspension *was* shot to hell. It was a 1973 Ford Capri with tinted windows, an air duct and a spoiler. It was a loser's car, with dark green nylon fur on the dashboard and the door panels. The wheel arches were history, long since eaten by rust. Yet every year without fail it passed its MOT. The coincidence was, the garage mechanic was a regular client of Daintry's.

"I could get a new car," Daintry said, "but it gets me from A back to A again, so what's the point?"

There was something in this. He seldom left the estate. He lived there, shopped there, he'd been born there and he'd die there. He never took a holiday, not even a weekend away, and he never ever ventured south of the river. He spent all his free time watching videos. The guy who runs the video shop reckoned Daintry had seen every film in the shop a dozen times over.

"He knows their numbers off by heart."

He did know lots about movies: running time, director, writer, supporting actor. He was always a hot contender when the club ran its trivia quiz. He sat in that smelly house of his with the curtains shut and a blue light flickering. He was a film junkie. And somehow, he managed to spend all his money on them. He must have done, or what else did he do with it? His Rolex was a fake, lighter than air when you picked it up, and probably his gold jewellery was fake too. Maybe somewhere there's a secret bank account with thousands salted away, but I don't think so. Don't ask me why, I just don't think so.

Roadworks. That's the information I passed on to Daintry. That's what he wanted to talk to me about. Roadworks. *Major* roadworks.

"You know the sort of thing," he'd say, "anywhere where you're digging a *big* hole. Maybe building a flyover or improving drainage. Major roadworks."

Sure enough, I had access to this sort of information. I just had to listen to the various crews talking about what they were working on and where they were doing the work. Over tea and biscuits in the canteen, I could earn myself a few drinks and a pint glass of goodwill.

"How deep does that need to be?" Daintry would ask.

"I don't know, eight maybe ten feet."

"By what?"

"Maybe three long, the same wide."

And he'd nod. This was early in the game, and I was slow catching on. You're probably much faster, right? So you know why he was asking. But I was puzzled the first couple of times. I mean, I thought maybe he was interested in the ... what's it, the infrastructure. He wanted to see improvements. Then it dawned on me: no, what he wanted to see were big holes. Holes that would be filled in with concrete and covered over with huge imovable objects, like bridge supports for example. Holes where bodies could be hidden. I didn't say anything, but I knew that's what we were talking about. We were talking about Human Resources Disposal.

And Daintry knew that I knew. He'd wink from behind his cigarette smoke, using those creased stinging eyes of his. Managing to look a little like his idol Robert de Niro. In *Goodfellas*. That's what Daintry would say. He'd always be making physical comparisons like that. Me, I thought he was much more of a Joe Pesci. But I didn't tell him that. I didn't even tell him that Pesci isn't pronounced pesky.

He knew I'd blab about our little dialogues, and I did, casually like. And word spread. And suddenly Daintry was a man to be feared. But he wasn't really. He was just stupid, with a low flashpoint. And if you wanted to know what sort of mood he was going to be in, you only had to visit the video shop.

"He's taken out *Goodfellas* and *Godfather 3*." So you knew there was trouble coming. Now you really didn't want to cross him. But if he'd taken out soft core or a Steve Martin or even some early Brando, everything was going to be all right. He must have been on a gangster high the night he went round to speak with Mr. and Mrs. McAndrew. In his time, Mr. McAndrew had been a bit of a lad himself, but he was in his late seventies with a wife ten years younger. They lived in one of the estate's nicer houses. They'd bought it from the council and had installed a fancy front door, double-glazed windows, you name it, and all the glass was that leaded criss-cross stuff. It wasn't cheap. These days, Mr. McAndrew spent all his time in the garden. At the front of the house he had some beautiful flower beds, with the back garden given over to vegetables. In the summer, you saw him playing football with his grandchildren.

"Just like," as somebody pointed out, "Marlon Brando in *The Godfather*." This was apt in its way since, like I say, despite the gardening Mr. McAndrew's hands were probably cleaner these days than they had been in the past.

How he got to owe Daintry money I do not know. But Daintry, believe me, would have been only too happy to lend. There was McAndrew's reputation for a start. Plus the McAndrews seemed prosperous enough, he was sure to see his money and interest returned. But not so. Whether out of sheer cussedness or because he really couldn't pay, McAndrew had been holding out on Daintry. I saw it as a struggle between the old gangster and the new. Maybe Daintry did too. Whatever, one night he walked into the McAndrews' house and beat up Mrs. McAndrew in front of her husband. He had two heavies with him, one to hold Mr. McAndrew, one to hold Mrs. McAndrew. Either one of them could have dropped dead of a heart attack right then and there.

There were murmurs in the street the next day, and for days afterwards. Daintry, it was felt, had overstepped the mark. He was out of order. To him it was merely business, and he'd gotten the money from McAndrew so the case was closed. But he now found himself shorter of friends than ever before. Which is probably why he turned to me when he wanted the favour done. Simply, he couldn't get anyone else to do it.

"You want me to what?"

He'd told me to meet him in the children's play-park. We walked around the path. There was no one else in the park. It was a battlefield, all broken glass and rocks. Dog shit was smeared up and down the chute, the swings had been wrapped around themselves until they couldn't be reached. The roundabout had disappeared one night, leaving only a metal stump in place. You'd be safer sending your kids to play on the North Circular.

"It's quite simple," Daintry said. "I want you to get rid of a package for me. There's good money in it."

"How much money?"

"A hundred."

I paused at that. A hundred pounds, just to dispose of a package . . .

"But you'll need a deep hole," said Daintry.

Yeah, of course. It was *that* kind of package. I wondered who it was. There was a story going around that Daintry had set up a nice little disposal operation which dealt with Human Resource Waste from miles around. Villains as far away as Watford and Luton were bringing "packages" for him to dispose of. But it was just a story, just one of many.

"A hundred," I said, nodding.

"All right, one twenty-five. But it's got to be tonight."

I KNEW JUST THE HOLE.

They were building a new footbridge over the North Circular, over to the west near Wembley. I knew the gang wouldn't be working night-shift: the job wasn't that urgent and who could afford the shift bonus these days? There'd be a few deep holes there all right. And while the gang might notice a big black bin-bag at the bottom of one of them, they wouldn't do anything about it. People were always dumping rubbish down the holes. It all got covered over with concrete, gone and quite forgotten. I hadn't seen a dead body before, and I didn't intend seeing one now. So I insisted it was all wrapped up before I'd stick it in the car-boot.

Daintry and I stood in the lock-up he rented and looked down at the black bin liner.

"It's not so big, is it?" I said.

"I broke the rigor mortis," he explained. "That way you can get it into the car."

I nodded and went outside to throw up. I felt better after that. Curried chicken never did agree with me.

"I'm not sure I can do it," I said, wiping my mouth.

Daintry was ready for me. "Ah, that's a pity." He stuck his hands in his pockets, studying the tips of his shoes. "How's your old mum by the way? Keeping well is she?"

"She's fine, yeah . . ." I stared at him. "What do you mean?"

"Nothing, nothing. Let's hope her good health continues." He looked up at me, a glint in his eye. "Still fancy Brenda?"

"Who says I do?"

He laughed. "Common knowledge. Must be the way your trousers bulge whenever you see her shadow."

"That's rubbish."

"She seems well enough, too. The marriage is a bit shaky, but what can you expect? That Harry of hers is a monster." Daintry paused, fingering his thin gold neck-chain. "I wouldn't be surprised if he took a tap to the skull one of these dark nights."

"Oh?"

He shrugged. "Just a guess. Pity you can't . . ." He touched the bin-bag with his shoe. "You know." And he smiled.

We loaded the bag together. It wasn't heavy, and was easy enough to manoeuvre. I could feel a foot and a leg, or maybe a hand and arm. I tried not to think about it. Imagine him threatening my old mum! He was lucky I'm not quick to ignite, not like him, or it'd've been broken nose city and hospital cuisine. But what he said about Brenda's husband put thought of my mum right out of my head.

We closed the boot and I went to lock it.

"He's not going to make a run for it," Daintry said.

"I suppose not," I admitted. But I locked the boot anyway.

Then the car wouldn't start, and when it did start it kept cutting out, like the engine was flooding or something. Maybe a block in the fuel line. I'd let it get very low before the last fill of petrol. There might be a lot of rubbish swilling around in the tank. After a couple of miles it cut out on me at some traffic lights in Dalston. I rolled down my window and waved for the cars behind me to pass. I was content to sit for a few moments and let everything settle, my stomach included. One car stopped alongside me. And Jesus, wouldn't you know it: it was a cop car.

"Everything all right?" the cop in the passenger seat called.

"Yeah, just stalled."

"You can't sit there forever."

"No."

"If it doesn't start next go, push your car to the side of the road."

"Yeah, sure." He made no move to leave. Now the driver was looking at me too, and traffic was building up behind us. Nobody sounded their horn. Everyone could see that a cop car was talking with the driver of another vehicle. Sweat tickled my ears. I turned the ignition, resisting the temptation to pump the accelerator. The engine rumbled, then came to life. I grinned at the cops and started forwards, going through an amber light.

They could probably arrest me for that. It was five minutes before I stopped staring in the rearview mirror. But I couldn't see them. They'd turned off somewhere. I let all my fear and tension out in a rasping scream, then remembered the window was still rolled down. I wound it back up again. I decided not to go straight to the bridge-site, but to drive around a bit, let all the traffic clear along with my head.

I pulled into a bus-stop just before the North Circular and changed into my work clothes. That way I wouldn't look suspicious. Good thinking, eh? It was my own idea, one Daintry had appreciated. I had a question for him now, and the question was: why wasn't he doing this himself? But he wasn't around to answer it. And I knew the answer anyway: he'd rather pay someone else to do dangerous jobs. Oh yes, it was dangerous; I knew that now. Worth a lot more than a hundred and twenty-five nicker, sixty of which were already in my pocket in the shape of dirty old pound notes. Repayments, doubtless, from Daintry's punters.

Grubby money, but still money. I hoped it hadn't come from the McAndrews.

I sat at the bus-stop for a while. A car pulled in behind me. Not a police car this time, just an ordinary car. I heard the driver's door slam shut. Footsteps, a tap at my window. I looked out. The man was bald and middle-aged, dressed in suit and tie. A lower executive look, a sales rep maybe, that sort of person. He was smiling in a friendly enough sort of fashion. And if he wanted to steal my car and jemmy open the boot, well that was fine too.

I wound down my window. "Yeah?"

"I think I missed my turning," he said. "Can you tell me where we are, roughly?"

"Roughly," I said, "roughly we're about a mile north of Wembley."

"And that's west London?" His accent wasn't quite English, not southern English. Welsh or a Geordie or a Scouser maybe.

"About as west as you can get," I told him. Yeah, the wild west.

"I can't be too far away then. I want St. John's Wood. That's west too, isn't it?"

"Yeah, not far at all." These poor sods, you came across them a lot in my line of work. New to the city and pleading directions, getting hot and a bit crazy as the signposts and one-ways led them further into the maze. I felt sorry for them a lot of the time. It wasn't their fault. So I took my time as I directed him towards Harlesden, miles away from where he wanted to be. ·

"It's a short cut," I told him. He seemed pleased to have some local knowledge. He went back to his car and sounded his horn in thank you as he drove off. I know, that was a bit naughty of me, wasn't it? Well, there you go. That was my spot of devilry for the night. I started my own car and headed back onto the road.

There was a sign off saying "Works Access Only," so I signalled and drove between the two rows of striped traffic cones. Then I stopped the car. There were no other cars around, just the dark shapes of earth-moving equipment and cement mixers. Fine and dandy. Cars and lorries roared past, but they didn't give me a second's notice. They weren't about to slow down enough to take in any of the scene. The existing overpass and built-up verges hid me pretty well from civilization. Before unloading the package, I went for a recce, taking my torch with me.

And of course there were no decent holes to be found. They'd been filled in already. The concrete was hard, long metal rods poking out of it like the prongs on a fork. There were a few shallow cuts in the earth, but nothing like deep enough for the purpose. Hell's teeth and gums. I went back to the car, thinking suddenly how useful a car-phone would be. I wanted to speak to Daintry. I wanted to ask him what to do. A police car went past. I saw its brake lights glow. They'd noticed my car, but they didn't stop. No, but they might come back round again. I started the car and headed out onto the carriageway.

Only a few minutes later, there was a police car behind me. He sat on my tail for a while, then signalled to overtake, drawing level with me and staying there. The passenger checked me out. They were almost certainly the ones who'd seen me parked back at the bridge-site. The passenger saw that I was wearing overalls and a standard issue work-jacket. I sort of waved at him. He spoke to the driver, and the patrol car accelerated away.

Lucky for me he hadn't seen the tears in my eyes. I was terrified and bursting for a piss. I knew that I had to get off this road. My brain was numb. I couldn't think of another place to dump the body. I didn't want to think about it at all. I just wanted rid of it. I think I saw the travelling salesman hurtle past, fleeing Harlesden. He was heading out of town.

I came off the North Circular and just drove around, crawling east-wards until I knew the streets so well it was like remote control. I knew exactly where I'd effected repairs, and where repairs were still waiting to be carried out. There was one pot-hole on a sharp bend that could buckle a wheel. That was down as a priority, and would probably be started on tomorrow. I calmed myself a little with memories of holes dug and holes filled in, the rich aroma of hot tarmac, the jokes yelled out by the Driller Killer. I'd never worked out why he'd try telling jokes to someone wearing industrial ear protectors beside a pneumatic drill.

Seeking safety, I came back into the estate. I felt better immediately, my head clearing. I knew what I had to do. I had to face up to Daintry. I'd give him back the money of course, less a quid or two for petrol, and I'd explain that nowhere was safe. Mission impossible. I didn't know what he'd do. It depended on whether tonight was a *Goodfellas* night or not. He might slap me about a bit. He might stop buying me drinks.

He might do something to my mum.

Or to Brenda.

I'd have to talk to him. Maybe we could do a deal. Maybe I'd have to kill him. Yeah, then I'd just have the *two* bodies to worry about. In order to stop worrying about the first, I stopped by the lock-up. This was one of a cul-de-sac of identical garages next to some wasteland which had been planted with trees and was now termed a Conservation Area. The man in the High Street had certainly conserved his energy thinking up that one.

There were no kids about, so I used a rock to break the lock, then hauled the door open with my crowbar. I stopped for a moment and wondered what I was going to do now. I'd meant to leave the body in the garage, but I'd had to break the locks to get in, so now if I left the body there anybody at all could wander along and find it. But then I thought, this is *Daintry's* garage. Everybody knows it, and nobody in their right mind would dare trespass. So I hauled the package inside, closed the door again, and left a rock in front of it. I was confident I'd done my best.

So now it was time to go talk with Daintry. The easy part of the evening was past. But first I went home. I don't know why, I just wanted to see my mum. We used to be on the eleventh floor, but they'd moved us eventually to the third because the lifts kept breaking and mum couldn't climb eleven flights. I took the stairs tonight, relieved not to find any of the local kids shooting up or shagging between floors. Mum was sitting with Mrs. Gregg from along the hall. They were talking about Mrs. McAndrew.

"Story she gave her doctor was she fell down the stairs."

"Well I think it's a shame."

Mum looked up and saw me. "I thought you'd be down the club."

"Not tonight, mum."

"Well that makes a change."

"Hallo, Mrs. Gregg."

"Hallo, love. There's a band on tonight, you know."

"Where?"

She rolled her eyes. "At the club. Plenty of lovely girls too, I'll bet."

They wanted rid of me. I nodded. "Just going to my room. Won't be long."

I lay on my bed, the same bed I'd slept in since I was . . . well, since before I could remember. The room had been painted and papered in the last year. I stared at the wallpaper, lying on one side and then on the other. This room, it occurred to me, was probably the size of a prison cell. It might even be a bit smaller. What was it, eight feet square? But I'd always felt comfortable enough here. I heard my mum laughing at something Mrs. Gregg said, and pop music from the flat downstairs. These weren't very solid flats, thin walls and floors. They'd knock our block down one of these days. I liked it well enough though. I didn't want to lose it. I didn't want to lose my mum.

I decided that I was probably going to have to kill Daintry.

I packed some clothes into a black holdall, just holding back the tears. What would I say to my mum? I've got to go away for a while? I'll phone you when I can? I recalled all the stories I'd heard about Daintry. How some guy from Trading Standards had been tailing him and was sitting in his car at the side of the road by the shops when a sawn-off shotgun appeared in the window and a voice told him to get the hell out of there pronto. Guns and knives, knuckle-dusters and a machete. Just stories . . . just stories.

I knew he wouldn't be expecting *me* to try anything. He'd open his door, he'd let me in, he'd turn his back to lead me through to the living room. That's when I'd do it. When his back was turned. It was the only safe and certain time I could think of. Anything else and I reckoned I'd lose my bottle. I left the holdall on my bed and went through to the kitchen. I took time at the open drawer, choosing my knife. Nothing too grand, just a simple four-inch blade at the end of a wooden handle. I stuck it in my pocket.

"Just nipping out for some fresh air, mum."

"Bye then."

"See you."

And that was that. I walked back down the echoing stairwell with my mind set on murder. It wasn't like the films. It was just . . . well, *ordinary.* Like I was going to fetch fish and chips or something. I kept my hand on the knife handle. I wanted to feel comfortable with it. But my legs were a bit shaky. I had to keep locking them at the knees, holding on to a wall or a lamppost and taking deep breaths. It was a five-minute walk to Daintry's, but I managed to stretch it to ten. I passed a couple of people I vaguely knew, but didn't stop to talk. I didn't trust my teeth not to chatter, my jaw not to lock.

And to tell you the truth, I was relieved to see that there was someone standing on the doorstep, another visitor. I felt my whole body relax. The man crouched to peer through the letter box, then knocked again. As I walked down the path towards him, I saw that he was tall and well-built with a black leather jacket and short black hair.

"Isn't he in?"

The man turned his head slowly towards me. I didn't like the look of his face. It was grey and hard like the side of a house.

"Doesn't look like it," he said. "Any idea where he'd be?"

He was standing up straight now, his head handing down over mine. Police, I thought for a second. But he wasn't police. I swallowed. I started to shake my head, but then I had an idea. I released my grip on the knife.

"If he's not in he's probably down the club," I said. "Do you know where it is?"

"No."

"Go back down to the bottom of the road, take a left, and when you come to the shops it's up a side road between the laundrette and the chip shop."

He studied me. "Thanks."

"No problem," I said. "You know what he looks like?"

He nodded in perfect slow motion. He never took his eyes off me.

"Right then," I said. "Oh, and you might have to park outside the shops. The car-park's usually full when there's a band on."

"There's a band?"

"In the club." I smiled. "It gets noisy, you can hardly hear a word that's said to you, even in the toilets."

"Is that so?"

"Yes," I said, "that is so."

Then I walked back down the path and gave him a slight wave as I headed for home. I made sure I walked home too. I didn't want him thinking I was on my way to the club ahead of him.

"Short walk," mum said. She was pouring tea for Mrs. Gregg.

"Bit cold."

"Cold?" squeaked Mrs. Gregg. "A lad your age shouldn't feel the cold."

"Have you seen my knife?" mum asked. She was looking down at the cake she'd made. It was on one of the better plates and hadn't been cut yet. I brought the knife out of my pocket.

"Here you are, mum."

"What's it doing in your pocket?"

"The lock on the car-boot's not working. I'd to cut some string to tie it shut."

"Do you want some tea?"

I shook my head. "I'll leave you to it," I said. "I'm off to bed."

IT WAS THE TALK of the estate the next morning, how Daintry had been knifed to death in a toilet cubicle, just as the band were finishing their encore. They were some Sixties four-piece, still performing long past their sell-by. That's what people said who were there. And they'd compensated for a lack of ability by cranking the sound system all the way up. You not only couldn't hear yourself think, you couldn't *think*.

I suppose they have to make a living as best they can. We all do.

It was the assistant manager who found Daintry. He was doing his nightly check of the club to see how many drunks had managed to fall asleep in how many hidden places. Nobody used the end cubicle of the gents' much; it didn't have any toilet seat. But there sat Daintry, not caring any more about the lack of amenities. Police were called, staff and clientele interviewed, but no one had anything much to say.

Well, not to the police at any rate. But there was plenty of gossip on the streets and in the shops and in the lifts between neighbours. And slowly a story emerged. Mr. McAndrew, remember, had been a lad at one time. He was rumoured still to have a few contacts, a few friends who owed him. Or maybe he just stumped up cash. Whatever, everyone knew Mr. McAndrew had put out the contract on Daintry. And, as also agreed, good riddance to him. On a Friday night too. So anyone who'd tapped him for a loan could see the sun rise on Monday morning with a big wide smile.

Meantime, the body was found in Daintry's lock-up. Well, the police knew who was responsible for that, didn't they? Though they did wonder about the broken locks. Kids most likely, intent on burglary but doing a runner when they saw the corpse. Seemed feasible to me too.

Mr. McAndrew, eh? I watched him more closely after that. He still looked to me like a nice old man. But then it was only a story after all, only one of many. Me, I had other things to think about. I knew I could do it now. I could take Brenda away from Harry. Don't ask me why I feel so sure, I just do.

Liz Holliday is another crossover writer, one whose primrary career has been in science fiction. A Londoner who has sold to a variety of magazines and anthologies, Liz launched her mystery career quite notably: the following is her first mystery story, and it was shortlisted as a Golden Dagger nominee.

And She Laughed
LIZ HOLLIDAY

"I reckon it took all the luck in the world to get me this flat," Jane Martin said. "Probably means I'll never get another job, or win the pools, or anything."

She was sitting in the darkness in the hall, with the telephone receiver cradled on her shoulder. She took a piece of meat from the kebab open on the floor in front of her. "I mean," she went on, "how many other single people do you know who have council flats to themselves, Paula?"

Her friend's voice crackled down the line at her, saying something congratulatory, but Jane's attention was on the cans of paint she had bought that morning: painting the whole flat white wasn't really cheap, just cheaper than any other idea she had been able to come up with.

"I'll see you about noon then?" Paula said. "You provide the lunch and I'll provide the labour."

"Greater love hath no woman than that she paint her best friend's new flat," Jane said. By the time she put the phone down, they were both giggling. She picked a chilli out of the kebab and munched on it. Something made her turn towards the door. A pair of blue eyes was staring at her through the letter-box.

Her heart thumped once. She shouted, "What are you doing, you bastard?"

The letter-box swung silently shut. She thought she heard a single footstep. Then there was silence. Her whole body was rigid, and her breath was unsteady. She stared into the darkness with her hand on the phone. After a few moments, when she was calmer, she thought: I should phone the police. But it was too late. By the time they arrived, he would be gone.

She stood near to the door, listening, but heard nothing. Curious, she touched the letter-box. It was slightly open, but shut easily beneath her fingers. If she hadn't known better she might have thought the wind had opened it. But she did know better. She imagined him standing on the other side. He was probably laughing at her, laughing at her fear.

She went into the living room. The room was almost empty, but moonlight illuminated the floor cushions and the sofa, her one decent piece of furniture. She went and looked out of the bare windows. *I ought to get some curtains*, she thought; but she didn't really want to. She loved the way the spring sunlight flooded into the room, and the sense the openness gave her of being part of a living community. *What's the point of living near Portobello Road if you're going to shut yourself away?* That was what she had said to Paula, when they had been making a list of essentials. Sometimes Paula was just too practical for her own good.

A car door slammed somewhere. Jane's head jerked round. She realized she had been listening for . . . *something* the whole time.

Before she went to bed that night she jammed a chair up against the front door, but as she lay sleepless in her bed she was still listening, listening.

"YOU SHOULD HAVE SHOVED A KNIFE in the guy's face." Paula stabbed at the door with a brushful of white gloss.

"And get done for manslaughter, knowing my luck? Yeah, right." Jane pulled the roller down the wall with more vigour than was strictly necessary. Paint splattered everywhere. "He was probably just looking for a flat to squat. Now he knows someone's here, he won't be back."

"Well, at least call the police. What do you think they're there for?"

"Oh sure. He ran off the second I shouted at him. He could have been at Marble Arch by the time they arrived."

"For God's sake . . . you have to stop thinking like a victim." Paula started to fill in around the doorhandle.

"Great. Now it's my fault."

"I'm not saying that. I'm just saying you have to do *something*. Don't let the bastard win, you know?" She laid the brush across the top of the can. "Hell with this. I'm going to make a cup of tea."

Jane watched Paula's retreating back. *Damn*, she thought. *Now she's pissed off with me.* "Milk, no sugar," she called, just to keep the conversation going. "I'll get a chain for the door tomorrow, OK?"

"And report last night to the police?"

"OK, OK." Jane took another swipe at the wall. It was almost finished.

After a moment Paula came back out of the kitchen. "And promise you'll phone them the instant he comes back?"

"That too."

"Promise?"
"Promise."

NOTHING THAT NIGHT. Nothing the night after. Jane started to think it had been a one off. The night after that she was putting a poster up by the front door when she heard the noise again.

She turned and saw his eyes. Blue eyes in a strip of white skin. She got an impression of thick eyebrows, heavy cheekbones. The moment dragged on. *I'm out of his line of sight*, she thought. The chain, purchased the day before, lay on the kitchen table; despite her promise to Paula, she had forgotten to fit it. *Idiot*, she thought fiercely at herself.

She heard him saying something, but the door muffled the sound. It was enough to break the spell, though.

"Fuck off, you bastard!" she shouted, and was pleased at how strong her voice sounded.

The letter-box swung shut. She reached for the phone and punched 999, was appalled at how long it took first to get an answer, then to be put through. *What do I say*, she wondered as she waited. *Please, someone just came and looked through my letter-box, but he's gone now, so it's all right?*

"I think someone is trying to break into my flat," she said when they would let her. She listened numbly as the police telephonist told her someone would be there soon, that she must not let anyone in.

She stood by the door until the police arrived: three of them, two men and a woman, not much older than she was.

"Not much we can do without a description, love," one of the men said.

"Once you've got the chain fitted, you could try opening the door to get a look at him," said the other.

Sure, Jane thought. *Sure.*

"If you could keep him talking for a while, we might have a chance to get here before he goes," said the first man. "The main thing is to keep calm and not do anything that might make him angry. I don't want to frighten you, but if he decides to hang about . . ."

Christ, that never even occurred to me . . . Jane made a conscious effort to unclench her fists, noting the sharp look the woman gave him.

"We'll catch him sooner or later, love," the woman said. "We've got a very strong presence on this estate. Just give us time."

THAT NIGHT SHE DREAMED of him. His eyes, caught by the moonlight, stared out of the darkness at her. Giant shadows jumped on the green walls behind him as he came towards her. Light glinted on the knife he carried . . .

Her foot slid on the stair and she fell, twisting, towards him. His mouth opened, and he started to speak, but she knew she must not listen. Her scream cut the night. She woke, trembling and sweating, and did not sleep again.

JANE SLEPT LATE THE NEXT DAY. When she did get up she was gritty-eyed and irritable. She wandered from room to room in the flat as if it were a cage. She couldn't bring herself to do any more panting or unpacking, and she knew she ought to fit the chain on the door. She ended up slumped in the sofa drinking cup after cup of tea. All her energy had gone. A job application stared up at her from the coffee table. There were vacancies for assistants at the local library. She had been really excited when she saw the advert. Now she felt that even trying to fill out the form was tantamount to asking for a kick in the teeth.

She was supposed to meet Paula in the pub at seven. She thought about calling her to cancel, but she knew it would lead to an argument. Paula would ask about the chain. She knew it. She hauled herself up and forced herself to fit it. It took far longer than she had expected, what with trying to line the two halves of it up and sorting out the right screws.

"Oh sod this," she muttered; then wondered if *he* were on the other side of the door listening.

She did get it done in the end, and immediately felt much more secure. At least the door was the only way into the flat. She grinned: she'd make it a fortress if she had to.

The hallway outside was empty. Jane shivered as she fumbled to double lock her door. The fluorescent light cast harsh, multiple shadows on the institutional green walls. *It's like a prison corridor*, she thought; and then: If I screamed for help, I wonder if anyone would come. A vision flashed through her mind. She was lying on the floor, T-shirt stained with blood. But then her eyes opened, turned from brown to blue: blue eyes set in a wide-cheekboned face. In her dream he had tried to speak to her. Now his mouth hung slackly open. She bit her lip and the vision passed.

Determinedly, she set off down the corridor. Her footsteps rang around the hall as if it were an echo chamber. *Bloody prison*, she thought.

The dog in the flat opposite started to bark; by the sound of it, a Doberman or a Rottweiler, maybe even a pitbull. Jane was out in the stairwell before she realized just how used to that sound she had become in a short space of time. The damned dog barked every time anyone walked past. But when her visitor came, it had made no sound at all.

She tried not to think about it as she got outside, as she pushed past the two old men sharing a bottle of cider on the steps, as she crossed the road to avoid the knot of kids outside the chip shop.

The others were already in the pub. She got herself a half of bitter and a stool in that order.

"Hi, Paula. Kath ... Dave." She never had liked him. She turned to talk to some of the others. She felt much more secure now she was surrounded by friends. "How you doing, Phil? Anita?"

"Hi, Jane," Dave said from behind her. "How's your midnight crawler, then?"

Sensitive as a brick wall, as always Jane thought. "You'd probably have more idea than I do," she said, wishing she could come up with a wittier put-down. "I've been thinking. Maybe he lives in the block."

"Oh surely not." That was Kath. She always had been too innocent for her own good.

"Well, the dog opposite didn't bark, and I didn't hear the stair doors slam, so—"

"This dog, does it bark at everyone?" It was Phil, being as reasonable as ever."

"I told you it does—" Jane snapped.

"What, the postman, the caretaker—"

"Yes," she said irritably. She sipped her beer. He had a point, she decided after a moment. He usually did. "No," she conceded. "Actually, it doesn't."

"So maybe it isn't one of your neighbours. Maybe the dog only barks at you because it isn't used to you yet . . . Get you another?" He pointed at her drink.

She shook her head. Phil went up to the bar.

"Still, this creep must have hung around for a while, if the dog's used to him," Dave said as soon as Phil had gone. Jane scowled. "Sorry. Just trying to cover all the bases." He took a pull at his lager before he went on, "But he must be a genuine weirdo, I mean, what the hell's he getting out of it? It isn't like he's watching your bedroom or anything . . ."

"Thanks a million, Dave," Jane said. She turned away from him deliberately.

"I reckon you ought to squirt an aerosol in the bastard's face. That'd convince him to look for easier pickings," Anita said.

"The police told me not to—" Jane began, but her voice was drowned out by all the others chipping in.

"Paint . . ."

"I still think jabbing a knife at his eyes . . ."

"Wire a battery up, give the so and so a good jolt."

"We could ambush him—"

"But paint . . ."

"—If there was somewhere to wait."

"You ought to tell the police."

". . . Or indelible ink . . ."

In the end she just sat there and let it all roll over her. A spontaneous silence fell, in which she became aware that her hands were clenched round her glass, that she was frowning.

"C'mon, Janie. Tell us what you're going to do about the son of a bitch." It was Dave. It would be Dave.

"I'll tell you what I'm going to do. I'm going to live my life. He'll get bored and go away eventually, I'm sure." She looked hard at Dave. "And I'll tell you what I'm not going to do. I'm not going to panic. I'm not going to let him scare me away. And I'm not going to let you lot hype me into doing something stupid that would end up with me in trouble." She slammed her glass down. Beer slopped over her hand.

"Jane, for God's sake listen. We're just worried about you—" Paula put her hand out toward Jane.

"No, you listen. Maybe you think I ought to be afraid, and maybe you're right. But all I know is as long as there's a solid door between him and me—and he runs off if I shout at him—I'm not as bothered as you all appear to want me to be. And that's just tough." She stood up. "Night everyone. See you around."

"Jane—" It was Paula. Jane ignored her. "Look, I've been thinking. Maybe you should ask your neighbours if they've seen anyone hanging around."

"No." The very thought appalled Jane, though she couldn't have explained why. "Supposing he does live there? I wouldn't want him to think he's got me rattled. That would probably just turn him on."

"And if you do nothing, that's playing into his hands too. But go ahead, be a victim. See if I care."

She always has known how to press my buttons, Jane thought. "Be a victim? You just don't ever listen, do you, Jane? Letting him think I'm running scared—now *that* would be giving in to him, and *that* would be being a victim."

"But you can't just let this go on. You have to do something—"

"'Cause if I don't, you're going to nag me to death?"

"If I have to," Paula said. Her eyes glinted dangerously. Jane knew she wasn't joking.

"OK, mama. Anything for a quiet life." *I can always plead self-defence,* Jane thought.

"Good. I'll come with you, if you like." It wasn't a question.

"Tomorrow," Jane said. She turned and walked away.

"Don't you want me to see you home?" Paula called.

"I'm all grown up. I'll manage," Jane said over her shoulder, then immediately wished she hadn't.

She stayed furious all the way home. Furious that they couldn't see that she was doing everything she could; furious at herself for not being certain of herself.

As she climbed the stairs, it occurred to her that he might be there—that she might catch him in the act. The way the corridor was arranged she could be almost on top of him before he noticed her. But there was only the echoing silence, the rasp of her own breathing. She went on, slowly at first. She came out into the hallway and made sure the stair door banged loudly: she wanted to give him time to get away. The dog began to bark. She almost ran to her flat. The letter-box was firmly shut.

She got inside and checked the locks. The chain too. She made a pot of tea and took it into the front room, intending to meditate before bed. Perhaps then she wouldn't dream. It seemed such a shame when getting the flat at all had been such a piece of luck. She stared at the bare windows. Curtains. In the circumstances maybe she ought to get some after all. Or perhaps blinds would be better ...

A few moments later she came to with a start, realizing she had drifted off. Something was moving on the balcony. Shadows made by car headlights, she told herself firmly. That's a very busy road out there. But no sound broke the silence. She did not move; realized she was scarcely breathing.

But something was out there. She was sure now: there was the outline of a head, an arm. A hand, surely holding something—a brick?—coming towards the pane of glass. A mouth, wide open to shout, indistinct through the glass. "Pah ... seh ..." *Prostitute?* she wondered. Does he think I'm one? She had heard of serial killers who had fixated on them.

She heard herself scream, then launched herself towards the balcony door. There was nothing there except the weeds in the window box, swaying gently in the night.

She slumped against the door for a long while, knowing she was crying and hating herself for it.

Eventually she dragged herself to bed. She did not undress. She kept thinking she would wake up to find him standing over her, with his blue eyes illuminated by the moonlight. She dozed, fitfully; confused dreams of the man—in the alley, with his mouth open to shout, and his hand coming towards her—and of something moving on the balcony. The last dream was the worst, and she woke knowing she had smelled blood, that it had covered her face and hands and T-shirt.

On her way to the bathroom she touched the letter-box—just out of curiosity, of course. It was open. *It's nothing*, she thought. *Nothing the wind couldn't have done.* But it wasn't the wind, and she knew it.

THAT EVENING PAULA came round and they went knocking on doors. Jane hung back at first, but so few people answered that she stopped worrying.

As they got closer to her flat, she started to get nervous again. The Rottweiler started to bark. It didn't help. There were six doors left; then four; then only the one opposite Jane's, where the dog was.

"Might as well get it over with," Paula said cheerfully as she went up to the door. Inside, they could hear the dog going wild. "Bet it bites my hand off."

Jane realized Paula was watching her. *To hell with her thinking I'm a wimp*, Jane thought. She pushed past Paula and knocked on the last door herself.

Nothing happened for a moment. Then a harsh male voice shouted something. Claws scrabbled on a hard surface, and the barking died away. The door opened. The man that stood there was six feet plus. His sleeveless T-shirt did nothing to conceal his body-builder's muscles.

Jane stared up at him, at the wild hank of greying hair and thick moustache; at the wide cheekbones. And he stared back out of blue, blue eyes.

With a jolt Jane realized he had spoken to her moments before. Paula answered, but it was as if she were in slow motion. The sounds were dragged out and unintelligible. The man replied. Jane saw his lips stretch out around the words. Then it was as if he split in two: the person she could see, and the figure from her dream, with blood splattered over him, and his mouth opening wide. "Prostitute," he called out. "Prostitute." The light glinted on his knife blade. She understood with sudden clarity that she was seeing the future: that she was bound to it, to the moment when he would come towards her, unavoidably come towards her with that knife, and that after that there would be no more future for her . . .

. . . but it wasn't his knife, it was his belt buckle, and already the door was closing, hiding his eyes from her. She stepped back, realized she was going to fall and put her hand out to stop herself.

"Well that's that, I guess." Paula's voice was shockingly normal. Jane couldn't speak. She stared at Paula, who frowned. "What's up? You look terrible."

"That was him." The wall was cool against Jane's back. She let herself rest against it. Her mouth had gone dry, and she felt as if she were floating three feet above her own skull.

"Don't be daft. You're letting this get to you."

"Inside," Jane said, suddenly realizing that he might be listening to every word they said. She pushed herself off from the wall, and by concentrating very hard, was able to get into her own flat without too much trouble.

Paula followed. "Tea," she said. It was a command, not a question, and without waiting for an answer she filled the kettle. Jane sat on the sofa with her head in her hands. She wondered if she was about to be sick; no doubt Paula would clean up very efficiently after her. Sometimes Paula was just too wonderful to be true.

"I'm telling you, that was him," she said a little later. "I *know*."

"You said you never got a good look at him."

"Not when he looked through the letter-box, no."

"Well, for God's—if you saw him some other time, why didn't you tell me? You'll have to phone the police you know."

"I can't," Jane said. She stared at Paula over her tea, then took a sip to steady herself. "I only saw him in a dream."

"A *dream*? Oh for pity's sake. Next you'll tell me your horoscope said to beware of a tall dark stranger—"

"Don't laugh at me. *Don't*. He was in my dream. Not just anyone. Him. Waiting for me on the stairs. He had a knife and there was blood everywhere. He called me a prostitute. It's going to happen, Paula. I know it. And there won't be anything you or I can do to stop it."

Paula put her hand on Jane's. "Sorry," she said. "I can see you're strung out. You should—"

Jane shrugged her hand away. "You can piss off if you're going to be so condescending. Anyway, maybe I'll go to the police tomorrow."

"Sorry," Paula repeated. "Are you sure that's a good idea?"

"I won't mention my dream then. Satisfied?"

JANE WOKE NEXT MORNING drenched in sweat and muggy from the echoes of fast fading dreams. She got up intending to go straight to the police station, but somehow the morning slipped by. It was only when she found herself sorting her books alphabetically that she admitted that she did not want to go out. Suppose he was watching out for her? Suppose he followed her?

Straight to the police station, you daft cow? she thought; and with that she put her coat on and left. There was no one around.

The police were politely dismissive. She would need more evidence, because it was such a serious charge, they said; phone them if anything happened. The duty officer had pale skin and spots. He looked about fifteen. Jane nodded at him, quite unable to speak. Then she turned and stumbled out of the claustrophobic reception, into the hazy sunshine.

Panic took her. She knew she couldn't go home. Not yet, when he might be waiting for her. Instead she went to a burger bar and nursed a cup of tea through a full hour.

She was calmer after that. The thought of climbing the stairs to her flat no longer made her pulse race. She went home by way of Portobello Road, where she found some old velveteen curtains on one of the stalls. They were pricey but worth it. A stall selling kitchen equipment caught her eye next. They had knives there. Big knives, little knives, all very sharp and very cheap: so the stallholder told her. She stood in the middle of the road with her arms crossed over her body and her head down, trying to think.

A knife would be good protection, but carrying one about with her didn't seem like a good idea. Perhaps she had been standing there too long, because suddenly the stallholder held a knife in a blister pack out to her. For a moment she thought of taking it; she could almost feel the extra confidence it would give her. But the moment passed quickly. Didn't they say attackers often turned knives on their owners? Maybe that's what would happen. Besides, there were probably laws against carrying a knife around in your pocket. She shook her head, ignoring the stallholder's scowl.

She went instead to the chemist, where she bought a can of hairspray. You can't get arrested for owning a can of hairspray.

SHE HUNG THE CURTAINS as soon as she got in. There was enough material to cover the front door as well as the windows. When she had finished, she went outside and looked through the letter-box. She could see nothing but a few square inches of lining material.

"Let's see you get your jollies now, you bastard," she said aloud, then looked around almost guiltily, convinced someone had heard.

When she went back inside she made sure she closed the flap again. *That's better*, she thought, as she looked at it. She wondered if she would hear him at all through it. The thought of him wandering around outside without her knowing made her feel quite ill.

She had plenty to do. There was the bathroom to paint and some boxes of books that needed unpacking; and she still hadn't filled out the application form for the library job. Nevertheless, she found herself mooching around, trying to read, failing to do the crossword, staring out of the window. And listening. All the time listening.

He's won, she thought. *I can't live my life like this.* Determinedly she picked up the application form. With a job she would be out of the flat in the day, and the money would mean she could go out at night. She worked at the form like nothing she had done in a long time. First she made a rough draft, then set about copying everything over. Between trying to remember her exact O-level grades and all the casual jobs she had done since she graduated, it took a long time.

She heard a faint metallic scraping. Her whole body jerked. The pen scrawled across the form, ruining it. She stared down at it and could have cried. All that work, all those dreams, all for nothing.

The noise came again. She ran to the door. The curtain billowed out, as if there were a breeze behind it; or perhaps as if *he* was trying to push it aside with a stick.

It took all her courage, but she grabbed hold of it and pulled it aside. Nothing. Gingerly, she touched the letter-box. It was firmly shut. Just the wind, blowing through the cracks around the door. Just the wind, and maybe she never had seen him in the first place. *I'm not crazy*, she thought. *I did see him. I did.* She slammed her hand against the door, once and then again and again. There had been no one there. How dare there be no one there when she had been so afraid?

*   *   *

THE NIGHTS THAT FOLLOWED were sleepless. She kept the hairspray on the bed beside her. She would lie in the dark, every muscle tense, not quite touching it, straining to hear: and if she heard something, she would fight against the urge to get up and go and stand by the door, or perhaps to touch the letter-box.

In the mornings, sometimes she would find he had been, sometimes not: it did not matter anymore, for just the act of passing the door on the way to the bathroom was enough to start her shaking.

She spent her days half-asleep. Sometimes she dreamed of him: moonlight on his eyes, on his bright knife (she was sure now that he carried a knife), blood on her T-shirt; and always, his mouth opening around a word: *puh . . . puh . . .* Not prostitute, she realized. *Please.* He was begging her. Begging her to give in to him, perhaps, or to stop him.

After that she started to take the spray with her whenever she had to go out. It was only small, and it fitted easily into the deep side pocket of her jacket. She kept her hand on it as she passed his flat; in fact she never let go of it until she was out on the street.

She knew she ought to phone the police when he came, if only she could be certain he was really there. But it seemed pointless, and she could not bring herself to do it, any more than she could make herself ring Paula, but instead she disconnected the phone so she could not be contacted. The weight of the other woman's concern would drag her down, she was sure. It would make what was happening more real, and if it was real she would have to be afraid of it. There would be no living with that fear.

There came a day when she was asleep on the sofa, and she woke to find him there. He was sprawled half over her, but his weight was nothing at all. His breath, strained through those big white teeth of his, was hot on her face. His hand pinioned her wrist, gripped it so hard she was sure the bones would grate together. There was something wet on her breasts. She twisted her head and saw that her shirt was covered in blood. She stared at it, stared at him. He was drenched in it. It covered his chest and arms and, she realized now, his hands. The spray was in the bedroom, where it could do her no good at all.

He opened his mouth, but before he could speak she began to scream. Her only chance was if she could scare him off. It didn't work. She could still hear him. "Please," he said. "Please don't." He held a knife in his free hand, and it was covered in gore. He brought it up in front of her face as if to show it off to her. His eyes were wide and staring, filled with anger. Or was that terror? He was crazy, impossible to read. Maybe he was scared of women. That would fit the pattern. She shoved hard, flailed with her legs to get some purchase on the cushions. If she could kick him in the groin—

Her eyes flickered open. Someone was banging on the door. No blood.

There was no blood. So she was awake now, and that other had been a dream. She looked at her wrist. There were no marks. The banging came again.

She pulled herself up and staggered to the door. "Who is it?" she called. "Who is it?" They would have to tell her their name. She wouldn't open the door unless they did. She didn't have to.

"Jane? It's me. Paula."

Jane started to unchain the door, when suddenly she realized that she had no way of being certain it really was Paula. Suppose it was him? Suppose he'd said, "It's Paul," not "It's Paula." Or he might have heard her call Paula by name. While he was watching her.

"Jane, for Christ's sake open the door."

Jane did so, reluctantly. She peered out of the two-inch slit the chain allowed her. Paula was standing there, arms folded, looking impatient. She opened her mouth to speak, but then her face twisted, became his. His lips stretching round the words she could not understand, his blue eyes hot with anger. Blood blossomed on his shirt. He fell forwards and slid down the door with his hand clawing out towards her . . . and then he had gone, and there was only Paula.

"God, you look awful, girl," Paula said. "Come on, let me in." Jane fumbled with the chain. She led Paula into the living room and sat down on the sofa.

"When was the last time you ate properly?" Paula stared down at Jane. She sounded angry. Jane didn't think she had a right to be angry.

"Couldn't be bothered," she muttered.

"You should have rung me—"

"I couldn't—"

"You should have told me—"

"You didn't believe me." Jane rubbed her eyes with the palms of her hands. It didn't help.

"What?" Paula sounded genuinely puzzled.

"I tried to tell you. About my dream. That it's him, over there."

"This is my fault," Paula said. "I should have seen this coming. I think maybe you should see someone. Someone who can help you—"

"The police said—"

"Not the police. A counsellor. Something like that. I could ask at the Citizen's Advice Bureau. Would you let me do that, Jane?"

"You think I'm nuts." Flat statement. What else was there to say. "But I'm not. It's him. Lurking around. He won't even leave me alone when I'm asleep, did you know that?" It was too much. The horror of it broke over her, and her tears exploded outwards so that there was no holding them back.

Paula held her hands while she cried, and rubbed her back and whispered to her as if she were a child.

*   *   *

PAULA STAYED THAT NIGHT. She slept on the sofa. It made no difference.
Jane lay staring into darkness illuminated only by the LED display on
her clock. She saw his face, but she no longer knew what was dream and
what was imagination. Had she ever seen that mole high up on his cheekbone before? She didn't know. In her dream, or vision, he tried to speak
to her. "Please," he said. "Please don't—"

"*Please don't* what?" she thought, as she woke to daylight and the
sound of Paula moving around in the living room. "Please don't come
near me and make me murder you." That made sense. She would be
happy to oblige. She got up, shrugged herself into a T-shirt and jeans.

"Place was a pig-sty," Paula said. "I've tidied up a bit. Made some
soup for lunch. You are going to eat, aren't you?"

"Yeah, yeah." Paula could be so unreasonable.

"Also, I made free with your phone. We're meeting the others at the
pub at seven, so dig out your gladrags, girl."

"No." That was too much.

"Yes. No arguments. I'll be with you on the way, and we'll all walk
you back."

"No, I said." She tried and failed to stare Paula down.

"You were the one that wasn't going to let this thing beat you." The
words were as effective as a slap in the face. Jane went to find a fresh
T-shirt. The night was cool enough that her jacket would not seem out
of place; and Paula didn't need to know that she had slipped the can of
hairspray in her pocket.

At the pub, no one mentioned the man, not even Dave. Jane hardly
spoke. She just sat sipping diet Coke. She wished it were whisky, but she
knew if she started on alcohol she wouldn't stop.

Halfway through the evening *he* walked in. Jane noticed him immediately. She tracked him as he went up to the bar and ordered a pint. The
barman obviously knew him. He picked up his bitter and turned to find
a seat. Even in the dim pub lighting his eyes were clear blue; and yes,
he had a mole on his cheek, just where she had dreamed it. He noticed
her. Looking away was impossible.

"Evening," he said, cool as you might like, and smiled. How could he
smile at her knowing what he knew? Then he disappeared off into the
shadows around the pool table.

Jane sat, as if frozen. She wanted to tell them—to tell Paula—that he
was there. But they would think she was being stupid. Besides, she might
break down again, and that would be intolerable in public. But when it
was time for the next round, she asked for a whisky, and got it. And a
couple more after that, too.

They left the pub a little after last orders. She felt warm and cheerful,
and though she knew it was the whisky, she didn't care. It was a beautiful

night, cool enough for comfort with a sickle moon riding high in a clear sky, and she was with her friends. Maybe there was a problem, but she could solve it. She said as much as they walked home, and was surprised when Kath shushed her, telling her it was late and people would be sleeping.

When they got to the flats Paula wanted to go upstairs with her, but that was just stupid. What could happen to her so close to home? Besides, they had left *him* behind at the pub. What did Paula think he was, a magician?

She shrugged Paula's hand away from her arm and went inside. As she closed the double doors she could see them drifting slowly away down the road. They were probably waiting for her to start yelling for help. Damn them.

There was something odd about the inner stairs. Something about the moonlight. She heard the door bang outside. She paused. There were footsteps on the steps below. Instantly she was dead sober. An old statistic flashed through her mind: eighty per cent of all rape occurs close to the victims' homes; she wondered what the rate for murder was and cursed herself for a fool all at the same time as her hand clutched the hairspray in her jacket pocket.

She started to run up the stairs, and as the footsteps came closer, began to take them two at a time.

"Wait," a male voice called out. *His* voice. She would have known it anywhere.

She was out of breath. There were too many stairs. Maybe Paula was right, and she should have been eating better. She grabbed the bannister to try and haul herself up. He touched her. She thought he did.

She had to see. She turned, and he was right behind her, staring at her out of blue eyes made bright by moonlight. He stretched his hand towards her and said something. Then it was as if the world split in two. She was both herself, and a shadow-Jane. Shadow-Jane pulled a knife out of her pocket. Jane felt the textured plastic of the handle superimposed on the cold smoothness of the can of hairspray as she took it out of her pocket, felt her heart thunder in double time, shadow-heart and real-heart slightly syncopated. Two men stood before her now, both holding out her purse like a peace-offering, both plainly caught in that moment before understanding turns to terror. She saw her hand holding the can of hairspray, and another, translucent as a ghost, holding the knife.

"Christ," she thought. "This is what was supposed to happen . . ."

But the man—the men—were speaking. "Please don't—"

And Jane thought, *He doesn't want to hurt me. My dream—I'm supposed to kill* him, *not the other way around*—She felt shadow-Jane lunge forward with the knife extended, felt her own fingers press down on the button of the can, all in the same instant that she thought, *I don't have to do this*—

She jerked the can up, away from the man's eyes. Hairspray hissed harmlessly into the dark, leaving the air pungent behind it. But the shadow-knife slid into the man's chest.

Blood spurted everywhere. Shadow blood. On her T-shirt, on her hands. She felt shadow-Jane bite back hysteria; staring down at his blue dying eyes with mingled terror and exultation—

But he's dying Jane thought. *No matter what he was going to do, that can't please you.*

—at what she had escaped. Jane felt her shadow think, *You can't hurt me now*, felt the laughter that was beginning to bubble out of her throat. She felt herself beginning to laugh too. *I don't have to*, she thought desperately. *I don't want to be a murderer*—

But she could have been. She felt that darkness within herself, and she knew it. The man—the real man—was coming towards her, hands holding out her purse, saying words she couldn't understand.

"Don't come near me," she said in panic. If he came near her, she would hurt him. Hadn't all the others said she should hurt him? She could do it. Shadow-Jane had. Shadow-Jane was laughing in delight about it. But shadow-Jane wasn't there anymore, she had slipped away into the darkness; the shadow-man too, and all his blood. Only the laughter remained, coming out of Jane's throat, harsh and echoing, squeezing out sanity, leaving no room for thought.

Yet she thought, *I could have done it I could I could I could.* There was no way to deny it. She was still laughing as he came over to her. She looked at him, but it was the shadow-man's blue, dying eyes that she saw. She knew that she would be seeing those eyes forever. And she laughed.

Reviewers have praised Jo Bannister's crime novels, A BLEEDING OF INNO-
CENTS and SINS OF THE HEART, as powerful examinations of contemporary
society. All the praise will make sense once you've read her story here, another Golden Dagger nominee.

Last of Kin
JO BANNISTER

At the mention of the words "sweet little old lady," everyone who knew
her immediately thought of Mrs. Nancy Budgens. Even people who didn't
know her got a mind's eye view of someone very *like* Nancy: someone
of about seventy with a soft powdery complexion, fluffy peach-white hair,
faded but still warm blue eyes, no great height and nothing you could
call a waist without setting off a lie detector. They pictured the way she
smiled, the blue eyes disappearing in a mass of crinkles pushed up by
the apple cheeks, and the way she walked, with a slight roll like a deep-
sea sailor. They knew her wardrobe consisted almost entirely of flower-
printed cotton dresses.

Asked to speculate further, they would have attributed to this arche-
typal Little Old Lady a large close-knit family of equally apple-cheeked
husband, children, grandchildren and quite possibly great-grandchildren
as well. It seemed somehow part of the package, that such a plainly
maternal figure should come with all the trimmings.

But in fact Nancy Budgens did not have the perfect family life which
would have completed the picture. Mr. Budgens, branch manager of a
local bank for twenty years, died at his desk just weeks short of retirement. Their daughter Sandra never married, though she did raise a child.
A dull woman, prematurely middle-aged, she seemed content in her un-
demanding job as an assistant librarian; until one morning she was found
hanging from a length of picture cord attached to the specially high shelf
for books of a certain artistic nature.

Which reduced the already small family to just two: Nancy and her
grandson Trevor. When anyone asked she would put on that brave smile

patented by little old ladies and say, "Trevor's all I have left." Then: "And I'm all he has."

This led some of her friends to suppose the relationship closer than in fact it was. Although alone, Sandra Budgens had managed to provide a home and a decent upbringing for her son without recourse to her parents. Young Trevor saw as much of his grandma and grandad as most boys—occasional holidays, birthdays, Christmas—and no more. There was an element of wishful thinking in what Nancy said. Though they were indeed next of kin after Sandra's sad meaningless departure, she and Trevor remained more amiable than close.

For one thing, Trevor wasn't Reliable. As the widow of a bank manager Nancy put a lot of stock in Reliability, which she judged by such things as having a Proper Job and a Nice Home and Nice Friends. Trevor disappointed on every count. He was an actor. He said he was quite a good one and made a decent living. All Nancy knew was that he visited her at times when people with Proper Jobs would be working, and he wore clothes she wouldn't have let Mr. Budgens put in their own dustbin. He shared a run-down Victorian house with several other Thespians of both traditional sexes and one or two others.

In spite of that, he seemed a kind young man. He brought her chocolates on her birthday, and flowers for no particular reason, and phoned her at intervals to check that she was keeping well.

And she was keeping well; but she was aware of the passing of time and the need to make proper provision for her old age. The family home, which had never felt a burden until recently, seemed to be getting bigger, the stairs steeper, the bathroom further down the landing with every month that passed. Once it had been her ambition to die in this house; now that seemed less a hope than a sentence. She thought there must be easier ways for an old lady with a little money to spend her last years.

She asked Trevor round to discuss the situation. He came willingly enough but puzzled, as if she'd asked for his advice on gerbils. All he knew about money was that if you didn't pay what you owed people came after you with pick-axe handles.

"I'm not a wealthy woman," Nancy began coyly. "Your grandfather, God bless him, left me comfortable, but that's getting to be a long time ago. Running this house has eaten into what he left. Then there was the inflation, and the recession . . ." She smiled apologetically.

Trevor glanced around him. It wasn't a big house but it was a considerable asset. He couldn't believe she was desperate enough to be asking him for money. "Grandma, of course I'd help if I could. But—"

But when Trevor said he was successful he meant he could live on what he earned as an actor, and didn't have to work in kitchens when he was "resting." It did not mean he had a numbered account in Switzerland that the Inland Revenue knew nothing about. His mother's estate had boiled down to a few thousand pounds in a building society, which he considered his insurance against destitution if the roles he specialized in—petty criminals, undesirable boyfriends and assorted Shakespearian gravediggers and sword-carriers whose first names were always Second—dried up. His only other assets were an elderly van—his ability to transport scenery had won him several parts—and a fifth share in a house that grew mushrooms.

Oh yes: and an elderly grandmother with a much nicer house of her own and no other relatives.

Nancy patted his hand absently. "Would you, dear? Bless you. But that's not quite what I had in mind.

"You and I are one another's only family, Trevor. When I die, what I have will naturally be yours. I've always hoped it would be enough to provide you with a little security.

"But if I do what I have in mind there won't be as much left as I'd like. I'm an old lady now, but I could live another twenty years. And nice residential accommodation doesn't come cheap. I'd have to sell this house and buy an annuity. On the credit side"—Nancy wasn't a bank manager's widow for nothing—"I'd never be a burden to you. On the debit side, there mightn't be much left for *your* old age. Before I burn any boats I'd like to know how you feel about that. Would it be a major blow?"

Trevor had never given it much thought. He knew he was his grandmother's only heir, and anticipated benefiting at some point, but he'd never worked out how much he could expect let alone how to use it. He thought about it now.

She was seventy-one: no great age by today's standards. She was fit, she had no history of illness—she might live to be a hundred. He'd be in his fifties then. There were an awful lot of fifty-year-old actors for whom "resting" had become a permanent state of affairs. Whatever the house was worth, whatever she got for the antiques that furnished it and whatever remained from his grandfather's investments, it would all be gone by then. Even if she didn't live to be a hundred; even if she only lived another ten years, say, which was nothing. Every week she would reduce his expectations by hundreds of pounds.

The mere fact that he wasn't able to brush it off unconsidered, with a gallant smile and a casual "Grandma, it's your money, use it how you want," told Nancy that however well he was doing in his own terms her grandson did not have the kind of financial reserves beside which her own paled to insignificance.

"Oh dear," she said anxiously, reaching for his hand, "it *would*, wouldn't it? You've been counting on it. You're a good boy, you've never asked me for money, even when you couldn't possibly have had enough. And now I'm proposing to spend your inheritance. No, it really won't do—I shall have to think again."

Trevor got a belated grip on his expression and clasped her hand in return. "Don't be silly, Grandma," he said. "It's your money—Grandad made it and he'd want you to use it in your best interests. Spend it and enjoy it. I've some money of my own: not a fortune but enough to see me through the odd sticky patch. Mum left me nearly ten thousand, and I've added a bit to it since I've been working. And hell, I'm only twenty-five: if I can't put together a comfortable stake over the next forty years I should have been a greengrocer instead! Now, tell me about your plans. Is there somewhere you've got your eye on?"

Nancy's face lit up with pleasure. If it was true that Sandra had never fulfilled the highest potential as a daughter, that she and her mother had in fact found it hard to like one another, she had at least raised a son to be proud of. "Trevor, you're a lovely lad." Nancy got up and bustled over to her bureau, coming back with a sheaf of envelopes made of expensively grained paper. "Yes, I have. I've been doing a bit of research, and there's a couple of wonderful places."

She spread the brochures in front of him, pointing out the lifts, the en-suite bathrooms, the extensive gardens with the enthusiasm of a child comparing holiday camps.

"I think Rosedale's the one I shall go for. Look at those *lovely* flowerbeds! And if you pay a little more for a room on this side of the house"—she tapped the illustration with a fingernail—"there's a view of the river. Oh, I did used to love the river when we were younger! I really think it would be worth finding a little more to be able to enjoy it again."

"What's this one?" asked Trevor, holding up a well-thumbed prospectus with a lot of gold-leaf on the cover.

Nancy's voice went schoolgirl breathy. "The Beeches. The Rolls-Royce of residential provision for the elderly—the sort of place you only get sent to if the family feel really guilty about the way they've treated you. I wish someone had treated *me* that badly! Even by selling this place I couldn't meet the fees at The Beeches." She smiled cheerily. "Still, it's nice to dream."

" 'Course it is, Gran," Trevor said bravely, well aware that her dreams were putting the boot into his. Even if he'd never thought of it in those terms, this house had been his insurance against having to play comic footmen in pantomime in Huddersfield. When it was gone he was on his own. Her news had given him much to think about.

As his had given Nancy. But they parted on the doorstep with their customary brief hug as if all was well.

"You are a *nice* boy, Trevor," his grandmother said again. "I've been quite worried, I don't mind saying. I'm glad we've had this talk."

"There's nothing to worry about," Trevor said firmly. "Like you always say, all we've got is each other. If we don't look out for one another, who else will?"

Normally they met every month or so. But there were practicalities to discuss so there was nothing odd about them going for a drive in Trevor's van just three days later. The inquest heard that it was Trevor's suggestion but that Nancy jumped at the idea.

They drove down to the river and parked where they could just see the roofs of the Rosedale Retirement Home across the municipal playing fields. "It's a nice area," said Trevor.

"Yes, it is pretty," agreed Nancy. "Not that I'll be able to walk this far, but it'll be nice to look at from the bedroom window. That's the advantage with The Beeches, you see." She turned and indicated the butter-coloured stone of a large house surrounded by tree-studded lawns that rolled down to the water's edge a quarter of a mile upstream. "No walking—it's an actual riverside property."

"I'd have thought that was a drawback for a retirement home. Don't the old dears keep sliding in?"

Nancy smiled. "There's a chicken-wire fence to catch them. I don't think they lose many."

Trevor grinned. "You and Grandad had a boat on the river, didn't you?" She nodded. "Mum used to try and make me come out with you sometimes: she said the fresh air would do me good. But I never did like being that close to water."

"I remember," murmured Nancy. "When your grandad tried teaching you to swim you screamed so much he had to give up. Such a pity."

Trevor shrugged. "There are worse handicaps for an actor. The only time it gives me a problem is in *The Tempest*."

Nancy chuckled. "You must favour your father's side. I can't think how a grandson of mine could *not* love the river. It's *beautiful*."

A man walking his dog along the far bank saw what happened next. The van doors opened and a young man and an elderly lady got out and strolled along the bank a few feet from the water, a brown torrent swollen by months of rain. As they walked the woman gestured up and down stream as if pointing out items of interest. Then they turned back to the van.

In doing so the old lady lost her footing on the rain-softened bank and fell with a startled squawk first to her knees and then, as she struggled to get up, down the muddy slope into the river. At once the young man threw himself full length on the bank in an effort to reach her. But her hand remained tantalizingly beyond his grasp. After only a brief hesitation he kicked off his shoes and slithered down the muddy bank into the water.

The witness was unable to say quite what followed. Poor Mr. Budgens reached his struggling grandmother and grasped her hand. But then either he lost his footing, or in her panic she unbalanced him, and he disappeared under the rolling flood. He surfaced yards out into the river, here even in normal weather there was depth enough for quite big boats, and yelled and waved his arms over his head until he disappeared again. Twice more he floundered to the surface, further from the bank each time, while the witness watched in helpless horror. After that he did not see him again.

By then help had reached Mrs. Budgens. Strong arms pulled her up the bank, wrapped coats and car-rugs around her, chafed her trembling hands. All she could say was, "Trevor. Where's Trevor? Where's Trevor?"

The inquest was a formality. Death by misadventure, and an eloquent tribute from the coroner for a courageous young man who braved an element he feared deeply in an attempt to rescue a frail old lady. It was the stuff of tabloid headlines, and Nancy Budgens was touched by the kindness paid by so many people who never knew him to poor Trevor's memory.

When it was all done, no one was surprised that Nancy sold her house and used the proceeds to move into residential accommodation. There were a few raised eyebrows that she chose a home so close to the scene of the tragedy. But as she pointed out, she had always loved the river; and in a sort of a way, there was something of Trevor in it now. Perhaps it was odd of her. Bereaved elderly ladies of seventy-one were entitled to be odd.

So she moved into The Beeches. It was worth every penny it cost. With poor Trevor gone there was no one left to consider but herself, so she spent the money with a clear conscience. Together, the proceeds of her house and Trevor's building society bought an annuity that would keep her in the state to which she meant to become accustomed for as long as she lived. It was, after all, what Trevor would have wished.

Trevor had been her last surviving blood-relation, her only heir. And she had been his.

Ed Gorman's work has won the Shamus, been nominated for the Edgar and Anthony, and now the Golden Dagger. While he's best known for his darker work, he points out that two of his first four novels were screwball comedies. He returns to that form here.

One of Those Days,
One of Those Nights
ED GORMAN

The thing you have to understand is that I found it by accident. I was looking for a place to hide the birthday gift I'd bought Laura—a string of pearls she'd been wanting to wear with the new black dress she'd bought for herself—and all I was going to do was lay the gift-wrapped box in the second drawer of the bureau . . .

. . . and there it was.

A plain number ten envelope with her name written across the middle in a big manly scrawl and a canceled Elvis Presley stamp up in the corner. Postmarked two days ago.

Just as I spotted it, Laura called from the living room, "Bye, honey, see you at six." The last two years we've been saving to buy a house so we have only the one car. Laura goes an hour earlier than I do, so she rides with a woman who lives a few blocks over. Then I pick her up at six after somebody relieves me at the computer store where I work. For what it's worth, I have an MA in English literature but with the economy being what it is, it hasn't done me much good.

I saw a sci-fi movie once where a guy could set something on fire simply by staring at it intently enough. That's what I was trying to do with this letter my wife got. Burn it so that I wouldn't have to read what it said inside and get my heart broken.

I closed the drawer.

Could be completely harmless. Her fifteenth high school reunion was coming up this spring. Maybe it was from one of her old classmates. And

122

maybe the manly scrawl wasn't so manly after all. Maybe it was from a woman who wrote in a rolling dramatic hand.

Laura always said that I was the jealous type and this was certainly proof. A harmless letter tucked harmlessly in a bureau drawer. And here my heart was pounding, and fine cold sweat slicked my face, and my fingers were trembling.

God, wasn't I a pitiful guy? Shouldn't I be ashamed of myself?

I went into the bathroom and lathered up and did my usual relentless fifteen-minute morning regimen of shaving, showering and shining up my apple-cheeked Irish face and my thinning Irish hair, if hair follicles can have a nationality, that is.

Then I went back into our bedroom and took down a white shirt, blue necktie, navy blazer and tan slacks. All dressed, I looked just like seventy or eighty million other men getting ready for work this particular sunny April morning.

Then I stood very still in the middle of the bedroom and stared at Laura's bureau. Maybe I wasn't simply going to set the letter on fire. Maybe I was going to ignite the entire bureau.

The grandfather clock in the living room tolled eight-thirty. If I didn't leave now I would be late, and if you were late you inevitably got a chewing out from Ms. Sandstrom, the boss. Anybody who believes that women would run a more benign world than men needs only to spend five minutes with Ms. Sandstrom. Hitler would have used her as a pin-up girl.

The bureau. The letter. The manly scrawl.

What was I going to do?

Only one thing I could think of, since I hadn't made a decision about reading the letter or not. I'd simply take it with me to work. If I decided to read it, I'd give it a quick scan over my lunch hour.

But probably I wouldn't read it at all. I had a lot of faith where Laura was concerned. And I didn't like to think of myself as the sort of possessive guy who snuck around reading his wife's mail.

I reached into the bureau drawer.

My fingers touched the letter.

I was almost certain I wasn't going to read it. Hell, I'd probably get so busy at work that I'd forget all about it.

But just in case I decided to . . .

I grabbed the letter and stuffed it into my blazer pocket, and closed the drawer. In the kitchen I had a final cup of coffee and read my newspaper horoscope. Bad news, as always. I should never read the damn things . . . Then I hurried out of the apartment to the little Toyota parked at the kerb.

Six blocks away, it stalled. Our friendly mechanic said that moisture seemed to get in the fuel pump a lot. He's not sure why. We've run it in three times but it still stalls several times a week.

*   *   *

AROUND TEN O'CLOCK, hurrying into a sales meeting that Ms. Sandstrom had decided to call, I dropped my pen. And when I bent over to pick it up, my glasses fell out of my pocket and when I moved to pick them up, I took one step too many and put all 175 pounds of my body directly on to them. I heard something snap.

By the time I retrieved both pen and glasses, Ms. Sandstrom was closing the door and calling the meeting to order. I hurried down the hall trying to see how much damage I'd done. I held the glasses up to the light. A major fissure snaked down the center of the right lens. I slipped them on. The crack was even more difficult to see through than I'd thought.

Ms. Sandstrom, a very attractive fiftyish woman given to sleek gray suits and burning blue gazes, warned us as usual that if sales of our computers didn't pick up, two or three people in this room would likely be looking for jobs. Soon. And just as she finished saying this, her eyes met mine. "For instance, Donaldson, what kind of month are you having?"

"What kind of month am I having?"

"Do I hear a parrot in here?" Ms. Sandstrom said, and several of the salespeople laughed.

"I'm not having too bad a month."

Ms. Sandstrom nodded wearily and looked around the room. "Do we have to ask Donaldson here any more questions? Isn't he telling us everything we need to know when he says 'I'm not having too bad a month'? What're we hearing when Donaldson says that?"

I hadn't noticed till this morning how much Ms. Sandstrom reminded me of Miss Hutchison, my fourth-grade teacher. Her favorite weapon had also been humiliation.

Dick Weybright raised his hand. Dick Weybright always raises his hand, especially when he gets to help Ms. Sandstrom humiliate somebody.

"We hear defeatism, when he says that," Dick said. "We hear defeatism and a serious lack of self-esteem."

Twice a week, Ms. Sandstrom made us listen to motivational tapes. You know, "I upped my income, Up yours," that sort of thing. And nobody took those tapes more seriously than Dick Weybright.

"Very good, Dick," Ms. Sandstrom said. "Defeatism and lack of self-esteem. That tells us all we need to know about Donaldson here. Just as the fact that he's got a crack in his glasses tells us something else about him, doesn't it?"

Dick Weybright waggled his hand again. "Lack of self-respect."

"Exactly," Ms. Sandstrom said, smiling coldly at me. "Lack of self-respect."

She didn't address me again until I was leaving the sales room. I'd knocked some of my papers on the floor. By the time I got them picked up, I was alone with Ms. Sandstrom. I heard her come up behind me as I pointed myself toward the door.

"You missed something, Donaldson."

I turned. "Oh?"

She waved Laura's envelope in the air. Then her blue eyes showed curiosity as they read the name on the envelope. "You're not one of those, are you, Donaldson?"

"One of those?"

"Men who read their wives' mail?"

"Oh. One of those. I see."

"Are you?"

"No."

"Then what're you doing with this?"

"What am I doing with that?"

"That parrot's in here again."

"I must've picked it up off the table by mistake."

"The table?"

"The little Edwardian table under the mirror in the foyer. Where we always set the mail."

She shook her head again. She shook her head a lot. "You are one of those, aren't you, Donaldson? So were my first three husbands, the bastards."

She handed me the envelope, brushed past me and disappeared down the hall.

THERE'S A PARK NEAR THE RIVER where I usually eat lunch when I'm downtown for the day. I spend most of the time feeding the pigeons.

Today I spent most of my time staring at the envelope laid next to me on the park bench. There was a warm spring breeze and I half-hoped it would lift up the envelope and carry it away.

Now I wished I'd left the number ten with the manly scrawl right where I'd found it because it was getting harder and harder to resist lifting the letter from inside and giving it a quick read.

I checked my watch. Twenty minutes to go before I needed to be back at work. Twenty minutes to stare at the letter. Twenty minutes to resist temptation.

Twenty minutes—and how's this for cheap symbolism?—during which the sky went from cloudless blue to dark and ominous.

By now, I'd pretty much decided that the letter had to be from a man. Otherwise, why would Laura have hidden it in her drawer? I'd also decided that it must contain something pretty incriminating.

Had she been having an affair with somebody? Was she thinking of running away with somebody?

On the way back to the office, I carefully slipped the letter from the envelope and read it. Read it four times as a matter of fact. And felt worse every time I did.

So Chris Tomlin, her ridiculously handsome, ridiculously wealthy, ridiculously slick college boyfriend was back in her life.

I can't tell you much about the rest of the afternoon. It's all very vague: voices spoke to me, phones rang at me, computer printers spat things at me—but I didn't respond. I felt as if I were scuttling across the floor of an ocean so deep that neither light nor sound could penetrate it.

Chris Tomlin. My God.

I kept reading the letter, stopping only when I'd memorized it entirely and could keep rerunning it in my mind without any visual aid.

Dear Laura,

I still haven't forgotten you—or forgiven you for choosing you-know-who over me.

I'm going to be in your fair city this Friday. How about meeting me at the Fairmont right at noon for lunch?

Of course, you could contact me the evening before it you're interested. I'll be staying at the Wallingham. I did a little checking and found that you work nearby.

I can't wait to see you.

Love,
Chris Tomlin.

Not even good old Ms. Sandstrom could penetrate my stupor. I know she charged into my office a few times and made some nasty threats—something about my not returning the call of one of our most important customers—but I honestly couldn't tell you who she wanted me to call or what she wanted me to say.

About all I can remember is that it got very dark and cold suddenly. The lights blinked on and off a few times. We were having a terrible rainstorm. Somebody came in soaked and said that the storm sewers were backing up and that downtown was a mess.

Not that I paid this information any particular heed.

I was wondering if she'd call him Thursday night. I took it as a foregone conclusion that she would have lunch with him on Friday. But how about Thursday night?

Would she visit him in his hotel room?

And come to think of it, why *had* she chosen me over Chris Tomlin? I mean, while I may not be a nerd, I'm not exactly a movie star, either. And with Chris Tomlin, there wouldn't have been any penny-pinching for a down payment on a house, either.

With his daddy's millions in pharmaceuticals, good ole Chris would have bought her a manse as a wedding present.

The workday ended. The usual number of people peeked into my office to say the usual number of good nights. The usual cleaning crew, high school kids in gray uniforms, appeared to start hauling out trash and run roaring vacuum cleaners. And I went through my usual process of staying at my desk until it was time to pick up Laura.

I was just about to walk out the front door when I noticed in the gloom that Ms. Sandstrom's light was still on.

She had good ears. Even above the vacuum cleaner roaring its way down the hall to her left, she heard me leaving and looked up.

She waved me into her office.

When I reached her desk, she handed me a slip of paper with some typing on it.

"How does that read to you, Donaldson?"

"Uh, what is it?"

"A Help Wanted ad I may be running tomorrow."

That was another thing Miss Hutchison, my fourth-grade teacher, had been good at—indirect torture.

Ms. Sandstrom wanted me to read the ad she'd be running for my replacement.

I scanned it and handed it back.

"Nice."

"Is that all you have to say? Nice?"

"I guess so."

"You realize that this means I'm going to fire you?"

"That's what I took it to mean."

"What the hell's wrong with you, Donaldson? Usually you'd be groveling and sniveling by now."

"I've got some—personal problems."

A smirk. "That's what you get for reading your wife's mail." Then a scowl. "When you come in tomorrow morning, you come straight to my office, you understand?"

I nodded. "All right."

"And be prepared to do some groveling and sniveling. You're going to need it."

WHY DON'T I JUST MAKE A LIST of the things I found wrong with my Toyota after I slammed the door and belted myself in.

A) The motor wouldn't turn over. Remember what I said about moisture and the fuel pump?

B) The roof had sprung a new leak. This was different from the old leak, which dribbled rain down on to the passenger seat. The new one dribbled rain down on to the driver's seat.

C) The turn signal arm had come loose again and was hanging down from naked wires like a half-amputated limb. Apparently after finding the letter this morning, I was in so much of a fog I hadn't noticed that it was broken again.

I can't tell you how dark and cold and lonely I felt just then. Bereft of wife. Bereft of automobile. Bereft of—dare I say it?—self-esteem and self-respect. And, on top of it, I was a disciple of defeatism. Just ask my co-worker Dick Weybright.

The goddamned car finally started and I drove off to pick up my goddamned wife.

The city was a mess.

Lashing winds and lashing rains—both of which were still lashing merrily along—had uprooted trees in the park, smashed out store windows here and there, and had apparently caused a power outage that shut down all the automatic traffic signals.

I wanted to be home and I wanted to be dry and I wanted to be in my jammies. But most of all I wanted to be loved by the one woman I had ever really and truly loved.

If only I hadn't opened her bureau drawer to hide her pearls . . .

She was standing behind the glass door in the entrance to the art deco building where she works as a market researcher for a mutual fund company. When I saw her, I felt all sorts of things at once—love, anger, shame, terror—and all I wanted to do was park the car and run up to her and take her in my arms and give her the tenderest kiss I was capable of.

But then I remembered the letter and . . .

Well, I'm sure I don't have to tell you about jealousy. There's nothing worse to carry around in your stony little heart. All that rage and self-righteousness and self-pity. It begins to smother you and . . .

By the time Laura climbed into the car, it was smothering me. She smelled of rain and perfume and her sweet tender body.

"Hi," she said. "I was worried about you."

"Yeah. I'll bet."

Then, closing the door, she gave me a long, long look. "Are you all right?"

"Fine."

"Then why did you say, 'Yeah. I'll bet'?"

"Just being funny."

She gave me another stare. I tried to look regular and normal. You know, not on the verge of whipping the letter out and shoving it in her face.

"Oh, God," she said, "you're not starting your period already are you?"

The period thing is one of our little jokes. A few months after we got married, she came home cranky one day and I laid the blame for her mood on her period. She said I was being sexist. I said I was only making an observation. I wrote down the date. For the next four months, on or around the same time each month, she came home crabby. I pointed this out to her. She said, "All right. But men have periods, too." "They do?" "You're damned right they do." And so now, whenever I seem inexplicably grouchy, she asks me if my period is starting.

"Maybe so," I said, swinging from outrage to a strange kind of whipped exhaustion.

"Boy, this is really leaking," Laura said.

I just drove. There was a burly traffic cop out in the middle of a busy intersection directing traffic with two flashlights in the rain and gloom.

"Did you hear me, Rich? I said this is really leaking."

"I know it's really leaking."

"What's up with you, anyway? What're you so mad about? Did Sandstrom give you a hard time today?"

"No—other than telling me that she may fire me."

"You're kidding."

"No."

"But why?"

Because while I was going through your bureau, I found a letter from your ex-lover and I know all about the tryst you're planning to set up.

That's what I wanted to say.

What I said was: "I guess I wasn't paying proper attention during another one of her goddamned sales meetings."

"But, Rich, if you get fired—"

She didn't have to finish her sentence. If I got fired, we'd never get the house we'd been saving for.

"She told me that when I came in tomorrow morning, I should be prepared to grovel and snivel. And she wasn't kidding."

"She actually said that?"

"She actually said that."

"What a bitch."

"Boss's daughter. You know how this city is. The last frontier for hard-core nepotism."

We drove on several more blocks, stopping every quarter block or so to pull out around somebody whose car had stalled in the dirty water backing up from the sewers.

"So is that why you're so down?"

"Yeah," I said, "Isn't that reason enough?"

"Usually, about Sandstrom, I mean, you get mad. You don't get depressed."

"Well, Sandstrom chews me out but she doesn't usually threaten to fire me."

"That's true. But—"

"But what?"

"It just seems that there's—something else." Then, "Where're you going?"

My mind had been on the letter tucked inside my blazer. In the meantime, the Toyota had been guiding itself into the most violent neighborhood in the city. Not even the cops wanted to to come here.

"God, can you turn around?" Laura said. "I'd sure hate to get stuck here."

"We'll be all right. I'll hang a left at the next corner and then we'll drive back to Marymount Avenue."

"I wondered where you were going. I should have said something." She leaned over and kissed me on the cheek.

That boil of feelings, of profound tenderness and profound rage, churned up inside of me again.

"Things'll work out with Sandstrom," she said, and then smiled. "Maybe she's just starting her period."

And I couldn't help it. The rage was gone, replaced by pure and total love. This was my friend, my bride, my lover. There had to be a reasonable and innocent explanation for the letter. There had to.

I started hanging the left and that's when it happened. The fuel pump. Rain.

The Toyota stopped dead.

"Oh, no," she said, glancing out the windshield at the forbidding blocks of falling-down houses and dark, condemned buildings.

Beyond the wind, beyond the rain, you could hear sirens. There were always sirens in neighborhoods like these.

"Maybe I can fix it," I said.

"But, honey, you don't know anything about cars."

"Well, I watched him make that adjustment last time."

"I don't know," she said skeptically. "Besides, you'll just get wet."

"I'll be fine."

I knew why I was doing this, of course. In addition to being rich, powerful and handsome, Chris Tomlin was also one of those men who could fix practically anything. I remembered her telling me how he'd fixed a refrigerator at an old cabin they'd once stayed in.

I opened the door. A wave of rain washed over me. But I was determined to act like the kind of guy who could walk through a meteor storm and laugh it off. Maybe that's why Laura was considering a rendezvous with Chris. Maybe she was sick of my whining. A macho man, I'm not.

"Just be careful," she said.

"Be right back."

I eased out of the car and then realized I hadn't used the hood latch inside. I leaned in and popped the latch and gave Laura a quick smile.

And then I went back outside into the storm.

*   *   *

I WAS SOAKED completely in less than a minute, my shoes soggy, my clothes drenched and cold and clinging. Even my raincoat.

But I figured this would help my image as a take-charge sort of guy. I even gave Laura a little half-salute before I raised the hood. She smiled at me. God, I wanted to forget all about the letter and be happily in love again.

Any vague hopes I'd had of starting the car were soon forgotten as I gaped at the motor and realized that I had absolutely no idea what I was looking at.

The mechanic in the shop had made it look very simple. You raised the hood, you leaned in and snatched off the oil filter and then did a couple of quick things to it and put it back. And *voilà*, your car was running again.

I got the hood open all right, and I leaned in just fine, and I even took the oil filter off with no problem.

But when it came to doing a couple of quick things to it, my brain was as dead as the motor. That was the part I hadn't picked up from the mechanic. Those couple of quick things.

I started shaking the oil filter. Don't ask me why. I had it under the protection of the hood to keep it dry and shook it left and shook it right and shook it high and shook it low. I figured that maybe some kind of invisible cosmic forces would come into play here and the engine would start as soon as I gave the ignition key a little turn.

I closed the hood and ran back through the slashing rain, opened the door and crawled inside.

"God, it's incredible out there."

Only then did I get a real good look at Laura and only then did I see that she looked sick, like the time we both picked up a slight case of ptomaine poisoning at her friend Susan's wedding.

Except now she looked a lot sicker.

And then I saw the guy.

In the back seat.

"Who the hell are you?"

But he had questions of his own. "Your wife won't tell me if you've got an ATM card."

So it had finally happened. Our little city turned violent about fifteen years ago, during which time most honest working folks had to take their turns getting mugged, sort of like a rite of passage. But as time wore on, the muggers weren't satisfied with simply robbing their victims. Now they beat them up. And sometimes, for no reason at all, they killed them.

This guy was white, chunky, with a ragged scar on his left cheek, stupid dark eyes, a dark turtleneck sweater and a large and formidable gun. He smelled of sweat, cigarette smoke, beer and a high sweet unclean tang.

"How much can you get with your card?"

"Couple hundred."

"Yeah. Right."

"Couple hundred. I mean, we're not exactly rich people. Look at this car."

He turned to Laura. "How much can he get, babe?"

"He told you. A couple of hundred." She sounded surprisingly calm.

"One more time." He had turned back to me. "How much can you get with that card of yours?"

"I told you," I said.

You know how movie thugs are always slugging people with gun butts? Well, let me tell you something. It hurts. He hit me hard enough to draw blood, hard enough to fill my sight with darkness and blinking stars, like a planetarium ceiling, and hard enough to lay my forehead against the steering wheel.

Laura didn't scream.

She just leaned over and touched my head with her long, gentle fingers. And you know what? Even then, even suffering from what might be a concussion, I had this image of Laura's fingers touching Chris Tomlin's head this way. Ain't jealousy grand?

"Now," said the voice in the back seat, "let's talk."

Neither of us paid him much attention for a minute or so. Laura helped me sit back in the seat. She took her handkerchief and daubed it against the back of my head.

"You didn't have to hit him."

"Now maybe he'll tell me the truth."

"Four or five hundred," she said. "That's how much we can get. And don't hit him again. Don't lay a finger on him."

"The mama lion fights for her little cub. That's nice." He leaned forward and put the end of the gun directly against my ear. "You're gonna have to go back out in that nasty ole rain. There's an ATM machine down at the west end of this block and around the corner. You go down there and get me five hundred dollars and then you haul your ass right back. I'll be waiting right here with your exceedingly good-looking wife. and with my gun."

"Where did you ever learn a word like exceedingly?" I said.

"What the hell's that supposed to mean?"

"I was just curious."

"If it's any of your goddamned business, my cell-mate had one of them improve your vocabulary books."

I glanced at Laura. She still looked scared but she also looked a little bit angry. For us, five hundred dollars was a lot of money.

And now a robber who used the word "exceedingly" was going to take every last dime of it.

"Go get it," he said.

I reached over to touch Laura's hand as reassuringly as possible, and that was when I noticed it.

The white number ten envelope.

The one Chris had sent her.

I stared at it a long moment and then raised my eyes to meet hers.

"I was going to tell you about it."

I shook my head. "I shouldn't have looked in your drawer."

"No, you shouldn't have. But I still owe you an explanation."

"What the hell are you two talking about?"

"Nothing that's exceedingly interesting," I said, and opened the door, and dangled a leg out and then had the rest of my body follow the leg.

"You got five minutes, you understand?" the man said.

I nodded and glanced at Laura. "I love you."

"I'm sorry about the letter."

"You know the funny thing? I was hiding your present, that's how I found it. I was going to tuck it in your underwear drawer and have you find them. You know, the pearls."

"You got me the pearl necklace?"

"Uh-huh."

"Oh, honey, that's so sweet."

"Go get the goddamned money," the man said, "and get it fast."

"I'll be right back," I said to Laura and blew her a little kiss.

IF I HADN'T BEEN SODDEN before, I certainly was now.

There were two brick buildings facing each other across a narrow alley. Most people drove up to this particular ATM machine because it was housed in a deep indentation that faced the alley. It could also accommodate foot traffic.

What it didn't do was give you much protection from the storm.

By now, I was sneezing and feeling a scratchiness in my throat. Bad sinuses. My whole family.

I walked up to the oasis of light and technology in this ancient and wild neighborhood, took out my wallet and inserted my ATM card.

It was all very casual, especially considering the fact that Laura was being held hostage.

The card would go in. The money would come out. The thief would get his loot. Laura and I would dash to the nearest phone and call the police.

Except I couldn't remember my secret pin number.

If I had to estimate how many times I'd used this card, I'd put it at probably a thousand or so.

So how, after all those times, could I now forget the pin number?

Panic. That's what was wrong. I was so scared that Laura would be hurt that I couldn't think clearly.

Deep breaths. There.

Now. Think. Clearly.

Just relax and your pin number will come back to you. No problem.

That was when I noticed the slight black man in the rain parka standing just to the left of me. In the rain. With a gun in his hand.

"You wanna die?"

"Oh, shit. You've got to be kidding. You're a goddamned thief?"

"Yes, and I ain't ashamed of it either, man."

I thought of explaining it to him, explaining that another thief already had first dibs on the proceeds of my bank account—that is, if I could ever remember the pin number—but he didn't seem to be the understanding type at all. In fact, he looked even more desperate and crazy than the man who was holding Laura.

"How much can you take out?"

"I can't give it to you."

"You see this gun, man?"

"Yeah. I see it."

"You know what happens if you don't crank some serious money out for me?"

I had to explain after all. ". . . so, you see, I can't give it to you."

"What the hell's that supposed to mean?"

"Somebody's already got dibs on it."

"Dibs? What the hell does 'dibs' mean?"

"It means another robber has already spoken for this money."

He looked at me carefully. "You're crazy, man. You really are. But that don't mean I won't shoot you."

"And there's one more thing."

"What?"

"I can't remember my pin number."

"Bullshit."

"It's true. That's why I've been standing here. My mind's a blank."

"You gotta relax, man."

"I know that. But it's kind've hard. You've got a gun and so does the other guy."

"There's really some other dude holdin' your old lady?"

"Right."

He grinned with exceedingly bad teeth. "You got yourself a real problem, dude."

I closed my eyes.

I must have spent my five minutes already.

Would he really kill Laura?

"You tried deep breathin'?"

"Yeah."

"And that didn't work?"

"Huh-uh."

"You tried makin' your mind go blank for a little bit?"

"That didn't work, either."

He pushed the gun right into my face. "I ain't got much time, man."

"I can't give you the money, anyway."

"You ain't gonna be much use to your old lady if you got six or seven bullet holes in you."

"God!"

"What's wrong?"

My pin number had popped into my head.

Nothing like a gun in your face to jog your memory.

I dove for the ATM machine.

And started punching buttons.

The right buttons.

"Listen," I said as I cranked away, "I really can't give you this money."

"Right."

"I mean, I would if I could but the guy would never believe me if I told him some other crook had taken it. No offense, 'crook' I mean."

"Here it comes."

"I'm serious. You can't have it."

"Pretty, pretty Yankee dollars. Praise the Lord."

The plastic cover opened and the machine began spitting out green Yankee dollars.

And that's when he slugged me on the back of the head.

The guy back in the car had hit me but it had been nothing like this. This time, the field of black floating in front of my eyes didn't even have stars. This time, hot shooting pain traveled from the point of impact near the top of my skull all the way down into my neck and shoulders. This time, my knees gave out immediately.

Pavement. Hard. Wet. Smelling of cold rain. And still the darkness. Total darkness. I had a moment of panic. Had I been blinded for life? I wanted to be angry but I was too disoriented. Pain. Cold. Darkness.

And then I felt his hands tearing the money from mine.

I had to hold on to it. Had to. Otherwise Laura would be injured. Or killed.

The kick landed hard just above my sternum. Stars suddenly appeared in the field of black. His foot seemed to have jarred them loose.

More pain. But now there was anger. I blindly lashed out and grabbed his trouser leg, clung to it, forcing him to drag me down the sidewalk as he tried to get away. I don't know how many names I called him, some of them probably didn't even make sense, I just clung to his leg, exulting in his rage, in his inability to get rid of me.

Then he leaned down and grabbed a handful of my hair and pulled so hard I screamed. And inadvertently let go of his leg.

And then I heard his footsteps, retreating, retreating, and felt the rain start slashing at me again. He had dragged me out from beneath the protection of the ATM overhang.

I struggled to get up. It wasn't easy. I still couldn't see. And every time I tried to stand, I was overcome by dizziness and a faint nausea.

But I kept thinking of Laura. And kept pushing myself to my feet, no matter how much pain pounded in my head, no matter how I started to pitch forward and collapse again.

By the time I got to my feet, and fell against the rough brick of the building for support, my eyesight was back. Funny how much you take it for granted. It's terrifying when it's gone.

I looked at the oasis of light in the gloom. At the foot of the ATM was my bank card. I wobbled over and picked it up. I knew that I'd taken out my allotted amount for the day but I decided to try and see if the cosmic forces were with me for once.

They weren't.

The only thing I got from the machine was a snotty little note saying that I'd have to contact my personal banker if I wanted to receive more money.

A) I had no idea who this personal banker was, and

B) I doubted if he would be happy if I called him at home on such a rainy night even if I did have his name and number.

Then I did what any red-blooded American would do. I started kicking the machine. Kicking hard. Kicking obsessively. Until my toes started to hurt.

I stood for a long moment in the rain, letting it pour down on me, feeling as if I were melting like a wax statue in the hot sun. I became one with the drumming and thrumming and pounding of it all.

There was only one thing I could do now.

I took off running back to the car. To Laura. And the man with the gun.

I broke into a crazy grin when I saw the car. I could see Laura's profile in the gloom. She was still alive.

I reached the driver's door, opened it up and pitched myself inside.

"My God, what happened to you?" Laura said. "Did somebody beat you up?"

The man with the gun was a little less sympathetic. "Where the hell's the money?"

I decided to answer both questions at once. "I couldn't remember my pin number so I had to stand there for a while. And then this guy—this black guy—he came out of nowhere and he had a gun and then he made me give him the money." I looked back at the man with the gun. "I couldn't help it. I told him that you had first dibs on the money but he didn't care."

"You expect me to believe that crap?"

"Honest to God. That's what happened."

He looked at me and smiled. And then put the gun right up against Laura's head. "You want me to show you what's gonna happen here if you're not back in five minutes with the money?"

I looked at Laura. "God, honey, I'm telling the truth. About the guy with the gun."

"I know."

"I'm sorry." I glanced forlornly out the window at the rain filling the kerbs. "I'll get the money. Somehow."

I opened the door again. And then noticed the white envelope still sitting on her lap. "I'm sorry I didn't trust you, sweetheart."

She was scared, that was easy enough to see, but she forced herself to focus and smile at me. "I love you, honey."

"Get the hell out of here and get that money," said the man with the gun.

"I knew you wouldn't believe me."

"You heard what I said. Get going."

I reached over and took Laura's hand gently. "I'll get the money, sweetheart. I promise."

I got out of the car and started walking again. Then trotting. Then flat out running. My head was still pounding with pain but I didn't care. I had to get the money. Somehow. Somewhere.

I didn't even know where I was going. I was just—running. It was better than standing still and contemplating what the guy with the gun might do.

I reached the corner and looked down the block where the ATM was located.

A car came from behind me, its headlights stabbing through the silver sheets of night rain. It moved on past me. When it came even with the lights of the ATM machine, it turned an abrupt left and headed for the machine.

Guy inside his car. Nice and warm and dry. Inserts his card, gets all the money he wants, and then drives on to do a lot of fun things with his nice and warm and dry evening.

While I stood out here in the soaking rain and—

Of course, I thought.

Of course.

There was only one thing I could do.

I started running, really running, splashing through puddles and tripping and nearly falling down. But nothing could stop me.

The bald man had parked too far away from the ATM to do his banking from the car. He backed up and gave it another try. He was concentrating on backing up so I didn't have much trouble opening the passenger door and slipping in.

"What the—" he started to say as he became aware of me.

"Stick up."

"What?"

"I'm robbing you."

"Oh, man, that's all I need. I've had a really crummy day today, mister," he said. "I knew I never should've come in this neighborhood but I was in a hurry and—"

"You want to hear about my bad day, mister? Huh?"

I raised the coat of my raincoat, hoping that he would think that I was pointing a gun at him.

He looked down at my coat-draped fist and said, "You can't get a whole hell of a lot a money out of these ATM machines."

"You can get three hundred and that's good enough."

"What if I don't have three hundred?"

"New car. Nice new suit. Maybe twenty CDs in that box there. You've got three hundred. Easy."

"I work hard for my money."

"So do I."

"What if I told you I don't believe you've got a gun in there?"

"Then I'd say fine. And then I'd kill you."

"You don't look like a stick-up guy."

"And you don't look like a guy who's stupid enough to get himself shot over three hundred dollars."

"I have to back up again. So I can get close."

"Back up. But go easy."

"Some goddamned birthday this is."

"It's your birthday?"

"Yeah. Ain't that a bitch?"

He backed up, pulled forward again, got right up next to the ATM, pulled out his card and went to work.

The money came out with no problem. He handed it over to me.

"You have a pencil and paper?"

"What?"

"Something you can write with?"

"Oh. Yeah. Why?"

"I want you to write down your name and address."

"For what?"

"Because tomorrow morning I'm going to put three hundred dollars in an envelope and mail it to you."

"Are you some kind of crazy drug addict or what?"

"Just write down your name and address."

He shook his head. "Not only do I get robbed, I get robbed by some goddamned fruitcake."

But he wrote down his name and address, probably thinking I'd shoot him if he didn't.

"I appreciate the loan," I said, getting out of his car.

"Loan? You tell the cops it was a 'loan' and see what they say."

"Hope the rest of your day goes better," I said, and slammed the door.

And I hope the rest of my day goes better, too, I thought.

"GOOD THING YOU GOT BACK here when you did," the man with the gun said. "I was just about to waste her."

"Spare me the macho crap, all right?" I said. I was getting cranky. The rain. The cold. The fear. And then having to commit a felony to get the cash I needed—and putting fear into a perfectly decent citizen who'd been having a very bad day himself.

I handed the money over to him. "Now you can go," I said.

He counted it in hard, harsh grunts, like a pig rutting in the mud.

"Three goddamned hundred. It was supposed to be four. Or five."

"I guess you'll just have to shoot us, then, huh?"

Laura gave me a frantic look and then dug her nails into my hands. Obviously, like the man I'd just left at the ATM, she thought I had lost what little of my senses I had left.

"I wouldn't push it, punk," the man with the gun said. "Because I just might shoot you yet."

He leaned forward from the back seat and said, "Lemme see your purse, babe."

Laura looked at me. I nodded. She handed him her purse.

More rutting sounds as he went through it.

"Twenty-six bucks?"

"I'm sorry," Laura said.

"Where're your credit cards?"

"We don't have credit cards. It's too tempting to use them. We're saving for a house."

"Ain't that sweet!"

He pitched the purse over the front seat and opened the back door. Chill. Fog. Rain.

"You got a jerk for a husband, babe, I mean, just in case you haven't figured that out already."

Then he slammed the door and was gone.

"YOU WERE REALLY GOING to tear it up?"

"Or let you tear it up. Whichever you preferred. I mean, I know you think I still have this thing for Chris but I really don't. I was going to prove it to you by showing you the letter tonight and letting you do whatever you wanted with it."

We were in bed, three hours after getting our car towed to a station, the tow truck giving us a ride home.

The rain had quit an hour ago. Now there were just icy winds. But it was snug and warm in the bed of my one true love and icy winds didn't bother me at all.

"I'm sorry," I said, "about being so jealous."

"And I'm sorry about hiding the letter. It made you think I was going to take him up on his offer. But I really don't have any desire to see him at all."

Then we kind of just laid back and listened to the wind for a time.

And she started getting affectionate, her foot rubbing my foot, her hand taking my hand.

And then in the darkness, she said, "Would you like to make love?"

"Would I?" I laughed. "Would I?"

And then I rolled over and we began kissing and then I began running my fingers through her long dark hair and then I suddenly realized that—

"What's wrong?" she said, as I rolled away from her, flat on my back, staring at the ceiling.

"Let's just go to sleep."

"God, honey, I want to know what's going on. Here we are making out and then all of a sudden you stop."

"Oh God," I said. "What a day this has been." I sighed and prepared myself for the ultimate in manly humiliation. "Remember that time when Rick's sister got married?"

"Uh-huh."

"And I got real drunk?"

"Uh-huh."

"And that night we tried—well, we tried to make love but I couldn't?"

"Uh-huh." She was silent a long moment. Then, "Oh, God, you mean, the same thing happened to you just now?"

"Uh-huh," I said.

"Oh, honey, I'm sorry."

"The perfect ending to the perfect day," I said.

"First you find that letter from Chris—"

And then I can't concentrate on my job—"

"And then Ms. Sandstrom threatens to fire you—"

"And then a man sticks us up—"

"And then you have to stick up another man—"

"And then we come home and go to bed and—" I sighed. "I think I'll just roll over and go to sleep."

"Good idea, honey. That's what we both need. A good night's sleep."

"I love you, sweetheart," I said. "I'm sorry I wasn't able to . . . well, you know."

"It's fine, sweetie. It happens to every man once in a while."

"It's just one of those days," I said.
"And one of those nights," she said.

BUT YOU KNOW WHAT? Some time later, the grandfather clock in the living room woke me as it tolled twelve midnight, and when I rolled over to see how Laura was doing, she was wide awake and took me in her sweet warm arms, and I didn't have any trouble at all showing her how grateful I was.

It was a brand-new day ... and when I finally got around to breakfast, the first thing I did was lift the horoscope section of the paper ... and drop it, unread, into the wastebasket.

No more snooping in drawers ... and no more bad-luck horoscopes.

Peter Straub's GHOST STORY is one of the classic horror novels of the century, a masterpiece of characterization, pace, and unpredictable plot turns. Straub has done equally well by the literary novel and the mainstream thriller, his books making him one of the most important and successful novelists of our time. The following story shows Peter fusing at least two different genres to create a mesmerizing novella that is truly one of the year's best.

Pork Pie Hat
PETER STRAUB

PART ONE

I

If you know jazz, you know about him, and the title of this memoir tells you who he is. If you don't know the music, his name doesn't matter. I'll call him Hat. What does matter is what he meant. I don't mean what he meant to people who were touched by what he said through his horn. (His horn was an old Selmer Balanced Action tenor saxophone, most of its lacquer worn off.) I'm talking about the whole long curve of his life, and the way that what appeared to be a long slide from joyous mastery to outright exhaustion can be seen in another way altogether.

Hat did slide into alcoholism and depression. The last ten years of his life amounted to suicide by malnutrition, and he was almost transparent by the time he died in the hotel room where I met him. Yet he was able to play until nearly the end. When he was working, he would wake up around seven in the evening, listen to Frank Sinatra or Billie Holiday records while he dressed, get to the club by nine, play three sets, come back to his room sometime after three, drink and listen to more records (he was on a lot of those records), and finally go back to bed around the time of day people begin thinking about lunch. When he wasn't working, he got into bed about an hour earlier, woke up about five or six, and listened to records and drank through his long upside-down day.

It sounds like a miserable life, but it was just an unhappy one. The unhappiness came from a deep, irreversible sadness. Sadness is different from misery, at least Hat's was. His sadness seemed impersonal—it did not disfigure him, as misery can do. Hat's sadness seemed to be for the universe, or to be a larger than usual personal share of a sadness already existing in the universe. Inside it, Hat was unfailingly gentle, kind, even funny. His sadness seemed merely the opposite face of the equally impersonal happiness that shone through his earlier work.

In Hat's later years, his music thickened, and sorrow spoke through the phrases. In his last years, what he played often sounded like heartbreak itself. He was like someone who had passed through a great mystery, who *was passing* through a great mystery, and had to speak of what he had seen, what he was seeing.

2

I brought two boxes of records with me when I first came to New York from Evanston, Illinois, where I'd earned a B.A. in English at Northwestern, and the first thing I set up in my shoebox at the top of John Jay Hill in Columbia University was my portable record player. I did everything to music in those days, and I supplied the rest of my unpacking with a soundtrack provided by Hat's disciples. The kind of music I most liked when I was twenty-one was called "cool" jazz, but my respect for Hat, the progenitor of this movement, was almost entirely abstract. I didn't know his earliest records, and all I'd heard of his later style was one track on a Verve sampler album. I thought he must almost certainly be dead, and I imagined that if by some miracle he was still alive, he would have been in his early seventies, like Louis Armstrong. In fact, the man who seemed a virtual ancient to me was a few months short of his fiftieth birthday.

In my first weeks at Columbia I almost never left the campus. I was taking five courses, also a seminar that was intended to lead me to a Master's thesis, and when I was not in lecture halls or my room, I was in the library. But by the end of September, feeling less overwhelmed, I began to go downtown to Greenwich Village. The IRT, the only subway line I actually understood, described a straight north-south axis that allowed you to get on at 116th Street and get off at Sheridan Square. From Sheridan Square radiated out an unimaginable wealth (unimaginable if you'd spent the previous four years in Evanston, Illinois) of cafes, bars, restaurants, record shops, bookstores, and jazz clubs. I'd come to New York to get an M.A. in English, but I'd also come for this.

I learned that Hat was still alive about seven o'clock in the evening on the first Saturday in October, when I saw a poster bearing his name on the window of a storefront jazz club near St. Mark's Place. My conviction that Hat was dead was so strong that I first saw the poster as an advertisement of past glory. I stopped to gaze longer at this relic of a historical period. Hat had been playing with a quartet including a bassist and drummer of his own era, musicians long associated with him. But the piano player had been John Hawes, one of *my* musicians—John Hawes was on half a dozen of the records back in John Jay Hall. He must have been about twenty at the time, I thought, convinced that the poster had been preserved as memorabilia. Maybe Hawes's first job had been with Hat—anyhow, Hat's quartet must have been one of Hawes's, first stops on the way to fame. John Hawes was a great figure to me, and the thought of him playing with a back number like Hat was a disturbance in the texture of reality. I looked down at the date on the poster, and my snobbish and rule-bound version of reality shuddered under another assault of the unthinkable. Hat's engagement had begun on the Tuesday of this week—the first Tuesday in October; and its last night took place on the Sunday after next—the Sunday before Halloween. Hat was still alive, and John Hawes was playing with him. I couldn't have told you which half of this proposition was the more surprising.

To make sure, I went inside and asked the short, impassive man behind the bar if John Hawes was really playing there tonight. "He'd better be, if he wants to get paid," the man said.

"So Hat is still alive," I said.

"Put it this way," he said. "If it was you, you probably wouldn't be."

3

Two hours and twenty minutes later, Hat came through the front door, and I saw what he meant. Maybe a third of the tables between the door and the bandstand were filled with people listening to the piano trio. This was what I'd come for, and I thought that the evening was perfect. I hoped that Hat would stay away. All he could accomplish by showing up would be to steal soloing time from Hawes, who, apart from seeming a bit disengaged, was playing wonderfully. Maybe Hawes always seemed a bit disengaged. That was fine with me. Hawes was *supposed* to be cool. Then the bass player looked toward the door and smiled, and the drummer grinned and knocked one stick against the side of his snare drum in a rhythmic figure that managed both to suit what the trio was playing and serve as a half-comic, half-respectful greeting. I turned away from the trio and looked back toward the door. The bent figure of a light-skinned black man in a long, drooping, dark coat was carrying a tenor saxophone case into the club. Layers of airline stickers covered the case, and a black porkpie hat concealed most of the man's face. As soon as he got past the door, he fell into a chair next to an empty table—really fell, as if he would need a wheelchair to get any farther.

Most of the people who had watched him enter turned back to John

Hawes and the trio, who were beginning the last few choruses of "Love Walked In." The old man laboriously unbuttoned his coat and let it fall off his shoulders onto the back of the chair. Then, with the same painful slowness, he lifted the hat off his head and lowered it to the table beside him. A brimming shot glass had appeared between himself and the hat, though I hadn't noticed any of the waiters or waitresses put it there. Hat picked up the glass and poured its entire contents into his mouth. Before he swallowed, he let himself take in the room, moving his eyes without changing the position of his head. He was wearing a dark gray suit, a blue shirt with a tight tab collar, and a black knit tie. His face looked soft and worn with drink, and his eyes were of no real color at all, as if not merely washed out but washed clean. He bent over, unlocked the case, and began assembling his horn. As soon as "Love Walked In" ended, he was on his feet, clipping the horn to his strap and walking toward the bandstand. There was some quiet applause.

Hat stepped neatly up onto the bandstand, acknowledged us with a nod, and whispered something to John Hawes, who raised his hands to the keyboard. The drummer was still grinning, and the bassist had closed his eyes. Hat tilted his horn to one side, examined the mouthpiece, and slid it a tiny distance down the cork. He licked the reed, tapped his foot twice, and put his lips around the mouthpiece.

What happened next changed my life—changed me, anyhow. It was like discovering that some vital, even necessary substance had all along been missing from my life. Anyone who hears a great musician for the first time knows the feeling that the universe has just expanded. In fact, all that happened was that Hat had started playing "Too Marvelous For Words," one of the twenty-odd songs that were his entire repertoire at the time. Actually, he was playing some oblique, one-time-only melody of his own that floated above "Too Marvelous For Words," and this spontaneous melody seemed to me to comment affectionately on the song while utterly transcending it—to turn a nice little song into something profound. I forgot to breathe for a little while, and goosebumps came up on my arms. Halfway through Hat's solo, I saw John Hawes watching him and realized that Hawes, whom I all but revered, revered *him*. But by that time, I did, too.

I stayed for all three sets, and after my seminar the next day, I went down to Sam Goody's and bought five of Hat's records, all I could afford. That night, I went back to the club and took a table right in front of the bandstand. For the next two weeks, I occupied the same table every night I could persuade myself that I did not have to study—eight or nine, out of the twelve nights Hat worked. Every night was like the first: the same things, in the same order, happened. Halfway through the first set, Hat turned up and collapsed into the nearest chair. Unobtrusively, a waiter put a drink beside him. Off went the pork pie and the long coat, and out from its case came the horn. The waiter carried the case, pork pie, and coat into a back room while Hat drifted toward the bandstand, often still fitting the pieces of his saxophone together. He stood straighter, seemed almost to grow taller, as he got on the stand. A nod to his audience, an inaudible word to John Hawes. And then that sense of passing over the border between very good, even excellent music and majestic, mysterious art. Between songs, Hat sipped from a glass placed beside his left foot. Three forty-five-minute sets. Two half-hour breaks, during which Hat disappeared through a door behind the bandstand. The same twenty or so songs, recycled again and again. Ecstasy, as if I were hearing *Mozart* play Mozart.

One afternoon toward the end of the second week, I stood up from a library book I was trying to stuff whole into my brain—*Modern Approaches to Milton*—and walked out of my carrel to find whatever I could that had been written about Hat. I'd been hearing the sound of Hat's tenor in my head ever since I'd gotten out of bed. And in those days, I was a sort of apprentice scholar: I thought that real answers in the form of interpretations could be found in the pages of scholarly journals. If there were at least a thousand, maybe two thousand, articles concerning John Milton in Low Library, shouldn't there be at least a hundred about Hat? And out of the hundred shouldn't a dozen or so at least begin to explain what happened to me when I heard him play? I was looking for *close readings* of his solos, for analyses that would explain Hat's effects in terms of subdivided rhythms, alternate cords, and note choices, in the way that poetry critics parsed diction levels, inversions of meter, and permutations of imagery.

Of course I did not find a dozen articles that applied a musicological version of the New Criticism to Hat's recorded solos. I found six old concert write-ups in the *New York Times*, maybe as many record reviews in jazz magazines, and a couple of chapters in jazz histories. Hat had been born in Mississippi, played in his family band, left after a mysterious disagreement at the time they were becoming a successful "territory" band, then joined a famous jazz band in its infancy and quit, again mysteriously, just after its breakthrough into nationwide success. After that, he went out on his own. It seemed that if you wanted to know about him, you had to go straight to the music: There was virtually nowhere else to go.

I wandered back from the catalogues to my carrel, closed the door on the outer world, and went back to stuffing *Modern Approaches to Milton* into my brain. Around six o'clock, I opened the carrel door and realized that *I* could write about Hat. Given the paucity of criticism of his work—given the virtual absence of information about the man himself—I virtually had to write something. The only drawback to this inspiration was that I knew nothing about music. I could not write the sort of article I had wished to read. What I could do, however, would be to interview the man. Potentially, an interview would be more valuable than analysis. I could fill in the dark places, answer the unanswered questions—why had he left both bands just as they began to do well? I wondered if he'd had problems with his father, and then transferred these problems to his next bandleader. There had to be some kind of story. Any band within smelling distance of its first success would be more than reluctant to lose its star soloist—wouldn't they beg him, bribe him, to stay? I could think of other questions no one had ever asked: who had influenced him? What did he think of all those tenor players whom he had influenced? Was he friendly with any of his artistic children? Did they come to his house and talk about music?

Above all, I was curious about the texture of his life—I wondered what his life, the life of a genius, tasted like. If I could have put my half-formed fantasies into words, I would have described my naive, uninformed conceptions of Leonard Bernstein's surroundings. Mentally, I equippied Hat with a big apartment, handsome furniture, advanced stereo equipment, a good but not flashy car, paintings ... the surroundings of a famous American artist, at least by the standards of John Jay Hall and Evanston, Illinois. The difference between Bernstein and Hat was that the conductor probably lived on Fifth Avenue, and the tenor played in the Village.

I walked out of the library humming "Love Walked In."

4

The dictionary-sized Manhattan telephone directory chained to the shelf beneath the pay telephone on the ground floor of John Jay Hall failed to provide Hat's number. Moments later, I met similar failure back in the library after having consulted the equally impressive directories for Brooklyn, Queens, and the Bronx, as well as the much smaller volume for Staten Island. But of course Hat lived in New York: Where else would he live? Like other celebrities, he avoided the unwelcome intrusions of strangers by going unlisted. I could not explain his absence from the city's five telephone books in any other way. Of course Hat lived in the Village—that was what the Village was *for*.

Yet even then, remembering the unhealthy-looking man who each night entered the club to drop into the nearest chair, I experienced a wobble of doubt. Maybe the great man's life was nothing like my imaginings. Hat wore decent clothes, but did not seem rich—he seemed to exist at the same oblique angle to wordly success that his nightly variations on "Too Marvelous For Words" bore to the original melody. For a moment, I pictured my genius in a slum apartment where roaches scuttled across a bare floor and water dripped from a rip in the ceiling. I had no idea of how jazz musicians actually lived. Hollywood, unafraid of cliché, surrounded them with squalor. On the rare moments when literature stooped to consider jazz people, it, too, served up an ambiance of broken bedsprings and peeling walls. And literature's bohemians—Rimbaud, Jack London, Kerouac, Hart Crane, William Burroughs—had often inhabited mean, unhappy rooms. It was possible that the great man was not listed in the city's directories because he could not afford a telephone.

This notion was unacceptable. There was another explanation—Hat could not live in a tenement room without a telephone. The man still possessed the elegance of his generation of jazz musicians, the generation that wore good suits and highly polished shoes, played in big bands, and lived on buses and in hotel rooms.

And there, I thought, was my answer. It was a comedown from the apartment in the Village with which I had supplied him, but a room in some "artistic" hotel like the Chelsea would suit him just as well, and probably cost a lot less in rent. Feeling inspired, I looked up the Chelsea's number on the spot, dialed, and asked for Hat's room. The clerk told me that he wasn't registered in the hotel. "But you know who he is," I said. "Sure," said the clerk. "Guitar, right? I know he was in one of those San Francisco bands, but I can't remember which one."

I hung up without replying, realizing that the only way I was going to discover Hat's telephone number, short of calling every hotel in New York, was by asking him for it.

5

This was on a Monday, and jazz clubs were closed. On Tuesday, Professor Marcus told us to read all of *Vanity Fair* by Friday; on Wednesday, after I'd spent a nearly sleepless night with Thackeray, my seminar leader asked me to prepare a paper on James Joyce's "Two Gallants" for the Friday class. Wednesday and Thursday nights I spent in the library. On Friday I listened to Professor Marcus being brilliant about *Vanity Fair* and read my laborious and dimwitted Joyce paper, on each of the five pages of which the word "epiphany" appeared at least twice, to my fellow-scholars. The seminar leader smiled and nodded throughout my performance and when I sat down metaphorically picked up my little paper between thumb and forefinger and slit its throat. "Some of you students are so *certain* about things," he said. The rest of his remarks disappeared into a vast, horrifying sense of shame. I returned to my room, intending to lie down for an hour or two, and woke up ravenous ten hours later, when even the West End Bar, even the local Chock Full O' Nuts, were shut for the night.

On Saturday night, I took my usual table in front of the bandstand and sat expectantly through the piano trio's usual three numbers. In the

middle of "Love Walked In" I looked around with an insider's fore-
knowledge to enjoy Hat's dramatic entrance, but he did not appear, and
the number ended without him. John Hawes and the other two musicians
seemed untroubled by this break in the routine, and went on to play
"Too Marvelous For Words" without their leader. During the next three
songs, I kept turning around to look for Hat, but the set ended without
him. Hawes announced a short break, and the musicians stood up and
moved toward the bar. I fidgeted at my table, nursing my second beer
of the night and anxiously checking the door. The minutes trudged by. I
feared he would never show up. He had passed out in his room. He'd
been hit by a cab, he'd had a stroke, he was already lying dead in a
hospital room—and just when I was going to write the article that would
finally do him justice!

Half an hour later, still without their leader, John Hawes and other
sidemen went back on the stand. No one but me seemed to have noticed
that Hat was not present. The other customers talked and smoked—
this was in the days when people still smoked—and gave the music the
intermittent and sometimes ostentatious attention they allowed it even
when Hat was on the stand. By now, Hat was an hour and a half late,
and I could see the gangsterish man behind the bar, owner of the club,
scowling as he checked his wristwatch. Hawes played two originals I
particularly liked, favorites of mine from his Contemporay records, but
in my mingled anxiety and irritation I scarcely heard them.

Toward the end of the second of these songs, Hat entered the club
and fell into his customary seat a little more heavily than usual. The
owner motioned away the waiter, who had begun moving toward him
with the customary shot glass. Hat dropped the pork pie on the table
and struggled with his coat buttons. When he heard what Hawes was
playing, he sat listening with his hands still on a coat button, and I
listened, too—the music had a tighter, harder, more modern feel, like
Hawes's records. Hat nodded to himself, got his coat off, and struggled
with the snaps on his saxophone case. The audience gave Hawes unusually appreciative applause. It took Hat longer than usual to fit the horn
together, and by the time he was up on his feet, Hawes and the other
two musicians had turned around to watch his progress as if they feared
he would not make it all the way to the bandstand. Hat wound through
the tables with his head tilted back, smiling to himself. When he got
close to the stand, I saw that he was walking on his toes like a small
child. The owner crossed his arms over his chest and glared. Hat seemed
almost to float onto the stand. He licked his reed. Then he lowered his
horn and, with his mouth open, stared out at us for a moment. "Ladies,
ladies," he said in a soft, high voice. These were the first words I had
ever heard him speak. "Thank you for your appreciation of our pianist,
Mr. Hawes. And now I must explain my absence during the first set. My

son passed away this afternoon, and I have been . . . busy . . . with details. Thank you."

With that, he spoke a single word to Hawes, put his horn back in his mouth, and began to play a blues called "Hat Jumped Up," one of his twenty songs. The audience sat motionless with shock. Hawes, the bassist, and the drummer played on as if nothing unusual had happened—they must have known about his son, I thought. Or maybe they knew that he had no son, and had invented a grotesque excuse for turning up ninety minutes late. The club owner bit his lower lip and looked unusually introspective. Hat played one familiar, uncomplicated figure after another, his tone rough, almost coarse. At the end of his solo, he repeated one note for an entire chorus, fingering the key while staring out toward the back of the club. Maybe he was watching the customers leave—three couples and a couple of single people walked out while he was playing. But I don't think he saw anything at all. When the song was over, Hat leaned over to whisper to Hawes, and the piano player announced a short break. The second set was over.

Hat put his tenor on top of the piano and stepped down off the bandstand, pursing his mouth with concentration. The owner had come out from behind the bar and moved up in front of him as Hat tiptoed around the stand. The owner spoke a few quiet words. Hat answered. From behind, he looked slumped and tired, and his hair curled far over the back of his collar. Whatever he had said only partially satisfied the owner, who spoke again before leaving him. Hat stood in place for a moment, perhaps not noticing that the owner had gone, and resumed his tiptoe glide toward the door. Looking at his back, I think I took in for the first time how genuinely *strange* he was. Floating through the door in his gray flannel suit, hair dangling in ringletlike strands past his collar, leaving in the air behind him the announcement about a dead son, he seemed absolutely separate from the rest of humankind, a species of one.

I turned as if for guidance to the musicians at the bar. Talking, smiling, greeting a few fans and friends, they behaved just as they did on every other night. Could Hat really have lost a son earlier today? Maybe this was the jazz of facing grief—to come back to work, to carry on. Still it seemed the worst of all times to approach Hat with my offer. His playing was a drunken parody of itself. He would forget anything he said to me; I was wasting my time.

On that thought, I stood up and walked past the bandstand and opened the door—if I was wasting my time, it didn't matter what I did.

HE WAS LEANING AGAINST A BRICK wall about ten feet up the alleyway from the club's back door. The door clicked shut behind me, but Hat did not open his eyes. His face tilted up, and a sweetness that might have been sleep lay over his features. He looked exhausted and insubstantial, too frail to move. I would have gone back inside the club if he had not produced a cigarette from a pack in his shirt pocket, lit it with a match, and then flicked the match away, all without opening his eyes. At least he was awake. I stepped toward him, and his eyes opened. He glanced at me and blew out white smoke. "Taste?" he said.

I had no idea what he meant. "Can I talk to you for a minute, sir?" I asked.

He put his hand into one of his jacket pockets and pulled out a half-pint bottle. "Have a taste." Hat broke the seal on the cap, tilted it into his mouth, and drank. Then he held the bottle out toward me.

I took it. "I've been coming here as often as I can."

"Me, too," he said. "Go on, do it."

I took a sip from the bottle—gin. "I'm sorry about your son."

"Son?" He looked upward, as if trying to work out my meaning. "I got a son—out on Long Island. With his momma." He drank again and checked the level of the bottle.

"He's not dead, then."

He spoke the next words slowly, almost wonderingly. "Nobody—told—me—if—he—is." He shook his head and drank another mouthful of gin. "Damn. Wouldn't that be something, boy dies and nobody tells me? I'd have to think about that, you know, have to really *think* about that one."

"I'm just talking about what you said onstage."

He cocked his head and seemed to examine an empty place in the dark air about three feet from his face. "Uh huh. That's right. I did say that. Son of mine passed."

It was like dealing with a sphinx. All I could do was plunge in. "Well, sir, actually there's a reason I came out here," I said. "I'd like to interview you. Do you think that might be possible? You're a great artist, and there's very little about you in print. Do you think we could set up a time when I could talk to you?"

He looked at me with his bleary, colorless eyes, and I wondered if he could see me at all. And then I felt that, despite his drunkenness, he saw everything—that he saw things about me that I couldn't see.

"You a jazz writer?" he asked.

"No, I'm a graduate student. I'd just like to do it. I think it would be important."

"Important." He took another swallow from the half pint and slid the bottle back into his pocket. "Be nice, doing an *important* interview."

He stood leaning against the wall, moving further into outer space with every word. Only because I had started, I pressed on: I was already losing faith in this project. The reason Hat had never been interviewed was that ordinary American English was a foreign language to him. "Could we do this interview after you finish up at this club? I could meet you anywhere you like." Even as I said these words, I despaired. Hat was in no shape to know what he had to do after this engagement finished. I was surprised he could make it back to Long Island every night.

Hat rubbed his face, sighed, and restored my faith in him. "It'll have to wait a little while. Night after I finish here, I go to Toronto for two nights. Then I got something in Hartford on the thirtieth. You come see me after that."

"On the thirty-first?" I asked.

"Around nine, ten, something like that. Be nice if you brought some refreshments."

"Fine, great," I said, wondering if I would be able to take a late train back from wherever he lived. "But where on Long Island should I go?"

His eyes widened in mock-horror. "Don't go nowhere on Long Island. You come see me. In the Albert Hotel, Forty-ninth and Eighth. Room 821."

I smiled at him—I had guessed right about one thing, anyhow. Hat did not live in the Village, but he did live in a Manhattan hotel. I asked him for his phone number, and wrote it down, along with the other information, on a napkin from the club. After I folded the napkin into my jacket pocket, I thanked him and turned toward the door.

"Important as a motherfucker," he said in his high, soft, slurry voice.

I turned around in alarm, but he had tilted his head toward the sky again, and his eyes were closed.

"Indiana," he said. His voice made the word seem sung. "Moonlight in Vermont. I Thought About You. Flamingo."

He was deciding what to play during his next set. I went back inside, where twenty or thirty new arrivals, more people than I had ever seen in the club, waited for the music to start. Hat soon reappeared through the door, the other musicians left the bar, and the third set began. Hat played all four of the songs he had named, interspersing them through his standard repertoire during the course of an unusually long set. He was playing as well as I'd ever heard him, maybe better than I'd heard on all the other nights I had come to the club. The Saturday night crowd applauded explosively after every solo. I didn't know if what I was seeing was genius or desperation.

AN OBITUARY in the Sunday *New York Times*, which I read over breakfast the next morning in the John Jay cafeteria, explained some of what had happened. Early Saturday morning, a thirty-eight-year-old tenor saxophone player named Grant Kilbert had been killed in an automobile accident. One of the most successful jazz musicians in the world, one of the few jazz musicians known outside of the immediate circle of fans, Kilbert had probably been Hat's most prominent disciple. He had certainly been one of my favorite musicians. More importantly, from his first record, *Cool Breeze*, Kilbert had excited respect and admiration. I looked at the photograph of the handsome young man beaming out over the neck of his saxophone and realized that the first four songs on *Cool Breeze* were "Indiana," "Moonlight in Vermont," "I Thought About You," and "Flamingo." Sometime late Saturday afternoon, someone had called up Hat to tell him about Kilbert. What I had seen had not merely been alcoholic eccentricity, it had been grief for a lost son. And when I thought about it, I was sure that the lost son, not himself, had been the important motherfucker he'd apothesized. What I had taken for spaciness and disconnection had all along been irony.

PART TWO

I

On the thirty-first of October, after calling first to make sure he remembered our appointment, I did go to the Albert Hotel, room 821, and interview Hat. That is, I asked him questions and listened to the long, rambling, often obscene responses he gave them. During the long night I spent in his room, he drank the fifth of Gordon's gin, the "refreshments" I brought with me—all of it, an entire bottle of gin, without tonic, ice, or other dilutants. He just poured it into a tumbler and drank, as if it were water. (I refused his single offer of a "taste.") I made frequent checks to make sure that the tape recorder I'd borrowed from a business student down the hall from me was still working, I changed tapes until they ran out, I made detailed backup notes with a ballpoint pen in a stenographic notebook. A couple of times, he played me sections of records that he wanted me to hear, and now and then he sang a couple of bars to make sure that I understood what he was telling me. He sat me in his only chair, and during the entire night stationed himself, dressed in his pork pie hat, a dark blue chalk-stripe suit, and white button-down shirt with a black knit tie, on the edge of his bed. This was a formal occasion. When I arrived at nine o'clock, he addressed me as "Mr. Leonard Feather" (the name of a well-known jazz critic), and when he opened his door at six thirty the next morning, he called me "Miss Rosemary." By then, I knew that this was an allusion to Rosemary Clooney, whose singing I had learned that he liked, and that the nickname meant he liked me, too. It was not at all certain, however, that he remembered my actual name.

I had three sixty-minute tapes and a notebook filled with handwriting that gradually degenerated from my usual scrawl into loops and wiggles that resembled Arabic more than English. Over the next month, I spent whatever spare time I had transcribing the tapes and trying to decipher my own handwriting. I wasn't sure that what I had was an interview. My carefully prepared questions had been met either with evasions or blank, silent refusals to answer—he had simply started talking about something else. After about an hour, I realized that this was his interview, not mine, and let him roll.

After my notes had been typed up and the tapes transcribed, I put everything in a drawer and went back to work on my M.A. What I had was even more puzzling than I'd thought, and straightening it out would have taken more time than I could afford. So the rest of that academic year was a long grind of studying for the comprehensive exam and getting a thesis ready. Until I picked up an old *Time* magazine in the John Jay lounge and saw his name in the "Milestones" column, I didn't even know that Hat had died.

Two months after I'd interviewed him, he had begun to hemorrhage on a flight back from France; an ambulance had taken him directly from the airport to a hospital. Five days after his release from the hospital, he had died in his bed at the Albert.

After I earned my degree, I was determined to wrestle something usable from my long night with Hat—I owed it to him. During the first seven weeks of that summer, I wrote out a version of what Hat had said to me, and sent it to the only publication I thought would be interested in it. *Downbeat* accepted the interview, and it appeared there about six months later. Eventually, it acquired some fame as the last of his rare public statements. I still see lines from the interview quoted in the sort of pieces about Hat never printed during his life. Sometimes they are lines he really did say to me; sometimes they are stitched together from remarks he made at different times; sometimes they are quotations I invented in order to be able to use other things he did say.

But one section of that interview has never been quoted, because it was never printed. I never figured out what to make of it. Certainly I could not believe all he had said. He had been putting me on, silently, laughing at my credulity, for he could not possibly believe that what he was telling me was literal truth. I was a white boy with a tape recorder, it was Halloween, and Hat was having fun with me. He was *jiving* me.

Now I feel different about his story, and about him, too. He was a great man, and I was an unworldly kid. He was drunk, and I was priggishly sober, but in every important way, he was functioning far above my level. Hat had lived forty-nine years as a black man in America, and I'd spent all of my twenty-one years in white suburbs. He was an immensely talented musician, a man who virtually thought in music, and I can't even hum in tune. That I expected to understand anything at all about him staggers me now. Back then, I didn't know anything about grief, and Hat wore grief about him daily, like a cloak. Now that I am the age he was then, I see that most of what is called information is interpretation, and interpretation is always partial.

Probably Hat was putting me on, jiving me, though not maliciously. He certainly was not telling me the literal truth, though I have never been able to learn what was the literal truth of this case. It's possible that even Hat never knew what was the literal truth behind the story he told me—possible, I mean, that he was still trying to work out what the truth was, forty years after the fact.

2

He started telling me the story after we heard what I thought were gunshots from the street. I jumped from the chair and rushed to the windows, which looked out onto Eighth Avenue. "Kids," Hat said. In the hard yellow light of the streetlamps, four or five teenage boys trotted up the Avenue. Three of them carried paper bags. "Kids shooting?" I asked. My amazement tells you how long ago this was.

"Fireworks," Hat said. "Every Halloween in New York, fool kids run around with bags full of fireworks, trying to blow their hands off."

Here and in what follows, I am not going to try to represent the way Hat actually spoke. I cannot represent the way his voice glided over certain words and turned others into mushy growls, though he expressed more than half of his meaning by sound; and I don't want to reproduce his constant, reflexive obscenity. Hat couldn't utter four words in a row without throwing in a "motherfucker." Mostly, I have replaced his obscenities with other words, and the reader can imagine what was really said. Also, if I tried to imitate his grammar, I'd sound racist and he would sound stupid. Hat left school in the fourth grade, and his language, though precise, was casual. To add to these difficulties, Hat employed a private language of his own, a code to ensure that he would be understood only by the people he wished to understand him. I have replaced most of his code words with their equivalents.

It must have been around one in the morning, which means that I had been in his room about four hours. Until Hat explained the "gunshots," I had forgotten that it was Halloween night, and I told him this as I turned away from the window.

"I never forget about Halloween," Hat said. "If I can, I stay home on Halloween. Don't want to be out on the street, that night."

He had already given me proof that he was superstitious, and as he spoke he glanced almost nervously around the room, as if looking for sinister presences.

"You'd feel in danger?" I asked.

He rolled gin around in his mouth and looked at me as he had in the alley behind the club, taking note of qualities I myself did not yet perceive. This did not feel at all judgmental. The nervousness I thought I had seen had disappeared, and his manner seemed marginally more concentrated than earlier in the evening. He swallowed the gin and looked at me without speaking for a couple of seconds.

"No," he finally said. "Not exactly. But I wouldn't feel safe, either."

I sat with my pen half an inch from the page of my notebook, uncertain whether or not to write this down.

"I'm from Mississippi, you know."

I nodded.

"Funny things happen down there. Whole different world. Back when I was a little kid, it was really a different world. Know what I mean?"

"I can guess," I said.

He nodded. "Sometimes people just disappeared. They'd be *gone.* All kinds of stuff used to happen, stuff you wouldn't even believe in now. I met a witch-lady once, a real one, who could put curses on you, make you go blind and crazy. I saw a dead man walk. Another time, I saw a mean, murdering son of a bitch named Eddie Grimes die and come back to life—he got shot to death at a dance we were playing, he was *dead,* and a woman went down and whispered to him, and Eddie Grimes stood right back up on his feet. The man who shot him took off double-quick and he must have kept on going, because we never saw him after that."

"Did you start playing again?" I asked, taking notes as fast as I could.

"We never stopped," Hat said. "You let the people deal with what's going on, but you gotta keep on playing."

"Did you live in the country?" I asked, thinking that all of this sounded like Dogpatch—witches and walking dead men.

He shook his head. "I was brought up in town, Woodland, Mississippi. On the river. Where we lived was called Darktown, you know, but most of Woodland was white, with nice houses and all. Lots of our people did the cooking and washing in the big houses on Miller's Hill, that kind of work. In fact, we lived in a pretty nice house, for Darktown—the band always did well, and my father had a couple of other jobs on top of that. He was a good piano player, mainly, but he could play any kind of instrument. And he was a big, strong guy, nice-looking, real light-complected, so he was called Red, which was what that meant in those days. People respected him."

Another long, rattling burst of explosions came from Eighth Avenue. I wanted to ask him again about leaving his father's band, but Hat once more gave his little room a quick inspection, swallowed another mouthful of gin, and went on talking.

"We even went out trick-or-treating on Halloween, you know, just like the white kids. I guess our people didn't do that everywhere, but we did.

Naturally, we stuck to our neighborhood, and probably we got a lot less than the kids from Miller's Hill, but they didn't have anything up there that tasted as good as the apples and candy we brought home in our bags. Around us, folks made instead of bought, and that's the difference." He smiled at either the memory or the unexpected sentimentality he had just revealed—for a moment, he looked both lost in time and uneasy with himself for having said too much. "Or maybe I just remember it that way, you know? Anyhow, we used to raise some hell, too. You were *supposed* to raise hell, on Halloween."

"You went out with your brothers?" I asked.

"No, no, they were—" He flipped his hand in the air, dismissing whatever it was that his brothers had been. "I was always apart, you dig? Me, I was always into my own little things. I was that way right from the beginning. I play like that—never play like anyone else, don't even play like myself. You gotta find new places for yourself, or else nothing's happening, isn't that right? Don't want to be a repeater pencil." He saluted this declaration with another swallow of gin. "Back in those days, I used to go out with a boy named Rodney Sparks—we called him Dee, short for Demon, 'cause Dee Sparks would do anything that came into his head. That boy was the bravest little bastard I ever knew. He'd wrassle a mad dog. He was just that way. And the reason was, Dee was the preacher's boy. If you happen to be the preacher's boy, seems like you gotta prove every way you can that you're no Buster Brown, you know? So I hung with Dee, because I wasn't any Buster Brown, either. This is all when we were eleven, around then—the time when you talk about girls, you know, but you still aren't too sure what that's about. You don't know what *anything*'s about, to tell the truth. You along for the ride, you trying to pack in as much fun as possible. So Dee was my right hand, and when I went out on Halloween in Woodland, I went out with *him*."

He rolled his eyes toward the window and said, "Yeah." An expression I could not read at all took over his face. By the standards of ordinary people, Hat almost always looked detached, even impassive, tuned to some private wavelength, and this sense of detachment had intensified. I thought he was changing mental gears, dismissing his childhood, and opened my mouth to ask him about Grant Kilbert. But he raised his glass to his mouth again and rolled his eyes back to me, and the quality of his gaze told me to keep quiet.

"I didn't know it," he said, "but I was getting ready to stop being a little boy. To stop believing in little boy things and start seeing like a grown-up. I guess that's part of what I liked about Dee Sparks—he seemed like he was a lot more grown-up than I was, shows you what my head was like. The age we were, this would have been the last time we actually went out on Halloween to get apples and candy. From then on, we would have gone out mainly to raise hell. Smash in a few windows. Bust up somebody's wagon. Scare the shit out of little kids. But the way it turned out, it was the last time we ever went out on Halloween."

He finished off the gin in his glass and reached down to pick the bottle off the floor and pour another few inches into the tumbler. "Here I am, sitting in this room. There's my horn over there. Here's this bottle. You know what I'm saying?"

I didn't. I had no idea what he was saying. The hint of fatality clung to his earlier statement, and for a second, I thought he was going to say that he was here but Dee Sparks was nowhere because Dee Sparks had died in Woodland, Mississippi, at the age of eleven on Halloween night. Hat was looking at me with a steady curiosity which compelled a response. "What happened?" I asked.

Now I know that he was saying *It has come down to just this, my room, my horn, my bottle.* My question was as good as any other response.

"If I was to tell you everything that happened, we'd have to stay in this room for a month." He smiled and straightened up on the bed. His ankles were crossed, and for the first time I noticed that his feet, shod in dark suede shoes with crepe soles, did not quite touch the floor. "And, you know, I never tell anybody everything, I always have to keep something back for myself. Things turned out all right. Only thing I mind is, I should have earned more money. Grant Kilbert, he earned a lot of money, and some of that was mine, you know."

"Were you friends?" I asked.

"I knew the man." He tilted his head and stared at the ceiling for so long that eventually I looked up at it, too. It was not a remarkable ceiling. A circular section near the center had been replastered not long before.

"No matter where you live, there are places you're not supposed to go," he said, still gazing up. "And sooner or later, you're gonna wind up there." He smiled at me again. "Where we lived, the place you weren't supposed to go was called The Backs. Out of town, stuck in the woods on one little path. In Darktown, we had all kinds from preachers on down. We had washerwomen and blacksmiths and carpenters, and we had some no-good thieving trash, too, like Eddie Grimes, that man who came back from being dead. In The Backs, they started with trash like Eddie Grimes, and went down from there. Sometimes, some of our people went out there to buy a jug, and sometimes they went there to get a woman, but they never talked about it. The Backs was *rough.* What they had was *rough.*" He rolled his eyes at me and said, "That witch-lady I told you about, she lived in The Backs." He snickered. "Man, they were a mean bunch of people. They'd cut you, you looked at 'em bad. But one thing funny about the place, white and colored lived there just the same—it was *integrated.* Backs people were so evil, color didn't make no difference to them. They hated everybody anyhow, on principle." Hat pointed his glass at me, tilted his head, and narrowed his eyes. "At least, that was what everybody *said*. So this particular Halloween, Dee Sparks says to me after we finish with Darktown, we ought to head out to The Backs and see what the place is really like. Maybe we can have some fun.

"Well, that sounded fine to me. The idea of going out to The Backs kind of scared me, but being scared was part of the fun—Halloween, right? And if anyplace in Woodland was perfect for all that Halloween shit, you know, someplace where you might really see a ghost or a goblin, The Backs was better than the graveyard." Hat shook his head, holding the glass out at a right angle to his body. A silvery amusement momentarily transformed him, and it struck me that his native elegance, the product of his character and bearing much more than of the handsome suit and the suede shoes, had in effect been paid for by the surviving of a thousand unimaginable difficulties, each painful to a varying degree. Then I realized that what I meant by elegance was really dignity, that for the first time I had recognized actual dignity in another human being, and that dignity was nothing like the self-congratulatory superiority people usually mistook for it.

"We were just little babies, and we wanted some of those good old Halloween scares. Like those dumbbells out on the street, tossing firecrackers at each other." Hat wiped his free hand down over his face and made sure that I was prepared to write down everything he said. (The tapes had already been used up.) "When I'm done, tell me if we found it, okay?"

"Okay," I said.

3

"Dee showed up at my house just after dinner, dressed in an old sheet with two eyeholes cut in it and carrying a paper bag. His big old shoes stuck out underneath the sheet. I had the same costume, but it was the one my brother used the year before, and it dragged along the ground and my feet got caught in it. The eyeholes kept sliding away from my eyes. My mother gave me a bag and told me to behave myself and get home before eight. It didn't take but half an hour to cover all the likely houses in Darktown, but she knew I'd want to fool around with Dee for an hour or so afterwards.

"Then up and down the streets we go, knocking on the doors where they'd give us stuff and making a little mischief where we knew they wouldn't. Nothing real bad, just banging on the door and running like hell, throwing rocks on the roof, little stuff. A few places, we plain and simple stayed away from—the places where people like Eddie Grimes lived. I always thought that was funny. We knew enough to steer clear of those houses, but we were still crazy to get out to The Backs.

"Only way I can figure it is, The Backs was *forbidden*. Nobody had to tell us to stay away from Eddie Grimes's house that night. You wouldn't even go there in the daylight, 'cause Eddie Grimes would get you and that would be that.

"Anyhow, Dee kept us moving along real quick, and when folks asked us questions or said they wouldn't give us stuff unless we sang a song, he moaned like a ghost and shook his bag in their faces, so we could get away faster. He was so excited, I think he was almost shaking.

"Me, I was excited, too. Not like Dee—sort of sick-excited, the way people must feel the first time they use a parachute. Scared-excited.

"As soon as we got away from the last house, Dee crossed the street and started running down the side of the little general store we all used. I knew where he was going. Out behind the store was a field, and on the other side of the field was Meridian Road, which took you out into the woods and to the path up to The Backs. When he realized that I wasn't next to him, he turned around and yelled at me to hurry up. *No, I said inside myself, I ain't gonna jump outta of this here airplane, I'm not dumb enough to do that.* And then I pulled up my sheet and scrunched up my eye to look through the one hole close enough to see through, and I took off after him.

"It was beginning to get dark when Dee and I left my house, and now it was dark. The Backs was about a mile and a half away, or at least the path was. We didn't know how far along that path you had to go before you got there. Hell, we didn't even know what it was—I was still thinking the place was a collection of little houses, like a sort of shadow-Woodland. And then, while we were crossing the field, I stepped on my costume and fell down flat on my face. Enough of this stuff, I said, and yanked the damned thing off. Dee started cussing me out, I wasn't doing this stuff the right way, we had to keep our costumes on in case anybody saw us, did I forget that this is Halloween, on Halloween a costume *protected* you. So I told him I'd put it back on when we got there. If I kept on falling down, it'd take us twice as long. That shut him up.

"As soon as I got that blasted sheet over my head, I discovered that I could see at least a little ways ahead of me. The moon was up, and a lot of stars were out. Under his sheet, Dee Sparks looked a little bit like a real ghost. It kind of glimmered. You couldn't really make out its edges, so the darn thing like *floated*. But I could see his legs and those big old shoes sticking out.

"We got out of the field and started up Meridian Road, and pretty soon the trees came up right to the ditches alongside the road, and I couldn't see too well anymore. The road looked like it went smack into the woods and disappeared. The trees looked taller and thicker than in the daytime, and now and then something right at the edge of the woods shone round and white, like an eye—reflecting the moonlight, I guess. Spooked me. I didn't think we'd ever be able to find the path up to The Backs, and that was fine with me. I thought we might go along the road another ten-fifteen minutes, and then turn around and go home. Dee was swooping around up in front of me, flapping his sheet and acting bughouse. *He* sure wasn't trying too hard to find that path.

"After we walked about a mile down Meridian Road, I saw headlights like yellow dots coming toward us fast—Dee didn't see anything at all, running around in circles the way he was. I shouted at him to get off the road, and he took off like a rabbit—disappeared into the woods before I did. I jumped the ditch and hunkered down behind a pine about ten feet off the road to see who was coming. There weren't many cars in Woodland in those days, and I knew every one of them. When the car came by, it was Dr. Garland's old red Cord—Dr. Garland was a white man, but he had two waiting rooms and took colored patients, so colored patients was mostly what he had. And the man was a heavy drinker, *heavy* drinker. He zipped by, goin' at least fifty, which was mighty fast for those days, probably as fast as that old Cord would go. For about a second, I saw Dr. Garland's face under his white hair, and his mouth was wide open, stretched like he was screaming. After he passed, I waited a long time before I came out of the woods. Turning around and going home would have been fine with me. Dr. Garland changed everything. Normally, he was kind of slow and quiet, you know, and I could still see that black screaming hole opened up in his face—he looked like he was being tortured, like he was in Hell. I sure as hell didn't want to see whatever *he* had seen.

"I could hear the Cord's engine after the tail lights disappeared. I turned around and saw that I was all alone on the road. Dee Sparks was nowhere in sight. A couple of times, real soft, I called out his name. Then I called his name a little louder. Away off in the woods, I heard Dee giggle. I said he could run around all night if he liked but I was going home, and then I saw that pale silver sheet moving through the trees, and I started back down Meridian Road. After about twenty paces, I looked back, and there he was, standing in the middle of the road in that silly sheet, watching me go. Come on, I said, let's get back. He paid me no mind. Wasn't that Dr. Garland? Where was he going, as fast as that? What was happening? When I said the doctor was probably out on some emergency, Dee said the man was going *home*—he lived in Woodland, didn't he?

"Then I thought maybe Dr. Garland had been up in The Backs. And Dee thought the same thing, which made him want to go there all the more. Now he was determined. Maybe we'd see some dead guy. We stood there until I understood that he was going to go by himself if I didn't go with him. That meant that I *had* to go. Wild as he was, Dee'd get himself into some kind of mess for sure if I wasn't there to hold him down. So I said okay, I was coming along, and Dee started swooping along like before, saying crazy stuff. There was no way we were going to be able to find some little old path that went up into the woods. It was so dark, you couldn't see the separate trees, only giant black walls on both sides of the road.

"We went so far along Meridian Road I was sure we must have passed it. Dee was running around in circles about ten feet ahead of me. I told him that we missed the path, and now it was time to get back home. He laughed at me and ran across to the right side of the road and disappeared into the darkness.

"I told him to get back, damn it, and he laughed some more and said I should come to *him*. Why? I said, and he said, Because this here is the path, dummy. I didn't believe him—came right up to where he disappeared. All I could see was a black wall that could have been trees or just plain night. Moron, Dee said, look down. And I did. Sure enough, one of those white things like an eye shone up from where the ditch should have been. I bent down and touched cold little stones, and the shining dot of white went off like a light—a pebble that caught the moonlight just right. Bending down like that, I could see the hump of grass growing up between the tire tracks that led out onto Meridian Road. He'd found the path, all right.

"At night, Dee Sparks could see one hell of a lot better than me. He spotted the break in the ditch from across the road. He was already walking up the path in those big old shoes, turning around every other step to look back at me, make sure I was coming along behind him. When I started following him, Dee told me to get my sheet back on, and I pulled the thing over my head even though I'd rather have sucked the water out of a hollow stump. But I knew he was right—on Halloween, especially in a place like where we were, you were safer in a costume.

"From then on in, we were in no-man's-land. Neither one of us had any idea of how far we had to go to get to The Backs, or what it would look like once we got there. Once I set foot on that wagon-track I knew for sure The Backs wasn't anything like the way I thought. It was a lot more primitive than a bunch of houses in the woods. Maybe they didn't even have houses! Maybe they lived in caves!

"Naturally, after I got that blamed costume over my head, I couldn't see for a while. Dee kept hissing at me to hurry up, and I kept cussing him out. Finally I bunched up a couple handfuls of the sheet right under my chin and held it against my neck, and that way I could see pretty well and walk without tripping all over myself. All I had to do was follow Dee, and that was easy. He was only a couple of inches in front of me, and even through one eyehole, I could see that silvery sheet moving along.

"Things moved in the woods, and once in a while an owl hooted. To tell you the truth, I never did like being out in the woods at night. Even back then, give me a nice warm barroom instead, and I'd be happy. Only animal I ever liked was a cat, because a cat is soft to the touch, and it'll fall asleep on your lap. But this was even worse than usual, because of Halloween, and even before we got to The Backs, I wasn't sure if what I heard moving around in the woods was just a possum or a fox or something a lot worse, something with funny eyes and long teeth that liked the taste of little boys. Maybe Eddie Grimes was out there, looking for whatever kind of treat Eddie Grimes liked on Halloween night. Once I thought of that, I got so close to Dee Sparks I could smell him right through his sheet.

"You know what Dee Sparks smelled like? Like sweat, and a little bit like the soap the preacher made him use on his hands and face before dinner, but really like a fire in a junction box—a sharp, kind of bitter smell. That's how excited he was.

"After a while we were going uphill, and then we got to the top of the rise, and a breeze pressed my sheet against my legs. We started going downhill, and over Dee's electrical fire, I could smell woodsmoke. And something else I couldn't name. Dee stopped moving so sudden, I bumped into him. I asked him what he could see. Nothing but the woods, he said, but we're getting there. People are up ahead somewhere. And they got a still. We got to be real quiet from here on out, he told me, as if he had to, and to let him know I understood I pulled him off the path into the woods.

"Well, I thought, at least I know what Dr. Garland was after.

"Dee and I went snaking through the trees—me holding that blamed sheet under my chin so I could see out of one eye, at least, and walk without falling down. I was glad for that big fat pad of pine needles on the ground. An elephant could have walked over that stuff as quiet as a beetle. We went along a little further, and it got so I could smell all kinds of stuff—burned sugar, crushed juniper berries, tobacco juice, grease. And after Dee and I moved a little bit along, I heard voices, and that was enough for me. Those voices sounded angry.

"I yanked at Dee's sheet and squatted down—I wasn't going any farther without taking a good look. He slipped down beside me. I pushed the wad of material under my chin up over my face, grabbed another handful, and yanked that up, too, to look out under the bottom of the sheet. Once I could actually *see* where we were, I almost passed out. Twenty feet away through the trees, a kerosene lantern lit up the greasepaper window cut into the back of a little wooden shack, and a big raggedy guy carrying another kerosene lantern came stepping out of a door we couldn't see and stumbled toward a shed. On the other side of the building I could see the yellow square of a window in another shack, and past that, another one, a sliver of yellow shining out through the trees. Dee was crouched next to me, and when I turned to look at him, I could see another chink of yellow light from someway off in the woods over that way. Whether he knew it or not, he'd just about walked us straight into the middle of The Backs.

"He whispered for me to cover my face. I shook my head. Both of us watched the big guy stagger toward the shed. Somewhere in front of us, a woman screeched, and I almost dumped a load in my pants. Dee stuck his head out from under his sheet and held it out, as if I needed *him* to tell me to be quiet. The woman screeched again, and the big guy sort of swayed back and forth. The light from the lantern swung around in big circles. I saw that the woods were full of little paths that ran between the shacks. The light hit the shack, and it wasn't even wood, but tarpaper. The woman laughed or maybe sobbed. Whoever was inside the shack shouted, and the raggedy guy wobbled toward the shed again. He was so drunk he couldn't even walk straight. When he got to the shed, he set down the lantern and bent to get in.

"Dee put his mouth up to my ear and whispered, *Cover up—you don't want these people to see who you are. Rip the eyeholes, if you can't see good enough.*

"I didn't want anyone in The Backs to see my face. I let the costume drop down over me again, and stuck my fingers in the nearest eyehole and pulled. Every living thing for about a mile around must have heard that cloth ripping. The big guy came out of the shed like someone pulled him out on a string, yanked the lantern up off the ground, and held it in our direction. Then we could see his face, and it was Eddie Grimes. You wouldn't want to run into Eddie Grimes anywhere, but The Backs was the last place you'd want to come across him. I was afraid he was going to start looking for us, but that woman started making stuck pig noises, and the man in the shack yelled something, and Grimes ducked back into the shed and came out with a jug. He lumbered back toward the shack and disappeared around the front of it. Dee and I could hear him arguing with the man inside.

"I jerked my thumb toward Meridian Road, but Dee shook his head. I whispered, *Didn't you already see Eddie Grimes, and isn't that enough for you?* He shook his head again. His eyes were gleaming behind that sheet. *So what do you want*, I asked, and he said, *I want to see that girl. We don't even know where she is*, I whispered, and Dee said, *All we got to do is follow her sound.*

"Dee and I sat and listened for a while. Every now and then, she let out a sort of whoop, and then she'd sort of cry, and after that she might say a word or two that sounded almost ordinary before she got going again on crying or laughing, the two all mixed up together. Sometimes we could hear other noises coming from the shacks, and none of them sounded happy. People were grumbling and arguing or just plain talking to themselves, but at least they sounded normal. That lady, she sounded like *Halloween*—like something that came up out of a grave.

"Probably you're thinking what I was hearing was sex—that I was too young to know how much noise ladies make when they're having fun. Well, maybe I was only eleven, but I grew up in Darktown, not Miller's Hill, and our walls were none too thick. What was going on with this lady didn't have anything to do with fun. The strange thing is, Dee didn't know that—he thought just what you were thinking. He wanted to see this lady getting humped. Maybe he even thought he could sneak in and get some for himself, I don't know. The main thing is, he thought he was listening to some wild sex, and he wanted to get close enough to see it. Well, I thought, his daddy was a preacher, and maybe preachers didn't do it once they got kids. And Dee didn't have an older brother like mine, who sneaked girls into the house whenever he thought he wouldn't get caught.

"He started sliding sideways through the woods, and I had to follow him. I'd seen enough of The Backs to last me the rest of my life, but I couldn't run off and leave Dee behind. And at least he was going at it the right way, circling around the shacks sideways, instead of trying to sneak straight through them. I started off after him. At least I could see a little better ever since I ripped at my eyehole, but I still had to hold my blasted costume bunched up under my chin, and if I moved my head or my hand the wrong way, the hole moved away from my eye and I couldn't see anything at all.

"So naturally, the first thing that happened was that I lost sight of Dee Sparks. My foot came down in a hole and I stumbled ahead for a few steps, completely blind, and then I hit a tree. I just came to a halt, sure that Eddie Grimes and a few other murderers were about to jump on me. For a couple of seconds I stood as still as a wooden Indian, too scared to move. When I didn't hear anything, I hauled at my costume until I could see out of it. No murderers were coming toward me from the shack beside the still. Eddie Grimes was saying *You don't understand*, over and over, like he was so drunk that one phrase got stuck in his head, and he couldn't say or hear anything else. That woman yipped, like an animal noise, not a human one—like a fox barking. I sidled up next to the tree I'd run into and looked around for Dee. All I could see was dark trees and that one yellow window I'd seen before. To hell with Dee Sparks, I said to myself, and pulled the costume off over my head. I could see better, but there wasn't any glimmer of white over that way. He'd gone so far ahead of me I couldn't even see him.

"So I had to catch up with him, didn't I? I knew where he was going—the woman's noises were coming from the shack way up there in the woods—and I knew he was going to sneak around the outside of the shacks. In a couple of seconds, after he noticed I wasn't there, he was going to stop and wait for me. Makes sense, doesn't it? All I had to do was keep going toward that shack off to the side until I ran into him. I shoved my costume inside my shirt, and then I did something else—set my bag of candy down next to the tree. I'd clean forgotten about it ever since I saw Eddie Grimes's face, and if I had to run, I'd go faster without holding on to a lot of apples and chunks of taffy.

"About a minute later, I came out into the open between two big old chinaberry trees. There was a patch of grass between me and the next stand of trees. The woman made a gargling sound that ended in one of those fox-yips, and I looked up in that direction and saw that the clearing extended in a straight line up and down, like a path. Stars shone out of the patch of darkness between the two parts of the woods. And when I started to walk across it, I felt a grassy hump between two beaten tracks. The path into The Backs off Meridian Road curved around somewhere up ahead and wound back down through the shacks before it came to a dead end. It had to come to a dead end, because it sure didn't join back up with Meridian Road.

"And this was how I'd managed to lose sight of Dee Sparks. Instead of avoiding the path and working his way around through the woods, he'd just taken the easiest way toward the woman's shack. Hell, I'd had to pull him off the path in the first place! By the time I got out of my sheet, he was probably way up there, out in the open for anyone to see and too excited to notice that he was all by himself. What I had to do was what I'd been trying to do all along, save his ass from anybody who might see him.

"As soon as I started going as soft as I could up the path, I saw that saving Dee Sparks's ass might be a tougher job than I thought—maybe I couldn't even save my own. When I first took off my costume, I'd seen lights from three or four shacks. I thought that's what The Backs was—three or four shacks. But after I started up the path, I saw a low square shape standing between two trees at the edge of the woods and realized that it was another shack. Whoever was inside had extinguished his kerosene lamp, or maybe wasn't home. About twenty-thirty feet on, there was another shack, all dark, and the only reason I noticed that one was, I heard voices coming from it, a man and a woman, both of them sounding drunk and slowed-down. Deeper in the woods past that one, another greasepaper window gleamed through the woods like a firefly. There were shacks all over the woods. As soon as I realized that Dee and I might not be the only people walking through The Backs on Halloween night,

I bent down low to the ground and damn near slowed to a standstill. The only thing Dee had going for him, I thought, was good night vision— at least he might spot someone before they spotted him.

"A noise came from one of those shacks, and I stopped cold, with my heart pounding away like a bass drum. Then a big voice called out, *Who's that?*, and I just lay down in the track and tried to disappear. *Who's there?* Here I was calling Dee a fool, and I was making more noise than he did. I heard that man walk outside his door, and my heart pretty near exploded. Then the woman moaned up ahead, and the man who'd heard me swore to himself and went back inside. I just lay there in the dirt for a while. The woman moaned again, and this time it sounded scarier than ever, because it had a kind of a chuckle in it. She was crazy. Or she was a witch, and if she was having sex, it was with the devil. That was enough to make me start crawling along, and I kept on crawling until I was long past the shack where the man had heard me. Finally I got up on my feet again, thinking that if I didn't see Dee Sparks real soon, I was going to sneak back to Meridian Road by myself. If Dee Sparks wanted to see a witch in bed with the devil, he could do it without me.

"And then I thought I was a fool not to ditch Dee, because hadn't he ditched me? After all this time, he must have noticed that I wasn't with him anymore. Did he come back and look for me? The hell he did.

"And right then I would have gone back home, but for two things. The first was that I heard that woman make another sound—a sound that was hardly human, but wasn't made by any animal. It wasn't even loud. And it sure as hell wasn't any witch in bed with the devil. It made me want to throw up. That woman was being *hurt*. She wasn't just getting beat up—I knew what that sounded like—she was being hurt bad enough to drive her crazy, bad enough to kill her. Because you couldn't live through being hurt bad enough to make that sound. I was in The Backs, sure enough, and the place was even worse than it was supposed to be. Someone was killing a woman, everybody could hear it, and all that happened was that Eddie Grimes fetched another jug back from the still. I froze. When I could move, I pulled my ghost costume out from inside my shirt, because Dee was right, and for certain I didn't want anybody seeing my face out there on *this* night. And then the second thing happened. While I was pulling the sheet over my head, I saw something pale lying in the grass a couple of feet back toward the woods I'd come out of, and when I looked at it, it turned into Dee Sparks's Halloween bag.

"I went up to the bag and touched it to make sure about what it was. I'd found Dee's bag, all right. And it was empty. Flat. He had stuffed the contents into his pockets and left the bag behind. What that meant was, I couldn't turn around and leave him—because he hadn't left me after all. He waited for me until he couldn't stand it anymore, and then he emptied his bag and left it behind as a sign. He was counting on me to see in the dark as well as he could. But I wouldn't have seen it at all if that woman hadn't stopped me cold.

"The top of the bag was pointing north, so Dee was still heading toward the woman's shack. I looked up that way, and all I could see was a solid wall of darkness underneath a lighter darkness filled with stars. For about a second, I realized, I had felt pure relief. Dee had ditched me, so I could ditch him and go home. Now I was stuck with Dee all over again.

"About twenty feet ahead, another surprise jumped up at me out of darkness. Something that looked like a little tiny shack began to take shape, and I got down on my hands and knees to crawl toward the path when I saw a long silver gleam along the top of the thing. That meant it had to be metal—tarpaper might have a lot of uses, but it never yet reflected starlight. Once I realized that the thing in front of me was metal, I remembered its shape and realized it was a car. You wouldn't think you'd come across a car in a down-and-out rathole like The Backs, would you? People like that, they don't even own two shirts, so how do they come by cars? Then I remembered Dr. Garland speeding driving away down Meridian Road, and I thought *You don't have to live in The Backs to drive there.* Someone could turn up onto the path, drive around the loop, pull his car off onto the grass, and no one would ever see it or know that he was there.

"And this made me feel funny. The car probably belonged to someone I knew. Our band played dances and parties all over the county and everywhere in Woodland, and I'd probably seen every single person in town, and they'd seen me, too, and knew me by name. I walked closer to the car to see if I recognized it, but it was just an old black Model T. There must have been twenty cars just like it in Woodland. Whites and coloreds, the few coloreds that owned cars, both had them. And when I got right up beside the Model T, I saw what Dee had left for me on the hood—an apple.

"About twenty feet further along, there was an apple on top of a big old stone. He was putting those apples where I couldn't help but see them. The third one was on top of a post at the edge of the woods, and it was so pale it looked almost white. Next to the post one of those paths running all through The Backs led back into the woods. If it hadn't been for that apple, I would have gone right past it.

"At least I didn't have to worry so much about being making noise once I got back into the woods. Must have been six inches of pine needles and fallen leaves underfoot, and I walked so quiet I could have been floating—tell you the truth, I've worn crepe soles ever since then, and for the same reason. You walk *soft*. But I was still plenty scared—back in the woods there was a lot less light, and I'd have to step on an apple to see it. All I wanted was to find Dee and persuade him to leave with me.

"For a while, all I did was keep moving between the trees and try to make sure I wasn't coming up on a shack. Every now and then, a faint, slurry voice came from somewhere off in the woods, but I didn't let it spook me. Then, way up ahead, I saw Dee Sparks. The path didn't go in a straight line, it kind of angled back and forth, so I didn't have a good clear look at him, but I got a flash of that silvery-looking sheet way off through the trees. If I sped up I could get to him before he did anything stupid. I pulled my costume up a little further toward my neck and started to jog.

"The path started dipping *downhill.* I couldn't figure it out. Dee was in a straight line ahead of me, and as soon as I followed the path downhill a little bit, I lost sight of him. After a couple more steps, I stopped. The path got a lot steeper. If I kept running, I'd go ass over teakettle. The woman made another terrible sound, and it seemed to come from everywhere at once. Like everything around me had been *hurt.* I damn near came unglued. Seemed like everything was *dying.* That Halloween stuff about horrible creatures wasn't any story, man, it was the way things really were—you couldn't know anything, you couldn't trust anything, and you were surrounded by *death.* I almost fell down and cried like a baby boy. I was lost. I didn't think I'd ever get back home.

"Then the worst thing of all happened.

"I heard her die. It was just a little noise, more like a sigh than anything, but that sigh came from everywhere and went straight into my ear. A soft sound can be loud, too, you know, be the loudest thing you ever heard. That sigh about lifted me up off the ground, about blew my head apart.

"I stumbled down the path, trying to wipe my eyes with my costume, and all of a sudden I heard men's voices from off to my left. Someone was saying a word I couldn't understand over and over, and someone else was telling him to shut up. Then, behind me, I heard running—heavy running, a man. I took off, and right away my feet got tangled up in the sheet and I was rolling downhill, hitting my head on rocks and bouncing off trees and smashing into stuff I didn't have any idea what it was. Biff bop bang slam smash clang crash ding dong. I hit something big and solid and wound up half-covered in water. Took me a long time to get upright, twisted up in the sheet the way I was. My ears buzzed, and I saw stars—yellow and blue and red stars, not real ones. When I tried to sit up, the blasted sheet pulled me back down, so I got a faceful of cold water. I scrambled around like a fox in a trap, and when I finally got so I was at least sitting up, I saw a slash of real sky out the corner of one eye, and I got my hands free and ripped that hole in the sheet wide enough for my whole head to fit through it.

"I was sitting in a little stream next to a fallen tree. The tree was what had stopped me. My whole body hurt like the dickens. No idea where I was. Wasn't even sure I could stand up. Got my hands on the top of the fallen tree and pushed myself up with my legs—blasted sheet ripped in half, and my knees almost bent back the wrong way, but I got up on my feet. And there was Dee Sparks, coming toward me through the woods on the other side of the stream.

"He looked like he didn't feel any better than I did, like he couldn't move in a straight line. His silvery sheet was smearing through the trees. *Dee got hurt, too*, I thought—he looked like he was in some total panic. The next time I saw the white smear between the trees it was twisting about teen feet off the ground. *No*, I said to myself, and closed my eyes. Whatever that thing was, it wasn't Dee. An unbearable feeling, an absolute despair, flowed out from it. I fought against this wave of despair with every weapon I had. I didn't want to know that feeling. I couldn't know that feeling—I was eleven years old. If that feeling reached me when I was eleven years old, my entire life would be changed, I'd be in a different universe altogether.

"But it did reach me, didn't it? I could say *no* all I liked, but I couldn't change what had happened. I opened my eyes, and the white smear was gone.

"That was almost worse—I wanted it to be Dee after all, doing something crazy and reckless, climbing trees, running around like a wildman, trying to give me a big whopping scare. But it wasn't Dee Sparks, and it meant that the worst things I'd ever imagined were true. Everything was dying. You couldn't know anything, you couldn't trust anything, we were all lost in the midst of the death that surrounded us.

"Most people will tell you growing up means you stop believing in Halloween things—I'm telling you the reverse. You start to grow up when you understand that the stuff that scares you is part of the air you breathe.

"I stared at the spot where I'd seen that twist of whiteness, I guess trying to go back in time to before I saw Dr. Garland fleeing down Meridian Road. My face looked like his, I thought—because now I knew that you really *could* see a ghost. The heavy footsteps I'd heard before suddenly cut through the buzzing in my head, and after I turned around and saw who was coming at me down the hill, I thought it was probably my own ghost I'd seen.

"Eddie Grimes looked as big as an oak tree, and he had a long knife in one hand. His feet slipped out from under him, and he skidded the last few yards down to the creek, but I didn't even try to run away. Drunk as he was, I'd never get away from him. All I did was back up alongside the fallen tree and watch him slide downhill toward the water. I was so scared I couldn't even talk. Eddie Grimes's shirt was flapping open, and big long scars ran all across his chest and belly. He'd been raised from the dead at least a couple of times since I'd seen him get killed at the dance. He jumped back up on his feet and started coming for me. I opened my mouth, but nothing came out.

"Eddie Grimes took another step toward me, and then he stopped and looked straight at my face. He lowered the knife. A sour stink of sweat and alcohol came off him. All he could do was stare at me. Eddie Grimes knew my face all right, he knew my name, he knew my whole family—even at night, he couldn't mistake me for anyone else. I finally saw that Eddie was actually afraid, like he was the one who'd seen a ghost. The two of us just stood there in the shallow water for a couple more seconds, and then Eddie Grimes pointed his knife at the other side of the creek.

"That was all I needed, baby. My legs unfroze, and I forgot all my aches and pains. Eddie watched me roll over the fallen tree and lowered his knife. I splashed through the water and started moving up the hill, grabbing at weeds and branches to pull me along. My feet were frozen, and my clothes were soaked and muddy, and I was trembling all over. About halfway up the hill, I looked back over my shoulder, but Eddie Grimes was gone. It was like he'd never been there at all, like he was nothing but the product of a couple of good raps to the noggin.

"Finally, I pulled myself shaking up over the top of the rise, and what did I see about ten feet away through a lot of skinny birch trees but a kid in a sheet facing away from me into the woods, and hopping from foot to foot in a pair of big clumsy shoes? And what was in front of him but a path I could make out from even ten feet away? Obviously, this was where I was supposed to turn up, only in the dark and all I must have missed an apple stuck onto a branch or some blasted thing, and I took that little side trip downhill on my head and wound up throwing a spook into Eddie Grimes.

"As soon as I saw him, I realized I hated Dee Sparks. I wouldn't have tossed him a rope if he was drowning. Without even thinking about it, I bent down and picked up a stone and flung it at him. The stone bounced off a tree, so I bent down and got another one. Dee turned around to find out what made the noise, and the second stone hit him right in the chest, even though it was really his head I was aiming at.

"He pulled his sheet up over his face like an Arab and stared at me with his mouth wide open. Then he looked back over his shoulder at the path, as if the real me might come along at any second. I felt like pegging another rock at his stupid face, but instead I marched up to him. He was shaking his head from side to side. *Jim Dawg,* he whispered, *what happened to you?* By way of answer, I hit him a good hard knock on the breastbone. *What's the matter?* he wanted to know. *After you left me,* I say, *I fell down a hill and ran into Eddie Grimes.*

"That gave him something to think about, all right. Was Grimes coming after me, he wanted to know? Did he see which way I went? Did Grimes see who I was? He was pulling me into the woods while he asked me these dumb-ass questions, and I shoved him away. His sheet flopped back down over his front, and he looked like a little boy. He couldn't figure out why I was mad at him. From his point of view, he'd been pretty clever, and if I got lost, it was my fault. But I wasn't mad at him because I got lost. I wasn't even mad at him because I'd run into Eddie Grimes. It was everything else. Maybe it wasn't even him I was mad at.

"*I want to get home without getting killed,* I whispered. *Eddie ain't gonna let me go twice.* Then I pretended he wasn't there anymore and tried to figure out how to get back to Meridian Road. It seemed to me that I was still going north when I took that tumble downhill, so when I climbed up the hill on the other side of the creek I was still going north. The wagon-track that Dee and I took into The Backs had to be off to my right. I turned away from Dee and started moving through the woods. I didn't care if he followed me or not. He had nothing to do with me anymore, he was on his own. When I heard him coming along after me, I was sorry. I wanted to get away from Dee Sparks. I wanted to get away from everybody.

"I didn't want to be around anybody who was supposed to be my friend. I'd rather have had Eddie Grimes following me than Dee Sparks.

"Then I stopped moving, because through the trees I could see one of those greasepaper windows glowing up ahead of me. That yellow light looked evil as the devil's eye—everything in The Backs was evil, poisoned, even the trees, even the air. The terrible expression on Dr. Garland's face and the white smudge in the air seemed like the same thing—they were what I didn't want to know.

"Dee shoved me from behind, and if I hadn't felt so sick inside I would have turned around and punched him. Instead, I looked over my shoulder and saw him nodding toward where the side of the shack would be. He wanted to get closer! For a second, he seemed as crazy as everything else out there, and then I got it: I was all turned around, and instead of heading back to the main path, I'd been taking us toward the woman's shack. That was why Dee was following me.

"I shook my head. No, I wasn't going to sneak up to that place. Whatever was inside there was something I didn't have to know about. It had too much power—it turned Eddie Grimes around, and that was enough for me. Dee knew I wasn't fooling. He went around me and started creeping toward the shack.

"And damnedest thing, I watched him slipping through the trees for a second, and started following him. If he could go up there, so could I. If I didn't exactly look at whatever was in there myself, I could watch Dee look at it. That would tell me most of what I had to know. And anyways, probably Dee wouldn't see anything anyhow, unless the front door was hanging open, and that didn't seem too likely to me. He wouldn't see anything, and I wouldn't either, and we could both go home.

"The door of the shack opened up, and a man walked outside. Dee and I freeze, and I mean *freeze*. We're about twenty feet away, on the side of this shack, and if the man looked sideways, he'd see our sheets. There were a lot of trees between us and him, and I couldn't get a very good look at him, but one thing about him made the whole situation a lot more serious. This man was white, and he was wearing good clothes— I couldn't see his face, but I could see his rolled-up sleeves, and his suit jacket slung over one arm, and some kind of wrapped-up bundle he was holding in his hands. All this took about a second. The white man started carrying his bundle straight through the woods, and in another two seconds he was out of sight.

"Dee was a little closer than I was, and I think his sight line was a little clearer than mine. On top of that, he saw better at night than I did. Dee didn't get around like me, but he might have recognized the man we'd seen, and that would be pure trouble. Some rich white man, killing a girl out in The Backs? And us two boys close enough to see him? Do you know what would have happened to us? There wouldn't be enough left of either one of us to make a decent shadow.

"Dee turned around to face me, and I could see his eyes behind his costume, but I couldn't tell what he was thinking. He just stood there, looking at me. In a little bit, just when I was about to explode, we heard a car starting up off to our left. I whispered at Dee if he saw who that was. *Nobody*, Dee said. Now, what the hell did that mean? Nobody? You could say Santa Claus, you could say J. Edgar *Hoover*, it'd be a better answer than Nobody. The Model T's headlights shone through the trees when the car swung around the top of the path and started going toward Meridian Road. *Nobody I ever saw before*, Dee said. When the headlights cut through the trees, both of us ducked out of sight. Actually, we were so far from the path, we had nothing to worry about. I could barely see the car when it went past, and I couldn't see the driver at all.

"We stood up. Over Dee's shoulder I could see the side of the shack where the white man had been. Lamplight flickered on the ground in front of the open door. The last thing in the world I wanted to do was to go inside that place—I didn't even want to walk around to the front and look in the door. Dee stepped back from me and jerked his head toward the shack. I knew it was going to be just like before. I'd say no, he'd say yes, and then I'd follow him wherever he thought he had to go. I felt the same way I did when I saw that white smear in the woods— hopeless, lost in the midst of death. *You go, if you have to*, I whispered to him, *it's what you wanted to do all along.* He didn't move, and I saw that he wasn't too sure about what he wanted anymore.

"Everything was different now, because the white man made it different. Once a white man walked out that door, it was like raising the stakes in a poker game. But Dee had been working toward that one shack ever since we got into The Backs, and he was still curious as a cat about it. He turned away from me and started moving sideways in a straight line, so he'd be able to peek inside the door from a safe distance.

"After he got about halfway to the front, he looked back and waved me on, like this was still some great adventure he wanted me to share. He was afraid to be on his own, that was all. When he realized I was going to stay put, he bent down and moved real slow past the side. He still couldn't see more than a sliver of the inside of the shack, and he moved ahead another little ways. By then, I figured, he should have been able to see about half of the inside of the shack. He hunkered down inside his sheet, staring in the direction of the open door. And there he stayed.

"I took it for about half a minute, and then I couldn't anymore. I was sick enough to die and angry enough to explode, both at the same time. How long could Dee Sparks look at a dead whore? Wouldn't a couple of seconds be enough? Dee was acting like he was watching a goddamn Hopalong Cassidy movie. An owl screeched, and some man in another shack said *Now that's over*, and someone else shushed him. If Dee heard, he paid it no mind. I started along toward him, and I don't think he noticed me, either. He didn't look up until I was past the front of the shack, and had already seen the door hanging open, and the lamplight spilling over the plank floor and onto the grass outside.

"I took another step, and Dee's head snapped around. He tried to stop me by holding out his hand. All that did was make me mad. Who was Dee Sparks to tell me what I couldn't see? All he did was leave me alone in the woods with a trail of apples, and he didn't even do that right. When I kept on coming, Dee started waving both hands at me, looking back and forth between me and the inside of the shack. Like something was happening in there that I couldn't be allowed to see. I didn't stop, and Dee got up on his feet and skittered toward me.

"*We gotta get out of here*, he whispered. He was close enough so I could smell that electrical fire stink. I stepped to his side, and he grabbed my arm. I yanked my arm out of his grip and went forward a little ways and looked through the door of the shack.

"A bed was shoved up against the far wall, and a woman lay naked on the bed. There was blood all over her legs, and blood all over the sheets, and big puddles of blood on the floor. A woman in a raggedy robe, hair stuck out all over her head, squatted beside the bed, holding the other woman's hand. She was a colored woman—a Backs woman— but the other one, the one on the bed, was white. Probably she was pretty, when she was alive. All I could see was white skin and blood, and I near fainted.

"This wasn't some white-trash woman who lived out in The Backs, she was brought here, and the man who brought her had killed her. More trouble was coming down than I could imagine, trouble enough to kill lots of our people. And if Dee and I said a word about the white man we'd seen, the trouble would come right straight down on us.

"I must have made some kind of noise, because the woman next to the bed turned halfway around and looked at me. There wasn't any doubt about it—she saw me. All she saw of Dee was a dirty white sheet, but she saw my face, and she knew who I was. I knew her, too, and she wasn't any Backs woman. She lived down the street from us. Her name was Mary Randolph, and she was the one who came up to Eddie Grimes after he got shot to death and brought him back to life. Mary Randolph followed my dad's band, and when we played roadhouses or colored dance halls, she'd be likely to turn up. A couple of times she told me I played good drums—I was a drummer back then, you know, switched to saxophone when I turned twelve. Mary Randolph just looked at me, her hair stuck out straight all over her head like she was already inside a whirlwind of trouble. No expression on her face except that look you get when your mind is going a mile a minute and our body can't move at all. She didn't even look surprised. She almost looked like she *wasn't* surprised, like she was expecting to see me. As bad as I'd felt that night, this was the worst of all. I liked to have died. I'd have disappeared down an anthill, if I could. I didn't know what I had done—just be there, I guess—but I'd never be able to undo it.

"I pulled at Dee's sheet, and he tore off down the side of the shack like he'd been waiting for a signal. Mary Randolph stared into my eyes, and it felt like I had to pull myself away—I couldn't just turn my head, I had to *disconnect*. And when I did, I could still feel her staring at me. Somehow I made myself go down past the side of the shack, but I could still see Mary Randolph inside there, looking out at the place I'd been.

"If Dee said anything at all when I caught up with him, I'd have knocked his teeth down his throat, but he just moved fast and quiet through the trees, seeing the best way to go, and I followed after. I felt like I'd been kicked by a horse. When we got on the path, we didn't bother trying to sneak down through the woods on the other side, we lit out and ran as hard as we could—like wild dogs were after us. And after we got onto Meridian Road, we ran toward town until we couldn't run anymore.

"Dee clamped his hand over his side and staggered forward a little bit. Then he stopped and ripped off his costume and lay down by the side of the road, breathing hard. I was leaning forward with hands on my knees, as winded as he was. When I could breathe again, I started walking down the road. Dee picked himself up and got next to me and walked along, looking at my face and then looking away, and then look-ing back at my face again.

"*So?* I said.

"*I know that lady*, Dee said.

"Hell, that was no news. Of course he knew Mary Randolph—she was his neighbor, too. I didn't bother to answer, I just grunted at him. Then I reminded him that Mary hadn't seen his face, only mine.

"*Not Mary*, he said. "The other one.

"He knew the dead white woman's name? That made everything worse. A lady like that shouldn't be in Dee Sparks's world, especially if she's going to wind up dead in The Backs. I wondered who was going to get lynched, and how many.

"Then Dee said that I knew her, too. I stopped walking and looked him straight in the face.

"*Miss Abbey Montgomery*, he said. *She brings clothes and food down to our church, Thanksgiving and Christmas.*

"He was right—I wasn't sure if I'd ever heard her name, but I'd seen her once or twice, bringing baskets of ham and chicken and boxes of clothes to Dee's father's church. She was about twenty years old, I guess, so pretty she made you smile just to look at. From a rich family in a big house right at the top of Miller's Hill. Some man didn't think a girl like that should have any associations with colored people, I guess, and decided to express his opinion about as strong as possible. Which meant that we were going to take the blame for what happened to her, and the next time we saw white sheets, they wouldn't be Halloween costumes.

"*He sure took a long time to kill her*, I said.

"And Dee said, *She ain't dead.*

"So I asked him, What the hell did he mean by that? I saw the girl. I saw the blood. Did he think she was going to get up and walk around? Or maybe Mary Randolph was going to tell her that magic word and bring her back to life?

"*You can think that if you want to*, Dee said. *But Abbey Montgomery ain't dead.*

"I almost told him I'd seen her ghost, but he didn't deserve to hear about it. The fool couldn't even see what was right in front of his eyes. I couldn't expect him to understand what happened to me when I saw that miserable ... that *thing*. He was rushing on ahead of me anyhow, like I'd suddenly embarrassed him or something. That was fine with me. I felt the exact same way. I said, *I guess you know neither one of us can ever talk about this*, and he said, *I guess you know it, too*, and that was the last thing we said to each other that night. All the way down Meridian Road Dee Sparks kept his eyes straight ahead and his mouth shut. When we got to the field, he turned toward me like he had something to say, and I waited for it, but he faced forward again and ran away. Just ran. I watched him disappear past the general store, and then I walked home by myself.

"My mom gave me hell for getting my clothes all wet and dirty, and my brothers laughed at me and wanted to know who beat me up and stole my candy. As soon as I could, I went to bed, pulled the covers up over my head, and closed my eyes. A little while later, my mom came in and asked if I was all right. Did I get into a fight with Dee Sparks? Dee Sparks was born to hang, that was what she thought, and I ought to have a better class of friends. *I'm tired of playing those drums, Momma,* I said, *I want to play the saxophone instead.* She looked at me surprised, but said she'd talk about it with Daddy, and that it might work out.

"For the next couple days, I waited for the bomb to go off. On the Friday, I went to school, but couldn't concentrate for beans. Dee Sparks and I didn't even nod at each other in the hallways—just walked by like the other guy was invisible. On the weekend I said I felt sick and stayed in bed, wondering when that whirlwind of trouble would come down. I wondered if Eddie Grimes would talk about seeing me—once they found the body, they'd get around to Eddie Grimes real quick.

"But nothing happened that weekend, and nothing happened all the next week. I thought Mary Randolph must have hid the white girl in a grave out in The Backs. But how long could a girl from one of those rich families go missing without investigations and search parties? And, on top of that, what was Mary Randolph doing there in the first place? She liked to have a good time, but she wasn't one of those wild girls with a razor under her skirt—she went to church every Sunday, was good to people, nice to kids. Maybe she went out to comfort that poor girl, but how did she know she'd be there in the first place? Misses Abbey Montgomerys from the hill didn't share their plans with Mary Randolph from Darktown. I couldn't forget the way she looked at me, but I couldn't understand it, either. The more I thought about that look, the more it was like Mary Randolph was saying something to me, but what? *Are you ready for this? Do you understand this? Do you know how careful you must be?*

"My father said I could start learning the C-melody sax, and when I was ready to play it in public, my little brother wanted to take over the drums. Seems he always wanted to play drums, and in fact, he's been a drummer ever since, a good one. So I worked out how to play my little sax, I went to school and came straight home after, and everything went on like normal, except Dee Sparks and I weren't friends anymore. If the police were searching for a missing rich girl, I didn't hear anything about it.

"Then one Saturday I was walking down our street to go to the general store, and Mary Randolph came through her front door just as I got to her house. When she saw me, she stopped moving real sudden, with one hand still on the side of the door. I was so surprised to see her that I was in kind of slow motion, and I must have stared at her. She gave me a look like an X ray, a look that searched around down inside me. I don't know what she saw, but her face relaxed, and she took her hand off the door and let it close behind her, and she wasn't looking inside me anymore. *Miss Randolph*, I said, and she told me she was looking forward to hearing our band play at a Beergarden dance in a couple of weeks. I told her I was going to be playing the saxophone at that dance, and she said something about that, and all the time it was like we were having two conversations, the top one about me and the band, and the one underneath about her and the murdered white girl in The Backs. It made me so nervous, my words got all mixed up. Finally she said *You make sure you say hello to your daddy for me, now*, and I got away.

"After I passed her house, Mary Randolph started walking down the street behind me. I could feel her watching me, and I started to sweat. Mary Randolph was a total mystery to me. She was a nice lady, but probably she buried that girl's body. I didn't know but that she was going to come and kill *me*, one day. And then I remembered her kneeling down beside Eddie Grimes at the roadhouse. She had been *dancing* with Eddie Grimes, who was in jail more often than he was out. I wondered if you could be a respectable lady and still know Eddie Grimes well enough to dance with him. And how did she bring him back to life? Or was that what happened at all? Hearing that lady walk along behind me made me so uptight, I crossed to the other side of the street.

"A couple days after that, when I was beginning to think that the trouble was never going to happen after all, it came down. We heard police cars coming down the street right when we were finishing dinner. I thought they were coming for me, and I almost lost my chicken and rice. The sirens went straight past our house, and then more sirens came toward us from other directions—the old klaxons they had in those days. It sounded like every cop in the state was rushing into Darktown. This was bad, bad news. Someone was going to wind up dead, that was certain. No way all those police were going to come into our part of town, make all that commotion, and leave without killing at least one man. That's the truth. You just had to pray that the man they killed wasn't you or anyone in your family. My daddy turned off the lamps, and we went to the window to watch the cars go by. Two of them were state police. When it was safe, Daddy went outside to see where all the trouble was headed. After he came back in, he said it looked like the police were going toward Eddie Grimes's place. We wanted to go out and look, but they wouldn't let us, so we went to the back windows that faced toward Grimes's house. Couldn't see anything but a lot of cars and police standing all over the road back there. Sounded like they were knocking down Grimes's house with sledge hammers. Then a whole bunch of cops took off running, and all I could see was the cars spread out across the road. About ten minutes later, we heard lots of gunfire coming from a couple of streets further back. It like to have lasted forever. Like hearing the Battle of the Bulge. My momma started to cry, and so did my little brother. The shooting stopped. The police shouted to each other, and then they came back and got in their cars and went away.

"On the radio the next morning, they said that a known criminal, a Negro man named Edward Grimes, had been killed while trying to escape arrest for the murder of a white woman. The body of Eleanore Monday, missing for three days, had been found in a shallow grave by Woodland police searching near an illegal distillery in the region called The Backs. Miss Monday, the daughter of grocer Albert Monday, had been in poor mental and physical health, and Grimes had apparently taken advantage of her weakness either to abduct or lure her to The Backs, where she had been savagely murdered. That's what it said on the radio—I still remember the words. *In poor mental and physical health. Savagely murdered.*

"When the paper finally came, there on the front page was a picture of Eleanore Monday, girl with dark hair and a big nose. She didn't look anything like the dead woman in the shack. She hadn't even disappeared on the right day. Eddie Grimes was never going to be able to explain things, because the police had finally cornered him in the old jute warehouse just off Meridian Road next to the general store. I don't suppose they even bothered trying to arrest him—they weren't interested in *arresting* him. He killed a white girl. They wanted revenge, and they got it.

"After I looked at the paper, I got out of the house and ran between the houses to get a look at the jute warehouse. Turned out a lot of folks had the same idea. A big crowd strung out in a long line in front of the warehouse, and cars were parked all along Meridian Road. Right up in front of the warehouse door was a police car, and a big cop stood in the middle of the big doorway, watching people file by. They were walking past the doorway one by one, acting like they were at some kind of exhibit. Nobody was talking. It was a sight I never saw before in that town, whites and colored all lined up together. On the other side of the warehouse, two groups of men stood alongside the road, one colored and one white, talking so quietly you couldn't hear a word.

"Now I was never one who liked standing in lines, so I figured I'd just dart up there, peek in, and save myself some time. I came around the end of the line and ambled toward the two bunches of men, like I'd already had my look and was just hanging around to enjoy the scene. After I got a little past the warehouse door, I sort of drifted up alongside it. I looked down on the row of people, and there was Dee Sparks, just a few yards away from being able to see in. Dee was leaning forward, and when he saw me he almost jumped out of his skin. He looked away as fast as he could. His eyes turned as dead as stones. The cop at the door yelled at me to go to the end of the line. He never would have noticed me at all if Dee hadn't jumped like someone just shot off a firecracker behind him.

"About halfway down the line. Mary Randolph was standing behind some of the ladies from the neighborhood. She looked terrible. Her hair stuck out in raggedy clumps, and her skin was all ashy, like she hadn't slept in a long time. I sped up a little, hoping she wouldn't notice me, but after I took one more step, Mary Randolph looked down and her eyes hooked into mine. I swear, what was in her eyes almost knocked me down. I couldn't even tell what it was, unless it was just pure hate. Hate and pain. With her eyes hooked into mine like that, I couldn't look away. It was like I was seeing that miserable, terrible white smear twisting up between the trees on that night in The Backs. Mary let me go, and I almost fell down all over again.

"I got to the end of the line and started moving along regular and slow with everybody else. Mary Randolph stayed in my mind and blanked out everything else. When I got up to the door, I barely took in what was inside the warehouse—a wall full of bulletholes and bloodstains all over the place, big slick ones and little drizzly ones. All I could think of was the shack and Mary Randolph sitting next to the dead girl, and I was back there all over again.

"Mary Randolph didn't show up at the Beergarden dance, so she didn't hear me play saxophone in public for the first time. I didn't expect her, either, not after the way she looked out at the warehouse. There'd been a lot of news about Eddie Grimes, who they made out to be less civilized than a gorilla, a crazy man who'd murder anyone as long as he could kill all the white women first. The paper had a picture of what they called Grimes's 'lair,' with busted furniture all over the place and holes in the walls, but they never explained that it was the police tore it up and made it look that way.

"The other thing people got suddenly all hot about was The Backs. Seems the place was even worse than everybody thought. Seems white girls besides Eleanore Monday had been taken out there—according to some, there were even white girls living out there, along with a lot of bad coloreds. The place was a nest of vice, Sodom and Gomorrah. Two days before the town council was supposed to discuss the problem, a gang of white men went out there with guns and clubs and torches and burned every shack in The Backs clear down to the ground. While they were there, they didn't see a single soul, white, colored, male, female, damned or saved. Everybody who had lived in The Backs had skedaddled. And the funny thing was, long as The Backs had existed right outside of Woodland, no one in Woodland could recollect the name of anyone who had ever lived there. They couldn't even recall the name of anyone who had ever gone there, except for Eddie Grimes. In fact, after the place burned down, it appeared that it must have been a sign just to say its name, because no one ever mentioned it. You'd think men so fine and moral as to burn down The Backs would be willing to take the credit, but none ever did.

"You could think they must have wanted to get rid of some things out there. Or wanted real bad to forget about things out there. One thing I thought, Doctor Garland and the man I saw leaving that shack had been out there with torches.

"But maybe I didn't know anything at all. Two weeks later, a couple things happened that shook me good.

"The first one happened three nights before Thanksgiving. I was hurrying home, a little bit late. Nobody else on the street, everybody inside either sitting down to dinner or getting ready for it. When I got to Mary Randolph's house, some kind of noise coming from inside stopped me. What I thought was, it sounded exactly like somebody trying to scream while someone else was holding a hand over their mouth. Well, that was plain foolish, wasn't it? How did I know what that would sound like? I moved along a step or two, and then I heard it again. Could be anything, I told myself. Mary Randolph didn't like me too much, anyway. She wouldn't be partial to my knocking on her door. Best thing I could do was get out. Which was what I did. Just went home to supper and forgot about it.

"Until the next day, anyhow, when a friend of Mary's walked in her front door and found her lying dead with her throat cut and a knife in her hand. A cut of fatback, we heard, had boiled away to cinders on her stove. I didn't tell anybody about what I heard the night before. Too scared. I couldn't do anything but wait to see what the police did.

"To the police, it was all real clear. Mary killed herself, plain and simple.

"When our minister went across town to ask why a lady who intended to commit suicide had bothered to start cooking her supper, the chief told him that a female bent on killing herself probably didn't care *what* happened to the food on her stove. Then I suppose Mary Randolph nearly managed to cut her own head off, said the minister. A female in despair possesses a godawful strength, said the chief. And asked, wouldn't she have screamed if she'd been attacked? And added, couldn't it be that maybe this female here had secrets in her life connected to the late savage murderer named Eddie Grimes? We might all be better off if these secrets get buried with your Mary Randolph, said the chief. I'm sure you understand me, Reverend. And yes, the Reverend did understand, he surely did. So Mary Randolph got laid away in the cemetery, and nobody ever said her name again. She was put away out of mind, like The Backs.

"The second thing that shook me up and proved to me that I didn't know anything, that I was no better than a blind dog, happened on Thanksgiving day. My daddy played piano in church, and on special days, we played our instruments along with the gospel songs. I got to church early with the rest of my family, and we practiced with the choir. Afterwards, I went to fooling around outside until the people came, and saw a big car come up into the church parking lot. Must have been the biggest, fanciest car I'd ever seen. Miller's Hill was written all over that vehicle. I couldn't have told you why, but the sight of it made my heart stop. The front door opened, and out stepped a colored man in a fancy gray uniform with a smart cap. He didn't so much as dirty his eyes by looking at me, or at the church, or at anything around him. He stepped around the front of the car and opened the rear door on my side. A young woman was in the passenger seat, and when she got out of the car, the sun fell on her blond hair and the little fur jacket she was wearing. I couldn't see more than the top of her head, her shoulders under the jacket, and her legs. Then she straightened up, and her eyes lighted right on me. She smiled, but I couldn't smile back. I couldn't even begin to move.

"It was Abbey Montgomery, delivering baskets of food to our church, the way she did every Thanksgiving and Christmas. She looked older and thinner than the last time I'd seen her alive—older and thinner, but more than that, like there was no fun at all in her life anymore. She walked to the trunk of the car, and the driver opened it up, leaned in, and brought out a great big basket of food. He took it into the church by the back way and came back for another one. Abbey Montgomery just stood still and watched him carry the baskets. She looked—she looked like she was just going through the motions, like going through the motions was all she was ever going to do from now on, and she knew it. Once she smiled at the driver, but the smile was so sad that the driver didn't even try to smile back. When he was done, he closed the trunk and let her into the passenger seat, got behind the wheel, and drove away.

"I was thinking, *Dee Sparks was right, she was alive all the time.* Then I thought, *No, Mary Randolph brought her back, too, like she did Eddie Grimes. But it didn't work right, and only part of her came back.*

"And that's the whole thing, except that Abbey Montgomery didn't deliver food to our church, that Christmas—she was traveling out of the country, with her aunt. And she didn't bring the food the next Thanksgiving, either, just sent her driver with the baskets. By that time, we didn't expect her, because we'd already heard that, soon as she got back to town, Abbey Montgomery stopped leaving her house. That girl shut herself up and never came out. I heard from somebody who probably didn't know any more than I did that she eventually got so she wouldn't even leave her room. Five years later, she passed away. Twenty-six years old, and they said she looked to be at least fifty."

4

Hat fell silent, and I sat with my pen ready over the notebook, waiting for more. When I realized that he had finished, I asked, "What did she die of?"

"Nobody ever told me."

"And nobody ever found who had killed Mary Randolph."

The limpid, colorless eyes momentarily rested on me. "Was she killed?"

"Did you ever become friends with Dee Sparks again? Did you at least talk about it with him?"

"Surely did not. Nothing to talk about."

That was a remarkable statement, considering that for an hour he had done nothing but talk about what had happened to the two of them, but I let it go. Hat was still looking at me with his unreadable eyes. His face had become particularly bland, almost immobile. It was not possible to imagine this man as an active eleven-year-old boy. "Now you heard me out, answer my question," he said.

I couldn't remember the question.

"Did we find what we were looking for?"

Scares—that was what they had been looking for. "I think you found a lot more than that," I said.

He nodded slowly. "That's right. It was more."

Then I asked him some question about his family's band, he lubricated himself with another swallow of gin, and the interview returned to more typical matters. But the experience of listening to him had changed. After I had heard the long, unresolved tale of his Halloween night, everything Hat said seemed to have two separate meanings, the daylight meaning created by sequences of ordinary English words, and another, nighttime meaning, far less determined and knowable. He was like a man discoursing with eerie rationality in the midst of a particularly surreal dream: like a man carrying on an ordinary conversation with one foot placed on solid ground and the other suspended above a bottomless abyss. I focused on the rationality, on the foot placed in the context I understood; the rest unsettling to the point of being frightening. By six thirty, when he kindly called me "Miss Rosemary" and opened his door, I felt as if I'd spent several weeks, if not whole months, in his room.

PART THREE

Although I did get my M.A. at Columbia, I didn't have enough money to stay on for a Ph.D., so I never became a college professor. I never became a jazz critic, either, or anything else very interesting. For a couple of years after Columbia, I taught English in a high school until I quit to take the job I have now, which involves a lot of traveling and pays a little bit better than teaching. Maybe even quite a bit better, but that's not saying much, especially when you consider my expenses. I own a nice little house in the Chicago suburbs, my marriage held up against everything life did to it, and my twenty-two-year-old son, a young man who never once in his life for the purpose of pleasure read a novel, looked at a painting, visited a museum, or listened to anything but the most readily available music, recently announced to his mother and myself that he has decided to become an artist, actual type of art to be determined later, but probably to include aspects of photography, videotape, and the creation of "installations." I take this as proof that he was raised in a manner that left his self-esteem intact.

I no longer provide my life with a perpetual sound track (though my son, who has moved back in with us, does), in part because my income does not permit the purchase of a great many compact discs. (A friend presented me with a CD player on my forty-fifth birthday.) And these days, I'm as interested in classical music as in jazz. Of course, I never go to jazz clubs when I am home. Are there still people, apart from New Yorkers, who patronize jazz nightclubs in their own hometowns? The concept seems faintly retrograde, even somehow illicit. But when I am out on the road, living in airplanes and hotel rooms, I often check the jazz listings in the local papers to see if I can find some way to fill my evenings. Many of the legends of my youth are still out there, in most cases, playing at least as well as before. Some months ago, while I was in San Francisco, I came across John Hawes's name in this fashion. He was working in a club so close to my hotel that I could walk to it.

His appearance in any club at all was surprising. Hawes had ceased performing jazz in public years before. He had earned a great deal of fame (and undoubtedly, a great deal of money) writing film scores, and in the past decade, he had begun to appear in swallowtail coat and white tie as a conductor of the standard classical repertoire. I believe he had a permanent post in some city like Seattle, or perhaps Salt Lake City. If he was spending a week playing jazz with a trio in San Francisco, it must have been for the sheer pleasure of it.

I turned up just before the beginning of the first set, and got a table toward the back of the club. Most of the tables were filled—Hawes's celebrity had guaranteed him a good house. Only a few minutes after the announced time of the first set, Hawes emerged through a door at the front of the club and moved toward the piano followed by his bassist and drummer. He looked like a more successful version of the younger man I had seen in New York, and the only indication of the extra years were his silver-gray hair, still abundant, and a little paunch. His playing, too, seemed essentially unchanged, but I could not hear it in the way I once had. He was still a good pianist—no doubt about that—but he seemed to be skating over the surface of the songs he played, using his wonderful technique and good time merely to decorate their melodies. It was the sort of playing that becomes less impressive the more attention you give it—if you were listening with half an ear, it probably sounded like Art Tatum. I wondered if John Hawes had always had this superficial streak in him, or if he had lost a certain necessary passion during his years away from jazz. Certainly he had not sounded superficial when I had heard him with Hat.

Hawes, too, might have been thinking about his old employer, because in the first set he played "Love Walked In," "Too Marvelous For Words," and "Up Jumped Hat." In the last of these, inner gears seemed to mesh, the rhythm simultaneously relaxed and intensified, and the music turned into real, not imitation, jazz. Hawes looked pleased with himself when he stood up from the piano bench, and half a dozen fans moved to greet him as he stepped off the bandstand. Most of them were carrying old records they wished him to sign.

A few minutes later, I saw Hawes standing by himself at the end of the bar, drinking what appeared to be club soda, in proximity to his musicians but not actually speaking with them. Wondering if his allusions to Hat had been deliberate, I left my table and walked toward the bar. Hawes watched me approach out of the side of his eye, neither encouraging nor discouraging me to approach him. When I introduced myself, he smiled nicely and shook my hand and waited for whatever I wanted to say to him.

At first, I made some inane comment about the difference between playing in clubs and conducting in concert halls, and he replied with the noncommittal and equally banal agreement that yes the two experiences were very different.

Then I told him that I had seen him play with Hat all those years ago in New York, and he turned to me with genuine pleasure in his face. "Did you? At that little club on St. Mark's Place? That was the only time I ever worked with him, but it sure was fun. What an experience. I guess I must have been thinking about it, because I played some of those songs we used to do."

"That was why I came over," I said. "I guess that was one of the best musical experiences I ever had."

"You and me both." Hawes smiled to himself. "Sometimes, I just couldn't believe what he was doing."

"It showed," I said.

"Well." His eyes slid away from mine. "Great character. Completely otherworldly."

"I saw some of that," I said. "I did that interview with him that turns up now and then, the one in *Downbeat*."

"Oh!" Hawes gave me his first genuinely interested look so far. "Well, that was him, all right."

"Most of it was, anyhow."

"You cheated?" Now he was looking even more interested.

"I had to make it understandable."

"Oh, sure. You couldn't put in all those ding-dings and bells and Bob Crosbys." These had been elements of Hat's private code. Hawes laughed at the memory. "When he wanted to play a blues in G, he'd lean over and say, 'Gs, please.' "

"Did you get to know him at all well, personally?" I asked, thinking that the answer must be that he had not—I didn't think that anyone had ever really known Hat very well.

"Pretty well," Hawes said. "A couple of times, around '54 and '55, he invited me home with him, to his parents' house, I mean. We got to be friends on a Jazz at the Phil tour, and twice when we were in the South, he asked me if I wanted to eat some good home cooking."

"You went to his hometown?"

He nodded. "His parents put me up. They were interesting people. Hat's father, Red, was about the lightest black man I ever saw, and he could have passed for white anywhere, but I don't suppose the thought ever occurred to him."

"Was the family band still going?"

"No, to tell you the truth, I don't think they were getting much work up toward the end of the forties. At the end, they were using a tenor player and a drummer from the high school band. And the church work got more and more demanding for Hat's father."

"His father was a deacon, or something like that?"

He raised his eyebrows. "No, Red was the Baptist minister. The Reverend. He ran that church. I think he even started it."

"Hat told me his father played piano in church, but . . ."

"The Reverend would have made a hell of a blues piano player, if he'd ever left his day job."

"There must have been another Baptist church in the neighborhood," I said, thinking this the only explanation for the presence of two Baptist ministers. But why had Hat not mentioned that his own father, like Dee Sparks's, had been a clergyman?

"Are you kidding? There was barely enough money in that place to keep one of them going." He looked at his watch, nodded at me, and began to move closer to his sidemen.

"Could I ask you one more question?"

"I suppose so," he said, almost impatiently.

"Did Hat strike you as superstitious?"

Hawes grinned. "Oh, he was superstitious, all right. He told me he never worked on Halloween—he didn't even want to go out of his room, on Halloween. That's why he left the big band, you know. They were starting a tour on Halloween, and Hat refused to do it. He just quit." He leaned toward me. "I'll tell you another funny thing. I always had the feeling that Hat was terrified of his father—I thought he invited me to Hatchville with him so I could be some kind of buffer between him and his father. Never made any sense to me. Red was a big strong old guy, and I'm pretty sure a long time ago he used to mess around with the ladies, Reverend or not, but I couldn't ever figure out why Hat should be afraid of him. But whenever Red came into the room, Hat shut up. Funny, isn't it?"

I must have looked very perplexed. "Hatchville?"

"Where they lived. Hatchville, Mississippi—not too far from Biloxi."

"But he told me—"

"Hat never gave too many straight answers," Hawes said. "And he didn't let the facts get in the way of a good story. When you come to think of it, why should he? He was *Hat*."

After the next set, I walked back uphill to my hotel, wondering again about the long story Hat had told me. Had there been any truth in it at all?

2

Three weeks later I found myself released from a meeting at our Midwestern headquarters in downtown Chicago earlier than I had expected, and instead of going to a bar with the other wandering corporate ghosts like myself, made up a story about a relative I had promised to visit. I didn't want to admit to my fellow employees, committed like all male business people to aggressive endeavors such as racquetball, drinking, and the pursuit of women, that I intended to visit the library. Short of a trip to Mississippi, a good periodical room offered the most likely means of finding out once and for all how much truth had been in what Hat had told me.

I hadn't forgotten everything I had learned at Columbia—I still knew how to look things up.

In the main library, a boy set me up with a monitor and spools of microfilm representing the complete contents of the daily newspapers from Biloxi and Hatchville, Mississippi, for Hat's tenth and eleventh years. That made three papers, two for Biloxi and one for Hatchville, but all I had to examine were the issues dating from the end of October through the middle of November—I was looking for references to Eddie Grimes, Eleanore Monday, Mary Randolph, Abbey Montgomery, Hat's family, The Backs, and anyone named Sparks.

The Hatchville *Blade*, a gossipy daily printed on peach-colored paper, offered plenty of references to each of these names and places, and the papers from Biloxi contained nearly as many—Biloxi could not conceal the delight, disguised as horror, aroused in its collective soul by the unimaginable events taking place in the smaller, supposedly respectable town ten miles west. Biloxi was riveted, Biloxi was superior, Biloxi was virtually intoxicated with dread and outrage. In Hatchville, the press maintained a persistent optimistic dignity: When wickedness had appeared, justice official and unofficial had dealt with it. Hatchville was shocked but proud (or at least pretended to be proud), and Biloxi all but preened. The *Blade* printed detailed news stories, but the Biloxi papers suggested implications not allowed by Hatchville's version of events. I needed Hatchville to confirm or question Hat's story, but Biloxi gave me at least the beginning of a way to understand it.

A black ex-convict named Edward Grimes had in some fashion persuaded or coerced Eleanore Monday, a retarded young white woman, to accompany him to an area variously described as "a longstanding local disgrace" (the *Blade*) and "a haunt of deepest vice" (Biloxi) and after "the perpetration of the most offensive and brutal deeds upon her person" (the *Blade*) or "acts which the judicious commentator must decline to imagine, much less describe" (Biloxi) murdered her, presumably to ensure her silence, and then buried the body near the "squalid dwelling" where he made and sold illegal liquor. State and local police departments acting in concert had located the body, identified Grimes as the fiend, and, after a search of his house, had tracked him to a warehouse where the murderer was killed in a gun battle. The *Blade* covered half its front page with a photograph of a gaping double door and a bloodstained wall. All Mississippi, both Hatchville and Biloxi declared, now could breathe more easily.

The *Blade* gave the death of Mary Randolph a single paragraph on its back page, the Biloxi papers nothing.

In Hatchville, the raid on The Backs was described as an heroic assault on a dangerous criminal encampment that had somehow come to flourish in a little-noticed section of the countryside. At great risk to themselves, anonymous citizens of Hatchville had descended like the army of the righteous and driven forth the hidden sinners from their dens. Troublemakers, beware! The Biloxi papers, while seeming to endorse the action in Hatchville, actually took another tone altogether. Can it be, they asked, that the Hatchville police had never before noticed the existence of a Sodom and Gomorrah so close to the town line? Did it take the savage murder of a helpless woman to bring it to their attention? Of course Biloxi celebrated the destruction of The Backs, such vileness must be eradicated, but it wondered what else had been destroyed along with the stills and the mean buildings where loose women had plied their trade. Men ever are men, and those who have succumbed to temptation may wish to remove from the face of the earth any evidence of their lapses. Had not the police of Hatchville ever heard the rumor, vague and doubtless baseless, that operations of an illegal nature had been performed in the selfsame Backs? That in an atmosphere of drugs, intoxication, and gambling, the races had mingled there, and that "fast" young women had risked life and honor in search of illicit thrills? Hatchville may have rid itself of a few buildings, but Biloxi was willing to suggest that the problems of its smaller neighbor might not have disappeared with them.

As this campaign of innuendo went on in Biloxi, the *Blade* blandly reported the ongoing events of any smaller American city. Miss Abigail Montgomery sailed with her aunt, Miss Lucinda Bright, from New Orleans to France for an eight-week tour of the Continent. The Reverend Jasper Sparks of the Miller's Hill Presbyterian Church delivered a sermon on the subject of "Christian Forgiveness." (Just after Thanksgiving, the Reverend Sparks's son, Rodney, was sent off with the blessings and congratulations of all Hatchville to a private academy in Charleston, South Carolina.) There were bake sales, church socials, and costume parties. A saxophone virtuoso named Albert Woodland demonstrated his astonishing wizardry at a well-attended recital presented in Temperance Hall.

Well, I knew the name of at least one person who had attended the recital. If Hat had chosen to disguise the name of his hometown, he had done so by substituting for it a name that represented another sort of home.

But, although I had more ideas about this than before, I still did not know exactly what Hat had seen or done on Halloween night in The Backs. It seemed possible that he had gone there with a white boy of his age, a preacher's son like himself, and had the wits scared out of him by whatever had happened to Abbey Montgomery—and after that night, Abbey herself had been sent out of town, as had Dee Sparks. I couldn't think that a man had murdered the young woman, leaving Mary Randolph to bring her back to life. Surely whatever had happened to Abbey Montgomery had brought Dr. Garland out to The Backs, and what he had witnessed or done there had sent him away screaming. And this event—what had befallen a rich young white woman in the shadiest, most criminal section of a Mississippi county—had led to the slaying of Eddie Grimes and the murder of Mary Randolph. Because they knew what had happened, they had to die.

I understood all this, and Hat had understood it, too. Yet he had introduced needless puzzles, as if embedded in the midst of this unresolved story were something he either wished to conceal or not to know. And concealed it would remain; if Hat did not know it, I never would. Whatever had really happened in The Backs on Halloween night was lost for good.

On the *Blade*'s entertainment page for a Saturday in the middle of November I had come across a photograph of Hat's family's band, and when I had reached this hopeless point in my thinking, I spooled back across the pages to look at it again. Hat, his two brothers, his sister, and his parents stood in a straight line, tallest to smallest, in front of what must have been the family car. Hat held a C-melody saxophone, his brothers a trumpet and drumsticks, his sister a clarinet. As the piano player, the Reverend carried nothing at all—nothing except for what came through even a grainy, sixty-year-old photograph as a powerful sense of self. Hat's father had been a tall, impressive man, and in the photograph he looked as white as I did. But what was impressive was not the lightness of his skin, or even his striking handsomeness: What impressed was the sense of authority implicit in his posture, his straightforward gaze, even the dictatorial set of his chin. In retrospect, I was not surprised by what John Hawes had told me, for this man could easily be frightening. You would not wish to oppose him; you would not elect to get in his way. Beside him, Hat's mother seemed vague and distracted, as if her husband had robbed her of all certainty. Then I noticed the car, and for the first time realized why it had been included in the photograph. It was a sign of their prosperity, the respectable status they had achieved—the car was as much an advertisement as the photograph. It was, I thought, an old Model T Ford, but I didn't waste any time speculating that it might have been the Model T Hat had seen in The Backs.

And that would be that—the hint of an absurd supposition—except for something I read a few days ago in a book called *Cool Breeze: The Life of Grant Kilbert*.

There are few biographies of any jazz musicians apart from Louis Armstrong and Duke Ellington (though one does now exist of Hat, the title of which was drawn from my interview with him), and I was surprised to see *Cool Breeze* at the B. Dalton in our local mall. Biographies have not yet been written of Art Blakey, Clifford Brown, Ben Webster, Art Tatum, and many others of more musical and historical importance than Kilbert. Yet I should not have been surprised. Kilbert was one of those musicians who attract and maintain a large personal following, and twenty years after his death, almost all of his records have been released on CD, many of them in multidisc boxed sets. He had been a great, great player, the closest to Hat of all his disciples. Because Kilbert had been one of my early heroes, I bought the book (for $35!) and brought it home.

Like the lives of many jazz musicians, I suppose of artists in general, Kilbert's had been an odd mixture of public fame and private misery. He had committed burglaries, even armed robberies, to feed his persistent heroin addiction; he had spent years in jail; his two marriages had ended in outright hatred; he had managed to betray most of his friends. That this weak, narcissistic louse had found it in himself to create music of real tenderness and beauty was one of art's enigmas, but not actually a surprise. I'd heard and read enough stories about Grant Kilbert to know what kind of man he'd been.

But what I had not known was that Kilbert, to all appearances an American of conventional northern European, perhaps Scandinavian or Anglo-Saxon, stock, had occasionally claimed to be black. (This claim had always been dismissed, apparently, as another indication of Kilbert's mental aberrancy.) At other times, being Kilbert, he had denied ever making this claim.

Neither had I known that the received version of his birth and upbringing were in question. Unlike Hat, Kilbert had been interviewed dozens of times both in *Downbeat* and in mass-market weekly news magazines, invariably to offer the same story of having been born in Hattiesburg, Mississippi, to an unmusical, working-class family (a plumber's family), of knowing virtually from infancy that he was born to make music, of begging for and finally being given a saxophone, of early mastery and the dazzled admiration of his teachers, then of dropping out of school at sixteen and joining the Woody Herman band. After that, almost immediate fame.

Most of this, the Grant Kilbert myth, was undisputed. He had been raised in Hattiesburg by a plumber named Kilbert, he had been a prodigy and high-school dropout, he'd become famous with Woody Herman before he was twenty. Yet he told a few friends, not necessarily those to whom he said he was black, that he'd been adopted by the Kilberts, and that once or twice, in great anger, either the plumber or his wife had told him that he had been born into poverty and disgrace and that he'd better by God be grateful for the opportunities he'd been given. The source of this story was John Hawes, who'd met Kilbert on another long Jazz at the Phil tour, the last he made before leaving the road for film scoring.

"Grant didn't have a lot of friends on that tour," Hawes told the biographer. "Even though he was such a great player, you never knew what he was going to say, and if he was in a bad mood, he was liable to put down some of the older players. He was always respectful around Hat, his whole style was based on Hat's, but Hat could go days without saying anything, and by those days he certainly wasn't making any new friends. Still, he'd let Grant sit next to him on the bus, and nod his head while Grant talked to him, so he must have felt some affection for him. Anyhow, eventually I was about the only guy on the tour that was willing to have a conversation with Grant, and we'd sit up in the bar late at night after the concerts. The way he played, I could forgive him a lot of failings. One of those nights, he said that he'd been adopted, and that not knowing who his real parents were was driving him crazy. He didn't even have a birth certificate. From a hint his mother once gave him, he thought one of his birth parents was black, but when he asked them directly, they always denied it. These were white Mississippians, after all, and if they had wanted a baby so bad that they had taken in a child who looked completely white but maybe had a drop or two of black blood in his veins, they weren't going to admit it, even to themselves."

In the midst of so much supposition, here is a fact. Grant Kilbert was exactly eleven years younger than Hat. The jazz encyclopedias give his birth date as November first, which instead of his actual birthday may have been the day he was delivered to the couple in Hattiesburg.

I wonder if Hat saw more than he admitted to me of the man leaving the shack where Abbey Montgomery lay on bloody sheets; I wonder if he had reason to fear his father. I don't know if what I am thinking is correct—I'll never know that—but now, finally, I think I know why Hat never wanted to go out of his room on Halloween nights. The story he told me never left him, but it must have been most fully present on those nights. I think he heard the screams, saw the bleeding girl, and saw Mary Randolph staring at him with displaced pain and rage. I think that in some small closed corner deep within himself, he knew who had been the real object of these feelings, and therefore had to lock himself inside his hotel room and gulp gin until he obliterated the horror of his own thoughts.

Sharyn McCrumb's first books included a very witty look at science fiction fandom (BIMBOS OF THE DEATH SUN, 1998), as well some traditional mysteries (if anything of Sharyn's can be traditional). But it has been her more serious novels about Appalachian culture (IF EVER I RETURN, PRETTY PEGGY-O, 1990; THE HANGMAN'S BEAUTIFUL DAUGHTER, 1992; and SHE WALKS THESE HILLS, 1994) that has brought her best reviews, and greatest readership. Not that she's deserted the traditional mystery, She remains one of its most colorful practitioners.

Old Rattler
SHARYN McCRUMB

She was a city woman, and she looked too old to want to get pregnant, so I reckoned she had hate in her heart.

That's mostly the only reasons I ever see city folks: babies and meanness. Country people come to me right along, though, for poultices and tonics for the rheumatism; to go dowsing for well water on their land; or to help them find what's lost, and such like; but them city folks from Knoxville, and Johnson City, and from Asheville, over in North Carolina—the skinny ones with their fancy colorless cars, talking all educated, slick as goose grease—they don't hold with home remedies or the Sight. Superstition, they call it. Unless you label your potions "macrobiotics," or "holistic," and package them up fancy for the customers in earth-tone clay jars, or call your visions "channeling."

Shoot, I know what city folks are like. I could'a been rich if I'd had the stomach for it. But I didn't care to cater to their notions, or to have to listen to their self-centered whining, when a city doctor could see to their needs by charging more and taking longer. I say, let him. They don't need me so bad nohow. They'd rather pay a hundred dollars to some fool boy doctor who's likely guessing about what ails them. Of course, they got insurance to cover it, which country people mostly don't—them as makes do with me, anyhow.

"That old Rattler," city people say. "Holed up in that filthy old shanty up a dirt road. Wearing those ragged overalls. Living on Pepsis and Twinkies. What does he know about doctoring?"

And I smile and let 'em think that, because when they are desperate enough, and they have nowhere to turn, they'll be along to see me, same as the country people. Meanwhile, I go right on helping the halt and the blind who have no one else to turn to. *For I will restore health unto thee, and I will heal thee of thy wounds, saith the Lord.* Jeremiah 30. What do I know? A lot. I can tell more from looking at a person's fingernails, smelling their breath, and looking at the whites of their eyes than the doctoring tribe in Knoxville can tell with their high-priced X rays and such. And sometimes I can pray the sickness out of them and sometimes I can't. If I can't, I don't charge for it—you show me a city doctor that will make you that promise.

The first thing I do is, I look at the patient, before I even listen to a word. I look at the way they walk, the set of the jaw, whether they look straight ahead or down at the ground, like they was waiting to crawl into it. I could tell right from looking at the city woman—what she had wrong with her wasn't no praying matter.

She parked her colorless cracker box of a car on the gravel patch by the spring, and she stood squinting up through the sunshine at my corrugated tin shanty (*I* know it's a shanty, but it's paid for. Think on that awhile.) She looked doubtful at first—that was her common sense trying to talk her out of taking her troubles to some backwoods witch doctor. But then her eyes narrowed, and her jaw set, and her lips tightened into a long, thin line, and I could tell that she was thinking on whatever it was that hurt her so bad that she was willing to resort to me. I got out a new milk-jug of my comfrey and chamomile tea and two Dixie cups, and went out on the porch to meet her.

"Come on up!" I called out to her, smiling and waving most friendly-like. A lot of people say that rural mountain folks don't take kindly to strangers, but that's mainly if they don't know what you've come about, and it makes them anxious, not knowing if you're a welfare snoop or a paint-your-house-with-whitewash conman, or the law. I knew what this stranger had come about, though, so I didn't mind her at all. She was as harmless as a buckshot doe, and hurting just as bad, I reckoned. Only she didn't know she was hurting. She thought she was just angry.

If she could have kept her eyes young and her neck smooth, she would have looked thirty-two, even close-up, but as it was, she looked like a prosperous, well-maintained forty-four-year-old, who could use less coffee and more sleep. She was slender, with a natural-like brownish hair—though I knew better—wearing a khaki skirt and a navy top and a silver necklace with a crystal pendant, which she might have believed was a talisman. There's no telling what city people will believe. But she smiled at me, a little nervous, and asked if I had time to talk to her. That pleased me. When people are taken up with their own troubles, they seldom worry about anybody else's convenience.

"Sit down," I said, smiling to put her at ease. "Time runs slow on the mountain. Why don't you have a swig of my herb tea, and rest a spell. That's a rough road if you're not used to it."

She looked back at the dusty trail winding its way down the mountain. "It certainly is," she said. "Somebody told me how to get here, but I was positive I'd got lost."

I handed her the Dixie cup of herb tea, and made a point of sipping mine, so she'd know I wasn't attempting to drug her into white slavery. They get fanciful, these college types. Must be all that reading they do. "If you're looking for Old Rattler, you found him," I told her.

"I thought you must be." She nodded. "Is your name really Rattler?"

"Not on my birth certificate, assuming I had one, but it's done me for a raft of years now. It's what I answer to. How about yourself?"

"My name is Evelyn Johnson." She stumbled a little bit before she said *Johnson.* Just once I wish somebody would come here claiming to be a *Robinson* or an *Evans.* Those names are every bit as common as Jones, Johnson, and Smith, but nobody ever resorts to them. I guess they think I don't know any better. But I didn't bring it up, because she looked troubled enough, without me trying to find out who she really was, and why she was lying about it. Mostly people lie because they feel foolish coming to me at all, and they don't want word to get back to town about it. I let it pass.

"This tea is good," she said, looking surprised. "You made this?"

I smiled. "Cherokee recipe. I'd give it to you, but you couldn't get the ingredients in town—not even at the health food store."

"Somebody told me that you were something of a miracle worker." Her hands fluttered in her lap, because she was sounding silly to herself, but I didn't look surprised, because I wasn't. People have said that for a long time, and it's nothing for me to get puffed up about, because it's not my doing. It's a gift.

"I can do things other folks can't explain," I told her. "That might be a few logs short of a miracle. But I can find water with a forked stick, and charm bees, and locate lost objects. There's some sicknesses I can minister to. Not yours, though."

Her eyes saucered, and she said, "I'm perfectly well, thank you."

I just sat there looking at her, deadpan. I waited. She waited. Silence.

Finally, she turned a little pinker, and ducked her head. "All right," she whispered, like it hurt. "I'm not perfectly well. I'm a nervous wreck. I guess I have to tell you about it."

"That would be best, Evelyn," I said.

"My daughter has been missing since July." She opened her purse and took out a picture of a pretty young girl, soft brown hair like her mother's, and young, happy eyes. "Her name is Amy. She was a freshman at East Tennessee State, and she went rafting with three of her friends on the Nolichucky. They all got separated by the current. When the other three met up farther downstream, they got out and went looking for Amy, but there was no trace of her. She hasn't been seen since."

"They dragged, the river, I reckon." Rock-studded mountain rivers are bad for keeping bodies snagged down where you can't find them.

"They dragged that stretch of the Nolichucky for three days. They even sent down divers. They said even if she'd got wedged under a rock, we'd have something by now." It cost her something to say that.

"Well, she's a grown girl," I said, to turn the flow of words. "Sometimes they get an urge to kick over the traces."

"Not Amy. She wasn't the party type. And even supposing she felt like that—because I know people don't believe a mother's assessment of character—would she run away in her bathing suit? All her clothes were back in her dorm, and her boyfriend was walking up and down the riverbank with the other two students, calling out to her. I don't think she went anywhere on her own."

"Likely not," I said. "But it would have been a comfort to think so, wouldn't it?"

Her eyes went wet. "I kept checking her bank account for withdrawals, and I looked at her past phone bill to see if any calls were made after July sixth. But there's no indication that she was alive past that date. We put posters up all over Johnson City, asking for information about her. There's been no response."

"Of course, the police are doing what they can," I said.

"It's the Wake County sheriff's department, actually," she said. "But the Tennessee Bureau of Investigation is helping them. They don't have much to go on. They've questioned people who were at the river. One fellow claims to have seen a red pickup leaving the scene with a girl in it, but they haven't been able to trace it. The investigators have questioned all her college friends and her professors, but they're running out of leads. It's been three months. Pretty soon they'll quit trying altogether." Her voice shook. "You see, Mr.—Rattler—they all think she's dead."

"So you came to me?"

She nodded. "I didn't know what else to do. Amy's father is no help. He says to let the police handle it. We're divorced, and he's remarried and has a two-year-old son. But Amy is all I've got. I can't let her go!" She set down the paper cup, and covered her face with her hands.

"Could I see that picture of Amy, Mrs.—Johnson?"

"It's Albright," she said softly, handing me the photograph. "Our real last name is Albright. I just felt foolish before, so I didn't tell you my real name."

"It happens," I said, but I wasn't really listening to her apology. I had closed my eyes, and I was trying to make the edges of the snapshot curl around me, so that I would be standing next to the smiling girl, and get some sense of how she was. But the photograph stayed cold and flat in my hand, and no matter how hard I tried to think my way into it, the picture shut me out. There was nothing.

I opened my eyes, and she was looking at me, scared, but waiting, too, for what I could tell her. I handed back the picture. "I could be wrong," I said. "I told you I'm no miracle worker."

"She's dead, isn't she?"

"Oh, yes. Since the first day, I do believe."

She straightened up, and those slanting lines deepened around her mouth. "I've felt it, too," she said. "I'd reach out to her with my thoughts, and I'd feel nothing. Even when she was away at school, I could always sense her somehow. Sometimes I'd call, and she'd say, 'Mom, I was just thinking about you.' But now I reach out to her and I feel empty. She's just—gone."

"Finding mortal remains is a sorrowful business," I said. "And I don't know that I'll be able to help you."

Evelyn Albright shook her head. "I didn't come here about finding Amy's body, Rattler," she said. "I came to find her killer."

I SPENT THREE MORE Dixie cups of herb tea trying to bring back her faith in the Tennessee legal system. Now, I never was much bothered with the process of the law, but, like I told her, in this case I did know that pulling a live coal from an iron pot-bellied stove was a mighty puny miracle compared to finding the one guilty sinner with the mark of Cain in all this world, when there are so many evildoers to choose from. It seemed to me that for all their frailty, the law had the manpower and the system to sort through a thousand possible killers, and to find the one fingerprint or the exact bloodstain that would lay the matter of Amy Albright to rest.

"But you knew she was dead when you touched her picture!" she said. "Can't you tell from that who did it? Can't you see where she is?"

I shook my head. "My grandma might could have done it, rest her soul. She had a wonderful gift of prophecy, but I wasn't trained to it the way she was. *Her* grandmother was a Cherokee medicine woman, and she could read the signs like yesterday's newspaper. I only have the little flicker of Sight I was born with. Some things I know, but I can't see it happening like she could have done."

"What did you see?"

"Nothing. I just felt that the person I was trying to reach in that photograph was gone. And I think the lawmen are the ones you should be trusting to hunt down the killer."

Evelyn didn't see it that way. "They aren't getting anywhere," she kept telling me. "They've questioned all of Amy's friends, and asked the public to call in for information, and now they're at a standstill."

"I hear tell they're sly, these hunters of humans. He could be miles away by now," I said, but she was shaking her head no.

"The sheriff's department thinks it was someone who knew the area. First of all, because that section of the river isn't a tourist spot, and secondly, because he apparently knew where to take Amy so that he wouldn't be seen by anyone with her in the car, and he has managed to keep her from being found. Besides"—she looked away, and her eyes were wet again—"they won't say much about this, but apparently Amy isn't the first. There was a high school girl who disappeared around here two years ago. Some hunters found her body in an abandoned well. I heard one of the sheriff's deputies say that he thought the same person might be responsible for both crimes."

"Then he's like a dog killing sheep. He's doing it for the fun of it, and he must be stopped, because a sheep killer never stops of his own accord."

"People told me you could do marvelous things—find water with a forked stick; heal the sick. I was hoping that you would be able to tell me something about what happened to Amy. I thought you might be able to see who killed her. Because I want him to suffer."

I shook my head. "A dishonest man would string you along," I told her. "A well-meaning one might tell you what you want to hear just to make you feel better. But all I can offer you is the truth: when I touched that photograph, I felt her death, but I saw nothing."

"I had hoped for more." She twisted the rings on her hands. "Do you think you could find her body?"

"I have done something like that, once. When I was twelve, an old man wandered away from his home in December. He was my best friend's grandfather, and they lived on the next farm, so I knew him, you see. I went out with the searchers on that cold, dark afternoon, with the wind baying like a hound through the hollers. As I walked along by myself, I looked up at the clouds, and I had a sudden vision of that old man sitting down next to a broken rail fence. He looked like he was asleep, but I reckoned I knew better. Anyhow, I thought on it as I walked, and I reckoned that the nearest rail fence to his farm was at an abandoned homestead at the back of our land. It was in one of our pastures. I hollered for the others to follow me, and I led them out there to the back pasture."

"Was he there?"

"He was there. He'd wandered off—his mind was going—and when he got lost, he sat down to rest a spell, and he'd dozed off where he sat. Another couple of hours would have finished him, but we got him home to a hot bath and scalding coffee, and he lived till spring."

"He was alive, though."

"Well, that's it. The life in him might have been a beacon. It might not work when the life is gone."

"I'd like you to try, though. If we can find Amy, there might be some clue that will help us find the man who did this."

"I tell you what: you send the sheriff to see me, and I'll have a talk with him. If it suits him, I'll do my level best to find her. But I have to speak to him first."

"Why?"

"Professional courtesy," I said, which was partly true, but, also, because I wanted to be sure she was who she claimed to be. City people usually do give me a fake name out of embarrassment, but I didn't want to chance her being a reporter on the Amy Albright case, or, worse, someone on the killer's side. Besides, I wanted to stay on good terms with Sheriff Spencer Arrowood. We go back a long way. He used to ride out this way on his bike when he was a kid, and he'd sit and listen to tales about the Indian times—stories I'd heard from my grandma—or I'd take him fishing at the trout pool in Broom Creek. One year, his older brother Cal talked me into taking the two of them out owling, since they were too young to hunt. I walked them across every ridge over the holler, and taught them to look for the sweep of wings above the tall grass in the field, and to listen for the sound of the waking owl, ready to track his prey by the slightest sound, the shade of movement. I taught them how to make owl calls, to where we couldn't tell if it was an owl calling out from the woods or one of us. Look out, I told them. When the owl calls your name, it means death.

Later on, they became owls, I reckon. Cal Arrowood went to Vietnam, and died in a dark jungle full of screeching birds. I felt him go. And Spencer grew up to be sheriff, so I reckon he hunts prey of his own by the slightest sound, and by one false move. A lot of people had heard him call their name.

I hadn't seen much of Spencer since he grew up, but I hoped we were still buddies. Now that he was sheriff, I knew he could make trouble for me if he wanted to, and so far he never has. I wanted to keep things cordial.

"All right," said Evelyn. "I can't promise they'll come out here, but I will tell them what you said. Will you call and tell me what you're going to do?"

"No phone," I said, jerking my thumb back toward the shack. "Send the sheriff out here. He'll let you know."

SHE MUST HAVE GONE to the sheriff's office, straightaway after leaving my place. I thought she would. I wasn't surprised at that, because I could see that she wasn't doing much else right now besides brood about her

loss. She needed an ending so that she could go on. I had tried to make
her take a milk jug of herb tea, because I never saw anybody so much
in need of a night's sleep, but she wouldn't have it. "Just find my girl
for me," she'd said. "Help us find the man who did it, and put him away.
Then I'll sleep."

When the brown sheriff's car rolled up my dirt road about noon the
next day, I was expecting it. I was sitting in my cane chair on the porch
whittling a face onto a hickory broom handle when I saw the flash of
the gold star on the side of the car door, and the sheriff himself got out.
I waved, and he touched his hat, like they used to do in cowboy movies.
I reckon little boys who grow up to be sheriff watch a lot of cowboy
movies in their day. I didn't mind Spencer Arrowood, though. He hadn't
changed all that much from when I knew him. There were gray flecks in
his fair hair, but they didn't show much, and he never did make it to six
feet, but he'd managed to keep his weight down, so he looked all right.
He was kin to the Pigeon Roost Arrowoods, and like them he was smart
and honest without being a glad-hander. He seemed a little young to be
the high sheriff to an old-timer like me, but that's never a permanent
problem for anybody, is it? Anyhow, I trusted him, and that's worth a
lot in these sorry times.

I made him sit down in the other cane chair, because I hate people
hovering over me while I whittle. He asked did I remember him.

"Spencer," I said, "I'd have to be drinking something a lot stronger
than chamomile tea to forget you."

He grinned, but then he seemed to remember what sad errand had
brought him out here, and the faint lines came back around his eyes. "I
guess you've heard about this case I'm on."

"I was told. It sounds to me like we've got a human sheep killer in
the fold. I hate to hear that. Killing for pleasure is an unclean act. I said
I'd help the law any way I could to dispose of the killer, if it was all
right with you."

"That's what I heard," the sheriff said. "For what it's worth, the TBI
agrees with you about the sort of person we're after, although they didn't
liken it to *sheep killing*. They meant the same thing, though."

"So Mrs. Albright did come to see you?" I asked him, keeping my
eyes fixed on the curl of the beard of that hickory face.

"Sure did, Rattler," said the sheriff. "She tells me that you've agreed
to try to locate Amy's body."

"It can't do no harm to try," I said. "Unless you mind too awful much.
I don't reckon you believe in such like."

He smiled. "It doesn't matter what I believe if it works, does it, Rattler? You're welcome to try. But, actually, I've thought of another way
that you might be useful in this case."

"What's that?"

"You heard about the other murdered girl, didn't you? They found her body in an abandoned well up on Locust Ridge."

"Whose land?"

"National forest now. The homestead has been in ruins for at least a century. But that's a remote area of the country. It's a couple of miles from the Appalachian Trail, and just as far from the river, so I wouldn't expect an outsider to know about it. The only way up there is on an old country road. The TBI psychologist thinks the killer has dumped Amy Albright's body somewhere in the vicinity of the other burial. He says they do that. Serial killers, I mean. They establish territories."

"Painters do that," I said, and the sheriff remembered his roots well enough to know that I meant a mountain lion, not a fellow with an easel. We called them painters in the old days, when there were more of them in the mountains than just a scream and a shadow every couple of years. City people think I'm crazy to live on the mountain where the wild creatures are, and then they shut themselves up in cities with the most pitiless killers ever put on this earth: each other. I marvel at the logic.

"Since you reckon he's leaving his victims in one area, why haven't you searched it?"

"Oh, we have," said the sheriff, looking weary. "I've had volunteers combing that mountain, and they haven't turned up a thing. There's a lot of square miles of forest to cover up there. Besides, I think our man has been more careful about concealment this time. What we need is more help. Not more searchers, but a more precise location."

"Where do I come in? You said you wanted me to do more than just find the body. Not that I can even promise to do that."

"I want to get your permission to try something that may help us catch this individual," Spencer Arrowood was saying.

"What's that?"

"I want you to give some newspaper interviews. Local TV, even, if we can talk them into it. I want to publicize the fact that you are going to search for Amy Albright on Locust Ridge. Give them your background as a psychic and healer. I want a lot of coverage on this."

I shuddered. You don't have to be psychic to foresee the outcome of that. A stream of city people in colorless cars, wanting babies and diet tonics.

"When were you planning to search for the body, Rattler?"

"I was waiting on you. Any day will suit me, as long as it isn't raining. Rain distracts me."

"Okay, let's announce that you're conducting the psychic search of Locust Ridge next Tuesday. I'll send some reporters out here to interview you. Give them the full treatment."

"How does all this harassment help you catch the killer, Spencer?"

"This is not for publication, Rattler, but I think we can smoke him out," said the sheriff. "We announce in all the media that you're going to be dowsing for bones on Tuesday. We insist that you can work wonders, and that we're confident you'll find Amy. If the killer is a local man, he'll see the notices, and get nervous. I'm betting that he'll go up there Monday night, just to make sure the body is well-hidden. There's only one road into that area. If we can keep the killer from spotting us, I think he'll lead us to Amy's body."

"That's fine, Sheriff, but how are you going to track this fellow in the dark?"

Spencer Arrowood smiled. "Why, Rattler," he said, "I've got the Sight."

YOU HAVE TO DO WHAT YOU CAN to keep a sheep killer out of your fold, even if it means talking to a bunch of reporters who don't know ass from aardvark. I put up with all their fool questions, and dispensed about a dozen jugs of comfrey and chamomile tea, and I even told that blond lady on Channel 7 that she didn't need any herbs for getting pregnant, because she already was, which surprised her so much that she almost dropped her microphone, but I reckon my hospitality worked to Spencer Arrowood's satisfaction, because he came along Monday afternoon to show me a stack of newspapers with my picture looking out of the page, and he thanked me for being helpful.

"Don't thank me," I said. "Just let me go with you tonight. You'll need all the watchers you can get to cover that ridge."

He saw the sense of that, and agreed without too much argument. I wanted to see what he meant about "having the Sight," because I'd known him since he was knee-high to a grasshopper, and he didn't have so much as a flicker of the power. None of the Arrowoods did. But he was smart enough in regular ways, and I knew he had some kind of ace up his sleeve.

An hour past sunset that night I was standing in a clearing on Locust Ridge, surrounded by law enforcement people from three counties. There were nine of us. We were so far from town that there seemed to be twice as many stars, so dark was that October sky without the haze of street lights to bleed out the fainter ones. The sheriff was talking one notch above a whisper, in case the suspect had come early. He opened a big cardboard box, and started passing out yellow and black binoculars.

"There are called ITT Night Mariners," he told us. "I borrowed ten pair from a dealer at Watauga Lake, so take care of them. They run about $2500 apiece."

"Are they infrared?" somebody asked him.

"No. But they collect available light and magnify it up to 20,000 times, so they will allow you excellent night vision. The full moon will give us all the light we need. You'll be able to walk around without a flashlight, and you'll be able to see obstacles, terrain features, and anything that's out there moving around."

"The military developed this technology in Desert Storm," said Deputy LeDonne.

"Well, let's hope it works for us tonight," said the sheriff. "Try looking through them."

I held them up to my eyes. They didn't weigh much—about the same as two apples, I reckoned. Around me, everybody was muttering surprise, tickled pink about this new gadget. I looked through mine, and I could see the dark shapes of trees up on the hill—not in a clump, the way they look at night, but one by one, with spaces between them. The sheriff walked away from us, and I could see him go, but when I took the Night Mariners down from my eyes, he was gone. I put them back on, and there he was again.

"I reckon you do have the *Sight*, Sheriff," I told him. "Your man won't know we're watching him with these babies."

"I wonder if they're legal for hunting," said a Unicoi County man. "This sure beats spotlighting deer."

"They're illegal for deer," Spencer told him. "But they're perfect for catching sheep killers." He smiled over at me. "Now that we've tested the equipment, y'all split up. I've given you your patrol areas. Don't use your walkie-talkies unless it's absolutely necessary. Rattler, you just go where you please, but try not to let the suspect catch you at it. Are you going to do your stuff?"

"I'm going to try to let it happen," I said. It's a gift. I don't control it. I just receive.

We went our separate ways. I walked a while, enjoying the new magic of seeing the night woods same as a possum would, but when I tried to clear my mind and summon up that other kind of seeing, I found I couldn't do it, so, instead of helping, the Night Mariners were blinding me. I slipped the fancy goggles into the pocket of my jacket, and stood there under an oak tree for a minute or two, trying to open my heart for guidance. I whispered a verse from Psalm 27: *Teach me thy way, O Lord, and lead me in a plain path, because of mine enemies.* Then I looked up at the stars and tried to think of nothing. After a while I started walking, trying to keep my mind clear and go where I was led.

Maybe five minutes later, maybe an hour, I was walking across an abandoned field, overgrown with scrub cedars. The moonlight glowed in the long grass, and the cold air made my ears and fingers tingle. When I touched a post of the broken split-rail fence, it happened. I saw the field in daylight. I saw brown grass, drying up in the summer heat, and flies making lazy circles around my head. When I looked down at the fence rail at my feet, I saw her. She was wearing a watermelon-colored T-shirt and jean shorts. Her brown hair spilled across her shoulders and twined with the chicory weeds. Her eyes were closed. I could see a smear of blood at one corner of her mouth, and I knew. I looked up at the moon, and when I looked back, the grass was dead, and the darkness had closed in again. I crouched behind a cedar tree before I heard the footsteps.

They weren't footsteps, really. Just the swish sound of boots and trouser legs brushing against tall, dry grass. I could see his shape in the moonlight, and he wasn't one of the searchers. He was here to keep his secrets. He stepped over the fence rail, and walked toward the one big tree in the clearing—a twisted old maple, big around as two men. He knelt down beside that tree, and I saw him moving his hands on the ground, picking up a dead branch, and brushing leaves away. He looked, rocked back on his heels, leaned forward, and started pushing the leaves back again.

They hadn't given me a walkie-talkie, and I didn't hold with guns, though I knew he might have one. I wasn't really part of the posse. Old Rattler with his Twinkies and his root tea and his prophecies. I was just bait. But I couldn't risk letting the sheep killer slip away. Finding the grave might catch him; might not. None of my visions would help Spencer in a court of law, which is why I mostly stick to dispensing tonics and leave evil alone.

I cupped my hands to my mouth and gave an owl cry, loud as I could. Just one. The dark shape jumped up, took a couple of steps up and back, moving its head from side to side.

Far off in the woods, I heard an owl reply. I pulled out the Night Mariners then, and started scanning the hillsides around that meadow, and in less than a minute, I could make out the sheriff, with that badge pinned to his coat, standing at the edge of the trees with his field glasses on, scanning the clearing. I started waving and pointing.

The sheep killer was hurrying away now, but he was headed in my direction, and I thought, *Risk it. What called your name, Rattler, wasn't an owl.* So just as he's about to pass by, I stepped out at him, and said, "Hush now. You'll scare the deer."

He was startled into screaming, and he swung out at me with something that flashed silver in the moonlight. As I went down, he broke into a run, crashing through weeds, noisy enough to scare the deer across the state line—but the moonlight wasn't bright enough for him to get far. He covered maybe twenty yards before his foot caught on a fieldstone, and he went down. I saw the sheriff closing distance, and I went to help, but I felt light-headed all of a sudden, and my shirt was wet. I was glad it wasn't light enough to see colors in that field. Red was never my favorite.

I OPENED MY EYES and shut them again, because the flashing orange light of the rescue squad van was too bright for the ache in my head. When

I looked away, I saw cold and dark, and knew I was still on Locust Ridge. "Where's Spencer Arrowood?" I asked a blue jacket bending near me.

"Sheriff! He's coming around."

Spencer Arrowood was bending over me then, with that worried look he used to have when a big one hit his fishing line. "We got him," he said. "You've got a puncture in your lung that will need more than herbal tea to fix, but you're going to be all right, Rattler."

"Since when did you get the Sight?" I asked him. But he was right. I needed to get off that mountain and get well, because the last thing I saw before I went down was the same scene that came to me when I first saw her car and walk toward my cabin. I saw what Evelyn Albright was going to do at the trial, with that flash of silver half hidden in her hand, and I didn't want it to end that way.

J. A. Jance once confessed that she gets tired of being called an "overnight success" because, in fact, she spent many years driving up and down the West Coast promoting her books long before she had a sizable audience. J. A. has been a high school teacher and a school librarian on an Arizona Indian reservation. It was this latter occupation that led to her writing Joanna Bradley novels (DESERT HEAT, 1993; and TOMBSTONE COURAGE, 1994), fine books about life in present-day Arizona.

Oil and Water
J. A. JANCE

I was headed into the precinct briefing room when Captain Waldron stopped me. "You're up, Detective Lanier. We've just had a 9-1-1 call reporting a homicide out in May Valley. Detective Barry's gassing up the car. He'll pick you up out front."

Of all the detectives who work for the King County Police Department, Detective James Joseph Barry was my least favorite possible partner. A recent transfer from Chicago P.D., Detective Barry shared his reactionary views with all concerned. Although barely thirty-five, his unbearably tedious monologues made Mike Royko's curmudgeonly rumblings sound like those of a lily-livered liberal.

But newly appointed to the Detective Division, I didn't dare question the captain when it came to handing out assignments. I shut my mouth, kept my opinions to myself, and headed for the door.

Moments after I stepped outside, the unmarked car skidded to a stop beside me. As I slipped into the rider's seat, Detective Barry made a big deal of checking out my legs. He was obvious as hell, but I ignored it.

"So," he said, ramming the car into gear and careening through the rain-slicked parking lot, "how come a great-looking babe like you isn't married?"

"Homicide dicks aren't much good in the marriage department," I told him evenly. "A fact of life your wife must have figured out all on her own."

Touché! The fleeting grimace on his face told me my remark had hit the intended target. "Shut up and drive, will you?" I said.

He did, for the time being. Meanwhile, I got on the horn to ask Records what they knew about where we were headed and what we'd be up against. From the radio I gathered that patrol officers were already on the scene. The victim was dead and the crime scene secure, so there was no need for either flashing lights or siren. Detective Barry made liberal use of both.

It was a chilly October night. After a delightful Indian-summer September, this was winter's first real rainstorm. The pavement was glassy and dangerously slick with mixed accumulations of oil and water. Instead of telling him to slow down, I made sure my seatbelt was securely fastened and thanked God for airbags.

Over the rhythmic slap of the windshield wipers, Barry launched off into one of his interminable stories about the good old days back in Chicago, this one featuring his late, unlamented, bowling partner—the beady-eyed Beady Dodgson.

"So I says to him, I says, 'Beady, you old billy goat. For chrissakes, when you gonna wash that damn shirt of yours?' And he says back, he says, 'Barry, you stupid mick, after the damn tournament. Whaddaya tink? You want I should wash away my luck?' "

Detective Barry liked nothing better than the sound of his own voice. However, boring tales of reminiscence were far preferable to questions about my current marital status which seemed to surface every time the two of us had any joint dealings. Detective Barry made no secret of the fact that he thought I should be home taking care of a husband and kids. He didn't approve of what he called *girl* detectives. Which is no doubt why Captain Waldron made sure he was stuck with me. Or vice versa.

"Turn here," I said. "Take the first right up the hill."

As we turned off the May Valley Highway and headed up a steep, winding incline, the headlights cut through sheets of slanting raindrops illuminating a yellow "Livestock" warning sign along the road. Detective Barry slowed the car to a bare crawl.

City born and bred, Detective Barry was in his element and totally at home when confronting a group of urbanized, street-toughened teenagers. It was strange to realize that he was petrified of encountering stray cattle or horses on one of King County's numerous rural roads.

At last the radio crackled back to life and the harried Records clerk's voice came over the air to deliver what scanty information was then available. The victim's name was de Gasteneau, Renée Denise de Gasteneau. A computer check of the de Gasteneau address in the 18500 block of Rainier Vista had turned up six priors in the previous six weeks—two domestics, one civil disturbance, and the rest noise complaints. Chances were Renée de Gasteneau was probably none too popular with her neighbors.

"One other thing," the operator from records added. "Her husband's there on the scene right now. Emile de Gasteneau."

The name was one I had seen in local society columns from time to time but most recently in the police blotter. "Is that as in Dr. de Gasteneau, the plastic surgeon?" I asked.

"That's the one. When officers responded to the first domestic, they let him go. The second time they picked him up. He's out on bail for that one."

"Three's the charm," I muttered.

Domestic disturbances are tough calls for all cops. For me personally they were especially disturbing. "Why do women stay with men like that?" I demanded. "Why the hell don't they get out while there's still time?"

Detective Barry shrugged. "Maybe they stay because they don't have anywhere else to go."

"That's no excuse," I said. And I meant it with every ounce of my being.

I left the very first time Mark hit me—the only time Mark hit me—and I never went back. It was less than six weeks after our wedding—a three-ring circus, storybook, church, and country-club affair with all the necessary trimmings. I came back to the Park and Ride after work late one Friday afternoon and discovered that someone had broken into my little Fiat and stolen both the stereo and the steering wheel.

That Fiat was my baby. It was the first car I had chosen, bought, and paid for all on my own. When I told Mark about it, I expected some sympathy. Instead, he lit into me. He said I should have had better sense than to leave it at the Park and Ride in the first place. The argument got totally out of hand, and before I knew what was happening, he hit me—knocked me out cold.

Once I picked myself up off the kitchen floor, I called the cops. I remember trying to keep the blood from my loosened teeth from dripping into the telephone receiver. The two patrol officers who responded were wonderful. One of them kept Mark out of the room while the other one stuck with me. He followed me around the house while I threw my clothes and makeup into suitcases and plastic trash bags. He helped amass an odd assortment of hastily collected household goods—dishes, silverware, pots, and pans. I made off with Aunt Mindy's wedding present waffle iron, one of the two popcorn poppers, and every single set of matching towels and washcloths I could lay hands on.

The two cops were more than happy to help me drag my collection of stuff downstairs and out the door where they obligingly loaded it into a waiting Yellow cab. Now that I'm a police officer myself, I know why they were so eager to help me. I was the exception, not the rule. Most women don't leave. Ever.

By then our car was rounding a tight curve on the winding foothills road called Rainier Vista, although any view of Mount Rainier was totally shrouded in clouds. Ahead of us the narrow right-of-way and the lowering clouds were brightly lit by the orange glow of flashing lights from numerous emergency vehicles—several patrol cars and what was evidently a now totally unnecessary ambulance.

The figure of a rain-slickered patrol officer emerged out of the darkness. The cop motioned for us to park directly behind one of the medical examiner's somber gray vans.

"How the hell did the meat wagon beat us?" Detective Barry demanded irritably.

"Believe me," I said, "it wasn't because you didn't try."

The uniformed deputy hurried over to our car. Detective Barry lowered his window. "What's up?"

"The husband's waiting out back. I let him know detectives were on the way; told him you'd probably want to talk to him."

Barry nodded. "I'm sure we do."

"That's his Jaguar over there in the driveway," the deputy added.

A Jag, I thought. That figured. Mark loved his Corvette more than life itself. Certainly more than he loved me. He beat the crap out of me, but as far as I know, he never damaged so much as a fender on that precious car of his.

By the time Detective Barry rolled his window back up, I was already out of the car and headed up the sidewalk. He caught me before I made it to the front porch.

"Let me handle the guy, Detective Lanier," Barry said. "I know where he's coming from."

"I don't give a damn where he's coming from," I returned. "Just as long as he goes to jail."

"Jumping to conclusions, aren't we?" Barry taunted.

His patronizing attitude bugged the hell out of me. Yes, he had been a cop a whole lot longer than I had, transferring out to Washington State after years of being a detective in Chicago. But as a transferring officer, he had been cycled through King County's training program all the same, and he had spent his obligatory time in Patrol right along with the new hires. When it was time to make the move from Patrol to Detective Division, the two of us did it at almost the same time. Since scores on training exams are posted, I knew I had outscored him on every written exam we'd been given.

I shoved my clenched fists out of sight in the pockets of my already dripping raincoat. "Cram it, Barry," I told him. "I'll do my best to keep an open mind."

Looking at it from the outside, the house was one of those you expect to find featured on the pages of *House Beautiful* or *Architectural Digest*— vast expanses of clear glass and straight up-and-downs punctuated here and there by unexpectedly sharp angles. The place was lit up like the proverbial Christmas tree with warmly inviting lights glowing through every window. Appearances can be deceiving. Once inside, it was clear the entire house was a shambles.

Even in the well-appointed entryway, every available surface—including the burled maple entryway table—was covered with an accumulation of junk and debris. There were dirty dishes and glasses everywhere, along with a collection of empty beer and soda cans, overflowing ashtrays, and unopened mail. Under the table was a mound of at least a month's worth of yellowed, unread newspapers, still rolled up and encircled by rubber bands.

The human mind is an amazing device. One glance at that hopeless disarray threw me back ten years to the weeks and months just after I left Mark. Once beyond the initial blast of hurt and anger, I closeted myself away in a tiny, two-room apartment and drifted into a miasma of despair and self-loathing. It was a time when I didn't do the dishes, answer the phone, open the mail, pay the bills, or take messages off the machine. Even the simplest tasks became impossibilities, the smallest decisions unthinkable.

If it hadn't been for Aunt Mindy and Uncle Ed, I might be there still. The telephone company had already disconnected my phone for lack of payment when Aunt Mindy and Uncle Ed showed up on my doorstep early one Saturday morning. They knocked and knocked. When I wouldn't open the door, Uncle Ed literally broke it down. They packed me up, cleaned out the place, and took me home with them. One piece at a time, they helped me start gluing my life back together. Six months later I found myself down at the county courthouse, filling out an application to become a police officer.

Thrusting that sudden series of painful memories aside, I took a deep breath and focused my attention on the dead woman lying naked in the middle of the parquet entryway floor. Her pale skin was spotlit by the soft light of a huge crystal chandelier that hung down from the soaring ceiling some three stories above us.

Careful to disturb nothing, I stepped near enough to examine her more closely. Renée Denise de Gasteneau was white, blonde, and probably not much more than thirty. She lay sprawled in an awkward position. One knee was drawn up and thrust forward—as though she had been struck down in mid-stride.

While I bent over the body, Detective James Barry moved farther into the entryway and glanced into the living room.

"I'll tell you one thing," he announced. "This broad was almost as shitty a housekeeper as my ex-wife."

"Believe me," I returned coldly, "housekeeping is the least of this woman's problems."

Tom Hammond, an assistant from the Medical Examiner's office, was standing off to one side, watching us quizzically. "What do you think, Tom?" I asked.

"I've seen worse—housekeeping, that is."

"Forget the damn housekeeping, for godssake! What do you think killed her?"

"Too soon to tell," he replied. "I can see some bruising on the back of the neck, right there where her hair is parted. Could be from a blow to the back of the head. Could be she was strangled. We won't know for sure until we get her downtown."

"How long's she been dead?" Barry asked.

"Hard to say. Ten to twelve hours at least. Maybe longer."

About that time one of the county's crime-scene techs showed up with their photography equipment as well as the Alternate Light Source box that can be used to locate all kinds of trace evidence from latent fingerprints to stray strands of hair or thread or carpet fuzz. What crime techs need more than anything is for people to get the hell out of the way and leave them alone.

"Let's go talk to her husband," I said.

"Suits me," Detective Barry said.

We found Dr. Emile de Gasteneau sitting in an Adirondack chair on a covered deck at the rear of the house. He sat there, sobbing quietly, his face buried in his hands. When he glanced up at our approach, his cheeks were wet with tears. "Are you the detectives?" he croaked.

I nodded and flashed my badge in front of him, but he barely noticed. "I didn't mean for it to end this way," he groaned.

"What way is that, Dr. de Gasteneau?" I asked.

"With her dead like this," he answered hopelessly. "I just wanted to get on with my life. I never meant to hurt her."

My initial reaction was to Mirandize the guy on the spot. It sounded to me as though he was ready to blurt out a full-blown confession, and I didn't want it disqualified in a court of law on some stupid technicality.

Evidently Detective Barry didn't agree. He stepped forward and moved me aside. "How's that, Dr. de Gasteneau? How'd you hurt your wife?"

"I left her," the seemingly distraught man answered. "I just couldn't go on living a lie. I told her I wanted out, but I offered her a good settlement, a fair settlement. I told her she could have the entire equity from the house on the condition she sell it as soon as possible. I thought she'd take the money and run—find someplace less expensive to live and keep the change.

"Instead, she just let the place go to ruin. You can see it's a mess. There's a For Sale sign out front, but as far as I know, no one's even been out here to look at it. I think the real estate agent is ashamed to bring anyone by. I don't blame her. Who would want to buy a $750,000 pigsty—"

"Excuse me, Dr. de Gasteneau," I interrupted. "It sounds to me as though you're more upset by the fact that your wife was a poor house-keeper than you are by the fact she's dead."

The widower stiffened and glared at me. "That was rude."

"So is murder," I countered.

Giving up on any possibility of a voluntary confession, I took my note-pad out of my pocket. "Are you the one who called 9-1-1?"

De Gasteneau nodded. "Yes."

"What time?"

He glanced at his watch—an expensive jewel-encrusted timepiece the size of a doorknob, with luminous hands that glowed in the dim light of the porch. "Right after I got here," he answered. "About an hour ago now."

Without a word, Detective Barry stepped off the porch and moved purposefully toward the Jaguar parked a few feet away in the driveway. He put his hand on the hood, checking for residual warmth, and then nodded in my direction.

"Since you and your wife were separated, why did you come here?"

"Mrs. Wilbur called me."

"Who's she?"

"A neighbor from just across the road. She was worried about Renée. She called my office and asked me to come check on her—on Renée."

"Why?"

"I don't know. She was worried about her, I guess. I told her I'd come over right after work."

"Why was she worried? Had she seen strange cars, heard noises, what?"

"I don't know. She didn't say, and I didn't ask. I came out as soon as I could. I had an engagement."

I was about to ask him what kind of engagement when Detective Barry sauntered back up onto the porch. "That's a pretty slick Jagwire you've got out there. Always wanted to get me one of those. What kind of gas mileage does that thing get?"

"It's not that good on gas," de Gasteneau admitted.

Jagwire! The man sounded like he'd just crawled out from under a rock. Renée de Gasteneau was dead, and here was this jerk of a Detective Barry sounding like a hick out kicking the tires at some exotic car dealership. How the hell did Captain Waldron expect me to work with a creep like that?

"How about if we step inside, Dr. de Gasteneau?" I said. "Maybe you can tell us whether or not anything is missing from your wife's house."

What I really wanted to do was to get inside where the light was better. I wanted to check out Emile de Gasteneau's arms and wrists and the backs of his hands to see if there were any scratches, any signs of a life-

and-death struggle that might have left telltale marks on the living flesh of Renée de Gasteneau's killer.

Without a word the good doctor de Gasteneau stood up and went inside. "Just wait," Detective Barry whispered over my shoulder as we followed him into the house. "Next thing you know, he's going to try telling us a one-armed man did it. You know—like in *The Fugitive.*"

"Please," I sighed. "I got it. You don't have to explain."

As we trailed Dr. de Gasteneau from one impossibly messy room to another, I stole several discreet glances in the direction of his hands and arms. I was more disappointed than I should have been when there was nothing to see.

Checking throughout the house, it was difficult to tell whether or not anything was missing. Several television sets and VCR's were in their proper places as were two very expensive stereo systems. The jewelry was a tougher call, but as far as de Gasteneau could tell, none of that was missing, either.

"When's the last time you saw your wife?" I asked as we left the upstairs master bedroom and headed back toward the main level of the house.

He paused before he answered. "Two weeks ago," he answered guardedly. "But you probably already know about that."

"You mean the time when you were arrested for hitting her?"

"Yes."

"And you haven't seen her since then?"

"No."

"What time do you get off work?"

"Between four and four-thirty. I'm my own boss. I come and go when I damn well please."

"But you told the neighbor, Mrs. Wilbur, that you'd come here as soon as you could after work. The 9-1-1 call didn't come in until a little after eight. Where were you between four and eight?"

"I already told you. I had an engagement."

"With whom?"

"I don't have to tell you that."

"Phyllis—" Detective Barry interjected, but I silenced him with a single hard-edged stare. I was on track, and I wasn't about to let him pull me away.

"You're right," I said easily. "You don't have to tell us anything at all. But if you don't, I guarantee you we'll find out anyway—one way or the other."

It was nothing more than an empty threat, but de Gasteneau fell for it all the same. "I was seeing my friend," he conceded angrily. "We met for a drink."

Just the way he answered triggered a warning signal in my mind, made me wonder if we were dealing with a lover's triangle. "What kind of friend?" I asked. "Male or female?"

"A male friend," he answered.

So much for the lover theory, I thought. I said, "What's his name?"

De Gasteneau looked at Detective Barry in a blatant appeal for help, but I wasn't about to be derailed. "What's his name?" I insisted.

"Garth," de Gasteneau answered flatly. "His name's Garth Homewood. But please don't call him. Believe me, he's got nothing to do with all this."

"Why would we think he did?" I asked.

We were descending the broad, carpeted stairway when, suddenly, de Gasteneau sank down on the bottom step.

"Garth and I are lovers," he answered unexpectedly. "He's the whole reason I left Renée in the first place. I guess that's one of the reasons she was so upset about it. Maybe if I'd left her for another woman, it wouldn't have bothered her so much."

These are the nineties. Detective Barry and I are both adults and we are both cops. I guess de Gasteneau's admission shouldn't have shocked or surprised either one of us, but it did. My partner looked stunned. I felt like someone who pokes something he thinks is a dead twig only to have it turn out to be a quick brown snake. Once again I was struck by an incredible feeling of kinship toward the dead woman. Poor Renée de Gasteneau. It occurred to me that learning her husband was gay was probably as much a blow to her self-esteem as Mark Lanier's punishing balled fist had been to mine.

"Why?" I said. Not why did you leave her? That much was clear. But why did you marry her in the first place?

The last question as well as the unspoken ones that followed were more reflex than anything else. I didn't really expect Emile de Gasteneau to answer, but he did.

"I tricked her," he admitted, somberly. "I wanted an heir, a child. Someone to leave all this to." His despairing glance encompassed the whole house and everything in it. "Except it didn't work out. I picked the wrong woman. Renée loved me, I guess, but I didn't care about her. Not the same way she did for me. And when it turned out she couldn't get pregnant, it was too much. After a while, I couldn't bring myself to try anymore. It was too dishonest. Now she's dead. Although I didn't kill her, I know it's my fault."

The tears came again. While Emile de Gasteneau sat sobbing on the bottom stair, Detective Barry tapped me on the shoulder.

"Come on," he said, jerking his head toward the door. "Leave the guy alone. Let's go talk to the woman across the street."

I thought it was uncharacteristically nice of Barry to want to give the poor man some privacy, but outside and safely out of earshot, James Joseph Barry, ex-Chicago cop, let go with an amazing string of oaths.

"The guy's a frigging queer!" he raged. "For all we know, he's probably dying of AIDS. Jesus Christ! Did he breathe on us? You got a breath spray on you?"

Detective Barry's only obvious concession toward society's current mania for political correctness was refraining from use of the N-word in racially mixed company. The word "gay" had neither entered his vocabulary nor penetrated his consciousness. I, too, had been shocked by Emile de Gasteneau's revelation, but not for the same reason my partner was.

We walked across the road together and made our way down a steeply pitched driveway to the house we had been told belonged to a family named Wilbur. This one was somewhat older than Renée de Gasteneau's had been, and slightly less showy, but it was still a very expensive piece of suburban real estate.

Detective Barry continued to mutter under his breath as he rang the doorbell. An attractive woman in her late sixties or early seventies answered the door and switched on the porch light.

"Yes?" she said guardedly. "Can I help you?"

I moved forward and showed her my badge. "We're Detectives Barry and Lanier," I explained. "We're investigating the incident across the street. Are you Mrs. Wilbur?"

She nodded but without opening the door any wider. "Inez," she said, "what do you want?"

"I understand you were the person who called Dr. de Gasteneau. Is that true?"

"Yes."

"Why did you call him? Did you hear something unusual? See something out of the ordinary?"

"Well, yes. I mean no. It's just that Renée was always on the go, rushing off this way or that. When her car didn't move all day long, I was worried."

I looked back over my shoulder. From where I stood on the front step of Inez Wilbur's porch, only the topmost gable of the de Gasteneau roof was visible over the crest of the hill. Inez Wilbur seemed to follow both my movements as well as my train of thought.

"You're right," she put in quickly. "It's not easy to see from where you are, but I can see her house from upstairs, from my room ..."

"Mama," a man's voice said from somewhere behind her. "Who is it?"

"It's nothing, Carl. Go back to your program. I'll be done here in a minute."

"But it's a boring program, Mama," he replied. "I don't like it."

The voice had the basso timbre of an adult, but the words were the whining complaints of a dissatisfied child.

"Please, Carl," Inez Wilbur said, with a tight frown. "Change channels then. I'll be done in a minute."

"Who's Carl?" I asked.

"He's my son," she answered. "He's not a child, but he's like a child, if you know what I mean. All this would upset him terribly."

"All what would upset him terribly?" I asked.

A look of anguished confusion washed over Inez Wilbur's delicately made-up face. "About Mrs. de Gasteneau."

"What about her?"

"She's dead, isn't she?"

"Mama," Carl said behind her, "who is it? Is it company? Are we going to have dessert now?"

Inez let go of the doorknob and covered her face with her hands. Slowly, as though being pushed by the wind, the heavy wooden door swung open.

A large, open-faced man with a wild headful of slightly graying hair stood illuminated in the vestibule behind her. He was wearing a short-sleeved shirt and expertly playing with a yo-yo. His muscular forearms were raked with long deep parallel scratches—a last desperate message from a dying woman.

"Hello, Carl," I said quietly. "My name's Detective Lanier and this is Detective Barry. We'd like to talk to you for a few minutes if you don't mind."

Inez stepped aside and let us into the house while Carl Wilbur's mouth broke into a broad, gap-toothed grin. "Detectives? Really? Do you hear that, Mama? They're cops, and they want to talk to me!"

Inez Wilbur's face collapsed like a shattered teacup, and she began to cry.

Detective Barry pulled his Miranda card out of his wallet. "I'll bet you've seen this on TV, Carl. It's called reading you your rights. You have the right to remain silent . . ."

IT WAS SIX O'CLOCK the next morning before we finally finished our paper. Inez Wilbur had tried to explain to Renée de Gasteneau that Carl was watching her, that she should always pull her curtains and be more careful about walking around the house without any clothes on. But Renée had ignored the warnings just as she had ignored Carl himself.

In the aftermath of Emile's defection, Renée de Gasteneau had searched for validation of her womanhood by taking on all comers. Carl Wilbur, her curious neighbor, had watched all the proceedings with rapt fascination, learning as he did so that there was more to life than he had previously suspected, that there were some interesting things that he wanted to try for himself. And when those things were denied him, he had responded with unthinking but lethal rage. He had thrown a lifeless Renée de Gasteneau to the floor, like a discarded and broken doll.

I was dragging myself out to the parking lot when Captain Waldron caught me by the front door. He hurried up to me, his kind face etched with concern.

"Are you all right?" he asked.

"Just tired. Worn out."

Detective Barry drove by out in the parking lot. He tapped on his horn and waved. I waved back.

"Tough case," Captain Waldron said, "but you handled it like a pair of champs. How do you like working with Detective Barry?"

"He's okay," I said.

Waldron nodded. "Good. I was worried about whether or not you two could get along."

I laughed. "Why? Because Barry's an asshole?"

"No, because of his divorce."

"What about his divorce?"

"You mean you don't know about that? It's common knowledge. I thought everyone knew. His wife left him because he beat her up and she turned him in. That's why he transferred out here from Chicago. Her father's a captain on the Berwyn P.D. somewhere outside of Chicago. I guess things got pretty sticky for a while, but with his track record for cracking serial-killer cases, the sheriff was willing to take him on."

"No questions asked?" I demanded.

Waldron shrugged. "I think he had to complete one of those anger-management courses."

"Did he?"

"As far as I know. I just wanted to let you know how glad I was that the two of you were able to get along."

"We got along, all right," I said. "Just like oil and water."

Jan Grape is one of today's best short-story writers, and will soon join the ranks of novelists, as well. Jan and her husband Elmer run a mystery bookstore in Austin, Texas. Jan also finds time to be the guiding spirit behind the Private Eye Writers of America, an organization begun by mystery novelist Robert J. Randisi.

No Simple Solution
JAN GRAPE

I

"It sounded like an open-and-shut case to me when I first heard about it. And besides, who can blame the guy?" I said. "If my five-year-old child had been killed in a drive-by shooting, I might have done the same thing Eloy Stewart did." The drive-by shooter had been tried and acquitted and that's when Mr. Stewart took matters into his own hands, allegedly killing Benito Alvarez, age twenty, three days ago. Also killed was a sixteen-year-old girl who'd been with Alvarez.

C. J. snorted. "No *might have* in my mind, Jenny. I'd have gone after the little turd with my bare hands," she said. Her full name is Cinnamon Jemima Gunn, but only close friends know her secret. When she gets that haughty look she reminds me of photos I've seen of Nefertiti.

C. J. and I have owned and operated a detective agency since my ex-cop-turned-private eye husband, Tommy Gordon, was killed three years ago. We had teamed up back then to catch the killer.

C. J.'s mind held no gray areas when it came to murdered children— the innocents—everything was in stark black and white. She'd learned this philosophy the hard way. Harsh maybe, but her own little girl had been killed a few years ago, along with her policeman husband, and anytime she heard of a child being killed she was immediately ready to hang the guilty herself. I'll admit I felt almost as strong as my partner did. And we don't always see eye-to-eye about a lot of things.

The Austin and national news had told and retold the story of how

Eloy Stewart, his wife, and little girl had gone to a downtown restaurant—a totally innocent evening out—and after eating had walked to the side parking lot on the way to their car.

Two rival gangs were chasing each other down the street, both groups in automobiles. The lead gang-banger's car stopped directly in front of the Mexican food restaurant and started firing at the approaching rival's car. A stray bullet hit the Stewart's little girl, killing her instantly. No one else had been injured.

Both gangs claimed the other side fired the fatal bullet. And too many questions about the bullet's trajectory mystified the jurors, so Benito Alvarez had won an acquittal.

The same day we'd been discussing the Alvarez case, Stewart's father came to see us at G & G Investigations, and asked for our assistance. We both agreed to talk to him.

Albert Stewart arrived shortly after lunch. "I ain't saying he wouldn't of killed that boy," he said. "Eloy admits he went over there with that in mind, but I'll never believe he'd of killed Alvarez's girlfriend."

"The police found him standing over the bodies with a gun in his hand," C. J. reminded him.

The older man was a smaller, diminished version of the son I'd watched during the local news coverage. His shoulders were stooped as if just carrying his head around was too much to bear, but there was still a fire in his brown eyes and a strength in his seventyish voice. And you could also see where the son got his good looks. Something in their manner reminded me of farming folks, raw-boned, sturdy people much like the pioneering Europeans—Germans, Slavs, Poles, or perhaps the Scandinavians—who had settled in central Texas in the early 1830s.

They weren't farmers, however, Albert Stewart was retired from managing an automotive parts store and Eloy had taught junior high school, at least until his daughter was killed.

"It weren't his gun." Mr. Stewart's speech was pure country.

"I spoke with Lieutenant Hayes of Homicide," I said. I'd called the lieutenant for details just before escorting Albert Stewart into the inner office.

Larry Hays and my late husband graduated from the Austin Police Academy in the same class, partnered for ten years on the force, and remained friends when Tommy left APD to become a private eye. Larry treated me like he was my big brother and I often asked his advice in police matters, although I didn't always take it.

I continued, "He says a second gun was taken from Eloy which hadn't been fired. But the one found in Eloy's hand was definitely the one used to kill Benito and Emily."

"I know how it looks. Bad as it can get, I guess. Eloy says Benito and Emily were already dead when he got there. But he also says just when he got out of his car, he saw a blond-haired girl dartin' out from behind a house two doors down from Alvarez's. When she got on the sidewalk and saw Eloy, she ran. He figures she saw who done the killing or maybe she was there and got skeered and ran. If you could find this girl, maybe she'd testify. Maybe she could verify that after seeing him, he didn't have time to do the killing before the police showed up."

"And what do the police say about the girl?" I asked and wondered why it didn't occur to the Stewarts that the running girl had done the killing.

"They didn't care to listen. Far as they're concerned they have their killer and the case's closed," Mr. Stewart said. "One officer did say if he knew something to clear Eloy, we oughta tell his lawyer."

"Who is your son's lawyer?" C. J. wanted to know.

"The court appointed this young gal. Eloy's flat broke since he ain't worked in over a year. My daughter-in-law went back up to St. Louis to stay with her family several months ago. She was here for Alvarez's trial but soon as that was over, she took off again. What little savings they had is gone. I'm trying to raise money for his bail myself, but my wife's in a nursing home. Her expenses are huge and Medicare doesn't pay for custodial care, so there's not much I can do."

The lines around the older man's mouth and eyes showed his grief. "This lady lawyer's a nice person," he said, "but she's overworked and don't have time to be bothered. She told Eloy to plead guilty to jus-ti-fi-able homicide and the judge'd probably go easy. Even that the prosecutor said he'd recommend leniency if Eloy pled guilty. Said Eloy'd probably only serve two, three years at the most."

"But he won't plead?" I looked at the old man and wondered how to get him to understand we probably couldn't help. What he was telling us was too vague, too iffy.

"No way. Eloy says he didn't do it, Miz Gordon, Miz Gunn," he said, looking at each of us in turn. "I'm just a countrified-foolish-old man, but I believe my son. I knowed if Eloy'd killed them two—he'd say so. He'd go to prison or take whatever punishment was handed out to him."

"I think you're trying to be a good father," I said, "and help your son." But I couldn't see a killer leaving the girl alive as a witness. "A man seeking revenge . . ."

He was nodding his gray head. "If Eloy'd walked in there and found Benito alone, he might not've hesitated pulling that trigger. But with that girl there—an innocent bystander—another child would die for no reason. He wouldn't do that to another mother. To another family. He's just not capable."

Maybe, maybe not, but we said we'd look into the matter for him. After a small argument—with us trying to give him a discount and him protesting weakly—he paid a reduced two-day retainer and left.

"Guess I was wrong about this being an open-and-shut case."

"You got that right, girlfriend," said my partner. She was thoughtful for a few moments. "Something about that old man bothers me. He's too, too ..."

"Too what? I'll swear, C. J., you'd be suspicious of your own grandmother."

"My grandmother was a bootlegger and a hooker. I wouldn't trust her as far as I could throw her."

"I don't believe that. Too bad she isn't alive to defend herself." C. J. and I have worked together three years and we're close, but she doesn't dwell in the past or talk about it much.

"Look it up in the newspapers if you don't believe me. Or better yet, ask my mother. She'll tell you."

"One of these days I just might," I told her, knowing full well I wouldn't. It was more fun to think her granny had been a character and added to C. J's mystique.

Since many police officers have a negative opinion of private investigators, it wasn't easy for us to get permission to visit Eloy Stewart in jail. Lieutenant Hays helped to arrange things from the police department's standpoint and then we talked Stewart's attorney, Jacqui Johnston. I don't know if it was because of her heavy work schedule or what, but for a moment she acted as if she didn't remember him. Hard to believe with all the media attention, but I gave her the benefit of a doubt when she got us on the visitor's list.

Travis County Jail is next door to the county courthouse. Some pretrial inmates are kept there, some are sent to the Del Valle jail out near Bergstrom Air Force Base, and some stay downtown at the city jail. The inmates placement has to do with certain aggressive cases going here and nonaggressives going there and attempting to keep a racial balance, but I'll never understand how it's determined who goes where.

Eloy Stewart was brought into a small interview room with a table and three folding chairs where we waited. He was wearing the dark-green clothing, made like a scrub suit with TCJ for Travis County Jail stenciled on the breast pocket, which is worn by inmates at this location.

Stewart was forty-one, around five-foot-ten, and weighed close to 180 pounds—most of it solid muscle. The dark-green scrub suit made his hazel eyes look greener. They were set too close together to be attractive, but his dark eyelashes were long and to die for. He smiled, but only with his mouth. I'd guess he didn't have much to smile about.

"It's like my father told you," he said in a monotone. "I went over there ready to punish Benito. I found him and the girl dead. I remember feeling angry because Benito had died and I didn't get to see his face when it happened."

Eloy had a three-day stubble and bloodshot eyes. "Someone beat me to it but only by a few minutes because the girl made a gurgling sound just as I entered the room. I felt her pulse and there wasn't any. That bothered me . . . a lot."

"Did you call 9-1-1?" I asked.

"No. She was dead and I, uh, I wasn't thinking too clearly."

"Why did you pick up that gun—the murder weapon?" C. J. asked.

"I don't remember doing it. The next thing I knew, the police charged in the front and back doors and told me to drop the gun and get down on the floor. I didn't even hear them drive up or knock or anything."

"Tell us about that girl," I said, taking out a notebook. "The one your father thinks might help clear you."

"She was just a girl. Blond hair put up in uh, a double ponytail thing— you know one bunch tied off near the top of her head and the long part tied off separately. She wore shorts and a pair of red cowboy boots. I couldn't see her face too well, but she looked young and pretty. At least that was my impression."

"How young?" I asked, making notes.

"About the same age as Emily Jimenez, sixteen, seventeen," he said, closing his eyes. They popped open quickly as if the memory was too vivid and he shivered. "It was horrible seeing them like that."

"Did you see this blond girl go into a house or getting into a car?" asked C. J.

"No, I didn't."

C. J. and I looked at each other and I knew we thought the same. We weren't getting much enlightenment here.

I asked about gunpowder residue and he said the tests were inconclusive.

"Uh, I guess I should tell you . . ." He hesitated.

"Anything you think that might help," I urged. "To be honest we don't have much that can—"

Eloy interrupted. "You should know how much I wanted Benito dead. I doubt you can understand that, but losing a child is something that'll make you totally crazy."

C. J. nodded—she understood. Her daughter had been killed ten years ago, back when she was working for the Pittsburgh police department. She had caused some heavy grief for an organized drug syndicate. They had retaliated by planting a bomb in her car one Sunday morning. Her husband decided to use her car when he went to buy doughnuts and took their little girl with him. There wasn't much of either one left to bury.

Since my husband had been murdered, I could sympathize, but I couldn't imagine the grief of losing a child.

"I couldn't eat or sleep. I couldn't give comfort to my wife, I couldn't take comfort from her or anyone. My life felt like it was over. I still don't have much of a life but I do feel some responsibility for my parents. If anything happens to me . . ." He let his voice trail off and began tracing his right index finger on the tabletop, making circles around and around in the same spot.

"We'd wanted a kid so much, we'd tried unsuccessfully for thirteen years and when my wife got pregnant, when Rachel Ann was finally born it was like a miracle." He kept tracing that circle and I wondered if he would wear a groove in the table.

"Rachel Ann was . . . precious," he said. "Smart and funny and the cutest little thing you ever saw."

His voice broke and his eyes filled. He shook his head and rubbed them with his left hand. I thought he was probably a man who couldn't handle anyone seeing him cry and, I was right. He got up and walked over to stand facing the wall.

When he was back in control and resumed speaking, his voice cracked but he stayed where he was—staring at the wall. "I have trouble even now believing she's dead and it's been thirteen months."

Neither C. J. nor I spoke. There was nothing for us to say, his wound was still too raw, too painful.

In a few seconds Eloy began a slow pace around the room, making a complete circuit and another and another. "I keep telling myself. I probably wouldn't have killed Benito if he'd been alive when I got there. But I just don't know because he was already dead. I didn't have to stand there and decide whether or not to pull the trigger. I know I wanted him dead. I thought it would ease my pain if he died but I was wrong. It didn't stop it and I guess it never will."

"But what about Emily, the girl with him?" I asked.

"No one wants to talk about that. The police think that I killed her to keep from leaving a witness. Even if she'd testified—it wouldn't have mattered—I still wouldn't have shot her. My plan all along was to confess and turn myself in."

He stopped pacing and looked at me without batting an eye and I believed him. "If I'd killed either of them," he stated, "I'd take my punishment because I don't much care what happens to me. But being accused when I'm innocent is a different story."

He laughed then, a hollow laugh, "Guess that sounds like I do care about something. A kind of survival instinct probably. And maybe eventually I really will care again."

I'd never have predicted what happened next in a million years. C. J. walked over to Eloy Stewart and talked quietly to him for some minutes, then said in a voice loud enough for me to hear, "Don't worry, Mr. Stewart, we'll find that girl and clear you."

She's the one usually accusing me of letting emotions get in the way of my good judgment, but I knew she'd been touched by his little girl's death. And yes, my emotions were involved too, what can I say? I'm a sentimental slob.

We were about to leave; Stewart was being escorted down a hallway by one of the deputies from the Sheriff's Department (they run the jails in Austin) and C. J. and I were partway through the security door when Eloy stopped and asked the guard if he could say one more thing to us. "Make it quick," the deputy replied.

"I just remembered. Something was weird about that girl."

"Weird? How?" I asked.

"I can't put my finger on it . . . maybe." He shook his head. "No, I just don't know . . ."

The deputy said, "Come along. You can talk again tomorrow."

"See if you can get permission to phone our office. Just give us anything else you might think of," C. J. called to Eloy.

"I'll call tomorrow," he said.

But something in his voice made me wonder if he would.

II

After a brief discussion we decided to canvass the neighborhood around the Alvarez house and see if we could turn up a witness who had seen the girl. The girl seemed to be Stewart's only chance. Maybe folks had remembered something they hadn't told the police last week or we might find someone who'd not wanted to get involved before. It happens more times than the police will ever admit.

C. J. likes to drive when we travel together but her new pickup was in the shop having its five-thousand-mile checkup. I'm a good driver, Tommy had raced cars in his youth and he'd taught me defensive driving, but she complained when I drove. I think it's a control thing with her. She grumbled while I unlocked my silver Omni, but she got in and we headed south on Loop 1, known to the locals as Mo-Pac (so named for its proximity to the Missouri-Pacific Railway).

The late afternoon sky was still so bright it hurt to look at it. The heat was never-ending this summer and although the Midwest was washing away in floods, we hadn't had a decent rain in months. Luckily, the Omni had a good air conditioner and I kept the blower on high while we listened to a Garth Brooks tape.

The neighborhood the Alvarez family lived in consisted of small frame houses on Austin's south side, not far from South Congress Avenue. It was a mixture of decent-looking little homes with others sliding into total neglect.

The corner house, the one young Alvarez had died in, fit the latter category. It was painted a pale green that reminded me of that sickly color that used to always be used for hospital walls. A water-cooled air-conditioning unit sat in the front window, dripping and leaving a limestone calcification on the wall.

An old car with no wheels, its headlights rusted and falling out, was on blocks at the side of the house next to the street. The grass was dead, but with the heat we'd had this summer, that wasn't unusual in any part of town.

C. J. and I parked and walked to the door on the south side of the Alvarez house. Logically, the girl must have gone through this backyard to come out two doors down. An attempt had been made to keep this house among the decent-looking. The white paint was probably no more than two years old. New porch steps made of treated lumber had been installed, but were as yet unpainted. Two ferns hung in baskets along the porch's outer edge and three pots of peppers were on the floor near the front door.

C. J. knocked. A lady with a face as wrinkled as an unironed cotton blouse pushed aside the lacy curtain at the front window and peered out. She must have been satisfied with what she saw because a moment later she opened the door. Her hair was iron gray, but her dark eyes sparkled with vitality. "Are y'all from the newspapers?" She had an artificial-looking smile pasted on her face.

"No, ma'am," said C. J. "We're private investigators. I'm C. J. Gunn and this is Jenny Gordon. Would you have a moment to talk?"

The woman frowned briefly before she said, "Oh, my, y'all better come inside before some of those gang boys see you out here, although I guess with Benito dead they won't be paying so much attention."

She said her name was Juanita Hidalgo and she led us into a front parlor with dark-wood paneling and velvet upholstered furniture. Crochet doilies were pinned to the backs and armrests of the chairs and sofa, and an afghan made of bright-colored yarn covered the back of a platform rocker. A small religious shrine stood in the far corner. C. J. and I sat on the sofa and Mrs. Hidalgo insisted we have some fresh lemonade she'd just made.

"I feel sorry for Mrs. Alvarez," she said. It had taken her only a moment to bring the refreshments as if the tray had already been prepared. "She's had a rough time. Her husband ran off and left her with six little ones. She does the best she can, works all the time, but that means her kids never have much supervision. The older ones are grown now and they're all good kids except for that one—Benito. He always was mean. Running with a bad crowd, getting in trouble with the police. I knew he'd cause his mother grief one day."

She handed over our glasses and offered homemade sugar cookies which looked too good to refuse. She placed the tray on the coffee table and sat in the rocker opposite us, rocking slowly. "It's been so exciting around here, neighbors, reporters, and policemen and, now, you young ladies. I haven't had so much company in years." The pasted-on smile was back in place. "What was it you wanted to ask?"

I glanced at C. J., and saw my partner's tiny shrug. "We're trying to help clear the man accused of killing Benito and his friend, Emily," I said. "Mr. Stewart says the boy and girl were already dead when he got there." Mrs. Hidalgo had been nodding as I spoke but didn't interrupt. It suddenly dawned on me that her weird smile had to do with the fact she wore dentures.

I continued, "Mr. Stewart saw a girl. He thinks she came from the Alvarez's house, crossed your backyard, and came out in front of the house on the other side of you. He's hoping the girl could say what time she saw him and help prove his story. Do you know a blond-haired girl who lives down that way?"

She shook her head. "No. But boys and girls always went in and out all the time visiting Benito."

"Were you at home the day the shooting took place?" C. J. asked. "Last Sunday?"

"Oh my, no. Saturday's my shopping day. My youngest son picked me up early and after shopping, took me back to his place for dinner. I never get home until late on Saturday." She glanced at the array of family photographs lined up on the credenza next to the sofa. "My children," she said, proudly. "They all live in Del Rio except for Tony, my youngest."

"Nice family," I said, sipping the lemonade. I realized I'd been counting on her, she was the type to see everything in the neighborhood. I swallowed my disappointment and it tasted like the drink, a little tart.

"I'd like to help clear that young man," she said. "I feel sorry for him losing his little girl like that and then being arrested for Benito's murder. Oh my, it just doesn't seem fair."

She stopped the rocker and looked at me. "I'll just bet he didn't do it—I'll bet it was one of those awful-looking boys that come around all the time that shot Benito. They have guns and knives and no telling what all. I'm sure they're all gangsters."

"Do they bother you?" C. J. asked. "Or do damage to your house?"

The old woman laughed out loud. "Oh, my goodness, no. You should see my Tony. He's big and strong and he warned Benito a long time ago. Told that boy he'd pull his head off and beat him with it if I ever got mistreated. They throw their beer cans and trash in my yard, but they know better than to cause me trouble."

Mrs. Hidalgo continued talking, telling about the gunshots that filled her neighborhood at night, especially on the weekends. "I'm sorry I haven't been much help." She stopped the rocker again and this time she wasn't smiling.

"Well," I said, "we need to visit some other neighbors and we probably shouldn't take any more of your time."

"Time is all I have most days and it gets lonesome when you're alone. I know Tony has his own life to live so I make sure I have other things to do: sewing, knitting, crocheting, reading, yard work, my baking, and housecleaning. I don't want to be a burden on anyone."

"I'm sure you'd never be a burden," I said.

"Your cookies were delicious," C. J. said as we stood.

"Would you like the recipe?" Mrs. Hidalgo asked.

"If it's not too much trouble," said C. J.

Mrs. Hidalgo went to the credenza and opened a drawer, taking out an index card. The recipe was already written under the heading of Juanita's Sugar Cookies. She handed the card to C. J. and walked with us to the front door.

"I wonder," she said. "Maybe the girl Mr. Stewart saw was that little blond-haired girl Benito dated for a while. I don't know why she doesn't come around anymore."

"Was Emily Jimenez his current girlfriend?" I asked.

"She might have been special, but Benito had many girlfriends. They were always chasing after him. But that blonde hung around here the longest, up until a few months ago."

"Do you know the girl's name?"

She furrowed her brow. "Seems like I heard them call her Stacy. But I don't know her last name. You could ask Mrs. Alvarez, she might know."

"Did Stacy ever wear cowboy boots?" I asked.

"She sure did, red ones. Wore them all the time. Looked funny too with her shorts, but young folks dress wild and crazy these days."

"Well, thanks for your help and for the refreshments."

"And for the recipe," said C. J. "I can't hardly wait to try it."

"They'll be good every time you make them," Mrs. Hidalgo promised. "Everybody raves about them."

"Thanks again," we said, and I felt sorry knowing she was going to be lonesome for the rest of the day.

"What a character," I said. "But the poor soul is starved for company."

"Might be you or I someday, girlfriend," commented C. J. and it was a sobering thought.

We walked across the lawn and knocked on the door at the Alvarez house, but no one answered. As we stepped off the porch, a dark-haired boy about nine or ten years old came riding up the driveway on a beat-up old bicycle. "Hi! Are you looking for my mother? Need some ironing or housework done?"

"Is Mrs. Alvarez your mom?" C. J. asked.

"Yeah. But she ain't home now." He had put one foot down on the concrete, stopping the bike and stood straddling it.

"When will she be back?" I inquired.

"Tomorrow. She's staying with my sister who's getting a new baby."

We laughed and C. J. said, "We'll try to come back tomorrow."

We had already started toward the car when I stopped and walked back to where the boy was trying to turn the bicycle around. "Maybe you could help. I'm looking for Stacy. She was a friend of your, uh, Benito." C. J. continued to walk to my car and leaned against the fender while she waited.

"Yeah. I know Stacy. She worked at the Dairy Queen, but I don't think she does anymore."

"The Dairy Queen down on Ben White Boulevard?"

"Yeah, that's the one."

"Thanks," I said. "And your name is. . . ?"

"George Alvarez."

"Thanks, George. By the way, you're not staying here all by yourself with your mother gone, are you?"

"No. I'm staying down there with her." He pointed to a house three doors down and across the street.

I guess I looked funny because he grinned. "My sister lives there."

He hopped back up on the bike and peddled out into the street. "See you." He waved.

"Yeah, see you, George."

I told C. J. what George had said and we drove to the Diary Queen, parked, and got out. "A hot-fudge sundae sounds good."

"You don't need one," C. J. said. "You just ate three large sugar cookies."

"I know I don't need one, but—"

"You don't have to explain it to me but remember if you do eat ice cream you'll have to do an extra workout tomorrow."

It wasn't fair. She stands six feet tall in her stocking feet and is blessed with a body that never puts an extra ounce on it even if she eats like a football player. I'm only five feet six and every time I smell food I add another half-pound to my 125-pound weight.

When we got to the counter, I resisted temptation and asked to speak to the manager. He was a plump young man wearing glasses and had a bad case of acne. He told us Stacy's last name was Carson and gave us the girl's address in Westlake Hills. We left right after that so I wouldn't have to suffer hot-fudge deprivation.

C. J. took an Austin city map from the glove compartment to look up Stacy Carson's address as I drove west to pick up Loop 1 and headed north again.

Westlake Hills is what its name implies: it's west Austin, has a lake and hills. It also has canyons, twisting roads, and prime real estate with huge price tags.

"Pretty ritzy neighborhood," said C. J. "Wonder how Stacy got hooked up with the likes of Benito Alvarez? And why was she working at a Dairy Queen over in that part of town? We're miles from her stomping grounds."

"Maybe when we talk to her we'll find out."

Stacy Carson's house was as we expected. It *was* ritzy—a two-story white brick with Colonial pillars holding up the front porch. A spot of rust wouldn't dare appear on the red Mustang convertible which sat in the circular drive. Magnolia, elm, oak, and mimosa trees shaded the house. Late summer roses bloomed in a diamond-shaped landscaped area on one side in front of a gazebo. A gardener was pruning shrubbery and a sprinkler twirled lazily on the lush green lawn. Only people with big bucks can afford the upkeep on such a yard with the drought we'd been having.

A girl who looked about sixteen with her blond hair gathered up in a double ponytail answered the doorbell. She was wearing shorts and red cowboy boots. Her face was pale as if she hadn't been outside all summer or maybe she'd been sick.

"Stacy?" I asked. When she nodded, I introduced us and said we were private investigators and would she be willing to answer a couple of questions.

"Private eyes like V. I. Warshawski, huh?" she asked. "I saw the movie."

"Well, not exactly," I said. "I'm not too crazy about baseball."

Stacy laughed and invited us inside.

"Who is it?" asked a soft voice coming from behind the girl. A young Mexican-American woman of about twenty-five came bustling up, her dark hair braided and hanging down her back. She wore a worried frown. "You shouldn't be up answering the door, Miss Stacy. That's my job and besides you shouldn't be out of bed yet." She turned to us. "We're not interested in buying anything today."

The woman reminded me of someone I'd seen recently and suddenly I realized she looked like an older version of George Alvarez, Benito's little brother. I glanced at C. J. and couldn't tell from her expression if she'd noticed or not.

"It's okay, Consuela," said Stacy. "They're private investigators not salespeople."

"Investigators?" The woman's concern was obvious. She placed a protective arm around the girl. "I don't know. I don't think your father . . ."

"Screw my father," said Stacy and shrugged off the arm. "Come along, Ms. Gordon, Ms. Gunn." We followed her across the huge entry hall and she said to the woman in passing. "We don't want to be disturbed, Consuela. Except you could bring something cold to drink."

"Nothing for me," I said and C. J. echoed my statement.

"Fine. We'll go to the sunroom." Stacy led the way. I tried not to stare at the exquisite furniture, paintings, and expensive antique art objects decorating the huge living and dining rooms we passed.

The sunroom with glass all around, including the roof, was carpeted in a pale shade of blue and was large enough to hold the living/kitchen area in my apartment. One end of the room was devoted to plants, some in hanging baskets. The other end held an arrangement of chairs and love seats, each decorated in various shades of blue and white.

Stacy Carson invited us to sit while she sat opposite and asked, "How did you find me? I'll bet that old busybody next door told you about me, didn't she? She's always snooping where she shouldn't."

"Stacy," I said, "we're trying to locate a witness who was seen leaving the scene where a murder was committed."

Her face flushed, and she wouldn't look at me. In a minute, she composed herself and said breathlessly, "Wow. You investigate murderers? How exciting."

"Murder isn't glamorous or exciting," stated C. J. "It's quite an ugly, serious business."

"Of course, how thoughtless of me." She sounded contrite, hooked one finger in a wisp of hair that hung in front of her ear, and began twisting it. "You do know that some people just deserve to die."

"I understand you spent a great deal of time at the home of Benito Alvarez," I said. "Did he deserve to die?"

She flinched when she heard his name but she kept her cool.

"Yes, I was there once or twice. Consuela is, was, Benito's older sister. But I know nothing about his death. I feel sorry for his family. I even feel sorry for the poor man who killed Benito." She stopped twisting her hair, and shrugged. "But this doesn't have anything to do with me."

"Were you at the Alvarez's house the day Benito was killed?" C. J. asked.

She fidgeted a moment, gave a small shudder, and I saw goose bumps pop out on her arms.

"No. I don't believe so." She stood. "Is that all the questions you have?"

"How well did you know Benito?" I asked, but she ignored me.

"I must ask you to leave now," she said. "My father is returning home from Russia the day after tomorrow. We're having a welcome-home party."

"Your father's in Russia?" I stood. "Where is your mother?"

Her mouth grimaced slightly and one large tear rolled down her cheek. But I couldn't tell if her feelings were fake or genuine.

"My mother died last year."

"I'm sorry," I said, and meant it. My own mother had died when I was twelve and I still miss her, almost every day. It's not easy being a young girl with only a father to take care of you, and it would be even more difficult if your father had to be away. "Does your father travel often?"

Stacy nodded. "This time he's been gone for six months and I've missed, well, never mind."

"You don't stay here alone, do you?" C. J. asked as Stacy led us toward the front of the house.

"No, Consuela's my companion. She keeps me from being lonely."

"Thanks for your time." I was frustrated but knew we couldn't force her if she refused to answer our questions.

"Sure, and I hope you find your witness."

"Oh, we will," C. J. said. "In fact, I think we've already found her."

Stacy gave us an odd look as we turned and walked to my Omni.

"What was that?" I asked C. J. "Is she for real?"

"She was there that day. And she knows something."

"You'll get no argument from me, but we need to get a photo and see if Eloy can identify her."

"We need to find out all we can about her father, too."

"Can your computer do us any good?"

"You just watch me."

It was late. Time to pack it in and start fresh in the morning. I dropped C. J. at her place and promised to pick her up tomorrow since she didn't have transportation.

After I'd eaten dinner I called Albert Stewart to update him on our progress. "We've located the girl. Her name is Stacy Carson. She denies being there naturally, but we think she's lying. We need proof. Corroboration from another person would be helpful."

Stewart sounded like a happy man when we hung up.

III

C. J. called early the next morning and said her truck was ready. The car dealer's van would pick her up and she wouldn't need to wait for me.

I made a few phone calls from home which led to a trip out to Westlake High School. I received permission to talk to several of Stacy's classmates and one of her counselors who gave me some insights into the girl, and I picked up a school yearbook which had Stacy's photo in it from the school library.

When I got to the office shortly after noon, I told C. J. what I'd learned. When the school semester began a few weeks ago the counselor noticed Stacy had gained weight and wondered if the girl might be pregnant, but Stacy denied it. "The counselor told me she wouldn't swear to it, but that in her opinion Stacy was pregnant. Her school chums say she definitely was pregnant," I said. "She tried to hide it by wearing a panty girdle and big shirts. She's missed school the last two days and the rumor is that she's off to have the baby. The talk is that Benito Alvarez is her baby's father.

"The counselor also mentioned Stacy's father was a tyrant who made the girl's life miserable," I continued. "The only joy the girl had had was taking drama classes. She appeared in several community productions and was gaining a reputation as an actress."

"No wonder she was so cool," C. J. said. She had been busy, too, and found out via computer that Mr. Carson owned a successful development company and was currently involved in negotiations to develop some property in Russia. "He's been arrested for being drunk and disorderly a couple of times. In this country, not over there."

"Any history of family abuse?"

"Nothing's showed up yet, but I'll stay with it."

I retreated to my desk to clear up the paperwork left over from an employee check we'd done for a savings and loan.

Three hours later C. J. came into my office. "Tadah." She was wearing a Cheshire cat smile. "You remember little George telling you yesterday about his mother helping his sister and her baby?"

I nodded.

"How does Stacy strike you as the one having a baby?"

"Are you serious?"

"Yeah. Mrs. Alvarez and a midwife delivered Stacy's baby, but get this: the oldest Alvarez daughter plans to adopt it."

"How did you find that out?"

"A birth certificate for a little boy born the day before yesterday was registered to Stacy and Benito Alvarez," said C. J., "but the baby's being adopted by Rudy and Mary Alvarez Cantu."

"Okay, but how does this information get us to who killed Benito and Emily Jimenez?"

"I don't know yet," C. J. admitted, "but we'll find out."

The rest of the day brought us nothing new and we felt the frustration of being against a nearly impossible situation.

It was quitting time when the telephone rang and C. J. answered and listened before exploding. "Larry, you don't seriously believe him, do you?"

"What?" I asked, but she motioned me to silence.

"But it's ridiculous and you know it." C. J. listened for what seemed like a long time before saying, "Okay, but we identified the girl who Stewart saw that day—what do you want us to do?"

She listened again for a time and then told him, "Okay." She hung up and turned to me. "Albert Stewart just confessed to killing Benito Alvarez and Emily Jimenez."

"You're kidding! They don't believe him, do they? He must be trying to save Eloy."

"I know it and you know it but the District Attorney says he has to take the confession seriously. Mr. Stewart gave so many details of what happened that they all believe him."

"He knows all these details because Eloy happened upon the scene."

"Right."

"How can he explain away the fact his son was there with the gun in his hand?"

"He says his son probably figured out that he planned to kill Benito. Mr. Stewart says he left immediately after the shooting and in the meantime, Eloy showed up. Then Eloy found the bodies and the cops found Eloy."

"I can't see the old man killing Emily—for the same reason that Eloy couldn't kill her. She was only guilty of being at the wrong place at the wrong time."

An hour later we were fresh out of ideas except I did call Larry to ask if Eloy knew of his father's plans to go to see Alvarez. Larry said Eloy believed his father shot Benito.

All of this heavy thinking made us hungry and we decided a trip to the LaVista restaurant at the Hyatt to eat fajitas was in order.

The hotel is on Town Lake in downtown Austin. LaVista not only serves superb food, but has a great view. Several office buildings across the lake from the hotel were outlined in white, red, and gold lights, while the Franklin Savings is trimmed in blue. Their reflection shimmered in the water, but C. J. and I had too many questions about our suddenly incarcerated client to appreciate the sight. We did manage to enjoy the food—mostly because we'd been too busy to eat lunch.

"Albert Stewart has convinced everyone except you and me that he is guilty," I said. "Maybe he is."

"It doesn't make sense, if he were guilty why didn't he confess earlier and clear his son? Why did he hire us?" She frowned and asked, "Did you tell Albert we'd found Stacy?"

"Yes. Remember? I told you I called last night and gave him a progress report. That we were on the verge of proving Stacy was there and clearing Eloy."

"So what happened between last night and when he walked in the police station today and confessed?"

She answered her own question. "Albert must've talked to Stacy Carson. You don't suppose she told him . . . Oh, shit."

"What, C. J.?"

"What if Albert went over there and begged her to help him get his son out of jail and she refused. I can see him threatening to tell her father that she'd been seeing Benito. Not exactly a young man her father would approve of, and I'm sure she wouldn't want Dad to know."

"A little emotional blackmail?"

"Possibly," C. J. said.

I counted back in my mind, "About the time Benito was killed had to be about the same time Stacy found out she was pregnant."

C. J. leaned back and thought briefly. "She goes to Benito, tells him she's pregnant with his child, and he doesn't even care. She was furious with him because he's dropped her and began going with other girls. She goes over there hoping for a commitment of marriage and he laughs at her. Emily was there and he flaunts Emily in Stacy's face. Stacy flips out. She decides if she can't have him no one else can either and she kills them both."

"Maybe that's why she said some people deserve to die," I said. "Okay, Albert is at Stacy's house. They're arguing or he's pleading or whatever and she accidentally lets it slip that she killed Benito and Emily. And she cries and begs him not to tell."

"I'm sure she appealed to his sympathy by telling him about the baby," said C. J. "And about how she'd had to give him up and how she'd never see her baby if she turned herself in and wound up in prison."

"But Albert's concerned about his son and he's caught in the middle," I said. "He tells her he feels sorry for her but he needs his son free and he also has a sick wife in a nursing home to think about."

I thought for a moment. "So Miss Stacy comes up with a plan. She tells Albert that if Eloy takes the blame for her she'll pay him. She'll pay enough to make it worth his time if he's convicted and goes to prison. He might even get off, she says.

"Albert refuses," I continued. "He wants his son's freedom, but suddenly he realizes Stacy has offered him a way he can get his hands on some big money. He says he'll take the blame for the killing except he wants a guarantee of X amount of money."

"It would have to be enough money for Mrs. Stewart's medical expenses with enough left over so his son could have a new start at putting his life back together," C. J. said. "Maybe something like a million bucks."

"Her father can afford it if she can convince him to pony up," I said. "And Stacy could even have money of her own. Inherited from her mother's estate."

We knew it was pure speculation, but it sounded good. We decided to have a talk with Larry Hays about the whole case. He answered his pager quickly and agreed to meet us at the LaVista in ten minutes. We ordered the coffee while we waited.

It was closer to fifteen minutes when I spotted Larry riding the escalator up to the second-floor restaurant. He's a tall, lanky man, pushing forty-five with sandy-colored hair, hazel eyes, and size thirteen shoes. Tonight, he looked about as tired as I'd ever seen him. "Rough day, huh?"

"I'd tell you about it, but none of it was pleasant." He sat next to me. "I haven't eaten all day or stopped more than five minutes for that matter."

After the waiter had taken his order for a cheeseburger and iced tea, he asked: "What's this new information you have?"

We explained our theory to him and to his credit he didn't interrupt or make smart remarks about our convoluted reasoning.

"You're probably close to being right about this," he agreed. "I had a gut feeling that old man was lying, but he's convinced everyone else and it's a done deal."

"You mean you won't reopen the case?" I asked.

"Not won't—can't. There's no evidence that disputes Albert's story. No fingerprints. No witnesses. And he wanted Benito punished about as much as his son did. The gun used to shoot both victims was sold to Albert. He had motive, means, and opportunity."

"He bought the gun?" C. J. asked.

Larry's food came and he wolfed it down like a starving hound. "I don't think so but he has this receipt from the flea market out on Highway 290."

"Of course, Stacy *gave* Albert that receipt," I said.

Larry drank huge swallows of tea to wash down his food. "The dealer says it's his receipt, but he doesn't remember the sale exactly. He says if Albert Stewart says he bought a gun from him, then he must have."

"Nothing can be done, then?" I asked Larry.

"Albert will stand trial. A jury will decide if he's telling the truth. He might even get off, who knows?"

"Albert Stewart is willing to sacrifice himself for money?" C. J.'s voice sounded husky.

"Sure," said Larry. "Albert's getting up there in years. Probably thinks he won't live much longer. Big money can ease all his worries. And Stacy Carson has given him an out."

"He's a nice old man caught up in lies and murder," I said. "But it still seems unfair to me."

"I agree, but no one ever said life was fair," said Larry.

"And Stacy gets away with murder. Isn't there some way to prove she was there?"

"Who knows?" said Larry. "But it would have to be strong evidence : to get the D.A. to reopen the investigation, and we don't have it. The D.A. wanted this case wrapped up and in his view, it is."

"Stacy's going to have to live with all of it for the rest of her life," said C. J. "And don't forget she gave up her baby. It might not matter now, but on down the line she might have regrets." She cleared her throat. "Sometimes, there's no simple solution to murder."

I didn't have an answer to that. It still didn't feel right, but the case was closed as far as we were concerned. Whatever might happen legally was totally out of our hands.

Dana Stabenow was best known as a science fiction writer until she won the Edgar for best paperback with her first mystery A COLD DAY FOR MURDER (1992), which featured Aleut Kate Shugak, a likable sleuth who guides us through contemporary Alaska. There have been four more Shugaks to date: A FATAL THAW (1993), DEAD IN THE WATER (1993), COLD-BLOODED BUSINESS (1994), and PLAY WITH FIRE (1995).

Nooses Give
DANA STABENOW

The bodies had fallen around the table like three cards from a spent deck. Jeremy Mike, the jack of spades. Sally Jorgenson, queen of hearts. Ted Muktoyuk, the king of diamonds. The King of the Key, they called him from the bleachers, at five feet ten the tallest center Bernie Koslowski had ever had the privilege of coaching.

Bernie's mouth was set in a grim line. "What happened?"

Billy Mike had a mobile moon face, usually beaming with good nature and content. This morning it was grim and tired. The jack of spades had been a nephew, his youngest sister's only child. She didn't know yet, and he didn't know how he was going to tell her. He told Bernie instead. "They were drunk. It's Jeremy's pistol."

"How do you know?"

Billy's face twisted. "I gave it to him for Christmas." Bernie waited, patient, and Billy got himself under control. "He must have brought it from home. Sally's parents are in Ahtna for a corporation conference, so they came here to drink."

"And play Russian roulette."

Billy nodded. "Looks like Ted lost. He was left-handed—remember that hook shot?"

"Remember it? I taught it to him."

"Sally was on his right. She couldn't have shot him in the left side of his head from where she sat." He pointed at the pistol, lying on the table a few inches from Sally's hand. "You know Ted and Sally were going together?"

236

Bernie grunted. "You figure Sally blamed Jeremy? For bringing the gun?" "Or the bottle, or both." The tribal chief's nod was weary. "Probably grabbed the gun and shot Jeremy, then herself." He stooped and picked up a plastic liquor bottle from the floor.

He held it out, and Bernie examined the label. "Windsor Canadian. The bootlegger's friend. Retail price in Anchorage, seven-fifty a bottle. Retail price in a dry village, a hundred bucks easy."

"Yeah." The bottle dropped to the table, next to the gun.

"You talk to him?"

"I tried. He shot out the headlights on my snow machine."

"Uh-huh."

"Town's tense. You know the DampAct passed by only five votes. There's plenty who think he's just doing business, that he's got every right to make a living, same as the rest of us."

"No," Bernie said, "not the same as the rest of us."

"No," Billy agreed. "Bernie. The trooper's chasing after some nut who shot up a bank in Valdez, and the tribal police ... well, hell, the tribal policemen are okay at checking planes for booze and getting the drunks home safe from the Roadhouse. Like I said, the town's tense. Anything could happen." A pause. "We're not going to be able to handle this on our own."

"No." Bernie's eyes met Billy's. "But we know someone who can."

The tribal chief hesitated. "I don't know, Bernie. There's some history there."

Bernie gave the bodies a last look, a gaze equal parts sorrow and rage. "All the better."

THE NEXT MORNING Bernie bundled himself into parka, gauntlets, and books, kissed his wife and children goodbye, and got on his snow machine. There had been a record amount of snow that winter, drifting twenty feet deep in places. Moose were unable to get at the tree bark that was their primary food source and were starving to death all over the Park, but the snow machining had never been better. An hour and thirty-five minutes later, his cheeks frostbitten and his hands and feet numb, he burst into a small clearing. He cut the engine and slid to a stop six feet from the log cabin.

It sat at the center of a half circle of small buildings, including a garage, a greenhouse, a cache, and an outhouse. Snow was piled high beneath the eaves of the cabin, and neat paths had been cut through it from door to door and to the woodpile between cabin and outhouse. Beyond the buildings were more trees and a creek. Beyond the creek the ground fell away into a long, broad valley that glittered hard and cold and white in what there was of the Arctic noon sun, a valley that rose again into the Teglliq foothills and the Quilak mountain range, a mighty upward thrust of earth's crust that gouged the sky with 18,000-foot spurs until it bled ice-blue glaze down their sharp flanks.

It was a sight to steal the heart. Bernie Koslowski would never have seen any of it if he hadn't dodged the draft all the way into British Columbia in 1970. From here it was but a step over the border into Alaska and some fine, rip-roaring years on the TransAlaska Pipeline. By the time the line was finished, he had enough of a stake to buy the Roadhouse, the only establishment legally licensed to sell liquor in the twenty-million-acre Park, and he settled down to marry a local girl and make babies and boilermakers for the rest of his life.

He sold liquor to make a living. He coached basketball for fun. He had so much fun at it that Niniltna High School's Kanuyaq Kings were headed for the Class C State Championship. Or they had been until Ted Muktoyuk's resignation from the team. Bernie's eyes dropped from the mountains to the clearing.

She hadn't been off the homestead in the last four feet of snow; he'd had to break trail with the machine a quarter of a mile through the woods. The thermometer mounted next to the door read six below. He knocked. No answer. Smoke was coming from both chimneys. He knocked again, harder.

This time the door opened. She stood five feet tall and small of frame, dwarfed by the wolf-husky hybrid standing at her side. The wolf's eyes were yellow, the woman's hazel, both wary and hostile. The woman said, "What?"

"What 'what'?" Bernie said. "What am I doing here? What do I want? Whatever happened to this thing called love?" He gave a hopeful smile. There was no response. "Come on, Kate. How about a chance to get in out of the cold?"

For a minute he thought she was going to shut the door in his face. Instead she stepped to one side. "In."

The dog curled a lip at him, and he took this as tacit permission to enter. The cabin was a twenty-five-foot square with a sleeping loft. Built-in bookshelves, built-in couch, table and chairs and two stoves, one oil, one wood, took up the first floor. Gas lamps hissed gently from brackets in all four corners. She took his parka and hung it next to hers on the caribou rack mounted next to the door. "Sit."

He sat. She poured out two mugs of coffee and gave him one. He gulped gratefully and felt the hot liquid creep all the way down his legs and out into his fingertips, and as if she had only been waiting for that, she said, "Talk."

Her voice was a hoarse, croaking whisper, and irresistibly his eyes were drawn to the red, angry scar bisecting the smooth brown skin of her throat, literally from ear to ear. None of the Pack rats knew the whole story, and none of them had had the guts to ask for it, but the scar marked her throat the way it had marked the end of her career seven months before as an investigator on the staff of the Anchorage district attorney's office. She had returned to her father's homestead sometime last summer. The first anyone knew about it was when her mail started being delivered to the Niniltna post office. Old Abel Int-Hout picked it up and presumably brought it out to her homestead, and the only time anyone else saw her was when she came into Niniltna for supplies in October, the big silver wolf-husky hybrid walking close by her side, warning off any and all advances with a hard yellow stare.

Her plaid shirt was open at the throat, her long black hair pulled back into a loose braid. She wasn't trying to hide the scar. Maybe it needed air to heal. Or maybe she was proud of it. Or maybe it was only that she wasn't ashamed of it, which wasn't quite the same thing. He looked up from the scar and met eyes beneath an epicanthic fold that gave her face an exotic, Eastern flavor. She was an Aleut icon stepped out of a gilt frame, dark and hard and stern. "I've got a problem," he said.

"So?"

"So I'm hoping you'll make it your problem too." He drank more coffee, preparing for a tough sell. "You know about the DampAct?" She shook her head. "In November the village voted to go dry. You can bring in booze for your own consumption but not in amounts to sell." He added, "I'm okay because the Roadhouse is outside tribal boundaries." She didn't look as if she'd been worrying about him or his business. "Well, Kate, it ain't working out too good."

There was a brief pause. "Bootlegger," she said.

"Yeah."

She doubled her verbal output. "Tell me." He told her. It must have been hard to hear. She was shirttail cousin to all three of the teenagers. Hell, there weren't very many people in the village of Niniltna or the entire Park for that matter she couldn't call cousin, including himself, through his wife. It was the reason he was here. One of them.

"You know who?" she said.

He snorted into his coffee and put the mug down with a thump. "Of course I know who. Everybody knows who. He's been flying booze into remote villages, wet or dry, for thirty years. Wherever there isn't a bar— shit, wherever there is a bar and somebody'd rather buy their bottle out of the back of a plane anyway—there's Pete with his hand out. God knows it's better than working for a living."

Her face didn't change, but he had the sudden feeling that he had all her attention, and remembered Billy Mike's comment about history. "Pete Liverakos," she said. He gave a gloomy nod. "Stop him. The local option law says the state can seize any equipment used to make, transport, sell or store liquor. Start confiscating."

This time a gloomy shake. "We don't know where to start."

A corner of the wide mouth turned down. "Gee, maybe you could try his plane. You can pack a lot of cases of booze into the back of a 180, especially if you pull all the seats except the pilot's."

"He's not using it," Bernie said. "Since the DampAct passed, the tribal council has been searching every plane that lands at gunpoint. Pete's been in and out in his Cessna all winter, Billy Mike says clean as a whistle every time."

"How often?"

"Once a week, sometimes twice." He added, "He's not even bringing in anything for personal use, which all by itself makes me suspicious, because Pete and Laura Anne are a couple what likes a little caribou with their cabernet."

"Get the trooper."

"Kate. You know and I know the trooper's based in Tok, and his jurisdiction is spread pretty thin even before he gets within flying distance of Niniltna. Besides, he's already in pursuit of some yo-yo who shot up a bank in Valdez and took off up Thompson Pass, on foot, no less. So much for state law. The DampAct—" He shrugged. "The DampAct is a local ordinance. Even if they catch him at it, all the council can do is fine him a thousand bucks. Like a speeding ticket. In any given year Pete spends more than that on olives for martinis."

"He got somebody flying it in from Anchorage?"

Bernie gave a bark of laughter. "Sure. MarkAir." At her look, he said, "Shit, Kate, MarkAir runs specials with the Brown Jug in town. Guy endorses his permanent dividend fund check over at the local MarkAir office, MarkAir carries it to Anchorage and expedites it to the Brown Jug warehouse, Brown Jug fills the order, MarkAir picks it up and takes it out to the airport and flies it to the village."

"Competition for you," she said.

He met her eyes levelly. "That isn't what this is about, and you know it. I serve drinks, not drunks, and I don't sell bottles."

She looked away. "Sorry."

He gave a curt nod.

There was a brief silence. She broke it. "What do you want me to do?"

He drained his mug and set it on the table with a decisive snap. "I got a state championship coming up. I need sober players who come to practice instead of out earning their next bottle running booze for that asshole. Preferably players who have not previously blown their brains out with their friend's gun. I want you to find out how Pete's getting the booze in, and stop him."

THE NEXT MORNING she fired up the Polaris and followed Bernie's tracks up the trail to the road that connected Niniltna and Ahtna and the Richardson Highway. The Polaris was old and slow, and the twenty-five miles between her homestead and the village took the better part of an hour, including the ten-minute break to investigate the tracks she spotted four miles outside the village. A pack of five wolves, healthy, hungry, and hunting. The 30.06 was always with her, and there was always a round in the chamber, but she stopped and checked anyway. One wolf was an appetite with attitude. Five of them looked like patrons of a diner, with her as the blue-plate special.

The tracks were crusted hard, a day old at least. Mutt's sniff was interested but unalarmed, and Kate replaced the rifle and continued up the road. It wasn't a road, really; it was the remains of the gravel roadbed of the Kanuyaq and Northwestern Railroad, built in 1910 to carry copper from the mine outside Niniltna to freighters docked in Cordova. In 1936 the copper played out, the railroad shut down, and locals began ripping up rails to get to the ties. It was an easy load of firewood, a lot easier than logging out the same load by hand.

The rails and ties were all gone now, although in summertime you could still pick up the odd spike in your truck tires. Twice a year, once after breakup, again just before the termination dust started creeping down the mountains, the state ran a grader over the rough surface to smooth over the potholes and the washouts. For the rest of the time they left itself to itself, and to the hundreds of Park rats who used it as a secondary means of transportation and commerce.

In the Alaskan bush, the primary means was ever and always air, and it was to the village airstrip Kate went first, a 4,800-foot stretch of hard-packed snow, much better maintained than the road. A dozen planes were tied down next to a hangar. Across the strip was a large log cabin with the U.S. flag flying outside, which backed up the wind sock at the end of the runway. Both hung limp this morning, and smoke rose straight up into the Arctic air from a cluster of rooftops glimpsed over the tops of the trees.

Kate stopped the snow machine next to the hangar, killed the engine, and stripped off her fur gauntlets. The round white thermometer fixed to the wall read twelve below. Colder than yesterday. She worked her fingers. It felt like it. Mutt jumped down and went trotting inside. A moment later there was a yell. "God*damn!*" Kate followed the sound.

A tall man in a gray coverall leaned up against the side of a Cessna 206 that looked as if it had enough hours on the Hobbs to put it into lunar orbit. The cowling was peeled back from the engine, and there were parts laid out on a canvas tarp. Both man and parts were covered with black grease. He scowled at her. "The next time that goddamn dog sticks her nose in my crotch from behind, I'm going to pinch her head off!"

"Hi, George."

Mutt nudged his hand with her head. He muttered something, pulled a rag out of a hip pocket, wiped his hands, and crouched down to give her ears a thorough scratching. She stood stock-still with an expression of bliss on her face, her plume of a tail waving gently. She'd been in love with George Perry since she was a puppy, and George had flown Milk-Bones into the set-net site Kate fished during her summer vacations. Kate had been in love with George since he'd flown Nestlé's Semi-Sweet Morsels into that same site.

The bush pilot gave Mutt a last affectionate cuff and stood to look at Kate. "I heard you were back."

She nodded in answer to his question, without offering an explanation. He didn't ask for one. "Coffee?"

She nodded again, and he led the way into his office, a small rectangular corner walled off from the rest of the building, furnished with a desk, a chair, and a Naugahyde couch heavily patched with black electrician's tape. The walls were covered with yellowing, tattered maps mended with Scotch tape. George went into a tiny bathroom and came out with a coffeepot held together with three-inch duct tape. He started the coffee and sat down at the desk. "So—how the hell are you, Shugak? Long time no see." His eyes dropped briefly to the open collar of her shirt. "*Long* time. You okay?" She nodded. "Good. Glad you're back anyway. Missed you."

"Me too."

"And the monster." He rummaged through a drawer for Oreo cookies and tossed one to Mutt. The coffeemaker sucked up the last of the water, and he poured out. Handing her a mug, he said, "What brings you into town?"

She nodded at the wall. "Wanted to take a look at your maps."

His eyebrows rose. "Be my guest." Mug in hand, she rose to her feet and began examining the maps beneath his speculative gaze, until she found the right one. Pete Liverakos's homestead was on Beaver Creek, about a mile downstream from the village. She traced a forefinger down the Kanuyaq River until she found it. The map indicated the homestead had its own airstrip, but then what self-respecting Alaskan homestead didn't?

George's voice sounded over her shoulder. "What are you looking for?"

She dropped her hand. "Just wanted to check something, and my maps are all about fifty years out of date."

"So are mine." He paused. "Dan O'Brien's bunch just did a new survey of the Kanuyaq. Source to delta, Copper Glacier to Kolinhenik Bar. They did the whole thing this summer. I thought those fucking—excuse me, Mutt—those frigging choppers never would leave."

"Have they got the new maps yet?" Though her voice was still harsh and broken, and according to the doctors always would be, the more she talked, the less it hurt. The realization brought her no joy.

He shook his head. "They're printing 'em this winter. They'll be selling 'em in the spring." He paused. "Dan's probably got the originals at Park Headquarters."

She drained her mug and set it on the desk. "Can I bum a ride up to the Step?"

He set his mug next to hers. "Sure. The Cub's prepped and ready to fly."

GEORGE TOOK OFF HOT, as straight as he could with only 150 horsepower under the hood. The sky was clear and the air was still and it was CAVU all the way from the Quilak Mountains to the gulf of Alaska. He climbed to 2,000 feet and stayed there, the throttle all the way out, a typical taxi driver whose sole interest was in there and back again. All rubbernecking did was burn gas. Twenty minutes later they landed on a small plateau in almost the exact geographical center of the Park. The north end of the airstrip began at the base of a Quilak mountain; the south end fell off the tip of a Teglliq foothill into the long river valley below. The airstrip on the Step was approximately 3,800 feet shorter than the one in Niniltna, and George stood on the pedals the instant the Super Cub touched down. They roared to a halt ten feet from the front door of the largest building in the group of prefabricated buildings huddled together at the side of the runway. They climbed out, and Mutt vanished into the trees. "I won't be long," Kate said.

George nodded. "I'll go down to the mess hall and scare up a free meal."

Dan O'Brien had dodged alligators in the Everglades and a'a in Kilauea with enough success to be transferred to the Park on December 3, 1980, the day after Jimmy Carter signed the d-2 lands bill, which added over a hundred million acres to already existing park lands in Alaska. Dan was fiercely protective of the region under his jurisdiction, and at the same time respectful of the rights of the people around whose homesteads and fish camps and mines and villages the Park had been created, which was why he was the only national park ranger in the history of the state never to get shot at, at least not while on park duties. Ranger by day, he was a notorious rounder by night. He'd known Kate since she was in college, and he'd been trying to lay her for at least that long.

The news of her return hadn't reached the Step, and he started around the desk with a big grin and open arms, only to skid to a halt as she unzipped her parka and he saw the scar. "Jesus Christ, Shugak," he said in a shaken voice, "what the hell did you do to your neck?"

She shrugged open the parka but kept it on. "George Perry tells me your boys have been making some new maps of the Kanuyaq."

Her harsh voice grated on his ears. He remembered the guitar, and thought of all the long winter evenings spent singing sea chanteys, and he turned his back on the subject and walked away. It might be the only thing he could do for an old friend, but he would by God do it and do it right. He did ask one question. "Mutt okay?"

"She's fine. She's chasing lunch down outside. About those maps."

"Maps?" he said brightly. "You bet we got maps. We got a map that shows every hump and bump from Eagle to Anchorage. We got a census map that shows the location of every moose bull, cow, and calf from here to the Kanuyaq River delta. We got maps that show where every miner with a pickax sunk a hole more than a foot deep anywhere within two hundred miles. We got maps that show the spread of spruce beetles north of Ikaluq. We got—"

"I need a map that show me any airstrips there might be around Beaver Creek."

"Pete Liverakos' place? Sure, he's got a strip. About twelve hundred feet, I think. Plenty long enough for his Cessna, but he lands her at Niniltna." His brow puckered. "Been curious about that myself. Why walk a mile downriver in winter when you can land on your own front doorstep?"

She nodded, although she wasn't curious; she knew why. "Is there another airstrip further up the creek, say halfway between his homestead and Ahtna?"

He thought. "Yeah, I think there's an old mine up there somewheres. Let's take a look." He led the way into a map room, a place of large tables and cabinets with long, wide, shallow drawers. He consulted a key, went to a drawer, and produced a map three feet square, laying it out on a table with a double-jointed lamp bolted to the side. He switched on the light, and they leaned over the map. A stubby forefinger found Niniltna and traced the river from the village to Beaver Creek, and from there up the creek to the homestead. He tapped once. "Here's Pete's place. A twelve-hundred-foot strip just sitting there going to waste. And Ahtna's up this way, to the northwest, about a hundred miles from Niniltna," adding apologetically, "The scale's too large to show it on this map." He marked the spot with an eraser and produced a yardstick, laying it on the map, one end pointing at Beaver Creek, the other at the eraser. With his hand he traced the length of the yardstick. "And presto chango, there it is. Like I thought, it's an airstrip next to a gold mine. Two thousand footer. Probably needed the extra to land heavy equipment. Abandoned in ... oh, hell 'long about '78? Probably about the time Carter declared most of the state an antiquity." He patted her on the ass and leered when her head snapped up. "Just think what you'd be missing if he hadn't."

"Just think," she agreed, moving the target out of range. "Is the strip maintained?"

He made a face. "I doubt it. Never was much gold there to begin with, and too fine to get out in commercial quantities anyway. Myself, I think the mine was just an excuse to come in and poach moose."

Her finger came back down the yardstick. "Beaver Creek runs right up to it."

"Uh-huh." Showing off, he produced another map, with a flourish worthy of Mandrake the Magician. "This shows the estimated animal population in the same area." They studied it. "Neat, huh? a couple moose moved in five years ago, been real good about dropping a calf or two every spring. There's half a dozen pairs of eagles. Beaver, mostly on the creek." He snapped his fingers. "Sure. I remember one time I was at the Roadhouse and Pete brought in a beaver hide. Said he was running a trapline up the creek." His lip lifted in a sneer. "Said he'd cured it himself. Shape it was in, nobody doubted it for a minute."

He looked up from the map. The hazel eyes had an edge sharp enough to cut. He remembered a time when those eyes could laugh. "Hell of a trapper and hunter," he said, "that Pete. That is, if you don't count him joining in that wolf hunt the state had last year." He grinned. "Nobody else does."

"Why not?"

"He got three inches off the prop of his plane, running out to draw a bead on a running female."

"He wreck the plane?" Dan shook his head. "Too bad. Okay. Dan. Thanks."

He followed her out of the room. "Okay'? 'Thanks'? Is that it? Is that all I get? Of all the ungrateful—"

The front door shut on the rest of it.

George flew back to Niniltna by way of a stop at Ahtna to pick up the mail, fresh off the daily MarkAir flight from Anchorage. Kate waited by the Cub, watching cargo unload from the 737. Ahtna, at the junction of the Park road with the Richardson Highway, was a wet town, with a population of a thousand and three flourishing bars. An entire pallet of Olympia beer was marked for the Polar Bar, a case of Jose Cuervo gold and another of assorted liqueurs for the Midnight Sun Lounge. The 737 took off, and a Northern Air Cargo DC-6 landed in its place, off-loading an igloo of building supplies from Spenard Lumber and a pallet of Rainier beer, this one marked for the Riverside Inn.

No Windsor Canadian in either cargo, but then she didn't see Pete or his 50 Papa around anywhere, either. Once a week, Bernie had said. This wasn't the day.

Ahtna, like Niniltna, was on the Kanuyaq. Downriver was Niniltna. Farther downriver was Prince William Sound. Upriver was a state highway maintenance camp. Last year during a spring storm a corner of the yard had crumbled into the river, taking a barrel of methanol with it. The barrel had floated downriver; to wash ashore outside Ahtna. Four high school kids, who sixteen, one fifteen, one fourteen, already drunk, had literally stumbled across it and instead of falling in the river and drowning tapped the barrel and died of poisoning.

George returned with the bag as the pallet of Rainier was loaded onto the back of a flatbed. He read her silence correctly and said, "They're a common carrier, Kate, just like me. We fly anything, anywhere, anytime, for cash money. That's how we make a living."

"You don't fly booze."

He shrugged. "Not up to me. The town voted to go dry."

"And if it hadn't?"

He shrugged again. A half hour later they were back in Niniltna.

THE LAND, LOW AND FLAT near the river, began to rise soon after she left it. Blueberry bushes, cottonwoods, and scrub spruce were left behind for currants, birches, and hemlocks. The snow was so deep and was packed down so well beneath its own weight that the Polaris skimmed over it, doing better than forty miles an hour. In spite of the wide swing to avoid the homestead, she reached the abandoned gold mine at four-thirty, with more than an hour of twilight left.

She ran the machine into some birches, the nose pointing downhill, and cut branches for camouflage and to sweep the snow free of tracks. Strapping on the snowshoes that were part of the standard winter survival kit she kept beneath the Polaris's seat, she shouldered her pack, slung the 30.06, and hiked the quarter of a mile to the mine entrance that gaped blackly from halfway up the hill next to the creek. It was dark inside until she got out the flashlight. The snow in the entrance was solidly packed down, as if something heavy had been stacked there.

Kate explored and found a branching tunnel, where she pitched the tent and unrolled the sleeping bag. Taking the ax and a collapsible bucket, she went down to the creek and chopped a hole in the ice beneath an overhanging bush. She filled the bucket with ice and water. Back at the tent, she lit the Sterno stove. The exertion and the cold had left her hungry, and she ate two packages of Top Ramen noodles sitting at the entrance to the mine, surveying the terrain in the fading light.

The airstrip ran parallel to the creek, which ran southeast-northwest around the hill of the mine. A narrow footpath led from the mine to one end of the airstrip. She squinted. A second, wider trail started at the other end of the trip, going in the opposite direction. Birches and scrub spruce clustered thickly at the edges of the strip and both trails. The creek was lined with cottonwoods and diamond willow. Mutt visited them all, sniffing, marking territory.

Kate went back for a Chunky and sat again at the mine entrance, gnawing at the cold, hard chocolate as she waited for the moon to come up. An hour later it did, full and bright. By Agudar's light she walked down the footpath. Mutt trotted out of the woods and met her on the strip. It was as hard and smooth as the strip at Niniltna. The second, wider trial was a snow machine track. It followed the creek southwest, dodging back and forth, taking the easiest way through the trees and undergrowth without coming too close to the bank.

The creek itself was frozen over. No snares. No holes cut into the ice in any of the likelier places Kate spotted for snares.

She went back to the mine and crawled into her sleeping bag, Mutt next to her. Mutt didn't dream. Kate did, the same dream as always, children in pain. In the night she moved, restless, half waking, moaning a little. In the night Mutt moved closer to her, the animal's 140-pound weight warm and solid. Kate slept again.

The next morning the sun was up by nine, and Kate and Mutt were on the creek trail as the first rays hit and slid off the hard surface of the frozen landscape. Kate kept to the trail to minimize the track she left behind. She moved slowly, ears cocked for the sound of an airplane engine, eyes on the creek side of the trail. Again there were no holes, and no snares for holes. There was nothing more to see. Old habits are hard to break, especially the habit of verification instinctive in every good investigator. It had compelled her to give Pete the benefit of the doubt. Now there was none. She went back to the mine.

THEY WAITED, camping in the tunnel, carrying water from the creek, Mutt grazing the local rabbit population, for three days. Every morning she broke down the camp and packed it down the hill to the Polaris, and every evening she packed it back up again.

She'd had worse stakeouts. The first morning a pair of eagles cruised by overhead, flying low and slow, eyes alert for any movement on the ground. A gaunt and edgy moose cow and her two calves passed through the area on the second day, moving like they had a purpose. That night they heard the long-drawn-out howl of a wolf. Purpose enough. Down by the creek, a gnawed stand of diamond willow confirmed the presence of Dan's beavers, although the winter's heavy snowfall kept Kate from spotting the dam until the second day. The third afternoon a fat black raven croaked at them contemptuously on his way to make mischief elsewhere. That evening Kate ran out of Top Ramen and had to fall back on reconstituted freeze-dried spaghetti. Some prices are almost too high to pay.

Late on the afternoon of the fourth day, as she was thinking about fetching her camp up again from the Polaris, Mutt's ears went forward and she got to her feet and pointed her muzzle west. Kate faded back into the mine, one hand knotted in Mutt's ruff, the other gripping the handle of her ax, as the Cessna 180 with the tail numbers marking 50 PAPA came into view over the trees. It touched down and used up all of the strip on the runout, bright shiny new in its fresh-off-the-assembly-line coat of red and white. Only bootleggers could afford new planes in the Alaskan bush.

The pilot was tall and rangy and well-muscled, and the unloading was easy and practiced. All the seats save the pilot's had been removed and the remaining space filled up with case after case of Windsor Canadian whiskey, in the plastic bottles. Glass bottles weighed more and took more gas to get into the air. Glass bottles cut into the profit margin.

When he had all the boxes out on the ground, he tucked one box beneath his arm and started up the path toward the mine. Kate and Mutt retreated farther into the darkness.

He made the trip up and back six times, twelve cases in all, stacking them inside the mouth of the mine where the snow was packed down all nice and hard, where he'd stacked different cases many times before. He whistled while he worked, and when he was done he paused in the mine entrance to remove his cap and wipe his forehead on his sleeve. In the thin sun of an Arctic afternoon, his fifty-year-old face was handsome, although his nose and chin were a little too sharp, like his smile.

He replaced his cap and started down the hill, whistling again. He wasn't halfway to the plane before he heard it, and the sound spun him around on his heels.

Kate stood in front of the stack of boxes, swinging from the hips. The blade of the ax bit deep. A dark-brown liquid spurted out when she pulled it free. The smell of alcohol cut through the air like a knife.

"Hey!" he yelled. "What the hell!" He started back up the slope.

Without a break in her swing, Kate said one word. "Mutt."

A gray blur streaked out of the mine to intercept him, and he skidded to a halt and almost fell. "Shit!"

The blade bit into another case. More whiskey gushed out.

"Goddamn it! Kate!"

"Hello, Pete," she said, and swung.

"Kate, for chrissake cut that out—that stuff's worth a hundred bucks a bottle to me!"

The ax struck again. He made as if to move, but Mutt stood between them, lips drawn back from her teeth, head held low, body quivering with the eagerness to attack.

"You fly to Ahtna and pick up your shipment," Kate said, torn voice harsh in the still afternoon air. The ax bit into the sixth case. "You drop it here and store it in the mine entrance. You fly back to Niniltna, landing at the village strip so the tribal policemen can see how squeaky clean you are. You hike back down to your homestead and spend the next week running your trapline. You were catching beavers, you told everybody at the Roadhouse one night. You even showed them a pelt."

Cardboard and plastic crunched. "Only you don't have a trapline. There isn't a hole in the ice between here and your homestead, or a single snare to drop down a hole. You're not trapping beaver—you're using your snow machine to bring the booze down a case at a time."

He shifted from one foot to the other and tried a disarming smile. "Well, shit, Kate. Guy's got to make a living. Listen, can we talk about this? Don't!" he shouted when she swung again. "Goddamn it. I'll just buy more!"

"No, you won't."

"You can't stop me!"

"No?" She swung. The ax chunked.

It took fifteen minutes in all. Kate had always been very good with an ax. He cursed her through every second of it, unable to walk away. When she was finished, she struck a wooden match on the thigh of her jeans and tossed it into the pile of broken boxes. There was a whoosh of air and a burst of flame. She shouldered the ax and walked down the hill. Mutt followed, keeping between Kate and Pete, hard, bright gaze watching him carefully.

When she approached the Cessna, Pete's voice rose to a scream. "You fucking bitch, you lay a hand on that plane and I'll—"

Mutt snarled. He shut up. Kate raised the ax and swung with all her strength. The blade bit deep into the airframe just above the gear where the controls were located. She pulled the blade free, raised the ax for another swing, and several things happened at once.

A bottle she'd missed exploded in the mine entrance and everybody jumped. Mutt barked, a single, sharp sound, and kept barking. There was a scramble of feet behind Kate. The ax twisted out of her hands and thudded into the snow six feet away, and she whirled to face a blade that gleamed in the reflection of the whiskey fire. She halted in a half crouch, arms curved at her sides.

Where was Mutt? A bark answered the question somewhere off to her right. She couldn't look away from the blade to see what Mutt had found more important than guarding her back. They would discuss the matter, in detail. Later.

The bootlegger's grin taunted her, and he wasn't looking so handsome anymore. "Sorry, Kate." He gestured at her scar with the knife. "Guess I get to finish what one of your baby-rapers started. No offense," he added. "I'm just making me too much money to let you walk away from this one."

"No offense," she agreed, and as he took a step forward dropped to her hands, kicked out with her right foot, hooked his ankle, and yanked his feet out from under him. He landed hard on his back, hard enough to jolt the knife out of his grip. She snagged it out of the air and in one continuing smooth motion had the point under his chin. The grin froze in place.

She pressed up with the blade. Very slowly and very carefully he got to his feet. She kept pressing, and he went all the way up on tiptoe. "What is this," she said, "a six-inch blade?" A bead of bright-red blood appeared, and he gave an inarticulate grunt. "I personally think your brain is too small for the blade to reach if I stick it in from under your chin." She pressed harder. "What do you think?"

His voice broke on a sob. "Jesus, Kate, don't, please don't."

Disgusted, she relaxed enough for him to come down off his toes. The point of the knife shifted, and he jerked back out of range. Blood dripped from his chin. He wiped at it and gave his hand an incredulous look. "You cut me! You bitch, you cut me!" He backed away from her as if he could back away from the blood too. His heel caught on something, and he lost his balance and fell over the bank of the creek. It was short but steep, and momentum threw him into a heavy, awkward backward somersault. He landed on a fallen log. Kate heard the unmistakable crack of breaking bone from where she stood. The whiskey fire was high enough to show the white gleam of bone thrusting up through the fabric covering his left thigh.

Becoming aware of a low rumble of sound, she turned. Mutt stood in the middle of the airstrip, legs stiff, hackles raised, all her teeth showing as she stared into the trees. A steady, menacing growl rumbled up out of her throat. Kate followed her gaze. Five pairs of cold, speculative eyes met her own. Five muzzles sniffed the air, filled with the scents of burning whiskey, leaking hydraulic fluid, broken flesh, the rust-red smell of fresh blood.

Behind them Pete clawed his way up the creekbank and saw. "Kate." His voice sweated fear.

She turned her head to look at the man lying on the frozen creekbank, and she did not see him. She saw instead eight kids in Alakanuk, drunk and then dead drunk. She saw a baby drowned in Birch Creek, left on a sandbar by parents too drunk to remember to load him into the skiff with the case of beer they had just bought, and just opened.

She saw her mother, cold and still by the side of the road, halfway to a home to which she never returned and a husband and a daughter she never saw again.

Kate picked up the ax and took a step back. Five pairs of eyes shifted from the prone man to follow her progress. "Mutt," she said, her torn voice low.

The steady rumble of Mutt's growl never ceased as she, too, began to retreat, one careful step at a time.

"Kate," Pete said. "That thing with your mother, that was business. A guy has a right to make a living, you know?"

Her camp was already packed and stowed. The ax went in with it. The brush concealing the Polaris was easily cleared, and she'd left the machine pointed downhill for an easy start. She straddled the seat.

"Kate!" His voice rose. "Your mother would fuck for a bottle! Shit, after a while she'd fuck for a drink! Goddamn you, Kate, you can't leave me here! Kate!"

The roar of the engine drowned out his scream.

Gathering clouds hid the setting sun. It would snow before morning. It was sixty miles across country to her homestead. Time to go. Mutt jumped up on the seat behind her, and Kate put the machine in gear.

Max Collins's series about detective Nathan Heller is one of the great *noir* creations of this century. Max has overhauled the historical mystery and made it entirely his own, as is easy to see in such novels as TRUE DETECTIVE (1983) and NEON MIRAGE (1988). Most recently, his Heller novel CARNAL HOURS won praise from virtually every major mystery reviewer, and added to Max's long string of Shamus wins and nominations. Max has also written the Nolan, Quarry, and Mallory series. He is also, as is evidenced here, a short-story writer of the first order.

His Father's Ghost
MAX ALLAN COLLINS

The bus dropped him off at a truck stop two miles from Greenwood, and Jeff had milk and homemade cherry pie before walking the two miles to the little town. It was May, a sunny cool afternoon that couldn't make up its mind whether to be spring or summer, and the walk along the blacktop up and over rolling hills was pleasant enough.

On the last of these hills—overlooking where the undulating Grant Wood farmland flattened out to nestle the small collection of houses and buildings labeled "Greenwood" by the water tower—was the cemetery. The breeze riffled the leaves of trees that shaded the gravestones; it seemed to Jeff that someone was whispering to him, but he couldn't make out what they were saying.

Nobody rich was buried here—no fancy monuments, anyway. He stopped at the top and worked his way down. The boy—Jeff was barely twenty-one—in his faded jeans and new running shoes and Desert Storm sweatshirt, duffel bag slung over his arm, walked backward, eyes slowly scanning the names. When he reached the bottom, he began back up the hill, still scanning, and was threading his way down again when he saw the name.

Carl Henry Hastings—Beloved Husband, Loving Father. 1954–1992.

Jeff Carson studied the gravestone; put his hand on it. Ran his hand over the chiseled inscription. He thought about dropping to his knees for a prayer. But he couldn't, somehow. He'd been raised religious—or any-way, Methodist—but he didn't have much faith in any of that, anymore.

And he couldn't feel what he wanted to feel; he felt as dead as those around him, as cold inside as the marble of the tombstone.

The wind whispered to him through the trees, but he still couldn't make out what it said to him, and so just walked on into the little town, stopping at a motel just beyond the billboard announcing NEW JERSEY'S CLEANEST LITTLE CITY and a sign marking the city limits and population, six thousand.

He tapped the bell on the counter to summon a woman he could see in a room back behind there, to the right of the wall of keys, in what seemed to be living quarters, watching a soap opera, the volume so loud it was distorting. Maybe she didn't want to hear the bell.

But she heard it anyway, a heavyset woman in a floral muumuu with black beehive hair and Cleopatra eye makeup, hauling herself out of a chair as overstuffed as she was; twenty years ago she probably looked like Elizabeth Taylor. Now she looked more like John Belushi *doing* Elizabeth Taylor.

"Twenty-six dollars," she informed him, pushing the register his way. "Cash, check, or credit card?"

"Cash."

She looked at him for the first time, and her heavily mascaraed eyes froze.

"Jesus Christ," she said.

"What's wrong, lady?"

"Nuh . . . nothing."

He signed the register, and she stood there gaping at him. She hadn't returned to her soap opera when he exited, standing there frozen, an obese Lot's wife.

In his room he tossed his duffel bag on the bureau, turned on the TV to CNN just for the noise, and sat on the bed by the nightstand. He found the slim Greenwood phone book in the top drawer, next to the Gideon Bible, and he thumbed through it, looking for an address. He wrote it down on the notepad by the phone.

It was getting close enough to supper time that he couldn't go calling on people. But small-town people ate early, so by seven or maybe even six-thirty he could risk it. He'd been raised in a small town himself, back in Indiana—not this small, but small enough.

He showered, shaved, and after he'd splashed cold water on his face, he studied it in the bathroom mirror as if looking for clues: gray-blue eyes, high cheekbones, narrow nose, dimpled chin. Then he shrugged at himself and ran a hand through his long, shaggy, wheat-colored hair; that was all the more attention he ever paid to it.

Slipping back into his jeans and pulling on a light blue polo shirt, he hoped he looked presentable enough not to get chased away when he showed up on a certain doorstep. He breathed deep—half sigh, half determination.

He'd not be turned away.

Greenwood wasn't big enough to rate a McDonald's, apparently, but there was a Dairy Freez and a Mr. Quik-Burger, whatever that was. He passed up both, walking along a shady, idyllic residential street, with homes dating mostly to the 1920s or before he'd guess, and well-kept up. Finally, he came to the downtown, which seemed relatively prosperous: a corner supermarket, video store, numerous bars, and a café called Mom's.

Somebody somewhere had told him that one of the three rules of life was not eating at any restaurant called Mom's; one of the others was not playing cards with anybody named Doc. He'd forgotten the third and proved the first wrong by having the chicken-fried steak, American fries with gravy, corn, and slaw, and finding them delicious.

The only thing wrong with Mom's was that it was fairly busy—farm families, blue-collar folks—all of whom kept looking at him. It was as if he were wearing a KICK ME sign, only they weren't smirking; they had wide, hollow eyes and whispered. Husband and wives would put their heads together; mothers would place lips near a child's ear for a hushed explanation.

Jeff's dad, back in Indiana, was not much of a man's man; Dad was a drama teacher at a small college, and if it hadn't been for Uncle Fred, Jess would never have learned to hunt and fish and shoot. But Jeff's dad's guilty pleasure (Dad's term) was John Wayne movies and other westerns. Jeff loved them, too. *The Searchers* he had seen maybe a million times—wore out the video tape.

But right now he felt like Randolph Scott or maybe Audie Murphy in one of those fifties westerns where a stranger came to town and everybody looked at him funny.

Or maybe it was just his imagination. He was sitting in the corner of the café, and to his left, up on the wall, after all, was a little chalkboard with the specials of the day.

His waitress was looking at him funny; she was a blonde of perhaps fifteen, pretty and plump, about to burst the buttons of her waitress uniform. She wanted to flirt, but Jeff wasn't in the mood.

When she brought the bill, however, he asked her directions to the address he'd written on the note paper.

"That's just up the street to Main and two blocks left and one more right," she said. "I could show you ... I get off at eight."

"That's okay. How old are you?"

"Eighteen. That little pin you're wearing ... were you really in Desert Storm?"

He'd forgotten it was on there. "Uh, yeah."

"See any action?"

He nodded, digging some paper money out of his pocket. "Yeah, a little."

Her round pretty face beamed. "Greenwood's gonna seem awful dull, after that. My name's Tabitha, but my friends call me Tabby."

"Hi, Tabby."

"My folks just moved here, six months ago. Dad works at Chemco."

"Mmmm," Jeff said, as if that meant something to him. He was leaving a five-dollar bill and an extra buck, which covered the food and a tip.

"Jenkins!" somebody called.

It was the manager, or at least the guy in shirt and tie behind the register up front; he was about fifty with dark hair, a pot belly, and an irritated expression.

"You got orders up!" he said, scowling over at the girl.

Then he saw Jeff and his red face whitened.

"What's with him?" Tabby asked under her breath. "Looks like he saw a ghost. . . ."

The pleasantly plump waitress swished away quickly, and Jeff, face burning from all the eyes on him, got the hell out of there.

AT DUSK IN THE COOL BREEZE, Greenwood seemed unreal, like something Hollywood dreamed up; as he walked back into the residential neighborhood—earlier he must have walked by within a block of the address he was seeking—he was thinking how perfect it seemed, when a red pickup rolled by with speakers blasting a Metallica song.

He hated that shit. Heavy metal was not his style, or drugs, either. His folks liked to joke about being "old hippies," and indeed he'd grown up used to the smell of incense and the sweet sickening aroma of pot. They weren't potheads or anything, but now and then, on a weekend night at home, they'd go in the den and put on Hendrix and Cream (music Jeff didn't care for in the least) and talk about the good old days.

Jeff loved his parents, but that Woodstock crap made him sick. He liked country western music—Garth Brooks, Travis Tritt—and found his folks' liberal politics naive. Some of his views came from Uncle Fred, no question; and maybe, like most kids, Jeff was just inclined to be contrary to his parents.

But a part of him had always felt apart from them. A stranger.

If it hadn't been for Dad liking western movies—Mom hated them and never had a kind word for "that fascist, John Wayne"—they might not have bonded at all. But when his father was a kid, *Gunsmoke* and *Have Gun Will Travel* were on TV, and that bug had bit his dad before the Beatles came along to screw up Jeff's parents' entire generation.

The streetlamp out front was burned out, but a light was on over the door of the one-and-a-half-story 1950s era brick bungalow, with its four steps up to a stoop and its lighted doorbell. It was as if he were expected.

But he wasn't.

And he stood on the stoop the longest time before he finally had the nerve to push the bell.

The door opened all the way—not just a protective crack; this was still a small enough, safe enough town to warrant such confidence, or naivete. The cheerful-looking woman standing there in a yellow halter top and red shorts and yellow-and-red open-toed sandals was slender and redheaded with pale freckled-all-over skin; she was green-eyed, pug-nosed, with full lips—attractive but not beautiful, and probably about thirty.

"Danny," she began, obviously expecting somebody else, a bottle of Coors in a red-nailed hand, "I—"

Then her wide smile dissolved, and her eyes widened and saying "Jesus Christ!," she dropped the Coors; it exploded on the porch, and Jeff jumped back.

Breathing hard, she looked at him, ignoring the foaming beer and the broken glass between them.

"What ... what is ... who ..."

Her eyes tightened and shifted, as if she were trying to get him in focus.

"Mrs. Hastings, I'm sorry to jump drop in on you like this."

Her voice was breathless, disbelieving: "Carl?"

"My name is Jeff Carson, Mrs. Hastings. We spoke on the phone?"

"Step into the light. Mind the glass."

He did.

Her eyes widened again and her mouth was open, her full lips quivering. "It's not possible."

"I called inquiring about your husband. And you told me he had died recently."

"Six months ago. I don't understand ..."

"Is there somewhere we could talk? You seem to be expecting somebody. ..."

She nodded; then swallowed. "Mr. Carson ... Jeff?"

"Please."

"There's a deck in back; I was just relaxing there. Would you mind walking around and meeting me there? I don't ... don't want you walking through the house just yet. My son is playing Nintendo and I ... don't want to disturb him."

That made as little sense as anything else, but Jeff merely nodded.

In back, up some steps onto the wooden sun deck, Jeff sat in a white metal patio chair by a white metal table under a colorful umbrella; dusk was darkening into evening, and the backyard stretched endlessly to a break of trees. A bug light snapped and popped, eating mosquitoes; but a few managed to nibble Jeff, just the same.

In a minute or so she appeared through a glass door. She had two beers this time; she handed him one and took a manlike gulp from the other.

"So you're the one who called," she said.

"That's right."

"I almost forgot about that. All you did was ask for Carl, and when I said he'd died, you just said 'oh,' and asked when, and I said not long ago, and you said you were very sorry and hung up. Right? Wasn't that the conversation?"

"That was the conversation."

"Are you his son?"

That surprised Jeff, but he nodded and said, "How did you know? Is there . . . a resemblance?"

She had a mouthful of beer and almost spit it out. "Wait here."

She went inside the house and came back with a framed color photograph of a man in sheriff's uniform and hat—gray-blue eyes, high cheekbones, narrow nose, dimpled chin. Jeff might have been looking into a mirror of the future, showing him what he would look like in twenty-one years.

"No wonder everybody's been looking at me weird," he said. He couldn't stop staring at the picture; his hand shook.

"You never met him?"

"No. Except for this afternoon."

"This afternoon?"

"At the cemetery."

And then Jeff began to cry.

Mrs. Hastings rose and came over and put her arm around him; she patted his shoulder, as if to say, "There, there." "Listen . . . what's your name?"

"Jeff."

She moved away as Jeff dried his eyes with his fingertips. "Jeff, I never knew about you. Carl never told me. We were married a long time, but he never said anything about you."

"He was the local sheriff?"

"Yes. City, not county. For twelve years. You don't know much about your dad, do you?"

"My dad . . . my dad is a man named Stephen Carson."

"I don't understand."

"I was adopted." He said the obvious: "Carl Hastings was my natural father."

She was sitting again. She said, "Oh," drawing it out into a very long word. Then she pointed at him. "And the mother was Margie Holdaway!"

"That's right. How did you know?"

"Carl and Margie were an item in high school. Oh, I was just in grade school at the time, myself, but I've heard all about it. Not from Carl . . . from the gossips in this town that wanted to make sure I knew all about the Boy Most Likely and his hot affair with the Homecoming Queen. I just never knew anything had . . . come of it."

"Tell me about him."

"You . . . you don't know anything about him, do you, Jeff?"

"No. I always wanted to know who my real parents were. My *folks* knew . . . they didn't get me from an agency. There was some connection between Dad, that is, Stephen Carson, and a lawyer who went to school with Margie Holdaway's father. Anyway, that's how the adoption was arranged. My parents told me that when I turned twenty-one, if I still wanted to know who my natural parents were, they'd tell me. And they did."

"And you came looking for your dad."

"Six months too late, it looks like. Tell me about him."

She told him Carl Hastings was an only child, a farm boy from around Greenwood who was one of the little town's favorite sons—a high-school football star (All-State), he had gone on a scholarship and a successful run of college ball that led to pro offers. But in his senior year Carl had broken his leg in the final game of the season. He had returned to Greenwood where he went to work for a car dealership.

"My *daddy's* business," Mrs. Hastings said, and she sipped her Coors. "I was ten years younger than Carl . . . your daddy. I was working in the Greenwood Pontiac sales office, just out of high school, and things just sort of developed." She smiled and gazed upward and inward, then shook her head. "Carl was just about the handsomest man I ever saw. Least, till you came to my door."

"When did he become sheriff?"

She smirked a little, shook her head. "After we got married, Carl felt funny about working for his wife's daddy. Shouldn't have, but he did. When he got promoted to manager, he just . . . brooded. He was a funny sort of guy, your daddy—very moral. Lots of integrity. Too much, maybe."

"Why do you say that?"

"Oh, I don't know. It was his only fault, really . . . he could be kind of a stuffed shirt. Couldn't roll with the flow, or cut people much slack."

"Did that make him a good sheriff or a bad one?"

"He was re-elected five times, if that answers your question. He was the most dedicated lawman you can imagine."

"Is that what got him killed?"

The words hit her like a physical blow. She swallowed; her eyes began to go moist. She nodded. "I . . . I guess it was."

"I know it must be painful, ma'am. But what were the circumstances?"

Her expression froze, and then she smiled. "The way you said that
... you said it, *phrased* it, just like Carl would have. Right down to
the 'ma'am.' "

"How did my father die?"

"It *is* painful for me to talk about. If you wait a few minutes, Danny
Simmons is stopping by—"

As if on cue, a man in the uniform of the local sheriff came out through
the house via the glass doors. He was not Carl Hastings, of course: he
was a tall, dark-haired man with angular features, wearing his sunglasses
even though darkness had fallen.

"I let myself in, babe—I think Tim's gone numb from Nintendo ...
Judas Priest!"

The man in the sheriff's uniform whipped off his sunglasses to get a
better look; his exclamation of surprise was at seeing Jeff.

"Danny, this is Carl's son." She had stood and was gesturing to Jeff,
who slowly rose himself.

"Jesus, Annie." Simmons looked like he'd been pole-axed. "I didn't
know Carl had a son, except for Tim."

"Neither did I," she said.

"He was my natural father," Jeff said, extending his hand, and the two
men shook in the midst of the explanation.

"Adopted, huh? I'll bet I know who the mother was," Simmons said
tactlessly, finding a metal patio chair to deposit his lanky frame in. "Margie Sterling."

"I thought her name was Holdaway," Jeff said.

"Maiden name," Mrs. Hastings explained. "Margie married Al Sterling
right after college."

"Al Sterling?"

"His Honor Alfred Sterling," Simmons said, with a faint edge of nasty
sarcasm. "Circuit judge. Of course, he wasn't a judge when Margie married him; he was just the golden boy who was supposed to take the legal
profession by storm."

"And didn't?" Jeff asked.

Sheriff Simmons leaned forward, and Jeff could smell liquor on the
man's breath, perhaps explaining the obnoxious behavior. "Fell on his
ass in New York City with some major firm. Came crawling back to
Greenwood to work in his daddy's law office. Now he's the biggest tight-
ass judge around. You got a beer for me, babe?"

A little disgusted, a little irritated, Mrs. Hastings said, "Sure you need
it, Danny?"

"I'd have go some, to match that lush Sterling." He turned to Jeff and
shrugged and smiled. "Have to forgive me, kid. I had a long day."

"No problem. Did you work with my father?"

"Proud to say I did. I was his deputy for five, no, six years. Stepping into his shoes was the hardest, biggest thing I ever had to try to do."

"Mrs. Hastings suggested I ask you about how he died."

Simmons lost his confident, smirky, expression; he seemed genuinely sorrowful when he said, "Sorry, kid—I thought you knew."

"No. That's why I'm here. I'm trying to find out about him."

Simmons seemed to be tasting something foul. "Punks . . . goddamn gang scum."

"Gangs? In a little town like this?"

"Oh, they're not local. They come in from the big cities, looking for farmhouses to rent and set up as crack houses—quiet rural areas where they can do their drug trafficking out of and don't have big-city law enforcement to bother 'em."

"You've got that kind of thing going on here?"

Mrs. Hastings smiled proudly as she said, "Not now—Carl chased 'em out. He and Danny shot it out with a bad-ass bunch and chased 'em out of the county."

"No kidding," Jeff said. He felt a surge of pride. Had his real dad *been* John Wayne?

"That was about two weeks before it happened," Simmons said softly.

"Before what happened?"

Mrs. Hastings stood abruptly and said, "I'm getting myself another beer. Anybody else?"

"No thanks," Jeff said.

"I already asked for one and didn't get it," Simmons reminded her.

She nodded and went inside.

Simmons leaned forward, hands folded, elbows on his knees. "It wasn't pretty. Classic urban-style drive-by shooting—as he come out of the office, some nameless faceless asshole let loose of a twelve-gauge shotgun and . . . sorry. Practically blew his head off."

Jeff winced. "Anybody see it?"

"Not a soul. It was three in the morning; we'd had a big accident out on the highway and he worked late. Office is downtown, and about then, it's deserted as hell. Practically tumbleweed blowin' through."

"Then how do you know it was that gang retaliating?"

Simmons shrugged. "Just the M.O., really. And we did have a report that a van of those Spic bastards was spotted rolling through town that afternoon."

"It was an Hispanic gang?"

"That's what I said."

"Nobody else had a motive?"

"You mean, to kill your dad? Kid, they would have elected that man president around here if they could. Everybody loved him."

"Not quite everybody," Jeff said.

Mrs. Hastings came back out and sat down with her Coors in hand. She still hadn't brought Simmons one.

"Sorry," she said. "I just didn't want to have to hear that again."

"I don't blame you," Jeff said. "I need to ask you something, and I don't mean for it to be embarrassing or anything."

"Go ahead," she said guardedly.

"Were my father and Margie Sterling still . . . friends?"

Her expression froze; then she sighed. She looked at the bottle of beer as her thumb traced a line in the moisture there. "You'll have to ask her that."

"You think she'd be around?"

"Probably. I can give you the address."

"I'd appreciate that."

Then she smiled one-sidedly, and it was kind of nasty. "Like to see the expression on her face when she gets a load of *you*. Excuse me a second—I'll go write that address down for you."

She got up and went inside again.

Simmons lounged his scarecrowlike body back in the patio chair and smiled affably. "So how long you going to be in town?"

"As long as it takes."

"To do what?"

"Find out why my father was killed."

The smile disappeared. "Look . . . kid. We investigated ourselves; plus, we had state investigators in. It was a gang shooting."

"Really? What gang exactly?"

"We didn't take their pedigree when Carl and me ran 'em off that farm!"

"You must have had a warrant."

"We did. It was a John Doe. Hey, hell with you, kid. You don't know me, and you don't know our town, and you didn't even know your damn father."

"Why do you call my father's wife, 'babe'?"

"What?"

"You heard me."

Mrs. Hastings came back out with the address on a slip of paper. She handed it to Jeff.

"Good luck," she said, and then, suddenly, she touched his face. Her hand was cold and moist from the beer bottle she'd been holding, but the gesture was overwhelmingly warm. He looked deep into the moist green eyes and found only love for his late father.

"You can answer my question later," he said to the sheriff, and walked down the steps and away from the deck."

THE STERLING HOUSE was as close to a mansion as Greenwood had. On the outskirts of town in a housing development of split-level homes that looked as expensive as they did similar, dominating a circular cul-de-sac, it was a much larger structure, plantationlike, white, with pillars; through a large multipaned octagonal window high above the entry, a chandelier glimmered.

He rang the bell, and an endlessly bing-bonging theme played behind the massive mahogany door; a tall narrow row of windows on either side of the door provided a glimpse of a marble-floored entryway beyond.

He half expected a butler to answer, but instead it was a woman in a sweatshirt and slacks; at first he thought she was the housekeeper, but she wasn't.

She was his mother.

She was small and attractive. She had been cute, no doubt, when his father had dated her a lifetime ago; now she was a pixie-woman with short brown hair and wideset eyes and a thin, pretty mouth. The only sign of wealth was a massive glittering diamond on the hand she brought up to her mouth as she gasped at the sight of him.

". . . Carl?" Her voice was high-pitched, breathy, like a little girl's.

"No," Jeff said.

"You're not Carl. Who . . ."

Then she knew.

She didn't say so, but her eyes told him, *she knew*, and she stepped back and slammed the door in his face.

He stood staring at it for a while, and was just starting to get angry, finger poised to press the bell again, and again, for an hour, for forever if he had to, when the door opened, slowly, and she looked at him. She had gray-blue eyes, too. Maybe his eyes had come from her, not his father.

Then the little woman threw herself around him. Held him. She was weeping. Pretty soon he was weeping, too. They stood outside the mansionlike home and held one another, comforting one another, until a male voice said, "What *is* this?"

They moved apart, then turned to see a man who could have been forty or fifty, but his dark eyes seemed dead already—a thin, gray-haired individual whose once-handsome features were tightened into a clenched fist of a face. He wore a cardigan sweater over a pale blue shirt with a tie. He had a pipe in one hand and a large cocktail glass in the other.

"What the hell is this about?" he demanded, but his voice was thin and whiny.

She pulled Jeff into the light. "Al, this is my son." Then she turned to Jeff and asked, "What's your name?"

SOON JEFF AND MRS. STERLING were seated on high chrome stools at the ceramic-tile island in the center of a large kitchen with endless dark-wood cabinets, appliance-loaded countertops, and stained-glass windows. She had served him chocolate chip cookies and tea; the pot was still simmering on one of the burners opposite them on the ceramic island.

Judge Sterling had, almost immediately, gotten out of their way, saying morosely, "You'll be wanting some privacy," and disappearing into a study.

"I told Al all about my youthful pregnancy," she said. "We're both Catholic, and I like to think he respects my decision to have you."

"I'm certainly glad you did," Jeff said, and smiled. This should have felt awkward, but it didn't. He felt he'd always known this pretty little woman.

"I didn't show at all," she said. "When we graduated, I was six months along, and no one even guessed. I had you late that summer, and then started college a few weeks later ... never missed a beat."

She had a perky way about her that endeared her to him immediately.

"I hope ... I hope you can forgive me for never getting in touch with you. That's just the way it was done in those days. I don't know how it is now, but when you gave up a baby back then, you gave him up. His new parents *were* his parents."

"I don't hold any grudge. Not at all. I had good parents. I had a fine childhood."

She touched his hand; stroked it, soothingly. "I hope so. And I want to hear all about it. I hope we can be ... friends, at least."

"I hope so, too."

He told her about his parents' pledge to reveal his true parentage to him at his twenty-first birthday.

"My only regret ... my only resentment toward my folks ... is that, by making me wait, they cost me knowing ... or even meeting ... my real father."

She nodded, and her eyes were damp. "I know. That's a terrible thing, I know everyone's already told you, but you're a dead ringer for your dad. Poor choice of words. "I'm sorry."

"That's why I'm here, actually. The main reason."

"What do you mean?"

"To find out why and how my father died."

"Who have you spoken to?"

He filled her in.

"Terrible thing," she said, "what those gang kids did."

"You believe he died that way?"

"Oh, yes. We were proud of him, locally"—she lowered her voice—"although the board of inquiry into the farmhouse shooting, which my husband oversaw, was pretty hard on Carl and Dan."

"Really?"

"They were both suspended without pay for a month. Excessive use of force. Overstepping certain bounds of legal procedure. I don't know what, exactly. I'm afraid . . . nothing."

"What?"

She leaned close. "I'm afraid Alfred may have used the situation to get back at Carl."

"Your . . . romance with my father—it was strictly a high-school affair, wasn't it?"

She scooted off the chrome stool to get the tea kettle and pour herself another cup. Her back was to him when she said, "It wasn't entirely a . . . high-school affair."

He nibbled at a chocolate chip cookie; it was sweet and good. He wondered if it was homemade, and if so, if a cook had made it, or if his mother had.

She was seated again, stirring sugar into her tea. "For a lot of years, we didn't even speak, your father and I. Both our parents had made sure we were kept apart. We went to different colleges. The pregnancy—please don't take this wrong—but it was tragedy in our lives, not the joy it should have been. The baby . . . you . . . broke us apart instead of bringing us together, like it should." She shook her head. "Times were different."

"You don't have to apologize. I don't need explanations. I just want to know the basic facts. The . . . truth."

"The truth is, your dad and I would see each other, around town—I moved back here, oh, ten years ago, when Al's New York law practice didn't work out—and when we passed at the grocery store or on the street, Carl and me, we'd smile kind of nervously, nod from a distance, never even speak, really."

"I understand. Kind of embarrassed about it."

"Right! Well, last year . . . no, it was a year and a half ago . . . Al and I were separated for a time. We have two children, both college age, boy and a girl—they're your half brother and sister, you know. You *do* have some catching up to do."

That was an understatement.

"Anyway, when the kids moved out, I moved out. It's . . . the details aren't important. Anyway, we were separated, and as fate would have it, Carl and Annie were having some problems, too. Carl and I, we ran into each other at one of the local bars one night, kind of started crying into each other's beer . . . and it just happened."

"You got romantic again."

She nodded: studied her tea, as if the leaves might tell her something about the future—or the past. "It was brief. Like I said, I'm Catholic and have certain beliefs, and Al and I decided to go to marriage counseling, and Carl and Annie got back together, and ... that was the end of it."

"I see."

She touched his hand again; clutched it. "But it was a sweet two weeks, Jeff. It was a reminder of what could have been. Maybe, what should have been."

"I see. The trouble my father and his wife were having, did it have anything to do with his deputy?"

"That weasel Danny Simmons? How did *you* know?"

"He was over at her house tonight. Calling her 'babe.' "

She laughed humorlessly. "She and Danny did have an affair. Cheap fling is more like it. Danny was the problem between her and Carl. Your father ... he was too straight an arrow to have ever run around on her—anyway, before she had run around on him."

"But they got back together?"

"They did. And just because Annie and Danny have drifted back together, don't take it wrong. I truly believe she loved your father, and that they'd found their way back to each other."

"Well, she's found her way back to Simmons, now."

"You shouldn't blame her. People make wrong choices sometimes ... particularly when they're at a low ebb, emotionally."

"Well ... I suppose she can use a man in her life, with a son to raise. Was there any sort of pension from my father being sheriff, or some kind of insurance? I mean, he was shot in the line of duty."

"I'm sure there is. But don't worry about Annie Hastings, financially. Her father's car dealership is one of the most successful businesses in the county, and she's an only child."

He slid off the stool. "Well, thank you, Mrs. Sterling. You've been very gracious."

"Must you go?"

"I think I should." He grinned at her. "The cookies were great. Did you make them?"

"I sure did." She climbed off her stool and came up and hugged him. "Any time you want some more, you just holler. We're going to get to know each other, Jeff. And Jeff?"

"Yes?"

"Would you work on something for me?"

"What's that?"

"See if you can work yourself up to calling me 'mom'—instead of Mrs. Sterling."

"Okay," he said.

She saw him to the door. Before he left, she tugged on his arm, pulling him sideways, and pecked his cheek. "You be good."

He started to say something, but then noticed her face was streaked with tears, and suddenly he couldn't talk. He nodded and walked away.

It was approaching ten o'clock now, and he walked back downtown; he wanted to see where his father worked, and around the corner from Mom's café—now closed—he found the County Sheriff's office, a one-story tan brick building. He stood staring at the sidewalk out front, heavily bathed in light from a nearby streetlamp. He knelt, touched the cement, wondering where his father's blood had been. Heavy bushes stood to the right and left of the sidewalk and Jeff squinted at them. Then he looked up at the streetlamp and squinted again.

THE SHERIFF'S BROWN-AND-WHITE VEHICLE was still parked in front of the Hastings home. Jeff leaned against the car, waiting, hoping Simmons wouldn't be spending the night.

At a little after eleven, the tall sheriff came loping around from behind the house—apparently, they'd stayed out on the deck this whole time.

"Who is that?"

"Can't you see me?"

He chuckled, hung his thumbs in his leather gun belt. "The Hastings kid. No, I couldn't see you—streetlight's out."

"Actually, my name is Carson. The streetlight wasn't out in front of my father's office, was it?"

Simmons frowned; his angular face was a shadowy mask in the night. "What are you talking about?"

"Annie Hastings stands to come into her share of money, one of these days, doesn't she? Her father owns that car dealership and all."

"Yeah. So?"

"So I figure she wasn't in on it."

"On what?"

"Murdering my father."

Silence hung like a curtain. Crickets called; somewhere tires squealed.

"Your father was killed by street-gang trash."

"He was killed by trash, all right. But it wasn't a street gang. Out in front of the sheriff's office, my father couldn't have been cut down in a drive-by shooting; he'd have dived for the bushes, or back inside. He'd have got a shot off in his own defense, at least."

"That's just nonsense."

"I think it was somebody who knew him—somebody who called to him, who he turned to, who shot his head off. I think it was you. You wanted his job, and you wanted his wife."

"You're just talking."

"All I want to know is, was she in on it?"

Simmons didn't answer; he went around the car to the driver's side door.

Jeff followed, grabbed the man's wrist as he reached for the car-door handle. "Was his wife in on it? Tell me!"

Simmons shoved him away. "Go away. Go home!" Go back to Iowa or wherever the hell."

"Indiana."

"Wherever the hell! Go home!"

"No. I'm staying right here in Greenwood. Asking questions. Poking my nose in. Looking at the files, the autopsy, the crime-scene report, talking to the state cops, putting it all together until you're inside a cell where you belong."

Simmons smiled. It seemed friendly. "This is just a misunderstanding," he said and slipped his arm around Jeff's shoulder, all chummy, when the gun was out of its holster in Jeff's midsection *now*.

"Let's take a walk," Simmons said, softly; the arm around Jeff's shoulder had slipped around his neck and turned into a near choke hold. "There's some trees behind the house. We'll—"

Jeff flipped the man and the sheriff landed hard on the pavement on his back, but dazed or not, Simmons brought the gun up, his face a thin satanic grimace, and fired, exploding the night.

The car window on the driver's side spiderwebbed as Jeff ducked out of the way, and with a swift martial-art kick he sent the gun flying out of Simmons's hand, and it fell, nearby, with a *thunk*. The sheriff was getting to his feet but another almost invisible kick put him back down again, unconscious.

The night was quiet. Crickets. An automobile somewhere. Despite the shot, no porch lights were popping on.

Jeff walked over to where the gun had landed. He picked it up, enjoying the cool steel feel of the revolver in his hand, walked back to the unconscious Simmons, cocked it, pointed it down, and studied the skinny son of a bitch who had killed his father.

"It's not what your father would have done," she said.

Jeff turned, and Annie Hastings was standing there. At first he thought she had a gun in her hand, but it was only another Coors.

He said, "Did you hear any of that?"

She nodded. "Enough."

"He killed your husband."

"I believe he did."

"You didn't know?"

"I didn't know."

"You weren't part of it?"

"No, I wasn't."

"Can I trust you?"

"You'll know as much," she said, swigging the beer, then smiling bitterly, "when I back you up in court."

*   *   *

HE STOOD AT THE GRAVESTONE in the cemetery on the hillside. He studied the words: *Carl Henry Hastings—Beloved Husband, Loving Father. 1954–1992.* He touched the carved letters: *Father.* He said a silent prayer.

The wind whispered a response through the trees.

"What was he like?" he asked. "What was he *really* like?"

His mother smiled; her pretty pixie face made him happy.

"He was like you," she said. "He was just like you."

Poet, novelist, mystery writer, critic, Julian Symons served all these callings admirably. When he died this year, he left behind a major legacy for future generations of crime-novel readers to enjoy. His best books, THE THIRTY-FIRST OF FEBRUARY (1950) and THE COLOUR OF MURDER (1957) display his fascination with contemporary evil, and his ability to come to grim terms with it. The following is one of his last stories, and one of the his best.

The Man Who Hated Television
JULIAN SYMONS

You say it may help if I tell the story of my father's tragedy as I saw it, and I will try to do that. The origin of it was that my father, Jacob Pryde, hated television.

There was a reason for this. His own father was an insurance salesman who cheated his employers by claiming commission on nonexistent sales which he justified by forged orders and invoices. When this could not be covered up any longer, he took his wife out in their car, stopped in a quiet country road, and shot first her and then himself.

My father was small, I believe five years old. He was taken away from home by an aunt and told his parents had gone on holiday. He learned of their deaths because he was watching the TV news when an item was shown with pictures of the car and their bodies. I'm told that for some time after that he screamed whenever the television was switched on. So it is not surprising that he refused to have a set in our home.

Television was not the only thing father hated. I think he also hated his wife Susan, and perhaps he hated the people to whom he sold the rare books in which he dealt, books he sometimes said he would sooner have kept on his own shelves in the extension added to our little house in Wandsworth, which is a district in southwest London. The extension was called the library, but really it was just a brick addition to the house, joined to it by a covered passageway.

So did my father hate everybody? Not quite. He loved one person, his daughter Elvira. Me.

These were the characters in the tragedy, one that seems to me in retrospect inevitable. There was also Doctor Finale, but of course he did not exist. Let me tell the story.

There was a time—the pictures in my mind flicker uncertainly like those in an old film—when father was a lover, not a hater. I remember, or *think* I remember, for it is hard to be sure about such scenes from early years, a time when father was happy, and loving not only to me but also to Susan. I see him bending over my cot, lifting me out, his moustache tickling my neck so that I scream with laughter, and he laughs too. I see him holding my mother, they are performing a kind of dance across the room, then they collapse onto a bed. I am standing up in my cot watching, she shrieks something, he cries out, and I cry out too because I think he is hurting her. Later they hold me, pass me from one to the other, make cooing encouraging sounds.

There are other pictures, similarly fuzzy, particularly of Susan in the kitchen. She loved the kitchen, and was a great cook. I see her busy with a fruitcake, making pancakes on Shrove Tuesday and throwing them up and catching them in the pan, putting a joint of beef in the oven. She is always cheerful, often laughing. Sometimes she sang, out of tune, a snatch of a popular song. Father was in the extension or library, cataloguing his old dark books, cleaning them, perhaps even reading them. She would send me in to tell him when a meal was ready.

I remember the day when her laughter stopped. I was very young, four or five, but I remember it.

She was cooking something, I don't know what, something in a pan with hot fat. I was playing beside the kitchen table near her, perhaps putting a doll to bed, I can't remember. She was singing. Then suddenly her song changed to a scream. I saw there were flames in the pan, bright yellow, and some fat had splashed onto her hand. My father ran in from the extension. His first thought was for me, that I might be splashed by the burning fat. He picked me up, and as he did so he or I must have knocked against the pan. The fat in it went straight into my mother's face. Then there were screams and screams.

When she came out of hospital after the skin grafts, one side of her face was stiff and unreal as if it was made of wood or hard wax, and the left side of her mouth was fixed in what looked like a sneering grin. When I first saw her I cried, ran away and hid.

From that time our life changed. My father could not bear ugly things. Susan was ugly now, and I think he blamed her for it. He spoke to her as little as possible, and would sometimes ask if she couldn't look at him without that grin on her face. She had changed too. She was very silent now, never sang, looked after the house as before, and cooked, but took no pleasure in it. She rarely left the house, never with him. I don't think he offered to take her.

His attention now was focused almost exclusively on me. We spent hours together in the library where he told me about the books, which were valuable and why, showed me how to distinguish between typefaces and tell which was appropriate for a particular kind of book or size of page, the way in which he described books when he sent out lists to attract the interest of possible clients.

The whole of his business was carried on through these lists or catalogues, which he prepared with immense care. When he received an order he would be both pleased and upset, upset because he hated to part with any of the books. Orders would be packed first in tissue paper, then plastic wrapping, cardboard, and finally thick brown paper. He tried vainly to teach me what he called the art of packing. In part this was because my fingers seemed all thumbs when I tried to put the wrapping round, but also I felt that to take such care about packing a book was ridiculous. Not until I was thirteen or fourteen did I realise that all those evenings and weekends spent in the library were preparation for the time when he expected me to carry on the business. One day he showed me a sheet of the writing paper headed *Jacob Pryde, Fine Books,* and said: "The time will come when this will be *Jacob and Elvira Pryde,* and then just *Elvira.*"

I knew then that this would not be so. I had little interest in books, none in bookselling. Those hours spent in the library or extension were time wasted for me, hours of boredom. Why did I not say so? Because I both admired and feared my father. He was a handsome man, rather above the ordinary height, slim, hair and moustache iron grey, face lean, nose aquiline, expression generally stern.

He had only two recreations in life apart from his books. One was his car, an old Mercedes which he cared for as if it were a child, washing, leathering, and polishing it weekly. The other was a local club for those who, like him, had been in the Territorial army. He had somehow managed to retain the revolver used by his own father, and he used it to practice in the club's little shooting gallery. He took me to the club once, but I did not care for the beer-drinking, back-slapping atmosphere, and perhaps he realised this. Certainly he never suggested I should pay another visit.

And my mother, she who had laughed and sung? She was like a lamed bird, trying always to hide the damaged part of her face with its unintended sneer. Are you thinking I should have pitied her, loved her? No doubt I ought to have done, but in truth her appearance repelled me and I took no pains to conceal the fact. Of course she noticed my behaviour, and it must have pained her.

This may sound like a miserable household, yet when young one becomes accustomed to any way of life. What I missed most was the lack of a television set. At school all the girls talked about the programmes, the sexy women and the hunky men ("hunky" was a great word at the time among my friends—"He's really hunky" meant more than sexy, rather like "macho" but intelligent and understanding as well). I hadn't seen the hunky men on TV, couldn't talk about them. I felt deprived, and illogically blamed my mother, and not my father.

At fourteen I began smoking pot and using amphetamines. I also had my first sexual coupling, with a boy who acted with me in the school play. These were experiments. I found them pleasant and continued experimenting. The boys were callow, not hunky, the drugs soothing rather than exciting. I know psychiatrists attribute what they call the early resort to sex and drugs to the nature of my home life. Personally I put it down to being deprived of TV. If I'd seen hunky men on the screen I don't think I'd have started experimenting with a schoolboy.

One day, under the soothing influence of speed (I know it's supposed to excite, but can only say I *felt* perfectly calm), I told Jacob my name would never be on the writing paper. For a moment he seemed not to have heard, then he asked what I meant. He was in the midst of a tedious exposition about the qualities of some rare editions he had recently bought. I picked up the book—though it was not really a book but a pamphlet, something to do with Swinburne or Rossetti or one of that lot—and said I wasn't interested, everything to do with his business bored me. As I spoke the pamphlet drifted away and sank slowly to the floor, yet some of it remained in my hand. I had torn it in two, an act performed quite unconsciously and at the time causing me no alarm. I repeat that speed *felt* soothing.

Jacob—it was at this moment he changed in my perception from *Father* to *Jacob*—at first looked unbelievingly from what remained in my hand to the papers on the floor. Then I saw his hand raised, heard the sound as it struck my cheek (the sound, though, faint and fading like an echo). The paper I held was removed from my grasp, and then he was on the floor picking up the rest of the pamphlet, saying something I failed to hear or understand. But I could not mistake the look in his dark eyes as we stood close together, the pages still in his trembling hand. It was a look of hatred.

I ran out of the library, my feet seeming to bounce lightly on the ground, and spent the rest of the evening in my room. It had been my custom to kiss Jacob's cheek, and that of my mother—the good side of course—when I came down to breakfast, but on the next morning my lips brushed only her cheek. Then I sat down. Jacob stared at me. I stared back. Then he spoke, not to me nor to Susan, simply a ruler laying down the law in his kingdom.

"Elvira has been stupidly disobedient. She had destroyed a valuable first edition. She says also that she does not wish to do the work for which I have trained her, as my assistant and eventual partner. She must be taught obedience. Elvira will receive no allowance for a month, nor leave this house in the evening without my permission. Her evenings will be spent with me in the library, learning more about her future occupation."

But, you will say, how could anybody talk like that? This was the twentieth century, the place London and not some rural area where time had stood still. I was fifteen years old. I can only say that strange things happen in the heart of great cities, and that Jacob Pryde was an unusual, an extraordinary man. The fixity of his dark gaze was compelling, it excluded any possibility of doubt that he would be obeyed. He drove me to school that day in the Mercedes, sitting bolt upright, immovable as a statue. When we arrived he said he would be waiting for me in the afternoon. I saw the future stretching before me, as it seemed endlessly, long days in classrooms and longer evenings in the library forced to learn more about the world of book dealing I had come to detest. That evening my mother, the wounded bird, said in a moment when we were alone that she was sorry, there was nothing she could do. I knew this was true. Jacob had bent her to his will, as he now meant to bend me.

Yet this *was* the twentieth century, I *was* fifteen years old and not literally a prisoner. There were people I knew through the drugs circuit, and through the school play I had met one or two students at RADA. On the third night spent under Jacob's Law, I took money from my mother's purse, left a note in my bedroom saying I was not coming back but would be in touch, and shinned down a drainpipe outside my bedroom window. I spent that night on the sofa of a girl at RADA.

I don't want to describe the next six years in detail. I slept around (contracting neither AIDS nor any venereal disease), worked in shops, got hooked on drugs, and then unhooked myself when I realised what they were doing to me—and I made a career in TV. I had hated those old smelly books Jacob caressed with such pleasure, and was bored by the theatre, yet I wanted some sort of career connected with the arts, modern arts, and what is more modern than TV? It's here today and forgotten next week, and I like that too. I hate the sort of stuff Jacob loved, that lingers on and on, stuff people like simply because it's old.

Anyway, I made a career on the box, first with the help of the RADA student, who introduced me to her agent. I'm supposed to have a wistful little-girl-lost look, and I played mostly what you might call victim parts in sitcoms and thrillers, never a lead player. I supposed I was typecast, but typecasting can have its advantages. If you're lucky it can keep you in steady work. And I was lucky. At twenty-one I had my own little flat, a bit of money in the bank, no steady boyfriend.

I used my own name, Elvira Pryde, why not? I talked quite often to Susan on the phone, but Jacob would never speak. Soon after I started appearing on the box I paid for a set and had it sent to her. Of course I knew Jacob would never buy her one, but I couldn't have imagined his reaction. When I rang to ask if she enjoyed seeing me, she told me Jacob had been angry when he saw the set, and had been beside himself when he heard it came from me. He made her look while he smashed it up with a hammer, then threw it away. Perhaps I should have realised then that he was crazy.

Susan told me about this without apparent emotion. The accident had changed not only her face but also her voice, making it dry and thin. I asked why she didn't leave Jacob, come and live with me. She said she was his wife, what would he do without her? I was going to say what I thought of that when she added: "He's a good man, you know. He only wanted the best for you."

"The *best*." I couldn't believe what I heard.

"He loves you. You know that."

"He's mad. He must be, to hate television the way he does."

"He wants you to come back. He would make you a partner at once. And I would be pleased."

She said it in that same dry voice. Suppose she had pleaded with me, would it have made a difference? I don't suppose so.

Then I got the job as Doctor Finale's assistant. That was a real boost for me, regular work in a thirteen-part series, and a bigger part than anything I'd had. After the tragedy, of course the show came off the air. It's never mentioned now, and I don't suppose anything like it will be done again. So I'd better describe it briefly.

It was called a horror soap, and that's about right. Doctor Finale, as his name suggests, was a kind of last resort. One man came to him because he was dying of AIDS and believed his heir had deliberately arranged his infection, a woman wanted revenge on the man who'd killed her young daughter in a car accident and been acquitted on trial, a man whose family had been wiped out by a terrorist bomb wanted Doctor Finale's help in turning himself into a living bomb that would blow up the terrorist state's embassy.

Mostly these were revenge stories, always they were violent. Doctor Finale, whose degree was in psychology and not medicine, had no regard for the law and was absolutely ruthless. Once he discovered a client had been trying to trick him, and arranged a trap that left him financially ruined and physically damaged. Doctor Finale respected only money and power. He was an emotional sadist who treated everybody, clients, opponents, and his own assistants, with contempt. Those who did not hate him worshipped him, and I was one of the worshippers. He was played by Lester Morton, a handsome actor in his forties made up to look suitably sinister. I was his secretary Jennifer, a prissy worshipper who was the subject of constant sneers at her accent, love life, and lack of clothes sense.

Lester was apologetic. "I've never played such an A-one bastard," he said. "I don't know why you stay with him."

He laughed, and I did too. "It's your psychic magnetism, Doctor. That and the viewing figures." Lester was undeniably an attractive man, everybody said so. And we all knew the show was a success. There had been a short series before I came into it, starting as a cult oddity admired by a few critics. Then it had shot up in the ratings, gaining more viewers every week. One producer, asked to explain its success, said: "Sadism and violence, how can it fail?" It's always nice to be associated with success, although something about my scenes with Lester made me faintly uneasy.

One day when I rang Susan her voice seemed duller and drier than usual. I asked her if something was wrong.

"This play you are in—"

"Not really a play, it's a series. About someone called Doctor Finale, and people who come to him with problems."

"This Doctor Finale, what is he like?"

"He's a monster."

"But what does he look like?" Before I could reply, she went on: "Does he look like your father?"

The question stunned me. Lester was balding a little and wore a grey wig, he was made up round the eyes and had a way of opening them wide and then half-closing them that was frightening, his complexion was dark and his nose aquiline—was it a likeness to Jacob that had made me feel uneasy when playing scenes with him? My mother went on to say that at one of the book sales Jacob attended, somebody had congratulated him on my success as a TV actress. That would have been sufficiently uncongenial to him, but the man went on to say the principal actor had been made up to look exactly like Jacob. He added that other dealers had noticed it and it had caused much amusement.

Susan was upset. She said Jacob thought I had arranged deliberately that the actor should look like him, that I was sneering at him by making an odious character recognisable as Jacob. I tried to make her understand how absurd it was to suppose an unimportant actress like me could have had any part in the casting.

"This actor who is playing Doctor Finale, how well do you know him?" I did not reply. How well I knew Lester was not her business. "Does he look like your father?"

I said I could see no resemblance, but when I put down the telephone I wondered. When I left home I had taken with me a photograph of Jacob, and now I compared it with one of Lester as Doctor Finale. At times it seemed to me there was no likeness, at others the two faces seemed to blend into each other and become one. I found Jennifer's scenes with Doctor Finale disturbing, especially those when the doctor touched her and, on one occasion when she had made a mistake, hit her so that she fell and lay whimpering in a corner of the room. The director was pleased with the scene but Lester was concerned, said he hoped he hadn't hurt me. I replied that he couldn't possibly have hurt *me*, he would have hurt Jennifer, and since she had recovered enough to be in a car chasing a pair of graverobbers a few minutes later, she had not been hurt. Lester laughed, but I'm not sure he understood what I meant, which was that Jennifer is one person, I am another.

When I rang Susan again three or four days later, she surprised me by saying Jacob had hired a television and a video recorder. He had taped the last two Doctor Finale programmes, including the one in which Jennifer was knocked across the room, and played them again and again. She said he was beside himself, at one moment raging against my betrayal of him by putting him on the screen, the next saying he must protect me against the way I was being treated. She wanted me to come home and talk to him. I asked how she thought that would help. I was very calm.

"He believes this Doctor Finale is made up to look like him, and it's your doing." I repeated that this was ridiculous. "The men at the club all think it's a great joke, they've started calling him Doctor Finale. If you could explain to him—"

"There's nothing to explain." But there was something I wanted to know. "You saw the programmes, did you think she was good, Jennifer? Did she convince you?"

"Good? Oh yes, I suppose so." She spoke in that strangled voice, as if she didn't mean it. "I wish you would talk to him. He's not himself. He hates the television, but he sits in front of it playing those scenes with you in them, sometimes shouting at you and at the man. I'm afraid of what he'll do."

I didn't take her seriously. I should have done. I said I had no intention of coming home or talking to Jacob. I repeated what I had said before, she should leave Jacob and come and live with me. That might have been awkward, because Lester had moved in with me, but I suppose I really knew she would never leave Jacob.

So I come to the last scene of the tragedy.

The episode in production was based on what was said to be an actual plot by the CIA to assassinate Castro by poisoning the wet suit he used. The intended victim here was a Middle East dictator who had already foiled several assassination attempts, the most recent being shown in a violent opening scene where two agents were caught trying to fix limpet bombs to the dictator's yacht and then tortured to death. Doctor Finale, approached by the government, produces the plan for the poisoned wet suit, then gains the dictator's confidence by revealing the plan to him. The doctor plans with the dictator to blow up the House of Commons and install a friendly prime minister. The dictator fancies Jennifer, and attempts to rape her. Doctor Finale, who has appeared to arrange the rape, breaks in before the dictator has his wicked way, shoots him with a poisoned dart from a cigarette lighter, and escapes with Jennifer in a submarine lurking off the coast, mission accomplished.

Tosh, with plenty of action, lots of nastiness, scenes with the dictator's other women, etcetera.

We were shooting a scene between the doctor and Jennifer, in which he tells her she must go to the dictator's bedroom and do whatever he asks. Jennifer at first refuses but finally agrees, compelled by the mesmeric power of Doctor Finale's malevolent gaze. At one moment she says he wouldn't care if she was given to the guards to be raped and brutalised. She waits for him to contradict her. "Would you care? Would you?" she asks, and he replies calmly: "Not in the least."

It was a difficult scene to do—not to mention the over-the-top dialogue—and Joe Frawley, the director, was on his fourth take when there was a lot of noise from the dark area at the back of the set. It sounded as if props were being knocked over, then there were voices. After that, silence. And then Jacob Pryde came out of the darkness onto the studio floor.

Joe said: "Who the hell are you?" Then he was silent as Jacob moved towards Lester. The revolver, that fatal revolver, was in his hand. Jacob said: "You are Doctor Finale. You have corrupted my daughter."

Lester muttered something about it being just a play, shrank away. Seeing the two together, I recognized the likeness discovered by Jacob's friends. It was not just that they were physically of a size. The shape of the lean head, the bell-like ring of the voice and its contemptuous tone, the look that pierced the personality of the person it was aimed at and punctured self-confidence and self-belief—that look to which I had been exposed daily during my most susceptible years—those were the similarities I recognised. There was this difference, that Lester was an actor assuming such qualities, while in Jacob they were real.

I knew what I had to do. "Jacob," I said. "Father."

He turned. That gaze of fire and ice was bent on me. "I have come to take you home," he said, and I replied that I would come home. I said he should give me the revolver. He came very close to me, held out the blue shining thing, and I took it. His arms were spread wide, wide as those of a fallen angel, as I moved into his embrace. But then, as he looked over my shoulder, he must have seen Lester again. He shouted something incoherent about corrupting and saving me and struggled to get the revolver. I knew why he wanted it, to kill Lester—I suppose that would have been in a way to kill himself—and I did my best to keep hold of it when I felt his hand on mine. The rest of them seemed to stay still, like figures in a tableau, as Jacob and I struggled. I heard a crack, another crack. I could not have said where it came from. Then Jacob sighed, and said something again about our going home together. And that was all. It seemed somehow right that he should have died in my arms—or was it in Jennifer's arms? Now that I think about it afterwards, I believe he really was Doctor Finale.

"INTERESTING, but I'm afraid not very satisfactory," Dr. Margetson said. Her eyes behind the large square glasses were gentle as a gazelle's. "The idea of suggesting to patients that they should write about the experiences in the outer world that have brought them here is to see how near they get to facing what actually happened."

"Does that really matter?" the visitor asked.

On Dr. Margetson's desk there was a telephone, a diary pad, a paperweight in the shape of a lion's head, and a jar of red and yellow roses. She paused for a moment as if giving the visitor's novel idea consideration before she answered. "Oh yes. Yes, I think it matters if they are unable to accept reality." Her voice was delicate, light, comforting, although the words were not. "Elvira is happy here at Fernley Park. She has made friends, I don't think she really wants to leave. It may even be possible to use her acting abilities in the Christmas play."

"Nobody can like being shut up."

"We try to make patients feel they are not shut up but cared for. But in any case—you've read this?" She indicated the exercise book written in a round, almost childish hand. "Or rather, you've read a typed copy of it. What did you think?"

"It's very vivid. And quite clear, quite coherent."

"But not accurate."

"Oh yes, I thought so. Leaving home, getting out of the window—"

"But not about the reason for leaving. Elvira didn't leave because her father smacked her face. Nor because she was bored with what she learned about the book trade. In our conversations, long friendly conversations in which Elvira spoke freely, with no constraint or inducement, she told me of the many occasions when her father sexually abused her in the extension or library, whichever you call it. And Elvira consented; when she was a girl she was in love with her father. He was a handsome man, and she liked handsome men. Then she fully realised what she was doing and felt revulsion from it—"

"There is no proof, no proof anything happened at all. It's only what she says now. She said nothing at the time."

Softly Dr. Margetson said: "And you never asked questions?"

"Why should I have done?" Susan Pryde's hands were clasped tightly. "If there had been any proof—"

"Positive proof is often lacking in such matters. But we know, you and I, that Elvira was capable of deceit. And that she could be vicious. What she says here about your own tragedy is not the truth."

Susan Pryde had been sitting, as she always tried to do, with the good side of her face turned towards Dr. Margetson, but now she turned to show the waxen half of her features with their curious smiling sneer. "It was an accident. I have always said so."

The doctor's voice was dulcet. "I don't mean to criticise you in any way. But Elvira is not telling the truth. She says she was four or five years old, and perhaps playing with a doll. In fact she was eight, and perhaps already being molested."

"It was a long time ago. I've tried to put it all out of my mind."

"Elvira says you tried to stop her going into the library one day, perhaps because you suspected what happened there. There was an argument, and she caught hold of the pan of fat and threw it in your face."

"Why should you believe her? It's her word against mine."

"I believe what she tells me, that she felt the need to atone for what she had done. That was partly why she telephoned so often. For that, and to have news of her father. He had never got over her departure, longed for her to come back. Isn't that so?"

"Perhaps."

Miriam Margetson's gaze was friendly through the square lenses. "But he wanted the girl he had known, not the woman who appeared on a television screen. So he destroyed the television." She waited for a comment, but none came. "He wanted to resume their relationship, something Elvira contemplated with horror at the same time that she desired it."

"All this is simply something you are inventing."

"Did you notice her hints about Lester? First that she knew him well, then the casual remark that he had moved in with her. He was a replacement for the father she loved and feared."

"She happened to mention him, that's all. You make too much of everything."

Dr. Margetson shook her head. "Such remarks are never accidental, they have meaning. And so does what she says about the final scene, blending fact with invention. It's true your husband went to the studio with the idea that he could persuade or force Elvira to give up her work as an actress and return to him. And she agreed, so why should he want to fire the revolver?"

"To hurt the actor, Lester Morton, Doctor Finale."

"Why should he do that when he thought Elvira had agreed to go with him? Is it really likely that the shots that killed him were fired by accident? Elvira says that when his arms closed on her she tried to keep hold of the revolver. And she did keep hold, her prints were on it."

"It was the pressure of his hand that fired the shots." Now Susan looked steadily, full face, at the doctor. "I want my daughter home again. To live with me. Perhaps eventually to resume her career."

"I have to remind you that it was to avoid the trauma of appearing in court with all it would have entailed that Elvira became a voluntary patient here at Fernley Park."

"Until she might be ready for release. That was three years ago."

"She is not ready yet."

"Let me judge for myself. It's over a year since I have seen her. I want to see my daughter."

"As you wish." The doctor picked up the telephone, murmured words. Her gentle eyes looked at Susan sympathetically.

Any doubt Susan Pryde felt about her daughter's health was dispelled by the sight of her. She wore a bright print dress, her bare arms were brown, she was smiling. A uniformed nurse stood beside the door. Elvira's voice was clear and high as she said, "Miriam, I didn't know I was going to see you this afternoon." She stopped. "Who's this?"

She shrank back as Susan came towards her and said: "It's me. Your mother."

"No." Elvira shook her head. "You're ugly. My mother isn't ugly. Ask my father, he knows my mother isn't ugly."

Dr. Margetson said: "Elvira, be quiet and listen. Your mother wants—"

Elvira shrieked, "No," again, picked up the paperweight, and threw it at Susan. There was a tinkle of broken glass as it hit a picture on the wall. Elvira moaned with distress, launched herself at Dr. Margetson. They grappled for a moment, then the nurse pinned Elvira's arms behind her back and took her away.

The doctor retrieved her glasses, which had been knocked off. "You see."

"Is she often like that?"

"She lives in the present, which is Fernley Park, some other patients, me. She has eliminated the past. But if she is to leave here she must come to terms with it, remember it as it was." She tapped the exercise book. "This was a trial run. It is disappointing, but we shall try again, perhaps in another form. One day she will be ready to come out. But not yet."

"She seems to like you."

"Affections are often transferred. One must be careful not to reject them. But also not to accept. If you understand me." The doctor permitted herself a small smile.

"You believe she did this to my face, killed her father. Those things are not true. I *know* it, I tell you." She turned the waxen side of her face to the doctor, the lip curled in its sneer.

"You are her mother. I respect your feelings."

Susan Pryde's voice rose. "You have institutionalised her, turned her into a zombie. You are the guilty one."

"Perhaps it helps you to think so. But I am glad you've seen Elvira." She picked up the lion's head paperweight, replaced it on the desk. "And whatever you think, no harm has been done. Except, of course, for a little broken glass."

John Lutz has written virtually every kind of crime novel, from the Jim Thomp-sonesque THE TRUTH OF THE MATTER (1971) to the quietly brilliant small-town thriller BONEGRINDER (1977), to the riveting contemporary suspense novel SINGLE WHITE FEMALE (1992). He has also excelled at series fiction, his Alo Nudger and Fred Carver mysteries being among the best crime novels of the past two decades. During all this productivity, Lutz has also found time to become a master short-story writer.

With Anchovies
JOHN LUTZ

This guy, Joey Longo, laid a deluxe pizza box on the table and slipped into the booth to sit down across from Hamish. He drummed his thick fingers on the low, flat box and said, "Lemme get right to the point."

Hamish, who was on his second lite beer and had thought he'd finally get to eat when the pizza was placed on the table, said, "Please do." The spicy aroma rising from the box was making him even hungrier.

Except for one thing. Anchovies. He was certain he smelled anchovies, and if they were on the pizza he was sure he'd ordered with pepperoni and cheese only, he wouldn't be able to eat supper for a long time. Anchovies were for Hamish something of an allergy. He responded to them the way some people responded to penicillin or bee venom. He was almost swelling up and itching now, just catching a whiff of the unfortunate little fish.

Longo introduced himself despite the plastic name tag on his white chef's uniform, then glanced around as if to make sure there was no one else in Longo's Pizzeria, so they could talk privately. He was a medium-height, muscular guy with wavy black hair and a dark dusting of beard. Women might find him attractive despite the fact that he had a pattern of moles with hair growing out of them on one side of his nose.

When Hamish extended his hand and said, "Ralph Hamish," Longo ignored the hand and said, "I know who and what you are, Hamish."

"What I am is a customer," Hamish said, getting irritated. "And what I smell is anchovies. I'm sure I told the waitress no—"

"This isn't your pizza," Longo said, smiling with what seemed to be strained tolerance. "Yours ain't quite ready. This pizza"—he drummed the box with his fingertips again—"is for a job I want to hire you to do."

It took a second for Hamish to recover from his surprise. "I came in here for supper, not a job."

"Don't waste my time with pride, Hamish. You came in here because of the coupon in this morning's paper and because you can't afford to eat at a higher-price restaurant. I've checked into you very carefully, my friend, and you ain't got a pot to plant petunias in. And that's why I figured you gotta be interested in this job. In fact, there's no way a loser like you's gonna turn down this little piece of action, hey? So, you hired?"

"No. Still hungry, though."

Longo smiled. The warts looked particularly nasty when he did that. "What I want you to do will take less than an hour, my friend, and the pay is excellent."

Hamish considered the stack of unpaid bills on his desk. Then there was the collection agency that was making his life hell. Then there was the mounting sum he was discovering his medical insurance didn't cover after his prostate operation. Then there was his former wife ... well, there was more. "So what is the pay?" he asked.

"It's worth fifty to me. You do it, then you get the money."

"When and how do I get paid?"

"Don't worry, I'll get it to you."

"It's not a bad hourly wage," Hamish admitted.

Longo grinned. "Not for a guy like you. Middle age, losing your hair, getting a fat gut and a thin bank account to take you into your old age. You're a private dick, Hamish, and that's a sleazy profession, hey? You guys'll do anything even when you're not desperate. And you're desperate, my friend."

Who did this guy think he was? "You aren't paying so much I'll endure insults," Hamish said. He started to slide from the booth.

"Okay, okay," Longo told him, smiling hard. "So I was too rough on you, and I apologize. But on the other hand, you shouldn't be too proud, Hamish. Too much false pride is how you got where you are, hey?"

Hamish couldn't deny it. "Hey," he said. He settled back down in the booth. "So what's the job?"

"I want you to deliver this," Longo said, pressing his palm lightly on the pizza box.

"There's gotta be more to it than that."

"There is. When the guy opens the door to reach for the pizza, instead of handing it to him, you give it to him right smack in the face."

"A joke, huh?"

"You might say that. He's home alone, so he'll open the door."

"What's he look like?"

"Guy in his sixties, gray hair, kinda short and wiry."

"Like he just got a haircut?"

"I mean the *guy* is short and wiry."

"He a good sport?"

"What the hell's that matter? You just do your job—splat! in the face—then you collect your pay, and that'll be that, hey?"

"Not quite," Hamish said.

"Oh?"

"We got a deal only if you throw in a free pizza. And one without anchovies."

"You serious?"

"Everything *but* anchovies," Hamish said. Despite what Longo might think, he had his pride.

"You got a deal," Longo said. He fished a stubby yellow pencil from a shirt pocket and scribbled an address on a napkin. Then he stood up from the booth and grinned down at Hamish. "Deliver the pizza your special way anytime within the next hour."

"Soon as I'm finished with my supper," Hamish said.

Longo laughed. "Sure. I'll send the waitress right out with it."

"Wanna take this pizza back and keep it warm till I go?"

Longo laughed even harder. "Sure, why not, hey?" He swaggered back toward the kitchen, carrying the flat pizza delivery box. "You guys are something," he called back over his shoulder.

"Us guys like to eat when we're hungry," Hamish said. But even as he spoke, the waitress appeared with his pizza and a third bottle of lite beer on a tray. She was smiling at him a little nervously, maybe treating him with new respect because he was a fellow employee.

THE ADDRESS LONGO HAD GIVEN him belonged to a sprawling English Tudor house in Ladue. There was a gate with an intercom. Hamish parked his rusty ten-year-old Plymouth and climbed out. He pressed the button on the intercom box, and a voice said, "Yeah?"

"Pizza," Hamish said.

"This a quiz?"

"I'm delivering a pizza," Hamish told the box.

"I didn't order no goddamn pizza."

Hamish didn't think this guy sounded like a good sport, but he forged ahead. "It's from Longo's Pizzeria."

"Huh? You sure?"

"Yep. I was told to deliver it here to this address. No mistake about it."

After a pause the voice in the box said, "Drive on in."

The tall chain-link gates glided open as Hamish got back in the Plymouth. The pizza's anchovy smell had tainted the air inside the car, making his entire body itch slightly. Well, he'd drive home with the windows open, as soon as he was finished here.

He steered the Plymouth up a long blacktop driveway lined with identical small pine trees, then parked in the shade of a portico. He got the flat white box from the backseat, removed the pizza and hefted it until he felt comfortable holding it in his right hand, then went to a door that looked as if it belonged on a castle. With his left hand he worked a big brass knocker in the shape of a lion's head.

Hamish widened his stance and drew back his right arm, balancing the pizza. He was ready.

There was a faint sound from inside the house; then the big, heavy door swung open.

A small man, probably in his late sixties, stood there looking curious. He had gray hair and a wiry build and the face of a wary accountant. Hamish recognized his target with the instantaneousness and intelligence of a smart bomb. He struck with the pizza.

The little guy opened his mouth, starting to say something, but *splat!*— too late.

There the guy stood, cheese and tomato sauce stuck to his face and running down his white shirt. Anchovies dotting the mess like nasty little sequins. Surprised, all right.

Hamish realized he'd better not take too much time admiring his work. He turned away from the astounded man, got in his car, and was just closing the door when he heard the man yell, "I'll kill you, you bastard!"

Whoa! Longo had this guy wrong. He was no sport. He was furious, wiping the colorful goo from his face, stepping toward the car and waving his fist like some character in a cartoon before the feature film.

Hamish was glad he'd left the engine running. He slammed the gearshift lever into drive and tromped the accelerator. Fortunately the driveway made a circle up near the house. He jockeyed the old Plymouth in a tight turn, then sped down the driveway toward the street.

As the car jounced over the curb and he made a screeching left turn, he glanced in the rearview mirror and saw the tall gates gliding shut behind him.

His heart was beating hard, and his stomach was grinding.

Then, half a mile from the house, he cranked down all the windows and sat in the rush of wind, giggling, then laughing so hard he had trouble steering. It hadn't worked out exactly as Longo had told him, but by now the old guy was probably in the shower and had calmed down and was thinking the whole thing was kind of funny at that. Maybe he'd done something similar to Longo and Longo owed him one. Maybe they were even now, or the old guy would get Longo back. Order a bunch of pizzas to be delivered to some nonexistent address. That kind of thing.

Anyway, Hamish thought, parking in front of his apartment, it was an easy fifty dollars, and he no longer itched.

It wasn't until the next morning that he noticed the bullet hole in the car's trunk.

THAT GAVE HIM PAUSE FOR THOUGHT. He drove immediately to the Fifth District station house to see his friend Police Lieutenant Will Malloy.

Malloy, a tall man who was a spiffy dresser and had known Hamish since childhood, sat patiently and listened, then adjusted his cuff links and said, "You are in so deep that whales have never been there, Ralph."

Hamish stared at him. Malloy actually appeared modestly worried, and that in turn worried Hamish. Not much bothered Malloy as long as he could wear his expensive civilian shirts on duty.

"The old guy you hit in the face with the pizza is Paul Marin."

The name was remotely familiar to Hamish, but he couldn't remember from where.

Malloy was gazing at him with disbelief. "You really don't get *it*, do you?"

"That's why I'm here," Hamish said.

"Marin doesn't get much publicity because he doesn't want it, but he controls all organized crime in the city," Malloy said.

Now Hamish did have a vague recollection of seeing the name in the papers, on TV news during some story about ... *half a dozen bodies fished from the river*. Ho, boy! "You mean he's kind of like the Godfather?"

"Very much like."

Hamish swallowed. It might have been heard out in the hall.

"Joey Longo is Marin's archrival, Ralph. You misunderstood him. He hired you to hit Marin all right. But not with a pizza."

Hamish sat motionless for a long time, listening to the sounds of the station house sifting into the office, the distant chatter of a police radio, voices from the booking area, laughter from the squad room. "Maybe if I went back and explained everything to Marin."

Malloy leaned forward and locked gazes with him. "Ralph, you hit the kingpin of organized crime in the face with a pizza. Marin can't let that pass. He won't be satisfied until ... well, just until."

"What would you do if you were me?" Hamish asked.

Malloy stared into space and touched his tie knot lightly, absently checking to make sure it was tight and neat. "You got a passport?"

"No. What about if you have me locked up for a while, for safekeeping?"

"Ha! You think you're in danger on the outside, Ralph, think about a prison. Any con in there would be set for life if he did the guy hit the Godfather with a pizza. Protective custody's outa the question. Inside, you're good as dead. Who you gotta watch out for on the outside—besides Joey Longo, of course—are Marin's two sons."

Exactly like the Godfather in the movie, Hamish thought. "I guess one son's gentle and sensitive and the other's a hotheaded killer," he said.

"No," Malloy told him, "they're both cold-blooded killers."

Hamish got up from his chair and started for the door.

"Where you going, Ralph?"

"To hide out in some other city. Maybe—"

"Don't tell me where," Malloy interrupted. "I mean, in case I'm, uh, asked persuasively, it'd be better if I didn't know your whereabouts."

"You're a friend," Hamish said, going out the door.

Behind him Malloy said, "Please forget that for a while."

HAMISH'S PHONE WAS RINGING when he opened the door to his office. He lifted the receiver tentatively and identified himself.

"You made a fool outa me," Longo's voice said, in a tone as flat and cold as yesterday's pizza. "People don't do that and live, my friend. I trusted you, hey? I thought we was chums with a business arrangement, even paid you the money before I knew the job was done."

"I never got any money."

"Look on your desk."

Hamish leafed through his unopened mail, and there it was, an envelope containing fifty thousand-dollar bills. He dropped it as if it were hot. "I'll give the money back. Really."

"I don't want the money. What I'm gonna do is make you earn it the hard way. Gonna hang you by your bozongos with piano wire and listen to you beg—"

Hamish slammed down the receiver. His stomach was bucking, and he was trembling. He'd been paid not fifty dollars but fifty thousand, and these were hard people he'd gotten mixed up with. Piano wire! His hand floated to his neck, then dropped lower. Bozongos! He shivered and started getting everything out of his desk drawers he might want to take with him to . . . oh, say, Cincinnati. He might be safe in a city he couldn't spell.

"Don't be in a rush," a voice said.

Hamish jumped, whirled, and stood motionless, listening to his heart.

Two men stood just inside the door. One was tall and dark, with reptilian eyes and a cruel slash of a mouth. The other looked exactly like him only squashed down to slightly over five feet tall. They were wearing identical black suits, white shirts, red ties with tiny, tiny knots, lots of glittery gold jewelry, and the expressions of sadists contemplating a party.

"I'm Jack Marin," the tall one said. "This is my brother, Curtis. Every-body calls him Crush. Maybe that's because he couldn't pronounce his name when he was two ... I'm not sure."

Crush smiled. "I think it's for some other reason."

From beneath their suit coats both men drew steel-blue semi-automatics with silencers attached. Jack said, "Bet you can guess why we're here."

"Paul Marin is your father?" Hamish said.

"Unfortunately for you," Crush said, "that's true. He's a man would kill either one of us if we hit him in the face with a pizza. I mean, he put me in the hospital for a week when I was sixteen 'cause I put a dent in the car. You can imagine what he wants done with you."

"He'd rather not imagine," Jack said. He leveled his gun and casually blasted Hamish's telephone. The shattering plastic made more noise than the shot.

"That thing under warranty or anything?" Crush asked.

Hamish shook his head no.

"My brother had some trouble with federal people tapping his phone," Crush explained. " 'Cause of that, he doesn't like phones, so whenever he gets a chance, he drills one. I guess that's better'n where his next shot might go, huh?"

Hamish didn't know what to say, so he said nothing. Merely trembled.

"We talked to Pop," Jack said. "He agreed to give you the chance to go on living, but only under a certain condition."

"Like ... maimed?"

"No, no, nothing like that. A business condition. A job. For you to stay alive, Joey Longo has to be dead within twenty-four hours."

It took Hamish a few seconds to realize what they were saying. De-manding. They were telling him he had to hit Longo—and not with a pizza.

"It's your only chance," Crush said, "so there shouldn't be much hesi-tation. You turn us down, or you don't get the job done, and we come see you and kill you slow."

"I hope you do the hit on Longo," Jack said. "Crush has got this thing he likes to do with a pair of pliers, and I don't want to have to see that again."

Both men nodded, unsmiling. Crush winked at Hamish. Then they silently slipped out the door.

Somehow they made no noise descending the creaking stairs, but Ham-ish heard the street door open and close.

Hamish looked at the ceiling and said, "For God's sake, now what?"

Twenty-four hours.

Pliers.

Piano wire.

Hamish sat paralyzed with terror until almost noon, when the phone rattled beside him, startling him.

It wasn't a death rattle, the damaged instrument was actually ringing. Or trying to ring.

He lifted the receiver and pressed it to his ear. Said hello.

"Hamish, this is Longo. I been thinking things over. You got twenty-four hours to do what you was hired to do, or you're gonna be the next guy to get it in the face, anchovies and all. You understand? Hey?"

"Hey," Hamish said, and hung up. The receiver split into two sections, buzzed loudly, then was silent.

Hamish looked out the window, thinking, Cincinnati.

HE WAS PACKING HIS LEAST THREADBARE CLOTHES that evening when he saw it on local TV news: A crowd of shocked onlookers. Police cars and ambulances. Yellow crime-scene ribbons. A pretty blond anchorwoman said, "Two local crime kingpins were killed just hours ago."

The handsome anchorman next to her said, "Paul Marin was shot and killed at his home around noon today."

"And Joseph 'Joey' Longo, another infamous hoodlum—"

"—was strangled a few hours later," the anchorman finished for her. "Police have no leads—"

"—nor are they releasing any details of the crimes," said the anchorwoman.

"—either to the press—"

"—or to the public—"

"—regarding either death."

"Speaking of dead, Bob, the wind has sure died down out there. What's our weather got in store for us?"

Hamish switched off the TV. He was interested in the weather only in Cincinnati, where he would sit down and try to figure all this out.

UNDER THE NAME of his old algebra teacher in high school, Hamish reserved a seat on the next flight to Cincinnati. He was preparing to carry his packed suitcases down to the car when there was a soft knock on the door.

He went to the door but didn't open it. Instead he stood listening, marveling that his knees were actually knocking. He hadn't thought such a thing was possible.

"Mr. Hamish?" The voice from the hall was soft, respectful.

"Mr. Hamish?"

Hamish opened the door an inch and peered out.

He wished he hadn't.

Four men were standing in the hall. They were all huge and looked like gorillas who'd been shaved and sent to a skillful tailor.

"We wanna talk, is all, sir," said the one with greased back hair and a wilted carnation in his lapel.

Somewhat stunned, Hamish stepped back, and they filed into the apartment.

They introduced themselves. They had names like Knuckles, Meathook, Big Lou, Bigger Lou. Bigger Lou, with the wilted carnation and crude-oiled hair, seemed to be the spokesman.

He said, "We can't work for Jack Marin."

Hamish, feeling trapped in a kind of dark Damon Runyon piece, said, "What's that mean?"

"It means now that you've hit the old man and Joey Longo, we got problems. It's no secret how loyal me and Big Lou was to the old man, and Knuckles and Meathook was close to Joey, in a business sense."

Hamish understood. "So the Marin brothers don't trust you."

"Which means they'll hit us," Bigger Lou said. "It's just a matter of time, like with you."

Hamish's stomach plunged. "Me?"

"Sure. You don't think they'll let a loose end like you walk around forever, do you? Not to mention, if you got the bozongos to hit people like Joey and the old man, you might get ideas about running the show yourself."

More understanding pushed its way through Hamish's fear. "Now wait a minute!"

When he raised his voice, all three huge men backed away. He scratched beneath his arm. Even Bigger Lou turned pale.

Hamish said, "I think I understand. You want me to beat them to the punch, to take over the city's criminal operations before I'm killed."

"That's about the only choice you got," Bigger Lou said. "And we can make everything easier for you. As a kind of act of future loyalty on our part. All we ask is you do nothing while we make our moves. After we do away with the competition, you're in charge and you get your cut of all the action." He beamed. "Whaddya say, boss?"

Hamish stared at them. All four men were grinning as if the primate cage had been left unlocked.

Hamish finally fully grasped his position. Jack and Crush had murdered their father and then Joey Longo, using Hamish as the patsy. Hamish had a powerful motive for both murders: his survival. A few words in the right ears, and word had gotten around. Hamish the hit man was the most feared individual in the city. And he was trapped. If he claimed his innocence, he wouldn't be believed. And the Marins would never change their story. If the brothers exposed him as a phony and not a hit man, they'd be nailed for the murders either by the police or by elements who were loyal to Paul Marin or Joey Longo. The police wouldn't be able to prove anything, but they probably thought he was the killer, too.

Hamish didn't want to be a kingpin of crime, but there he was. Almost.

"Just don't say no, Mr. Hamish," Bigger Lou pleaded. "That's all we ask. All we need."

Hamish walked to the window and stood staring out at the starkly shadowed buildings across the street. A row of pigeons on a ledge seemed to stare back at him, as if they and Hamish had something in common.

After a few minutes Meathook rasped, "He ain't gonna say no, I think."

Bigger Lou said, "Fine, boss. That's plenty good enough for us."

When Hamish turned around, he found himself alone.

THE GANG WAR WAS BRUTAL and far-reaching. Within a week the death toll had reached a dozen. A few of the casualties' names were familiar. Hamish had run into the soldiers and hangers-on of the organization or heard or read about them in the news. He couldn't tell by reading the Cincinnati newspapers who was winning.

Then he read that Crush Marin had been found dead in a culvert with a meat hook in his throat. That ruined Hamish's breakfast.

It also suggested he might be able to return home. The war was winding down. He'd soon be the king of the underworld.

He should stay in Cincinnati and be king of nothing, he knew. But there was something in him, perhaps something perverse, that made him call the airport and book a flight for that afternoon. Not using his real name, of course. The warring factions might be watching the airlines; people like that, they had connections. John Bigg, he told the reservationist on the phone. Mr. Bigg.

This king-of-the-underworld idea was growing on him.

THE FIRST THING HE NOTICED when he walked into his office was the new phone. Probably a gift, he figured, a gesture of respect from his men. The second thing he noticed was the envelope containing the fifty thousand dollars. He picked it up, stared at it for a while, then stuffed it toward the back of a file cabinet door.

Then he sat down behind his desk, clasped his hands behind his head, leaned back, and wished he had a cigar. Cuban and hand-rolled. The king of the underworld deserved no less.

The phone rang. Sort of chimed, actually. A chime of respect.

Hamish picked up the clean white receiver, noticing it was heavy. An expensive phone. He said hello.

"This is Jack Marin, Hamish."

"Shtill alive, hey?" Hamish said. He was imagining the cigar in his mouth, even though he didn't have it yet.

"You won't feel so tough by the time I hang up, you phone gonzolla."

Hamish wondered what that meant. Had he been called a Venetian boat?

"Your boys got me backed in a corner," Marin said. "I'm jittery even going out and starting my car, afraid I'll get blown up the way you're gonna."

"Me?" Hamish stared at the phone. The heavy receiver. Was it possible the thing was packed with explosives? That it could somehow be detonated through the phone lines by Marin? Surely not!

"Your life won't last long after I pass the word you didn't hit my old man and Joey Longo."

"If you do that," Hamish reminded him, "*your* life won't last long."

"Not if I tell everybody it was Crush did the hits," Jack said smugly.

"You'd blame your own brother for that?"

"I killed my own father, jerkhead, so why don't you think I'd hang the rap on my brother? Besides, he's dead, so what the hell's he gonna care?"

Those were both pretty good points, Hamish had to admit to himself.

"So long, Hamish," Jack said with a nasty little chuckle. "Either here or in Cincinnati, where you thought you were hiding out, you're a dead man that just needs a place to lie down. Or maybe you should try some other city. You don't think Bigger Lou can track you down within hours, you're dead wrong." He laughed. "It don't matter if he can spell the place or not, he's got ways to find you wherever you go."

Click. Buzz.

The connection was broken.

Hamish slowly replaced the receiver. He was scared. No longer Mr. Bigg. Mr. Frightened-out-of-His-Wits now.

Grateful he hadn't unpacked, he drove to his apartment and tossed his suitcases into the trunk of the Plymouth. Then he got in the car and drove south. He didn't even bother considering a destination. He simply drove. Distance was what he craved. Distance between himself and immediate danger.

But not for a second did he forget the more distant danger. Organized crime was called that for a reason. He knew Jack Marin was right: Bigger Lou would find him wherever he went.

And if Bigger Lou didn't, Jack Marin would.

HAMISH DIDN'T GET A CHANCE to run far. The next morning, as he unfolded a newspaper in his cheap motel room, he read that Jack Marin had been arrested and charged with the murders of his father and Joey Longo.

Hamish phoned Malloy and asked him what it was all about.

"It's all about you, Ralph," Malloy said. "The case against Jack Marin is based on the wiretap recording of his phone conversation with you."

"Me?" Then Hamish remembered the new phone in his office, replacing the one Jack Marin had shot. "So it was the law that replaced my phone," he said, "not my men."

"I don't know anything about that," Malloy said. "I figured it was the guy who tipped us to put a tap on it."

Hamish sat down on the edge of the mattress. "What guy was that?"

"One Louis Willard Davidson."

"Big Lou?"

"Nope. Bigger Lou. The war's over, Ralph. There's a cease-fire, and it's Bigger Lou who's left standing, now that Jack Marin's up on a murder charge."

"Then it's safe for me to come back?"

"I'd say so. Bigger Lou's lost some respect for you as a tough guy, but he no doubt regards you as a friend. Insofar as guys like Bigger Lou have friends."

Hamish wasted no time. He was tired of hotels and motels, of fear and greasy restaurant food. Especially fast food. He didn't want to eat any of it ever again.

He did make an exception when the pizza, which he hadn't ordered, was delivered to him his first night back home.

The box was lettered "Bigger Lou's Pizzeria."

The pizza was the deluxe with everything on it.

Except anchovies.

Barbara Collins's short stories combine the narrative drive of the well-made story with some very idiosyncratic (and hilarious) social observation. There is virtually no subject that Barb can't find a wry side to, as in this story of one cat's plight. Barb is presently working on her first novel, and producing more short stories as well.

The Ten Lives of Talbert
BARBARA COLLINS

At 8:00 A.M. on Rodeo Drive, the immaculate street was devoid of its native Jaguars, Rolls-Royces and Ferraris. The only vehicles, prowling or parked, were of the dreary domestic variety—Ford, Chevrolet, Dodge—but for the occasional Japanese, which were only a marginal step up.

The sidewalks, too, were deserted, except for a few shoppers hovering near the fashionable storefronts, waiting for the doors to open.

Tourists.

Charles watched them from inside the locked glass door of his exclusive boutique, Chez Charles. He could tell they were tourists, no matter how well they dressed, because the real people of Beverly Hills simply never came out until the sun burned the haze out of the air.

He hated them. The *touristes*. Clopping into his shop in their *vulgaire* shoes and *prêt-à-porter* clothing, carrying bourgeois bags, smelling of cheap *eau de toilette* . . . Why, they couldn't even afford a simple bauble, let alone a creation from his chic spring *haute couture*!

So when the *racaille*—the riff-raff—came in, he would raise his eyebrows in surprise and look down his nose at them disdainfully and say, *"Oui?"*, drawing the word out as if it were three. That was enough to make most flee.

But every once in a while some stupid woman would pretend she was actually interested in purchasing a ten-thousand-dollar, hand-beaded gown. When that happened, Charles would gaze at her appraisingly, then state condescendingly that his creations did not come in *grande* sizes.

Charles made a disgusted sound with his lips as he stood waiting by

294

the front glass door; just the thought of some ... *paysan* ... trying on
one of his magnificent gowns made his skin crawl. His designs were only
for the rich and famous!

A sleek white limousine pulled up.

Instantly excited, Charles unlocked the door with a trembling hand
and stepped out into the pleasant spring morning.

Even now, he couldn't believe his luck! When the call had come in a
month ago, he thought it a hoax: a woman claiming to be the great Simone
Vedette, enduring icon of the silver screen of the thirties. He nearly
slammed the phone receiver down. Because, except for some fleeting tabloid snapshots taken of the actress on a beach somewhere, and a trashy un-
authorized biography written by the woman's adopted daughter, the
reclusive star had avoided contact with the public for over forty years!

But as Charles listened to the woman's low, sensual voice, laced with
aristocratic breeding, the more he believed the call was authentic.

She told him she was being honored at the Academy Awards, and had,
after much coaxing, agreed to personally accept the Oscar for Lifetime
Achievement. She needed a gown—a beautiful dress—like the ones she
had recently spotted in his store window. Could she see him some morning before hours?

And now, the aged immortal star—really the only legend left alive
since the deaths of Dietrich and Garbo—was about to exit the limo, its
windows darkened for privacy, to purchase a gown from him! From Chez
Charles! Elusive fame would at last be his. Once he leaked the news to
the tabloids, that is.

The chauffeur, a middle-aged man with graying temples, smartly
dressed in uniform and cap, opened the car's back door.

Charles wiped his sweating palms on the sides of his tailored trousers.
Moved closer to the curb.

But instead of the living legend, out of the back of the limo climbed
a plain-faced woman of Mexican descent who could have been thirty, or
forty or fifty years old, wearing a cotton print housedress, horn-rimmed
glasses and oversized headscarf.

This was not Simone Vedette!

Perhaps under different circumstances, Charles would have laughed at
the ludicrousness of such a common woman getting out of a limousine;
but instead, he stood frozen in disappointment and confusion.

But then the peasant woman turned and bent slightly and extended a
hand into the car.

A long, slender gold-braceleted arm appeared, taking that hand, then
a shapely black-nyloned leg extended outward toward the curb, as the
great Simone Vedette was helped from the limo.

Charles sighed with relief, then grinned with pleasure. The grande
dame of the cinema was still quite beautiful!

She was small, perhaps five foot three, not the five foot seven or eight he had imagined. She wore a simple black dress (too short) and a large, wide-brimmed black hat (too big). A gold necklace (too heavy) graced her surprisingly firm and unwrinkled neck. In one hand she carried a red quilted Chanel bag (too overpowering); the other arm held a white cat (too furry).

Charles moved closer to the great movie star, catching the scent of her perfume (too floral), and bowed as if to royalty. *"Bonjour, madame,"* he gushed.

"Good morning," she responded in a voice that was low and warm. But her face was cold, chiseled: thin, arched eyebrows, large deep-set eyes, high hollow cheekbones, long straight nose, narrow bowed lips. She did, however, look like a woman in her fifties, instead of someone in her eighties. Her plastic surgeon must be *fantastique!*

"This is my housekeeper, Lucinda Lopez," the actress said, introducing the peasant woman who stood quietly nearby. "And my cat Talbert." She scratched the animal's neck, and it undulated in her arms. "Both go everywhere with me."

Charles gave the housekeeper a cursory look, then smiled at the cat as genuinely as he could, for a man who abhorred such creatures.

"Entrer?" he said with a flourish of a gesture.

Charles opened the glass door, and Simone Vedette went in, the housekeeper in tow. He followed, shutting and locking the door behind them.

"Elle est là-bas," he instructed, as the two women hesitated just inside; he pointed toward the back of the shop.

The movie star and the Mexican woman headed that way, through the outer room which was just for the general public.

Charles had spent hours arranging this outer room, knowing Simone would pass through it, displaying his creations just so ... but the actress took no notice as she made her way along.

The housekeeper, however, ooohed and aaahed at this and that, which only caused him great irritation.

They went through a thick red-velvet curtain, tied back to one side.

"Asseyez-vous à la chaise, s'il vous plaît," Charles smiled.

Simone Vedette looked at him blankly. "I don't speak French, young man," she said. "And I wish you'd stop."

Charles blinked. "But, I thought ... I mean, your name ..."

"I was born in Brooklyn," she said simply.

Charles stood dumbfounded, then recovered and gestured grandly to a gilded satin-covered French Empire chair. "Won't you please sit down," he said.

The great star sat, the cat curled on her lap.

He didn't bother to offer the housekeeper a chair; she found herself a place next to a rack of clothes.

Charles stood before the actress, bending slightly toward her, pressing his hands together, prayerlike.

"I have designed for you the most incredibly exquisite gown!" he exclaimed, then paused for effect. "And after you wear it at the Academy Awards, the media will dispense with their traditional fashion dissection—what did Cher wear? Who designed Geena Davis's gown? Who cares? *No one,* not once you have been seen wearing ..."

"Yes, yes," the actress interrupted impatiently, but her curiosity was clearly piqued. "Please, bring it out!"

The white, fluffy cat on her lap looked up at him with bored blue eyes.

Eagerly Charles disappeared behind a large dressing screen, where the gown was hidden, displayed on a platformed mannequin. He gazed at the dress, his eyes gleaming like the six thousand sequins and pearls he had sewed by hand onto the sheer beige silk soufflé.

The gown was worth twenty thousand; he would charge her forty.

Carefully, tenderly, Charles covered up the mannequin with a large gold lamé cloth. Then he rolled the platform out from behind the screen, positioning the statue in front of the actress.

With a smile, he slowly pulled on one end of the gold material, teasingly, exposing the bottom of the drop-dead gorgeous gown, and then, with a *snap,* yanked it completely off.

Simone Vedette gasped.

Charles beamed, looking at the dress. It truly was his finest work. A masterpiece that would soon make his name synonymous with the likes of Dior, Valentino and Galtier!

His eyes went back to the actress, who was still gasping, leaning forward, but now clutching her chest. The cat on her lap rose to its feet, struggling to keep from falling.

"Madame!" Charles cried out, alarmed. Something was wrong with the woman!

From behind him, the housekeeper shrieked, further terrifying the cat, which leapt from his mistress's lap onto the mannequin, claws bared, clinging, ripping as it slid down the delicate material, sequins and pearls popping and dropping onto the floor, where the last of the legends now lay—but no longer living.

Charles stared at shock and disbelief at the dead woman at his feet. Had he been foiled by his own brilliance? Had he finally done it?

Created a dress to die for?

BRENDA VEDETTE SAT IN A LEATHER CHAIR in a posh office on Wilshire Boulevard in Beverly Hills.

The woman, in her mid-thirties, attractive, with straight, shoulder-length blond hair, was dressed in a dark gray suit, an inexpensive copy of a Paris original. Across from her, behind a massive mahogany desk, was Mitchell Levin, a slender, bespectacled man in his sixties, who was her late mother's lawyer.

Brenda pulled a pack of cigarettes from her purse. "Mind if I smoke?" she asked.

By way of an answer, the lawyer pushed a glass ashtray toward her on the desk.

She lit the cigarette, took a puff, and blew the smoke out the side of her mouth. Then she asked, "So, am I cut out of the will, or what?"

Mitchell Levin looked down at the document before him. "No," he said cautiously, "you aren't. However, there are a few provisions ..."

Brenda laughed hoarsely. "Like what? I find a job, get married, quit smoking?"

The corners of the lawyer's mouth turned up slightly, but more from disgust, Brenda thought, than amusement.

"These provisions," he explained, "have to do with your mother's cat, Talbert, and housekeeper, Lucinda Lopez."

A sickening feeling spread slowly through Brenda's body. *That crazy old broad hadn't left the bulk of everything to them, had she?*

Brenda took another puff of the cigarette and said as blandly as she could, "Go on."

Mitchell studied the papers in his hands. "It was your mother's wish that Talbert remain at her home in Malibu in the comfort he has been used to, and under the care of Lucinda, until his death, at which time the estate will go to you."

Brenda sat numbly and said nothing.

Mitchell said, "Now, you can *try* to contest the will, but I'm warning you ..."

"Mr. Levin!" Brenda snapped, working indignation into those two words, and the ones that followed. "I have no intention of going against my mother's wishes!"

Most likely prepared for a fight, the lawyer looked a little stunned.

Brenda leaned forward and forcefully stubbed out her cigarette in the ashtray. "My mother and I may not have seen eye to eye, but she certainly has the right to do whatever she wants with her money."

Brenda sat back in her chair, lowered her voice. "And she was correct in being concerned about Talbert ... I wouldn't have wanted him. And I'd have sold the house. It holds nothing but painful memories for me." Her voice cracked at the end.

There was an awkward silence. Tears sprang to her eyes.

"Do you think it was *easy* being raised in the shadow of the great Simone Vedette?" Brenda blurted. "She *never* should have adopted me ... she just didn't have the right temperament! And she was *too old*."

Brenda looked down at her hands in her lap and shook her head slowly. "My mother expected so much from me, yet gave so little in return. I guess that was why I wrote the book ... Any attention I could get from her, no matter how negative, was better than nothing."

"It hurt her deeply," the lawyer said.

"Well, *she* hurt *me*!"

Brenda sobbed into her hands.

Mitchell Levin reached into his coat pocket and pulled out a handkerchief. "Here," he said softly, giving it to her. "Use this."

Brenda dabbed at her eyes with the cloth. Composed herself. Looked at the lawyer. "I just want you to know, I did love my mother, and I'm sorry that book was ever published. And I'll certainly comply with any of her last wishes."

Mitchell gave Brenda a little smile; it seemed genuine. "Your mother would have been proud to hear you say that," he told her.

Brenda nodded. Then, as an afterthought, she asked, "Oh ... my monthly stipend ... will it continue?"

"The same as usual."

The young woman stood. "Then if there's nothing else ..."

Mitchell rose from behind his desk. "Goodbye, Brenda," he said, extending one hand. "I'll be in touch. Take care of yourself."

"Thank you," she returned warmly, and shook his hand.

Out on the street, Brenda got into her five-year-old Ford Escort convertible, which was parked at the curb. She plucked any old cassette from the many tapes scattered on the seat next to her, and inserted it into the dash. Then with dated disco music throbbing, pulled out into the traffic.

She looked at herself in the visor mirror.

Her mother wasn't the *only* Vedette who could give an Academy Award performance ...

So she wouldn't get her inheritance until the cat was dead? Fine. How long could a cat live, anyway?

After all, accidents did happen.

A DARK-HAIRED WOMAN in sunglasses, T-shirt, backpack and jeans walked her dog along the beach in Malibu, where expensive ocean-front homes crowded so close together they almost touched, with barely enough room between them for the fences that separated these patches of precious, puny real estate.

It was early afternoon, and anyone who might notice the young lady would not give her a second thought—even though the dog on the leash was a vicious pit bull—because the woman was carrying two socially and ecologically correct items: a pooper-scooper and a sack.

The dog seemed well behaved, stopping occasionally to sniff at this and that. The man the woman had bought the pit bull from had said the animal liked people ... it was just *cats* the dogs hated.

Bewigged Brenda let the dog lead her down a narrow passageway between the tall wooden fences of two homes.

She stopped by the fence belonging to the house on the right. Quietly she pulled back a board she had loosened late the night before.

She peeked through.

Talbert—that fat, lazy puss—was having his usual afternoon nap on the patio. He lay on his side, in the shade of a tall potted plant, legs stretched out, dead to the world—as he soon would be. The housekeeper was nowhere in sight.

Brenda unleashed the pit bull and gently pushed its head toward the opening in the fence.

The dog resisted at first, but then suddenly it caught sight of the sleeping cat, and with powerful legs propelled itself through the opening, splintering the wood, leaving an outline of its massive body on the remaining boards, moving like a freight train into the yard.

Brenda wanted to watch, but didn't dare. She stayed only long enough, hidden behind the wooden fence, to hear the snarls of the dog, and yowls of the cat, and then screams of the housekeeper, who must have come running out of the house . . .

Brenda hurried along the passageway between the fences, putting on a red nylon jacket. The pooper-scooper and leash, along with the black wig, she stowed in the backpack.

Quickly she moved down the beach—just a pretty, blonde power-walker out for some exercise. Half a mile away, off Pacific Coast Highway, was her parked convertible.

Throwing the backpack in the back seat, she got in and started the car. She grabbed a tape from off the passenger seat and struck it in the player.

Think I'll go over to Cartier and get that diamond tennis bracelet I've always wanted, she mused to herself.

"After all," she said aloud, smiled, driving off, the music of the Bee Gees blaring, "I can afford it now."

LATER THAT NIGHT, under a sky bedecked with a million dazzling stars (though not as dazzling as the diamonds on her wrist), Brenda pulled the convertible into the driveway of her late mother's house.

She got out and pressed a buzzer on the gate of the wooden fence.

After a moment an intercom speaker crackled and Lucinda's voice said, "Yes? Who is it?"

The housekeeper sounded weary.

"It's Brenda. I've come to get a book."

There was a long pause. Then, "Okay. I let you in."

Brenda waited for the buzzer and pushed open the gate.

She walked slowly by the patio, which was awash in outside lighting.

Everything appeared normal. No disturbed deck furniture or overturned potted plants. Even the fence had been repaired. It was as if nothing had ever happened.

But as Brenda approached the back door of the beach house, she noticed a dark stain on the patio cement.

Blood, perhaps?

She repressed a smile as the housekeeper opened the door for her.

"Hello, Lucinda," Brenda said, as she entered the house. She was standing in a comfortable, tastefully decorated TV room. It was where her mother had spent most of her time.

"I need to find a book a friend loaned me," Brenda explained. "She wants it back, and I think I gave it to my mother."

The housekeeper stared at her with large, liquid eyes behind her old-fashioned glasses.

"Is something wrong?" Brenda asked, feigning concern. "You don't look well."

"This ... this afternoon," the woman began haltingly, "a terrible thing happened."

"What?"

"A big dog got through the fence and attacked little Talbert!"

"No!" Brenda said, aghast. "How awful!"

"I called the police, and they had to *shoot* the dog."

"How horrible!" Lucinda shook her head slowly, then looked down at the floor. "That poor, poor cat ... What a cruel way for it to die."

"Oh, Talbert's not dead," the housekeeper said.

"Not dead?"

Lucinda pointed to the other side of the room, where Brenda now saw the cat, sleeping on a pet bed on the floor next to a chair. Several of his paws were bandaged.

"He got away from the bad dog," Lucinda explained, "and climbed the ... what do you call it? On the side of the house?"

"Challis," Brenda said flatly.

"*Sí.* The challis. We're lucky it was there."

"Yes," Brenda replied slowly. "Lucky."

The room fell silent.

"You don't have to worry about Talbert, Miss Brenda," Lucinda said firmly. "From now on, I'm not letting him out of my sight."

Brenda smiled weakly.

The housekeeper smiled back. "Now, what was the name of that book you wanted?"

IT WAS HOT IN THE TINY, dingy apartment on Alameda Street, but the air conditioner in the window wasn't plugged in.

Brenda stood by the dirt-streaked window looking down on the filthy street below. She had rented the third-floor room, directly over the building's entrance, three weeks ago, under an assumed name.

She stepped back a little from the window as a limousine pulled up at the curb.

The chauffeur got out and went around to the side of the car, where he helped Lucinda out of the back seat. She was wearing her usual cotton housedress and headscarf and was carrying a sack of groceries, which she brought every Saturday morning to her elderly mother, who lived below, on the first floor. Looped around one arm was a green leash, and at the end of the leash, was Talbert.

The housekeeper made her way leisurely up the sidewalk of the apartment building.

She climbed the short flight of steps, bag in both arms, the leashed Talbert trailing behind.

Brenda, her head pressed against the dirty window pane, watched until the moment Lucinda disappeared from view into the building, Talbert bringing up the rear; then Brenda opened the window further and shoved the massive air conditioner out.

It crashed on the steps below, making a terrible, metallic racket, the leash winding out from under it like a green tail.

Brenda shut the window, gently.

IN THE LATE AFTERNOON, as the sun descended on Malibu, shimmering on the ocean like tinsel on a tree, Brenda wheeled her convertible into the driveway of her mother's house.

She got out, carrying a small basket, and rang the buzzer.

She had a present for Talbert, Brenda told the housekeeper, and could she come in?

Inside the TV room, Brenda's eyes darted to the little cat bed on the floor by the chair, but it was empty.

"The pet store around the corner from me is going out of business," Brenda said to Lucinda, "and everything was half-price." She paused and held up the basket in her hand. "I thought Talbert might like these treats and catnip and stuff."

Lucinda looked at her sadly.

Brenda let her mouth fall open. "Don't tell me something *else* has happened to Talbert!" she said incredulously.

The housekeeper nodded.

"What?"

"An air conditioner fell down on him."

"An *air conditioner*?"

Lucinda told her what had happened.

"That is so incredible!" Brenda said, then added sadly, "I'm going to miss that sweet little animal . . ."

"Oh, he's all right," the housekeeper said.

"All right?"

"Because the air conditioner fell on the steps," Lucinda explained, "there was a little space for him. It did hurt his tail, though."

Perhaps hearing his name, the white Persian entered the room from the kitchen. His front paws were still bandaged, and now so was his tail.

Brenda glared at the cat.

Lucinda bent down, gently picked up the animal, and kissed his diffident face.

"It must be true what they say," the housekeeper said, speaking more to the animal than Brenda. "A cat does have nine lives."

In her convertible, Brenda ejected the cassette out of the player, snatched another off the passenger seat, and shoved it inside.

"That mangy beast doesn't have nine lives," she fumed, "he has ten!"

She tore out of the driveway, tires squealing, music cranked.

Maybe she needed something so lethal it would snuff out every last life fat Talbert had left. It was time to stop playing Wile E. Coyote to his Road Runner.

Time for something a little more high tech ...

BRENDA BOUGHT A MODEM AND HOOKED it up to her home computer. Then she joined Internet and, going through an anonymous server known as a double-blind to protect her identity, posted this message: LOOKING FOR WAY TO KILL NEIGHBOR'S EVIL, ANNOYING CAT. WILL PAY $1,000 SIGNED, SLEEPLESS IN LA.

Within hours, her computer began to beep as hundreds of responses poured in from all over the world; evidently, a lot of cat haters traveled the information highway in cyberspace.

She heard from a terrorist group in Tangier who wanted the money for guns, and a Russian physicist suggesting she use red mercury—the latest in modern warfare, and some nut from New York who offered to do the job for free ...

But the message that intrigued her the most read: ACME ELECTRONICS 555 ACME RD., CUPERTINO (SILICON VALLEY). COME AFTER HOURS. BRING TAPE OF THE CAT'S MEOWING.

This person seemed serious.

"BUT IT'S A MOUSE!" Brenda said disappointedly, looking at the small brown rodent on the workbench in the cluttered back room of the electronic store.

"A *robot* mouse," corrected the middle-aged man who had introduced himself as Steve. He was about average height and weight, with sandy hair and a close-cropped beard; not the skinny, nerdy type with glasses Brenda had expected.

Brenda's eyes widened. "*That's* a robot?"

The man nodded. "You've heard of robot bugs?" he asked.

Brenda shook her head, no.

"They're miniature robots used mostly for espionage, but they don't really look like bugs." He paused and affectionately caressed the mouse's back. "This is my genius. It can squeeze under doors, scurry around in the heat ducts, hide under the furniture—just like a real mouse—only there's one little difference . . . this one explodes."

"Cool," Brenda said.

He looked at her sharply, eyes as brown as the mouse. "Did you bring the cassette?" he asked.

She nodded and dug into her purse and handed him the tape she had made of the cat meowing; she had recorded it the day before when she went over to sunbathe on the patio.

"Oh, and I have the money," Brenda added. She reached in her jacket pocket and pulled out ten one-hundred-dollar bills and put them on the workbench.

He smiled, but the smile was lopsided. "That's good," he said, "but it won't be enough . . . Brenda."

A chill went up her back. She hadn't given him her real name. And her identity on her computer message was supposed to have been kept secret!

"I cracked your anonymous ID," he shrugged. "Anyone who hides behind a double-blind has something to hide, I always say. Next time protect yourself with a password."

Brenda felt her face grow hot. She didn't know what to say.

"I also accessed your home computer files," he continued.

"*Which* files?" she demanded.

" 'Dear Monica, I won't get my inheritance until the cat is dead . . .' "

Brenda grabbed the money off the workbench and bolted for the door. But the man beat her to it, blocking the exit.

"Get out of my way, or I'll scream!" she shouted.

He put both hands up in the air. "Whoa! I'm not going to touch you . . . I just want a little more money, that's all."

She backed away from him. Narrowed her eyes. "How much more?"

He lowered his hands. "Ten thousand."

"Ten thousand!" she said, almost choking on the words. "I haven't got that kind of money!"

"But you *will* have," he said slyly. "That and a lot more . . ."

She stared at him.

"Look," he explained, his voice softer, "that robot is worth five grand, easy. I'll need to replace it. And then I want to build another."

She considered that, vacillating. The robot mouse *was* a neat gizmo, she thought, and would certainly do the trick.

But then she had a few more thoughts. Blowing the cat to kingdom come wouldn't exactly look like an accidental death. She would certainly be suspected . . .

Brenda looked at Steve, who was grinning at her smugly.

But the authorities could only get to her through him . . . and he *already* knew too much.

"Okay," she agreed, "I'll pay you ten thousand. But not until I get my money. Then you'll get *yours*."

That would give her enough time to figure out how to kill him.

She made a mental note to remember to ask for the tape of the cat back . . . wouldn't want any evidence left behind.

"Deal." He smiled and held out his hand for her to shake, which she did. "Now, let me show you how this cute little mouse works."

A TINY SLIVER OF MOON hung high in the sky, like the slit of a sleeping cat's eye, as Brenda drove her convertible slowly along the highway in front of her mother's house.

She parked the car in the mouth of the driveway and got out.

In the stillness of the night, she crept along the garage. She bent to the ground and carefully removed the mouse from her jacket pocket and placed the small robot on the cement, underneath the fence, between the boards and the ground.

There the mouse would stay, tucked away, for however long it took, until the cat meowed. The robot would then identify that particular sound, and with the guidance of a heat-seeking device, zero in on the animal and blow it to smithereens.

She smiled at the irony of a mouse chasing a cat—and killing it.

Brenda walked back to her car and slid in behind the wheel. She stuck a tape in the player, started the car.

"MEOW!" said the speakers.

Brenda froze, realizing what she had done. She looked over quickly to the space under the fence where she had put the mouse.

Even in the darkness she could see the small rodent move out of its hiding place and cut a path right toward her.

Brenda floored the car's accelerator, and with tires squealing and rubber smoking, backed out of the driveway and sped off.

She could outrun it, she thought. *After all, how fast could a little mouse go?*

Brenda flew down the highway, then suddenly she slammed on her brakes and made a U-turn, her tires squealing, as she bumped up on the curb, nearly running over a derelict who was sifting through a garbage can.

That should throw the little vermin off, she thought.

Furtively, she glanced over her shoulder. Under the bright street lights, she saw the small brown mouse make a tiny U-turn of its own, still tracking her, closing in.

Brenda went faster, her car careening, taking Malibu Canyon Road at a dangerous speed, the vehicle twisting and turning as it slid sideways into a pole.

The impact knocked Brenda nearly unconscious. But she did manage to say, "Oh, shit."

And there wasn't time for another word, before her world flashed white, then red, then black . . .

"MAS VINO, MADRE?" Lucinda asked, a wine decanter in her hand.

"Por favor," her mother answered. The woman, slender, with short, silver-gray hair, leaned forward in her lounge chair on the patio and held out a crystal goblet toward her daughter.

Lucinda filled the glass with Château Latour, and as she did, her mother told her in Spanish how beautiful Lucinda looked in the dress that she was wearing.

Lucinda smiled. She *did* feel like a movie star in the beige gown with sequins and pearls! If Talbert hadn't ripped it, she never would have owned the dress. So upset was Mr. Charles that he just *gave* it to her! And the rips that she herself had sewed shut hardly even showed, much.

Whenever she wore the dress—usually with one of her colorful head-scarfs and sandals—she proudly told whoever would listen that the gown was designed by Chez Charles on Rodeo Drive. It was the least she could do for that nice man!

Lucinda looked over at the sleeping white cat, stretched out on the patio. Held in its paws was the little pouch of catnip that Brenda had given him.

Poor Brenda, thought the housekeeper, *whatever had the girl been up to the night she died in the fiery crash just a few miles away?*

The police said there had been a witness. A poor man without a home saw the whole thing. He claimed Brenda was killed by a mouse that chased her down the highway! But, of course, that was silly.

A portable phone on the patio table rang and Lucinda picked it up.

"Hello?" she said.

"Miss Lopez?" a male voice asked.

"Yes?"

"This is Harold Davis, from Harold's Pet Emporium," he said. "Got a male white Persian for you."

"Gracias," Mr. Davis," Lucinda replied, "but I won't be needing the cat now." She paused, then added, "However, if I *should* want another in the future, can you get me one as fast as you got me the other two?"

Now that we are about to present four Edgar-nominated stories, mention should be made of two remarkable women, Janet Hutchings of *Ellery Queen* and Cathleen Jordan of *Alfred Hitchcock*. These editors have not simply made a home for the short crime story, they have also nurtured and shaped it. Janet has worked at a book club, edited a prize-winning line of mystery novels, and moved over to *Queen* a few years ago. Cathleen has not only edited mysteries, she's written a crime novel of her own. She has been at *Hitchcock* for several years. These editors play a key role largely responsible for its many shapes, sounds, and hues. We'd like to thank them here for their distinguished service to our field.

Brendan DuBois has been distinguishing himself for several years with first-rate crime stories. He is able to develop original themes and characters within the parameters of the traditional mystery story, and to do so with a slant very much his own. Brendan is also a novelist, his books DEAD SAND (1994) and BLACK TIDE (1955) wining favor with critics and readers alike. Brendan currently works in communications but is making the transition to full-time writing.

The Necessary Brother
BRENDAN DUBOIS

I still have the problem of last evening's phone call on my mind as I wait for Sarah to finish her shower this Thursday holiday morning in November. From my vantage point on the bed I see that the city's weather is overcast, and I wonder if snow flurries will start as I begin the long drive that waits for me later in the morning. The bedroom is large and is in the corner of the building, with a balcony that overlooks Central Park. I pause between the satin sheets and wait, my hands folded behind my head, as the shower stops and Sarah ambles out. She smiles at me and I smile back, feeling effortless in doing that, for we have no secrets from each other, no worries or frets about what the future may bring. That was settled months ago, in our agreement when we first met, and our arrangement works for both of us.

She comes over, toweling her long blond hair with a thick white towel, smile still on her face, a black silk dressing gown barely covering her model's body. As she clambers on the bed and straddles me, she drops the towel and leans forward, enveloping me in her damp hair, nuzzling my neck.

"I don't see why you have to leave, Carl," she says, in her breathless voice that can still make my head turn. "And I can't believe you're driving. That must be at least four hours away. Why don't you fly?"

"It's more like five," I say, idly caressing her slim hips. "And I'm driving because flying is torture this time of year, and I want to travel alone."

She gently bites me on the neck and then sits back, her pale blue eyes laughing at me. With her long red fingernails she idly traces the scars along my side and chest, and then touches the faint ones on my arms where I had the tattoos removed years ago. When we first met and first made love, Sarah was fascinated by the marks on my body, and it's a fascination that has grown over the months. At night, during our loveplay, she will sometimes stop and touch a scar and demand a story, and sometimes I surprise her by telling her the truth.

"And why are you going?" she asks. "We could have a lot of fun here today, you and me. Order up a wonderful meal. Watch the parades and old movies. Maybe even catch one of the football games."

I reach up and stroke her chin. "I'm going because I have to. And because it's family."

She makes a face and gets out of bed, drawing the gown closer to her. "Hah. Family. Must be some family to make you drive all that way. But I don't understand you, not at all. You hardly ever talk about them, Carl. Not ever. What's the rush? What's the reason?"

I shrug. "Because they're family. No other reason."

Sarah tosses the towel at my head and says in a joking tone, "You're impossible, and I'm not sure why I put up with you."

"Me too," I say, and I get up and go into the steamy bathroom as she begins to dive into the walk-in closet that belongs to her.

I STAY IN THE SHOWER for what seems hours, luxuriating in the hot and steamy water, remembering the times growing up in Boston Falls when showers were rationed to five minutes apiece because of the creaky hot water that could only stand so much use every cold day. Father had to take his shower before going to the mills, and Brad was next because he was the oldest. I was fortunate, being in the middle, for our youngest brother, Owen, sometimes ended up with lukewarm water, if that. And Mother, well, we never knew when she bathed. It was a family secret.

I get out and towel myself down, enjoying the feel of the warm heat on my lean body as I enter the bedroom. Another difference. Getting out of the shower used to mean walking across cold linoleum, grit on your feet as you got dressed for school. Now it means walking into a warm and carpeted bedroom, my clothes laid out neatly on my bed. I dress quickly, knowing I will have to move fast to avoid the traffic for the day's parade. I go out to the kitchen overlooking the large and dark sunken living room, and Sarah is gone, having left breakfast for me on the marbletop counter. The day's *Times* is there, folded, and I stand and eat the scrambled eggs, toast, and bacon, while drinking a large glass of orange juice and a cup of coffee.

When I unfold the *Times* a note falls out. It's in Sarah's handwriting. *Do have a nice trip,* it says. *I've called down to Raphael. See you when you get back. Yours, S.*

Yours. Sarah has never signed a note or a letter to me that says love. Always it's "yours." That's because Sarah tells the truth.

I wash the dishes and go into the large walk-in closet near the door that leads out to the hallway. I select a couple of heavy winter jackets, and from a combination-lock box similar to a fuse box, take out a Bianchi shoulder holster, a 9mm Beretta, and two spare magazines. I slide on the holster and pull a wool cardigan on and leave and take the elevator down, whistling as I do so.

Out on the sidewalk by the lobby Raphael nods to me as I step out into the brisk air, his doorkeeper's uniform clean and sharp. My black Mercedes is already pulled up, engine purring, faint tendrils of exhaust eddying up into the thick, cold air. Raphael smiles and touches his cap with a brief salute. There is an old knife scar on his brown cheek, and though still a teenager, he has seen some things that could give me the trembling wake-ups at two A.M. In addition to his compensation from the building, I pay Raphael an extra hundred a week to keep his eyes open for me. The doorkeepers in this city open and close lots of doors, and they also open and close a lot of secrets, and that's a wonderful resource for my business.

Raphael walks with me and opens the door. "A cold morning, Mr. Curtis. Are you ready for your drive?"

I slip a folded ten-dollar bill into his white-gloved hand, and it disappears effortlessly. "Absolutely. Trunk packed?"

"That it is," he says as I toss the two winter coats onto the passenger's seat and buckle up in the warm interior. I always wear seatbelts, a rule that, among others, I follow religiously. As he closes the door, Raphael smiles again and says, *"Vaya con Dios,"* and since the door is shut, I don't reply. But I do smile in return and he goes back to his post.

I'm about fifteen minutes into my drive when I notice the thermos bottle on the front seat, partially covered by the two coats I dumped there. At a long stoplight I unscrew the cap and smell the fresh coffee, then take a quick drink and decide Raphael probably deserves a larger Christmas bonus this year.

*   *   *

AS I DRIVE I LISTEN to my collection of classical music CDs. I can't tell you the difference between an opus and a symphony, a quartet or a movement, or who came first, Bach or Beethoven. But I do know what I like, and classical music is something that just seems to settle into my soul, like hot honey traveling into a honeycomb. I have no stomach for, nor interest in, what passes as modern music. When I drive I start at one end of my CD collection and in a month or so I get to the other end, and then start again.

The scenery as I go through the busy streets and across the numbered highways on my way to Connecticut is an urban sprawl of dead factories, junkyards, tenements, vacated lots, and battered cars with bald tires. Not a single pedestrian I see looks up. They all stare at the ground, as if embarrassed at what is around them, as if made shy by what has become of their country. I'm not embarrassed. I'm somewhat amused. It's the hard lives in that mess that give me my life's work.

I drive on, humming along to something on the CD that features a lot of French horns.

THROUGH CONNECTICUT I DRIVE in a half-daze, listening to the music, thinking over the phone call of the previous night and the unique problem that it poses for me. I knew within seconds of hanging up the telephone what my response would be, but it still troubles me. Some things are hard to confront, especially when they're personal. But I have no choice. I know what I must do and that gives me some comfort, but not enough. Not nearly enough.

While driving along the flat asphalt and concrete of the Connecticut highways, I keep my speed at an even sixty miles per hour, conscious of the eager state police who patrol these roads. Radar detectors are still illegal in this state and the police here seem to relish their role as adjuncts to the state's tax collection department. They have the best unmarked cars in the region, and I am in no mood to tempt them as I drive, drive along.

Only once do I nap out of my reverie, and that's when two Harley-Davidson motorcycles rumble by, one on each side, the two men squat and burly in their low seats, long hair flapping in the breeze, goggles hiding their eyes, their denim vests and leather jackets looking too thin for this weather, their expressions saying they don't particularly care. The sight brings back some sharp memories: the wind in my face, the throb of the engine against my thighs, the almost Zen-like sense of traveling at high speed, just inches away from the asphalt and only seconds away from serious injury or death, and the certainty and comfort of what those motored bikes meant. Independence. Willing companions. Some sharp and tight actions. I almost sigh at the pleasurable memory. I have not ridden a motorcycle for years, and I doubt that I ever will again.

I'm busy with other things.

SOMEWHERE IN MASSACHUSETTS the morning and midmorning coffee I have drunk has managed to percolate through my kidneys and is demanding to be released, and after some long minutes I see a sign that marks a rest area. As I pull into the short exit lane I see a smaller sign that in one line sums up the idiocy of highway engineering: No Sanitary Facilities. A rest area without a rest room. Why not.

There's a tractor-trailer parked at the far end of the lot, and the driver is out, slouched by the tires, examining something. Nearly a dozen cars have stopped and it seems odd to me that so many drivers have pulled over in this empty rest area. All this traffic, all these weary drivers, at this hour of this holiday morning?

I walk past the empty picnic tables, my leather boots crunching on the two or three inches of snow, when a man comes out from behind a tree. He's smoking a cigarette and he's shivering, and his knee-length leather coat is open, showing jeans and a white T-shirt. His blond hair is cut quite short, and he's to the point: "Looking for a date?"

The number of parked and empty cars now makes sense and I feel slightly foolish. I nod at the man and say, "Nope. Just looking for an empty tree," and keep on going. Some way to spend a holiday.

I find my empty tree and as I relieve myself against the pine trunk, I hear footsteps approach. I zip up and turn around and two younger men are there. One has a moustache and the other a beard, and both are wearing baseball caps with the bills pointed to the rear. Jeans, short black leather jackets, and sneakers mark their dress code. I smile and say, "No thanks, guys. I'm all set," as I walk away from the tree.

The one with the scraggly moustache laughs. "You don't understand, faggot. We're not all set."

Now they both have knives out, and the one with the beard says, "Turn over your wallet, 'fore we cut you where it counts."

I hold up my empty hands and say, "Jeez, no trouble, guys." I reach back and in a breath or two, my Beretta is in my hand, pointing at the two men. Their pasty-white faces deflate, like day-old balloons losing air, and I give them my best smile. They back up a few steps but I shake my head, and they stop, mouths still open in shock.

"Gee," I say. "Now I've changed my mind. I guess I'm not all set. Both knives, toss them behind you."

The knives are thrown behind them, making clattering noises as they strike tree branches and trunks before hitting the ground. The two young men turn again, arms held up, and the bearded one's hands are shaking.

"Very good," I say. I move the Beretta back and forth, scanning, so that one of the two is always covered. "Next I want those pants off and your wallets on the ground, and your jackets. No arguing."

The one with the moustache says, "You can't—"

I cock the hammer back on the Beretta. The noise sounds like a tree branch cracking from too much snow and ice.

"You don't listen well," I say. "No arguing."

The two slump to the ground and in a matter of moments the clothing is in a pile, and then they stand up again. Their arms go back up. One of the two—the one with the moustache—was not wearing any underwear and he is shriveled with cold and fear. Their legs are pasty white and quivering and I feel no pity whatsoever. I say, "Turn around, kneel down, and cross your ankles. Now."

They do as they're told, and I can see their bodies flinch as their bare skin strikes the snow and ice. I swoop down and pick up the clothing and say, "Move in the next fifteen minutes and you'll disappear, just like that."

I toss the clothing on the hood of my car and pull out a set of car keys and two wallets. From the wallets I take out a bundle of bills in various denominations, and I don't bother counting it. I just shove it into my pants pocket, throw everything into the car, and drive off.

After a mile I toss out the pants and jackets, and another mile after that, I toss out the car keys and wallets.

Too lenient, perhaps, but it is a holiday.

NINETY MINUTES LATER I pull over on a turn-off spot on Route 3, overlooking Boston Falls, the town which gave me the first years of my life. By now a light snow is falling and I check my watch. Ten minutes till one. Perfect timing. Mother always has her Thanksgiving dinner at three P.M., and I'll be on time, with a couple of free hours for chitchat and time for some other things. I lean against the warm hood of the Mercedes and look at the mills and buildings of the town below me. Self-portrait of the prodigal son returning, I think, and what would make the picture perfect would be a cigarette in my hand, thin gray smoke curling above my head, as I think great thoughts.

But I haven't smoked in years, and the thoughts I think aren't great, they're just troubled.

I wipe some snow off the fender of the car. The snow is small and dry, and whispers away with no problem.

A FEW MINUTES LATER I pull up to 74 Wall Street, the place where I grew up, a street with homes lining it on either side. The house is a small Cape Cod which used to be a bright red and now suffers a covering of tan vinyl siding. In my mind's eye, this house is always red. It's surrounded by a chain-link fence that Father put up during the few years of retirement he enjoyed before dying ("All my life, all I wanted was a fence to keep those goddamn dogs in the neighborhood from pissing on my shrubs, and now I'm going to get it."). I hope he managed to enjoy it before coughing up his lungs at Manchester Memorial. Father never smoked a cigarette in his life, but the air in those mills never passed through a filter on its journey to his lungs. Parked in front of the house is the battered tan Subaru that belongs to my younger brother Owen and the blue Ford pickup truck that is owned by older brother Brad.

On Owen's Subaru there is a sticker on the rear windshield for the Society for the Protection of New Hampshire Forests, and on Brad's Ford is a sticker for the Manchester Police Benevolent Society. One's life philosophy, spelled out in paper and gummed labels. The rear windshield of my Mercedes is empty. They don't make stickers for what I do or believe in.

Getting out of the car, I barely make it through the front door of the house before I'm assaulted by sounds, smells, and a handful of small children in the living room. The smells are of turkey and fresh bread, and most of the sounds come from the children yelling, "Uncle Carl! Uncle Carl!" as they jump around me. There are three of them—all girls—and they belong to Brad and his wife Deena: Carey, age twelve; Corinne, age nine; and the youngest, Christine, age six. All have blond hair in various lengths and they grasp at me, saying the usual kid things of how much they miss me, what was I doing, would I be up here long, and of course, their favorite question:

"Uncle Carl, did you bring any presents?"

Brad is standing by the television set in the living room, a grimace pretending to be a smile marking his face. Deena looks up to him, troubled, and then manages a smile for me and that's all I need. I toss my car keys to Carey, the oldest.

"In the trunk," I say, "and there's also one for your cousin."

The kids stream outside and then my brother Owen comes in from the kitchen holding his baby son Todd, and he's followed by his wife Jan, and Mother. Owen tries to say something, but Mother barrels by and give me the required hug, kiss, and why-don't-you-call-me-more look. Mother's looking fine, wearing an apron that one of us probably gave her as a birthday gift a decade or two ago, and her eyes are bright and alive behind her glasses. Most of her hair is gray and is pulled back in a bun, and she's wearing a floral print dress.

"My, you are looking sharp as always, Carl," she says admiringly, turning to see if Owen and Brand agree, and Owen smiles and Brad pretends to be watching something on television. Jan looks at me and winks, and I do nothing in return.

Mother goes back into the kitchen and I follow her and get a glass of water. When she isn't looking I reach up to a shelf and pull down a sugar bowl that contains her "mad money." I shove in the wad that I liberated earlier this day, and I return the bowl to the shelf, just in time to help stir the gravy.

As she works about the stove with me Owen comes in, still holding his son Todd, and Jan is with him. Owen sits down, looking up at me, holding the baby and its bottle, and it gurgles with what seems to be contentment. Owen's eyes are shiny behind his round, wire-rimmed glasses, and he says, "How are things in New York?"

"Cold," I say. "Loud. Dirty. The usual stuff."

Owen laughs and Jan joins in, but there's a different sound in her laugh. Owen is wearing a shapeless gray sweater and tan chinos, while Jan has on designer jeans and a buttoned light pink sweater that's about one button too many undone. Her brown hair is styled and shaped, and I can tell from her eyes that the drink in her hand isn't the first of the day.

"Maybe so," she says, "but at least it isn't boring, like some places people are forced to live."

Mother pretends to be busy about the stove and Owen is still smiling, though his eyes have faltered, as if he has remembered some old debt unpaid. I give Jan a sharp look and she just smiles and drinks, and I say to Owen, "How's the reporting?"

He shrugs, gently moving Todd back and forth. "The usual. Small-town stuff that doesn't get much coverage. But I've been thinking about starting a novel, nights when I get home from meetings. Something about small towns and small-town corruption."

Jan clicks her teeth against her glass. "Maybe your brother can help you. With some nasty ideas."

I finish off my water and walk past her. "Oh, I doubt that very much," I say, and I go into the living room, hearing the sound of Jan's laughter as I go.

THE THREE GIRLS HAVE COME BACK and the floor is a mess of shredded paper and broken boxes, as they ooh and aah over their gifts. There's a mix of clothing and dolls, the practical and the playful, because I know to the penny how much my older brother Brad makes each year and his budget is prohibitively tight.

His wife Deena is on the floor, playing with the girls, and she gives me a happy nod as I come in and sit down on the couch. She is a large woman and has on black stretch pants and a large blue sweater. I find that the more I get to know Deena, the more I like her. She comes from a farm family and makes no bones about having dropped out of high school at age sixteen. Though she's devoted utterly and totally to my brother, she also has a sharp rural way of looking at things, and though I'm sure Brad has told her many awful stories about me, she has also begun to trust her own feelings. I think she likes me, though I know she would never admit that to Brad.

Brad is sitting in an easy chair across the way, intent on looking at one of the Thanksgiving Day parades. He's wearing sensible black shoes, gray slacks, and an orange sweater, and pinned to one side is a turkey button, probably given to him by one of his daughters. Brad has a thin moustache and his black hair is slicked back, for he started losing it at age sixteen. He looks all right, though there's a roll of fat beginning to swell about his belly.

"How's it going, Brad?" I ask, sending out the first peace feeler.

"Oh, not bad," he says, eyes not leaving the screen.

"Detective work all right? Got any interesting cases you're working on?"

"Unh hunh," and he moves a glass of what looks like milk from one hand to the other.

"Who do you think will win the afternoon game?" I try again.

He shrugs. "Whoever has the best team, I imagine."

Well. Deena looks up again, troubled, and I just give her a quiet nod, saying with my look that everything's all right, and then I get up from the couch and go outside and get my winter coats and overnight bag and bring them back inside. I drop them off upstairs in the tiny room that used to be my bedroom so many years and memories ago, and then I look into a mirror over a battered bureau and say, "Time to get to work," and that makes me laugh. For the first time in a long time I'm working gratis.

I go downstairs to the basement, switching on the overhead fluores-cents, which *click-click-hum* into life. Father's old workbench is in one corner, and dumped near the workbench is a pile of firewood for the living room fireplace. The rest of the basement is taken up with boxes, old bicycles, and a washer and dryer. The basement floor is concrete and relatively clean. I go upstairs fast, taking two steps at a time. Brad is in the living room, with his three girls, trying to show some enthusiasm for the gifts I brought. I call out to him and he looks up.

"Yeah?" he says.

"C'mere," I say, excitement tingeing my voice. "You won't believe what I found."

He pauses for a moment, as if debating with himself whether he should ever trust his younger brother, and I think his cop curiosity wins out, for he says, " 'Scuse me," to his daughters and ambles over.

"What's going on?" he says in that flat voice I think cops learn at their service academy.

"Downstairs," I say. "I was poking around and behind Father's work-bench there's an old shoebox. Brad, it looks like your baseball card collection, the one Mother thought she tossed away."

For the first time I get a reaction out of Brad and a grin pops into life. "Are you sure?"

"Sure looks like it to me. C'mon down and take a look."

Brad brushes by me and thunders downstairs on the plain wooden steps, and I follow close behind, saying, "You've got to stretch across the table and really take a close look, Brad, but I think it's them."

He says, "My God, it's been almost twenty years since I've seen them. Think of how much money they could be worth . . . ."

In front of the workbench Brad leans over, casting his head back and forth, his orange sweater rising up, treating me to a glimpse of his bare back and the top of his hairy buttocks, and he says, "Carl, I don't see—"

And with that I pick up a piece of firewood and pound it into the back of his skull.

BRAD MAKES A COUGHING SOUND and falls on top of the workbench, and I kick away his legs and he swears at me and in a minute or two of tangled struggle, he ends up on his back. I straddle his chest, my knees digging into his upper arms, a forearm pressed tight against his throat, and he gurgles as I slap his face with my free hand.

"Do I have your attention, older brother?"

He curses some more and struggles, and I press in again with my forearm and replay the slapping. I'm thankful that no one from upstairs has heard us. I say, "Older brother, I'm younger, faster, and stronger, and we need to talk; if you'll stop thrashing around, we'll get somewhere."

Another series of curses, but then he starts gurgling louder and nods, and I ease up on the forearm and say, "Just how stupid do you have to be before you stop breathing, Brad?"

"What the hell are you doing, you maniac?" he demands, his voice a loud whisper. "I'm gonna have you arrested for assault, you no-good—"

I lean back with the forearm and he gurgles some more and I say, "Listen once, and listen well, older brother. I got a phone call last night from an old friend saying my police-detective brother is now in the pocket of one Bill Sutler. You mind telling me how the hell that happened?"

His eyes bug out and I pull back my forearm and he says, "I don't know what the hell you're talking about, you lowlife biker."

Two more slaps to the face. "First, I'm no biker and you know it. Second, I'm talking about Bill Sutler, who handles the numbers and other illegal adventures for this part of this lovely state. I'm talking about an old friend I can trust with my life telling me that you now belong to this charming gentleman. Now. Let's stop dancing and start talking, shall we?"

Brad's eyes are piggish and his face is red, his slick black hair now a tangle, and I'm preparing for another struggle or another series of denials, and then it's like a dam that has been ruptured, a wall that has been breached, for I feel his body loosen underneath me, and he turns his face. "Shit," he whispers.

"Gambling?" I ask.

He just nods. "How much?" I ask again.

"Ten K," he says. "It's the vig that's killing me, Carl, week after week, and now, well, now he wants more than just money."

"Of course," I say, leaning back some. "Information. Tip-offs. Leads on some investigations involving him and his crew."

Brad looks up and starts talking and I slap him again, harder, and I lean back into him and say in my most vicious tone, "Where in hell have you been storing your brains these past months, older brother? Do you have even the vaguest idea of what you've gotten yourself into? Do you think a creature like Bill Sutler is going to let you go after a couple of months? Of course not, and if he ever gets arrested by the state or the feds, he's going to toss you up for a deal so fast you'll think the world is spinning backwards."

He tries to talk but I keep plowing on. "Then let's take it from there, after you get turned over. Upstairs is a woman who loves you so much she'd probably go after this Sutler guy with her bare hands if she could, and you have three daughters who think you're the best daddy in the Western Hemisphere. Not to mention a woman who thinks you're the good son, the successful one, and a younger brother who wishes he could be half the man you pretend you are. Think of how they'll all do, how they'll live, when they see you taken away to the state prison in orange overalls."

By now Brad is silently weeping, the tears rolling down his quivering cheeks, and I feel neither disgust nor pity. It's what I expected, what I planned for, and I say, "Then think about what prison will be like, you, a cop, side by side with some rough characters who would leap at a chance to introduce you to some hard loving. Do I have your attention now, older brother? Do I?"

He's weeping so much that he can only nod, and then I get off his chest and stand up and he rolls over, in a fetal position, whispering faint obscenities, over and over again, and I don't mind since they're not aimed at me.

"Where does this guy Sutler live?" I ask.

"Purmort," he says.

"Get up," I say. "I'm going to pay him a visit, and you're going to help."

Brad sits up, snuffling, and leans back against the wooden workbench. "You're going to see him? Now? An hour before Thanksgiving dinner? You're crazy, even for a biker."

I shrug, knowing that I will be washing my hands momentarily. They look clean, but right now they feel quite soiled. "He'll talk to me, and you're going to back me up, because I'm saving your sorry ass this afternoon."

Brad looks suspicious. "What does that mean?"

"You'll find out, soon enough."

Before Brad can say anything, the door upstairs opens up and Deena calls down, "Hey, you guys are missing the parade."

I look at Brad and he's rubbing at this throat. I reply to Deena, "So we are, so we are."

FIFTEEN MINUTES LATER I pull into Founder's Park, near the Bellamy River, in an isolated section of town. Of course it's deserted on this special day and I point out an empty park bench, near two snow-covered picnic tables. "Go sit there and contemplate your sorry life."

"What?"

"I said, get out there and contemplate your sorry life. I'm going to talk to this Sutler character alone."

"But—"

"I'm getting you out of trouble today, older brother, and all I ask from you is one thing. That you become my alibi. Anything comes up later today or next week that has to do with me, you're going to swear as a gentleman and a police officer that the two of us were just driving around at this time of the day, looking at the town and having some fond recollections before turkey dinner. Understand?"

Brad looks stubborn for a moment and says, "It's cold out there."

I reach behind me and pull out the thermos bottle that Raphael had packed for me, so many hours and places ago. "Here. I freshened it up at the house a while ago, before we left. Go out there and sit and I'll be back."

That same stubborn look. "Why are you doing this for me?"

I lean over him and open the door. "Not for you. For the family. Get out, will you? I don't want to be late."

At last he steps out and walks over to the park bench, the thermos bottle in his humiliated hands, and he sits down and stares out at the frozen river. He doesn't look my way as I pull out and head to Purmort.

I'VE PARKED THE MERCEDES on a dirt road that leads into an abandoned gravel pit, and I have a long wool winter coat on over my cardigan sweater. The air is still and some of the old trees still have coverings of snow looking like plastic casts along the branches. There's a faint maze of animal tracks in the snow, and I recognize the prints of a rabbit and a squirrel. I'm leaning against the front hood of the Mercedes as a black Ford Bronco ambles up the dirt path. It parks in front of my car and I feel a quick tinge of unease: I don't like having my escape routes blocked, and then the unease grows as two men get out of the Bronco. I had only been expecting one.

The man on the right moves a bit faster than his companion and I figure that he's Bill Sutler. My guess is correct, and it is he who begins to chatter at me.

"Let me start off by saying I don't like you already for two reasons," he says in a gravelly tone that's either come from throat surgery or too many cigarettes at an early age. He's just a few inches shorter than me, and though his black hair is balding, he has a long strip at the back tied in a ponytail. Fairly fancy for this part of the state. His face is slightly pockmarked with old acne scars, and he has on a bright blue ski jacket with the obligatory tattered ski passes hanging from the zipper. Jeans and dull orange construction boots finish off his ensemble.

"Why's that?" I say, arms and legs crossed, still leaning against the warm hood of my Mercedes, my boots in the snow cover.

"Because you pulled me out of my house on Thanksgiving, and because of your license plates," he says, pointing to the front of my Mercedes, talking fast, his entire face seemingly squinting at me. "You're from New York, and I hate guys from New York who think they can breeze in here and throw their weight around. You're in my woods now, guy, and I don't care what games you've played back on your crappy island. We do things different up here."

His companion has stepped away from the passenger's side of the Bronco and is keeping watch on me. He seems a bit younger but he's considerably more bulky, with a tangle of curly hair and a thick beard. He's wearing an army fatigue coat and the same jeans/boot combination that Sutler is sporting. I note that the right pocket of his coat is sagging some, from the weight of something inside.

I nod over to the second man. "That your muscle, along to keep things quiet?"

Sutler turns his head for a moment. "That there's Kelly, and he's here because I want him here. I tell him to leave, he'll leave. I tell him to break every finger on your hands, he'd do that, too. So let's leave him out of things right now. Talk. You got me here, what do you want?"

I rub at my chin. "I want something that you have. I want Brad Curtis's *cojones*, and I understand you have them in your pocket."

Sutler smirks. "That I do. What's your offer?"

This just might be easy. "In twenty-four hours, I settle his gambling debt," I say. "I also put in a word to a couple of connected guys, and some extra business gets tossed your way. You get your money, and get some business, and I get what I want. You also never have any contact or dealings with him again, any time in the future."

"You're a relation, right?"

I nod. "His brother."

"Younger or older?"

"Younger."

Sutler smirks again, and I decide I don't like the look. "Isn't that sweet. Well, look at this, younger brother. The answer is no."

I cock my head. "Is that a real no, or do you want a counteroffer? If it's a counter offer, mention something. I'm sure I can be reasonable."

He laughs and rocks back on his heels a bit and says, "Little one, this isn't a negotiation. The answer is no."

"Why?"

That stops him for a moment, and there's a furtive gesture from his left hand, and Kelly steps a bit closer. "Because I already told you," he says. "I don't like you New York guys, and I don't trust you. Sure, you'd probably pay off the money, but everything else you say is probably crap. You think I'm stupid? Well, I think you're stupid, and here's why. I got something good in the nitwit detective, and you and your New York friends aren't going to take it away. I got him and my work here on my own, and I don't need your help. Understand?"

"Are you sure?"

Another laugh. "You think I'm giving up a detective on the largest police force in this state for you? The stuff he can feed me is pure gold, little one, and it's gonna set me for life. There's nothing you have that can match that. Nothing."

He gestures again. "And I'm tired of you, and I'm tired of this crap. I'm going back home."

"Me too," I say, and I slide my hand into the cardigan, pull out my Beretta, and blow away Kelly's left knee.

KELLY IS ON THE GROUND, howling, and the echo of the shot is still bouncing about the hills as I slam the Beretta into the side of the Sutler's head. He falls, and I stride over to Kelly. Amid his thrashings on the now-bloody snow, I grab a .357 revolver from his coat and toss it into the woods. In a matter of heartbeats I'm back to Sutler, who's on the ground, fumbling to get into his ski jacket. I kick him solidly in the crotch. He yelps and then I'm on him, the barrel of the Beretta jamming into his lips until he gags and has a couple of inches of the oily metal in his mouth. His eyes are very wide and there's a splotch of blood on his left cheek. I take a series of deep breaths, knowing that I want my voice cool and calm.

"About sixty seconds ago I was interested in negotiating with you, but now I've lost interest. Do you understand? If you do, nod your head, but nod it real slow. It's cold and my fingers are beginning to get numb."

His eyes are tearing and he nods, just like I said. "Very good," I say, trying to place a soothing tone in my voice. "I came here in a good mood, in a mood to make a deal that could help us both, and all you've done since we've met is insult me. Do you think I got up early this morning and drove half the day so a creature like you can toss insults my way? Do you?"

Though I didn't explain to him the procedure for shaking his head, Sutler shows some initiative and gently shakes it. Kelly, some yards away, is still groaning and occasionally crying. I ignore him because I want to, and I think Sutler is ignoring him because he has to.

"Now," I continue. "If you had some random brain cells in that sponge between your ears, I think you would have figured out that because this matter involves my brother, I might have a personal interest in what was going on. But you were too stupid to realize that, correct?"

Another nod of the head, and saliva and blood is beginning to drip down the barrel of the Beretta. "So instead of accepting a very generous offer, you said no and insulted me. So you left me no choice. I had to show you how serious I was, and I had to make an impression."

I gesture over to the sobbing hulk of his companion. "Take a look at Kelly if you can. I don't know the man, I have nothing against him, and if the two of us had met under different circumstances, we might have become friends."

Well, I doubt that, but I keep my doubts to myself. I am making a point. "But I had to make an example," I continue, "and in doing so, I've just crippled Kelly for life. Do you understand that? His knee is shattered and he'll never walk well again for the next thirty or forty years of his life because of your ill manners and stubbornness. Now. You having rejected my offer, here's my counteroffer. Are you now interested?"

Another nod, a bit more forceful. "Good. Here it is. You forget the gambling debt. You forget you ever knew my brother, and you take poor Kelly here to a hospital and tell them that he was shot in a hunting accident or something. I don't care. And if you ever bother my brother or his family, any time in the future, I'll come back."

I poke the Beretta in another centimeter or two, and Sutler groans. "Then I'll find out who counts most in your life—your mother, your wife, your child, for all I know—and I'll do the same thing to them that I did to Kelly. Oh, I could make it permanent, but a year or two after the funeral, you usually get on with life. Not with this treatment. The person suffers in your presence, for decades to come, because of you. Now. Is the deal complete?"

Sutler closes his teary eyes and nods, and I get up, wiping the Beretta's barrel on his ski jacket. Sutler is grimacing and the crotch of his pants is wet and steaming in the cold. Kelly is curled up on his side, weeping, his left leg a bloody mess, and I take a step back and gently prod Sutler with my foot.

"Move your Bronco, will you?" I ask politely.

*   *   *

MY BROTHER'S FACE IS A MIX of anger and hope as he climbs back into my Mercedes, rubbing his hands from the cold. His face and ears are quite red.

"Well?" he asks.

"Piece of cake," I say, and I drive back to the house.

DINNER IS LONG AND WONDERFUL, and I have a sharp appetite and eat well, sitting at the far end of the table. My nieces good-naturedly fight over the supposed honor of sitting next to me, which makes Mother and Deena laugh, and even Brad attempts a smile or two. I stuff myself and we regale each other with stories of holidays and Christmases and Thanksgivings past, and Owen bounces Todd on his knee as Jan smiles to herself and sips from one glass of wine and then another.

I feel good belonging here with them. Though I know that none of them quite knows who I am or what I do, it's still a comfortable feeling. It's like nothing else I experience, ever, and I cherish it.

LATER, I TAKE A NAP in my old bedroom, and feeling greasy from the day's exertions and the long meal, I take a quick shower, remembering a lot of days and weeks and years gone past as I climb into the tiny stall. It seems fairly humorous that I am in this house taking a weak and lukewarm shower after having remembered this creaky bathroom earlier this morning, back at my Manhattan home. That explains why I am smiling when I go back into my old bedroom, threadbare light green towel wrapped around my waist, and I find Jan there, waiting for me, my brother Owen's wife.

Her eyes are aglitter and her words are low and soft, but there's a hesitation there, as if she realizes she has been drinking for most of the day and she has to be careful in shoosing each noun and verb. She's standing by an old bureau, jean-encased hip leaning up against the wood, and she has something in her hands.

"Look at this, will you," she says. "Found it up here while I was waiting for you."

I step closer and I can smell the alcohol on her breath, and I also smell something a bit earthier. I try not to sigh, seeing the eager expression on her face. I take her offering and turn it over. It's an old color photograph, and it shows a heavyset man with a beard and long hair in a ponytail sitting astride a black Harley-Davidson motorcycle. He's wearing the obligatory jeans and leather vest. His arms are tattooed. The photo is easily a decade old, and in those years the chemicals on the print have faded and mutated, so that there's an eerie yellow glow about everything, as if the photo were taken at a time when volcanic ash was drifting through the air.

I look closely at the photo and then hand it back to my sister-in-law. About the only thing I recognize about the person is the eyes, for it's the only thing about me that I've not changed since that picture was taken.

"That's really you, isn't it?" she asks, that eager tone in her voice still there. With her in my old room, everything seems crowded. There's a tiny closet, the bureau, a night table, and lumpy bed with thin blankets and sheets. A window about the size of a pie plate looks out to the pale green vinyl siding of the house next door.

"Yes, that's me," I say. "Back when I was younger and dumber."

She licks her lips. "Asking questions about you of Owen is a waste of time, and your mother and Brad aren't much help either. You were a biker, right?"

I nod. "That's right."

"What was it like, Carl?" she asks, moving a few inches closer to me. I know I should feel embarrassed, standing in my old bedroom with my sister-in-law, just wearing a towel, but I'm not sure what I feel. I just know it's not embarrassment. So instead of debating the point, I answer her question.

"It was like moving to a different country and staying at home, all at the same time," I say. "There was an expression, something about being free and being a citizen. Being free meant the bike and your friends and whatever money you had for gas and food, and the time to travel any-where you wanted, any time, with no one to stop you, feeling the wind in your hair and face. Being a citizen meant death, staying at home, paying taxes, and working a forty-hour week. That's what it was like."

She gives me a sharp-toothed smile. "You almost make it sound like a Boy Scout troop. Way your older brother talks, I figure you've been in trouble."

I shrug. "Comes with the territory. It's something you get used to. Being free means you run into a lot of different people, and sometimes their tempers are short and their memories are long. Sometimes you do some work for some money that wouldn't look good on a job applica-tion form."

"So that explains the scars?" she asks.

"Yeah, I guess it does."

"So why did you change? What happpened? From the picture, I can tell you've had your tattoos taken off."

I look around and see that my clothes are still on the bed where I left them. "I got tired of having my life depend on other people. Thing is, you run with a group, the group can sometimes pull you down. What the group accomplishes can come back at night and break your windows, or gnaw on your leg. And I didn't want to become a citizen. So I chose a bit of each world and made my own, and along the way I changed my look."

"And what do you do now? Everyone says consulting work, but they always have an uncomfortable look on their face when they mention that, like they have gas or something. So what's your job?"

I pause and say, "Systems engineer."

Her eyes blink in amusement. "A what?"

"Systems engineer. Sometimes a system needs an outside pressure or force to make a necessary change or adjustment. That's what I do. I'm an independent contractor."

"Sounds very exciting," she says, arching an eyebrow this time. "You should talk some to your younger brother. Maybe pass some of the excitement along. Or maybe you're the brother who got it all in this family."

I now feel an aching sorrow for Owen, and I try not to think of what their pillow talk must be like at night. "Guess you have to work with what you've got."

"Unh-hunh," she says. "Look, you must be getting cold. Are you going to get dressed, or what?"

I decide she wants a show, or wants something specific to happen, so I say, "Or what, I suppose." I turn to the bed and drop the towel and get dressed, and I hear a hush of breath coming from her. After the underwear, pants, and boots, I turn, buttoning my shirt, and she's even closer and I reach to her and she comes forward, lips wet, and then I strike out and put a hand around her throat. And I squeeze.

"Jan," I say, stepping forward and looking into her eyes, "you and I are about to come to an agreement, do you understand?"

"What are you doing, you—" and I squeeze again, and she makes a tiny yelping sound, and her nostrils begin to flare as she tries to breathe harder. She starts to flail with her hands and I grab one hand and press her against the bureau. It shakes and she tries to kick, but I'm pushing at her at an uncomfortable angle, and she can't move.

"This won't take long, but I ask that you don't yell. You try to yell and I'll squeeze hard enough to make you black out. Do you understand? Try blinking your eyes."

She blinks, tears forming in her eyes. My mind plays with a few words and then I say, "Owen and my family mean everything to me. Everything. And right now, by accident of marriage and the fact of my brother's love, you're part of this family. But not totally. My mother and Owen and even Brad come before you. You're not equal in my eyes, do you understand?"

She moves her head a bit, and I'm conscious that I might have to take another shower when I'm finished. "So that's where I'm coming from when I tell you this: I don't care if you love my brother or hate my brother, but I do demand this. That you show him respect. He deserves that. Stay with him or leave him tonight, I don't care. But don't toss yourself to those random men that manage to cross your path, especially ones related to him. If you can't stand being with him, leave, but do it with dignity. Show him respect or I'll hurt you, Jan."

"You're hurting me now," she whispers.

"No, I'm not," I explain. "I'm not hurting you. I'm getting your attention. In an hour you'll be just fine, but in a hundred years you're always going to remember this conversation in this dingy bedroom. Am I right?"

She nods and I say, "So we've reached an understanding. Agreed?"

Another nod and I let her go and back away, and Jan rubs at her throat and coughs. Then she whispers a dark series of curses and leaves, slamming the door behind her, and what scares me is that she isn't crying, not one tear, not one sign of regret or fear.

I finish getting dressed, trying not to think of Owen.

DESPITE A LUMPY BED and too-silent surroundings of Boston Falls, I sleep fairly well that night, with none of those disturbing dreams of loud words and sharp actions that sometimes bring me awake. I get up with the sun and slowly walk through the living room to the kitchen. Sprawled across the carpeted floor in sleeping bags are my three nieces—Carey, Corinne, and Christine—and their shy innocence and the peacefulness of their slight breathing touches something inside of me that I wasn't sure even existed anymore.

Mother is in the kitchen and I give her a brief hug and grab a cup of coffee. I try not to grimace as I sip the brew; Mother, God bless her, has never made a decent cup of coffee in her life. I've been dressed since getting up and Mother is wearing a faded blue bathrobe, and as she stirs a half-dozen eggs in a mixing bowl she looks over at me through her thick glasses and says, "I'm not that dumb, you know."

I gamely try another sip of coffee. "I've always know that, ever since you found my collection of girlie magazines when I was in high school."

"Bah," she says, stirring the whisk harder. "I knew you had those for a while, and I knew boys always get curious at that age. I didn't mind much until your younger brother Owen was snooping around. Then I couldn't allow it. He was too young."

She throws in a bit of grated cheese and goes back to the bowl and says, "Are you all right, Carl?"

"Just fine."

"I wonder," she says. "Yesterday you were roaming around here like a panther at the zoo, and then you and Brad go off for a mysterious trip. You said it was just a friendly trip, but the two of you haven't been friends for years. You do something bad out there?"

I think about Kelly with the shattered leg and Bill Sutler with his equally ruined day, and I say, "Yeah, I suppose so."

Her voice is sharp. "Was it for Brad?"

Even Mother probably can see the surprise on my face, so I say, "Yes, it was for Brad."

"You hurt someone?"

I nod. "But he deserved it, Mom."

Then she puts down her utensils and wipes her hands on her apron and says, "That's what you do for a living, isn't it, Carl? You hurt people."

Right then I wish the coffee tasted better, for I could take a sip and gain a few seconds for a response, but Mother is looking right through me and I say, "You're absolutely right."

She sighs. "But yesterday was for Brad. And the money you send me, and the gifts for your nieces, and everything else, all comes from your job. Hurting people."

"That's right."

Mother goes back to the eggs, starts whisking again with the wire beater, and says, "I've known that for a very long time, ever since you claimed you quit being a biker. I just knew you went on to something different, something probably even worse, though you certainly dressed better and looked clean."

She looks over again. "Thank you for the truth, Carl. And I'll never ask you again, you can believe that. Just tell me that what you do is right, and that you're happy."

So I tell her what she wants to hear, and she gives me another hug, and then there's some noise as the kids get up.

AND THEN AFTER BREAKFAST it's time to go, and though Jan hangs back and says nothing, the kids are all over me, as is Mother, and even Deena—Brad's wife—gives me a peck on the cheek. Owen shakes my hand and I tell him to call me, anytime, making sure that Jan has heard me. And then there's the surprise, as Brad shakes my hand for the first time in a very long year or five.

"Thanks," he says. "And, um, well, come by sometime. The girls do miss you."

With that one sentence playing in my mind, I drive for over an hour, not bothering with the music on my CD player, for I'm hearing louder music in my head.

LATER THAT NIGHT I'm in my large sunken tub, a small metal pitcher of vodka martinis on the marble floor. Sarah is in the tub with me, suds up to her lovely and full chest, and her hair is drawn up around her head, making her look like a Gibson Girl from the turn of the century. I talk for some minutes and she laughs a few times and then reaches out with a wet and soapy foot and caresses my side. Like myself, she's holding a glass full of ice cubes and clear liquid.

"Only a guy like you, Carl, could travel hours to your family's home on a holiday weekend and bring your work with you," she says.

I sink a bit in the tub, feeling the hot water relax my back muscles. It had snowed some on the way back, and I'm still a bit tense from the drive.

"It wasn't work," I say. "It was a favor, a family thing."

"Mmmm," she says, sipping from her glass. "So that makes it all right?"

I shrug. "It just makes it, I guess."

"A worthwhile trip, then?"

"Very," I say, drinking from my own glass, enjoying the slightly oily bite of the drink. She sighs again and says, "You never really answered me, you know."

I close my eyes and say, "I didn't know I owed you an answer."

She nudges me with her foot. "Brute. From Thursday morning. When I asked you why you went there. And all you could say was family. Is that it, Carl? Truly?"

I know the true answer, which is that the little group of people in that tiny town are the only thing I have that is not bought or paid for in blood, and that keeping that little tie alive and well is important, very important to me. For if that tie was broken, then whatever passes for a human being in me would shrivel up and rot away, and I could not allow that. That is the truth, but I don't feel like debating philosophy tonight.

So I say, "Haven't you heard the expression?"

"What's that?"

I raise my drink to her in a toast. "Even the bad can do good."

Sarah makes a face and tosses the drink's contents at me, and then water starts slopping over onto the floor, and the lovely evening gets even lovelier, and there's no more talk of family and obligations, which is just fine.

Brenda Melton Burnham lives in Arizona, is just starting to become known in mystery circles, and wrote the following, which is one of the best stories your editors read all year.

The Tennis Court
BRENDA MELTON BURNHAM

I settle into the familiar contours of the wicker chair as the first sliver of sun appears over the eastern mountains. The screen door squeals its usual complaint, and Leah steps onto the porch, her entire concentration focused on the tray in her hands.

She arrives at the table and sets her burden down without spilling it, always a triumph to be savored, then pours my coffee and hands me the mug before dropping into the chair beside me. She reminds me of myself at twelve, all legs and eagerness; physically racing to catch up with her mind while emotionally still clinging to childhood.

"Gonna be another hot day," Leah says, using her grownup voice as she picks up her glass of milk.

"A scorcher," I agree.

We sip our refreshments in our best tea party manner. I can usually last longer than my granddaughter at this game of Let's Pretend; I've had years of adulthood in which to practice.

Sixty yards in front of us, across the slope of grass turning brown in the August heat, the men of the family bend their energies—and their backs—to the cause of tearing out the old tennis court. The noise of the heavy jackhammers echoes against the foothills.

"I was your age when my grandfather built this court," I say, even though I know I've said it many times before.

NINETEEN FORTY-TWO SAW COUNTRIES AT WAR and families in turmoil. Our family was no different. My father and Uncle Theo joined the army in the spring. When they left for training, my mother and my aunt packed up their children and returned here, to their father's farm.

I fell asleep to the sound of my mother and her three sisters as they laughed and talked among themselves. I woke in the morning to the same sounds—as though they had continued, unceasing, throughout the night. Bras and panties hung from the clothesline in the mud room. Lipsticks and powder lay atop the dresser scarves, next to the old inlaid brushes and tortoiseshell combs. Chinese checkers and dominoes decorated the side table in the living room, always ready and waiting for a quick game.

In the early mornings, before the sun reached the valley, my grandfather went fishing on the river at the back of the farm. Often one or more of his daughters accompanied him as they had done when they were young.

In the evenings, after dinner, we sat on the porch to catch the air and listen to Gabriel Heater on the radio. I helped turn the crank on the ice cream maker. We watched my seven-year-old sister and Aunt Marge's five-year-old twins chase fireflies.

Always, *always* my grandfather had dominated this house, these lives. Even when he wasn't present, his shadow was. But 1942, in the Krueger household, was to be the year of the women.

"C'mon, Sonia," they would call to me. "If you want to go with us you'd better hurry."

And of course I wanted to go with them. Every morning I examined my fat child's chest for signs of a bosom. I tried to brush my hair in a pageboy the way Aunt Trudy, the youngest of the sisters, did. Aunt Inga taught me to play cribbage and the strategy for winning at dominoes. Aunt Marge showed me how to use her nail polish. My mother let me stay up after the younger kids had been put to bed.

"I'm coming," I would call with one last glance in the mirror.

"Have you got the rackets, Inga?"

"Don't forget the balls this time, Liz."

Every afternoon we headed for the park in town where I watched my sister and the twins while the four women played tennis. I had never realized how beautiful they were with their blond hair and white teeth and strong, healthy bodies.

Soldiers and civilian personnel from the nearby military base realized it as well. There was always a contingent of them waiting to challenge the Krueger women. My mother, Marge, and Inga had no favorites and soundly defeated most comers, but Trudy was soft on a thin, dark, intense young man named Ira Glass.

It was a day like all other days as we headed home. Early June, perhaps, when the sun still promised a summer that would last forever. The car seats burned the backs of my legs, and my throat tasted of dust. The other women were teasing Trudy.

"You should've had the last point. Trudy. Don't give away the game just because you give away your heart."

"Tennis matches start with love. They don't always end that way."

"Oh, Ira, my wonderful one."

Trudy protested loudly and they all laughed.

When we got home, Grandfather waited on the porch. "Where have you been?" he shouted in German.

"Speak English, Poppa," Marge said.

"Playing tennis," Inga said. "At the park."

"Tramps! Strumpets! Parading yourselves in front of those men!"

I huddled back with the little kids, trying to be ignored.

"WAS IT HOT THAT SUMMER, Gram?" Leah asks.

"Hotter even than now," I reply.

The heavy pounding of the jackhammers ceases just as the sun pops over the ridge. My daughter comes out of the house with a pitcher of lemonade to refresh the laboring men before they begin the effort of removing the moss-stained chunks of concrete.

TRUDY HAD WORKED as a druggist's assistant in town and Inga as a secretary. Within a week of each other they were fired from their jobs. I was shooed from the room both times and was forced to listen at the door.

"... a sympathizer," Trudy sobbed.

"Silly man," my mother said.

"If only Poppa wouldn't insist on aggravating them."

"They're afraid," Marge scoffed. "That's all. It's the war."

"Besides," Inga said, "it gives us more time to be together."

And always the young men waited at the courts. More and more now Trudy and Ira were a pair. He gave her a pin, a gold tennis racket with a tiny ball of glittering stones. She gave him a silver ring she'd worn as a child; he wore it on a chain around his neck.

Some nights Trudy slipped out the side door after everyone had gone to bed, and I knew she went to meet Ira. I discovered this by accident one night when I got up to go to the bathroom. When I came out, my mother was waiting in the hall.

"What's wrong?" I whispered.

"Nothing. Go back to bed."

"But I saw Trudy ..."

My mother focused a hard look on me. "Yes? What did you see?"

"Nothing."

My mother put her arm around my shoulder and kissed the top of my head. "It isn't easy growing up, *liebchen*," she murmured into my hair.

"WERE YOU HAPPY THAT SUMMER?" my granddaughter asks.

"Oh yes," I reply. "Yes, I was happy."

*   *   *

THROUGHOUT THE WHOLE TIME my grandmother cooked. A short, round woman, she left the sanctuary of her kitchen only to feed her precious birds, calling to them in her native tongue. "Come, my pretty ones, come see what I have for you. Come, come."

July days melted one into the other. The temperature continued to soar. My grandfather seemed to shrivel with the heat while the women plumped out and grew taller and stronger. On the court their faces shone with perspiration. The tennis dresses whipped around their thighs. They were Valkyries . . . Amazons. I thought they were indomitable.

One day, as we walked to the car, a woman ran up and spat in Inga's face. "Nazi bitch!" she screamed, her face twisting with the ugly words.

Inga calmly wiped her cheek with the towel she had been carrying while my mother and Marge marched along beside her, their expressions closed and inscrutable. Trudy and I and the little kids stumbled alongside, silent with shock.

Another time, as we were driving past, a gang of boys threw rocks at us.

"You mustn't let it upset you, Sonia," Marge said to me. "They don't know who to take their anger out on."

"But we're Americans. Aren't we?"

"Of course we are."

"Even though some people forget it," Inga added.

"WERE YOU SURPRISED when your grandpa decided to build the tennis court?" Leah asks.

"You might say that," I acknowledge.

Out on the lawn the men finish their lemonade and bend to their labors once again. They tie handkerchiefs about their heads to keep the sweat out of their eyes. Their bodies glisten with moisture.

WHEN WE CAME DOWN to breakfast that morning in early August, Grandfather was outside, astride his tractor. Behind him the huge discs chopped up the once-green lawn.

"What's he doing?"

"What in the world . . ."

"He's tearing up the whole yard."

"You want to play tennis, *ja?*" he called out to them. "Fine. I build you a tennis court."

The women looked at each other and said things with their eyes.

The next day the Gruener brothers arrived and agreed to pour a concrete slab when Grandfather had the ground ready.

"Does this mean we won't be going to town anymore?" I asked. The women glared at me.

"No need," Grandfather said.

Our outings took on a desperate air those last days.

"We can always invite people over to play," Inga suggested.

"Can't you see it?" Marge said. "Poppa standing at the gate, checking everyone as they come through?" She laughed.

"He'll never let Ira come," Trudy said. She nibbled at the corners of her stubby red fingertips.

Her sisters didn't answer.

"Oh god, what'll I do?" she cried out.

"EVERYONE MUST'VE BEEN PRETTY EXCITED," Leah remarks.

"It was a pretty exciting time."

Already the heat is building. In front of us, their muscles bulge as the younger men load the concrete pieces on the flatbed truck.

EVERY DAY GRANDFATHER WORKED, harrowing, leveling, then building the forms for the concrete slabs. Every day the women's voices grew shriller.

"You really needn't tear up the yard like this for us," my mother, being the eldest, said at dinner. "Why don't you put in a flowerbed for Momma?"

"Momma has enough flowerbeds."

"We don't mind going into town."

"Even when someone spits on you?"

The women darted glances at one another. "We do have friends there," Marge said.

"Invite them here."

"Poppa," my mother said, "we *like* going to the park."

"I will not have my family spit on." Grandfather's fist crashed onto the table. Dishes rattle. One of the twins began to cry. Grandmother decided to make coffee cake so it would be ready for breakfast the next morning. "I will not have my daughters behaving like sluts. Do you hear me? You will play here or you will play nowhere."

Trudy jumped up and ran from the room.

In town the next day Trudy and Ira took the car while the others played tennis. Afterwards, as we were driving home, she said, 'It's decided. We'll go tonight and be married over in Slocum County." Her eyes glittered, and she bit her lip nervously.

"Trudy, are you sure?"

"Of course I'm sure. I love him. He loves me."

"Then bring him home. Poppa will give in when he knows you're serious."

"No. He won't. And you know it. He still has one foot on German soil."

"But you can't sneak off . . ."

"If you don't want to help me, you don't have to. I'll do it by myself."

"We'll help you," Inga said.

"I'LL BET YOU COULDN'T WAIT until the court was finished, right?" Leah prompts.

"It seemed to happen very fast." I close my eyes and let the heat seep into my bones.

"HOW DO I LOOK?" Trudy twirled, fluffing her hair, showing off her soft white dress. The little gold racket pin gleamed at her breast.

"You look beautiful," I said. The others nodded.

They all hugged each other, then my mother and Trudy slipped out the bedroom door and down the dark stairs. I rushed to the window and watched my youngest aunt disappear across the lawn.

And saw the other figure step out of the barn behind her.

"Someone else is out there," I whispered.

The others rushed over. "You're seeing things, *liebchen*," Inga said.

"No, no, I'm not!"

The door opened and my mother came in, her face pale. "Poppa was waiting by the barn. He's following her. He must've known about them all along."

"How could he know?"

"How did he know about the spitting? It's a small town. I tell you he knows."

"What'll we do?"

"What can we do?"

"Why didn't you go after her?"

"It was too late." My mother shrugged her shoulders and shook her head. "It was too late the minute Trudy stepped out the door."

We sat in the silent bedroom and waited, our ears straining to hear a strange noise among the night sounds, afraid to speak for fear of missing it.

There was no missing it when it came. Trudy raced back across the wet grass, slamming the screen door behind her, pounding up the stairs and into the room. Her hair hung in tangles. A huge red mark ran across her cheek. Dark stains covered her dress. The bodice was ripped and the tiny pin gone.

"Oh, Liz," she cried, "I'll never see him again," and fell into my mother's arms.

"Trudy, did you and Ira—" Inga paused. "You aren't pre—"

Marge turned to me, bumping Inga with her elbow. "Go to bed, Sonia."

"But I want . . ."

"Go to bed," my mother said.

* * *

"I STILL DON'T UNDERSTAND why you never played tennis, Gram," my granddaughter says.

One of the men—is it Max? or Charley? I can't tell—stops digging and kneels to work at the dirt with his hands.

I NEVER HEARD GRANDFATHER COME BACK. I woke late the next morning. No air moved through the silent house. Dressing was an effort. My clothes felt heavy on my body as I walked down the stairs. Mother and Marge and Inga were down by the dock. My sister and the twins dug ditches in the mud, something they weren't normally allowed to do. The women talked of the heat and answered the little kids' questions about bugs and dirt and trees. From the front yard we could hear the sounds of the Gruener brothers pouring the concrete slab for the tennis court.

"I'VE ALWAYS HATED THIS COURT," I whisper. To Leah? To myself? To the past? "Always."

The kneeling man—it is Max; I can see the bright cloth tied about his head—calls to the other men. They gather around him. I hear their exclamations but can't make out the words.

MY MOTHER DISCOVERED TRUDY'S BODY when she went upstairs to check on her. The coroner's report said "suicide while of an unsound mind." It was assumed she had gotten the sleeping pills when she was working at the drugstore.

Two MP's from the army base came to the house a week later. Ira Glass had gone AWOL, and they were trying to locate him.

"BUT I DON'T UNDERSTAND," Leah persists, her eyes full of the innocence of youth. "If you hated it so much, why did you wait until now to tear it out?"

All the men scrape at the earth with their hands.

"Pour me another cup of coffee, will you, dear?" I say.

THE MORNING THE HEAT WAVE BROKE, my mother and Inga went fishing with my grandfather. When the boat returned to the dock two hours later, only the women were aboard. They came ashore silently, their backs erect, their wet clothes dripping on the soft green grass.

"Poppa had a strike and had started to reel it in," they said, "when he dropped his pole and clutched at his chest."

"He must've had a heart attack," they said.

"He was overboard before we could catch him," they said.

"It was downstream where the current was strongest. That was where he always liked to fish, you remember," they said.

"We went in to help him, but he never came up," they said.

The police decided against dragging the river. His body surfaced four days later several miles away. He was buried in the family plot next to Trudy.

THEY'RE ALL GONE NOW . . . Trudy . . . Mother . . . Marge. Inga, who never married, died a week ago. After the funeral I asked my son Karl and my son-in-law Max, Leah's father, both stalwart, upright men, to tear out the tennis court.

Now the men walk up to the porch in a group. They let Karl lead.

"We found—" he begins, then stops to take a deep breath. "There were bones under the concrete, Mother." He holds out something. "And this." A set of dog tags. And a tiny silver ring.

I take the small objects in my hands. They are still cool from the dark, damp soil. I am aware of so many things. The heat from the sun, the river singing in the distance. The contours of the old wicker chair. Of debts owed and the debts paid.

My granddaughter, unusual for her, sits silent beside me.

"Mother," Karl says softly, fearful of startling me. "We'd better call the police, don't you think?" He looks at me. Waits. A good son.

"Yes," I answer. "You're right. We must."

Justin Scott has written several bestselling thrillers, including SHIPKILLER. Most recently, he has done two novels in the acclaimed Benjamin Abbot mystery series. His appearance here marks one of his rare appearances as a short story writer, though he's clearly got the knack. Hopefully we'll see more short stories of his in the future.

An Eye For a Tooth
JUSTIN SCOTT

Hagopian waited for the shooting to stop before he ventured out of his Amsterdam Avenue Luggage Repair Shop. On the sidewalk lay one body only: Ramos, selling crack, cheating his supplier. Hagopian—who was thirty-eight, looked a wizened sixty with three days' beard on his sunken cheeks, and felt seventy—was astonished at how long it had taken someone to shoot the fool.

A small boy knelt over the body, weeping. He scrambled into the crowd as the first of many police cars came screaming like artillery shells. Enormous blue-coated officers demanded to know who'd seen it happen.

Hagopian hesitated, torn between his instinct to hide and a powerful fear that if the police came into his shop to interrogate him they might discover his illegal apartment. If only he had a green card. The eight thousand he had already paid the immigration lawyer—who also happened to be his landlord—brought no peace of mind when a huge policeman asked, "Wha'd you see, Pop?"

Hagopian froze. His English, not yet reliable, failed him under pressure. He couldn't remember "Pop." His first language was Armenian; his second, the Russian they'd beaten into him in the Soviet Army; his third and fourth, the Afghan people's Peshto and Dari. The lawyer-landlord had laughed, "You sound like a Polack."

"You see anything? . . . Hey, Pops? Wake up! This your store?"

"Inside, I am fixing," Hagopian managed at last.

"You saw out the window."

Hagopian shook his head. The window of the basement shop was barred, the glass filthy, with luggage heaped behind it.

336

"What happened when you heard the shots?"

Hagopian gestured at the body. "Is kill-ed."

"Hey, detective?" the cop called. "Got a live one here."

Hagopian felt his blood congeal. Uniformed militia were one thing, detectives quite another. But he got a pleasant surprise when a pretty blonde flashed her badge and said, "Detective Dee. How are you doing, sir? A little shook up?"

"Shooking," Hagopian agreed.

"What is your name, please?"

"Hagopian," Hagopian admitted, swiftly reassessing his predicament. Detective Dee spoke gently, but she had eyes like a blizzard in the Hindu Kush.

"It would appear this gentleman was shot right outside your shop. I wonder if you can help me in my investigation. This *is* your shop?"

Hagopian nodded.

"You repair luggage," she prompted, reading the signs on the railing and the door.

"Luggage. Handbags. Zippers. I am fixing zippers many times."

"What's a 'trank'?"

"Trank? Ah!" Hagopian smiled and for a moment he looked more like the young man he might have been had he made it to Manhattan a decade earlier. "I am drawing—writing—sign when I come-ed," he explained. "Old sign." He pointed at the yellow sign on the stair railing he had hand-lettered in black print. Then he directed the detective's attention to the nearly identical sign on his battered tin door. "New sign. I am meaning 'trunk.' No 'trank.' You get?"

She smiled. But Hagopian was soon back in the ice fields. "Do you know the name of the victim?"

He was careful to first look at Ramos, who had bled into the gutter. "No."

"Never seen him before?" she persisted.

Conditioned by a lifetime of dodging officially generated misery, Hagopian hunched deep inside the quilted jacket he wore indoors and out, and commenced a drift into anonymity. His body seemed to shrink. His eyes emptied. His cheeks sunk deeper.

"Mr. Hagopian, did you see who shot that man?"

"No."

"Did you hear the shots?"

"No."

"Mr. Hagopian, five shots were heard blocks away. Are you sure you didn't hear them ten feet in front of your shop?"

The detective misinterpreted Hagopian's cringe as a shrug. "Let's see some ID, sir. Driver's license? Visa?"

Hagopian swept an apologetic arm over the front of his shop, the barred window blocked by luggage, the bent tin door, the yellow signs with block lettering. "Trank" was the only misspelling. Although every time he saw the squeezed-in "HANDbags," he was reminded that he was no longer a man who planned ahead.

She wrote his name down in her book and lectured him like a school teacher: "This isn't a bad neighborhood, yet. But it's gonna get worse until people like you help cops like me. Now come on, Mr. Hagopian. You're a neighborhood businessman, after all, and . . ."

As she scolded and cajoled, Hagopian stared at his feet. He watched from the corner of his eye the body, the ambulance attendants, the cops questioning his neighbors. For relief, he allowed his attention to settle on Consuela, the round and lovely Spanish woman who belonged to Eduardo, dispatcher of the Bolívar Car Service. Consuela tossed him a kind smile. Sadly, Eduardo carried a knife.

"Urban violence won't be stopped until good people stand up and be counted," Detective Dee was going on.

Hagopian almost smiled. Urban violence? One body? Urban violence was a Russian tank shelling the ground-floor supports of an apartment building until the people upstairs were spilled into the street. Urban violence was a gunship strafing city buses. Urban violence was . . . many things this pretty little American would never know.

She droned on. He let his mind wander to happier things—to the pleasures of his new home. He could buy cooked food from a dozen nationalities in this one block. Bookstores sold tens of thousands of books. The library lent them for free.

Around the corner, ballerinas served as waitresses in the Café Lalo. He could splurge three dollars for a cappuccino, heap it with sugar, steep himself in the warm talk around him, the music, the bakery smells, celebrate the winter light streaming in and pretend he was in Moscow, inside a Party-only café he had only seen through the window.

Too skinny, the ballerinas. Better this voluptuous policewoman. Or Consuela. Best, the beautiful daughter of the proprietor of the Amsterdam Afghanistan Restaurant. He couldn't bear to go in, but through the window he admired her long black hair and violet eyes—exactly like the girl he had married in the war.

"Oh, god," said Detective Dee, patting Hagopian on the arm. "Please don't cry."

"Excusing, please," he asked, and struggled in a trembling voice to explain. "A person remembered."

Detective Dee looked like she wished she hadn't reported to work that day. "Here's my card, Mr. Hagopian. If you remember anything about the dead gentleman shot outside your shop, please call me immediately."

Hagopian promised he would, to make her go away, and escaped at last into his shop. It was dim as a cave, ten feet wide and twelve feet deep, heaped floor to ceiling with bags repaired, bags awaiting repair, and bags forgotten—some by his customers, some by Hagopian.

Through these leather and vinyl mountains twisted a narrow ravine. Hagopian followed it past his workbench and through a curtain into his living quarters, a windowless storeroom that contained a single bed, a hotplate and a humming refrigerator he had found on the sidewalk.

He set his tea kettle on the hotplate and shuffled out to his sewing machine. The boy who had grieved for Ramos was crouched in the shadows of the shop with tears in his eyes and a gun in his hand.

ROBBERY? Hagopian looked without looking. His money was safe in the scuffed backpack that seemed to be waiting its turn at the sewing machine.

The gun—a cheap and serviceable rust-pitted 9 mm auto pistol, Hagopian noted—looked enormous in the little hand. But it pointed so steadily at his face that gun, hand, and the scrawny child himself might have been stamped from the same metal.

Wire-thin arms poked from a dirty red sweatshirt that read "Ralph Lauren POLO" and hung like an empty garment bag. His skin was gray, his nose as aquiline as a Spanish grandee's, his hair black and shiny as that of the South American Indians who delivered for the Korean liquor store. His eyes were red rimmed, wet, and determined.

Hagopian recognized him from the neighborhood and attempted a cautious smile. "Are kite boy? Yes?"

His little jaw dropped. His eyes narrowed. "Say what? How you know that?"

"Is not pointing gun . . ."

"Why you call me kite boy?"

Hagopian explained that he had seen him flying kites on Eighty-third Street.

"I got no money for kites."

Hagopian asked the boy's name. It was Hector.

". . . Gun, I am thinking . . ."

The gun stayed right where it was, while Hagopian explained how much he had admired the kites little Hector made from plastic straws and tissue paper. The other children had kites from the stationery shop. Hector's flew higher. "Like eagle. Great airplane engineer when grown. Gun is pointing—"

"I got business when the cops split."

"Cops . . . Perhaps I am locking door. Perhaps pointing gun elsewhere."

"Don't move!"

"Please, Hector. I am not telling. I am locking door so cop aren't walking in."

"If you run I'll bang holes in your back."

Hagopian promised that would not be necessary and walked slowly down the ravine, carefully keeping his hands in sight, and turned the massive Fox Lock. "All safe. See? Safe."

"Stay where I can see you, man. *What's that?*" Hector jumped down from the bags, and leveled the weapon at the whistling behind the curtain. Frightened, he looked even younger.

"Tea boil-ed," Hagopian assured him. "Wanting tea?"

"Got any food?"

"Perhaps we are looking inside refrigerator."

"You got candy?"

"Cookies."

"Get 'em."

Hagopian edged past the gun, poured boiling water on a tea bag in a mug and grabbed the boy a half-eaten bag of Oreos, rustling the plastic first to rout the roaches.

Hector finished the cookies before Hagopian's tea had cooled enough to drink. "What business you are having?" he asked.

"Justice."

"Justice? What is this justice? Police?"

"Not cops. *Justice.* Do right from wrong."

"What wrong?"

"The son-of-a-bitch Luis shot Ramos."

Hagopian covered his ears. "No, no, no. I am not hearing." Hot-tempered Luis Carbona, the most vicious thug in the neighborhood, was a customer. Hagopian was holding a fancy leather bag he had repaired for him.

"I saw him. Luis shot him in the back. Ramos didn't even get to pull his gun."

"That gun?"

"I took it off Ramos before the cops came. So I can bang Luis."

"Why you?"

"Ramos and me, I think we have the same father."

"Wait, wait, wait," said Hagopian. "You're a boy, you can't—"

"Who's going to stop me? You?"

The contempt in his eyes mirrored a helpless old man, but Hagopian persisted. "That not justice. What do you call it? Reverse—? No. Revenge."

"You got it, man."

"Eye for eye, is saying in my country."

"Same here."

"Now everybody blind."

Hector shrugged. "Here, guy bangs you, you bang him back."

"No, no, no. Here—" Hagopian could hardly believe the thought he was about to express; he expressed it anyway because, as much as he feared government, chaos was worse—"Here, seeing murder, you tell cop."

"No way. Cops'll lock him up, two years he's out. I got a cousin, shot in the Bronx? They catch the guy on video? Security camera? Cops a plea? Judge gives him two years in Rikers. He's out in nine months 'cause they got no room. Killed my cousin and he's back on the street. I got another cousin? Amelia? Customs catches her with a little coke at Kennedy Airport. Federal offense. Ten years. Hard time. My mom said she won't get out of jail 'til she's *thirty*. For a little coke? And the guy who kills my cousin, he gets out in nine months?" He stroked the gun. "Luis ain't gonna get out of *this* in no months."

Hagopian shook his head, struggling to explain that even if revenge was justice, it was not practical. "This Luis is very bad?"

"He kills for the drug dealers."

"He has friends?"

"Yeah?"

"Maybe they are coming to you for 'justice'?"

"I don't care, man. They come after me, I'll bang them too."

"How old are you?"

Hector claimed to be twelve. Outside on Amsterdam a police siren whooped. The boy looked out that way and Hagopian took the opportunity to snap the gun out of his hand.

"Hey! You bastard. You fu—. Hey, what are you doin', man?"

Hagopian's fingers flew and before the boy's astonished eyes the gun disintegrated into a tidy heap of metal parts.

"How you do that?"

"Practice."

Hagopian could have added, but hadn't the English, that skills mastered at night, in the rain, while people were shooting, were never forgotten. Just as he would never forget a child, lost on such a night. Shuffling sear spring, main spring, and recoil spring, he emptied the magazine and poked disdainfully at the dirty slide.

"Rust-ed." Hagopian snapped his fingers. "Behind you. WD-40!"

Hector, round-eyed, passed him the spray can Hagopian used to free corroded zippers and snaps. Quickly, methodically, he cleaned the gun and reassembled the now-glistening parts.

It was the first gun he had touched since 1991 when he abandoned his own in the men's room of De Gaulle Airport—a weapon he had carried four years in Afghanistan, home to Armenia, through the Azerbaijan War, all the way across Europe to Paris, fifty feet from the airport security metal detectors.

He wished he could tell Hector how frightening the last fifty feet had been, walking like a naked man. Then maybe the boy would know what "justice" cost.

Suddenly, a fist pounded the tin door. "Hey, open up! You got my bag, man. It's Luis. Open up or I'll kick the door down."

Hector whipped the gun off the worktable.

"No," said Hagopian.

"I'll bang that fucker right through the door. You try and stop me, I'll bang you too."

"Already you are stop-ed."

"Say what?"

Hagopian held up a tiny steel stud. "How you call? Fire pin."

"You fucker."

"You hiding."

"I'll get another gun, man. You can't stop me."

"Yes, yes, yes. But first, hiding . . . There!" He shooed Hector through the back room curtain. Luis resumed pounding, but Hagopian paused at his workbench before he shuffled to the door. He unlocked it and blinked out at Luis Carbona, a Latin with the dead gaze of a mountain wolf.

"Yes?"

"My bag, man. Give me my bag."

As usual, he had left his BMW with the door open and the motor running—a contemptuous dare that Hagopian likened to the custom in his part of the world of massing tanks at the border to remind neighbors who was dangerous.

"Receipt, please?"

"Screw that, man. You know my bag. Black leather. Strap came loose."

Hagopian cast a dubious look into the darkness behind him, then shuffled through the bag mountain, returning with Luis's many-zippered carry-all dangling by the broken strap.

"Is not ready."

"What?" He seized Hagopian's collar and lifted him off his feet. "I tole you a week ago. You tole me she be ready."

"Is very hard fixing inside. Putting down, please. I show." Luis flung him down and stood over him, his eyes hot, as Hagopian demonstrated how the strap had to be sewn from within. "Is good bag."

"Shit! I'm on a eight o'clock outta Kennedy. I'm leaving *here* at five-thirty. You got two hours or—" he shoved Hagopian against the stack of luggage "—or mine won't be the only bag 'is not ready'."

Hagopian believed him. Drugs, of course, paid for Luis's airline tickets between North and South America—not that he carried himself, Consuela had assured Hagopian during one of their chats in the morning sun. She called Luis a "mule driver," an overseer of the peasant women so often arrested at Customs, like Hector's cousin. *"Muy malo,"* the liquid Spanish had poured like honey from her lips. *Malo,* for sure. Ask Ramos on the sidewalk.

Cursing his impulse to save Hector from himself, Hagopian hurried to his workbench. He had no illusions about children—not in a world where eleven-year-olds rolled hand grenades into markets—but he did have hope.

Had his son survived, he'd have been Hector's age. And yet the connection he felt with this little boy ran deeper, into his own childhood, when the world had still seemed boundless. Was it possible, he wondered grimly, that Ramos was not the only fool on Amsterdam Avenue?

"Is gone-ed," he called.

Hector pushed through the curtain. "Fix the gun."

"Later."

"I told you, you don't fix it, I'll get another. I know where."

Hagopian did not look up from his sewing machine. "Later."

"When?"

"Eight o'clock. In airport."

"Say what?"

"So neighborhood not seeing you shooting. Yes?"

"Yes!"

Hagopian told him to find out what airplane Luis Carbona flew on. Hector hesitated in the doorway.

"What are you doing?"

"I do what I do." He hunched over his machine.

"Don't forget the firing pin."

TWO HOURS LATER, Luis Carbona slung his bag on his shoulder, told Hagopian he'd pay him when he got back to Manhattan, and raced off in his BMW. Hagopian hurried next door to the Bolívar Car Service. He fidgeted nervously behind a customer who asked for a receipt, and finally reached the bulletproof window that protected the dispatcher's desk.

"¿Cómo está, Eduardo? I am hiring car."

"Got any money?"

"How much?"

"Where you goin'?"

"Kennedy Airport."

"Twenty-five bucks plus tolls."

"As I am coming both directions, perhaps we are agreeing forty bucks."

"Fifty bucks—plus waiting—plus tolls."

Hagopian had sixty in his tattered change purse. The zipper stuck. Eduardo sneered.

Hagopian apologized: "How you say? 'Shoemaker's children get no Adidas. . . .' Ah, here! We go now."

"You gotta wait. Rush hour. I got no drivers."

Hagopian snatched back his money. "No waiting. Taking taxi."

"I'll drive him," said a honey voice, and there was Consuela, all round and dark, shiny white smile, red lips and fingernails, lush hair like a twist of night. And there was Eduardo, caught between greed for the fifty dollars and his suspicions. "Gimme the money."

As he followed her tight jeans to the car, Hagopian felt years slide from his body like melting snow. Hector ran from Caesar's Pizza clutching a greasy bag.

"Where you going?" demanded Consuela.

"I'm with him."

"Hector, if Eduardo finds pizza on his seats, you're dead meat."

"Where's the gun?" Hector whispered.

"Gun fine. Where's change?"

Hector returned fifty cents. As soon as he finished his slice, he started whispering to see the gun, despite Hagopian's warning nods in the direction of Consuela, who was cursing a fluent stream through the rush-hour traffic. To shut him up, Hagopian asked, "What is Uncle Sam?" He explained how the customer ahead of him at the car service had needed a receipt for "Uncle Sam."

"Don't you know nothing? IRS. Taxes."

Hagopian, ignorant of much in his new land, and glad of any means to distract Hector from out-loud outbursts of "Bang that fucker," asked, "Eduardo pay tax?"

Hector laughed. "You joking, man?" He repeated this absurdity in Spanish. Consuela giggled. Finally, as they passed under the Long Island Expressway, God smiled: Hector, lulled by food and the warm car, fell asleep.

"So where you going?" asked Consuela.

"American Airlines."

"I *know* that. Then where? Who you meeting?"

"We are seeing sights."

"Okay, don't tell me." She pouted, prettily, and Hagopian racked his brain for things to say. But whenever he hit on a subject, he couldn't come up with the words, and they drove mostly in silence into the airport and up to American departures.

Hector woke up fast, eyes glittering. He tried to dip his tiny hands into Hagopian's pockets. "Gimme the gun."

"Later," Hagopian whispered, slapping his hands away, terrified that Consuela had heard. She looked perplexed. "You wait?" said Hagopian.

"Not here. They'll bust me. I'll park and wait for you inside."

"No, no, no. We find you in parking." He looked around the moving maze of cars and buses and hurrying people and spotted the walkway to the parking lot. "By there!" he said, suddenly firm.

Consuela looked surprised. "Okay, if that's what you want."

The car clock read seven-twenty. "Coming," he said to the boy. "Hurry!"

Through electric doors and up the escalator Hector kept pestering him for the gun. But while repairing Luis's bag, Hagopian had rehearsed what he would tell the boy at this point, and had cobbled together some unusually coherent sentences.

"You are knowing what is hit man?"

"Me. Soon as you give me the gun."

"You know hot hit man work?"

"I'll bang the fucker second I see him. We split up. Meet at the car."

"No, no, no. This is not rap video. Real hit man is having . . . uuuhhhhh . . . what you call—*teammate*. I am being teammate. Hit man *not* carrying gun. Teammate carrying gun. See target, teammate giving hit man gun."

"Then you watch my back while I bang the fucker."

"Very good, Hector. Now we are finding gate."

They perused a departures screen and located Luis's flight.

"Gate six. Gimme the gun."

Hagopian strode off, following signs. The boy scampered after him, pleading for the gun. Hagopian watched for Luis. He felt his skin begin to crawl, his heart speed up. People rushing with bags, a thousand shoes— clinking, scuffling, rustling—voices from the ceiling, all hurled him back to Paris, back to those last fifty feet.

Blocking the corridor was a security checkpoint, beyond which only passengers with boarding passes were allowed. It funneled the passengers through X-ray machines and metal detectors. Agents stood in front, directing the flow. Others frisked those who set off the detector. Those studying the X-rays stopped the machines for closer looks, and opened bags that didn't pass. In addition, Hagopian noticed a plainclothes agent, an apparent passenger, whose shoulder bag, he would have bet a night with Consuela, contained an assault weapon.

"Gimme the gun."

Hagopian led Hector into the foyer of the men's room, which gave them a clear view of the checkpoint. Hector gasped. Luis came striding out of the men's room, running a comb through his hair.

Hagopian whirled to the wall, lifting one foot as if to tie a shoelace, and enveloped the boy in the folds of his quilted jacket. Luis brushed past them. His shoulderbag skimmed Hagopian's arm, but he did not turn to apologize and the next instant he was on the line forming at the checkpoint.

"Gimme the gun."

"Here."

"Hey, what are you doing?"

Hector tried to squirm away from the barrel pressing his belly, but Hagopian jammed his other hand behind his back, holding him hard against the weapon.

"You are not moving, or you are gut shot. You know what is gut shot? Maybe crack spine."

Hector looked up into the deadest eyes he had ever seen.

"But, but—You son of—But why? Luis buy you off? He pay you to stop me?"

"You want justice?"

"Yeah, man. You said you'd help."

"Watching."

"Hey, no fair, you banging him. *I* bang the guy who killed my brother, not you."

"Watching."

Luis's turn had come. A seasoned traveler, he laid his shoulder bag on the X-ray conveyor and passed through the metal detector, after first depositing his keys and coins in a tray. Flashing a smile at one of the prettier agents, Luis went to retrieve his shoulder bag. But as Luis's bag emerged, an agent took it and beckoned Luis to a table.

"What's he doing?" asked Hector.

Another agent ducked his head to speak into a shoulder mike.

"Watching."

The agent opened Luis's bag, zipper by zipper. Luis Carbona checked his watch. A second smile to the pretty agent got a look of stone, and now, as Hagopian held the boy, a swiftly moving cadre of plainclothes agents approached the checkpoint, while uniformed police officers suddenly appeared to steer passengers away.

"I can't see," Hector protested. To his amazement, Hagopian pocketed the penlight he had been pressing to his belly and hoisted him in a swift, sure motion to his shoulder.

"Watching."

He saw Luis arguing, refusing to face the wall, until two burly agents turned him around and slammed him against it.

"What do you see?"

"He had a gun in the bag. It has a false bottom. The X-ray machine nailed it."

"And more?"

Hector watched the agents remove the gun. "Hey, that's Ramos's gun—Wow, Luis tried to get away. This huge cop banged his face on the wall. There's blood all over. Excellent. They cuffed him."

Hagopian lowered him to the floor, stretched his aching back, and headed quickly for the escalator. "We gone-ed. Now!"

FROM THE TRIBORO BRIDGE, it appeared as if every light in Manhattan was burning. Hagopian remembered the Milky Way pierced by ice-capped mountains.

"Man, that was great! The Feds'll lock him up forever."

Not so great, thought Hagopian. It would have been greater for him if the hot-blooded Luis had fought to the death.

"Better justice than nine months, yes?"

For the rest of the drive, Hagopian and Hector discussed the possible penalties for the Federal crime of smuggling a gun onto an airliner. If cousin Amelia got ten Federal years for a little coke, it stood to reason that Luis would receive many more.

Suddenly Hector said, "He's gonna get you, man. He's going to know you put the gun—"

"Jail-ed."

"He's got friends. They know where to find you."

Hagopian had already concluded that he had put too much hope in Luis's fighting back. Worse, he had mistakenly assumed that American security agents would open fire like Russians.

"Better justice than small boy killing man. Yes?"

Hector said, "Watch your ass on the street, man."

"No kites in jail," Hagopian persisted. "No airplane engineer. Yes?"

"You better get a gun."

"I don't want a gun." Drained, Hagopian tipped Consuela his last two dollars and went to bed in the back of his shop.

THE NEXT DAY HE JUMPED whenever the door opened. Luis's arrest was on page two of both the *News* and the *Post*. He was pleased to see that his and Hector's estimates of jailtime had been conservative. But of course Luis had friends. Sadly, wishing he didn't have to, he asked Consuela if she knew someone who would sell him a gun.

From the many offered, he chose a man-stopping .45 automatic, discounted for a frozen slide which he easily repaired. It was a big weapon, but he had room in the folds of his quilted jacket. No one saw it when he had his cappuccino. But Café Lalo didn't feel the same.

That night, as he was closing, the door swung open.

"Close-ed," Hagopian called.

"It's me."

Hector's little face was round in smiles. "Boy, is Luis pissed. He's so mad he's banging his head on the bars."

"How are you knowing?"

"They got him down at Manhattan Correctional. My cousin's uncle is in there. I sent Luis a message."

"What message?"

"Told him I put the gun in the bag when you weren't looking."

Hagopian was appalled. "Why?"

"For Ramos."

"But we make-ed justice for Ramos. Now Luis's friends are hunting you."

"Hey, man, it weren't justice 'til Luis knew I banged him."

The Dancing Bear
DOUG ALLYN

The inn was a sorry place with walls of wattle and daub and a lice-ridden thatch roof in dire need of repair. The light within was equally poor, no proper candles, only tallow bowls and even a few Roman lamps that were probably cast aside when the last legions abandoned these Scottish borderlands to the Picts six hundred years ago. Still, logs were blazing in the hearth, the innkeeper had recently slaughtered a hog, and there were guests to entertain. I was content to strum my lute and sing for sausages and a place near the fire. The few coins to be earned in such a hovel weren't worth the risk. With five kings contending in Scotland and the Lionheart aboard, banditry ruled the roads.

The guests were a mixed lot, a pedlar of tinware, an elderly man and his wife on a pilgrimage to Canterbury, a crew of thatchers drifting south in search of work, two farmboys taking an ox to market.

The only person of any substance was a young soldier, a returned crusader from the boiled look of him. He wore a well-crafted chain mail shirt beneath his linen surcoat, and his broadsword was German steel, carried in a bearskin sheath across his back in the old Scottish style. He was tall with unkempt, sandy hair and a scraggly blond beard. His skin was scorched scarlet as a slab of beef, and his eyes were no more than slits. Perhaps they'd been narrowed by the desert sun. Or perhaps they'd seen too much.

He kept to himself, away from the camaraderie of the fire, though he did applaud with the others when I made up a roundelay that described each of the guests in a verse. But his countenance darkened again when I sang "The Cattle Raid at Cooley," an Irish war ballad popular in this border country. The innkeeper was an affable fellow, but I noticed he kept a weather eye on the moody young soldier. As did I.

But he was no trouble. As I gently plucked the opening notes to "The Song of Roland," the crusader lowered his head to the table and dozed off. The ballad is a hymn to the fallen stalwarts of mighty Charlemagne who died for honor. It's a song I sing well, but barely a quarter through it, I noticed the eyes of my listeners straying. Annoyed, I followed their glances.

In the shadows in the corner, the young soldier was on his feet. And he was dancing, shuffling round and round in the smoky darkness. At first I thought he was responding to my music, but his eyes were clenched tight and his steps were graceless. If he was hearing music, it was not mine. My voice died away, but still he danced, lost within himself. And we watched, in silence, bewitched. And for just a moment I felt a feather touch of a memory. There was something familiar about his movements, something I'd seen before. But I could not call it to mind. After a time I quietly took up my song again, though to little effect. I doubt anyone heard a word.

The young crusader stumbled back into his seat and his slumber before I finished singing, but the sense of fellowship around the fire was gone. Uneasy, avoiding each other's eyes, we each of us found places, wrapped our cloaks about us and so to sleep. But not for long.

Living on the road has sharpened my senses, if not my wits. Sometime in the night I heard a muffled footstep and snapped instantly awake, my glance flicking about the room like a bat.

Movement. In the corner. As my eyes adjusted to the dark, I could see the young soldier. Dancing. His eyes were partly open, but there was no light in them, no awareness. And his face was a twisted mask of anguish. And yet he danced shuffling in a mindless circle like a ...

Bear.

And I remembered where I'd seen this dance before. In the market-place of Shrewsbury when I was a boy. It was a feast day and there was a fair, with jugglers and minstrels and a puppet show. And near the village gate was a man with a chained bear, a great brown hulk of a brute with a mangy coat. The man would prod it with a stick and sing a doggerel verse, and the bear would rear upright and shuffle in a circle, pawing the air. And the man would swat it and caper about as though the two were dancing.

I was enchanted, awed by the power this ragamuffin minstrel had over his monstrous beast. When he worked the crowd, I paid him my only copper to see the bear dance again. And I gradually lost my fear of the animal and moved closer. Only then did I realize why the minstrel had no fear of it. The bear's claws had been ripped out, and his eyes seared with coals. He was blind.

I cried all the way home and poured out my heart to my father. Who cuffed me for whining. Perhaps rightly. But later that night I hid a blade beneath my jerkin and skulked back to the marketplace, determined to rescue the bear somehow. But the fair was finished and they were gone. I never saw him again. Until tonight. For the young soldier's dance reminded me strongly of the ghost bear of my boyhood. He too shuffled in his circle, blind to his surroundings. The difference was that if the soldier opened his eyes, he could see.

When I opened mine again, he was gone. As were the thatchers and the farmboys and even their ox. Only the old pilgrims and I had slept past the dawn, and they were packing to leave as I stirred myself. Perhaps I could have stayed another night, earned another meal, but the inn felt haunted to me now. I slung my lute o'er my shoulder, bade the innkeeper good day, and set out.

The day was fine, a brassy October morn, heather crunching beneath my shoes and curlews crying. I'd summered to the north in Strathclyde, singing in inns and village fairs, but winter was on the wing, and I wished to be far south of these border hills when it came. In England. Perhaps even at home in Shrewsbury.

Or perhaps not. A mile or so from the inn, I came to a fork in the trail. The young soldier was resting there, seated comfortably on a knoll above the path, his blade across his knees.

"Good morning, minstrel," he nodded. "I've been waiting for you."

"Good morning to you," I said. In the light of day he seemed older. Not his face, which despite his beard was boyish and unseamed, but his eyes.... "Waiting?" I said. "Why?"

"To offer you employment," he said. "I journey west to the Clyde, to a town called Sowerby. A small place, but lively. I should like to hire you to perform there, and a troubador of your skill will surely find other work as well."

"Thank you, no," I said. "I'm traveling south."

"To those of us who drift on the wind, one road is much like another, is it not? Come with me. I have need of your talent, and I can pay. In advance if you like." He rose, blotting out the sun with his shoulders. And for a moment he was again the blinded bear of my boyhood. And my dreams. And he was asking for my help.

"Keep your money," I said with a shrug, offering him my hand. "I'm Tallifer of Shrewsbury, minstrel and poet. And the price of my company is a riddle. Why does a man dance like a bear in the dark when no music plays?"

"I am Arthur Gunn," he said, accepting my hand. "Of Clyde, and the Holy Land. I, ah, danced last night?"

"That you did. A curious thing to see," I said as we set off on the path to the west. "Tell me the story of it."

"You should have taken the coins," he smiled. "There's nought wondrous about it. I followed the cross and King Richard to Acre, and I was captured by Saracens in a raid in '91 south of Caesarea, myself and a dozen more."

"People say they are cruel captors."

"Not unlike ourselves," he said dryly. "They led us east, into the wastes. By chance, one of the captured was a bastard son of Hugh of Burgundy, and so a band of French horse dogged us like hounds.

"And after a few days, the Saracens began to kill us. Not from malice, but to save water. Each night when we camped the guards would look us over and slaughter those who looked too weak to go on before giving water to the rest. I was young and very afraid, so when they approached me, I would rise and shuffle about to show I was hale. And worthy of a sip of water. Of living another day. As the chase stretched on, we all went half mad from thirst and exhaustion. And if a man fell on the trail and was killed, I would dance over him. To prove I was stronger, you see. That I was still alive. So my friends died, and I ... danced."

He fell silent, his face dark with memories.

"It must have been terrible," I said. "What happened?"

"On the twelfth day, young Burgundy died, and I knew the pursuit would end when they found him. I had wasted a bit so my shackles were not so tight, nor did the guards check as closely as before, for they were exhausted, too. That night I chewed my arm and dripped blood onto my ankle till it was oily enough to slip my chain. I must've fled into the desert, though I honestly don't remember. The French said I was dancing when they found me. Alone, on the sand."

"Perhaps it will pass now that you are returned?"

"It has abated somewhat," he agreed. "It only happens when I drink too much, or get overtired. With luck the winds of Scotland will blow my ghosts away altogether."

"I hope so," I said earnestly. "A happier question. What song do you wish me to sing? To your family? Or a lass, perhaps?"

"I've no family, and as for a lass, I'm not sure," he said, brightening. "Before I left, my best friend and I fought over a woman, a tanner's daughter we'd both lain with. Nearly killed each other, but by God she was worth the fight. Hair dark as a raven's wing, eyes like opals, and a heat about her ..."

"You still care for her, then?"

"Who knows?" He shrugged. "It's been long years. I lost to Duncan fair and square and went off crusading. I expect they are married now with a brood. Whatever their situation, I want you to make up a song to suit it as you did last night. And whether it's a wedding gift or a peace offering, say the trouble between us is forgotten, and I would be his friend again."

"And if he chooses not to forget the trouble?"

"Then perhaps you'll have to sing a dirge for one of us," he said mildly.

"That's all very well for you," I grumbled. "But dirges are difficult to sing. And if you kill each other, who will pay me?"

SOWERBY WAS LARGER THAN I EXPECTED, a walled market town sprawled haphazard along a riverbank, with a branch of the Clyde running through it. The village gate was guarded but open, and we passed through without being challenged. Within, all was abustle. There were two smithies with hammers ringing and sparks dancing aloft, a tannery, an alehouse, and a pottery shop with goods displayed on planks in front. A water-driven gristmill was built into the town's outer wall, rumbling like distant thunder as its great wheel turned.

The village houses were mostly thatch or wattle and daub, with a few built of stone. In the south corner, the castle keep loomed above all, a crude but substantial blockhouse built of stone atop a natural hill in the Norman style. Its corners were outset so archers could sweep its walls.

Two herds of horses were tethered just outside the inner ward gate, with guardsmen and merchants looking them over.

"Horse traders," Arthur offered, "from Menteith and Lennox if I recall their livery right. We've come at a good time, minstrel. There will be celebrating—"

"Arthur! Arthur Gunn?" A guards captain stepped away from a group of traders and strode toward us. He was a striking man, half a head taller than Gunn, bearded and dark as a Saracen. He wore a brimmed steel helmet and the livery of Sowerby over a mailed coat. His fist grasped the hilt of his broadsword as he came, from habit, I hoped.

He halted in front of Arthur, looking him over, his face unreadable. And then before Arthur could react, the captain seized him by the waist and lifted him aloft.

"God's eyes, Arthur," he grinned, "I thought you'd be dead with your head on a pike by now."

"I may be yet," Arthur said. "Or have you forgotten what happened the last time we spoke?"

The smile remained on the captain's face, but it no longer lit his eyes. "No," he said, lowering Arthur to the ground. "I've not forgotten. A word, Arthur, alone."

They wandered off a few paces, heads together, the captain whispering earnestly. I busied myself examining a row of pots, trying to appear uninterested, but I whirled about with my hand on my dirk when I heard Arthur shout.

But he was laughing. Both of them were, arm in arm, tears streaming, laughing like boys at the greatest joke in the world. I think Arthur would've fallen if the captain hadn't held him up. It appeared my song of peace wouldn't be needed. Just as well. Yet I'd have felt better about it if the burly guard captain's laughter had been less fierce.

"Tallifer, this is the old friend I told you about, Duncan Pentecost. A captain now, Duncan?"

"Aye. Promotion comes easy when the best men are off to the Holy Land. You've come at a good time, minstrel. Laird Osbern and his lady have come down from Pentland to look at stock. There's a feast tonight, and our steward's beside himself trying to organize an entertainment. His name's Geoffrey. Tell him I sent you and that you come highly recommended."

"You're most kind," I said.

"Not at all. Arthur says you're a fine singer, and his word has always been good with me. And now I'd best get back to the mounts before Simon of Lennox skins my lord's marshal out of his house and first-born daughter. I'll see you both tonight at the feast. And, Arthur, welcome home."

He strode back to the horse traders.

"A fair-sized man," I observed.

"So he is," Arthur agreed. "If we'd had trouble, it might have ended as it did before. Still, I was glad for your company, Tallifer. And I wish to pay you for the song, even though you didn't have to sing it."

"No need," I said. "With your friend's help I'll find profit enough to make my trip worthwhile. And as you said, to those who drift with the wind, one road's the same as another. I'd better be off in search of Geoffrey the steward."

"And I'll find our lodging," Arthur said. "Duncan offered us beds in a barracks room in the castle. You'll stay with me?"

"Are you sure you want me to? Isn't there someone else here you must see?"

"Someone else?"

"The woman, you clot. The one you and Duncan fought over. Is she his wife now?"

"No," he said, trying not to grin and failing. "He's unmarried. And the woman ... is dead, minstrel. Forget her. I'll see you later."

He strode off, chuckling quietly to himself. Crazed by grief over his lost love, no doubt. Hair dark as a raven's wing ... I shook my head and set off to find Laird Osbern's steward.

THE EVENING FEAST WAS A SMALL ONE, a courtesy to the traders who'd gathered rather than a display of wealth by the Laird Of Pentland and Sowerby, Solmund Osbern. There was food aplenty, but plain. Cold plates of venison and hare and partridge, wooden bowls of thick bean porridge flavored with leeks and garlic. The laird and his family sat at the linen-draped high table, a small army of them, four grown sons, their wives, the local reeve, and a priest. Two low tables of rude planks extended from the corners of the high table to form a rough horseshoe shape, which was appropriate since horses were the topic of the day.

In England, strict protocols of station would have been rigidly observed, but these Scots were more like an extended family, with jests and jibes flying back and forth between high and low tables. Indeed, I'd seen Laird Osbern himself that afternoon haggling like a fishmonger with a red-bearded trader from Lennox over a yearling colt. The laird was on in years, nearly sixty, folk said. He was gaunt of face and watery-eyed, but still formidable for all that. He'd gotten the best of the bargaining without adding the weight of his title to the scales.

His sons were a dour crew, wary and hard-eyed as bandits. They were dressed in coarse wools, little better than commoners'. They conversed courteously enough with their guests but kept wary eyes on them. They were fiercely deferential to their sire, though less so to his lady, I thought.

Lady Osbern was clearly not the laird's first wife, for she was a strikingly handsome woman younger than his sons. Richly clad in fur-trimmed emerald velvet, she had the canny eyes and grace of a cat. She stayed demurely at Osbern's elbow, saying little and that only to her husband, but I doubt there was a man in the room who wasn't aware of her. Or a woman either.

As I'd been hired last, I sang last, for such are the protocols of minstrelsy. I wasn't displeased at the order of things, since Scots afeeding can be a damned surly audience. Later, with full bellies and oiled with ale, they're a ready and roisterous crowd. I won them over early with a maudlin love ballad I'd learned in Strathclyde, then followed with "The Cattle Raid at Cooley." Even Laird Osbern joined in at the last chorus, with a full, if unsteady, baritone, and the guests roared their approval at the finish.

To a wandering singer like myself, such times are the true compensation for my craft, fair payment for the chancy life of the road, the loneliness, the lack of home and family. I was glowing like a country bridegroom, singing at my best, the circle of rowdy Scots cheering me on. And so chose my best tune next, "The Song of Roland." A mistake.

Half through it I began to hear murmurs and muffled laughter. I glanced behind me as I strolled the room. It was Arthur. He'd been sitting at low table with Duncan Pentecost, but now he was up, his face flushed with wine, eyes closed, dancing his mindless shuffle, round and round, my bear on a chain. It would've been funny if it were not for the agony so plain in his face. I skipped to the last verse of the song, thinking that if I ended it quickly, he might end his dance. But I was too late.

A trader from Menteith, a wiry rat of a man, staggered from his seat and began capering about Arthur, making sport of him. With a roar, Duncan Pentecost vaulted a table, seized the wretch by the throat, and hurled him back amongst his friends.

In a flash men were up, blades drawn, squaring off, ready for slaughter.

"Hold!" Laird Osbern roared. "I'll hang the first man who draws blood in my hall. Sheath your blades, sirs, or by God's eyes, ye'll answer to me and my sons."

"Your captain struck me for no good reason," the rat-faced trader complained.

"You were mocking a better man than you'll ever be," Duncan said. "And if you and your lot want satisfaction, come ahead on, one at a time or all together—"

"Shut your mouth, Duncan," Osbern snapped. "These men are guests. I've given you no leave to fight anyone. Now, what's wrong with this lad? Is he mad?"

"No, my lord," I said hastily, seizing Arthur's arm. He had stopped circling and was looking about, confused. "He's newly home from the Holy Land. He has no head for wine."

"Then see him to bed and let him sleep it off. As for you, Duncan, hie yourself up to keep tower and relieve the watchman there. The night air will cool your temper."

For a moment I thought Pentecost was going to refuse and charge into the traders. But he didn't. He visibly swallowed his anger, then nodded. "Yes, my lord. As you say." He wheeled and stalked out.

"And that, sirs, is the end to it. We can't fall to brawling in front of our good ladies like a pack of damned Vikings. We're friends here. So," he said, raising his tankard, "will you join me, gentlemen? Here's tae us. Wha's like us?"

In the hallway I heard the roar of approval as Osbern's guests answered his toast. The din seemed to startle Arthur into awareness.

"What's happened?" he mumbled, blinking.

"Nothing," I said, leading him into the barracks room and easing him down on a pallet. "Everything's all right."

"The laird was shouting at Duncan," he said, frowning, trying to remember. "Was there trouble because of me?"

"Nothing that can't be mended. Go to sleep, Arthur, we'll put things right in the morning."

But apparently he couldn't wait. Later that night, I woke to the scuff of a footstep, and saw Arthur go out.

IN THE MORNING HIS BED WAS EMPTY. I stirred myself and set off for the kitchen, in search of news and perhaps a crust of bread. But before I reached it, I heard shouts of alarm, and a guardsman pounded down the corridor past me. I followed him at a walk. Trouble finds me quick enough without hurrying toward it.

A crowd was clustered near the milltower in the outer bailey wall. I threaded through them close enough to see. It was Arthur, my bear. He lay crumpled against the stone wall, his limbs twisted at impossible angles, his body broken like a crushed insect in the muddy street. His cloak was torn and bloodstained, and his poor face was shattered, bits of bone and teeth gleaming bloody in the morning sun.

There was a stir behind me as Duncan Pentecost thrust his way through the crowd. He was hatless and bleary-eyed, doubtless roused from sleep after his long nightwatch. He knelt beside Arthur's body and gently closed his friend's eyes with his fingertips. Then he tugged Arthur's bloody cloak up to cover his head and turned to face the crowd. And those near him took a step back at the killing rage in his eyes. The others parted as Laird Osbern strode up with two of his sons and several of the Lennox and Menteith traders. "What's happened here?" Osbern asked.

"My friend's been beaten to death," Duncan said coldly. "And I tell you now, my lord, the cowards who did this will not see their pigsty homes again."

"You accuse us of this killing, captain?" the redbearded Lennoxman said, outraged.

"Perhaps not you personally, Simon of Lennox. But my friend was a soldier. It would take several men to break him like this. And he had no enemies here but your lot."

"We had no trouble with him, Pentecost. Only with you."

"But I was out of your reach last night. Perhaps some of you chanced on Arthur and took out your anger on him."

"Gentlemen," I interjected quietly. "Before this goes further, I think you should look at the body more closely. Arthur was not killed here."

"What do you mean?" Duncan said, whirling to face me as I knelt near the corpse. "Of course he was. And what would a singer know of such matters anyway?"

"I was a soldier before I was a singer," I said, rising. "I've seen death many times in many guises. And I tell you Arthur was not killed where he lies now."

"I don't care if he was killed in Araby," Simon of Lennox said. "I'll not have my men accused of murder by—"

"Curb your tongues and tempers a moment," the laird snapped. "You, minstrel, why do you say he was not killed here?"

"He's been brutally savaged, my lord, and his limbs are broken. If it had happened here, there would be blood spattered on the wall and the ground. But only his cloak is bloodsoaked."

"He's right," Laird Osbern's eldest son put in. "There is no blood about, or at least not enough for the damage done."

"True enough," the laird said, eyeing me shrewdly. "You arrived with the dead man, didn't you, minstrel? He was your friend?"

"Yes, my lord, he was."

"And you know no one else here, no friends or kinsmen?"

"No, lord."

"Then perhaps I see a way past this," Osbern nodded. "The traders planned to leave at midday. If I delay them, it might be said I'm making an excuse to seize their property. Since you are a stranger here, with neither friends *nor* allies," he added pointedly, "perhaps you can be relied on to give a fair accounting. My son Ruari will stay with you to lend you authority. Go where you like, question whom you like. If you discover who has done this to your friend, they shall pay dearly for it. But, minstrel, take care not to accuse anyone falsely. For that would be as great an offense as this. Do you understand?"

"Yes, my lord," I said, swallowing. "I will do what I can."

"And do it quickly," Osbern said. "I'll not risk war with Lennox over one death, however unfortunate. At midday, we'll have done with this whether you discover anything or no. And now, shall we see to our breakfast, gentlemen? I'd hate to hang a man on an empty stomach."

He strode off, trailed by the others. Duncan held back a moment, but at Osbern's pointed glance, he followed.

Young Osbern and I looked each other over warily. He was a bull of a youth, beetle-browed and round-shouldered, with a shaggy mane of dark hair. He wore the plain leather jerkin and pants of a yeoman. Save for his boots, which were finely made, he looked quite ordinary. He'd spoken up boldly about the blood, though, and his eyes were clever as a ferret's.

"So, minstrel," he said, "whom shall we talk to first?"

"The dead man," I said, kneeling beside Arthur's body. I pulled his cloak away from his face and swallowed. It was terrible to see. His skull was crushed, the bone showing clearly through the gash.

"His face has been smashed like a melon," Ruari said, wincing.

"And yet there's very little bleeding from it," I said. "I think he was probably dead already when this occurred."

"His cloak is quite soaked," Ruari said, reaching past me to tug the cloak from beneath the body. Beneath it his coat of mail gleamed dully, except in the small of his back, where it was darkly stained. "Odd. His armor appears intact."

"So it does," I said, tugging the mailed shirt up above the bloodstain, to reveal a puncture wound in the small of his back. "There. That is how he was killed."

Ruari knelt, gingerly touching the hole with his fingertips, in part, I think, to show he wasn't afraid. "I've seen this sort of wound before," he said slowly, "or one similar to it. A spike dagger, needle-bladed to slide through chain mail. That's why his armor is unmarred."

"Who would have such a blade?"

"I don't know," Ruari said. "It's an uncommon weapon. I doubt any of the traders own one."

"What about your father's men?"

"Nor them either," he said. "The blade's too thin to be of use in a fight. A man at arms might carry one into battle to finish a fallen enemy, but it's good for little else."

"Aye," I said. "And Arthur wore no helmet. Since he was struck from behind, he could have been killed as easily with a broadsword, or even with a cudgel. Why use a dagger at all?"

"Or break his bones after? Someone must have hated him greatly."

"Perhaps not. Perhaps he wasn't beaten. His bones could have been broken in a fall."

"From the milltower, you mean? Not likely. A man might break a limb, but not much more."

"But suppose he fell from the castle keep, and struck hard on the slope above us? He might tumble outward to land where he lies now."

"The keep? But what would he be doing there?"

"I don't know. What's directly above us?"

"The armory. But it would've been locked last night."

"Then perhaps I'm wrong. But if he did fall from above, there should be a mark of some kind on the rocks. He would have struck with great force."

"Aye, so he would," Ruari nodded thoughtfully, looking up at the rocky face that slanted steeply down from the stone towers above. "And it would have to be somewhere near the foot of the wall. . ."

He was climbing before he finished his thought, scrambling up the cliff face like a Barbary ape. A few rods below the ashlar facing of the wall he paused, glanced down to get his bearings, then began inching to his left among the rocks.

And then he stopped. He turned cautiously and looked down at me. And raised his hand. And even in the deep shadows of the keep above, I could see his palm was stained with blood.

IT WAS STILL AN HOUR UNTIL NOON when Ruari and I strode together into the great hall. The tables were as generously laden with cold game and trenchers as they had been the previous evening, but the mood was taut as a strung bow and no one was eating much. The traders from Lennox and Menteith were seated together, shoulder to shoulder, as though they were ringed by wolves.

And perhaps rightly, for there were a half dozen men at arms arrayed behind Laird Osbern, Duncan Pentecost was guarding the door, and armed yeomen were posted at intervals around the room. Save for Lady Osbern, who sat at her husband's left, no women were present at all.

"Father, gentlemen," Ruari began, but the laird waved him to silence.

"Have you discovered the truth of what happened to the crusader?" he asked.

"I'm not sure. Perhaps."

"Then let the minstrel tell it. If trouble comes from what is said here, on his head be it. Come, stand by me."

Ruari glanced at me, shrugged, and did as he was bid. Leaving me alone in the center of the room. "Now, minstrel, what did you find?"

"We found, my lord, that Arthur Gunn was murdered, struck from behind with a thin blade. A spike dagger."

"A spike dagger?" Osbern echoed, frowning.

"Yes, my lord. And further, he was not killed in the street where he was found. He was killed in the keep, either in the armory or near it, and his body thrown from the wall there."

"The keep? But there was no one up there, save my family and—"

"And Duncan Pentecost," I finished, "who was on duty there." I sensed a movement from behind me, where Duncan stood at the door.

"But Duncan was the lad's friend," Osbern scoffed. "He stood up for him at the feast, ready to fight half the room on his behalf."

"That is true, my lord. Duncan was his friend. In fact, he was the only close friend he had here. And thus the only one he would likely have gone to visit in the night. Where Duncan stood watch. In the keep tower."

"But the stairway guard—"

"Admitted to me that he had a bit too much ale last night," Ruari put it. "He likely was asleep when the crusader went past."

"But even so, Duncan and the crusader were friends."

"And sometimes even friends can fall out," I said quietly. "Over a woman."

"Enough!" Lady Osbern's voice cracked like a whip. "Duncan, will you just stand there and let this English vagabond dirty your name with his lies? He's all but called you murderer—"

"Gentlemen, I am not armed," I said, backing away. "Nor have I accused anyone."

"Duncan! Hold your place, sir!" Laird Osbern snapped. "Madam, forgive me for being such a lout. You're quite right, our hall is no fit place for such talk. And as you gentlemen of Lennox and Menteith have been found blameless, you are no doubt eager to be on your way, are you not?"

"Yes, my lord," Simon of Lennox said hastily, arising. "We have imposed on your hospitality too long already. By your leave we shall be off straightaway."

"Of course. Godspeed to you, Simon, and to all of you. My dear," Osbern said, smiling benignly at his lady, "all this talk has upset you. Perhaps you should retire and rest a bit. Alwyn! See your stepmother to her rooms. As to this other matter, Ruari, minstrel, Duncan, come with me."

He turned and stalked from the hall. I followed, and Ruari pointedly fell into step between Pentecost and myself. Osbern led us a considerable distance from the great hall to a tower guard room with arrow slits for windows and an oaken door.

"Ruari, wait out here and see we're not interrupted. By anyone." He closed the door and turned slowly to face us.

"And now, sirs, we are quite alone. And I will have the truth, from both of you. Minstrel, what did you find up there?"

"Bloodstains on the stones, my lord, near the armory. And on the wall. Arthur was killed there, and his body thrown down."

"I see. And you, Duncan, what have you to say?"

"It was . . . as the minstrel says, my lord," Pentecost said, swallowing. "Arthur and I fell out years ago, before he went crusading. And last night . . . we argued again."

"And you stabbed him from behind? Dishonorably? With a spike dagger? Is that what you are telling me?"

"Yes, my lord."

"I see. And you carry such a blade ordinarily, do you?"

"No, lord, I was . . . he found me in the armory, and we argued, and as he turned to leave, I, ah, I seized the dagger from a workbench. And struck him."

"You seized the dagger. You didn't draw your own blade and order your friend to defend himself? And yet a few hours earlier you were ready to fight *for* him. But never mind. This Arthur Gunn came upon you in the armory, you argued, and you killed him. From behind," Laird Osbern said, moving closer to Pentecost until their faces were only inches apart. "And was there, by chance, a witness to any of this, Duncan?"

"Witness, my lord?"

"I'm asking if you were alone when he found you?"

"Yes, my lord," Pentecost said, avoiding the old man's eyes. "Quite alone. I'd gone there to get out of the wind."

"Enough," Osbern said, turning away. "You've killed a man who was my guest, Duncan. I could have you gutted in the courtyard for that alone. But that would only cause my—family further upset. So I offer you a sporting chance, Pentecost. Go from this place, now. Take a mount, but no weapons. In two hours' time, armed men will follow. With orders to kill you on sight. Unless, of course, you have something further to offer in your defense. A mitigating circumstance, perhaps?"

"No, my lord. I have nothing more to say. Now or ever."

"Then be off. Forgive me if I don't wish you luck."

Duncan turned without a word and stalked out. Osbern eyed me for a moment in silence, then shrugged. "So, minstrel, are you satisfied that justice has been done for your friend's death?"

"Yes, my lord. And he wasn't a friend, really, only a companion of the road."

"I see. He behaved strangely last night, but he seemed harmless enough. People tell me you've been at court, minstrel. In London?"

"Yes, lord."

"Then you must have seen many beautiful women. And what do you think of my lady?"

I hesitated a heartbeat. I've been wounded in battle and once I was trapped in a burning stable, but I've never felt nearer death than at that moment. It was in the old man's eyes. I wondered if I would leave the room alive.

"Your wife is truly lovely, my lord. Her hair gleams like a raven's wing, her eyes glow like opals."

"Spoken like a poet," Osbern said dryly, "but that wasn't my point. Any fool can see she's beautiful. It's her ... deportment that troubles me. Speaking out of turn as she did today, for example. She's not nobly born, you see. She was only a tanner's daughter. But as my sons are grown and the succession is assured ... I indulged myself and married for love. And even now, God help me, I do not regret it. Still, a man of my station must maintain certain standards, must he not?"

"As you say, my lord."

"I have an aunt," he said, musing to himself more than to me. "A horse-faced old crone, married to the church. She is abbess of a grim little convent in the highlands north of Pentland. Perhaps I'll send my lady there for a rest. And to learn proper behavior. A few months with my aunt would teach a mule manners. As to the matter of your friend's death, there's still one minor point that troubles me. This woman Duncan and his friend fought over. What do you know of her?"

"Only that she is dead," I said carefully. "Arthur told me she died long ago."

"Did she indeed? What a pity. She must have been very comely to cause all this trouble from beyond the grave."

"We do not know for certain that the argument *was* over the woman, my lord. We have only Duncan's word for that. Perhaps they fought over something else. Men sometimes kill each other over a penny or a look. Or nothing at all."

"So they do," he nodded, satisfied. "You've a glib tongue, minstrel. And you're quick with a song as well. And will you sing of what happened here?"

"No, my lord," I said positively. "A friend murdering a friend over a trifle is no fit subject for a song. It's best forgotten."

"Truly," he said, gazing out the arrow slit. "Best forgotten. Will you be tarrying long in this country, do you think?"

"No, lord. My home is far to the south, and winter is coming on. I'd best be on my way."

"Very wise," he said, without looking at me. "Godspeed to you, minstrel."

I STROLLED OUT OF SOWERBY that afternoon at a leisurely pace, whistling as I went. Until I was out of sight of the watchtower. Then I plunged into the wood and struck hard to the east, running full out as long as I could, then slowing to a steady, mile-eating trot. I found a stream just at dusk, but instead of using the ford, I waded downstream until well after moonrise, finally leaving it many miles below where I'd entered.

Was I being overcautious? Perhaps. But I'd seen Ruari and a band of men-at-arms set out after Duncan in far less time than the two hours the old laird had promised. And I had little doubt that when they'd finished with him, they'd be hunting me.

The old laird knew damned well Duncan hadn't killed his friend over nothing. Arthur had gone to the keep looking for Duncan in the middle of the night. And found him in the armory. But not alone. He was almost certainly with Lady Osbern. Perhaps she'd even struck the blow that killed him. And now Arthur was dead, and Duncan soon would be. And I was the last one who might spread the tale. A proud old man with a young passionate wife fears the sound of laughter more than death itself. He will do anything, even murder, to stop it.

I maintained my killing pace all through the night and the next day. Late that evening, I forded the Tweed into England. Perhaps Osbern's men would not pursue me so far south, but the Tweed is only a river and the border only a line on a map. And Laird Osbern was a tall man with a long reach. I pushed on through the night.

The morning broke clear, a golden October dawn that melted away the shadows and my fears. As the sun climbed slowly through the morn, my spirits rose with it. I was exhausted but too numb to feel much pain. And so I walked on.

And just before midday, a breeze came wafting out of the east, swirling leaves and dirt into a dust devil that seemed to dance ahead of me on the road, leading me on. On a whim, I tried to join in with it, whirling round and round, capering about like a mating partridge. Or a dancing bear.

I shuffled in a circle until my legs finally gave way and I sank to my knees in the road. Still the dust devil danced on ahead. Beckoning me to follow. But not to the south and home.

To the west. Toward Ireland. A land of poets, they say.

I knew of no towns that lay in that direction. But there was a path of sorts. And to those who drift with the wind, one road is much like another.

As Jon Breen remarks in the introduction to this volume, this seems to be the year of Lawrence Block. After more than three decades of producing a steady output of novels and short stories, Block has finally come into his own. The following story is one of his most enjoyable, and displays all the skills that have made him such a favorite of mystery readers everywhere.

Keller on Horseback
LAWRENCE BLOCK

At the airport newsstand Keller picked up a paperback western. The cover was pretty much generic, showing a standard-issue Marlboro man, long and lean, walking down the dusty streets of a western town with a gun riding his hip. Neither the title nor the author's name meant anything to Keller. What drew him was a line that seemed to leap out from the cover.

"He rode a thousand miles," Keller read, "to kill a man he never met."

Keller paid for the book and tucked it into his carry-on bag. When the plane was in the air, he dug it out and looked at the cover, wondering why he'd bought it. He didn't read much, and when he did, he never chose westerns.

Maybe he wasn't supposed to read this book. Maybe he was supposed to keep it for a talisman.

All for that one sentence. Imagine riding a thousand miles on a horse for any purpose, let alone the killing of a stranger. How long would it take, a thousand-mile journey on horseback? A thoroughbred got around a racecourse in something like two minutes, but it couldn't go all day at that pace any more than a human being could string together twenty-six four-minute miles and call it a marathon.

What could you manage on a horse, fifty miles a day? A hundred miles in two days, a thousand miles in twenty? Three weeks, say, at the conclusion of which a man would probably be eager to kill anybody, stranger or blood kin.

Was Ol' Sweat 'n' Leather getting paid for his thousand miles? Was he in the trade? Keller turned the book over in his hands, read the paragraph on the back cover. It did not sound promising. Something about a drifter in the Arizona Territory, a saddle tramp, looking to avenge an old Civil War grievance.

Forgive and forget, Keller advised him.

Keller, riding substantially more than a thousand miles, albeit on a plane instead of a horse, was similarly charged with killing a man as yet unmet. And he was drifting into the Old West to do it, first to Denver, then to Casper, Wyoming, and finally to a town called Martingale. That had been reason enough to pick up the book, but was it reason enough to read it?

He gave it a try. He read a few pages before they came down the aisle with the drinks cart, read a couple more while he sipped his V-8 and ate the salted nuts. Then he evidently dozed off because the next thing he knew the stewardess was waking him to apologize for not having the fruit place he'd ordered. He told her it didn't matter, he'd have the regular dinner.

"Or there's a Hindu meal that's going begging," she said.

His mind filled with a vision of an airline tray wrapped in one of those saffron-colored robes, extending itself beseechingly and demanding alms. He had the regular dinner instead and ate most of it, except for the mystery meat. He dozed off afterward and didn't wake up until they were making their descent into Stapleton Airport.

Earlier he'd tucked the book into the seat pocket in front of him, and he'd intended to let it ride off into the sunset wedged between the airsickness bag and the plastic card with the emergency exit diagrams. At the last minute he changed his mind and brought the book along.

HE SPENT AN HOUR ON THE GROUND in Denver, another hour in the air flying to Casper. The cheerful young man at the Avis counter had a car reserved for Dale Whitlock. Keller showed him a Connecticut driver's license and an American Express Card, and the young man gave him a set of keys and told him to have a nice day.

The keys fitted a white Chevy Caprice. Cruising north on the interstate, Keller decided he liked everything about the car but its name. There was nothing capricious about his mission. Riding a thousand miles to kill a man you hadn't met was not something one undertook on a whim.

Ideally, he thought, he'd be bouncing along on a rutted two-lane blacktop in a Mustang, say, or maybe a Bronco. Even a Pinto sounded like a better match for a rawboned, leathery desperado like Dale Whitlock than a Caprice.

It was comfortable, though, and he liked the way it handled. And the color was okay. But forget white. As far as he was concerned, the car was a palomino.

*   *   *

IT TOOK ABOUT AN HOUR to drive to Martingale, a town of around ten thousand midway between Casper and Sheridan on I-25. Just looking around, you knew right away that you'd left the East Coast far behind. Mountains in the distance, a great expanse of sky overhead. And, right in front of you, frame buildings that could have been false fronts in a Randolph Scott film. A feedstore, a western wear emporium, a run-down hotel where you'd expect to find Wild Bill Hickok holding aces and eights at a table in the saloon, or Doc Holliday coughing his lungs out in a bedroom on the second floor.

Of course, there were also a couple of supermarkets and gas stations, a two-screen movie house and a Toyota dealership, a Pizza Hut and a Taco John's, so it wasn't too hard to keep track of what century you were in. He saw a man walk out of the Taco John's looking a lot like the young Randolph Scott, from his boots to his Stetson, but he spoiled the illusion by climbing into a pickup truck.

The hotel that inspired Hickok-Holliday fantasies was the Martingale, located right in the center of things on the wide main street. Keller imagined himself walking in, slapping a credit card on the counter. Then the desk clerk—Henry Jones always played him in the movie—would say that they didn't take plastic. "Or p-p-paper either," he'd say, eyes darting, looking for a place to duck when the shooting started.

And Keller would set a silver dollar spinning on the counter. "I'll be here a few days," he'd announce. "If I have any change coming, buy yourself a new pair of suspenders."

And Henry Jones would glance down at his suspenders, to see what was wrong with them.

He sighed, shook his head, and drove to the Holiday Inn near the interstate exit. It had plenty of rooms and gave him what he asked for, a nonsmoking room on the third floor in the rear. The desk clerk was a woman, very young, very blond, very perky, with nothing about her to remind you of Henry Jones. She said, "Enjoy your stay with us, Mr. Whitlock." Not stammering, eyes steady.

He unpacked, showered, and went to the window to look at the sunset. It was the sort of sunset a hero would ride off into, leaving a slender blonde to bite back tears while calling after him, "I hope you enjoyed your stay with us, Mr. Whitlock."

Stop it, he told himself. Stay with reality. You've flown a couple of thousand miles to kill a man you never met. Just get it done. The sunset can wait.

HE HADN'T MET THE MAN, but he knew his name. Even if he wasn't sure how to pronounce it.

The man in White Plains had handed Keller an index card with two lines of block capitals hand-printed.

"Lyman Crowder," he read, as if it rhymed with louder. "Or should that be Crowder?"—as if it rhymed with loader.

A shrug in response.

"Martingale, WY," Keller went on. "Why indeed? And where, besides Wyoming? Is Martingale near anything?"

Another shrug, accompanied by a photograph. Or a part of one; it had apparently been cropped from a larger photo and showed the upper half of a middle-aged man who looked to have spent a lot of time outdoors. A big man, too. Keller wasn't sure how he knew that. You couldn't see the man's legs, and there was nothing else in the photo to give you an idea of scale. But somehow he could tell.

"What did he do?"

Again a shrug, but one that conveyed information to Keller. If the other man didn't know what Crowder had done, he had evidently done it to somebody else. That meant the man in White Plains had no personal interest in the matter. It was strictly business.

"So who's the client?"

A shake of the head. Meaning that he didn't know who was picking up the tab or that he knew but wasn't saying? Hard to tell. The man in White Plains was a man of few words and master of none.

"What's the time frame?"

"The time frame," the man said, evidently enjoying the phrase. "No big hurry. One week, two weeks." He leaned forward, patted Keller on the knee. "Take your time," he said. "Enjoy yourself."

On the way out he'd shown the index card to Dot. He said, "How would you pronounce this? As in 'crow' or as in 'crowd'?"

Dot shrugged.

"Jesus," he said, "you're as bad as he is."

"Nobody's as bad as he is," Dot said. "Keller, what difference does it make how Lyman pronounces his last name?"

"I just wondered."

"Well, stick around for the funeral," she suggested. "See what the minister says."

"You're a big help," Keller said.

THERE WAS ONLY ONE CROWDER listed in the Martingale phone book. Lyman Crowder, with a telephone number but no address. About a third of the book's listings were like that. Keller wondered why. Did these people assume everybody knew where they lived in a town this size? Or were they saddle tramps with cellular phones and no fixed abode?

Probably rural, he decided. Lived out of town on some unnamed road, picked up their mail at the post office, so why list an address in the phone book?

Great. His quarry lived in the boondocks outside a town that wasn't big enough to have boondocks, and Keller didn't even have an address for him. He had a phone number, but what good was that? What was he supposed to do, call him up and ask directions? "Hi, this here's Dale Whitlock, we haven't met, but I just rode a thousand miles and—"

Scratch that.

HE DROVE AROUND AND ATE at a downtown café called the Singletree. It was housed in a weathered frame building just down the street from the Martingale Hotel. The café's name was spelled out in rope nailed to the vertical clapboards. For Keller the name brought a vision of a solitary pine or oak set out in the middle of vast grasslands, a landmark for herdsmen, a rare bit of shade from the relentless sun.

From the menu he learned that a singletree was some kind of apparatus used in hitching up a horse, or a team of horses. It was a little unclear to him just what it was or how it functioned, but it certainly didn't spread its branches in the middle of the prairie.

Keller had the special, a chicken-fried steak and some french fries that came smothered in gravy. He was hungry enough to eat everything in spite of the way it tasted.

You don't want to live here, he told himself.

It was a relief to know this. Driving around Martingale, Keller had found himself reminded of Roseburg, Oregon. Roseburg was larger, with none of the Old West feel of Martingale, but they both were small western towns of a sort Keller rarely got to. In Roseburg Keller had allowed his imagination to get away from him for a little while, and he wouldn't want to let that happen again.

Still, crossing the threshold of the Singletree, he had been unable to avoid remembering the little Mexican place in Roseburg. If the food and service here turned out to be on that level—

Forget it. He was safe.

AFTER HIS MEAL KELLER STRODE out through the bat-wing doors and walked up one side of the street and down the other. It seemed to him that there was something unusual about the way he was walking, that his gait was that of a man who had just climbed down from a horse.

Keller had been on a horse once in his life, and he couldn't remember how he'd walked after he got off it. So this walk he was doing now wasn't coming from his own past. It must have been something he'd learned unconsciously from movies and TV, a synthesis of all those riders of the purple sage and the silver screen.

No need to worry about yearning to settle here, he knew now. Because his fantasy now was not of someone settling in but passing through, the saddle tramp, the shootist, the flint-eyed loner who does his business and moves on.

That was a good fantasy, he decided. You wouldn't get into any trouble with a fantasy like that.

BACK IN HIS ROOM Keller tried the book again but couldn't keep his mind on what he was reading. He turned on the TV and worked his way through the channels, using the remote control bolted to the nightstand. Westerns, he decided, were like cops and cabs, never around when you wanted them. It seemed to him that he never made a trip around the cable circuit without running into John Wayne or Randolph Scott or Joel McCrea or a rerun of *Gunsmoke* or *Rawhide* or one of those spaghetti westerns with Eastwood or Lee Van Cleef. Or the great villains—Jack Elam, Strother Martin, the young Lee Marvin in *The Man Who Shot Liberty Valance.*

It probably said something about you, Keller thought, when your favorite actor was Jack Elam.

He switched off the set and looked up Lyman Crowder's phone number. He could dial it, and when someone picked up and said, "Crowder residence," he'd know how the name was pronounced. "Just checking," he could say, cradling the phone and giving them something to think about.

Of course, he wouldn't say that; he'd mutter something harmless about a wrong number, but was even that much contact a good idea? Maybe it would put Crowder on his guard. Maybe Crowder was already on his guard, as far as that went. That was the trouble with going in blind like this, knowing nothing about either the target or the client.

If he called Crowder's house from the motel, there might be a record of the call, a link between Lyman Crowder and Dale Whitlock. That wouldn't matter much to Keller, who would shed the Whitlock identity on his way out of town, but there was no reason to create more grief for the real Dale Whitlock.

Because there *was* a real Dale Whitlock, and Keller was giving him grief enough without making him a murder suspect.

It was pretty slick the way the man in White Plains worked it. He knew a man who had a machine with which he could make flawless American Express cards. He knew someone else who could obtain the names and account numbers of bona fide American Express cardholders. Then he had cards made which were essentially duplicates of existing cards. You didn't have to worry that the cardholder had reported his card stolen because it hadn't been stolen; it was still sitting in his wallet. You were off somewhere charging the earth, and he didn't have a clue until the charges turned up on his monthly statement.

The driver's license was real, too. Well, technically, it was a counterfeit, of course, and the photograph on it showed Keller, not Whitlock. But someone had managed to access the Connecticut Bureau of Motor Vehicles' computer, and thus the counterfeit license showed the same number as Whitlock's, and gave the same address.

In the old days, Keller thought, it had been a lot more straightforward. You didn't need a license to ride a horse or a credit card to rent one. You bought or stole one, and when you rode into town on it, nobody asked to see your ID. They might not even come right out and ask your name, and if they did, they wouldn't expect a detailed reply. "Call me Tex," you'd say, and that's what they'd call you as you rode off into the sunset.

"Good-bye, Tex," the blonde would call out. "I hope you enjoyed your stay with us."

THE LOUNGE DOWNSTAIRS turned out to be the hot spot in Martingale. Restless, Keller had gone downstairs to have a quiet drink. He walked into a thickly carpeted room with soft lighting and a good sound system. There were fifteen or twenty people in the place, all of them either having a good time or looking for one.

Keller ordered a Coors at the bar. On the jukebox Barbara Mandrell sang a song about cheating. When she was done, a duo he didn't recognize sang a song about cheating. Then came Hank Williams's oldie, "Your Cheating Heart."

A subtle pattern was beginning to emerge.

"I love this song," the blonde said.

A different blonde, not the perky young thing from the front desk. This woman was taller, older, and fuller-figured. She wore a skirt and a sort of cowgirl blouse with piping and embroidery on it.

"Old Hank," Keller said, to say something.

"I'm June."

"Call me Tex."

"Tex." Her laughter came in a sort of yelp. "When did anybody ever call you Tex, tell me that?"

"Well, nobody has," he admitted, "but that's not to say they never will."

"Where are you from, Tex? No, I'm sorry, I can't call you that; it sticks in my throat. If you want me to call you Tex, you're going to have to start wearing boots."

"You see by my outfit that I'm not a cowboy."

"Your outfit, your accent, your haircut. If you're not an easterner, then I'm a virgin."

"I'm from Connecticut."

"I knew it."

"My name's Dale."

"Well, you could keep that. If you were fixing to be a cowboy, I mean. You'd have to change the way you dress and talk and comb your hair, but you could hang on to Dale. There another name that goes with it?"

In for a penny, in for a pound. "Whitlock," he said.

"Dale Whitlock. Shoot, that's pretty close to perfect. You tell 'em a name like that, you got credit down at the Agway in a New York minute. Wouldn't even have to fill out a form. You married, Dale?"

"What was the right answer? She was wearing a ring herself, and the jukebox was now playing yet another cheating song.

"Not in Martingale," he said.

"Oh, I like that," she said, eyes sparkling. "I like the whole idea of regional marriage. I *am* married in Martingale, but we're not *in* Martingale. The town line's Front Street."

"In that case," he said, "maybe I could buy you a drink."

"You easterners," she said. "You're just so damn fast."

THERE HAD TO BE a catch.

Keller didn't do too badly with women. He got lucky once in a while. But he didn't have the sort of looks that made heads turn, nor had he made seduction his life's work. Some years ago he'd read a book called *How to Pick Up Girls*, filled with opening lines that were guaranteed to work. Keller thought they were silly. He was willing to believe they would work, but he was not able to believe they would work for him.

This woman, though, had hit on him before he'd had time to become aware of her presence. This sort of thing happened, especially when you were dealing with a married woman in a bar where all they played was cheating songs. Everybody knew what everybody else was there for, and nobody had come to dawdle. So this sort of thing happened, but it never seemed to happen to him, and he didn't trust it.

Something would go wrong. She'd call home and find out her kid was running a fever. Her husband would walk in the door just as the jukebox gave out with "You Picked a Fine Time to Leave Me, Lucille." She'd be overcome by conscience or rendered unconscious by the drink Keller had just bought her.

"I'd say my place or yours," she said, "but we both know the answer to that one. What's your room number?" Keller told her. "You go on up," she said. "I won't be a minute. Don't start without me."

He brushed his teeth, splashed on a little aftershave. She wouldn't show, he told himself. Or she'd expect to be paid, which would take a little of the frost off the pumpkin. Or her husband would turn up and they'd try to work some variation of the badger game.

Or she'd be sloppy drunk, or he'd be impotent. Or something.

*　　*　　*

"WHEW," SHE SAID. "I don't guess you need boots after all. I'll call you Tex or Slim or any damn thing you want me to, just so you come when you're called. How long are you in town for, Dale?"

"I'm not sure. A few days."

"Business, I suppose. What sort of business are you in?"

"I work for a big corporation," he said. "They fly me over to look into situations."

"Sounds like you can't talk about it."

"Well, we do a lot of government work," he said. "So I'm really not supposed to."

"Say no more," she said. "Oh, Lord, look at the time!"

While she showered, he picked up the paperback and rewrote the blurb. He killed a thousand miles, he thought, to ride a woman he never met. Well, sometimes you got lucky. The stars were in the right place; the forces that ruled the universe decided you deserved a present. There didn't always have to be a catch to it, did there?

She turned off the shower, and he heard the last line of the song she'd been singing. " 'And Margie's at the Lincoln Park Inn,' " she sang, and moments later she emerged from the bathroom and began dressing.

"What's this?" she said. " 'He rode a thousand miles to kill a man he never met.' You know, that's funny, because I just had the darnedest thought while I was runnin' the soap over my pink and tender flesh."

"Oh?"

"I just said that last to remind you what's under this here skirt and blouse. Oh, the thought I had? Well, something you said, government work. I thought maybe this man's CIA, maybe he's some old soldier of fortune, maybe he's the answer to this maiden's prayer."

"What do you mean?"

"Just that it was already a real fine evening, Dale, but it would be heaven on earth if what you came to Martingale for was to kill my damn husband."

CHRIST WAS *SHE* THE CLIENT? Was the pickup downstairs a cute way for them to meet? Could she actually be that stupid, coming on in a public place to a man she was hiring to kill her husband?

For that matter, how had she recognized him? Only Dot and the man in White Plains had known the name he was using. They'd have kept it to themselves. And she'd made her move before she knew his name. Had she been able to recognize him? I see by your outfit that you are a hit man? Something along those lines?

"Yarnell," she was saying. "Hobart Lee Yarnell, and what he'd like is for people to call him Bart, and what everybody calls him is Hobie. Now what does that tell you about the man?"

That he's not the man I came here to kill, Keller thought. This was comforting to realize but left her waiting for an answer to her question. "That he's not used to getting his own way," Keller said.

She laughed. "He's not," she said, "but it's not for lack of trying. You know, I like you, Dale. You're a nice fellow. But if it wasn't you tonight, it would have been somebody else."

"And here I thought it was my aftershave."

"I'll just bet you did. No, the kind of marriage I got, I come around here a lot. I've put a lot of quarters in that jukebox the last year or so."

"And played a lot of cheating songs?"

"And done a fair amount of cheating. But it doesn't really work. I still wake up the next day married to that bastard."

"Why don't you divorce him?"

"I've thought about it."

"And?"

"I was brought up not to believe in it," she said. "But I don't guess that's it. I wasn't raised to believe in cheating either." She frowned. "Money's part of it," she admitted. "I won't bore you with the details, but I'd get gored pretty bad in a divorce."

"That's a problem."

"I guess, except what do I care about money anyway? Enough's as much as a person needs, and my daddy's got pots of money. He's not about to let me starve."

"Well, then—"

"But he thinks the world of Hobie," she said, glaring at Keller as if it were his fault. "Hunts elk with him, goes after trout and salmon with him, thinks he's just the best thing ever came over the pass. And he doesn't even want to hear the word 'divorce.' You know that Tammy Wynette song where she spells it out a letter at a time? I swear he'd leave the room before you got past *R.* I say it'd about break Lyman Crowder's heart if his little girl ever got herself divorced."

WELL, IT WAS TRUE. If you kept your mouth shut and your ears open, you learned things. What he had learned was that "Crowder" rhymed with "powder."

Now what?

After her departure, after his own shower, he paced back and forth, trying to sort it all out. In the few hours since his arrival in Martingale, he'd slept with a woman who turned out to be the loving daughter of the target and, in all likelihood, the unloving wife of the client.

Well, maybe not. Lyman Crowder was a rich man, lived north of town on a good-size ranch that he ran pretty much as a hobby. He'd made his real money in oil, and nobody ever made a small amount of money that way. You either went broke or got rich. Rich men had enemies: people they'd crossed in business, people who stood to profit from their death.

But it figured that Yarnell was the client. There was a kind of poetic inevitability about it. She picks him up in the lounge, it's not enough that she's the target's daughter. She also ought to be the client's wife. Round things out, tie up all the loose ends.

The thing to do ... well, he knew the thing to do. The thing to do was get a few hours' sleep and then, bright and early, reverse the usual order of affairs by riding off into the sunrise. Get on a plane, get off in New York, and write off Martingale as a happy little romantic adventure. Men, after all, had been known to travel farther than that in the hope of getting laid.

He'd tell the man in White Plains to find somebody else. Sometimes you had to do that. No blame attached, as long as you didn't make a habit of it. He'd say he was blown.

As, come to think of it, he was. Quite expertly, as a matter of fact.

IN THE MORNING he got up and packed his carry-on. He'd call White Plains from the airport or wait until he was back in New York. He didn't want to phone from the room. When the real Dale Whitlock had a fit and called American Express, they'd look over things like the Holiday Inn statement. No sense leaving anything that led anywhere.

He thought about June, and the memory made him playful. He checked the time. Eight o'clock, two hours later in the East, not an uncivil time to call.

He called Whitlock's home in Rowayton, Connecticut. A woman answered. He identified himself as a representative of a political polling organization, using a name she would recognize. By asking questions that encouraged lengthy responses, he had no trouble keeping her on the phone. "Well, thank you very much," he said at length. "And have a nice day."

Now let Whitlock explain that one to American Express.

He finished packing and was almost out the door when his eye caught the paperback western. Take it along? Leave it for the maid? What?

He picked it up, read the cover line, sighed. Was this what Randolph Scott would do? Or John Wayne, or Clint Eastwood? How about Jack Elam?

No, of course not.

Because then there'd be no movie. A man rides into town, starts to have a look at the situation, meets a woman, gets it on with her, then just backs out and rides off? You put something like that on the screen, it wouldn't even play in the art houses.

Still, this wasn't a movie.

Still ...

He looked at the book and wanted to heave it across the room. But all he heaved was a sigh. Then he unpacked.

HE WAS HAVING A CUP of coffee in town when a pickup pulled up across the street and two men got out of it. One of them was Lyman Crowder. The other, not quite as tall, was twenty pounds lighter and twenty years younger. Crowder's son, by the looks of him.

His son-in-law, as it turned out. Keller followed the two men into a store where the fellow behind the counter greeted them as Lyman and Hobie. Crowder had a lengthy shopping list composed largely of items Keller would have been hard put to find a use for.

While the owner filled the order, Keller had a look at the display of hand-tooled boots. The pointed toes would be handy in New York, he thought, for killing cockroaches in corners. The heels would add better than an inch to his height. He wondered if he'd feel awkward in the boots, like a teenager in her first pair of high heels. Lyman and Hobie looked comfortable enough in their boots, as pointy in the toes and as elevated in the heels as any on display, but they also looked comfortable in their string ties and ten-gallon hats, and Keller was sure he'd feel ridiculous dressed like that.

They were a pair, he thought. They looked alike, they talked alike, they dressed alike, and they seemed uncommonly fond of each other.

BACK IN HIS ROOM Keller stood at the window and looked down at the parking lot, then across the way at a pair of mountains. A few years ago his work had taken him to Miami, where he'd met a Cuban who'd cautioned him against ever taking a hotel room above the second floor. "Suppose you got to leave in a hurry?" the man said. "Ground floor, no problem. Second floor, no problem. Third floor, break your fockeen leg."

The logic of this had impressed Keller, and for a while he had made a point of taking the man's advice. Then he happened to learn that the Cuban not only shunned the higher floors of hotels but also refused to enter an elevator or fly on an airplane. What had looked like tradecraft now appeared to be nothing more than phobia.

It struck Keller that he had never in his life had to leave a hotel room, or any other sort of room, by the window. This was not to say that it would never happen, but he'd decided it was a risk he was prepared to run. He liked high floors. Maybe he even liked running risks.

He picked up the phone, made a call. When she answered, he said, "This is Tex. Would you believe my business appointment canceled? Left me with the whole afternoon to myself."

"Are you where I left you?"

"I've barely moved since then."

"Well, don't move now," she said. "I'll be right on over."

* * *

AROUND NINE THAT NIGHT Keller wanted a drink, but he didn't want to have it in the company of adulterers and their favorite music. He drove around in his palomino Caprice until he found a place on the edge of town that looked promising. It called itself Joe's Bar. Outside, it was nondescript. Inside, it smelled of stale beer and casual plumbing. The lights were low. There was sawdust on the floor and the heads of dead animals on the walls. The clientele was exclusively male, and for a moment this gave Keller pause. There were gay bars in New York that tried hard to look like this place, though it was hard for Keller to imagine why. But Joe's, he realized, was not a gay bar, not in any sense of the word.

He sat on a wobbly stool and ordered a beer. The other drinkers left him alone, even as they left one another alone. The jukebox played intermittently, with men dropping in quarters when they could no longer bear the silence.

The songs, Keller noted, ran to type. There were the tryin'-to-drink-that-woman-off-of-my-mind songs and the if-it-wasn't-for-bad-luck-I-wouldn't-have-no-luck-at-all songs. Nothing about Margie in the Lincoln Park Inn, nothing about heaven being just a sin away. These songs were for drinking and feeling really rotten about it.

" 'Nother damn day," said a voice at Keller's elbow.

He knew who it was without turning. He supposed he might have recognized the voice, but he didn't think that was it. No, it was more a recognition of the inevitability of it all. Of course it would be Yarnell, making conversation with him in this bar where no one made conversation with anyone. Who else could it be?

" 'Nother damn day," Keller agreed.

"Don't believe I've seen you around."

"I'm just passing through."

"Well, you got the right idea," Yarnell said. "Name's Bart."

In for a pound, in for a ton. "Dale," Keller said.

"Good to know you, Dale."

"Same here, Bart."

The bartender loomed before them. "Hey, Hobie," he said. "The usual?"

Yarnell nodded. "And another of those for Dale here." The bartender poured Yarnell's usual, which turned out to be bourbon with water back, and uncapped another beer for Keller. Somebody broke down and fed the jukebox a quarter and played "There Stands the Glass."

Yarnell said, "You hear what he called me?"

"I wasn't paying attention."

"Called me Hobie," Yarnell said. "Everybody does. You'll be doing the same, won't be able to help yourself."

"The world is a terrible place," Keller said.

"By God, you got that right," Yarnell said. "No one ever said it better. You a married man, Dale?"

"Not at the moment."

" 'Not at the moment.' I swear I'd give a lot if I could say the same."

"Troubles?"

"Married to one woman and in love with another one. I guess you could call that trouble."

"I guess you could."

"Sweetest, gentlest, darlingest, lovingest creature God ever made," Yarnell said. "When she whispers 'Bart,' it don't matter if the whole rest of the world shouts 'Hobie.' "

"This isn't your wife you're talking about," Keller guessed.

"God, no! My wife's a round-heeled meanspirited hardhearted tramp. I hate my damn wife. I love my girlfriend."

They were silent for a moment, and so was the whole room. Then someone played "The Last Word in Lonesome Is Me."

"They don't write songs like that, anymore," Yarnell said.

The hell they didn't. "I'm sure I'm not the first person to suggest this," Keller said, "but have you thought about—"

"Leaving June," Yarnell said. "Running off with Edith. Getting a divorce."

"Something like that."

"Never an hour that I don't think about it, Dale. Night and goddamn day I think about it. I think about it, and I drink about it, but the one thing I can't do is do it."

"Why's that?"

"There is a man," Yarnell said, "who is a father and a best friend to me all rolled into one. Finest man I ever met in my life, and the only wrong thing he ever did in his life was have a daughter, and the biggest mistake I ever made was marrying her. And if there's one thing that man believes in, it's the sanctity of marriage. Why, he thinks 'divorce' is the dirtiest word in the language."

So Yarnell couldn't even let on to his father-in-law that his marriage was hell on earth, let alone take steps to end it. He had to keep his affair with Edith very much backstreet. The only person he could talk to was Edith, and she was out of town for the next week or so, leaving him dying of loneliness and ready to pour out his heart to the first stranger he could find. For which he apologized, but—

"Hey, that's all right, Bart," Keller said. "A man can't keep it all locked up inside."

"Calling me Bart, I appreciate that, I truly do. Even Lyman calls me Hobie, and he's the best friend any man ever had. Hell, he can't help it. Everybody calls me Hobie sooner or later."

"Well," Keller said. "I'll hold out as long as I can."

ALONE, Keller reviewed his options.

He could kill Lyman Crowder. He'd be keeping it simple, carrying out the mission as it had been given to him. And it would solve everybody's problems, June and Hobie could get the divorce they both so desperately wanted.

On the downside, they'd both be losing the man each regarded as the greatest thing since microwave popcorn.

He could toss a coin and take out either June or her husband, thus serving as a sort of divorce court of last resort. If it came up heads, June could spend the rest of her life cheating on a ghost. If it was tails, Yarnell could have his cake and Edith, too. Only a question of time until she stopped calling him Bart and took to calling him Hobie, of course, and next thing you knew she would turn up at the Holiday Inn, dropping her quarter in the slot to play "Third-Rate Romance, Low-Rent Rendezvous."

It struck Keller that there ought to be some sort of solution that didn't involve lowering the population. But he knew he was the person least likely to come up with it.

If you had a medical problem, the treatment you got depended on the sort of person you went to. You didn't expect a surgeon to manipulate your spine, or prescribe herbs and enemas, or kneel down and pray with you. Whatever the problem was, the first thing the surgeon would do was look around for something to cut. That's how he'd been trained; that's how he saw the world; that's what he did.

Keller, too, was predisposed to a surgical approach. While others might push counseling or twelve-step programs, Keller reached for a scalpel. But sometimes it was difficult to tell where to make the incision.

Kill 'em all, he thought savagely, and let God sort 'em out. Or ride off into the sunset with your tail between your legs.

FIRST THING IN THE MORNING Keller drove to Sheridan and caught a plane to Salt Lake City. He paid cash for his ticket and used the name John Richards. At the TWA counter in Salt Lake City he bought a one-way ticket to Las Vegas and again paid cash, this time using the name Alan Johnson.

At the Las Vegas airport he walked around the long-term parking lot as if looking for his car. He'd been doing this for five minutes or so when a balding man wearing a glen plaid sport coat parked a two-year-old Plymouth and removed several large suitcases from its trunk, affixing them to one of those aluminum luggage carriers. Wherever he was headed, he'd packed enough to stay there for a while.

As soon as he was out of sight, Keller dropped to a knee and groped the undercarriage until he found the magnetized hide-a-key. He always looked before breaking into a car, and he got lucky about one time in five. As usual, he was elated. Finding a key was a good omen. It boded well.

Keller had been to Vegas frequently over the years. He didn't like the place, but he knew his way around. He drove to Caesars Palace and left his borrowed Plymouth for the attendant to park. He knocked on the door of an eighth-floor room until its occupant protested that she was trying to sleep.

He said, "It's news from Martingale, Miss Bodine. For Christ's sake, open the door."

She opened the door a crack but kept the chain fastened. She was about the same age as June but looked older, her black hair a mess, her eyes bleary, her face still bearing traces of yesterday's makeup.

"Crowder's dead," he said.

Keller could think of any number of things she might have said, ranging from "What happened?" to "Who cares?" This woman cut to the chase. "You idiot," she said. "What are you doing here?"

Mistake.

"Let me in," he said, and she did.

Another mistake.

THE ATTENDANT BROUGHT KELLER'S PLYMOUTH and seemed happy with the tip Keller gave him. At the airport someone else had left a Toyota Camry in the spot where the balding man had originally parked the Plymouth, and the best Keller could do was wedge it into a spot one aisle over and a dozen spaces off to the side. He figured the owner would find it and hoped he wouldn't worry that he was in the early stages of Alzheimer's.

Keller flew to Denver as Richard Hill, to Sheridan as David Edwards. En route he thought about Edith Bodine, who'd evidently slipped on a wet tile in the bathroom of her room at Caesars, cracking her skull on the side of the big tub. With the Do Not Disturb sign hanging from the doorknob and the air conditioner at its highest setting, there was no telling how long she might remain undisturbed.

He'd figured she had to be the client. It wasn't June or Hobie, both of whom thought the world revolved around Lyman Crowder, so whom did that leave? Crowder himself, turned sneakily suicidal? Some old enemy, some business rival?

No, Edith was the best prospect. A client would either want to meet Keller—not obliquely, as both Yarnells had done, but by arrangement— or would contrive to be demonstrably off the scene when it all happened. Thus the trip to Las Vegas.

Why? The Crowder fortune, of course. She had Hobie Yarnell crazy about her, but he wouldn't leave June for fear of breaking Crowder's heart, and even if he did, he'd go empty-handed. Having June killed wouldn't work, either, because she didn't have any real money of her own. But June would inherit if the old man died, and later on something could always happen to June.

Anyway, that was how he figured it. If he'd wanted to know Edith's exact reasoning, he'd have had to ask her, and that had struck him as a waste of time. More to the point, the last thing he'd wanted was a chance to get to know her. That just screwed everything up when you got to know these people.

If you were going to ride a thousand miles to kill a man you'd never met, you were really well advised to be the tight-lipped stranger every step of the way. No point in talking to anybody, not the target, not the client, and not anybody else either. If you had anything to say, you could whisper it to your horse.

HE GOT OFF THE FOURTH PLANE of the day at Sheridan, picked up his Caprice—the name was seeming more appropriate with every passing hour—and drove back to Martingale. He kept it right around the speed limit, then slowed down along with everyone else five miles outside Martingale. They were clearing a wreck out of the northbound lane. That shouldn't have slowed things down in the southbound lane, but of course it did; everybody had to slow down to see what everyone else was slowing down to look at.

Back in his room he had his bag packed before he realized that he couldn't go anywhere. The client was dead, but that didn't change anything; since he had no way of knowing that she was the client or that she was dead, his mission remained unchanged. He could go home and admit an inability to get the job done, waiting for the news to seep through that there was no longer any job to be done. That would get him off the hook after the fact, but he wouldn't have covered himself with glory, nor would he get paid. The client had almost certainly paid in advance, and if there'd been a middleman between the client and the man in White Plains, he had almost certainly passed the money on, and there was very little likelihood that the man in White Plains would even consider the notion of refunding a fee to a dead client, nor that anyone would raise the subject. But neither would the man in White Plains pay Keller for work he'd failed to perform. The man in White Plains would just keep everything.

Keller thought about it. It looked to him as though his best course lay in playing a waiting game. How long could it take before a sneak thief or a chambermaid walked in on Edith Bodine? How long before news of her death found its way to White Plains?

The more he thought about it, the longer it seemed likely to take. If there were, as sometimes happened, a whole string of intermediaries involved, the message might very well never get to García.

Maybe the simplest thing was to kill Crowder and be done with it.

No, he thought. He'd just made a side trip of, yes, more than a thousand miles—and at his own expense yet—solely to keep from having to kill this legendary Man He Never Met. Damned if he was going to kill him now, after all that.

He'd wait a while anyway. He didn't want to drive anywhere now, and he couldn't bear to look at another airplane, let alone get on board.

He stretched out on the bed, closed his eyes.

HE HAD A FRIGHTFUL DREAM. In it he was walking at night out in the middle of the desert, lost, chilled, desperately alone. Then a horse came galloping out of nowhere, and on his back was a magnificent woman with a great mane of hair and eyes that flashed in the moonlight. She extended a hand, and Keller leaped up on the horse and rode behind her. She was naked. So was Keller, although he had somehow failed to notice this before.

They fell in love. Wordless, they told each other everything, knew each other like twin souls. And then, gazing into her eyes, Keller realized who she was. She was Edith Bodine, and she was dead; he'd killed her earlier without knowing she'd turn out to be the girl of his dreams. It was done, it could never be undone, and his heart was broken for eternity.

Keller woke up shaking. For five minutes he paced the room, struggling to sort out what was a dream and what was real. He hadn't been sleeping long. The sun was setting; it was still the same endless day.

God, what a hellish dream.

He couldn't get caught up in TV, and he had no luck at all with the book. He put it down, picked up the phone, and dialed June's number.

"It's Dale," he said. "I was sitting here and—"

"Oh, Dale," she cut in, "you're so thoughtful to call. Isn't it terrible? Isn't it the most awful thing?"

"Uh," he said.

"I can't talk now," she said. "I can't even think straight. I've never been so upset in my life. Thank you, Dale, for being so thoughtful."

She hung up and left him staring at the phone. Unless she was a better actress than he would have guessed, she sounded absolutely overcome. He was surprised that news of Edith Bodine's death could have reached her so soon, but far more surprised that she could be taking it so hard. Was there more to all this than met the eye? Were Hobie's wife and mistress actually close friends? Or were they—Jesus—*more* than just good friends?

Things were certainly a lot simpler for Randolph Scott.

*   *   *

THE SAME BARTENDER was on duty at Joe's. "I don't guess your friend Hobie'll be coming around tonight," he said. "I suppose you heard the news."

"Uh," Keller said. Some backstreet affair, he thought, if the whole town was ready to comfort Hobie before the body was cold.

"Hell of a thing," the man went on. "Terrible loss for this town. Martingale won't be the same without him."

"This news," Keller said carefully. "I think maybe I missed it. What happened anyway?"

HE CALLED THE AIRLINES from his motel room. The next flight out of Casper wasn't until morning. Of course, if he wanted to drive to Denver—

He didn't want to drive to Denver. He booked the first flight out in the morning, using the Whitlock name and the Whitlock credit card.

No need to stick around, not with Lyman Crowder stretched out somewhere getting pumped full of embalming fluid. Dead in a car crash on I-25 North, the very accident that had slowed Keller down on his way back from Sheridan.

He wouldn't be around for the funeral, but should he send flowers? It was quite clear that he shouldn't. Still, the impulse was there.

He dialed 1-800-FLOWERS and sent a dozen roses to Mrs. Dale Whitlock in Rowayton, charging them to Whitlock's American Express account. He asked them to enclose a card reading, "Just because I love you—Dale."

He felt it was the least he could do.

TWO DAYS LATER he was on Taunton Place in White Plains, making his report. Accidents were always good, the man told him. Accidents and natural causes, always the best. Oh, sometimes you needed a noisy hit to send a message, but the rest of the time you couldn't beat an accident.

"Good you could arrange it," the man said.

Would have taken a hell of an arranger, Keller thought. First you'd have had to arrange for Lyman Crowder to be speeding north in his pickup. Then you'd have had to get an unemployed sheepherder named Danny Vasco good and drunk and sent him hurtling toward Martingale, racing his own pickup—Jesus, didn't they drive anything but pickups?— racing it at ninety-plus miles an hour, and proceeding southbound in the northbound lane. Arrange for a few near misses. Arrange for Vasco to brush a school bus and sideswipe a minivan, and then let him ram Crowder head-on.

Some arrangement.

If the man in White Plains had any idea that the client was dead as well or even who the client was, he gave no sign to Keller. On the way out Dot asked him how Crowder pronounced his name.

"Rhymes with 'chowder,' " he said.

"I knew you'd find out," she said. "Keller, are you all right? You seem different."

"Just awed by the workings of fate," he said.

"Well," she said, "that'll do it."

ON THE TRAIN BACK to the city he thought about the workings of fate. Earlier he'd tried to tell himself that his side trip to Las Vegas had been a waste of time and money and human life. All he'd had to do was wait a day for Danny Vasco to take the game off the boards.

Never would have happened.

Without his trip to Vegas, there would have been no wreck on the highway. One event had opened some channel that allowed the other to happen. He couldn't explain this, couldn't make sense out of it, but somehow he knew it was true.

Everything had happened exactly the way it had had to happen. Encountering June in the Meet 'n' Cheat, running into Hobie at the Burnout Bar. He could no more have avoided those meetings than he could have kept himself from buying the paperback western novel that had set the tone for everything that followed.

He hoped Mrs. Whitlock liked the flowers.

Bill Pronzini is most often associated with his Nameless detective, a long-running series of novels that has the feel and depth of serious autobiography. HARDCASE (1995) is the most recent addition to the Nameless collection, and it is one of the two or three best in the series. His forthcoming novel BLUE LONESOME, which will be out by the time this book appears, is his masterpiece and should be read by mystery readers of all tastes. It is a remarkable and powerful tour-de-force, unlike anything Bill has ever done. "Out of The Depths" demonstrates why, when the dust settles and the fads fade, Pronzini's work will not simply stand but endure.

Out of the Depths
BILL PRONZINI

He came tumbling out of the sea, dark and misshapen, like a being that was not human. A creature from the depths; or a jumbee, the evil spirit of West Indian superstition. Fanciful thoughts, and Shea was not a fanciful woman. But on this strange, wild night nothing seemed real or explicable.

At first, with the moon hidden behind the running scud of clouds, she'd seen him as a blob of flotsam on a breaking wave. The squall earlier had left the sea rough and the swells out toward the reef were high, their crests stripped of spume by the wind. The angry surf threw him onto the strip of beach, dragged him back again; another wave flung him up a little farther. The moon reappeared then, bathing sea and beach and rocks in the kind of frost-white shine you found only in the Caribbean. Not flotsam—something alive. She saw his arms extend, splayed fingers dig into the sand to hold himself against the backward pull of the sea. Saw him raise a smallish head above a massive, deformed torso, then squirm weakly toward the nearest jut of rock. Another wave shoved him the last few feet. He clung to the rock, lying motionless with the surf foaming around him.

Out of the depths, she thought.

The irony made her shiver, draw the collar of her coat more tightly around her neck. She lifted her gaze again to the rocky peninsula farther south. Windflaw Point, where the undertow off its tiny beach was the most treacherous on the island. It had taken her almost an hour to marshal her courage to the point where she was ready—almost ready—to walk out there and into the ocean. *Into* the depths. Now . . .

Massive clouds sealed off the moon again. In the heavy darkness Shea could just make him out, still lying motionless on the fine coral sand. Unconscious? Dead? I ought to go down there, she thought. But she could not seem to lift herself out of the chair.

After several minutes he moved again: dark shape rising to hands and knees, then trying to stand. Three tries before he was able to keep his legs from collapsing under him. He stood swaying, as if gathering strength; finally staggered onto the path that led up through rocks and sea grape. Toward the house. Toward her.

On another night she would have felt any number of emotions by this time: surprise, bewilderment, curiosity, concern. But not on this night. There was a numbness in her mind, like the numbness in her body from the cold wind. It was as if she were dreaming, sitting there on the open terrace—as if she'd fallen asleep hours ago, before the clouds began to pile up at sunset and the sky turned the color of a blood bruise.

A new storm was making up. Hammering northern this time, from the look of the sky. The wind had shifted, coming out of the northeast now; the clouds were bloated and simmering in that direction and the air had a charged quality. Unless the wind shifted again soon, the rest of the night would be even wilder.

Briefly the clouds released the moon. In its white glare she saw him plodding closer, limping, almost dragging his left leg. A man, of course— just a man. And not deformed: what had made him seem that way was the life jacket fastened around his upper body. She remembered the lights of a freighter or tanker she had seen passing on the horizon just after nightfall, ahead of the squall. Had he gone overboard from that somehow?

He had reached the garden, was making his way past the flamboyant trees and the thick clusters of frangipani. Heading toward the garden door and the kitchen: she'd left the lights on in there and the jalousies open. It was the lights that had drawn him here, like a beacon that could be seen a long distance out to sea.

A good thing she'd left them on or not? She didn't want him here, a cast-up stranger, hurt and needing attention—not on this night, not when she'd been so close to making the walk to Windflaw Point. But neither could she refuse him access or help. John would have, if he'd been drunk and in the wrong mood. Not her. It was not in her nature to be cruel to anyone, except perhaps herself.

Abruptly Shea pushed herself out of the chair. He hadn't seen her sitting in the restless shadows, and he didn't see her now as she moved back across the terrace to the sliding glass doors to her bedroom. Or at least if he did see her, he didn't stop or call out to her. She hurried through the darkened bedroom, down the hall, and into the kitchen. She was halfway to the garden door when he began pounding on it.

She unlocked and opened the door without hesitation. He was propped against the stucco wall, arms hanging and body slumped with exhaustion. Big and youngish, that was her first impression. She couldn't see his face clearly.

"Need some help," he said in a thick, strained voice. "Been in the water ... washed up on your beach...."

"I know, I saw you from the terrace. Come inside."

"Better get a towel first. Coral ripped a gash in my foot ... blood all over your floor."

"All right. I'll have to close the door. The wind...."

"Go ahead."

She shut the door and went to fetch a towel, a blanket, and the first-aid kit. On the way back to the kitchen she turned the heat up several degrees. When she opened up to him again she saw that he'd shed the life jacket. His clothing was minimal: plaid wool shirt, denim trousers, canvas shoes, all nicked and torn by coral. Around his waist was a pouch-type waterproof belt, like a workman's utility belt. One of the pouches bulged slightly.

She gave him the towel, and when he had it wrapped around his left foot he hobbled inside. She took his arm, let him lean on her as she guided him to the kitchen table. His flesh was cold, sea-puckered; the touch of it made her feel a tremor of revulsion. It was like touching the sin of a dead man.

When he sank heavily onto one of the chairs, she dragged another chair over and lifted his injured leg onto it. He stripped off what was left of his shirt, swaddled himself in the blanket. His teeth were chattering.

The coffeemaker drew her; she poured two of the big mugs full. There was always hot coffee ready and waiting, no matter what the hour—she made sure of that. She drank too much coffee, much too much, but it was better than drinking what John usually drank. If she—

"You mind sweetening that?"

She half-turned. "Sugar?"

"Liquor. Rum, if you have it?"

"Jamaican rum." That was what John drank.

"Best there is. Fine."

She took down an open bottle, carried it and the mugs to the table, and watched while he spiked the coffee, drank, then poured more rum and drank again. Color came back into his stubbled cheeks. He used part of the blanket to rough-dry his hair.

He was a little older than she, early thirties, and in good physical condition: broad chest and shoulders, muscle-knotted arms. Sandy hair cropped short, thick sandy brows, a long-chinned face burned dark from exposure to the sun. The face was all right, might have been attractive except for the eyes. They were a bright off-blue color, shielded by lids that seemed perpetually lowered like flags at half-mast, and they didn't blink much. When the eyes lifted to meet and hold hers something in them made her look away.

"I'll see what I can do for your foot."

"Thanks. Hurts like hell."

The towel was already soaking through. Shea unwrapped it carefully, revealing a deep gash across the instep just above the tongue of his shoe. She got the shoe and sock off. More blood welled out of the cut.

"It doesn't look good. You may need a doctor—"

"No," he said, "no doctor."

"It'll take stitches to close properly."

"Just clean and bandage it, okay?"

She spilled iodine onto a gauze pad, swabbed at the gash as gently as she could. The sharp sting made him suck in his breath, but he didn't flinch or utter another sound. She laid a second piece of iodined gauze over the wound and began to wind tape tightly around his foot to hold the skin flaps together.

He said, "My name's Tanner. Harry Tanner."

"Shea Clifford."

"Shea. That short for something?"

"It's a family name."

"Pretty."

"Thank you."

"So are you," he said. "Real pretty with your hair all windblown like that."

She glanced up at him. He was smiling at her. Not a leer, just a weary smile, but it wasn't a good kind of smile. It had a predatory look, like the teeth-baring stretch of a wolf's jowls.

"No offense," he said.

"None taken." She lowered her gaze, watched her hands wind and tear tape. Her mind still felt numb. "What happened to you? Why were you in the water?"

"That damn squall a few hours ago. Came up so fast I didn't have time to get my genoa down. Wave as big as a house knocked poor little *Wanderer* into a full broach. I got thrown clear when she went over or I'd have sunk with her."

"Were you sailing alone?"

"All alone."

"Single-hander? Or just on a weekend lark?"

"Single-hander. You know boats, I see."

"Yes. Fairly well."

"Well, I'm a sea tramp," Tanner said. "Ten years of island-hopping and this is the first time I ever got caught unprepared."

"It happens. What kind of craft was *Wanderer?*"

"Bugeye ketch. Thirty-nine feet."

"Shame to lose a boat like that."

He shrugged. "She was insured."

"How far out were you?"

"Five or six miles. Hell of a long swim in a choppy sea."

"You're lucky the squall passed as quickly as it did."

"Lucky I was wearing my life jacket, too," Tanner said. "And lucky you stay up late with your lights on. If it weren't for the lights I probably wouldn't have made shore at all."

Shea nodded. She tore off the last piece of tape and then began putting the first-aid supplies away in the kit.

Tanner said, "I didn't see any other lights. This house the only one out here?"

"The only one on this side of the bay, yes."

"No close neighbors?"

"Three houses on the east shore, not far away."

"You live here alone?"

"With my husband."

"But he's not here now."

"Not now. He'll be home soon."

"That so? Where is he?"

"In Merrywing, the town on the far side of the island. He went out to dinner with friends."

"While you stayed home."

"I wasn't feeling well earlier."

"Merrywing. Salt Cay?"

"That's right."

"British-owned, isn't it?"

"Yes. You've never been here before?"

"Not my kind of place. Too small, too quiet, too rich. I prefer the livelier islands—St. Thomas, Nassau, Jamaica."

"St. Thomas isn't far from here," Shea said. "Is that where you were heading?"

"More or less. This husband of yours—how big is he?"

"... Big?"

"Big enough so his clothes would fit me?"

"Oh," she said, "yes. About your size."

"Think he'd mind if you let me have a pair of his pants and a shirt and some underwear? Wet things of mine are giving me a chill."

"No, of course not. I'll get them from his room."

She went to John's bedroom. The smells of his cologne and pipe tobacco were strong in there; they made her faintly nauseous. In haste she
dragged a pair of white linen trousers and a pullover off hangers in his
closet, turned toward the dresser as she came out. And stopped in
midstride.

Tanner stood in the open doorway, leaning against the jamb, his half-
lidded eyes fixed on her.

"*His* room," he said. "Right."

"Why did you follow me?"

"Felt like it. So you don't sleep with him."

"Why should that concern you?"

"I'm naturally curious. How come? I mean, how come you and your
husband don't share a bed?"

"Our sleeping arrangements are none of your business."

"Probably not. Your idea or his?"

"What?"

"Separate bedrooms. Your idea or his?"

"Mine, if you must know."

"Maybe he snores, huh?"

She didn't say anything.

"How long since you kicked him out of your bed?"

"I didn't kick him out. It wasn't like that."

"Sure it was. I can see it in your face."

"My private affairs—"

"—are none of my business. I know. But I also know the signs of a
bad marriage when I see them. A bad marriage and an unhappy woman.
Can't tell me you're not unhappy."

"All right," she said.

"So why don't you divorce him? Money?"

"Money has nothing to do with it."

"Money has something to do with everything."

"It isn't money."

"He have something on you?"

"No."

"Then why not just dump him?"

*You're not going to divorce me, Shea. Not you, not like the others. I'll
see you dead first. I mean it, Shea. You're mine and you'll stay mine until
I decide I don't want you anymore....*

She said flatly, "I'm not going to talk about my marriage to you. I
don't know you."

"We can fix that. I'm an easy guy to know."

She moved ahead to the dresser, found underwear and socks, put them on the bed with the trousers and pullover. "You can change in here," she said, and started for the doorway.

Tanner didn't move.

"I said—"

"I heard you, Shea."

"Mrs. Clifford."

"Clifford," he said. Then he smiled, the same wolfish lip-stretch he'd shown her in the kitchen. "Sure—Clifford. Your husband's name wouldn't be John, would it? John Clifford?"

She was silent.

"I'll bet it is. John Clifford, Clifford Yacht Designs. One of the best marine architects in Miami. Fancy motor sailers and racing yawls."

She still said nothing.

"House in Miami Beach, another on Salt Cay—this house. And you're his latest wife. Which is it, number three or number four?"

Between her teeth she said, "Three."

"He must be what, fifty now? And worth millions. Don't tell me money's not why you married him."

"I won't tell you anything."

But his wealth wasn't why she'd married him. He had been kind and attentive to her at first. And she'd been lonely after the bitter breakup with Neal. John had opened up a whole new, exciting world to her: travel to exotic places, sailing, the company of interesting and famous people. She hadn't loved him, but she had been fond of him; and she'd convinced herself she would learn to love him in time. Instead, when he revealed his dark side to her, she had learned to hate him.

Tanner said, "Didn't one of his other wives divorce him for knocking her around when he was drunk? Seems I remember reading something like that in the Miami papers a few years back. That why you're unhappy, Shea? He knock *you* around when he's drinking?"

Without answering, Shea pushed past him into the hallway. He didn't try to stop her. In the kitchen again she poured yet another cup of coffee and sat down with it. Even with her coat on and the furnace turned up, she was still cold. The heat from the mug failed to warm her hands.

She knew she ought to be afraid of Harry Tanner. But all she felt inside was a deep weariness. An image of Windflaw Point, the tiny beach with its treacherous undertow, flashed across the screen of her mind—and was gone again just as swiftly. Her courage, or maybe her cowardice, was gone too. She was no longer capable of walking out to the point, letting the sea have her. Not tonight and probably not ever again.

She sat listening to the wind clamor outside. It moaned in the twisted branches of the banyan tree; scraped palm fronds against the roof tiles. Through the open window jalousies she could smell ozone mixed with the sweet fragrances of white ginger blooms. The new storm would be here soon in all its fury.

The wind kept her from hearing Tanner reenter the kitchen. She sensed his presence, looked up, and saw him standing there with his eyes on her like probes. He'd put on all of John's clothing and found a pair of Reeboks for his feet. In his left hand he held the waterproof belt that had been strapped around his waist.

"Shirt's a little snug," he said, "but a pretty good fit otherwise. Your husband's got nice taste."

Shea didn't answer.

"In clothing, in houses, and in women."

She sipped her coffee, not looking at him.

Tanner limped around the table and sat down across from her. When he laid the belt next to the bottle of rum, the pouch that bulged made a thunking sound. "Boats too," he said. "I'll bet he keeps his best designs for himself; he's the kind that would. Am I right, Shea?"

"Yes."

"How many boats does he own?"

"Two."

"One's bound to be big. Oceangoing yacht?"

"Seventy-foot custom schooner."

"What's her name?"

"*Moneybags.*"

Tanner laughed. "Some sense of humor."

"If you say so."

"Where does he keep her? Here or Miami?"

"Miami."

"She there now?"

"Yes."

"And the other boat? That one berthed here?"

"The harbor at Merrywing."

"What kind is she?"

"A sloop," Shea said. "*Carib Princess.*"

"How big?"

"Thirty-two feet."

"She been back and forth across the Stream?"

"Several times, in good weather."

"With you at the helm?"

"No."

"You ever take her out by yourself?"

"No. He wouldn't allow it."

"But you can handle her, right? You said you know boats. You can pilot that little sloop without any trouble?"

"Why do you want to know that? Why are you asking so many questions about John's boats?"

"John's boats, John's houses, John's third wife." Tanner laughed again, just a bark this time. The wolfish smile pulled his mouth out of shape. "Are you afraid of me, Shea?"

"No."

"Not even a little?"

"Why? Should I be?"

"What do you think?"

"I'm not afraid of you," she said.

"Then how come you lied to me?"

"Lied? About what?"

"Your husband. Old John Clifford."

"I don't know what you mean."

"You said he'd be home soon. But he won't be. He's not in town with friends, he's not even on the island."

She stared silently at the steam rising from her cup. Her fingers felt cramped, as if she might be losing circulation in them.

"Well, Shea? That's the truth, isn't it."

"Yes. That's the truth."

"Where is he? Miami?"

She nodded.

"Went there on business and left you all by your lonesome."

"It isn't the first time."

"Might be the last, though." Tanner reached for the rum bottle, poured some of the dark liquid into his mug, drank, and then smacked his lips. "You want a shot of this?"

"No."

"Loosen you up a little."

"I don't need loosening up."

"You might after I tell you the truth about Harry Tanner."

"Does that mean you lied to me too?"

"I'm afraid so. But you 'fessed up and now it's my turn."

In the blackness outside the wind gusted sharply, banging a loose shutter somewhere at the front of the house. Rain began to pelt down with open-faucet suddenness.

"Listen to that," Tanner said. "Sounds like we're in for a big blow, this time."

"What did you lie about?"

"Well, let's see. For starters, about how I came to be in the water tonight. My bugeye ketch didn't sink in the squall. No, *Wanderer*'s tied up at a dock in Charlotte Amalie."

She sat stiffly, waiting.

"Boat I was on didn't sink either," Tanner said. "At least as far as I know it didn't. I jumped overboard. Not long after the squall hit us."

There was still nothing for her to say.

"If I hadn't gone overboard, the two guys I was with would've shot me dead. They tried to shoot me in the water but the ketch was pitching like crazy and they couldn't see me in the dark and the rain. I guess they figured I'd drown even with a life jacket on. Or the sharks or barracuda would get me."

Still nothing.

"We had a disagreement over money. That's what most things come down to these days—money. They thought I cheated them out of twenty thousand dollars down in Jamaica, and they were right, I did. They both put guns on me before I could do anything and I thought I was a dead man. The squall saved my bacon. Big swell almost broached us, knocked us all off our feet. I managed to scramble up the companionway and go over the side before they recovered."

The hard beat of the rain stopped as suddenly as it had begun. Momentary lull: the full brunt of the storm was minutes away yet.

"I'm not a single-hander," he said, "not a sea tramp. That's another thing I lied about. Ask me what it is I really am, Shea. Ask me how I make my living."

"I don't have to ask."

"No? Think you know?"

"Smuggling. You're a smuggler."

"That's right. Smart lady."

"Drugs, I suppose."

"Drugs, weapons, liquor, the wretched poor yearning to breathe free without benefit of a green card. You name it, I've handled it. Hell, smuggling's a tradition in these waters. Men have been doing it for three hundred years, since the days of the Spanish Main." He laughed. "A modern freebooter, that's what I am. Tanner the Pirate. Yo ho ho and a bottle of rum."

"Why are you telling me all this?"

"Why not? Don't you find it interesting?"

"No."

"Okay, I'll give it to you straight. I've got a problem—a big problem. I jumped off that ketch tonight with one thing besides the clothes on my back, and it wasn't money." He pulled the waterproof belt to him, unsnapped the pouch that bulged, and showed her what was inside. "Just this."

Her gaze registered the weapon—automatic, large caliber, lightweight frame—and slid away. She was not surprised; she had known there was a gun in the pouch when it made the thunking sound.

Tanner set it on the table within easy reach. "My two partners got my share of a hundred thousand from the Jamaica run. I might be able to get it back from them and I might not; they're a couple of hard cases and I'm not sure it's worth the risk. But I can't do anything until I quit this island. And I can't leave the usual ways because my money and my passport are both on that damn ketch. You see my dilemma, Shea?"

"I see it."

"Sure you do. You're a smart lady, like I said. What else do you see? The solution?"

She shook her head.

"Well, I've got a dandy." The predatory grin again. "You know, this really is turning into my lucky night. I couldn't have washed up in a better spot if I'd planned it. John Clifford's house, John Clifford's smart and pretty wife. And not far away, John Clifford's little sloop, the *Carib Princess*."

The rain came again, wind-driven with enough force to rattle the windows. Spray blew in through the screens behind the open jalousies. Shea made no move to get up and close the glass. Tanner didn't seem to notice the moisture.

"Here's what we're going to do," he said. "At dawn we'll drive in to the harbor. You do have a car here? Sure you do; he wouldn't leave you isolated without wheels. Once we get there we go onboard the sloop and you take her out. If anybody you know sees us and says anything, you tell them. I'm a friend or relative and John said it was okay for us to go for a sail without him."

She asked dully, "Then what?"

"Once we're out to sea? I'm not going to kill you and dump your body overboard, if that's worrying you. The only thing that's going to happen is we sail the *Carib Princess* across the Stream to Florida. A little place I know on the west coast up near Pavilion Key where you can sneak a boat in at night and keep her hidden for as long as you need to."

"And then?"

"Then I call your husband and we do some business. How much do you think he'll pay to get his wife and his sloop back safe and sound? Five hundred thousand? As much as a million?"

"My God," she said. "You're crazy."

"Like a fox."

"You couldn't get away with it. You *can't*."

"I figure I can. You think he won't pay because the marriage is on the rocks? You're wrong, Shea. He'll pay, all right. He's the kind that can't stand losing anything that belongs to him, wife or boat, and sure as hell not both at once. Plus he's had enough bad publicity; ignoring a ransom demand would hurt his image and his business and I'll make damned sure he knows it."

She shook her head again—a limp, rag-doll wobbling, as if it were coming loose from the stem of her neck.

"Don't look so miserable," Tanner said cheerfully. "I'm not such a bad guy when you get to know me, and there'll be plenty of time for us to get acquainted. And when old John pays off, I'll leave you with the sloop and you can sail her back to Miami. Okay? Give you my word on that."

He was lying: his word was worthless. He'd told her his name, the name of his ketch and where it was berthed; he wouldn't leave her alive to identify him. Not on the Florida coast. Not even here.

Automatically Shea picked up her mug, tilted it to her mouth. Dregs. Empty. She pushed back her chair, crossed to the counter, and poured the mug full again. Tanner sat relaxed, smiling, pleased with himself. The rising steam from the coffee formed a screen between them, so that she saw him as blurred, distorted. Not quite human, the way he had first seemed to her when he came out of the sea earlier.

Jumbee, she thought. Smiling evil.

The gale outside flung sheets of water at the house. The loose shutter chattered like a jackhammer until the wind slackened again.

Tanner said, "Going to be a long wet night." He made a noisy yawning sound. "Where do you sleep, Shea?"

The question sent a spasm through her body.

"Your bedroom—where is it?"

Oh God. "Why?"

"I told you, it's going to be a long night. And I'm tired and my foot hurts and I want to lie down. But I don't want to lie down alone. We might as well start getting to know each other the best way there is."

No, she thought. No, no, no.

"Well, Shea? Lead the way."

No, she thought again. But her legs worked as if with a will of their own, carried her back to the table. Tanner sat forward as she drew abreast of him, started to lift himself out of the chair.

She pivoted and threw the mug of hot coffee into his face.

She hadn't planned to do it, acted without thinking; it was almost as much of a surprise to her as it was to him. He yelled and pawed at his eyes, his body jerking so violently that both he and the chair toppled over sideways. Shea swept the automatic off the table and backed away with it extended at arm's length.

Tanner kicked the chair away and scrambled unsteadily to his feet. Bright red splotches stained his cheeks where the coffee had scalded him; his eyes were murderous. He took a step toward her, stopped when he realized she was pointing his own weapon at him. She watched him struggle to regain control of himself and the situation.

"You shouldn't have done that, Shea."

"Stay where you are."

"That gun isn't loaded."

"It's loaded. I know guns too."

"You won't shoot me." He took another step.

"I will. Don't come any closer."

"No you won't. You're not the type. I can pull the trigger on a person real easy. Have, more than once." Another step. "But not you. You don't have what it takes."

"Please don't make me shoot you. Please, please don't."

"See? You won't do it because you can't."

"Please."

"You won't shoot me, Shea."

On another night, any other night, he would have been right. But on this night—

He lunged at her.

And she shot him.

The impact of the high-caliber bullet brought him up short, as if he had walked into an invisible wall. A look of astonishment spread over his face. He took one last convulsive step before his hands came up to clutch at his chest and his knees buckled.

Shea didn't see him fall; she turned away. And the hue and the cry of the storm kept her from hearing him hit the floor. When she looked again, after several seconds, he lay face down and unmoving on the tiles. She did not have to go any closer to tell that he was dead.

There was a hollow queasiness in her stomach. Otherwise she felt nothing. She turned again, and there was a blank space of time, and then she found herself sitting on one of the chairs in the living room. She would have wept then but she had no tears. She had cried herself dry on the terrace.

After a while she became aware that she still gripped Tanner's automatic. She set it down on an end table; hesitated, then picked it up again. The numbness was finally leaving her mind, a swift release that brought her thoughts into sharpening focus. When the wind and rain lulled again she stood, walked slowly down the hall to her bedroom. She steeled herself as she opened the door and turned on the lights.

From where he lay sprawled across the bed, John's sightless eyes stared up at her. The stain of blood on his bare chest, drying now, gleamed darkly in the lamp glow.

Wild night, mad night.

She hadn't been through hell just once, she'd been through it twice. First in here and then in the kitchen.

But she hadn't shot John. She hadn't. He'd come home at nine, already drunk, and tried to make love to her, and when she denied him he'd slapped her, kept slapping her. After three long hellish years she couldn't take it anymore, not anymore. She'd managed to get the revolver out of her nightstand drawer ... not to shoot him, just as a threat to make him leave her alone. But he'd lunged at her, in almost the same way Tanner had, and they'd struggled, and the gun had gone off. And John Clifford was dead.

She had started to call the police. Hadn't because she knew they would not believe it was an accident. John was well liked and highly respected on Salt Cay; his public image was untarnished and no one, not even his close friends, believed his second wife's divorce claim or that he could ever mistreat anyone. She had never really been accepted here—some of the cattier rich women thought she was a gold digger—and she had no friends of her own in whom she could confide. John had seen to that. There were no marks on her body to prove it, either; he'd always been very careful not to leave marks.

The island police would surely have claimed she'd killed him in cold blood. She'd have been arrested and tried and convicted and put in a prison much worse than the one in which she had lived the past three years. The prospect of that was unbearable. It was what had driven her out onto the terrace, to sit and think about the undertow at Windflaw Point. The sea, in those moments, had seemed her only way out.

Now there was another way.

Her revolver lay on the floor where it had fallen. John had given it to her when they were first married, because he was away so much; and he had taught her how to use it. It was one of three handguns he'd bought illegally in Miami.

Shea bent to pick it up. With a corner of the bedsheet she wiped the grip carefully, then did the same to Tanner's automatic. That gun too, she was certain, would not be registered anywhere.

Wearily she put the automatic in John's hand, closing his fingers around it. Then she retreated to the kitchen and knelt to place the revolver in Tanner's hand. The first-aid kit was still on the table; she would use it once more, when she finished talking to the chief constable in Marrywing.

We tried to help Tanner, John and I, she would tell him. And he repaid our kindness by attempting to rob us at gunpoint. John told him we kept money in our bedroom; he took the gun out of the nightstand before I could stop him. They shot each other. John died instantly, but Tanner didn't believe his wound was as serious as it was. He made me bandage it and then kept me in the kitchen, threatening to kill me too. I managed to catch him off guard and throw coffee in his face. When he tried to come after me the strain aggravated his wound and he collapsed and died.

If this were Miami, or one of the larger Caribbean islands, she could not hope to get away with such a story. But here the native constabulary was unsophisticated and inexperienced because there was so little crime on Salt Cay. They were much more likely to overlook the fact that John had been shot two and a half hours before Harry Tanner. Much more likely, too, to credit a double homicide involving a stranger, particularly when they investigated Tanner's background, than the accidental shooting of a respected resident who had been abusing his wife. Yes, she might just get away with it. If there was any justice left for her in this world, she would—and one day she'd leave Salt Cay a free woman again.

Out of the depths, she thought as she picked up the phone. Out of the depths. . . .